IF IT LOOKS
TOO GOOD TO BE TRUE...

Feel & Look Young Again!

DE LEON LIFE EXTENSION CENTER
Coral Key, Florida

Revolutionary Antiaging Therapies

IT IS.

PLEASE NOTE: Treatments considered nonessential will not be covered by most insurance policies. Payment required at time of visit. Results may vary.

The De Leon Clinic will not be held responsible for unpleasant side effects.

MORTALITY

STEVEN FORD

BERKLEY BOOKS, NEW YORK

MORTALITY

A Berkley Book / published by arrangement with
the author

PRINTING HISTORY
Berkley edition / May 2003

Contact the author at
writestevenford@yahoo.com

ISBN: 0-425-18989-9

BERKLEY®
Berkley Books are published by The Berkley Publishing Group,
a division of Penguin Group (USA) Inc.,
375 Hudson Street, New York, New York 10014.
BERKLEY and the "B" design
are trademarks belonging to Penguin Group (USA) Inc.

PRINTED IN THE UNITED STATES OF AMERICA

10 9 8 7 6 5 4 3 2 1

For Belinda
again and always

PROLOGUE

JUSTIN PIKE HELD Britany's hand as the Air France jet pulled away from the terminal at JFK. Flying frightened her. This was their second flight together, so he knew that the takeoffs and landings were the worst; if he could just get her into the air, she'd be all right until they reached Paris.

As the plane rolled onto the runway she gripped his hand tightly. She was nineteen, just a kid. Naïve in so many ways. Which was one of the qualities he liked about her. She was less than half his age, with the most disarming smile he had ever seen, and the kind of body men go to war over. Her innocence did not carry over into the bedroom, though. There, she had no inhibitions at all. Sometimes he had to pinch himself to make sure this was real, that she was actually his. He had to be the envy of every man on earth.

He'd been with Britany for only a month, a whirlwind romance, yet he couldn't imagine going to France without her. She did so much for his ego. As if starring in his first movie wasn't enough. Well, not exactly *starring*. More like a supporting role, but a *major* supporting role. The actor they'd originally cast had taken sick yesterday. His scenes were scheduled to start shooting tomorrow and the producers didn't want to shut down the production. Of course Justin's agent told the producers he'd be there. This was the break he'd been working toward for twenty years. He'd get there even if he had to swim all the way to France.

He'd paid his dues, now it was time to reap the rewards. Britany. The movie role. The promise of a future. All of it. If he'd known this would be the result, he'd have gone to De Leon much sooner.

At forty-four, he looked better and felt better than he had in fifteen years. He'd lost the body fat he had gained since college. He'd kept fairly fit, but he had gotten a little softer around the middle, especially since turning forty. Now, though, he had the same physique he'd had as a point guard at NYU twenty-some-odd years ago. His skin, too, looked the way it had in his early twenties. The damage from all the years of careful tanning was gone. He was still surprised when he looked in the mirror—he looked like a much younger man. Which explained Britany. Unfortunately girls her age have short attention spans. She'd probably move on soon. But he was sure as hell going to enjoy her while she lasted.

As the jet's tires rose off the runway, Britany's grip tightened around his fingers, cutting off the blood. He put his arm around her and drew her close. "It's all right, baby," he said. "We're in the air now. Everything's okay."

As soon as the plane leveled out, he had the flight attendant bring Britany a glass of white wine. That quickly eased her nervousness. He told her to call her friends and tell them she was on her way to Paris—a little showing off on his part, but what the hell? While she made some calls on the Skyfone, he took out the script FedEx had delivered that morning and flipped through the pages. He'd read it through once already and highlighted his scenes. He planned to use this flight to memorize his lines. They expected him to go straight to the set as soon as the plane arrived, and he wanted to be sure he had his lines down cold.

He'd barely started reading his first scene when the pilot's voice came over the speaker. "I've got some bad news, folks." He had a southern accent, calm, casual. "We've got a slight problem with the heating system so we're going to have to make a quick stop in Boston to get that taken care of."

"That's not serious, is it?" Britany asked.

Justin didn't answer. He barely heard her. The pilot went on about agents waiting at Logan to assist passengers, but Justin wasn't listening to him either. He felt something strange inside his head. More than worry, more than anxiety. A weird kind of focused confusion. His thoughts began whirling out of control—Paris, the movie role, his big chance slipping away. He couldn't hear what was going on around him, couldn't see or feel or think of anything other than what he was about to lose.

He had to get to Paris in time for the beginning of shooting. He couldn't be late. The director was not going to stand around waiting for him to arrive. Movies didn't shut down for new actors. They'd hired him to replace a guy who got sick—they would hire someone else to replace him if he didn't get there on time. His big break would be lost, just like that. Twenty years of work would be gone, just like that. He could not let that happen.

"No," he said out loud. "We can't do that."

He started to stand up. Britany grasped his arm.

"What are you doing, Justin? What's wrong? The pilot said it was just the heater. That's not serious, is it?"

Justin glared at her. "We can't go to Boston."

She stared back at him, looking confused and worried. Why on earth couldn't she understand? But he couldn't waste time explaining to her. He had to take action.

He hurried up the aisle toward the cockpit, not thinking through what he was going to do, but knowing he had to do something.

One of the flight attendants scurried over as he reached the cockpit door. "Sir, the Fasten Seat Belts sign is illuminated," she said. "I'm going to have to ask you to sit down."

"I have to talk to the pilot." Justin tried the doorknob. It was locked.

"The pilot can't talk to you right now. We're getting ready to land."

"But we can't land in Boston," Justin said. "I have to get to Paris."

"You'll get to Paris. We won't be in Boston long."

"Are you sure?"

"It doesn't sound like it's anything major. Just the heater. I don't think it will take long to fix it."

"But are you *sure?*" he said again.

"Please, sir. I need you to take your seat," she said, gently removing his hand from the cockpit door and easing him back up the aisle.

Why didn't she answer? What was she hiding? He turned around and grasped her by the shoulders. "I have to get to Paris, don't you understand?"

She looked surprised by his physicality. She stepped back. Another flight attendant, an older woman, hurried up behind him. "Sir. Please take your seat," she said firmly. "The plane is landing."

Justin twisted his head around and glared at her. Did she know something? Was she hiding something, too? Just then Britany pulled on his sweater, drawing his attention away. When he looked down at her, he saw worry in her eyes. She was frightened. Part of it was his fault. The poor kid. She needed him to keep her calm.

The turmoil in his head calmed, like a switch being turned off. He took his seat and held Britany, feeling his own heartbeat gradually slowing down to normal. He couldn't believe he'd lost control that way. Flying didn't frighten him. And the problem was only a heater. They'd be on their way in no time. His life was not about to crash.

They waited at Logan for forty minutes. It was close to ten P.M. and the terminal was nearly empty, except for the passengers waiting for the flight to Paris. Finally the announcement came. All passengers on the flight from JFK to Paris were to go to the ticket counter to be rerouted. The mechanical problem could not be fixed so their plane was not leaving Boston tonight.

The switch in Justin's brain suddenly flipped on again. He rushed to the counter, Britany hurrying to keep up. Several other passengers were already in line ahead of him. But he couldn't help himself. He couldn't wait. He pushed past the other passengers and glared at the ticket agent behind the counter.

"I have to get on a plane for Paris!" he said.

"I understand, sir. We're going to make sure everyone gets on a flight, first thing in the morning. If you wouldn't mind getting in line," the agent said, pointing to the others already waiting, "I'll take care of you when—"

"In the morning!" Justin said. He couldn't believe what he was hearing. Wasn't this guy listening to him? "Are you crazy?" Justin said. "The morning's no good. That means I won't get to Paris until tomorrow night. That's too late. I have to *be there* by morning."

"There are no flights tonight, sir. We're going to put everyone up in hotels and make sure you're on the very first flight tomorrow. That's the best we can do at this point. We'll get you to Paris as soon as possible."

"This is a special situation. I have to be there by morning."

"I understand, sir, but there are no—"

"No, you *don't* understand!" Justin wanted to grab this guy by the shoulders and shake some sense into him.

A man in line behind Justin said, "Hey, pal, wait your turn like the rest of us."

Justin ignored the voice, which sounded more like a buzz than someone actually speaking. Britany pulled on Justin's arm, trying to get him to go back in line. He jerked his arm away from her and glared at the ticket agent.

"I have to be in Paris by tomorrow morning. I don't care how you get me there, just get me there. I'll go through London or Frankfurt or Iceland or anywhere. Just get me there."

"I'm sorry, sir. There's nothing I can do. There are no more flights to Europe at all tonight."

"The pilot said you could fix the plane!"

"Sir—"

"Don't *sir* me anymore! Just get me on a plane to Paris, damn it!"

Two more agents came over to the counter now, to help with the rerouting. One stood behind a computer terminal and gestured for another passenger to come to the counter. The other, a woman who was obviously a supervisor, came up beside Justin.

"I'm going to have to ask you to keep your voice down," she told Justin.

"Then get me to Paris," he said, intentionally keeping his voice up.

Britany grabbed his arm again. "Justin, calm down. Everything will be all right."

He snapped his arm away from her. Why was she siding with them, against him? "No, everything won't!" he said. Why the hell couldn't she understand? Why the hell couldn't any of them understand? He glared at the airline supervisor. "I have to leave for Paris tonight!" he said.

"Do you understand that there are no flights leaving tonight?"

"That's your problem," he said. "You took my money to get me to Paris by morning, so get me there!"

The woman sighed, frustrated. And that angered Justin more. He wasn't a nuisance. He had a serious problem and he wanted it dealt with seriously. She glanced back at the line of passengers stretching away behind them.

"Why don't we step over here," she said, gesturing to the side near the glass.

"Why?" he said. He looked toward the window. Outside stood the jet that should have been taking him to Paris. The sight of it angered him even more. "If I stand over there," he said, "are you going to be able to get me on a flight tonight?"

"If we stand over there," she said, struggling to keep her cool, "then these other people can get their vouchers and get to their hotels while we try to figure out what to do with your situation."

"Fine," Justin said, still angry, still loud. He followed her toward the window. "Just hurry up and figure this out."

"Justin, please," Britany said, keeping close to him. "They're going to take care of this. Don't worry."

He blew out a loud breath of frustration. Naïve and *stupid*. Better she just keep her mouth shut and let him handle this. He turned back to the airline supervisor. "All right, I'm here. Now let's do something about this."

"Sir, if there were a flight leaving for Europe, on any airline, we'd put you on it. Unfortunately there isn't one. Not until tomorrow. That's the best we can do at this point. So please—"

"That's what I stepped over here for? That's your way of figuring out how to fix things? That's bullshit!"

Behind her, through the crowd of passengers, he saw two security guards rushing in his direction. He glared at the counter, at the agent who must have called them. *The bastard!* That's what they were doing all along. Stalling him. They never intended to get him to Paris at all. *Sons of bitches!*

"I asked you to calm down," the supervisor said. Suddenly she was brave now that two uniforms were hurrying up behind her. "I'm not going to continue—"

Something snapped inside Justin. He felt a sudden loss of control. His body acted without him. He felt his fist land against the woman's jaw without even realizing that he was throwing a punch. Her face shattered beneath his knuckles. She collapsed to the floor in a blur of blood, screaming. *It felt so good.*

The security guards were on him instantly. He flailed his arms, landing several blows. One guard fell away. The other swung. Justin kicked at him. Then he felt someone grab him from behind. He whirled around and flung the body away with all his strength, not even realizing it was Britany that he had thrown off until he saw her stumbling backward toward the glass. She screamed as she broke through.

"No!" he shouted, horrified.

The switch inside him snapped off. Suddenly he was there again, rational. He rushed toward the cold air and broken glass but he was too slow. Britany was gone. The guards tackled him from behind. He fell hard to the floor, his face inches from the broken window. They wrenched his arms behind him. One of them pressed a knee down on his head, forcing his face harder into the carpet.

He didn't try to get away now. His energy was completely gone. The realization of what he'd done settled into his stomach, leaving him nauseated. This sense of being connected to what was happening had been missing an instant earlier; all he had felt was impulse, pure instinct.

Now he shivered in fear of what he was capable of.

He glared out the window at the tarmac below. Britany's motionless body lay in a splatter of blood. Two baggage handlers rushed to her. One of them touched her face then quickly pulled away. He looked at the other baggage handler and shook his head in horror. Britany was dead.

1

"HERE'S THE PROBLEM," Steve Polaski told her.

He was always direct, which was one of the reasons Alicia liked working for him, and one of the reasons a lot of other people didn't. It was a remnant of his New York upbringing and his days on the NYPD.

"Mrs. Bodges was very clear when she hired us," he said. "Her husband goes for young, model types. You're a good-looking woman and all, but let's be real—you're about as much a model type as I am. No offense."

How could she not take offense? "Look, I can get this guy to hit on me," Alicia said. "It takes more than just looks."

"No, for this guy, it takes looks."

"All right, so I'll wear a tight dress and I'll tease my hair up and act like an airhead. I know how to attract a man, don't worry."

Steve blew out a breath of exasperation. "Alicia, how old are you? Forty?"

That stung. "Thirty-five," she said. Those five years really mattered all of a sudden.

"Exactly," Steve said.

"Exactly *what?*" She felt insecure about her age and her looks, and it came out as irritation. "What's your point?" she said. "Thirty-five is young."

"To me it is. But then again I'm an old fart in his fifties. This guy's in his late twenties. According to his wife, he goes for coed types, girls right out of school who wanna become starlets."

He came around the desk. This kind of talk coming from a man with a large, round gut and a bald spot the size of California offended her even more. Who was he to tell her she wasn't pretty enough for this job?

He put his arm around her. "You should be flattered that I don't think of you that way," he said.

"Oh, great," she said. "I'm flattered that you think of me as a troll."

He chuckled. "I don't think of you as a troll. But you just don't fit the bill for this particular guy. You're a great investigator, Alicia—the best I've ever seen, aside from me. But for this case, ability comes second. Kristin looks like one of those girls on sorority row at UCLA. That's what this case needs. And that's not you."

"I wouldn't know," Alicia said, sniping at him. "I don't cruise UCLA looking for sorority girls."

"Ouch," he said. He went back around the desk and plopped down. "Anyway," he said, "Kristin's exactly what Bodges is looking for. That's what I need on this case."

"This isn't a modeling shoot," she said. "It takes a lot more than looks to do this kind of work."

"Nah. It's pretty straightforward. She walks up, shakes her ass, he propositions her, we get it on tape, and we're outta there. No problem."

"It's never that simple, Steve. How much experience does she have?"

"Shaking her ass? Probably a lot."

"That's real funny. I'm serious. Things can go wrong."

"It's a guy double-dipping on his wife, not the damn 'Hollywood Slasher.' "

"You never know what's going to happen on a case like this," she said. "It could get real ugly, real quick. You know that."

He grinned. "That's why you'll be there to back her up."

"Oh, come on."

Alicia didn't want to play second banana to someone whose highest qualification was her ability to shake her ass—she'd been a licensed private detective since she was nineteen. She'd tried to be a cop, but she learned in the first few months that she wasn't cut out for that. Her superiors didn't appreciate her penchant for bending the rules to get at the truth. That caused problems for the DA's office once the cases got to court.

As a private investigator she could bend the rules a lot more. Most of the cases weren't destined for court, and the way she got the information was definitely secondary to getting the information. That fit her personality much better. And she was good at what she did. She quickly became Steve's primary investigator, getting his most important cases.

That made Steve's insistence that she couldn't handle a simple case like this even more of an insult.

"Don't do this to me, Steve," she said.

"What am I doing?"

"Don't make me second banana to a . . . a Kristin."

Steve scratched his chin and thought about it a moment. Finally he said, "For what it's worth, I'd go for you before I'd go for Kristin. But I'm not Bodges and I promised the client I'd use a model type, so that's what I'm going to do. Sorry."

Alicia sat at a table in the corner of Shanahan's Pub, waiting for Kristin to come in. A few minutes earlier, parked outside on Sunset Boulevard, they'd reviewed what Kristin was supposed to do. Alicia had made sure the recorder worked and that Kristin knew how to turn it on, and she'd gone over the signals Kristin would use if she felt she was in danger. Alicia was being extra careful, even though she knew Steve was right: this was a simple operation, as long as Kristin did what she was supposed to.

Kristin came in the bar now. Alicia checked her watch. Ten minutes exactly, just as they'd discussed outside. When she walked across the barroom, she shook her ass, just like Steve said she would. She was good at it, too. Several of the men in this pub, businessmen throwing back a few stiff ones before heading home, turned to watch her make her way to the bar.

She sauntered up and climbed onto the stool next to

Bodges. He was tall and lean, average looking, except that his clothes, his haircut, his mannerisms all said he had money. That made his average looks seem irresistible. And he seemed a little more tactful than some of the other men in the place, the gawkers. He glanced over and checked Kristin out with a quick sweep of his eyes, then went back to his drink, as if he'd actually seen an attractive woman before.

Kristin was wearing a tight black dress that showed nearly everything. When she sat down, she was all legs and cleavage. And she had the body to pull it off. Alicia knew she couldn't have worn something like that without looking like an over-the-hill hooker. Kristin, on the other hand, looked like a hot little coed who could have any man in the bar and knew it. Alicia hated her guts.

Kristin quickly struck up a conversation with Bodges. Alicia couldn't hear what they were saying, but Kristin laughed at Bodges's remarks as though he were the funniest man on earth. As obvious as it was, he ate it up. The more interest she showed in him, the more he swelled with pride.

Bodges bought Kristin a drink. It looked like a margarita. He was drinking straight shots of bourbon. Alicia hoped Kristin had enough sense not to get sauced while on the job, and she hoped Kristin had remembered to turn on the tape recorder in her purse. If she didn't record Bodges's pass, his wife wouldn't have the evidence she needed when she took him to divorce court.

The waitress came over to Alicia's table now, blocking Alicia's view of the bar. She placed another tonic and lime on the table. Alicia had barely made a dent in the one she'd ordered.

"It's from him," the waitress said, gesturing toward the end of the bar.

A man who must have been sixty, with bad teeth, a comb-over hairstyle that barely covered his shiny scalp, and a tweed suit that looked like it came from Goodwill, smiled at her and lifted his glass of beer.

"You've got to be kidding," Alicia said to the waitress.

She pushed the tonic away and said, "Can you take it back?"

The waitress giggled. "When he comes over, tell him you're married," she said.

"Like that's really going to work."

"Then tell him you're gay."

"I think that'd turn him on."

"It's not easy being beautiful," the waitress said, with just enough sarcasm that Alicia wasn't sure if the girl was sympathizing with her or making fun of her.

When the waitress walked away, Alicia's thoughts were dark. She hated these cases—and there were many more than she cared to remember. Not only didn't she consider this real investigative work, but it also depressed the hell out of her. Nearly all the husbands went for the bait. If they weren't already cheating, as soon as the opportunity presented itself they were usually willing to start. Was it that all men were dogs? Or was it just that wives had a way of knowing when their husbands stopped loving them?

A wife who didn't trust her husband. A husband who couldn't be trusted. What kind of relationship was that? Alicia wanted no part of it. Opening your heart up to someone only gives that person the chance to hurt you. People cheat. People abandon you. People die. . . .

Sometimes, when she closed her eyes, she could still see the remnants of the burned-out airplane in Mexico that had taken her parents' lives twenty-one years ago. Alicia had spent eight years searching and made more than a dozen trips to Mexico before she finally uncovered the hidden maintenance records that proved that the company that owned the plane was negligent.

No money had come out of it; but that wasn't why she'd done it. She'd hoped it would provide some closure, and perhaps it did, to a certain extent. At least the questions were answered. But her parents were still gone. And even at age twenty-two, she'd still felt like a fourteen-year-old, suddenly facing the world without a mother and father. If it hadn't been for Nikki, her older sister, she would not have been able to make it. Nikki, who had just turned eighteen when their parents died, became Alicia's parent, the one and only person Alicia let herself depend on, let herself love.

Twenty-one years later, Nikki was still the only one.

Was losing her parents at such a young age what made her so strong and independent? Having to find out for herself what really happened had certainly helped make her a good investigator. It gave her the doggedness to continue looking until the hidden answers were uncovered. But had her loss also burdened her with an impenetrable shield of self-preservation? Alicia knew that she protected herself by not letting anyone in too close, not risking the kind of pain that came with losing people who meant the world to her. No, never again.

She put that out of her mind and focused on her work.

Kristin and Bodges got up from the bar. He carried their drinks to a table in a dark part of the room. Obviously the guy wanted privacy. His wife was right about him—*the unfaithful jerk!*

As Kristin sat down, she glanced over at Alicia. Her expression said, *Look at me. I got him to bite.* Alicia was thinking, *Just get the jerk on tape propositioning you so we can get out of here.*

"Hello there."

The voice startled Alicia. Standing beside her table was the gargoyle who'd sent her the tonic. He leered down at her like the big, bad wolf eyeing one of the three little piggies.

"I noticed you sitting here all alone," he said.

"Did you think that maybe there's a reason for that?" Alicia hoped her sarcastic tone would leave no doubt that she didn't want his company.

He chuckled. "I get it. Playing hard to get."

"No. Playing impossible to get."

His grin turned into a grimace. "You think you're hot shit. I just felt sorry for you. Good luck with the liposuction," he said and walked away, muttering, "ugly bitch."

Alicia didn't need that. Even though the guy was a hideous old moron, his comment still bothered her, coming directly on the heels of Steve's insistence on Kristin for this job.

No, she didn't need this tonight at all.

She tried to wipe the thought of that jerk out of her head and concentrate on the other jerk, the one she was being paid to concentrate on. She turned to see how Kristin was doing in her efforts to lure Bodges into divorce.

Their table was empty. She and Bodges were gone.

Alicia felt a twinge of anxiety. She glanced around to see if they had moved back to the bar or to another table. She was supposed to be keeping an eye on them. Kristin was inexperienced. It was Alicia's responsibility to make sure nothing went wrong.

But Kristin and Bodges weren't at the bar or anywhere else in the place.

Alicia saw the cocktail waitress and called her over. "Did you see where the two people who were at that table went?" she asked, pointing.

"Oh, yeah, the woman was practically falling asleep." The waitress pointed to the dark hallway that led to the restroom and the parking lot in the rear of the building. "They just left. I think she had too much to drink."

Alicia got up and headed toward the hallway. As she passed the table where Kristin and Bodges had been sitting, she noticed that Kristin's margarita was still half full. Unless Kristin passed out on half a glass of margarita, something strange was going on. She stopped and sniffed the drink. Tequila was all she smelled but she did notice some sediment in the bottom of the glass and it did not look like salt.

"Oh, shit!" she said and rushed down the hallway toward the rear exit.

When she threw open the door, she saw Kristin's Miata pull away. Bodges was driving. Kristin was slumped over in the passenger's seat. The car pulled out into the traffic of Sunset Boulevard.

By the time Alicia got to her car and sped up Sunset, the Miata was nowhere to be seen. Alicia was trying not to panic.

The worst-case scenario popped into her mind. The sediment in Kristin's margarita . . . could that have been "roofies"? She'd read the stories in the paper every few months—female victim found mutilated in the Hollywood Hills, signs of sexual assault, the tranquilizer Rohypnol in the victim's bloodstream. The Hollywood Slasher. Bodges?

Alicia had to find them. She took out her cell phone as she turned off Sunset Boulevard and headed up into the hills. She gave all the information to the 911 dispatcher, who told her not to take chances, the police would be there momentarily. Alicia hung up and continued weaving her way past the homes that dotted the heavily wooded hillside overlooking Los Angeles. If there was any chance Bodges was the serial killer, Kristin didn't have time to wait for the police. Alicia had to act herself, and quickly.

Going on instinct, she turned onto another road, peering into the brush on the side as she drove along. Kristin had counted on Alicia to back her up, to be there if there was any trouble. Alicia couldn't fail her.

She turned onto another road, hearing a distant siren far below. She was lost now, trying to think like a man who doesn't want to be found. She drove through a valley, from which she could no longer see the lights of L.A. There were very few houses around here because of the slope and rockiness of the terrain. The road wound up toward the HOLLYWOOD sign far above.

Alicia maneuvered around a curve and was nearly to the next turn when she glimpsed a tiny opening in the brush that marked the beginning of a dirt road. She backed up enough to see down there and peered into the darkness. With her window rolled down, she heard the creak of insects, the far-off whisper of city traffic, the hum of her own car's motor. No sign of any life down that road. She was about to continue on when she heard the quiet clack of a car door being eased shut.

That's it!

She turned hard and floored the gas pedal. Her car bounced off the paved road and down the dirt road, scraping the bushes and branches as she plowed through. The road rose up momentarily then suddenly crested and sloped down. As soon as she reached the crest, she saw the Miata at the bottom of the slope. Bodges was naked and kneeling over Kristin, clutching a knife in his hands.

He froze when Alicia's headlights illuminated him. For an instant he just knelt there, doing nothing. Alicia stomped on the accelerator. Her car lurched forward and flew down the decline toward him. He jumped up, abandoning Kristin, and ran down the road. Alicia swerved around the Miata and sped after Bodges. The stories she'd read in the newspaper about the things this guy had done flashed into her head, along with the few images of the victims that the newspapers had been able to print.

He veered toward a small path that Alicia knew her car couldn't go down. She couldn't let him get away. Just as he was about to duck down the path, she rammed him. He bounced off the fender and landed on the road, skidding on the dirt. He started to get up.

"No way," Alicia said out loud.

She steered the car toward him and drove over his left leg. He screamed out in pain. She stopped the car on top of him, pinning him there, letting him suffer the way he'd made so many others suffer, until the cops arrived.

Alicia spent the night being questioned by the police and by Steve, then hanging around the hospital to see Kristin. When Kristin's parents arrived from San Francisco early in the morning, she slipped out.

Outside the lobby doors was a line of newspaper boxes, and the front page of the *Los Angeles Times* caught her eye. Above the fold, taking up almost the entire section, was the headline PI CATCHES HOLLYWOOD SLASHER. Beneath it was a photo of Alicia speaking with the police up on the hillside, shortly after they'd come and arrested Bodges.

She was stunned; she remembered the newspeople arriving, but she didn't realize they'd taken a picture of her. She felt embarrassed about having her picture on the front page of the *L.A. Times,* for everyone to see. At the same time, she was ecstatic that she was on the front page of the *L.A. Times, for everyone to see!*

She bought all the papers in the box and piled them into her car, wondering if she had enough, then wondering what the heck she was going to do with all of them.

With the morning sun rising behind her, she headed toward Nikki's place in Venice. Nikki was supposed to have returned last night from that week-long swimsuit shoot in Miami. Even though Alicia was exhausted, she wanted to see her sister, show her the newspaper. Whenever something good, or bad, happened in her life, Nikki was the only person she sought out.

She was sure her sister would be up by now. Nicole ran along the boardwalk every morning at sunrise, then did yoga on the beach. She had an entire routine that kept her looking and feeling young. She was one of those people who always did the "healthy" thing, who got plenty of sleep and watched what she ate, and her lifestyle worked for her. At thirty-nine, she still had a thriving modeling career that was beginning to get her jobs as an actress. In two industries that favored women half her age, Nicole consistently earned a good living. She was always trying to get Alicia to take better care of herself, to work out, to eat properly, to pay more attention to defeating the aging process. Always looking out for her kid sister.

But appearance didn't matter as much to Alicia as it did to Nikki, who made her living by the way she looked. At least that was what Alicia had told herself until Steve told her she wasn't young and pretty enough. Now she couldn't wipe away the worry that she was letting herself go and needed to do something about it.

She looked down at her picture in the newspaper. She did look old and weathered. Well, that was a bit of an exaggeration, but she didn't look stunning, the way Nikki did in her photos. She never had. Only now it mattered to her. Perhaps Nikki could help her fix that.

She looked at the clock on the dashboard: 7:31. Nicole was probably done with her exercise routine by now, and the two of them could go out for breakfast. It might be a good day to start eating healthy. Nicole knew all the good restaurants for fruit and tofu.

As she got off the Santa Monica Freeway, Alicia picked up her cell phone and dialed Nicole's number. She was only ten minutes away. Maybe Nicole could meet her downstairs. Alicia didn't feel like going all the way up to Nikki's condo on the sixteenth floor just to come right back down again.

Nicole answered on the second ring. "Hello." Her voice was soft and unsteady, as if the phone had awakened her. That was strange. Even when Nicole traveled, she never missed her workout. She must have gotten in late last night. Maybe her plane was delayed.

"Hey, have you seen the front page of the paper this morning?" Alicia asked, sure Nikki hadn't.

"They don't want me," Nicole said, her voice a low murmur. She sounded hung over, but Alicia knew that Nicole didn't drink, not even wine with dinner. It wasn't part of her healthy lifestyle. So why did she sound so bad?

"Who doesn't want you?" Alicia asked.

"They said they wanted someone younger."

Alicia realized Nicole was talking about some acting or modeling job she'd been up for. She'd lost jobs before; it was the nature of the business. But she'd never taken it this hard before. It must have been a really important role to her.

"Come on, Nikki," Alicia said. "There'll be others. You know that. Let's go get some breakfast and talk about it."

"No, there won't be other roles," Nicole said. "Not good ones. Not like this. They're right. I'm too old."

"What are you talking about? No, you're not. For goodness' sake, you just came back from modeling bikinis in Florida. People who are too old don't get paid to do that. Okay?"

"You don't know . . ."

"I know that whoever didn't give you this other job because you're supposedly too old is an idiot, plain and simple. Now come on, Nikki. Snap out of it."

The phone went dead—Nicole had hung up.

Alicia sighed, frustrated. This wasn't like Nikki at all. She had always been the Rock of Gibraltar; she had always been the one who comforted Alicia, not the other way around; she had always been the one who'd said not to let other people's impressions of you rule your life. Why the sudden change this morning?

Alicia was already in Venice Beach, a couple of blocks from Nikki's condo. She made up her mind that she was going over there and finding out what was wrong with her sister. She dialed Nikki's number again. This time the answering machine picked up. Alicia decided that telling Nikki to snap out of it wasn't a very empathetic approach. Nicole would definitely get over this, but perhaps she needed a little TLC this morning.

After the beep Alicia said, "Nikki, pick up the phone, okay? Listen, I'm sorry. I know it sucks, what happened. And I know it's important to you. But I also know you'll get more roles. Listen, you're a beautiful woman."

Alicia rounded the corner and stopped in front of Nicole's building. Nikki still hadn't picked up the phone.

"Listen, I'm right outside," she said, glancing up toward Nikki's unit on the sixteenth floor. "I'm going to count to ten. If you don't pick up the phone by the time I get to ten, I'm going to—"

Just then she noticed Nicole walk out onto the balcony. She was wearing a white bathrobe that fluttered in the breeze.

"Nikki, I see you," Alicia said. "I'm down below. See my car?"

Nikki stepped to the railing and stared out toward the Pacific Ocean in the distance.

"No, down in the parking lot," Alicia said. "Can you hear me out there?"

Nicole didn't move, and didn't look down either.

"Listen, Nikki, I don't know if you can hear me or not, but I'm coming up there right now and—"

Before she could finish, she saw Nikki lean forward. It seemed to happen in slow motion. Nikki's feet left the balcony, her body folded over the railing, her head went down. Alicia suddenly realized what was happening.

"*No!*" she screamed as Nicole rolled over the railing and plummeted toward the parking lot, the white robe falling off her naked body. "*Nooooo!*"

2

"WOULD YOU LIKE wine with your dinner?" the flight attendant asked.

"Just coffee," Paul said.

He thought he caught her looking at him a little funny. She must have figured it out by now. This was the third time he'd declined a drink. A forty-three-year-old man, drinking coffee and Pepsi the whole flight. How could she not know? What's the point of flying first class if you're not going to take advantage of the free drinks? But first class hadn't been his idea. And as for drinks, he hadn't taken as much as a sip in twenty-six months and he didn't plan to start now. Sure, the cravings were still there. He wondered if they'd ever go away. Whether they did or not, drinking had cost him too much already; he was not going to let it ruin what was left of his life, ruin his chances of putting his family back together again.

When the flight attendant walked away, Paul Tobin reached for his silverware. He paused a moment, holding out his hands. This was a ritual he performed several times a day. *Still steady.* He hadn't lost it. He picked up the knife and held it as though he were going to make an incision. Not a flicker of unsteadiness. As bad as the drinking had gotten, he still had what it took to operate. And that was important to him, even though he doubted he'd ever perform surgery again. His license had been revoked and his chances of getting it reinstated were about as good as the chances of the cravings going away. But he had defined himself for so long by his profession, he needed to know that he still had what it took, that he still had value. So he continued to check the steadiness of his hands, and continued to cling to hope.

Just as he clung to the possibility of reuniting with Beth and the kids.

When the plane landed in Key West, Paul felt a disorienting sense of being out of place. He was wearing a gray suit, and his complexion showed that he was from New York and spent far too much time indoors. All around him were T-shirts, shorts, sandals, skin-destroying tans. Jimmy Buffett wanna-bes. *What on earth am I doing here?*

He was here because Beth's brother, Ethan Granier, had sent him a ticket and had convinced him that it would be worth his while to make the trip. Ethan had refused to explain any further. Paul wasn't the type of person who got into things without knowing exactly what he was getting into, but he trusted Ethan. And he felt he owed him. Not only had they been on staff together at Manhattan General, but Ethan had defended Paul when the incident occurred. He'd been the only member of the hospital's board who voted not to fire Paul. He'd even resigned in protest to the hospital's action against Paul. He had been a good friend as well as a brother-in-law.

Now they hadn't spoken in almost three years. Ethan was Beth's brother, so it was only right that his loyalty remain with her. And Ethan had his own tragedy to deal with. His son, Zachary, was afflicted with a form of progeria called Hutchinson-Gilford syndrome, a rare genetic disorder that caused his body to age prematurely. He had been eleven when Paul saw him last, but had looked like a sixty-year-old man, with a withered face, hunched body, no hair. It was a horrible, devastating illness with no known cure. To make matters worse, Ethan's wife hadn't been able to cope. She'd left him. Ethan had committed his life to his son.

Paul had kept his distance over the last three years, so why the phone call now? Why did Ethan insist Paul make the trip to Florida?

Paul had a notion why. Ethan knew that Paul had never wanted the divorce. Beth was the one who filed. Maybe Ethan wanted to help them get back together. But why? Paul couldn't imagine. Unless Ethan knew that Beth was finally willing to consider a reconciliation. That hope, almost too good to believe, was what had gotten Paul on the plane to Florida.

Beth and the kids had moved to Palm Beach a year ago, into her parents' house. Her parents were living in Europe somewhere. For Paul to make a reconciliation happen, he'd need to be in Florida, too. Ethan must have understood that, and he must have understood that Paul's financial situation made the trip a hardship. Which explained the airline ticket he'd sent and the offer of a place to stay. If Ethan was this willing to help, Paul was certainly willing to try. He wanted Beth to take him back. He would do whatever was necessary to make that happen.

The walk to baggage claim left Paul winded. He stopped to catch his breath and see if Ethan was waiting for him. When he'd quit drinking, he'd replaced that bad habit with bad eating habits. And he had no time to work out anymore. Since he could no longer practice medicine, he had to scramble to make a living. Rent in New York was astronomical. He owed a small fortune in legal bills from the incident at the hospital. His malpractice insurance had paid the settlement with the patient's family, but he had to pay the lawyer who had represented him before the state licensing board. Add to all that his child support payments, which he would sell his kidney to pay if he had to, and his alimony. He worked practically every waking hour. Between the two biology classes at Long Island Community College and the research he did for medical writers, he had no time and even less initiative to take better care of himself.

"Paul!" Ethan said, coming over. Paul realized that he had seen Ethan standing over there but hadn't recognized him. Ethan was tanned and athletic looking in his khaki pants and white polo shirt. He looked much younger than fifty-one, younger than Paul remembered him. Living in Florida seemed to have taken ten years off his looks.

"How are you?" Ethan said, pumping Paul's hand. "I'm really glad you came."

"It's good to see you again," Paul said.

The plastic surgeon in him secretly scrutinized Ethan's face. His skin definitely looked younger, more elastic, less wrinkled. Considering the deep tan he had, that didn't make sense. The sun should have had the opposite effect. But Paul couldn't see any signs that Ethan had undergone surgery, and the improvement was deeper than just Ethan's skin. Ethan had a youthful look in his eyes, a vital energy about him.

"Life down here certainly seems to agree with you," Paul said. "Somewhere along the way, you became younger than me. How did that happen?"

Ethan chuckled. "Actually, that's kind of the reason I asked you to come here," he said.

"What do you mean?"

"I'll explain on the drive. Where're your bags?" Paul reached for his suitcase going around on the belt. Ethan grabbed it and started walking. "Come on."

"Where are we going?"

"The fountain of youth."

3

THEY LEFT KEY West and drove across a few smaller keys, catching up a bit on how each of them was doing. Paul lied and said, "Fine." He didn't ask about Zack. He figured Ethan would say something if he wanted to talk about him. Paul did ask how Beth was doing.

"She's in Palm Beach, you know," Ethan said.

"Yes, I know. How long does it take to drive up there from here?" Paul asked.

"About three or four hours. Why? You thinking about going?" Ethan seemed a bit surprised. It didn't sound like that was the reason he had invited him down here. So if that wasn't the reason, what was?

"I don't know," Paul said. He wanted to know how Ethan thought Beth would react, but he didn't want to come right out and ask. "If there's time, maybe."

"Do you fish?" Ethan asked. "The spearfishing is great here."

"Spearfishing?" Paul laughed. "When did you become Lloyd Bridges?"

Ethan chuckled. "We'll go tomorrow. You'll have a blast, you'll see."

Paul was a little confused. "That's not why you brought me here, is it?" he asked. "To go spearfishing?"

Ethan just laughed again. Paul didn't think that was why he was here.

Ethan turned onto a bridge that stretched above a couple hundred yards of turquoise water. It was low, the roadway almost sitting in the surf. Ahead of them, palm trees waved from the island. The sun began to set behind it, coloring the sky in a dazzling palate of reds and oranges. Pelicans skimmed above a wave. A sign was carved into a large block of coral: DE LEON CENTER.

"I got a great deal on the lease," Ethan said.

"Lease for what?"

"This island. Coral Key."

"You leased the whole island?"

Ethan laughed. "It isn't *that* big."

They crossed the bridge and drove down a narrow road beneath a canopy of tropical growth. Paul realized that the island really wasn't that big. From some points on the road, when the brush thinned, he could see beach on either side. Still, it was large enough to have its own name. What on earth was Ethan doing with an island? Was his practice down here *that* successful? Was there that much of a call for hematologists?

"There used to be a Club Med–type place here," Ethan told Paul. "Until Andrew."

Paul didn't quite understand. "Who's Andrew?"

"Andrew is a what, not a who. It was a hurricane that came through several years ago. Did a lot of damage down here. Especially this key. The resort decided it was too expensive to rebuild and reopen. But they still had more than twenty years on their lease. They just wanted to cut their losses. This was perfect for what I needed. I got it for a song."

"What do you need an island for?" Paul asked. It sounded like a strange question to ask, but it was also the obvious one. As was his next question. "And what is the De Leon Center?"

"De Leon is my clinic," Ethan said. "And it's also the reason I asked you here."

Ethan parked in front of a small building with a portico that looked like the entrance to a tropical resort. The lobby, too, looked more like a vacation spot than a medical center. To one side were what used to be a gift shop and a beauty salon. The signs remained but the shops were empty. Some rattan chairs and couches were arranged on the other side. In the center, behind the former hotel front desk, a middle-aged woman sat, speaking to someone on the phone about available appointments in November. A small placard in front of her said RECEPTION. After she hung up, Ethan introduced her as Annie Parson.

"It's so nice to meet you," she said with the sweetest southern accent.

"Annie does all of our scheduling, provides information to prospective patients, and even takes care of the billing. I don't know what I'd do without her."

"Go out of business, probably," she said, teasing him.

Ethan laughed. "Probably."

"So, y'all know each other from New York City, *rot*?" she asked Paul. It took him a moment to figure out that "rot" meant "right."

"Yes, that's right," he said.

"Dr. Tobin is the best plastic surgeon in Manhattan," Ethan said.

"And Dr. Granier is the best exaggerator."

They chatted with Annie for a few minutes. She asked about New York like it was a different country. She was fascinated. She volunteered that she had never even left Florida but she hoped someday to visit New York, second in line after the trip to Graceland.

Paul liked her right off.

They left the reception area and continued through the lobby. Paul noticed a swimming pool out back and the beach beyond that. A handful of guests or patients or whatever they were called—the strange mixture of impressions that this place elicited made it confusing—were lounging in bathing suits, taking in the sunset.

"Some clinic," he said.

"I meant for it not to look like a medical facility," Ethan said. "I wanted it to have the feel of a vacation resort. I want De Leon's patients to feel relaxed and at ease while they're here. I think that's part of the reason they come."

"And what is the reason they come?" Paul asked.

Ethan's specialty was hematology. Paul couldn't imagine how that applied to this place. "What kind of clinic is this?" he asked.

Ethan stepped a little closer to Paul. He spoke this next word as though he were revealing some divine revelation. "Rejuvenation," he whispered. "De Leon makes its patients young again."

Ethan led Paul down a pathway of unusual coral stone that wound past a dozen or so bungalows.

"These are where patients stay when they come here for therapy," he explained. Paul noticed that each bungalow had a view of the beach.

"There was a ten-story hotel building," Ethan said, "but it was too severely damaged in the hurricane to repair. I had to tear it down." He pointed to a small building. "That was one of the resort's nightclubs," he said. "Now it's De Leon's medical building."

Ethan took Paul inside. Here, nothing of the nightclub remained; it could have been any small medical practice on Long Island. A reception desk, several examination rooms, some offices. "Patients come here for their exams and blood work," Ethan said. "And this is where I prescribe the therapies."

It was four in the afternoon. The medical assistant and nurse were gone. Most of the patients were out on the beach or by the pool. "The workdays here are short," Ethan explained. "Nothing like MGH—ten to twelve hours a day, remember?"

"On a good day," Paul said.

"There's a little more sanity here."

"What kind of therapies do you prescribe?" Paul asked. He still didn't understand what Ethan meant by making "its patients young again."

"Well, basically, De Leon's philosophy involves a three-tier approach to antiaging therapies," he told Paul. "The first tier is hormonal. Every patient who comes here is assessed to determine where their deficiencies lie. Through the use of antiaging hormonal therapies—such as human growth hormone, testosterone, estrogen to a lesser extent, DHEA, melatonin, and others—we can literally halt the body's natural aging process and in many cases actually reverse it."

Ethan's explanation was a bit anticlimactic. "That's nothing new," Paul said, skeptical. "Those things have been used for years as so-called antiaging drugs. I know hGH and testosterone can reduce body fat and add muscle mass. And maybe they can offer some minor benefit to skin elasticity, but that's about it. Hormone therapy can't *reverse* aging. It's just not possible."

"In the right doses and combinations, it certainly is possible. This is much more than just growth hormone and testosterone. This is a complete balanced and holistic approach, nothing like what's been done in the past. And it does work."

Paul sighed, not buying the hype. He was surprised that Ethan was even trying to sell it.

Ethan could see that he wasn't convinced. "Look," he said, "you asked me at the airport why I looked so much younger than you remembered. Well, what we're doing here is the reason why. It's the therapies we provide. I've been on the regimen myself. They really do work, Paul. I'm living proof."

Paul was still skeptical, but he could not deny that Ethan did look younger. Was it possible that there was some truth to what he was claiming? It seemed improbable. Aging was a part of life. It simply could not be stopped. People got older, their bodies deteriorated, period.

"You look great, but hormones don't do what you're claiming, Ethan," Paul said.

"I told you, it's a lot more complicated than just prescribing hormones. It has to be done in a certain way. Look, I didn't just jump into this. I've done a lot of research into this, because of Zack. I've spent my entire career since he was born researching aging. Believe me, Paul, I know what works."

"You've got Zack on this program?" Paul asked.

"Zachary is the reason I developed this program in the first place. Yes, he's on it. And he's doing well."

If he was still alive, then he was doing well. Life expectancy for children suffering his affliction was extremely short. He should have been dead by now. Maybe there was something to what Ethan was saying, after all.

"What we're doing is different from those other so-called antiaging clinics," Ethan said. "They rely mainly on human growth hormone. Hormone therapy is a part of what we do, but what we're advocating is complete lifestyle change. Remember I said it was a three-tier approach? Hormone therapy is just one tier. Come on, I'll show you the rest."

Paul followed Ethan outside to another building. His skepticism was beginning to weaken—especially if Ethan was telling the truth about Zack. Paul was curious to see Zack, and curious what else Ethan was doing here to make people younger.

He was also curious why Ethan was showing all this to him, trying to sell him on the place. Was he looking for an investor? If so, he was in for a big disappointment. Investors had to have money. All Paul had was debts.

"This used to be the resort's recreation building," Ethan said, taking Paul inside. The air-conditioning was strong in here, masking the faint odor of sweat. It still resembled a recreation building after you got past the small waiting room. Most of the building was a large studio filled with exercise equipment.

"We got rid of the Ping-Pong tables and video games," Ethan said. "Now it's our EPN center."

"What's that?" Paul asked.

"Exercise physiology and nutrition. This is where patients come for diet and exercise assessment and education."

Along the back wall was a treadmill, and running on it was a tall, athletic woman a few years older than Paul. She wore spandex shorts and a sports bra, leaving much of her body uncovered, a body rippling with long cords of muscle. Electrodes were attached to her chest. Over her mouth and nose was a mask, connected by a tube to a computer console. She glanced at Ethan and Paul, checked her watch, then gestured for them to wait one minute.

"That's Karla Weiss," Ethan said. "She's our exercise physiologist and nutritionist. She's also training for the 2004 Olympics."

"What Olympics?" Paul asked. She was much too old to be competing with the world's best athletes.

Ethan smiled. "*The* Olympics."

Paul leaned close to him and whispered, "She has to be fifty years old."

"She's younger than that, but not much," Ethan whispered. "I told you, what we're doing here is nothing short of incredible. Karla's been on the program since the beginning. Take a good look at her and tell me antiaging doesn't work."

Ethan was bragging. But if what he was saying was true, maybe he had good reason to brag. Unless she was competing in chess or archery.

"Anyway," Ethan said, gesturing around the room, "this is where we test our patients for strength and body composition, assess their diets, determine where they could stand improvement. Then we put them on an individually tailored program of exercise and nutrition. Diet and physical activity play a major role in maintaining a youthful body. It's an important complement to the hormone therapy program. The second tier of our approach here at De Leon."

Karla finished running. She removed the monitoring devices attached to her body, grabbed a towel, and came over.

"Karla, I'd like you to meet Dr. Paul Tobin," Ethan said.

"Nice to meet you."

Karla had a slight German accent and a stiff, powerful handshake. Up close, watching her wipe the perspiration off her biceps, Paul was impressed by her physique. Fitness-wise, she was perfect. But the plastic surgeon in him made him focus on her flaws. Her breasts were very small, barely noticeable with all the muscle on her chest plate. She also had two scars on her left cheek, what looked like lacerations from many years ago. She had good cheekbones and a wide jaw, a pretty face if it weren't for those scars and the wrinkles around her eyes. But the steel gray eyes themselves were difficult to look away from, and commanded attention.

"Ethan tells me you're training to compete in the Olympics," he said. "That's incredible. What's your event?" He was sure it wasn't one of the heavy physical competitions.

"Swimming," she said. That surprised him.

"She's going to compete in five events," Ethan said. "She'll make history, you'll see. The oldest woman to win five gold medals. The oldest woman ever to win any medal in swimming. The first woman to—"

"Ethan, Ethan," she said, stopping him. "Please. No more." She laughed and turned to Paul. "Meet my publicist, ya? He has me already on the podium, accepting the medals, and the Olympics are still two years away."

"Hey, I think it's great that you're doing it," Paul said, impressed. "Now I can say I know someone who's going to be in the Olympics."

"You don't know me yet," she said with a coy grin.

He laughed, but he didn't know if she was flirting with him.

"And he won't get to know you right now," Ethan said. "Maybe some other time. Right now I'm sure he'd like to get settled in." He looked at Paul and said, "And then we have some business we need to take care of."

When they got outside, Ethan pointed across the clinic grounds and said, "My house is just over there." He started walking in that direction, but Paul grasped his arm and stopped him. Ethan had brought him here for a reason. He was interested in finding out what it was.

"Ethan. I think it's time you told me why you asked me to come here."

"You mean you haven't figured it out yet? I told you there was a three-tier approach at De Leon. You've seen the first two."

"Yeah, so?"

"Aren't you curious about the third tier?"

He was more curious why Ethan had brought him here. But he humored him. "Okay, what's the third tier?"

"*You* are."

4

ETHAN'S HOUSE WAS Spanish-style and spacious, built on a jetty overlooking the ocean. The setting sun turned the water a deep purple. Lights from distant fishing boats sparkled on the horizon.

Ethan brought Paul inside. The house was silent and seemed empty—and strange, somehow. Paul felt uncomfortable. As he followed Ethan down a hallway and past the living room, he detected a woman's touch in the house. The vase of fresh flowers near one window. A fluffy afghan placed carefully over the back of a chair. The hint of perfume.

Had Ethan remarried? It seemed unlikely—not the Ethan Paul remembered from three years ago. Ethan hadn't gotten over his wife's leaving, and it had seemed he never would. Not that he loved her anymore. It was obvious he didn't; he hated her for abandoning Zachary. But it was just as obvious that he would never again let anyone that close—not to him and especially not to Zachary. Besides, from what Paul remembered, all Ethan's waking hours were devoted to his son and to his work. He didn't have time for a relationship.

Maybe that's why Paul still felt a connection to him, even though they hadn't spoken in years. Both of them had suffered when their marriages ended, unable to move on with their lives. And even though Paul wanted to put his marriage back together and Ethan never wanted to see his ex-wife again, the two of them really weren't so different. They both had empty, lonely lives.

"I have something for you," Ethan said. He gestured for Paul to follow him into his study.

Before they reached the room, Paul heard a slow clacking sound. He turned and saw Zachary struggling through the doorway of his bedroom. Braces supported his knees, and he leaned on two crutches. When he walked, he dragged one foot along the tile floor and swung the other in an awkward arc. His eyes squinted in pain with every movement.

The sight was shocking, even though Paul had seen him before: a child of fourteen, with all of his hair gone, his face withered, his body bent as though he were a grandfather. The smile he gave to his father showed that most of his teeth were gone. It was impossible not to pity him.

"Zack, what are you doing up?" Ethan said.

"I waited for you, Dad." His voice was as thin as his body, but still there was incredible will behind it.

A short, thin Hispanic woman came out of the room behind Zack and said, "Sorry, Dr. Granier. He insisted on staying up."

"That's okay, Carmen." Ethan smiled at Zack and said, "You didn't have to stay up. You know I would've come in later."

"I wanted to wait." Zack looked proud of himself for having succeeded at staying awake.

He noticed Paul now and grinned. "Uncle Paul!"

He struggled to come toward Paul, wincing with each step. Paul hurried over, wanting to save Zack the pain. In an awkward moment, Paul started to extend his hand, but Zack leaned into him and wrapped his arms around him, making it obvious that a hug was the only appropriate greeting. When Paul put his arms around his nephew, he felt just how gaunt and fragile Zachary was, as though if held too tightly, his bones would snap.

Paul hadn't seen Zack in three years, and though Ethan had told him that Zack was doing well on the program, Paul was still surprised. Zack's condition had worsened, but not nearly as much as Paul would have expected. Whatever therapy Ethan had developed for Zack was, to a certain extent, working. He was slowing the progression of the illness, keeping his son alive. Maybe there was something to his antiaging therapies.

Now Paul's interest was stirred.

"How's it going, champ?" Paul said.

"I went on a Jet Ski yesterday!" Zack said.

"You did?"

"Dad took me!"

Paul was surprised, considering how fragile Zack was. Ethan must have noticed this in Paul's face because he said, "Just in the lagoon."

"We went real fast!" Zack said.

"That's great!" Paul glanced at Ethan, who was watching his son with such love that it touched Paul's heart. A new energy seemed to fill Ethan now that Zack was present. He gently scooped Zack up and whirled him around, giving him a ride in the air, carefully yet playfully. Zack giggled, enthralled.

"I know what you were waiting for," Ethan said. "Your good-night flight. Weren't you?"

Zack was in seventh heaven as Ethan flew him around the room. Finally Ethan said, "Time for a landing in bed, young man. Say good night to Uncle Paul."

"Good night, Uncle Paul."

"Good night."

Ethan whisked Zack off down the hall. Carmen collected Zack's crutches and followed. Before ducking into the bedroom, Ethan glanced back at Paul and gestured toward the study. "Go on in. I'll be right there."

Ethan came in a few minutes later. Paul was staring out the window, thoughts of Zachary still in his head. Seeing Ethan's son reminded him of his own sons, Kenny and Pete. He hadn't seen them in eight months, since their last trip up north. He had tried to convince Beth to let him come down to Palm Beach to see them, but she'd refused. Visitation had to be on her terms, at her discretion, and she made it difficult. But she had the court system backing her. The judge had been quick to limit Paul's access when he had the drinking problem, but slow to lift it now that Paul was sober. Beth was very protective of their sons. Maybe that was why she'd moved down here. She, like the judge, was reluctant to accept that Paul had turned his life around. But he intended to prove it to her. He intended to be an important part of his sons' lives again.

"This is for you," Ethan said. He went straight to his desk and handed Paul a document from the top drawer.

"What's that?" Paul asked.

"Read it."

Paul peered down at the paper. He had read no more than a few words when he stopped, shocked. He couldn't believe what he was looking at. For several seconds he just stared at the forms of the letters on the page. He knew exactly what it was, but he still couldn't understand how this could be so.

Finally he looked up at Ethan. Before he could ask, Ethan answered. "Yes," he said. "It's on the level."

"But . . . I don't understand. How?"

"One of my patients is an attorney who represents a gentleman who happens to serve on the state's licensing board here in Florida. The attorney spoke with him. I spoke with him myself. It took some lobbying, a good deal of explaining, and even a bit of arm twisting, but in the end we made a strong case. We got them to approve it."

"But . . . why?" Paul still had difficulty getting the words out. He never would have expected this—*ever.* "Why did you do this for me?" he asked Ethan.

"It was the right thing to do," Ethan said, certainty in his voice.

He gestured toward the sofa, and he and Paul sat.

"Listen," he said. "We both know that you never should have lost your license in the first place. That was a travesty. What happened to Linda Wilkenson wasn't your fault. The drinking, well . . . that's a separate matter altogether. You've paid for that. God knows you've paid. And I know from talking to Beth that you've cleaned up your act."

"She said that?" Paul asked. That would be a huge breakthrough in winning her back.

"She said you've been trying. She's not a hundred percent convinced you've stopped drinking completely."

Ethan's words hit like a blow to the gut, deflating his hope.

"But I know there's no such thing as a little bit sober," Ethan said. "I know it's all or nothing. You've come a long way in that respect. But the Wilkenson thing, that was handled wrongly from the beginning. The hospital was wrong for not standing up for you. The licensing board in New York was wrong for revoking your license. The lawsuit that Wilkenson's family brought was wrong. All of it was wrong. I just think it's about time something was done to rectify that. This, I hope, is a start."

Paul just stared down at his medical license, still at a loss for words. "I don't know what to say," he murmured.

"Then let me do the talking," Ethan said. He stood up and walked to a cabinet in the corner of the room. When he opened it, Paul saw that it was filled with liquor. "Can I fix you a—" Ethan started to say, then stopped himself, looking embarrassed.

"It's all right," Paul said. "You can drink. It doesn't bother me. And I'm not going to start drinking again, don't worry."

Ethan hesitated but then poured himself a glass of scotch. "I've got soda, some juice . . ."

"Nothing, thanks."

Ethan turned and looked across the room at Paul. "Remember I told you that you were the third tier of what I want to offer patients here at De Leon? I meant it. I want you to join the staff as our plastic surgeon."

Paul was astonished, not just that he was being offered a job, but that Ethan had this much faith in him.

"I want this to be a one-stop, full-service antiaging center," Ethan said. "I've got the medical side covered. Karla has the nutrition and exercise. I need a surgeon to repair the outward signs of aging. No matter how good the therapies we offer are, they can't get rid of the deep wrinkles, the droopy eyelids, the imperfect noses, and the rest of it. Some of our patients need surgery. I want to offer that. I need a good surgeon, someone who can do the job, someone I can trust. I want you, Paul."

Paul was overwhelmed. This was all coming at him so fast. "I haven't operated in more than three years," he said, his confidence a little shaky.

"I know you can still do it," Ethan said. "I saw you work for many years. I know you still have it. This is a chance to get back to doing what you do best, immediately. The compensation is going to be well worth it for you, I guarantee it. I know you're in a little trouble financially at the moment. This will get you out of that quickly."

Ethan came over to the sofa and sat beside Paul. Paul could smell the scotch on his breath. For an instant he felt the cravings, but he suppressed them as he had done so many times before.

"And it will give you a chance to be close to Beth and the kids," Ethan said. "Palm Beach isn't that far away. If she sees you operating again, making a new start, it's bound to change the way she thinks. This is a great opportunity for you, Paul. Don't pass it up, okay? You need this. And I need you. It's as simple as that."

Paul stared at him, knowing that everything he was saying was true, but feeling caught in a tide. It still seemed unreal. This could not be happening. Not this easily.

"I don't know what to say," he said.

"Just say yes," Ethan told him.

Paul considered it for only a moment. An opportunity to be a surgeon again. And the chance to be close to Beth and the kids. The answer was pretty obvious.

"You just hired yourself a surgeon."

5

STEVE POLASKI PARKED the car and shut off the engine. Alicia started to open the door but Steve reached across and stopped her.

"Wait. Why don't you let me do this?" he said.

"No. I want to know the results of the autopsy." Alicia stared across the parking lot at the medical examiner's building. Even though she had been in there a few times before, the thought of going in today made her uneasy. In the past she had gone in as an investigator, to find out about people she didn't know. This was different. This was Nikki.

"It's okay not to go," Steve whispered.

"I said I want to go."

She started to get out but he grasped her arm again. "Alicia," he said, staring sympathetically at her. "Look, this is me here. You don't have to be the tough guy around me. It's okay to let your emotions go."

Alicia felt a sudden rush of anger. She didn't like Steve challenging her this way, telling her how she was supposed to act, what she was supposed to feel.

"She's my sister," she said. "I want to know what happened."

"You know already," he said.

"No, I don't. I don't know *why*."

"The autopsy's not going to tell you that."

"We haven't even seen the results and you're already deciding that." She was getting angrier at him. Why was he doing this to her? "A lot of help you're going to be," she said.

Steve let out a breath of frustration. "Okay, you win. If it's easier for you to focus on the details of the autopsy, rather than on what you're feeling about what happened, who am I to interfere."

She glared at him, really pissed now. "Listen to me, Steve. I don't need an amateur psychologist. If that's why you came—"

"I came because I'm your friend."

"Then act like one and stop giving me such a hard time. Or let me go alone."

"Okay. I'm sorry," he said.

She was still angry—because Steve was probably right. She hadn't let herself cry since Nikki's death. She hadn't even talked about it with anyone, talked about how she felt, and she certainly wasn't going to start now, not with him or anyone else. The only person she opened up to about things like this was Nikki—and Nikki was gone.

She got out of the car and headed into the building. Steve hurried behind.

Alicia hoped that by coming here she could make sense of all this. Her head was swirling with confusion. Why would Nicole kill herself? That made no sense at all. Nikki was a survivor. When their parents died, Nikki was the one who kept Alicia going. Nikki was the one who never lost the will to live. When they struggled just to keep a roof over their heads and some food on the table, Nikki was the one who wouldn't give up, the one who did everything in her power to keep the social workers from taking Alicia. That's how she'd gotten into modeling. Her looks were the one sure way for them to have enough money to keep the family together, to provide a good life.

No, Nicole was not the kind of person to kill herself. And that was what made this so difficult for Alicia to accept. This wasn't right. An illness, she might be able to understand. But this . . . No.

In the back of her head, she clung desperately to the

hope that there had been a big mistake and Nikki hadn't really killed herself, she wasn't really dead. She'd come back soon and life could resume as before.

Reality hit her hard as she and Steve took seats in Dr. Susan Polk's office. She knew the medical examiner fairly well, having conferred with her extensively on a case involving the hazing death of a fraternity pledge at Cal State. They'd even had lunch together a couple of times. Alicia liked her. She was professional, unemotional, all business.

Today, Alicia didn't see an acquaintance across the desk. She saw a doctor, someone who could provide details, an explanation. Susan seemed to realize that. She opened the file on the desk in front of her.

"I'm very sorry about your sister, Alicia," she said.

Alicia nodded. She didn't want to talk about Nicole that way, to deal with condolences. That was too difficult. As with her parents' death, she needed to focus instead on the black and white, on the details, on the facts. Leave the emotional aspects alone. No benefit came from concentrating on that.

Steve was right about her repressing the hurt, the sadness. But that was the only way she could get through this. That's what she had to do. Concentrate on the autopsy report, on the details.

"What did you find in the autopsy?" she asked Susan, and braced herself.

"Nicole's death was caused by massive trauma from the fall," Susan said.

The image of Nikki plummeting from her balcony to the pavement below flashed into Alicia's head. She winced and tried to force that video from her brain. *Focus on the cause, on the reason.* That way she wouldn't have to keep seeing the death replayed in her head, over and over.

"What else did the autopsy show?" she asked. "Was there any alcohol in Nicole's system?" She needed to answer the *Why?* question. Alcohol seemed like the only rational explanation.

"Her tox screen was negative for alcohol, and for narcotics and opiates," Susan said.

Alicia felt let down. She had been hoping for an easy explanation—maybe Nikki had been intoxicated and didn't know what she was doing. But now Susan had eliminated that possibility.

"Was there any indication of her having taken any prescription drugs, medications, anything like that?" Alicia asked. Nicole had sounded deeply depressed. Could she have been on some medication that caused her to react this way?

"I did find one odd thing," Susan said carefully. "There were remnants of needle marks on both of Nicole's thighs."

Alicia was stunned and confused. She couldn't bring herself to ask the obvious next question, so Steve did it for her.

"You mean from drugs, heroin, something like that?"

"No. Like I said, the tox screen showed no opiates. Besides, heroin is injected into veins. This was into muscle tissue. Nicole wasn't a diabetic, was she?" Susan asked Alicia.

"No," Alicia said.

"Was she on any kind of hormone therapy?"

"I don't know." Nicole never really discussed her medical problems. Having been thrust into the role of de facto parent at such a young age, Nikki had always kept whatever problems she had to herself, never wanting to worry Alicia.

But could there have been something that had contributed to Nicole's suicide?

"You mean estrogen replacement therapy or birth control pills, that type of thing?" Alicia asked, trying to think of what hormones Nikki might have taken.

"Not exactly, no."

"Then what exactly? You found hormones in her blood, is that it? What did you find?"

"Well, it's not that straightforward. The problem is, hormones are a tricky thing. The levels differ from individual to individual. One person could have very high levels of a particular hormone and another person very low levels of the same hormone, and that could be normal for both of them. I don't know what Nicole's normal levels were. I can tell you that for the most part, her levels fell within the normal range for a woman her age, but there were some unusual results."

"Unusual in what way?"

"Well, for instance, her testosterone seemed rather high."

"What does that mean?"

"I don't know that it means anything," Susan admitted. "I'm going to have to check with her doctor to find out if your sister had had any tests done in the past. That would give me some results to compare these against. Do you know who her doctor was?"

"No. But I'll find out and let you know."

Susan nodded, then looked down at the file again. Alicia could tell that she had something else on her mind. "What is it?" she asked Susan.

"Do you know if Nicole had cancer, either recently or in the past?"

Again Alicia was stunned. "*Cancer?* No. Why? What did you find?"

Susan took an X ray out of the file and showed it to Alicia. Alicia didn't know what it was at first—just that it was part of Nikki—but Susan pointed to a dark mark on the X ray. "This is a scar on her right pelvic bone, indicative of a possible bone marrow transplant."

"A bone marrow transplant?" Alicia was sure that if Nikki had undergone such a procedure, she would have said something. That's serious. Cancer wasn't something Nikki would have been able to hide from her—was it?

"How old is the scar?" Alicia asked, staring at the spot. "Can you tell?"

"It was relatively recent—a few months."

"It has to be from something else," Alicia said. "I would have known if Nikki had cancer." She had to believe she would have known. She couldn't have been so wrapped up in her own life not to have noticed something like that. What kind of sister would that make her? No, she would have known. She couldn't bear to think of Nikki going through something like that alone.

"What else could it be from?" she asked Susan.

"I don't want to try to guess," Susan said. "I think this is something else I can address with her doctor. Perhaps there is another explanation."

"There has to be."

6

ETHAN FELT A tinge of worry, bringing Paul in, but he knew this was something he had to do in order to continue developing a treatment for Zack. He needed the money that offering cosmetic surgery would bring in. Hiring Paul was the safest way to go. Paul would be grateful for being given a second chance. He'd owe Ethan. If, somehow, he found out about Rejuvenol, his loyalty would keep him from exposing what was happening here.

Paul had gone back to New York to settle his affairs and prepare for the move to Florida. Meanwhile, Ethan was having the largest bungalow repainted and had ordered new furniture for Paul's arrival. He'd also printed up revised brochures for De Leon, featuring the newly added cosmetic surgery options, as well as changing the ads he'd been running in *Health & Beauty* magazine and *USA Today*. Karla was updating the website.

He had a pretty good idea which patients would be interested in surgery, so he made personal calls, pitching Paul's services. Everything was set for De Leon to become the full-service, one-stop antiaging center that he'd originally envisioned, the center he needed to complete the work that would save Zachary's life.

When Paul arrived three weeks later, Ethan already had several appointments scheduled. Ethan took him spearfishing the first afternoon on the island. Spearing had become an important outlet for his frustration and stress. Maybe it was the feeling of power that it gave him. Maybe it was the total concentration that it required, forcing him to forget his troubles. Whatever it was, Ethan tried to go every couple of weeks, to maintain his sanity.

This day he speared two groupers. Paul missed on all his shots. "It takes a little practice to get good at it," Ethan said.

"I'm not sure this is something I want to be good at."

They had dinner at Ethan's house that night, along with Zachary and Carmen. Later, after Ethan tucked Zack in for the night and Carmen went to her room to read, Ethan and Paul sat outside on the patio, talking at length about the various procedures they'd offer at De Leon. They settled on the financial aspects of Paul's employment, with which Paul seemed pleased. As long as De Leon made money, Paul would make money.

Then Ethan brought up a touchy subject. It needed to be mentioned. There was no easy way to do it. He just hoped Paul would be all right with it.

"Patients are going to ask you about your experience," Ethan said.

Paul nodded. Ethan saw by the troubled look on Paul's face that Paul realized where this was going and had probably thought about it himself. Paul had very high ethical standards. This was obviously something that bothered him. But Ethan needed him to cooperate if this collaboration was to be successful.

"You do have almost twenty years of experience," Ethan said. "And that is what should matter most to our patients."

"And what about the last three years?" Paul asked. "And the suspension?"

"Patients need to be at ease with their surgeon. Your skills are there. They haven't been affected by what occurred over the last three years. If I thought your abilities were at all suspect, I wouldn't have brought you here."

"I'm not going to lie to my patients," Paul said.

Ethan didn't like the way Paul worded that. That wasn't what he was asking. And his tone also worried Ethan, for this was the first test of Paul's loyalty. How far would he go to show his gratitude to Ethan for giving him his career back?

"I don't want you to lie to your patients," Ethan said. "I just don't feel that the incident in New York and the temporary suspension are things you should bring up. Patients who are concerned about such things will certainly make the effort to find out for themselves. What I've discovered that patients want more than anything else is a sense of security that comes with believing in their surgeon. I don't see any reason to take that away. You're a good surgeon, Paul. Give yourself a chance to prove it to these patients."

Paul was silent for a few moments, clearly considering what Ethan had said. Finally he said, "I want this to work out just as much as you do. Probably more. I'm not going to lie to my patients, but I'm not going to give them undue reason to worry either."

"That's all I'm asking," Ethan said.

Paul fell silent again. Something else was on his mind.

"What is it?" Ethan asked.

"I'd like to ask you something," Paul said. "A favor. Something that's very important to me."

"Go ahead, ask me."

"I want to be able to do some pro bono work. I'm not trying to make this a charitable clinic or anything like that, but I just feel I need to take on a few patients who need reconstructive surgery but don't have the financial ability to pay for it."

"The state has surgeons who do that type of thing for the indigent."

"Well, there are some people who fall through the cracks. I don't know about Florida, but in New York, the state considers most cosmetic procedures elective and won't always approve them."

"You're right. Florida is probably the same."

"Those are the people I want to work with. Like children. Deformities for children can be extremely important to their emotional and psychological development. The state might not understand that, but I do. And I'm sure you do."

Of course Ethan did. Raising Zack made him keenly aware of how traumatic it was for a child to be "different."

"You'll have to keep it to some limit," Ethan said.

"How about one per month?"

Ethan extended his hand. "I think we have a deal."

Ethan walked with Paul back to his bungalow. It was a warm September night. The air smelled of the sea. The conversation shifted away from business.

"How's Beth doing?" Paul asked. "Do you see her often?"

"Occasionally," Ethan said. "She's doing okay."

He'd known this was going to come up, and he felt uneasy discussing Beth. He wasn't sure what to tell Paul, if he should explain what was going on with her. But that was for Beth to do, not him. Still, he felt badly talking about her and keeping the truth from Paul.

"Have you spoken with her yet?" Ethan asked. "Have you told her about your coming down here?"

"Not yet. I planned on calling her once I was settled in. Probably tomorrow. You haven't told her yet, have you?"

"No. I thought you'd want to do that."

"Thanks."

"Just have patience and try to be understanding," Ethan said, not knowing what else to tell him. "She went through a lot, you know."

Paul nodded silently, guilt showing in his eyes.

"You both did," Ethan added, hoping to assuage some of that guilt. "It's been a rough three years for both of you."

"It feels like ten years," Paul said with a tired sigh.

Ethan knew it was going to be devastating when Paul found out, but hopefully with his career back on track and a new life in the works, he'd be able to handle it. Getting everything on track here at the clinic was what mattered right now.

Ethan told Paul about the patients he already had lined up for the days to come. Paul looked a little uneasy when he heard that he'd be seeing his first patient within a week.

"What's wrong?" Ethan asked.

Paul hesitated, staring down. Finally he peered up at Ethan and whispered, "I hope I can do this. It's been so long."

"I know you can do it. I told you, I wouldn't have asked you to join me if I didn't know you could."

"I appreciate the vote of confidence, but . . ." Paul shook his head, still looking uncertain of himself. "It's just that it feels like I was a different person the last time I operated."

"You're still the surgeon I knew from Manhattan General. And that guy was damn good at what he did."

Paul let out a sad chuckle. "That guy was much younger."

"Not really."

"It sure feels like it."

"Well, you've come to the right place," Ethan said, realizing this was an opportunity to ensure Paul's loyalty.

"What do you mean?" Paul asked, not understanding.

"I want to see you at eight o'clock tomorrow morning, in my office."

"Why?"

"Just be there. Eight o'clock."

When Paul arrived the next morning, Ethan didn't give him a chance to refuse. He drew blood before Paul even realized what was going on.

"What's that for?" Paul asked.

"You're at an antiaging clinic, Paul. Take advantage of it. I need these levels to mark your progress and adjust the doses. I also need to do a PSA."

"PSA? I don't have prostate cancer. And doses of what?"

Ethan explained that he would be prescribing a regimen of hormones. "We're going to start with testosterone, DHEA, melatonin, and human growth hormone." He gave Paul a box containing thirty packets of Androgel testosterone gel. He had Paul put it on right then, rubbing it onto his shoulders. He'd do that once a day.

"What's the benefit of this?" Paul asked.

"Like the other hormones, your levels decrease as you

get older. The idea is to elevate them to the same level they were when you were younger. The Androgel will add muscle, improve bone strength, increase your libido."

Paul chuckled at the last benefit. "That's been so low for so long, I don't know."

"Don't worry, you'll see."

"How long does it take to see the benefits?" Paul asked.

"The muscle and bone improvements will begin to show in a couple weeks. The libido right away. A couple hours."

"Really? Now all I need is someone to use it on," he said with a weary laugh. Ethan could tell that he was hurting inside. He still held on to the hope that he and Beth could repair their marriage, the poor guy.

"The PSA is because of the testosterone," he explained. The hormone was perfectly safe unless a man had the beginnings of prostate cancer. Then the testosterone could accelerate it. The PSA was to rule out that danger. If the results were positive, they'd adjust the therapies accordingly.

Ethan then gave Paul a box of syringes and another box containing vials of synthetic human growth hormone. "You inject these intramuscularly," he said. "The thigh is where most patients do it. At least with you I won't have to explain how to use a syringe. These you inject every other day."

He explained the benefits of hGH. Along with muscle-building and bone-strengthening benefits similar to testosterone, hGH also decreased body fat, boosted energy levels, and improved skin elasticity.

The last two hormones came in pill form. DHEA and melatonin had fewer and less dramatic benefits. They should improve sleep, which indirectly benefited everything else. On their own they were only marginally effective, but in conjunction with the others, they helped round out the complete antiaging regimen.

Ethan stopped the therapy there. He had no intention of putting Paul on Rejuvenol, at least not yet. He trusted Paul, but not enough to tell him about Rejuvenol. The bone marrow extraction necessary to harvest the stem cells would be extremely dangerous. Not to Paul's health—but if he made the connection to Wilkenson, that'd be a huge problem.

That was the main reason he'd made Beth promise not to tell Paul about Kenny and Pete's having been bone marrow donors for Zack. As cousins, they were good genetic matches. And since Zack's cells were too damaged and hadn't responded in any of the early tests, Ethan needed donor cells. The only cell lines close enough genetically to Zack's so his body wouldn't reject them were Kenny's and Pete's.

Beth didn't understand enough about the Wilkenson incident to make the connection, to suspect anything. But Paul certainly would. Ethan had to be very careful how much he let Paul know.

Bottom line, he couldn't risk putting Paul on Rejuvenol at this point. Still, the hormone therapy he was prescribing would help Paul feel youthful again. That would make him a better surgeon, which would be better for De Leon, which would be better for Zachary.

When he finished setting up Paul's hormone therapy, Ethan sent him to see Karla.

7

KARLA WEISS WAS a realist.

Athletically, she had what it took. She was going to compete in five swimming events and she was confident she'd medal in at least one of them. She'd be the oldest woman ever to medal in a swimming event. But in the world of big-time sports, you could win a gold medal, or five gold medals, and be the oldest woman to do that, and still fade from the spotlight if you don't have the complete package.

She walked over to the mirror in her studio. The one thing she lacked was as important as her ability in the pool. Perhaps even more important. *The look*. Female athletes who made it big, who signed the endorsement deals that earned them serious money, who managed to maintain their stature in the public eye long after their achievement in their sport ended, were the ones who fit society's ideal of beauty. And she didn't fit that.

She stripped off her spandex shorts and sports bra, and studied herself as she'd done many times before. Her legs and ass were toned and had good shape. She had hard, flat abs. She liked to wear a belly button ring. It gave her a feeling of femininity. Because of her sport, her arms and shoulders were muscular, but not so much that she looked masculine. She was broad at the top, angling down to a narrow waist and hips. Society had come to accept athletic bodies on women. That much she was pleased with. But she saw two serious flaws.

First, her breasts were too small. That was an advantage athletically. Aesthetically, however, it was a weakness. And second, she had two hideous scars on her cheek and a road map of wrinkles from too many years of too much sun and wind. She looked older than her forty-nine years. Society favored a youthful appearance in its sports heroes—even its older sports heroes. It was a contradiction but it was fact.

She needed to correct her flaws, and for that she'd need some help.

If she'd known that Ethan was going to bring in a plastic surgeon, she would have made it part of her deal when she'd provided him the information he'd needed to complete his research. All she'd asked in return for stealing the research data from the East German Academy of Genetic Sciences was that he'd provide her with a steady supply of the by-product of that research.

The academy had been enlisted by the East German Olympic Committee to secretly provide a substance that would give their athletes an edge. They'd used prisoners to test it. As a former Olympic team member and a prisoner serving life for unspecified "crimes against the state," Karla had been a perfect research subject.

They had come extremely close to completing the project. Karla had recognized the improvements to her body and her abilities right away. Medically, the doctors raved about how healthy she'd become, even living under the terrible conditions of that prison, eating food devoid of nutrition. But then the wall came down and the system that had sustained the academy, the system by which Karla had lived all her life, the system that had created her and nurtured her and then sentenced her to spend the rest of her days behind bars, had vanished practically overnight. East Germany ceased to exist; its separate Olympic team ceased to exist; the academy and the secret program ceased to exist.

The geneticist who'd been working on it had kept his lab notes and experimental data, locking them in his home when his job disappeared along with his country. Karla, who'd been released with the other political prisoners, saw this as her chance to achieve what she'd been denied her entire life. She'd been willing to do whatever was necessary to see that the research be continued, and that she benefit from it.

So she made the arrangement with Ethan.

But she hadn't even considered surgery then; she hadn't lived in the West long enough to realize what really mattered. Now that she did, she was going to have to fill that gap.

And in the same way she'd done what was necessary to assure that she kept receiving the genetic sports enhancer, she would do what was necessary now to get the surgery that would complete the package and make her dreams come true.

She couldn't afford to pay for such surgery. She'd gotten no cash from Ethan and very little pay for her work here. But the money problem could be overcome if she handled Paul Tobin properly. Ethan had made an appointment for him for an EPN eval. She was interested in finding out what kind of man he was, what she'd have to do to get what she wanted. With luck, he'd be as easy to control as Ethan.

When Paul walked into her facility, Karla was soaking in the therapeutic whirlpool. She faked surprise to see him.

"Is it time for your appointment already?" she said.

He looked embarrassed. "I thought so, but I can come back later."

"No, no, that's okay. My apology. I lost track of the time." She pointed to the towel she'd left on the leg press machine. "Bring me that, ya?"

"Sure."

He brought the towel over, handed it to her, then turned around and moved away. She had him feeling uncomfortable and nervous. Advantage her.

"Are you sure you don't want me to come back in a little while?" he said.

"That's okay." She climbed out of the whirlpool. The walls of the studio were covered in full-length mirrors. She saw that he was checking her out. He passed the initial interest test. But she had a lot more work to do.

She pretended she didn't notice and took her time wrapping the towel around her. Then she walked past him to her office to dress, brushing him as she went by. "I'll just be a moment."

"Sure. No problem."

She put on black spandex shorts and a sports bra then came back out. After exchanging a few niceties, which she was never good at, she explained what the EPN eval entailed.

"We're going to start by assessing your body composition," she said. "Then we'll measure your muscle strength and muscle endurance, your cardiovascular endurance, how well your lungs process oxygen, basically everything about your conditioning, ya? From there I can develop an exercise program for you to follow and a diet that will meet your optimum nutritional needs."

"Sounds good."

"Let's get started. Take off your shirt, ya?"

He hesitated a moment, uneasy, but he did as she told him. He had a large frame, good genetics. Unfortunately he'd let himself go over the last few years. He looked like he used to be a lot more physical. She wondered what had happened.

She used calipers to measure his body fat, pinching his skin in several spots and recording the measurements on her clipboard. She did the calculations and said, "Nineteen percent body fat."

"Is that good or bad?"

She grinned and teased, "That depends on how much clothes you're wearing."

"Ouch. That hurt."

She chuckled. "Don't worry. You follow what I tell you, we'll cut that number in half. And *that* will be a good percentage. You can follow instructions, ya?"

"That depends on the instructions," he said.

He was flirting, and that pleased her. He was attracted to her. And that gave her power right from the start.

"By the way," he said, "what's your percentage of body fat?"

"Why? Do you see any part of my body that needs improvement?" She liked putting him on the spot, making him uncomfortable and seeing how he handled it.

"No," he said, looking a bit embarrassed. "I was just curious."

"Nine percent," she said.

"That's low."

"That's where I need to be. But I'm serious with my question. Do you?"

"Do I what?"

"See any part of my body that needs improvement? Be honest." She stepped back and stood there for him to look at. "You're a plastic surgeon," she said. "You're an artist, ya?"

He chuckled. "Not quite."

"A sculptor of the human body. That's an art. You have to have an eye for beauty. So, if you could sculpt me, what would you make different?"

She saw that he was uneasy again. "Nothing," he said.

She scoffed at him. "You're not being honest."

"How do you expect me to answer a question like that?" he said.

"Truthful. But if you can't . . ." She shrugged, letting her silence embarrass him. She had the edge in this exchange already. "It's good to know a man's limitations," she said and let that sink in. "Come, ya?" she said.

She took him over to the treadmill. She attached the electrodes to his chest, the oxygen tube over his mouth and nose, and the blood oxygen sensor to his finger. He remained silent, clearly affected by her remark about his truthfulness. It was wearing at his conscience. He obviously didn't want to be known as a man who couldn't be honest, even by her, a virtual stranger. She was pleased, and confident that he would come around soon.

She had him run at increasing speeds, measuring his body's efficiency and capacity for exercise. She made him go a little longer than she had to. Wear him down physically, he'd start to drop his defenses on every level.

After finishing the treadmill test, they moved over to the strength measuring equipment. He couldn't hold out any longer.

"Do you really want an honest assessment?" he asked.

"When you get to know me better, you'll realize that I don't ask something if I don't really want it. And I'm not a person who's afraid of the truth."

"That's a little unusual for most people."

"I'm not like most people," she said. "I'll give you a place to start." She pointed to her face and asked, "Can these scars be fixed?"

He leaned close and examined her. "I doubt they can be removed completely, but I'm sure they can be made less noticeable."

"And I'd look better without them, ya?" she asked, again testing him.

He hesitated a moment, but instead of backing down this time, he said, "Probably, yes."

"An honest answer. I like that. Okay, what else would you change?" she asked. "If I wanted to fit this society's ideal of beauty for a woman, what would I need to do? And I'm not talking about 'beauty is in the eye of the beholder' politically correct beauty. I'm talking about objective, movie star, public figure beauty. Can you be *that* honest with me?" she asked, making it a challenge for him.

"Well, if you're talking about that particular kind of look," he said, hedging a little, "most women who fit that bill probably have a little less muscularity, and maybe more curves."

She was impressed with his honesty. The muscularity wasn't changing, and she didn't see that as a deficit. So she focused on the curves. "Curves where?" she asked.

She watched him look her up and down, and tried to see if he had any reaction. He maintained a professional exterior, but what was going on inside? He had to feel a sexual stirring. He was human, a man. She had enough confidence and attitude to overcome any flaws in her appearance. She was comfortable with her sexuality and quite willing to use it, just as she would any other asset.

"Well?" she said, waiting for his assessment.

"Like you said, you have nine percent body fat. That doesn't allow for very much width in the hip area," he said.

"Really? Is there such a thing as hip implants?"

He chuckled. "The opposite is what's usually asked for, liposuction of the hips. I think most women would like to have your problem."

"But you think it's a problem, ya?" She liked the feeling of making him squirm.

"No, I don't. I'm just talking in relation to what you asked me, the movie star kind of image."

"Okay. What else is wrong with my body—in relation to the image we're talking about?"

"That ideal probably has more ample breasts," he told her.

"You think my breasts could be larger, ya?"

"For that particular body type," he said, hedging again, "yes."

"Do you think I would be a good candidate for that kind of surgery?" she asked.

"Why? Is that something you've been considering?"

"You mean before you told me that my breasts are too small?"

"I didn't—"

She laughed and decided to let him off the hook. "I'm just joking," she said, patting him on the shoulder as if it were part of the teasing. But she left her hand there a few moments, once again testing him, to see how he'd react. He didn't pull away, but he looked a bit uneasy. Sexual tension. *Excellent.*

"I've been considering it for a while," she said.

She squeezed past him to pick up the lifestyle questionnaire on the table. When she did, she intentionally brushed against the front of his pants. *Oh, yes.* She had gotten to him. She had him right where she wanted him. She just had to use what she had. That was what she'd done all her life.

She'd slept with her grizzly bear of a coach in school. That put her in a position to ruin his family life and career. For her silence, he gave her the extra attention she'd needed back then to develop as a swimmer. She'd gone down on that old gray cow who was in charge of selecting the women's Olympic swim team in 1984—for all the good that'd done. The boycott had kept all of the Soviet bloc countries away from L.A. that year, including East Germany, destroying her dream of being proclaimed the best female swimmer in the world. That disappointment had plagued her life ever since.

She'd slept with several of the prison guards. You had to, to survive. And that was what got her selected for the genetic experiment. Then she let that dinosaur from the academy, whose hands smelled like formaldehyde, finger her between the legs. He couldn't get it up to do anything else. All so she could have access to his lab, where he was developing the medical technology that Ethan was using today. And of course she'd fucked Ethan at that stem cell conference in Brussels.

He had been lonely at the beginning, almost desperate, and she played to that. Afterward, when she'd delivered what he wanted and moved down here, he lost interest in sex, focusing on his work like a man possessed. But she needed to maintain her control, so she persisted, eventually conquering him. They still got together from time to time, usually when she pushed him hard enough. That was part of her plan to keep him where she wanted.

And so, she would establish the same relationship with Tobin. She would get into his pants, or let him think he was getting into hers. Any reluctance he had now she could overcome. Maybe it'd take a little more effort than with Ethan, but Tobin was definitely susceptible. All men were. As were most women. It was just a matter of time and technique.

And then she'd get him to suggest she have the work done. It would come from him. A gift.

The last part of the evaluation involved a questionnaire about Tobin's eating and exercise habits. She gathered all the information and told him she'd work up an exercise and nutrition program.

"I'll bring it to you when it's ready," she said.

"I can pick it up."

"That's okay." She wanted it to be on her terms. She wanted to plan her next entry into his life carefully.

8

Paul left Karla's exercise physiology studio feeling a strange uneasiness.

He went back to his bungalow. He was scheduled to see his first patient tomorrow, a woman who was considering having some work done on her nose. Wanting to be prepared, he sat on the sofa with a stack of medical journals. He needed to be current before he started seeing patients again. In the three years since he lost his license, he hadn't kept up on the latest surgical techniques as well as he should have. He didn't have much time to catch up.

But as he started reading, his thoughts kept going back to the forty-five minutes he'd spent with Karla. Had she been making a pass at him? Or was that just her personality? He wasn't sure. Whether she was or not, he had to admit that she intrigued him. He'd even flirted a little with her. And that surprised him. He'd have thought a woman with that much muscle would have come across as masculine. She didn't—not at all. Strong, definitely. But still female. In fact, that aspect of her, the conditioning of her body, more than anything else, was what intrigued him.

She had a puzzling sexual appeal, a *What would it be like to be naked with her?* kind of allure. Obviously she had incredible awareness of her body. No physical limitations. And she went to extremes. No limits. No inhibition. Strength, flexibility, stamina. A woman who was that physical, who had that kind of mastery over her body, had to know how to use it in bed. A woman who pushed herself to the limits, who clearly did nothing passively, had to be a great lover.

But it stopped there with him—a curiosity that would never be satisfied. A little flirting was one thing. It was harmless. But anything more than that, no way. He wanted to get back together with Beth, to reunite his family, and he wasn't going to let anything get in the way.

He tried to refocus on the reading material but his thoughts kept going back to Karla. He couldn't get her out of his head. He'd love to know what she *felt* like. He remembered the hint of sweat about her, very subtle, not offensive at all. And the way she moved, the motion of the cords of muscle beneath her skin. Serpentlike.

He had to get up and splash some water on his face, hoping it'd help him refocus. The image of the serpent was appropriate, he thought. Very biblical. That made him think about Eve in the Garden of Eden. All Karla needed was an apple.

He remembered now what Ethan had told him about the Androgel, how the testosterone would boost his libido. Alcohol had had the opposite effect for years. So had the depression his drinking had caused, and the barrage of personal and professional problems that followed. So he hadn't felt any sexual interest in a very long time.

Hormones were powerful things. This particular one was definitely exerting its power today. At least he knew that one of the therapies Ethan gave him was working. He hoped the others would work as well. He'd aged a decade in the last three years—not a very good example for patients coming to an antiaging clinic. No wonder Ethan had insisted he start on De Leon's therapies.

Paul went back to the couch, feeling a little guilty that Karla had awakened a sexual excitement in him. Even though he attributed most of it to the Androgel, and even after three years of separation, he didn't think that excitement should be triggered by anyone but Beth.

But what mattered was what the body did. What mattered were his actions and his intentions, and in both of those aspects, Beth was it. He still had deep feelings of

love for her. Perhaps he didn't lust for her anymore, didn't
dream of what it would be like making love to her again.
But he was confident that those old feelings would return
once he became familiar with her body again.

He tried to read but that wasn't working; he couldn't
concentrate. So he took a break and called AA. He wanted
to find out where the meetings in the area were held. In
New York, he'd gone religiously. That had helped in his recovery and in maintaining his sobriety. He needed to keep
it up down here.

Key West had a few meetings. He'd have to try different
ones, see which one worked for him. Not every meeting fit
every individual. It took quite a bit of trial and error. Sitting
through half a dozen or more meetings that didn't do a
thing for him, before finding the right one, wasn't something he looked forward to, but that was part of relocating.
Change could be a trigger, he'd learned. Even change for
the better. So he needed to be mindful of that and continue
with what helped him stay sober.

The few meetings that fit his schedule best had been yesterday and the day before. That disappointed him. He'd try
to fit in one of the other meetings this week, but that was
going to be difficult. Not only had Ethan scheduled several
patients this week, but he had to get settled in, finish setting up the office and operating room, and just prepare
himself mentally to be a surgeon again. Plus he didn't have
a car so he'd have to find a way to get there. Probably a
taxi. One way or another, he'd make next week's meetings.
Until then, if he just kept going the way he had for the last
two years, he should be all right.

He read some more, managing to focus a little better,
then he took another break. He wanted to call the agency
he'd located in Key West that referred patients from Third
World countries to specialists who were willing to help
them free of charge. Paul had spoken with the agency
when he decided to come here almost a month ago. They'd
needed some time to check out his credentials. He called
today to find out if they had a referral yet.

They did, a five-year-old boy from the Dominican Republic who'd been bitten in the face by a police dog. He needed surgery to reduce the scarring and possibly rebuild some of the bone structure. He'd be coming to Miami in two days. Paul asked them to contact Annie and have her fit the boy into his schedule.

As it gradually sank in that he was actually going to start seeing patients tomorrow, he began to panic like a rookie doctor fresh out of medical school. Back when he was that rookie doctor and had felt this same anxiety, he'd found a technique that had helped quite a bit. The day before surgery, he'd take a long walk, visualizing whatever procedure he was scheduled to perform. He'd go through the entire operation in his head. It not only helped him to relax beforehand, but it would help him in the OR later; when he was actually performing the surgery he'd feel like he'd already done the procedure once. It gave him the confidence he'd needed as a young surgeon.

He'd stopped doing that after the operations became second nature for him. But now, after three years away, he'd lost that confidence. So he decided to take a walk now and use the technique all over again.

As he strolled along the water, he went through a simple rhinoplasty in his head. That was one of the procedures tomorrow's patient was interested in. He'd know better what she needed once he examined her, but for now, reviewing this procedure was good enough to get his head where he wanted it to be.

It worked. When he got back to his bungalow forty-five minutes later he was quite a bit more relaxed. He knew he wouldn't feel confident again until he actually performed a successful operation, but this was a start.

The walk also left him winded. He plopped down on the sofa to catch his breath, realizing just how much he'd let himself go. Maybe Ethan's antiaging therapies would reverse some of that neglect. If it worked half as well on him as it appeared to have worked on Ethan, he'd feel like a young man in no time. He'd settle for just feeling happy and alive again.

The program Karla was going to design for him would

be helpful, too. She obviously knew about fitness and could help him get back into shape. Performing surgery required strength and stamina in order to maintain a steady hand. Some procedures lasted hours. If he had to go into surgery right now, could he handle it? Physically, it'd be tough. He wouldn't want to be the patient.

Wilkenson flashed into his head. To this day he didn't understand how that had happened, what he'd done wrong. And that deeply troubled him. Because if he didn't realize what his mistake had been then, how was he going to prevent it from occurring again now?

He wasn't drinking now. That was the big difference. That was what would keep anything like that from happening again.

Fortunately, even though he'd see his first patient tomorrow, he wouldn't actually operate on anyone for a couple of weeks. By then, he'd make sure he was in shape, physically and mentally. He'd have his confidence, his stamina, his knowledge all in tune.

Someone knocked at his door. When he opened it, Karla stood outside in faded jeans, a white tank top cut short to reveal her waist and belly button ring, flip-flops. She had on a hint of perfume and a very light glaze of makeup. The sun was setting behind her, casting a shimmering gold on her hair. The scent of palms carried in on the breeze. The setting was perfect for a romantic stroll along the beach.

That thought suddenly made him feel very alone. He wished he and Beth were together again, longed to feel the kind of passion they'd once had, the kind of fulfillment that had been absent from his life since they split.

But Beth wasn't here. She wasn't his anymore.

Karla stood in front of him, looking good. He felt a primal energy awakening inside him. But that was something he was only supposed to feel for Beth. So he did his best to ignore it and try to think of Karla purely as a colleague.

"I have your EPN program," she said, holding up a large yellow envelope. "I'm heading over to the café now for dinner. Why don't you come along, ya? We can go over everything and I can answer any questions you might have."

Something told him that having dinner with her wasn't a good idea—probably the same thing in him that was intrigued by her. He still wondered about her intention. Was she coming on to him again? Is that why she wore perfume and makeup? Or was this how she went to dinner every night? After all, she was wearing jeans and flip-flops, not exactly seduction clothing. Maybe all she wanted was to explain the antiaging program. Maybe it was all in his head, not hers.

But that was reason enough to worry. Sitting in a tropical setting, with this sunset playing on his senses, Ethan's testosterone firing up his libido, feeling sad and lonely, and with his salacious, very physical curiosity about her, he might have difficulty focusing on diet and exercise.

"I'm pretty beat," he said. "I think I'm just going to turn in early tonight."

"Skipping meals is bad."

"I'll tell you what, I'll read through the program before I go to sleep and I'll start being good tomorrow."

She handed him the envelope, smiled, and said, "Don't be too good."

He managed an uneasy laugh. She was definitely coming on to him.

"A rain check then on the dinner, ya?" she said. "In case you have questions."

"If I have any questions, I'll let you know."

He should have just said no to the dinner and not left it open to a rain check, to any possibility of a misunderstanding. But he didn't know how to do that tactfully. He might be wrong about her intentions. And he still had to work with her. He didn't want to start things off on the wrong foot, by being either too rude or too friendly. A normal working relationship was what he needed to maintain.

After she left, he skimmed over the regimen she'd prepared for him. She'd given him a computer printout of a "nutritional program," with exact times for each of five meals and which foods to eat in what amounts. She included suggestions for snacks that fit into the program.

The workouts she'd designed varied each day, rotating between strength training one day and cardiovascular routines the next. She'd provided explanations of which part of the body each exercise benefited and options for the cardio workouts, such as running, swimming, rowing, and biking, so he wouldn't get bored. He had to admit, she did know her stuff. He was looking forward to beginning, to seeing results.

He had definitely come to the right place. Not only was he getting his professional life in order, but he was also going to be able to revitalize his body and his mind. Most importantly, he was closer to Beth and the boys so he could make himself a part of their lives again.

With everything else falling into place, it was time to focus on the most difficult part, reestablishing his family life.

He picked up the phone and dialed Beth's number. Beth answered on the first ring, sounding animated, like she was expecting a call. "Hello?" Maybe she and Ethan had spoken this afternoon and Ethan had told her that he was down here. Maybe she'd been looking forward to this call.

"Hi. It's me," he said, feeling bolstered.

"Oh, hi," she said. The excitement left her voice instantly. So did any illusion that she had been waiting for his call, that this was going to be easy. He didn't know who she was expecting with such anticipation, but was it so bad to hear from him instead?

He tried not to let her tone discourage him too much. *Be positive.* He asked how she was and how the boys were doing. Kenny and Pete had just begun school and seemed to like it. He waited for her to ask how he was so he could spring the news on her, but she didn't ask. Instead she said that she was kind of busy and had to leave; was there something important that he wanted?

Yes! "I'm going to be practicing medicine again," he

said, certain that it would make a difference if she knew, that she'd be eager to welcome him back into her life.

"What do you mean?" she said, sounding confused.

"My medical license was reinstated. I'm working again." What he meant was *I'm getting my life back in order and I want us to have another chance.* But he knew her well enough to realize that it would take time to earn back her trust.

Beth was silent for a long moment. Paul wondered what was going through her head. Did she think he was lying? He'd done his share of lying when he used to drink. That was part of the addiction. So he couldn't blame her for distrusting him now. But this was one thing that would be easy to prove to her.

"I'm working in Florida," he said.

Again, silence on her end. This began to unnerve him. He remembered that it was in her silent moments when her feelings were lowest. In all honesty, he hadn't expected this news to thrill her. But he was hoping it would at least interest her, start her thinking differently about him. And if he was closer to her and the kids, she might be more willing to let him back into their lives.

Finally she said, "Where in Florida?"

"I'm working down near Key West, with your brother at his clinic." *Close enough to see you and the boys more often.*

"With Ethan?" she said. Her voice had an angry edge to it. She let out an annoyed breath and said, "How did that happen?"

"It was the right opportunity at the right time," he said. "Ethan needed a surgeon, I needed a place to practice, to make a new start. And I thought that if I was closer to you and the kids—"

"Look, I really have to go," she said, cutting him off.

"Wait." He needed something positive to come out of this call. "Listen, I want to come up there and visit tomorrow afternoon," he said. He had the first patient in the morning. He could drive up to Palm Beach after that.

"No," she said, no explanation.

"Beth . . ."

"The kids have school."

"After school."

"I have to pick up Kenny after school."

"So, after that—"

"After that I have to take him to see his counselor."

This stunned Paul. "His counselor? Kenny's seeing a counselor?" As much as he wanted this conversation to go smoothly, he couldn't control his anger. "Why didn't you tell me he was seeing a counselor? Damn it, Beth!"

"I'm telling you right now," she shouted back. "And don't yell at me!"

He managed to calm himself, but he was still troubled about this news and by Beth's not telling him. "Why didn't you tell me before," he said, "when you first brought him to a counselor?"

"I didn't bring him before. This will be the first visit."

"Well, why are you bringing him? Why is he seeing a counselor?"

She let out a breath of annoyance. "He's having a difficult time right now."

"What do you mean?"

"What do you think? The divorce," she said. Then she added, ". . . And all the rest."

She didn't have to say what "all the rest" meant. He knew—an alcoholic father blamed for killing a patient. Paul felt sickening guilt.

"And he's at that age," Beth added, tempering her anger. "I don't know. . . . I just think he can benefit by talking to someone. We'll see what happens."

"You'll let me know, right?"

"I'll let you know. I've got to go now."

"I still want to come up there and see you and the boys. And I want to see what's going on with Kenny."

"Kenny's going to be all right."

"I'm his father, Beth."

She let out a long sigh, then said, "I have to drive down

to Key West in a couple weeks. I'll take Kenny and Pete. We'll stop and see you."

"Two weeks?" He didn't want to have to wait that long.

"That's the best I can do," she said, snapping back at him. "Take it or leave it."

9

Tonight was Carmen's regular night off. It was also the regular night Ethan gave Zachary his treatment.

Ethan waited until she drove away, heading to Miami to spend the night and next day with her mother and sister. When her Toyota disappeared into the evening mist, he took the black case that contained everything he needed into Zachary's room. Zack was still awake, in his pajamas, lying in bed, waiting. He knew the routine. Every Saturday night the same. Blood tests, urine specimen, injections, pills. Zack never complained. The needle sticks had to hurt. The pills were difficult to swallow. He always accepted whatever came to him. That always amazed Ethan.

And every Sunday was the same, too. Ethan would take Zack fishing. They'd cast a couple lines off the side of the boat and spend the entire day together. It was Ethan's chance to be alone with his son, to make him smile and give him the fullest life possible. It was the time Ethan valued the most.

"So, where would you like to go fishing tomorrow?" Ethan asked as he located a vein on Zack's arm and swabbed it with alcohol.

Zack shrugged. "I don't know."

He winced and bit his lip as the needle pierced his skin. But he didn't say a word. He'd endured so much anguish in his short years. How unfair life could be. Zack had done nothing to deserve this affliction, and yet here he was, bearing the pain every minute of his life. Life wasn't fair, not at all. Life could be downright cruel.

Ethan wanted desperately to make things right for him.

"How about we go over by Pelican Cove?" he suggested. "I'll bet the blues are biting over there."

Zack shrugged again, looking apathetic. "Do we have to go fishing tomorrow?" he asked.

This surprised Ethan. Zack loved fishing. "No, of course not," Ethan said. "We don't have to go if you don't want to."

"I'd rather just hang around the house, if that's okay." Zack seemed less energetic than usual tonight.

"Sure it's okay. We can stay here if you want," Ethan said. "Maybe we can watch the Dolphins game or a movie or something."

Zack just nodded.

Ethan wondered if he'd had an especially active day today. Carmen usually kept the activities down on Saturdays so Zack would have the energy to do things with Ethan on Sundays. She knew how important this was to Ethan. She wasn't the type of person to forget something like that.

"What did you do today?" Ethan asked.

Zack shrugged. "Just played Nintendo for a while and watched TV."

"You didn't go out?"

"I didn't feel like it."

Before Ethan had started Zack on the cocktail of hormones, Zack had had no energy at all. All he'd do all day was lie in bed. He'd been very close to the end. But that had changed once Ethan found the right combination. After that, Zack had been almost as active as any boy his age—almost. His energy level grew steadily. So did his strength and stamina. He had a better appetite, which meant he ate more and gained weight, something he'd desperately needed. With the hormone therapy, he had been on his way to a normal adolescent's life.

But that had only been a stopgap measure. It had worked well for a while, but the benefits were now starting to be reversed. Ethan had noticed a steady decline over the last several months. It was gradual, but it was definitely happening. Zack was losing energy and strength. That spark he'd had a few short months ago was becoming duller every day. Most troubling, his hyaluronic acid level was beginning to rise as was the amount of plaque deposits in his blood. His telomerase level was falling steadily, and there was a noticeable increase in neural damage on the molecular level. All that meant his internal organs were deteriorating. The downward spiral that marked his illness was resuming. He was, in a word, hyperaging again.

Ethan labeled the tube of blood and the urine specimen. He'd run the tests later, but he knew they were only going to show an even further deterioration in Zack's condition.

Ethan needed desperately to halt this. Zack was still better off than he'd been before he started taking the hormones, so Ethan was not going to discontinue them, but they weren't enough anymore. Zack was getting worse instead of better, and getting worse for Zack meant only one thing. Death.

Ethan couldn't bear to see his son die so young, without ever having had the chance to live.

Rejuvenol was the answer.

The current process had been through several versions, with varying success. He had the data from East Germany, plus the results of the genetic research he'd been doing for the last ten years. He was close to perfecting it to the point where it would be effective for Zack. The stem cell technology he used wasn't really revolutionary; cancer specialists and researchers had been experimenting with it for years. With one difference.

The East German scientist had isolated, in the blastocyst of bone marrow cells, an enzyme called glion-2. When combined with progenitor cells—cells primed to generate certain tissue growth—on which Ethan had focused his research, this acted like an "on" switch, turning on the body's ability to rejuvenate cells. Stimulating cell division and multiplication was like injecting millions of tiny repairmen into the bloodstream, sending them to work fixing the damage age caused to organs. In Zack's case, the damage that his disorder caused.

Ethan had tried to give Zack an earlier version of this therapy. He'd been stronger then, and still the treatment had made him terribly sick and weak. Ethan hadn't had the genetic modification right at the time—the potency of glion-2, the specific composition of the progenitor cells—but he had gone through several generations since then and he was sure he was close. But he couldn't risk giving it to Zack again until he knew it was safe for him. If Zack experienced another bad reaction, it would certainly kill him.

So he'd found other subjects to test it on. In the same way that Rejuvenol repaired and regenerated Zack's organs and body tissue, it could also repair and regenerate the organs and body tissue of otherwise healthy adults—men and women suffering from normal aging. It was the ultimate antiaging therapy.

It was also the ultimate sports-enhancing substance, since it quickly repaired the damage that training did to the body, making overtraining virtually impossible. It reversed injuries in record time, drastically improved the function of the lungs and heart, and built lean muscle mass far faster than any workout routine or even a regimen of anabolic steroids. That was why the East Germans had been working on it, and why he was testing it regularly on Karla. She knew the risks, but she was willing to take them. And the results spoke for themselves.

But Ethan couldn't use her as a benchmark for Rejuvenol's effectiveness or safety for Zack. Karla was taking an array of sports-enhancing drugs. In order to apply her test results to Zack's treatment, Ethan would need to regulate exactly what she took. Since she refused to let him do that, he had to test it on other subjects.

He'd offered it to a select few antiaging patients, ones he knew had enough money. He charged them five thousand dollars per injection for the privilege. He'd explained that the therapy wasn't FDA approved. And he only offered it if he was confident the patient would not tell anybody about it, that they would have too much to lose by violating the secrecy.

All Ethan's Rejuvenol patients were adults, so he had to interpolate their results to an adolescent subject, which left a considerable margin of error. Unfortunately he had no other choice. Children didn't come to antiaging clinics.

Recently he'd given the latest generation of Rejuvenol to a few adult patients. Their follow-up visits hadn't happened yet but he could not wait much longer for the results. He had to work quickly if he was to help his son.

He sat on the bed beside Zack and opened *The Hobbit* to where he'd left off last time. Before he could read half a chapter, Zack drifted off to sleep. Watching him lie there with his eyes closed, struggling to breathe, Ethan felt the cold fear of desperation.

He tucked Zack in, turned off the lamp, and went to his lab upstairs. As a precaution, he kept all the test data on the Rejuvenol patients here instead of with the rest of the patients' files in the medical building. He didn't want anyone else to have access to this information.

He'd given Rejuvenol to a patient a few weeks ago, a woman named Quinn. Her follow-up visit had been scheduled for yesterday but she hadn't kept her appointment. Ethan couldn't wait until she rescheduled. He needed to know how she'd responded.

He opened her file and found her telephone number. On the third ring a woman answered. Her voice was soft, tentative. It wasn't the voice he remembered Quinn having.

"Could I speak with Ms. Quinn, please?" he said.

The woman on the other end of the line hesitated a long moment. Ethan wasn't even sure the woman was still there or if they'd been cut off.

"Hello?" he said.

"Who's calling?" the woman asked.

Ethan knew that some patients didn't like anyone knowing that they were coming to De Leon. This kind of therapy had a certain stigma for some people, the way plastic surgery once did. He did not want to violate the trust his patients put in him.

"I'm her doctor," he told the woman.

"Thank goodness." The woman sounded relieved. "I've been trying to get hold of you," she said.

Why? Fear shivered through Ethan. *What on earth could have happened?* The phone suddenly felt hot and irritating against his ear. He shifted it to the other side. "Can I ask who is this?" he asked.

"Her sister," the woman said quietly.

"Is something wrong?" He already knew the answer. Something was definitely wrong. The question was, how wrong was it?

The woman hesitated again. Something bad had happened, Ethan realized. The Quinn woman must have had a negative reaction to the drug. But how sick had it made her? So sick that he wouldn't be able to give it to Zack? A setback like this would certainly raise the stakes for Zack.

"Doctor," the woman finally said. He could hear her take a breath, fortifying herself for what she was about to say. He held his own breath. "Nicole is dead."

As her words echoed in Ethan's head, he panicked. His thoughts raced. *Oh, my God! Rejuvenol killed her!* He didn't know what to say, what to do. *Hang up!* He hadn't given his name. She didn't know who he was. *Hang up!* But could she trace the call? Did her sister leave behind some evidence that would point to De Leon?

No, she doesn't know about De Leon. She had said she'd been trying to get hold of him. If she'd known about De Leon, she'd have called here. Nicole Quinn must have hidden her visits to De Leon, decided not to tell anyone that she was on antiaging therapies. Ethan allowed himself a thin breath of relief. The sister didn't know who he was or about the clinic.

But the woman was still dead. *Did Rejuvenol kill her? That can't be possible.* He'd been so careful about giving Rejuvenol to patients. He'd done it so gradually, taken precautions to make sure it was safe each step of the way. He did not want to harm anyone. Certainly he didn't want anyone to die. *It can't be Rejuvenol. It just can't.* Zack's life depended on Rejuvenol being safe and effective. If it killed a healthy adult, it would certainly kill Zack. *No, it can't be.*

Ethan needed to know for certain if Rejuvenol was deadly. He needed more information, so he said, "My God, that's terrible." The surprise and concern in his voice was quite genuine. "I'm so sorry to hear about that."

This sister of Nicole's thought he was Nicole's primary care doctor. Since the sister hadn't expected Nicole's doctor to know about her death, Ethan assumed it wasn't from a long-term illness or anything the doctor was involved in.

"Tell me what happened," he said.

The sister swallowed. Ethan was sure she was struggling not to cry. It took her a moment to answer.

"Nicole killed herself," the sister said.

Ethan's first reaction was shock. Hearing of such a young, beautiful woman taking her own life was very disturbing. But the implications of that were strangely consoling. He shut his eyes and let out a silent sigh of relief. Nicole Quinn hadn't died from Rejuvenol after all. She was dead just the same, and that was a horrible tragedy, but at least he hadn't killed her, Rejuvenol hadn't killed her. More importantly, her death did not mean Zack was going to die next.

Thank God. Rejuvenol might still be okay to give to Zack.

He was about to offer some appropriate expression of sympathy but the sister spoke first.

"Doctor," she said, "tell me, did Nicole have cancer?"

The question sent a shiver of fear through him. *They know.* There must have been an autopsy. It must have revealed the extraction. *Damn it!* Suddenly he realized just how vulnerable he was. If they knew that much, they might try to trace her visits to De Leon. And that could lead to discovering what he had been giving her, which would lead to all kinds of trouble from the FDA, which would definitely interfere with what he was trying to do to save Zack. *All because one bimbo was stupid enough to kill herself.*

He couldn't let that happen. He had to squash any suspicion right away, before it snowballed. They already attributed the scar to surgery for cancer. Let them believe that and put it to rest.

"Yes, she did," Ethan said.

"Oh, my goodness," the sister said. "I didn't even know."

"Don't feel bad. She didn't want anyone to know about it. Cancer still has a stigma in our society. Many patients would rather no one knew."

The sister let out a sad sigh. "If I had known," she said, "maybe I could have done something to prevent her . . ." She struggled with the last few words. "Her killing herself."

"You shouldn't think that way. I'm sure there was nothing anyone could have done." This was dragging out longer than Ethan wanted. The more he said, the greater the chance he'd say something that would raise her suspicions or she'd ask something he couldn't answer. It was time to end this, diplomatically. "I'm due in surgery shortly so I'm going to have to say good-bye," he said. "But again, please accept my condolences. Your sister was a wonderful—"

Before he could finish she asked, "Doctor, was she taking any medications that would have caused her to become depressed?"

This question rattled Ethan. She was searching for an explanation. "No," he said quickly. But she would need more. "I'm sure you can understand that her illness in and of itself would be devastating for anyone."

"Not Nicole," the sister said. "That wasn't like her at all."

Ethan did not like the direction this was taking. The sister was raising more questions, rather than letting it settle. Ethan had to get out of this conversation immediately.

"Yes, well . . ." he muttered. What else could he say? "Again, I'm sorry," he said. "I really do have to be in surgery."

"I understand."

He was about to hang up when she said, "Can we meet another time, to discuss this further? By the way, what was your name, Doctor?"

Ethan panicked. This was becoming dangerous. He had to separate from this—*right now!*

"Doctor?" she said when he didn't answer.

He hung up the phone and stepped back from it, fearful of what would happen now.

10

SOMETHING WAS VERY wrong.

Alicia hung up, feeling very uneasy about the conversation she'd just had with Nicole's doctor. And the sudden way it ended, being cut off so abruptly, was strange. Sure he'd call back, she sat on the sofa and waited. She'd been unable to ask everything she wanted to ask. How serious had Nikki's cancer been? What medications had she been taking? Was she being treated for anything else? Why in the world would Nikki kill herself? There were thousands of questions. She knew that many would never be answered, but she hoped Nikki's doctor could at least answer some.

It felt odd being here in Nikki's apartment. All of Nikki's things were just as Nikki had left them, the day she killed herself. It was as though Nikki would be back shortly. But she wasn't coming back. Alicia kept coming here, searching through Nikki's things, needing to find something that would explain why Nikki wanted to die. So far she'd found nothing that made the death any more understandable. And then this evening, when Nikki's doctor had called unexpectedly, she'd felt her first real hope. But then it ended just as unexpectedly, answering almost nothing.

A few moments passed and the phone didn't ring. Why wasn't he calling back? Was it possible they hadn't been cut off accidentally? Would Nicole's doctor have hung up intentionally? That made no sense at all. But that was exactly what it was beginning to feel like had happened. As soon as she'd asked him his name, he hung up.

Her suspicious mind was getting away from her. They'd been cut off and he was going to call right back.

Minutes passed. No call.

Her suspicions took over again. He'd sounded strange. Nothing specific he'd said. Just something about his voice, about the way he measured his words. Like he was being overly careful about what he said. Like he was hiding something. *Yes, that's it.* But what could he be hiding?

Was it that Nicole might have taken cancer medications that would cause her to kill herself? Had he prescribed something that had caused her depression? Was he trying to hide that now? Was he afraid that he'd be blamed? Afraid that he'd be sued?

Alicia needed to know. If he was to blame, she was going to make sure that he'd be punished.

She stared at the phone that would not ring. She wouldn't be able to put Nicole's death to rest until her questions were answered. But she couldn't call him to get those answers because she still didn't know his name. In the two weeks since Nicole's death, she'd gone through Nicole's apartment and hadn't been able to find the name of her primary care doctor or any prescription bottles with a name on them or anything that would point her in the right direction. This call was the only thing she had, and it turned out to be a dead end.

Suddenly she had an idea. She picked up the phone and dialed *69, hoping to learn his number. A recording came on. "The number you are trying to find is unavailable or private." She hung up, letting out a breath of frustration. Another dead end.

Alicia didn't know Nikki's friends. It had always been just the two of them. The only other person she knew who was close to Nikki was her agent, Steline Proulx. Her modeling agency, Élan, was on Wilshire Boulevard in Beverly Hills. Nikki called and asked Steline if she could meet with her the next morning.

• • •

The reception area of Élan was filled with women who looked like they'd been transported here from the pages of *Cosmo* and *Vogue*. Tall and thin. Unnaturally long legs. Hair, teeth, nails, all perfect. For Alicia it was surreal, and a bit intimidating. She felt strangely inadequate. She'd always considered herself to be smart, resourceful, tenacious. But here her intelligence and character didn't matter. All that counted was how a person looked, and in that respect she did not measure up to the women of Élan. She wanted to get out of here.

"Ms. Fernandes," the receptionist said. "Steline can see you now."

Nikki's agent's office looked like a luxurious living room with a glass-topped desk near the window. Steline was in her fifties but had taut skin and a fit body. She looked like she'd had extensive surgical help. She motioned to a sofa and offered Alicia some coffee.

"No, thanks."

"So, Alicia, what's on your mind?" They'd never met before, but Steline spoke as if she were Alicia's old friend.

"I was hoping you might be able to help me with something," Alicia said. "You knew Nikki pretty well, right?"

"I'd like to think so. To me, Élan is more of a family than a business. I consider all the girls my daughters."

Steline was already making Alicia sick to her stomach.

"I've been trying to find out a little about her medical history," she said. "I was wondering if you know who her doctor is."

Steline hesitated. Her silence interested Alicia. "You mean here in L.A.?" she asked.

"Did she have doctors somewhere else?"

"I guess she didn't tell you, then."

"Tell me what?" Alicia said.

Steline sighed. "She didn't want anyone to know. She only told me because she was worried that I might not renew her contract. She should have known better than that. That's not how we do things at Élan."

Alicia had no idea what this crazy woman was talking

about. "Nikki didn't want anyone to know what?" she asked.

"I guess I can tell you. You should know, you being her older sister."

Alicia just let the remark roll off her without correcting Steline. "I should know what?" she asked.

"I'll show you."

Steline brought Alicia into the bathroom adjoining her office. It was large enough to hold a conference in. There were a couple of chairs, a vanity table, mirrors all over. One of the cabinets had a lock on it. Steline unlocked it and said, "Nikki didn't want to keep it at home. I guess she felt strange about it. I'm not sure why. I think she thought it was something she shouldn't be doing."

"What was she doing?" Alicia asked.

Steline removed a plastic cosmetics box from the closet and held it out for Alicia to take. Alicia just stared at it, almost afraid to look inside. But she needed to know. Could this somehow explain Nikki's death?

Alicia took the box. It was heavy in her hands. The mystery of what might be inside made her shiver. She sat at the vanity table and slowly opened the box.

Neatly arranged inside were several glass vials and half a dozen disposable syringes. Her first thought was that Nikki had been on drugs, heroin or something like that. The medical examiner had been wrong.

She glanced up at Steline, who stood over her, just watching. Alicia took out one of the vials. The label said PROTROPIN (BIOSYNTHETIC HUMAN GROWTH HORMONE). Alicia had no idea why Nikki would be injecting this, but that would explain the needle marks the medical examiner had found. At least the ones on her thighs. But what about the mark in her hip bone?

Alicia replaced the vial and picked up a small foil packet the size of two NutraSweet packets attached end to end. The label on the foil said ANDROGEL (TESTOSTERONE 1%). The medical examiner had been right, after all. Nikki had been on some kind of hormone replacement therapy. But why had she kept it here? Why was this something to hide?

And why hadn't her doctor said anything about this on the phone yesterday? Could this have had something to do with her cancer, or with her suicide? Alicia needed to know what this meant.

She looked at the label again to see the name of the doctor who'd prescribed it, but there was no name. There were two pill bottles, as well. One was melatonin, which she'd vaguely heard of, though she didn't remember what it was. The other was DHEA, something she'd never heard of. They were over-the-counter pills, so there was no label to tell her who Nikki's doctor was.

She peered up at Steline. "What do you know about this? Do you know where Nikki got this stuff and what it's for?"

"Yes, I do," she said. She looked relieved to be telling someone, like she was unloading a great responsibility. "Nikki made me promise to keep it a secret. But I guess now . . ." Her words trailed off. There was no need to explain.

Steline took a breath and continued. "Nikki was going to a clinic in the Florida Keys."

"For her cancer?" Alicia asked.

"Cancer? Nikki didn't have cancer."

"Her doctor told me she did."

"What doctor?"

"I don't know his name." Alicia wanted to get back to what Steline was saying. "Tell me about the clinic in Florida," she said. "Why was Nikki going there?"

"Those," Steline said, pointing to the medications Alicia was holding. "It's an antiaging clinic. The hormones she was taking were supposed to restore her youth. It sounds far-fetched but it worked. I mean, it kept Nikki working, even at her age."

Alicia's first thought was that these hormones had driven Nikki to kill herself. Hormones could do a number on your emotions. She and Nikki both suffered mood swings during their periods. Could something like this have made Nikki's mood so low that she wanted to kill herself?

"What do you know about this clinic?" she asked Steline.

"Just that they specialize in antiaging treatments. Staying young was something Nikki had become obsessed with. She'd lost a few jobs because they wanted a younger look. I tried to tell her not to worry about it, that'd we'd rethink the direction we'd go with her career, maybe concentrating more on acting. But she was really adamant about keeping the modeling side viable as long as possible. A guy who used to be a client of mine told her about the clinic several months ago. He was getting older himself, and he started going there. The results were good. Nikki saw that, and she figured the clinic was the answer she was looking for."

"I want to talk to him, the guy who told Nikki about the clinic."

"He's not in L.A. anymore. He moved back east somewhere. I think he's trying to get into acting. I don't represent him anymore. I doubt he'd tell you much, even if I did know how to reach him."

"Why do you say that?"

"This is a cutthroat business. If someone finds something that'll give them an edge, they'd be crazy to share it."

"I'm not in this business. Besides, he shared it with Nikki."

Steline hesitated again. Finally she took Alicia by the hand and said, "Honey, your sister had to sleep with him. That's why he told her. Unless you intend to sleep with him, he's not going to talk to you. Sorry to be so blunt."

11

PAUL'S ASSISTANT, STACY, poked her head in the doorway. "Your patient is ready, Dr. Tobin."

Cold sweat dripped down Paul's forehead. He wiped his brow and swallowed hard. His stomach was a mess. He could barely breathe. He felt much the way he did on his first day as a resident a lifetime ago. Suddenly the urge to drink came over him with such intensity that he shivered with fear. The craving was stronger than it had been in a very long time. He wanted—no, *needed*—a taste to calm his nerves.

The incident that had destroyed his life three years ago flashed into his head. How he'd needed a shot of scotch before the liposuction procedure. How the shot became two, then three, but that was it, no more. But the effect was what he'd wanted—needed. Calming. Fortifying. He'd done it before other procedures. Three drinks, enough to steady him, but not so much that it'd depress his reflexes and abilities. It was as much a part of the surgery as scrubbing down or marking the patient's skin before cutting in.

And now he could taste the scotch on his tongue, taste the shots he'd swallowed three years ago. He could taste the mint he'd put in his mouth afterwards to conceal the smell of alcohol on his breath. He closed his eyes and in the darkness he saw himself scrubbing up, saw the patient on the table, saw the vital signs of the young Wilkenson woman crash. He replayed it in his head, how he'd tried to revive her. But there she lay, on the operating table, dead. *Dead.* What in God's name had happened?

He needed a shot of something right now to wash the memory away. But it wasn't going to go away. And he wasn't going to allow himself to drink, to start down that path again. He needed a different way to clear his head.

The ritual. He held his hands out in front of him and was surprised to see how steady they were. He focused on that. He still had it. He could still do it. He was not doomed to repeat the past. This would be different. He would make sure of it.

He took a deep breath and walked down the hallway to the examination room, to see his first patient in three years.

The woman sitting in the room was Lita Davis. Paul had already reviewed her chart before coming in. She'd been seeing Ethan for three months, and the results of his therapies were clear in her body composition. She'd lost twenty pounds and had experienced a visible increase in muscle tone. Her body fat had gone from twenty-two percent to sixteen. She was forty-nine years old, with striking good looks, except for her nose, which had the telltale signs of having been broken.

"Good morning, Ms. Davis," Paul said. He sat down across from her, her chart in his hands. He felt like a doctor this morning. And while it was awkward for him, it felt familiar, like returning to one's childhood home. It would take him a little time to fit back into this framework, but eventually he was going to fit nicely. This was where he belonged.

Lita Davis smiled, looking optimistic and happy to be here. "Good morning, Doctor," she said. "Dr. Granier tells me that you're the best." Her tone wasn't completely serious but she certainly seemed encouraged by whatever Ethan had told her.

"Well, I guess being the best is kind of a subjective opinion," Paul said, not sure how else to respond. "I've done many surgeries," he added, "and my patients have usually been very pleased."

"So you have been doing this for a long time?" She seemed reassured by this.

"Almost twenty years." Paul left it at that. If she asked about the last three years or about unsuccessful procedures, he would tell her. He'd even left the door open by saying that patients were "usually" pleased. But since she didn't pursue it any further, neither did he.

He began by examining her nose. "How did you break it?" he asked, studying the irregular line of the bones.

Her disposition suddenly changed. The smile disappeared. She lowered her eyes to the floor in a look of shame and embarrassment.

"My ex-husband," she said, bitterness in her quiet words. She didn't have to say any more. Paul understood.

She looked up now, her expression changing again. Now she looked proud. "The jackass was stupid enough to let me catch him fooling around with a twenty-year-old. My lawyer got nearly every cent out of him." She chuckled, a bittersweet laugh. "So as it turns out," she said, "his little escapade is paying for this surgery and for the hormone treatments Dr. Granier has been giving me. I'm going to look as good as his little twenty-year-old plaything. Even better."

As he continued the examination, his nervousness quickly disappeared. He felt like himself again, like the surgeon he had been years ago. Doing this felt natural. He ordered X rays, so he'd have a complete picture of her bone structure, then scheduled her for surgery.

When she walked out of the exam room, he closed the door and had to bite his lip to keep from cheering. He felt exhilarated. He was a surgeon again. He was doing what he was meant to do. At last his life was back on course.

12

MANY HOURS OF internet research later, Alicia found the clinic that she believed must be the one Nikki went to. She had been sure such a cutting-edge place would have its own website on the internet, and her hunch had paid off:

Feel & Look Young Again!

DE LEON LIFE EXTENSION CENTER
Coral Key, Florida

Revolutionary Antiaging Therapies

Unique 3-Tier Approach
Hormone Replacement
Nutrition & Exercise
Cosmetic Surgery

All therapies FDA approved. Most treatments considered nonessential and therefore not covered by most insurance policies. Payment required at time of visit. Results may vary.

Alicia clicked on "Hormone Replacement."

A new page appeared, explaining the hormones this clinic prescribed and the benefits attributed to each. The four Nikki had kept at Élan were mentioned. The combination of these hormones was supposed to restore patients to "physiological youth." Patients would feel much the way they had when they were thirty—with reduced body fat, more strength and energy, a stronger immune system, revitalized skin, and improved memory and overall cognitive ability.

Earlier today, Alicia had done a little research into the hormones she'd found at Élan. Human growth hormone was originally prescribed to children whose bodies didn't produce enough of the hormone naturally. It helped them grow to a more "normal" size. Researchers later discovered that if older adults took it, they would gain bone mass and lean muscle and lose body fat. Some doctors began prescribing hGH to seniors to make them stronger and less prone to injuries. From seniors, it trickled down to middle-aged patients and then to Baby Boomers.

The clinics that specialized in hGH used to be concentrated in Mexico and Europe. But in the last decade, more doctors in the United States had begun promoting this "off-label" use for the hormone. According to some research data, hGH also helped restore skin elasticity, improve memory, and increase energy. The list of benefits was long and impressive.

But not all experts in the field accepted this hormone, or the others that Nikki was taking, as antiaging magic bullets. The evidence supporting some of the claims, like the muscle gain and fat loss, was fairly solid. But for other claims, like the mental improvements, it was mainly anecdotal.

The doctors at De Leon seemed to come down on the side of accepting the claims. *Surely the profit motive doesn't have anything to do with it,* Alicia thought with disgust. Nothing worthwhile came easily. Aging was a fact of nature and could not be halted. She couldn't believe that Nikki had accepted the claims. She must have been so desperate that she'd believe anything that promised to make her young again.

Could she have been so desperate that when it didn't work, she no longer wanted to live?

These people had lied to Nikki. They gave her false hope. That enraged Alicia. She was sure the clinic had something to do with Nikki's suicide. She would make sure whoever was responsible would pay for what they did.

She clicked on "Nutrition & Exercise" and "Cosmetic Surgery" and read the claims. She had the same thought over and over: *How could anyone believe this crap? How could Nikki?* Even though Nikki had worked in a business based on illusion, she had always been securely grounded in reality. So why did she believe the hype about this place? And why would she sleep with a guy to find out about it?

Alicia clicked on the "Contact" button, jotted down the phone number, then logged off and called Florida. A woman with a southern drawl answered.

"De Leon," the woman said. "Can I help you?"

"Yes. I'm calling regarding my sister, who was a patient there. Nicole Quinn."

"Oh, you're Nikki's sister? It's nice to meet you."

She considered this a meeting? Alicia got to the point of the call. "I wanted to talk to someone about the medications Nikki was taking."

"Oh, I wouldn't be able to help with that," the woman said. "You'll have to speak to Nikki's doctor. I can transfer you to his office if you like."

"Thank you."

Alicia wondered if this was going to be the same doctor who'd called the other night, trying to reach Nikki. The conversation had been pretty short, so she wasn't sure she'd recognize his voice if she heard it again. But if it was him, she definitely had some questions to ask.

A man came on the line now. "This is Dr. Granier. Can I help you?" Alicia couldn't tell for sure if it was the voice from the other night, but it sounded like him.

"Hello, Doctor. My sister was a patient of yours. Nicole Quinn. I'm calling to find out some information about the medications she was taking and to see if any of the therapies—"

"Excuse me, miss," the doctor said, cutting her off. "I don't have a patient by that name."

"Quinn. Nicole Quinn. She *was* a patient there," Alicia said.

"I'm afraid you're mistaken." He was polite but firm. "I don't have a patient by that name. And even if I did, confidentiality laws would prohibit me from disclosing . . ."

He droned on. Alicia tuned him out. Her mind was still trying to make sense of the first thing he'd said, that Nikki wasn't a patient of his. Could Nikki have gone to a different antiaging clinic in Florida? But this was the only one Alicia had been able to find in the keys. And the woman who answered the phone and transferred her to Dr. Granier knew Nikki. This had to be the place.

"Maybe you could check your records, Doctor," she said. "My sister was a patient there."

"This is a small practice. I know all of my patients well, and I'm telling you, I don't have any patients by the name you gave."

"But the woman I just spoke to knew her. She said you're Nicole's doctor."

"She must have misunderstood you," he said, his tone showing irritation. "I'm sorry I can't be of more help to you. Anyway, I'm seeing patients right now, so I have to go."

Before she could say anything else, Dr. Granier hung up.

He was mistaken or he was lying. If he was the same doctor who called the other night, then he knew Nikki was dead. He could be trying to cover up what he'd done to her. The woman who answered the phone apparently wasn't in on the cover-up. She could confirm that Nikki was a patient and might even be talked into sharing a little information.

Alicia picked up the phone and hit redial. It rang several times before an answering machine picked up.

"Thank you for calling the De Leon Life Extension Center. Sorry to have missed your call, but our office is closed right now. Please leave your name and phone number, including the area code, and we'll call you back as soon as possible."

Alicia hung up without leaving a message. That was strange. The receptionist was there just a few minutes ago.

Thinking the woman might have stepped out for a moment, or might be on another line, Alicia decided to wait ten minutes before calling back. When she did, a different woman answered. This woman had a slight German accent and answered with a simple, "Hello. What can I do for you?" Alicia wondered if she'd dialed the wrong number.

"Is this the De Leon Life Extension Center?" she asked.

"Yes. What can I do for you?"

"I called a little while ago and spoke with another woman. I wonder if I could speak with her again."

"She left," the accented voice said abruptly. "What do you want?"

A chill ran through Alicia. What happened to the woman she'd spoken with? Could they have done something to her? She stopped herself from thinking these thoughts. She was letting her imagination run wild. The other receptionist had just finished her shift, that was all.

Alicia could tell by this woman's tone that she wasn't going to give out any information. There was no use even trying. So Alicia just hung up. But she had learned one important thing from this call: They were hiding something at that clinic. She didn't know what it was, didn't know if it had anything to do with Nikki's death, but she was determined to find out. And the only way to do that was to go there herself.

13

PAUL GOT UP early the next morning. He wanted to get started on the exercise program Karla had designed for him. Beth was coming down in two weeks, so that left him very little time to get himself back into shape. Three years of neglect wasn't easy to reverse.

He wasn't expecting miracles. He just wanted *some* improvement. If he could look a bit leaner, more energetic, more lively, more like the Paul she had fallen in love with so long ago, he might have a better chance of winning her back. Working out regularly, eating right, and following the same regimen of hormone replacement that had done wonders for Ethan might do the same for him.

The sun was just rising out of the turquoise waters as he walked down to the beach. The sand felt cool under his bare feet. A breeze came in off the sea, spicing the air with the scent of salt and tropical plants. According to Karla's program, he was to run for twenty minutes. He figured he'd do at least half an hour; maybe he'd get into shape more quickly. Before he'd starting drinking heavily, he had run for an hour every morning before work. That was his goal now.

As he ran this morning he used the visualization technique again, going through a basic facial reconstruction surgery, similar to the one the boy from the Dominican Republic might need. He still hadn't examined the boy, but he'd done procedures to repair dog bites in the past, so he had something to draw on. He called up the memory of one of those operations and went through it step by step in his mind.

He only ran for fifteen minutes before he became winded and had to slow to a walk. He was disappointed—he'd need stamina to go into surgery. While he was seeing several patients daily who were interested in surgery, his first procedure wouldn't be until next week, so at least he had some time to build his endurance back up.

He walked for five minutes to catch his breath, then started running again, making it another ten minutes before he was so spent he almost collapsed. He staggered out into the surf and flopped over. The water was cool and calm, invigorating beyond belief. *Now I know where I'll be spending my mornings.* He looked around. No one else was out yet. He had the whole beach to himself. It felt like he had the whole island to himself. The whole world.

He stood in the surf, the water up to his shoulders, and watched the sun climb above the palms. He was in paradise. *What a life. I could get used to this.* He could have stayed in the ocean all day, but he had to get to work. So he headed back up the beach toward his bungalow.

As he reached the edge of the sand and was about to head up the path toward the bungalows, he saw Ethan come out of his house, carrying Zack on his shoulders. Zack must have been having difficulty walking today, but Ethan was making it fun, probably not wanting Zack to feel bad. He brought him to the dock near the house and the two of them sat on the edge together.

Paul watched from the distance, not wanting to go over and disturb them. It was the perfect picture of a father and his son. He knew how much Ethan loved Zack and thought how difficult it was going to be when Zack died. Even as well as Zack was doing, as much as he'd defied the odds, he probably wouldn't live to be an adult.

Life was so fragile. How easy it was to lose the ones you love. In two weeks he would see Beth and his own sons, and try to be part of a family again.

• • •

After showering and dressing, Paul headed toward the dining room for breakfast, Karla's meal plan in hand. He ran into Lita Davis, just coming out of her bungalow, carrying her suitcase.

"Are you leaving?" he asked, surprised. She was scheduled for X rays today, and then an evaluation by Karla.

"Yes, unfortunately I have to." She sighed, annoyed and tired. She explained that her attorney had called; her ex-husband had filed some kind of emergency appeal regarding their divorce settlement. She had to go back for the hearing.

"Losing his money was harder for him than losing me," she said with a wry chuckle. "I picked a real loser, didn't I, Doctor?"

Paul wondered if Beth felt the same way. But he'd never struck her or abused her in any way. Or the boys. He'd always done everything he could for them. His problem had been more self-destructive.

Who are you kidding? It destroyed them as much as you.

Lita's surgery would be in three weeks. "I'm still going ahead with it," she told Paul. "He can file all the appeals and motions he wants; he's not getting a cent of the money back. I earned it, living with him. I'm fixing what he did to me, even if I have to take out a loan to do it."

"Well, I hope it won't come to that. But what about the X rays?"

He'd ordered films so he could examine her facial structure before her surgery.

"I'll come back and get those done, don't worry," she said. She told him she usually drove to Key West every couple of weeks anyway. She'd gotten their condo there in the divorce.

"Maybe that's what he wants now," she said. "Anyway, stopping back for the X rays won't be a problem."

"Great. I'll see you in three weeks."

He helped her with her suitcase, then went to the dining room. The buffet table was full of fresh pineapples, mangos, and melons. Karla's meal plan called for a bowl of oatmeal with skim milk and fruit, plus two tablespoon-sized scoops of powdered protein and a sixteen-ounce bottle of spring water. The oats and the protein were in glass canisters on the buffet table alongside the fruit and fresh-squeezed orange juice.

Paul had breakfast, then stopped by the lobby to see Annie and find out what his schedule was like for the next couple of weeks. He was wondering if he could get a long weekend to take the boys fishing or camping somewhere. That'd be the perfect opportunity for him to start forming a bond with them. Beth might come along, too.

He realized he was getting ahead of himself; Beth hadn't even let him take the kids for an afternoon yet. But he couldn't help himself. He had to remain positive. He was going to see if Annie could "coincidentally" leave him one Friday and the following Monday open.

When he walked through the lobby to the reception desk, he was surprised to see Ethan explaining the phones and the procedures to a different woman.

"Where's Annie?" Paul asked.

"She's no longer working here," Ethan said.

Paul was shocked. Annie practically ran all of the administrative aspects of the clinic. How was the place going to run without her? And why did she leave? He wanted to ask Ethan, but not in front of the new woman.

Ethan introduced Paul to the new receptionist, a temp named Donna, sent over by an agency in Key West. She'd be filling in until Ethan could find and train Annie's replacement.

He skimmed through his schedule. Somehow Ethan had found quite a few people interested in surgery and had them scheduled already. The long weekend might be difficult. He'd talk to Donna about it later, when Ethan wasn't around.

He walked out with Ethan, still thinking about Annie's departure. She'd never mentioned it and neither had Ethan.

"Did you know Annie was leaving?" he asked Ethan.

Ethan shook his head no.

"Why did she leave?" Paul asked. "She seemed happy here."

"She didn't leave on her own. I had to let her go."

"Really? Why? I thought she was good."

"She was. But I had a problem with her."

"What do you mean? What kind of problem?"

Ethan stopped walking and turned toward Paul. "Since you and I are more or less in this together, I should tell you. But it's between us."

"Of course." Who did Ethan expect him to tell, anyway? "What happened?" he asked.

"The one thing I take very seriously," Ethan said, "is patient confidentiality. When our patients come here, some of them don't want anyone knowing, not even their families. People can be very funny about this type of thing. You know that. You've done surgeries on patients who didn't want anyone knowing."

"Sure." When Paul had first started doing face-lifts and breast implants back in the early 1980s, most patients kept it a secret. Since then with many of them it had become something to brag about. But Paul understood Ethan's point.

"We have to be extremely careful," Ethan said. "Violating a patient's confidentiality not only hurts the patient but it can open us up to lawsuits, and none of us wants that. What Annie did is the one thing I can't tolerate here. From anybody." He looked directly into Paul's eyes. "I can't let anyone interfere with what we're doing here."

Paul understood what Ethan was telling him. Ethan wouldn't tolerate it from Annie, and he wouldn't tolerate it from Paul, either. But Paul felt a little hurt that Ethan would think he needed this little lecture. He had never violated a patient's confidentiality and wasn't about to start now. But he figured Ethan was within his rights, especially after the incident with Annie, whatever that was.

And he knew that this clinic made it possible for Ethan to afford to continue caring for Zack. That surely had a lot to do with the passion he was showing now.

Paul assured Ethan that he needn't have any concerns about something like that happening with him.

"I know," Ethan said. "You're not the type of person who forgets his responsibilities. Or his friends."

That was an odd remark—not so much the words as the way Ethan said them. Not as a threat, but almost as though he were making an accounting, pointing out their relative positions—kind of like a landlord warning a tenant who owed him back rent not to rock the boat by complaining about the leaky plumbing.

Paul tried to dismiss it as meaningless. He was already running a few minutes behind and he didn't want to keep his first patient waiting. But as he hurried across the clinic grounds Ethan's words echoed in his head.

You're not the type of person who forgets his responsibilities. Or his friends.

Paul did owe Ethan a lot. Ethan had gone out on a limb to bring him here. And Paul certainly appreciated it. But exactly what did Ethan expect in return?

That question troubled him.

For the first time since he accepted this position, he wondered if he was accumulating a debt that might be extremely difficult to repay.

The boy's name was Leonardo Pelez, but his parents called him Leito. His mother spoke English, but the boy and his father spoke only Spanish. Paul's Spanish was rudimentary at best. Manhattan General had had a full staff of interpreters so Paul never had to speak to patients in Spanish. De Leon didn't have that.

Leito looked nervous. Paul, thinking it might put the boy at ease a little if he spoke a few words in Spanish, said, *"Buenos días, Leito. ¿Cómo estás?"*

"Bien." Leito was tiny, even for a five-year-old. And shy, staying close to his mother. When he spoke, his voice was weak; he kept his head down, avoiding looking at Paul. He was obviously hiding his face, ashamed. It really saddened Paul to see the little boy like this.

"Me llamo Paul," he said. *"Soy tu doctor."*

Paul knelt down in front of Leito. He'd exhausted just

about all of his Spanish so he decided to let the boy's mother interpret. "Would it be all right if I took a look at your face?" he asked the boy.

His mother translated what Paul said, then Paul added, *"¿Puedo?"* Can I?

Leito slowly looked up. The bite was on his left cheek and part of his nose. It appeared that the damage went into the muscle and cartilage and possibly the bone. Paul had seen worse, but he had never seen anything sadder. Leito just stared up at him, as though his whole life depended on Paul making him normal again.

Paul smiled at him and pretended not to see anything wrong. *"¿Donde está el problema?"* he said, asking where the problem was.

Leito's father came over quickly and pointed to the scar on his son's face. He was very serious and he looked worried that Paul didn't notice.

"Oh, okay," Paul said, winking at Leito, who giggled. The boy's parents laughed now, too, lightening the mood just a bit.

Paul scheduled Leito's surgery for the end of the month, when Leito would make another trip from the Dominican Republic.

Paul saw two other patients before the day was over, both of whom were referred by Ethan. One of them wanted his chin reconstructed, saying that all of his life he looked like a chicken. But now, after the hormone therapy, he finally felt good enough about himself to do something about it. Paul did some reading that night, brushing up on some of the procedures he'd be doing in the coming weeks. He also picked up a few melons from the kitchen and a scalpel from the OR and practiced a bit, visualizing the melon as a patient and precisely cutting into the outer layer.

He went to bed early. When he woke up the next morning to go to the gym and start the weight-training program that Karla had designed, his legs were so sore he could barely walk. Yesterday's run had worked muscles that had been soft for years. He was paying for his past neglect.

When he limped into the gym, Karla was doing squats with a barbell across her shoulders. She saw him and started laughing, almost dropping the weights.

"Yeah, real funny," Paul said.

She racked the barbell and snatched her towel off the bench next to her. Wiping the sweat off her face and her abs, she came over. "I'll bet you didn't stretch after the run like the program says, ya?" she said.

"Like that really would have made much of a difference."

"You doctors think you know it all. Next time, listen to the experts, ya?"

"Ya," he muttered.

She laughed again. He wondered if she was laughing because he made fun of the way she talked or at the way he struggled to walk.

"I've got a workout to do," he grumbled.

"Over here," she said, walking to one of the larger benches.

"What?"

She pointed to the bench. "Lie down."

"Why?"

"We need to dissolve some of that lactic acid and limber up those muscles so you won't be complaining all day, and so your patients won't think you're handicapped. Lie down."

"What's wrong with a handicapped surgeon?"

"Just shut up and lie down," she said. "I have patients coming in later and I can't spend my whole day with you."

He came over and sat on the bench. "You have quite a bedside manner, you know that?" he said.

She pushed him backward so he was lying on the bench. "You haven't seen my bedside manner yet," she said with just enough rawness in her tone that he knew she wasn't talking about the way she dealt with patients. It was the last word, the *yet,* that unnerved him and at the same time fascinated him.

She began massaging his thighs. Her hands were powerful and she knew exactly how to work the muscles in a way that both hurt and relieved the stiffness at the same time.

"I can't have you walking around here like that," she

said. "Patients will think I did this to you. It makes me look bad."

"And I thought it was me you were concerned about."

She gripped hard into his thighs, sending a spike of pain through his legs. "Ouch!" he said. "That hurt. Take it easy."

"Maybe you won't be such a wiseass now, ya?"

"Ya. Anything you say."

She chuckled and continued massaging his legs. She pressed her palms down into his muscles and slowly slid them upward on his thighs. She stopped just shy of his crotch, her fingers almost brushing him. He suddenly started to get hard. The thin shorts he was wearing weren't going to hide his reaction. He panicked and quickly sat up.

"I'm not finished," she said.

"That's about all I have time for," he said. "I just remembered, I have an early patient to see so I have to get going."

"What about your workout?"

"I'll have to fit it in later, maybe this afternoon."

"At least let me work on the back of your legs, ya?"

He knew that if he said ya and let her start rubbing him again, he was going to be in trouble. Ethan's testosterone therapy was going right to his groin. He hadn't had urges like this in years. Karla wasn't the one he wanted to fulfill those urges, Beth was. But Karla was the one here, the one exciting him on a physical level, and he wasn't sure how much control he had over these new sensations.

"Thanks, but I'm fine now." He got up and walked to show her he was fine, forcing himself not to limp. "Yeah, that feels much better, thanks again." He hurried toward the door.

"Paul," she said, calling after him.

He stopped at the door. "Yeah?"

"Don't be embarrassed," she said.

He knew exactly what she meant. She'd noticed, and her pointing out that she'd noticed really embarrassed him. He was sure his face turned bright red. Well, so what. He'd gotten an erection when she rubbed his legs. He was a normal man, pumped with a lot of extra testosterone and other hormones. Any guy in the same situation would have had the same response. He had nothing to be embarrassed about.

But he was embarrassed. And even more, he felt guilty. He hadn't done a thing and yet he felt like he was being unfaithful to Beth, to whom he was no longer even married, with whom he hadn't been in a sexual way for more than three years.

But he still felt ashamed.

That morning he saw a patient who had come for a Botox injection in her forehead and collagen around her mouth. She wasn't interested in hormone replacement therapy and she didn't have time to work out regularly or to prepare special meals. She needed the type of quick fix that came in a syringe and worked instantly.

She was in her mid thirties, and had a few lines on her face, but really didn't look bad for her age. She just wanted to look twenty again. Paul didn't think she needed the injections, but she insisted, even knowing their effect was temporary. She explained that she was a lawyer from Atlanta, and at her firm, looks mattered. She'd noticed in her time there that the more attractive you were, the faster you made partner. She'd become a lawyer later in life than most, and so she had to preserve her youth while she proved herself in court.

"If it's that blatant, why don't you sue?" Paul said.

"If I could prove it, I would. But I can't prove it. I just know that's the way it is."

So she had decided to play the game. Once she made partner, she'd try to change things, but first she needed to make partner. If that meant coming here every six months, she'd gladly do it. She was also interested in liposuction, "some time in the future."

Paul gave her the injections. She left with renewed confidence. He'd done his job.

But it troubled him. The superficial nature of it had always disturbed him. What made him feel worse was the realization that by doing what he did, he was perpetuating this kind of conceit and discrimination. If he had his choice, he'd treat only patients like Leito, people who needed surgery to repair something that genuinely caused hardship. But just as this lawyer had to deal with the reality of her profession, Paul had to deal with the reality of his. Most patients came to a plastic surgeon out of vanity. All he could do was take solace in the fact that he made them feel better about themselves.

In the next few days he saw an average of four patients a day. The load was pretty light, but considering that he'd just started, he was impressed with how successfully Ethan attracted patients.

He scheduled several surgeries and a couple of micro-dermabrasions and laser peels. One of Ethan's patients, a man named Collins, came to find out about having some work done on his eyelids. The hormone therapy had done wonders for his appearance, but droopy eyelids or deep wrinkles could only be corrected with a scalpel. He also asked about hair transplants, but that was something Paul didn't do.

Collins did the weather on a TV station in Tampa and he said the camera seemed to show less mercy every month. He talked about the Japanese and how they aged grace-fully. He'd gone there on R and R when he was in the navy during the Vietnam War and had fallen in love with the place and visited at least once a year ever since.

"Aging isn't a negative thing there," he said. Then he chuckled and said, "But this isn't Japan."

Collins wasn't sure yet about having the surgery done; he just wanted Paul to evaluate him and explain the op-tions. He said he had to come back to De Leon in a couple of weeks. He'd decide by then.

Paul's first actual surgery was to be a liposuction, the same procedure Wilkenson had had. The night before the opera-tion, he didn't sleep a wink. He skipped his run that morn-ing and went to his office early so he could go through the procedure several times in his head. He even walked around the OR for a while, just trying to get comfortable in there. It felt strange, like somewhere he didn't belong—or rather, somewhere he used to belong but had lost the privilege of membership.

The urge to drink came on strong. He remembered the ritual and held out his hands. They were as steady as could be. He just held them there and silently repeated the serenity prayer he'd learned at AA. Taking deep breaths, he gradually calmed his nerves and fought off the desire to drink.

When the patient arrived and was prepped for surgery, Paul became nervous again. He scrubbed and went into the OR. He checked his hands. Steady. He took deep breaths and began with the tiny incision in the woman's hip. As he inserted the cannula, he was extremely careful about the path he took. He did not want to make the same mistake as his last surgery, three years ago. Back in New York, he'd gotten so proficient at this that he could do an entire procedure involving the thighs, waistline, and knees in thirty minutes. But today it took him over an hour. When he finished, he let out a long sigh. It was almost as if he'd been holding his breath the whole time.

When his assistant wheeled the patient into recovery, Paul went back to his office. The joy hit him suddenly. He wanted to scream. He'd done it. He was a surgeon again!

14

STILL FEELING HIGH from the successful liposuction, Paul left the office late in the afternoon and went down to the beach to take the run he'd skipped that morning. He was filled with energy and needed to burn some of it off.

A few patients were sitting in the sand, waiting for the sunset. He began jogging up the beach. Soon he was running. Funny how success can make you strong, he thought.

He had also noticed the difference that two weeks of regular exercise and hormone therapy made in the way he felt. He had more vigor and vitality. He'd even *seen* the change when he looked in the mirror. His love handles were shrinking. His shoulders and arms were filling out again. Maybe there was something to all of this. At the beginning, he hadn't been completely convinced, even after seeing Ethan. But now that he saw and felt the improvement in himself, he was becoming a believer.

Once around Coral Key was a mile and a half. He usually did two laps. This evening he decided to go for three. But halfway around, in a remote part of the island, he saw Karla swimming in the surf. She waved for him to stop and came out of the water.

She wore a sleek black two-piece Speedo designed for sport as much as for looks, the perfect accent for the hard, angular lines of her body.

"I thought you were a morning runner?" she said.

"Usually. But I couldn't make it this morning."

"Why? What were you doing last night?" she asked in a suggestive tone.

"Worrying. I had surgery this morning."

"It went well, ya?"

"Very well."

"So you missed sleep and you missed a workout for nothing." She shook her head. "What am I going to do about you?"

He chuckled. "I promise not to do it again."

"You should try a different cardio workout once in a while, instead of running all the time. Sometimes the body needs to be shocked, ya? Come on, we'll swim." She started back into the water. "We'll race."

"I don't have my swimsuit on," he said.

She pointed to his shorts. "That's fine."

"These are running shorts."

"Don't be such a baby," she teased. "I think you're afraid of losing, ya?"

"No, of course not."

"Then get your ass in here and we'll race."

Paul watched her walk deeper into the water. Something told him he shouldn't do it, but he felt himself taking off his shirt and following her into the surf. Something stronger was pulling him in her direction.

"There's a small key out there," she said, pointing. "See it?"

He did. A tiny dot of land with some trees and bushes.

"I usually swim there and back," she said. "It's a kilometer each way. You can make that, ya? Or will I have to rescue you halfway?"

"You just worry about losing the race," Paul said.

She laughed. "By the way," she said, pointing back up toward the beach. "You put your shirt too close to the water. The tide is going to take it away."

When he turned to look at it, she yelled, "Go!" and started swimming.

"Cheater!" Paul said and swam after her.

He shouldn't have been surprised at how strong a swimmer Karla was. But he was surprised. He'd thought he could keep close to her, but she got out so far in front of him so quickly that the only chance he had of catching up was if a speedboat came along and gave him a lift.

But he didn't want to let her beat him. The way she liked to tease him, she'd never let him live it down.

He had to play hardball. He stopped swimming and screeched in pain. When she turned around, he clutched his chest and bobbed under the water. She quickly swam back toward him, looking worried. He kept up the act until she reached for him, then he grabbed her shoulders and shoved her under. He began swimming full speed toward the island again.

"I can cheat as well as you!" he shouted back between strokes.

He glanced over his shoulder as he swam, to see how much of a lead he had. He'd need a lot to beat her. But he didn't see her. He took a couple more strokes then looked back again. She still wasn't there.

A shiver of panic ran through him. Could something have happened when he pushed her under? Why hadn't she come up?

"Karla?" he called out.

No answer. He scanned the water all around, just in case she'd come up somewhere else. But she was nowhere to be found. He started swimming back to where he'd pushed her under.

"Karla?" he called out.

He ducked underwater and squinted in the salty surf, looking for her. The water wasn't deep here, maybe ten feet. He could see the sand and coral at the bottom, but he couldn't see her. He came up for air.

"Karla?"

His panic grew. He looked toward shore, wishing someone was there to help him. But the beach was empty. The clinic was too far away for anyone there to hear him if he called for help. It was up to him. He had to find her. But where was she? She'd been under too long.

He took a deep breath so he could duck under again,

then suddenly felt a painful jab in his stomach that knocked the air out of him. Before he could even react, his shorts were ripped off of him. An instant later, Karla burst up through the surface of the water, gasping and laughing and waving his shorts over her head.

"Look what I found."

"Give me the shorts."

She shook her head.

"Stop playing games," he said. "Give me my shorts, okay?"

"I like games."

He let out a breath of frustration. This wasn't funny. "Karla, would you just give me my damn shorts?"

"Umm, getting angry, ya?"

"Give me my shorts!"

"Make me." She grinned at him, waved good-bye, and started swimming toward the island.

"It's not funny anymore, Karla!" he shouted.

She glanced back, laughing. "I think it is." She kept swimming.

"I swear to God, you better come back with my god-damn shorts!"

"Or else what? What are you going to do?"

He was really pissed now. He did not want to do this, but he needed his shorts. He couldn't exactly walk back to the clinic naked from the waist down. With his anger building, he swam after her, deciding that he was going to make her pay. See how she liked having to go back bare-assed.

She reached the island while he was still twenty yards offshore. She trudged up onto the beach, barely winded from the swim, still holding his shorts. She turned around and waved them at him.

"Come and get them, Doctor."

He lowered his feet and felt the bottom. Still ten yards out, he fought his way through the surf toward her. He stopped when the water was up to his waist. He was gasping for air.

"Okay, you had your fun," he said. "Now will you give me my shorts?"

She snickered. "No, I haven't had my fun yet." She turned and ran down a path that cut through the bushes in the center of the island.

"Hey! Come back! Goddamn it, Karla!"

She was gone in an instant. He didn't want to leave the water naked but he had no choice. He had to get his shorts back. He stormed up the beach, growing angrier by the second. A joke was one thing, but she was carrying this much too far.

He felt the cool wind on his skin. He hadn't done anything like this since he was a teenager. In a way, it felt invigorating. If he weren't so upset at Karla, he might have felt a thrill.

He glanced back toward Coral Key to make sure no one was watching him. The shore was too far away for anyone there to see him clearly anyway. He turned back toward the brush. He didn't see Karla, didn't hear her thrashing around in there. She was hiding, no doubt.

He crossed the beach, intent on finding her and teaching her a lesson. As he hurried down the path the sun was starting to set, and here under the trees there wasn't much light. But the path only went one way, so he continued ahead, finally coming out on the other side.

He looked across another beach that faced the endless Atlantic. Karla was nowhere around.

"Damn it," he said. He started to turn back when she jumped from behind a palmetto bush and rammed him, knocking the wind out of him again. She twisted her leg around his and tripped him, laying him out hard on the sand. She fell down on top of him, grabbed both of his hands, and shoved them down to the sand, pinning them there. She sat, straddling his chest. That's when he realized that her bathing suit was off now. She wore only the belly button ring and a look of defiance.

With each breath he drew, his lungs filled with the estrous scent of her body. He struggled to free himself, but it wasn't much of an attempt. He didn't really want to get away. He was exactly where he wanted to be. He noticed that she'd shaved all her pubic hair off, something he'd never seen before. The novelty excited him even more. He wanted her.

She held him down and glared at him, a look of depravity in her eyes. She slid down so her chest rubbed against his. Her pubis brushed his penis. He became so hard that her weight pressing down on his member sent a spike of pain through his pelvis. But it was good pain, pain he did not want to end. He hadn't been this aroused in years. The extra testosterone he was taking was supercharging his libido.

Karla wrapped him up with her powerful legs and smothered his mouth with hers. She didn't wait for his tongue; instead she went right in to find it. She let go of his hands and grabbed a fistful of his hair. She had such ardent passion that she began to claw at his shoulders and arms and neck. And he found himself doing the same. He could not control his desire for her. The feel of her toned, wet body slithering on top of him sent his hormones into a rage.

He wrapped his arms around her and grabbed her rock-hard ass. The precision of her moves, the utter control she had over every muscle in her body, the way he felt even the slightest movement she made ripple through her, drew him further into her spell. Her body screamed of what she could do with it.

He pulled her against him and slid his cock across the top of her clitoris, then he began rocking up and down. The friction sent shivers of pleasure through her body. As tough as she was, she gasped like a delicate girl. He kept it up until *she* decided it was enough. She pulled herself away and slithered down his body, kissing his chest, his stomach, and finally his cock. She took him in her mouth and gave him pleasure like he'd never felt before. She had a way of constricting her tongue around him then nipping him with her teeth. With one hand, she kneaded his balls and with the other tugged at his chest.

No, he'd never felt anything like this before. Beth had gone down on him, but it had felt very different. With Beth, it had seemed like obligation. Karla was doing it as much for herself as for him. She got off on it and that made it more exciting for him. She worked on him, slowing when he was getting close, letting the edge come off, then bringing him dangerously close all over again. She did this until he couldn't take it any more. She seemed to know exactly when that was. She pulled her lips and tongue off of him and crawled back up his body, looking like a feral cat closing in for the kill. She kissed him wildly again.

He grabbed her shoulders and rolled her over in the sand, then climbed onto her. It was his turn to show her that he could drive her crazy, too. His penis was still rock hard. He slid it over her clitoris as he licked and nipped at her breasts. There wasn't much there to bite, but what was there was enough to fire his hormones. Her nipples were erect and he pinched them between his teeth until he heard her moan.

"Yes," she hissed.

He slid his tongue down her breast, traced the grid of muscle on her abdomen, then licked a path between her legs. The smooth flesh was salty and pungent and new. Everything about her was new to him. She was hot and syrupy when he fluttered his tongue inside her. She gasped the first time he licked her clit. Then he went to work, starting slowly, gradually picking up speed and intensity. She moaned and dug her fingernails into his back as her passion flared.

She screamed the first time she came. The sound of her ecstasy excited him that much more. He imagined being deep inside her when she screamed like that. And he would be. Soon. But he wanted her completely ready. He brought her to orgasm again with his tongue. She screamed and writhed on the ground and nearly ripped the skin off his back. As she came out of the orgasm, she pulled him up toward her mouth. She'd had enough of the tongue and wanted the rest of him. This was the first time he felt just how strong she was. Even if he had wanted to, he could not have overpowered her. She wanted him inside her and nothing would stop her from getting what she wanted.

But he didn't want to stop her. He wanted to be inside

her as much as she wanted it. At this moment, he wanted it more than he'd ever wanted anything before. He thrust deep inside her. She wrapped her legs around him, digging her heels into his ass. She wanted him to do the work, which was fine with him. He got a rhythm going, and soon she was gasping again. The timing was perfect. They climaxed together, both howling into the darkening night. When he was through, he slowed and stopped, lowering his weight on top of her. She took a moment to catch her breath, then rolled him over, pulled him back inside her and rode him until she came one last time.

Being with her was like being with a savage creature. No restraint. Nothing held back. Nothing off limits. No shame or guilt or propriety to interfere with the pure, animalistic instincts. He was still shuddering, the aftershocks of coming inside her, when he felt the urge to fuck her again, fuck her as hard as he could. He'd never felt an urge like this before. It was stronger than the urges he used to have to drink. Sex with her was like alcohol, an addiction. He'd abstained for so long, and now she was allowing him to imbibe again, to taste the pleasure. He wanted every drop of it.

The hormones went right where he needed them. Hard again, he went at it with her. She had stamina like he'd never seen before, and she brought out a stamina in him he hadn't realized he had. He penetrated her and rode her like a wild mustang. She bit at his neck, drawing blood. But he didn't care, didn't even feel pain. He drove her down into the sand and fucked her until neither one could take it anymore. Then they sank down onto the beach, breathless.

"Um, that was so good," she said, staring up at the stars, her hand resting on his penis. "You liked it, ya?"

"Ya."

She laughed. "I know. I heard you."

He lay there in silence, soaked with sweat, sand sticking to his skin. His head began to clear of the wild thoughts of Karla, the rousing sensations of her naked body against his.

"Oh, ya," she said, laughing and rubbing him.

He tried to tune her out. Suddenly, through the intoxicating fog she'd left in his head, he remembered. A wave of nausea came over him. Tomorrow was the day he was supposed to get a visit from Beth and the kids.

Oh, my God. What have I done?

15

PAUL WAS ABLE to rearrange his appointments so he could spend the whole day with Beth and the kids. A lot was riding on today.

Nervously, he paced the lobby. Perspiration soaked his armpits and dripped down his neck. The urge to have one drink to steady his nerves came on him suddenly, stronger than ever before. He felt ashamed of what he'd done last night. He needed desperately to wash away the memory. He kept thinking Beth was going to find out. He kept thinking he was going to screw this up. He kept thinking that he wasn't ready to be reunited with his kids, that something was going to go wrong, that he should call and cancel and hide and get drunk.

No, be strong. He needed to go forward, not backward. He'd been able to see patients again; he'd been able to perform surgery. He could do this, too. He didn't have to drink. He didn't have to make a mistake. Beth didn't have to know about last night.

As he waited, he realized that he needed to find a twelve-step meeting. Maybe even get a sponsor down here. He'd let it slip to the bottom of his list of priorities. But he realized that was a mistake.

He had to be mindful. He had to avoid slipping up, at all costs. He'd already slipped up with Karla. But he'd cut that off immediately. He'd left that island sick with guilt and knowing exactly what he needed to do. Stay away from her. Keep all contact professional. As addictive as she

was—as sex with her was—he vowed to stay away from
her. He had to. More than anything else, he wanted to put
his family back together.

A few minutes before eleven, a maroon Ford Explorer
came down the roadway from the bridge. Paul recognized
Beth behind the wheel and Kenny in the front seat beside
her. Pete was in the back, poking his head over the seat.

It had been so long since he'd seen them. Too long. His
heart raced as the doors opened. Pete jumped out and ran
over to hug him. "Daddy!" Paul scooped him up. He was
eight now, much bigger than Paul remembered. They were
growing up without him. That realization hit him hard in
the heart. He couldn't bear to let that happen.

He saw Kenny get out of the SUV and just stand beside
it, scanning the surroundings. He was thirteen, already
taller than Beth, with the beginnings of peach fuzz under
his nose. He had the distant, independent look of a
teenager. Beth had said that Kenny was seeing a therapist.
Paul felt awful that his son was suffering so much inside.
Because of him.

"Kenny!" Paul said, waving him over.

Kenny nodded and motioned for Paul to calm down. He
let out an embarrassed sigh.

"He's just being weird," Pete said.

Paul realized that Kenny was just being a teenager. He
tried not to take it personally.

He looked toward the driver's seat of the SUV. Beth was
still inside, talking on the cell phone.

"Who's your mom talking to?" he asked Pete as he put
him down and the two of them walked toward the Ford.

Pete shrugged. Paul looked over at his other son.
"Kenny, do you know?"

"Does it matter?"

Kenny's voice was bitter. He did not want to be here.

"What do you say, Ken?" Paul said, extending his hand
to Kenny. "How are you doing?" He knew Kenny wouldn't
rush up for a hug, like Pete. He needed another tack to connect with him.

Kenny sighed, exasperated, and unhappily reached out

to shake Paul's hand. Paul quickly pulled him in for a hug before Kenny knew what was happening. Kenny squirmed away and groaned. "Come on, Dad. Grow up, will you?" He looked embarrassed and irritated. "Jeez . . ."

Pete laughed, which annoyed Kenny even more. "Shut up, twerp," Kenny told Pete.

From the other side of the SUV, Beth said, "Kenny, don't tell your brother to shut up, and don't call him a twerp."

Kenny rolled his eyes and looked off, muttering under his breath, "But that's what he is."

Paul looked over at Beth. She was off the phone now and standing beside the SUV. She closed the door and walked around to where the rest of them were standing. Her eyes were hidden behind sunglasses, her expression shaded beneath a wide-brimmed hat. But her lips were pursed tightly. Having been married to her for sixteen years, separated and divorced for another three, Paul could tell that she, like Kenny, wasn't too happy about coming here to see him. But at least she had come, which was a good sign, because she didn't have to. Paul tried to take confidence from that.

Maybe if she saw how well he was doing, she'd lighten up a bit—maybe even feel glad that she'd made the trip.

"Hi, hon," he said quietly, stepping close and quickly giving her a hug before she could pull a Kenny and avoid him. She patted him on the back in a way that felt very distant and detached.

Fear shivered up his neck when she touched him. Would she realize that he'd been with Karla last night? The feel of his body, a scent coming off him, the way he stood, something might expose him. Women had a way of sensing things.

He stepped back, needing safety.

The fear and guilt and uneasiness left him feeling unresponsive to her touch. He'd been so hard last night with Karla, so alive, but right now with Beth, he was completely flaccid. Even the hormones he was taking weren't enough to overcome his feelings of impotence.

"So, how was the ride down here?" he asked, needing to make small talk, to start connecting with her in a safe way.

"Fine." She glanced around at the expanse of buildings and grounds that made up the clinic. "I didn't realize you and Ethan had such a big place," she said, her voice without much emotion. But Paul did detect an edge of annoyance in her voice.

"Yeah, your brother built quite a clinic here," he said. "He's really committed to antiaging."

She nodded. "And to you," she said. He couldn't see her eyes behind the sunglasses, but he was certain she was glaring at him, certain he'd detected anger in her tone.

"I owe him a lot," he said.

She glanced at the two boys. "Stay here for a minute," she told them. "I want to talk to your father."

She and Paul started walking down the drive, back toward the bridge. She didn't say anything; she just stared ahead behind her sunglasses, remaining silent. Paul figured he should speak first.

"Look, I really appreciate you driving all the way down here," he said.

"I had to go to Key West anyway. This was on the way. So it's not a special trip."

She wanted him to know that he wasn't special in her life anymore. And it hurt him to hear that, to see how important it was to her that he know. But then she surprised him. "But I think it's good for the boys to see you . . . cleaned up," she said.

Paul felt another wave of nauseating guilt. His sons had seen him at his worst. He needed to show them that *that* wasn't him—*this* was him.

"Thanks," he said. He watched her for a moment as they walked, but he still couldn't see much expression. Finally he said, "It's good to see you, Beth."

She nodded. Then she stopped, took off her sunglasses, and studied him for a moment. "You look well." She sounded sincere. And not angry.

"Thanks." The antiaging regimen paid off after all.

"Obviously you're not drinking anymore," she said.

"I haven't touched a drop in over two years."

She nodded again, watching him. He could not read her face, could not tell what she was thinking. Was she considering giving him another chance? Or did she not believe that he'd been sober that long? Or maybe she didn't believe it would last. Whatever she was thinking, she kept it to herself. She put her sunglasses back on and started walking again.

It was still too soon, he realized. It would take time to convince her that he'd really changed. He didn't expect her to fall into his arms this morning. But he would do what was necessary to win her back, to prove that he'd turned his life around.

"So how are you doing?" he asked. "You look good." More small talk. He was trying to connect with her somehow.

"I'm doing okay." She turned her face toward him. All he saw were her sunglasses as she said, "I'm getting on with life."

Life without you . . . He wondered if that was what she was saying. But she left it at that, and he didn't have the guts to press her.

"By the way," he said, remembering their last conversation. "How's Kenny? What happened with the therapist?"

"Counselor," she said, as though the distinction mattered.

"Okay, what happened with the counselor?"

She sighed. "I think it's good for him to see her. He's going through some rough times, emotionally."

"What did she say?"

"I just told you," she said, snapping at him.

"Beth, he's my son, too. I really want to know what's going on with him."

"Then you shouldn't have—" She stopped herself. "Look, I didn't come here to fight with you."

"I don't want to fight, either."

"Kenny sees her once a week. They talk about what's going on with his life. I don't sit in on the sessions so I don't know what they say to each other, but I think it's go-

ing to help him. He's a good boy. He's just . . . confused
inside."

Paul sighed, feeling worried and ashamed. This, too,
was his fault. He felt so helpless to do anything for his son,
and that made it even worse.

"You'll let me know what happens?" he asked.

She nodded and kept walking.

There was a long moment of uncomfortable silence. Before Paul could say anything, Karla came jogging up the
road toward them. She was wearing her usual tight spandex shorts and sports bra. Her skin glistened with sweat.
She fixed her eyes right on Paul and veered toward him.

Oh, no. A nervous fear shuddered through him, center-
ing in his sphincter. He was terrified at what she was going
to do. He hadn't spoken to her since they'd left the island
last night. What if she came up and planted a kiss on his
lips, right here in front of Beth? Karla was just the type of
person to do that.

"What's *that*?" Beth whispered, noticing Karla coming
toward them.

Trouble. If only he'd realized it sooner. He braced himself.

Karla slowed to a walk. She was gasping for breath,
dripping with sweat as she approached. How was he going
to stop her from doing something that would ruin his
chances with Beth? He had to think quickly.

"Karla, hi. I want you to meet Beth, *my wife.*" He hoped
to God she'd get the message.

Beth glared at him. Obviously she didn't want to be introduced as his wife anymore.

Karla extended her hand. "Nice to meet you." She
glanced at Paul. He saw a wicked glint in her eyes. She was
going to do something bad.

"Karla works here," Paul said, speaking before Karla
could say anything harmful, like pointing out that they'd
had sex last night. "Karla is the clinic's nutritionist and
exercise physiologist."

"It's nice to meet you," Beth said to her.

"Dr. Tobin speaks of you often," Karla said.

"Really?" Beth glanced at Paul. He just smiled back. But inside he was in shock. Whatever Karla was up to, it wasn't good.

"Ya. He was talking about you last night. How much he was looking forward to coming."

With her accent, it sounded like she'd made an honest mistake with the language, but Paul knew better. She wanted to unnerve him, to make him sweat, and she succeeded.

Beth just nodded and glanced again at Paul.

There was a long, awkward silence.

Finally Karla said, "I'd love to stay and talk, but I have to go. So nice to meet you," she said to Beth. "We'll see more of you around here, ya?"

Beth didn't answer. Karla glanced at Paul, a dangerous look in her eyes, then started running. Beth watched her run down the road. She turned back to Paul. He was sure she knew.

"What was *that* supposed to be?" she asked, shaking her head in amazement.

"Your brother sure knows how to pick 'em," he said. He figured if he shifted the emphasis to Ethan, Beth wouldn't question him about his relationship with Karla.

She continued to watch as Karla ran past the boys. Kenny stared at her until she disappeared around the building. His teenage hormones were working overtime. *Like father, like son.*

Beth took off her sunglasses and looked at Paul. She spoke in a whisper now. "Do you think Ethan and she are . . . ?"

Inside, Paul let out a huge sigh of relief. Thank God she suspected her brother, not him. "Who knows?" he said. "Maybe."

She just shook her head, bewildered.

He needed to shift the subject away from Karla. "I wanted to ask you," he said. "What do you have to do in Key West?" He had an idea.

"Mom and Dad have a place there that they were renting out. The tenants are moving out. I have to make sure they

didn't destroy the place, then I have to close it up for hurricane season."

"How long will that take?" he asked.

"Not too long. A few hours."

"Do me a favor, Beth. Leave the boys here with me
while you do that. Let me spend some time with them. I
need this. And so do they."

She stared at him. He wished he knew what was going
on in her head, but they had been apart for so long that he
could no longer read her.

Finally she spoke. "Why couldn't you have sobered up
and straightened out while we were still together?" Her
voice was resentful.

He didn't know how to answer. He wasn't even sure she
really wanted an answer. Nothing he could say would
make any difference anyway.

"The boys need consistency," she said. "They need a father."

"They have one, Beth."

She hesitated again, silently assessing him. "This is your
last chance," she said. "Don't screw it up this time."

He took the boys fishing from the pier behind Ethan's
house. Kenny wasn't happy about it but he cast a line in the
water and sat there, staring blankly. Pete was thrilled. He
kept taking up the slack on his line, testing it to see if he
had a fish, asking Kenny if he had one. Paul felt good, seeing him so happy. If only he could make Kenny happy, too.
But that was going to be harder.

"Hey, Kenny," he said. "Do you like Jet Skis?"

Kenny turned, suddenly interested. "You have one?"

"Uncle Ethan has two. I'm sure he'll let us borrow them
later if you want to go for a ride."

"Are you kidding. When?"

"How about in an hour?"

"Me, too?" Pete said.

"You're too little," Kenny said.

"I am not."

"You and I'll ride it together," Paul told Pete.

"But I can go alone," Kenny said. "Right?"

"You can go alone. We'll fish for another hour then we'll go do that."

Kenny frowned. "I got to sit here *that* long?"

Paul heard footsteps on the dock behind him. He turned. Karla stood there, staring at them. She had changed out of her workout clothes and had on loose-fitting shorts and a T-shirt. She grinned at him. Something was on her mind.

"I'll be right back," he told his sons and went over to see what she wanted.

"Nice-looking boys," she said.

"Don't take this the wrong way, but I was hoping to spend some time alone with them."

She smiled. "You want me to leave, ya?"

He didn't answer but that was exactly what he wanted.

"Okay," she said. "But just remember, I did you a favor back there."

"What are you talking about?"

"With your wife. I didn't say anything about us."

Hearing her say that out loud terrified him. He peered back at his sons, worried they had heard. They didn't seem to have heard. He turned back to Karla and lowered his voice to a whisper. "There is no *us*, Karla. We were together last night, a one-time thing. It's over."

"I don't know . . ." she said. "You still owe me."

"What are you talking about? For last night?"

"No. For today. For not saying anything. You owe me."

What was this? Blackmail? "Just what do you want from me?" he asked, angry.

"Some work done," she said. "Surgically."

"I can't operate on you. That's a conflict of—"

She pressed her hand to his lips. "Don't bullshit me, Paul. If you don't want your wife—or them," she said, gesturing to Kenny and Pete, "to know what you and I do, you do the surgery I need. Simple as that, ya?"

"It's not something we *do*," he said, clenching his teeth to keep from exploding at her. "It's something we *did*. One time. It was a mistake and it's not going to happen again."

"You think your wife and kids will understand that?"

"Why are you doing this to me?"

She laughed. "I'll stop by your office tomorrow for an exam. We can talk about the surgery."

She turned and walked away before he could say anything else. He realized that he hadn't taken care of the problem he'd created last night. In fact it was only just beginning.

16

ETHAN PEERED THROUGH the microscope at Lita Davis's culture. He saw much greater cell regeneration than she'd had after being treated with the last formulation of Rejuvenol. The telomerase, the tips of the chromosomes, were beginning to be restored. The adjustments he'd made were working. He only cultured her blood cells for twenty-four hours, and he needed to do it for at least forty-eight to be certain, but this was great news.

If the improvement held true during the remainder of the culture period, and if the therapy could bring about the same type of cellular regeneration for Zack, his chances of improvement would be very high. But those were two big "ifs."

How well it would work on Zack was always the question. His size and physical frailty made giving him the right dosage extremely important. Too little would leave him weak and vulnerable. Too much would shock his system and kill him. Even with results as promising as these, doubt always remained. That doubt left Ethan fearing what he was doing every step of the way.

Ethan returned the culture to the Cultrex machine he'd purchased from BioGen Sciences in California. It had cost just over one hundred thousand dollars, money he didn't have. He'd taken out yet another loan. His monthly payments from all the loans were becoming difficult to meet. But he had no choice. He needed the money to pay for Zack's care. And he needed this machine to do the research.

It accelerated the culture process, allowing him to culture stem cells much faster than with the standard method. This made it possible for him to refine the process and test its efficiency more quickly. Hormone therapy was helping keep Zack's strength up, helping him live something resembling a normal life. But the benefits of that therapy were diminishing. The only thing that would help Zack now was stem cell therapy. Rejuvenol. But he couldn't hold out much longer. With time such a critical factor in saving Zack's life, Ethan had to have the best equipment available to complete his work.

He'd check Lita Davis's culture again tomorrow. Meanwhile he needed to enter Zack's lab results into the computer.

As he sat at his desk, his thoughts returned to the fashion model from Los Angeles. Ever since her death, his concern over the safety of Rejuvenol had increased. His fear that it might hurt Zack was very real. Rejuvenol hadn't killed Nicole Quinn; she'd committed suicide. But her death brought home the realization that something as powerful as stem cell therapy had the potential for adverse side effects. He hadn't seen any yet, but he'd only given it to healthy adults. What would it do to a tiny, frail boy like Zack?

Ethan finished updating Lita Davis's chart and poured himself a cup of coffee. He heard voices outside so he went to the window. Down below, Paul and his two sons were at the water's edge, getting ready to use the Jet Skis that Ethan had lent them.

He watched Paul interacting with his boys. He looked so happy to be with them. Seeing this, Ethan felt a sour twinge of envy in his stomach. He wished his son could be as healthy as Paul's. He wished Zack could run and play and ride a Jet Ski by himself like Kenny. But Zack had been denied that. He'd turned from a little boy into an old man, practically overnight. His problems weren't school, dating disappointments, all the normal angst of the teenage years. His problems were life and death. Ethan didn't have to worry about how often he would see his son and how he could reestablish their relationship, as Paul did. He had to worry about how long his son would be alive, about whether he'd even be alive at the end of the week.

Yes, he did envy Paul. He wished he could be so lucky as to have Paul's problems.

He watched Kenny drive off on the Jet Ski, cautious and slow at first, but eventually picking up speed and turning hard, enjoying himself. Paul drove off with Pete sitting in front of him. He didn't do as many drastic maneuvers as Kenny. Pete seemed happy just the same.

Kenny drove a little closer to shore now. Ethan noticed why. Lying on the beach in the sun was Denise Riggs, a sexy fifty-year-old stockbroker from New York who looked twenty years younger since first coming here eight months ago. She was one of the patients willing to pay for the extra therapy, one of the patients Ethan had been testing Rejuvenol on.

Paul swerved his Jet Ski by Kenny now, splashing him, which drew his attention away from Denise. He sped off after Paul and Pete, yelling something that Ethan couldn't hear. Ethan watched them playing and he thought again about Zachary back at the house.

The solution struck him as he watched Paul and his sons in the water. As Zack's cousins, Kenny and Pete had genetics similar to Zack's. Their bone marrow had been a perfect match, and it would be used to keep Zack alive once Rejuvenol was ready. They were the right age, the right size. They were the ideal subjects to test Rejuvenol.

But what were the chances that Paul and Beth would allow him to do that? Paul certainly owed him a lot for giving him a chance that no one else would and for defending him when no one else would. But was that enough for Paul to allow his sons to be guinea pigs? The way Paul talked about those kids, the way he adored them, he probably wouldn't go for it. And Beth, as overprotective as she was, would never allow anything that might endanger her sons. He'd barely convinced her to agree to the bone marrow extraction, and that hadn't even put her sons at risk. Getting her to allow either Kenny or Pete to receive an injection of something that was experimental would be impossible.

But what if she and Paul were assured that the tests would be done in a way that wouldn't endanger the boys? . . . And what if they understood that it might be Zack's only chance? . . . Maybe they'd put their own paranoia aside.

Just then the door opened, startling Ethan. Karla strode in, like an athlete entering Olympic Stadium. Ethan didn't like her coming here to his house. He preferred to deal with her elsewhere. Something about her being in his home, in the place where Zack lived, felt like a violation.

"This is going to have to wait," he said. "I'm busy right now."

"Really?" She came over to the window and peered out to see what Ethan was looking at. "Denise Riggs?" she said with a chuckle. "You like the old ones, ya? Should I be jealous?"

Ethan didn't even crack a smile. Karla had a way of pushing his buttons. She did it on purpose. She wanted him to react, but he wasn't going to give her the satisfaction today. She was his main regret about Rejuvenol. The fact that he needed her. For so many years, he'd tried to develop it on his own. Only when she procured the research data on glion-2 from the East Germans was he finally able to make real progress. Without Karla he wouldn't have had that research and Rejuvenol would never have existed.

His reliance on her gnawed at his sense of pride. He, a physician and scientist, could not succeed without the help of a muscle-bound athlete who never even finished college. And she never let him forget that, either. Right from the start, he'd been forced to do things on her terms, to enter into an agreement with her that practically put him at her mercy. She held the power to endanger the whole project. He had to be careful not to do anything to anger her. One word from her to the FDA or the FBI would put him in deep trouble, end the project forever, and, most importantly, sentence Zack to certain death.

He left the window and walked over to his desk. He hoped that if he ignored her, she'd get the hint and leave. He wasn't going to chat with her or give her the satisfaction of seeing that she was getting to him. When she didn't leave, he had to say something.

"What do you want, Karla? I told you, I'm busy right now." He started entering the data from Zack's tests into the computer, just to do something so he wouldn't have to look up at her.

"I saw how busy you were," she said. He glanced up. She was still by the window, peering out. "One of the fringe benefits of having a clinic where we make women beautiful, ya?"

"I mean it, Karla. I have a lot of work to do. So if you came here to chat we're going to have to make it another time."

She laughed. "No, I didn't come to chat. I came for my injections."

"You're up to date on all that," he said.

"No. It's time again."

She stripped off her T-shirt, leaving only her black sports bra. "I can tell by the way I feel," she said. She bent her arm, as if she were curling a dumbbell. Her biceps bulged. "I feel weak," she said.

Ethan didn't know if she flexed that way to intimidate him or to impress him. He didn't want to let her know that she was succeeding at both.

"Let me check your chart," he said.

As he took out her file from his desk, he glanced up at her. The change in her physique over the last twelve months was remarkable. She'd been in fair shape when she came here, definitely strong from a lifetime of competitive sports. But she'd put on a layer of fat. The hormone therapies had helped restore her body to a more athletic shape. But the amazing change came once she started on Rejuvenol.

All visible body fat disappeared, leaving only lean muscle. Her heart and lung function improved. She was able to train harder, longer. She needed less rest. At her age, injuries were a problem, but after Rejuvenol she sustained fewer injuries and she recovered more quickly from the ones she did get. Her body had the capacity of a twenty-year-old. Ethan had gone to one of her competitions, a small swim meet in Tallahassee. He watched in awe at how much better she was than the rest of the athletes, all of them college age. She'd gone from being a mediocre athlete, fairly good for her age, but not nearly good enough to compete with the top swimmers, to a world-class competitor with a real chance at getting to the Olympics.

She was quite a testament to the effectiveness of what he was doing.

He double-checked her chart. "No, you're not due for anything, not for another week and a half."

"That's all right. I'll take the shots now anyway, ya?" she said.

"No, that's not all right." Ethan didn't even try to conceal his annoyance with her now. He was the doctor—she wasn't. He tolerated a lot from her, but he wasn't going to tolerate her telling him how to practice medicine. "You stick with what you know, the physical training," he said. "I'll take care of the medical end."

Karla just chuckled. She was so damned sure of herself, it really annoyed him. And it made him uneasy. She always knew exactly what she wanted, and how to get it from him.

But not this time, he told himself. This time she'd have to do it his way.

He went back to entering Zack's data into the computer, ignoring her. Again she didn't get the hint and leave.

She walked over to the desk and shimmied in behind his chair. Her bare stomach brushed his neck, sending a shiver down his back. He felt the belly button ring pinch his skin. The scent of her body, a strangely sensual mixture of perspiration and perfume, gripped him. He knew it was the testosterone he was taking, but he couldn't help the way his body reacted to her. He pretended to ignore her and struggled to continue typing. But her nearness made him nervous, and he was sure it showed. And sure she sensed it. Like a predator toying with her prey.

"Are those the test results on your son?" she asked. "How's he doing?"

She was invading his and Zack's privacy now. She

shouldn't be asking that. She had her hand in everything else around here—he did not intend to let her get her talons into Zack's life.

He ignored her question and closed Zack's file. Nothing subtle now. He was certain she would get the message this time. But if she did, she didn't let it show. She put her hands on his shoulders and began massaging his muscles.

"Your traps are as tight as a rope," she said. "Why so tense?"

Because of you. "I'm fine," he said.

"No, you're not. Stop by my studio this afternoon, ya? I'll work on you, get some of these knots out."

He'd had enough. He swiveled around, freeing his shoulders from her hands. He faced her now and said, "Look, don't take this the wrong way, but I have a lot of work to do, so if you don't mind . . ."

"You want me to leave, ya?"

"Thank you for understanding." He managed to keep it from sounding sarcastic. He swiveled his chair back around, giving her his back, and pretended to be concentrating on the computer. He opened another patient's file and checked the data.

"I'll go," she said.

"Thank you."

"Just give me the injections."

"I told you," he said, gritting his teeth, struggling to hold his temper. "It's not time. You're not due for a week and a half."

She grabbed his arm and spun him around. Her toying was over. She glared down at him. "Listen to me, Ethan," she said. "The Olympic qualifiers are in three months. I know where my times should be three months out and they're not there. I need those injections now, *and* in a week and a half."

"You can't play with dosages like that," he said. What she was asking was not medically sound. "The amount you're taking now is the maximum safe dose. Make changes to your training if you have to, but we really can't play with the dosages."

"My training is exactly where it has to be. I know my body better than you do. Just give me the injections, Ethan."

"It's not that simple, Karla. There's blood work to do first. You'll have to have a liver function test and—"

"Whatever you have to do, do. Just give me the injections."

"That all costs money. The tests are expensive. The hormones are expensive. Producing Rejuvenol is expensive. You have to be realistic about this. Do you realize how much it's costing me to provide you with all this?"

"That's not my problem." She spoke in a cold, dispassionate tone. "We made an agreement," she said. "I fulfilled my part. I got you what you needed. Now you keep up your end."

"I am keeping up my end!" He was angry that she was accusing him of not doing what he'd agreed to do, angry at the threatening tone she was using.

"Good. Then don't give me any more shit, Ethan. Just give me the goddamn injections, ya?"

The way she glared at him, there was no refusing her. He wasn't sure what she would do if she didn't get what she wanted. He'd never seen her so heated, so menacing. She was very capable of trying something physical. But what concerned him even more was her going to the authorities. He could not afford to have her do that.

With no other option, he prepared the syringes and the infusion bag.

She became calm again, as though she'd never been upset or threatening at all. "By the way, I may need a few days off soon," she said.

"Why? Your schedule is pretty light already. You're only seeing—what?—two or three patients a day. You said you could do your training around the schedule."

He came over and swabbed her arm with alcohol where he was going to inject her. "Relax your arm," he said. Her muscles were so hard it always made it difficult to give her the shots.

"Not because of the training," she said. "Because of the surgery."

"What surgery?" He gave her the first injection, testosterone. She didn't even flinch when he jabbed the needle into her triceps. "What are you talking about?" he asked.

"Paul Tobin is going to do a little work on me."

"*What?* Who said?" Ethan needed Paul operating on paying patients. He needed money to fund the research, to pay for the equipment, to pay for Zack's care. What the hell was Paul doing?

"He and I made an agreement," Karla said. "So I'll need some time off."

"No. That won't do." Ethan still had to give her the Rejuvenol, but he started to walk away. He was going to go down to the beach right now and set Paul straight.

Karla grabbed his arm and pulled him back. She glared at him, the look of violence suddenly reappearing. "This is between Tobin and me. It has nothing to do with you."

"This is my clinic. He works for me. This has everything to do with me."

He tried to pull himself free but she tightened her grip and pulled him closer. She clenched her jaw and spoke in a menacing hiss. "Ethan, I'm having this done. You fuck it up, I'll fuck you up. You understand me?"

He understood very clearly.

17

ALICIA ARRIVED IN Miami and rented a car at the airport. The Avis agent helped her find Coral Key on the map. Two hours later, she turned off the highway and followed the road to a small bridge.

The sign said DE LEON CENTER. A shiver ran through her. What she felt wasn't so much fear as it was a strange uneasiness about what she was going to find here. The reason Nikki was dead lay somewhere on the island. How she was going to find out what caused Nikki to kill herself, or what she would do once she did, she didn't know. But she wasn't going to be able to put Nikki to rest until she found the truth.

She took a deep breath and drove past the sign and over the bridge.

The first thing that struck her as she drove up the palm tree–lined road to the front building was that this place looked more like a resort than a medical center. Was this place a legitimate medical facility? Or was it all antiaging hype? Just a slick way to take money from people whose livelihood depended on their looks? She hated to think of Nicole being ripped off by these people. Nikki had lived comfortably with her earnings from modeling and acting, but she wasn't wealthy by any standards. For these people to take advantage of her financially—

Alicia suddenly realized how ridiculous that thought was. Nicole was dead!

She parked the car and walked into the lobby. Through doors on the other side of the lobby was a patio. A dozen or so men and women were sitting by the pool. Beyond them, she could see the beach. Definitely looked like a resort.

Over the water, a line of charcoal-colored clouds crawled toward the island. Below them, reaching all the way to the horizon, was a thin sheet of lighter gray. Rain? A jagged line of lightning streaked through the gray, disappearing as suddenly as it appeared. Yes, rain. All this with blinding sunlight beating down on the pool area just outside the lobby. What a strange place.

The receptionist sat behind what looked like a hotel's front desk. She quickly took all the information to register Alicia as a De Leon patient. This was not the woman Alicia had spoken to over the phone, the one who knew Nikki. The voice was different.

"You understand that most medical insurances won't pay for the services we provide," the receptionist said as she finished doing the paperwork.

Alicia nodded. They had told her that when she made the appointment.

"I can take an imprint of your credit card," the receptionist said. "That way you won't have to leave a cash deposit."

More and more like a resort every minute.

Alicia gave the woman her American Express card. The woman handed her an information packet. On the diagram of the campus, she marked where Alicia's bungalow was located. She showed Alicia the listing of the nonmedical services offered, such as the dining options, free snorkeling equipment, and half-day tourist excursions.

Alicia was much more interested in the detailed explanations of the treatments and the biographical information about the clinicians. The receptionist went over some of it, but only briefly. She suggested Alicia skim through it when she had free time between appointments, perhaps on the beach or by the pool.

"You have about an hour before your blood work," the woman said. "Your first appointment will be right after that. You'll need to fill this out beforehand." She handed Alicia a questionnaire asking about her daily activities, dietary habits, and general health, as well as her goals.

Alicia had made appointments for every treatment the clinic offered. She wanted to meet everyone who might have had contact with Nicole.

Her first appointment was for an EPN evaluation with De Leon's exercise physiologist and nutritionist. The information packet explained this part of the program:

Nutrition and exercise physiology

De Leon offers extensive evaluation of each patient's physical conditioning and dietary tendencies. Under the guidance of a certified nutritionist/exercise physiologist, each patient is prescribed a goal-specific diet and exercise program, personally designed to fit their individual needs. The program utilizes proven techniques that retard, and in some cases reverse, the physiological symptoms of aging.

The person with whom Alicia had the appointment was named Karla Weiss. The brochure described her as a former Olympic athlete who held degrees in human kinetics and physical therapy and also had various "certifications," whatever that meant, in nutrition science, massage therapy, and personal training.

Alicia put her suitcase in her bungalow and filled out the questionnaire. While she was doing it, a technician came to the bungalow and drew blood. She told Alicia that the doctor would go over the results with her tomorrow.

As Alicia walked across the clinic grounds, the clouds she'd seen earlier overtook the island. The sun disappeared. The air suddenly felt much cooler. The patients by the pool scrambled to get inside. Alicia barely made it to the EPN center before the clouds dumped their rain.

The waiting room was empty. No receptionist. A sign on the door to another room said to press the button that looked like a doorbell, then have a seat. Alicia did. On the table were several fitness magazines. Alicia sat down and picked one up.

The door opened and a man came out. He looked a few years older than her, probably in his late thirties. He was wearing shorts and a polo shirt, which showed off an extremely fit body. He was very tanned and combed his hair forward, making his receding hairline slightly less obvious. He'd lost a lot of hair for someone his age, she thought. Still, he was a good-looking man.

"Karla asked me to tell you that she'll be out in a few minutes," he told Alicia.

"Oh, okay. Thanks."

He walked to the door and peered out at the downpour. "Talk about bad timing," he said. He peered up at the clouds. "Cumulonimbus. Shouldn't last long."

Alicia chuckled. "You sound like a weatherman."

"Is it that obvious?"

"You mean you *are* a weatherman?"

He held out his hand. "Doug Collins. WTSP, Channel Ten, Tampa."

He announced it like he was trying to impress her. Being on TV probably did impress some women. And maybe it would her, too, under different circumstances. She was flattered that he was trying to hit on her, but she wasn't here to meet men. Her thoughts were focused on Nikki.

She shook his hand and said, "Nice to meet you," but didn't tell him her name.

"Yeah, the rain will stop pretty quickly," he continued. "Now, if it had been a hurricane, then we'd be in serious trouble. Island this small, sticking this far out into the Caribbean, wouldn't stand a chance. Hurricane Andrew hit this island a few years back, you know."

"No, I didn't know that," Alicia said. Nor did she care.

"Yeah, quite a storm." He rambled on about wind velocity and sea height. "The eye actually hit just south of Miami, in Homestead," he said. "This area only got the outer bands. But if it had been centered over this place, it would have been curtains."

Alicia nodded. This was far more than she cared to

know. Probably his way of impressing women, step two after telling them he was on TV. He looked good, but he was as boring as hell to listen to. She hoped the rain would quickly stop so he'd leave.

"This is hurricane season, you know," he said. "It's pretty active off the coast of Africa right now. That's where hurricanes originate, you know. I predict we're going to see a level-three or -four storm before the season's over."

Borrrring.

"The worst storm I ever saw was when I was in Japan. They call them typhoons there. Man, it was something. I was on R and R from Vietnam, and I'll tell you what, that was some way to spend my week off."

He went on to tell her about the storm, but she wasn't listening to the details. What she found incredible was the time frame of his story. If he fought in Vietnam he had to be in his fifties now. She couldn't believe he was that old.

"Vietnam?" she said. "The *war* in Vietnam?"

He grinned. "I know what you're thinking. I don't look that old, do I?"

His gloating was annoying, but Alicia couldn't help but pursue this. "No, you don't."

"Let me show you something."

He took out his wallet and showed her a photograph of himself. What kind of man carries a picture of himself? A boring weatherman, that's who. But when she looked at the photo, she couldn't believe how different he looked in it. Like he was ten years older than he was now. He had more hair in the picture, but he was pale and flabby and tired-looking.

"This is really you?" she asked.

"Hard to believe, huh? It's really me. This was taken two years ago."

"What happened?"

"I started coming here."

Alicia was stunned. If he was typical, then whatever they did here actually worked. Maybe antiaging wasn't hype after all.

The door to the other room opened and a woman came out. "Still here?" she said to Doug Collins.

"Just waiting for the rain to let up."

"Afraid you're going to melt?" she said, teasing him. She came over to Alicia, extending her hand. "You must be Alicia Fernandes, ya?"

"Yes."

"I'm Karla Weiss. It's very nice to meet you."

Alicia recognized the accent. This was the woman who had answered the phone when Alicia wanted to reach the southern woman who knew Nikki. She was smiling now, and trying to sound kind, but she couldn't help coming across as hard and intimidating. Just as she had over the phone.

Much of that feeling, at least today, came from the way she looked. She was tall and muscular. It was impossible not to be intimidated by her. The brochure said she had competed in the Olympics in the early 1980s. She certainly had the physique of an athlete. But she looked too young to have been competing on that level twenty years ago. With the exception of two barely noticeable scars on one cheek, her face was smooth, flawless. Considering how old she must have been, she had to have had cosmetic surgery. Whoever did it certainly knew his or her stuff. She wondered if it was the surgeon here.

Karla pointed to the questionnaire Alicia had filled out. "This is for me, ya?" She took it and said, "Let's get started."

Karla put her through a series of tests to measure her strength, stamina, and cardiovascular fitness. The whole process took forty-five minutes. When it was done, Alicia was out of breath and soaked with sweat. She hadn't realized that she was going to have to work this hard when she came here. She might have gotten into better shape first.

Karla made a few notes on her clipboard then shook her head, looking unhappy.

"What's wrong?" Alicia asked.

"You don't exercise very much, ya?"

"I don't have time," Alicia said, feeling defensive. *Everyone can't be a gym rat like you.* "I have a very busy schedule," she added.

"Most people do these days. But not to worry, I'll design a routine that will fit into your schedule. Half an hour a day will make all the difference. You'll see. We want your muscles firmer." She flexed her arm and showed Alicia her biceps. She was showing off, which annoyed Alicia. "Like this, ya?" she said.

Amazing what steroids can do.

"I don't think I want to be *that much* firmer," Alicia said. "Nothing personal. I think you look fine. But that's not really the results I'm looking for."

"It takes a lot more than half an hour of exercise a day to look like this," Karla said, a note of narcissism in her voice.

Alicia saw an opening. "You mean you have to . . . take something to look like that?" She wondered if Karla gave patients steroids. Anabolic steroids were known to cause people to become violent. Could they cause someone to become violent against themselves? To become suicidal?

Karla said, "What I mean is, you have to be very dedicated to your workout, your diet, your entire lifestyle. It's not for everybody. And I don't think that's for you."

Alicia agreed. But it still offended her that Karla would say that, as though she wasn't good enough, wasn't dedicated enough. But she put her personal feelings aside and concentrated on getting as much information as possible.

"You don't recommend that patients take supplements and other things to help get results?" she asked.

"Anything like that comes from Dr. Granier. I deal with nutrition and exercise. This can do much to improve your body. Let me show you."

Karla took Alicia by the hand and brought her over to a mirror. She stood behind Alicia. "What we need to do"— she placed her hands on Alicia's shoulders—"is develop this area here. Add some shape to the delts." She slid her hands down Alicia's arms. "Build up your biceps and triceps a little, too." She brought her hands down to Alicia's waist. "That'll make this area look more narrow, give you a sexy shape. Someone as pretty as yourself," she said, "you want to be sure your body is as good as can be, ya?"

Karla kept her hands on Alicia's hips, staring at her in the mirror. She stood so close that Alicia felt her breath on her neck. It made her uneasy. Then Karla moved to the side, her thighs brushing Alicia's leg. Alicia spun around and stepped away. She didn't know if that contact was accidental or intentional, and she didn't want to find out.

If it weren't for her need to find out if Karla bore any responsibility for Nikki's death, Alicia would have left immediately. Instead, she walked to one of the exercise machines, putting some distance and a large piece of equipment between herself and Karla.

She got right to the reason she was here. "You know, I met a woman on a flight," she said. "The one who recommended this clinic to me. She told me she had such good results, I was hoping to get the same type of therapies she got."

"Each person's therapies are specific to their bodies and their needs," Karla said. "Hormone therapies as well as nutrition and exercise."

"I understand. But I was just wondering if maybe you could tell me whether the program you're going to design for me is similar to hers. Her name is Nicole Quinn."

Karla didn't answer. She stared at Alicia, the look on her face changing. She seemed to be assessing Alicia in a different way, no longer just for her strength and stamina. She now looked suspicious. Alicia feared she'd made a mistake.

Finally Karla said, "I told you, each patient is different."

Alicia wasn't going to push it any further. "Oh, okay, I see."

Karla walked to her desk and said, "Remove your shirt, ya?"

"Excuse me?"

Karla came back, holding calipers. "I have to measure your body. It won't be accurate through your shirt."

Alicia didn't want to do it, but she had to go along if she was to keep up the front of being a potential patient. She took off her shirt but left her bra on. She told herself this was a medical exam, that was all. It was okay. Then Karla stepped behind her and the feeling of uneasiness returned. She held her breath as Karla pinched a fold of her skin between her thumb and finger then measured it with the calipers.

"You have very nice skin," Karla said.

Alicia felt Karla's fingers smooth out the area she had just measured. A shiver ran up her back. She stood motionless. This was just part of the skin fold test. It would be over soon.

"I can tell that you stay out of the sun, ya?" Karla said. "That's good. I've been too much in the sun."

Then she'd definitely had surgery, Alicia realized. It helped to think about something other than what Karla was doing.

Karla moved to Alicia's side and measured another fold of skin, this time on Alicia's upper arm. As she did it, the back of her hand brushed Alicia's bra. Alicia flinched.

"Are you all right?" Karla asked.

"I'm just a little ticklish there."

Karla laughed and asked, "Anywhere else?" Her tone made Alicia squirm.

"Are you done with that?" she asked, pointing to the calipers.

"One more measurement."

Karla came around in front of Alicia and went down on one knee, her face so close to Alicia's waist that she felt Karla's breath on her skin. As Karla gently took a fold of skin just below Alicia's navel, she said, "The woman you mentioned . . . she's not a patient here."

"No? Are you sure?"

"I'm sure. She must have meant another clinic."

Alicia wasn't going to push it. "Oh, okay." But at least she now knew that Karla was covering up something having to do with Nikki.

"That's it," Karla said, finishing with the calipers. She stood up and wrote the measurements on the clipboard. "I'm going to compile the data and design a program for you. You can come back tomorrow at ten, ya?"

"Yeah." She'd be back. She'd keep coming back until she uncovered what Karla, and whoever else was involved, had done to Nikki.

18

ALICIA'S NEXT APPOINTMENT was with De Leon's plastic surgeon, Paul Tobin.

As far as she knew, Nicole hadn't had surgery, but she couldn't be certain of anything anymore, not after discovering Nikki's "secret life." Maybe she had undergone some kind of cosmetic procedure. If so, could that have driven her to kill herself? Alicia didn't know how it could, but she had to explore every possibility.

The doctor knocked at the door then came into the examination room. He looked to be in his mid to late forties, very serious, straightlaced, the kind of man who inspired confidence. He looked the part of a surgeon.

"Good afternoon. I'm Paul Tobin," he said. They shook hands and exchanged niceties, then he said, "So, what brings you here today, Ms. Fernandes?"

She couldn't pass a newsstand without seeing magazine covers teasing her about how cosmetic surgery could change her life. The morning news shows featured stories every couple of months, putting on some "renowned" doctor extolling the benefits and simplicity of the latest methods of removing cellulite and wrinkles. It was impossible to avoid the subliminal and not-so-subliminal messages about plastic surgery and about what she was "supposed" to look like. It was as though society was making a concerted effort to persuade every woman alive to surgically alter her body.

She had never fallen victim to that, though.

Until recently. Maybe it was being mistaken for Nikki's *older* sister. Maybe it was Steve Polaski's comments about her not being able to lure a client's husband into cheating on his wife. Whatever the reason, she considered that perhaps at some point in her life surgery might not be totally out of the question.

Society valued youth. She had to function in society. It didn't mean she was vain or insecure. It meant she was pragmatic.

But that wasn't why she was here now.

She told Paul Tobin she was considering liposuction to make her legs, hips, and buttocks smaller, and perhaps some work on her face to reduce the wrinkles. He nodded quietly and began his examination. First he looked closely at her face, positioning her under a special light. He made a few notes but didn't say much.

She wondered if he had done the work on Karla. If so, he was good. She also needed to ask him about Nikki. He didn't seem like the kind of doctor who would discuss one patient with another, but she had to try anyway.

"You know, this clinic comes highly recommended," she said. "I met a woman who told me this place works miracles."

He chuckled. "I'm not sure about miracles, but we do what we can."

"Well, she looked great," Alicia said. "Maybe you know her. Nicole Quinn."

"No," he said. No hesitation like Karla. No change in his expression. Either he was a much better liar than Karla or he really didn't know Nikki. "She didn't have surgery here," he said. "We just opened the surgical wing a few weeks ago."

"Oh." That would explain his not knowing her. But that didn't mean he wasn't part of whatever Karla was covering up. "So you're new?" she asked.

"New to De Leon," he said. "But I've been a plastic surgeon for more than twenty years."

He asked her to change into a hospital gown and excused himself so she could undress alone. When he returned a few minutes later, he brought his female assistant with him. He was definitely proper.

He asked her to stand up so he could examine her lower body. The exam was quick. He didn't touch her legs or buttocks, didn't open her gown very much. It was far more comfortable than the exam Karla had done. For that, Alicia was thankful.

He asked her to get dressed and come to his office so they could discuss her options. She doubted he could tell her anything about Nicole but she had to go through with the rest of the consultation. When she sat in his office, he surprised her.

"Well, Miss Fernandes, I really don't think you're a good candidate for surgery at this point," he said. "You don't have the kind of wrinkles on your face that would warrant surgery or even a peel. Perhaps Botox if you're set on doing something, but that only lasts a few months. As for your lower body, I think you could achieve the results you're looking for with diet and exercise alone. Have you spoken with Karla Weiss?"

"Yes. She's supposed to design a program for me."

"That's good. That and perhaps hormone therapy would serve you better, I think."

She was surprised that he was recommending *against* surgery. She hadn't expected that at all. These people were here to make money. And these days it seemed that just about everybody was a candidate for something, liposuction at the very least.

His recommending against surgery earned him points with her. Clearly he had principles. His loyalties lay with his patients and not with his personal economy. But she was also flattered that he didn't think she needed surgery to look good.

She trusted her judgment of people, and she was sure he wasn't involved in any kind of cover-up here. She wondered if she should confide in him the real reason she was here. If he was as principled as she believed, he might be willing to help her. She could use an ally.

But she decided against it. She really didn't know him

well enough. She couldn't risk giving herself away. Besides, he was new here; he didn't know Nikki; he probably didn't know much about what had gone on when she was here.

There was still one more area to investigate. The hormone therapies. If something drove Nikki to kill herself, it was probably that. Her appointment with Ethan Granier was scheduled for tomorrow morning. She'd have to wait until then to find out. And to find out why he'd lied over the phone about knowing Nikki.

19

THE RESULTS OF the tests on Zack terrified Ethan. His
hyaluronic acid level had risen dramatically. The EKG
showed a marked deterioration of his cardiac function. His
telomerase level was falling. Plaque was forming in dangerously high amounts. Time was running out. Something
had to be done—*now!*

Paul wasn't the one to go to. Too much explaining. Plus,
the whole Wilkenson connection. Beth was the one he had to
ask. Even though she was overprotective of those kids, she
could be convinced. He'd done it once; he could do it again.

He finished his last patient of the day then hurried out to
his car to drive to Palm Beach. As he was pulling away,
Karla waved him down. She hurried to his window.

"I think we have a problem," she said.

Ethan's thoughts were on Zack and the tests he needed
to do. He didn't need any other problems right now. "For
God's sake, what's wrong?" he said.

"You said the Quinn woman has a sister, ya?"

"Yeah. So?"

"There's a new patient here, asking questions about her.
She may be the sister."

That sent a shiver through Ethan. "What is she asking?"

"If I knew her and what therapies she was on."

"Damn it!" That wasn't good. He really didn't need this
right now. "What did you tell her? You didn't say you knew
her, did you?"

"I'm not stupid."

"Where is she now? Is she still here?"

"Yes. I checked her schedule. She sees you tomorrow."

He didn't have time to deal with this right now. He had to get to Palm Beach. The woman couldn't do anything to hurt them today anyway. All the incriminating records concerning Nicole Quinn were locked in his house and Carmen certainly wasn't going to let her in.

"I'll take care of her tomorrow," he said.

He started to roll up his window to leave, but Karla held the window down. "Listen, Ethan. I don't want this woman screwing with us. I think she's trouble."

"Let me take care of it. I'll handle it tomorrow."

"Do that," she said, glaring at him with threatening eyes.

When he arrived at Beth's, she and the boys had just finished dinner. The boys went outside to the driveway to play basketball under the lights. He helped Beth load the dishwasher then they sat in the screened patio, watching the boys. She had some travel brochures of Greece and Turkey on the table.

"Going away?" he asked, sitting beside her.

"We're thinking about it. It might be a good chance for everyone to get to know each other."

Beth looked directly at him, annoyed. "And by the way, why didn't you tell me that you were hiring Paul?"

"I didn't know I was supposed to run my professional dealings by you for approval."

"Don't be cute, Ethan. That's not what I'm talking about. Don't you think I have a right to know something like that?"

This wasn't the time to get into an argument with her, not when he was going to ask her to let him use her sons to test Rejuvenol. Better to appease her.

"Maybe I should have mentioned it to you," he said.

"No kidding."

They watched the two boys playing basketball for a moment. It was an uneasy silence for Ethan, who was looking for a way to ease into asking her about the tests. Before he could find the words, she sighed and spoke.

"I'm going to tell him tomorrow night."

Ethan wasn't sure what she meant. She looked worried as she stared off. He waited for her to explain.

"There's no sense putting it off any longer," she said. "It'll only get more difficult." She turned to him. "He still thinks there's a chance we'll get back together, doesn't he?"

Now he understood. "I don't know," he said, even though he did know. "That's not something Paul and I talk about."

"Oh, come on, Ethan. I'm sure he said something to you."

"Beth, Paul and I have a professional relationship. That's all. I don't know what his thoughts are regarding the two of you. To be honest with you, I really don't have the time to sit around and talk about his personal life with him. With the clinic and with Zack, believe me, I have my hands full."

He knew she couldn't argue with that. And she didn't.

"Anyway," she said, "I'm going to see if he'll have dinner with me tomorrow night. Then I'll tell him."

This troubled Ethan. How would the news affect Paul? He depended on Paul bringing money into the clinic. Part of the reason Paul had accepted his offer was to be near Beth. If it was over between them, would he continue working here?

He had to. They had an agreement. Besides, where else would Paul be able to get work? No, he'd stay. Sure, the news would rock him. But he was a grown man. He could take it.

"Well, I hope it goes okay," he told Beth.

"Whether it does or not, I have to do it."

She let out a long sigh then changed the subject.

"You're a long way from home," she said. "To what do I owe the pleasure of your visit?"

He was still unsure how to ask her, remembering how difficult it had been to convince her to allow him to extract the bone marrow, something far less risky than what he was going to ask now. He took a breath and said, "I wanted to talk to you about something."

"What is it?"

"It's about Zack."

"How is he doing, Ethan?" She sounded genuinely concerned. He knew that she cared for Zack, which was why she had allowed the boys to be donors for him. But did she care for him enough to allow this?

"Not too well," he said.

"But it seemed like he was doing better."

"He was, for a while, but he's been deteriorating lately."

"Is there anything that can be done? What about the bone marrow? Did that help him?"

"That's kind of what I wanted to talk to you about," he said.

Her face turned white. "You don't need to do it again, do you? That was so hard on the boys. You know, after that, Pete couldn't—"

Just then Pete screamed from the driveway. Beth jumped up and rushed outside. Ethan ran after her. Pete was lying on the pavement, clutching his ankle, crying in pain. Kenny was standing over him, still holding the basketball.

"My God, what happened?" Beth said, falling to her knees beside Pete.

"He twisted his ankle," Kenny said, calm and unconcerned.

"Is it broken?" Beth sounded terrified. She peered up at Ethan. "We have to bring him to the hospital!"

Kenny blew out a breath of frustration. "Mom, he just twisted it. He's okay."

"Are you a doctor?" she barked at him. She turned back to Pete and wrapped her arms around him. "Does it hurt bad, sweetheart?"

Pete nodded.

Beth glared at Kenny. "See? He's not okay." Kenny just rolled eyes, which angered her. But right now she was more concerned with Pete. She looked at Ethan. "Will you drive us?"

"Wait a minute, slow down," Ethan said. "Let me take a look."

He knelt beside Pete and examined his ankle. He had Pete move his foot, then he helped him stand and put some weight on it. By the time he was finished, Pete had stopped crying and was limping around. Beth, though, was still a wreck.

"It's only a sprain," Ethan told her. "We'll put some ice on it, wrap an Ace bandage around it. He'll be fine."

"Maybe he should have X rays," Beth said.

"Beth, I'm a doctor. I know what I'm talking about. He doesn't need X rays."

"What if there's a hairline fracture and it doesn't heal right? He could limp for the rest of his life."

By now Kenny had heard enough. He moaned, turned away, and walked off, dribbling the basketball.

"He's not going to limp for the rest of his life," Ethan told Beth. "Pete twisted his ankle. That happens in basketball all the time. He'll be all right. Look," he said, pointing to Pete, who was barely limping now as he followed Kenny, trying to get the ball. "See?"

Beth let out a relieved sigh. But she looked like she had just waited out life-or-death surgery for Pete. Ethan realized as he watched her scrutinizing Pete's every move that there was no way she was going to let him test a drug on her kids, no way she was going to let him put them at risk, no matter how slight that risk, even if Zack's life did depend on it.

20

ALICIA FOUND DOUG Collins in the lounge. He was sitting at the bar with a Heineken in front of him, watching a small TV behind the bar. A baseball game was on. She walked over and slid up onto the stool next to him.

"See any good downpours lately?" she said. Not a great line but at least it got his attention.

"Hey, hi. How are you?" he said. He smelled of beer and he was already well on his way to a decent buzz. "Can I buy you a drink?"

She ordered a glass of wine, and they started talking. Within a few minutes she knew that Collins had only three interests: weather, Japan, and sex. She also knew that he'd jump her bones if she let him. Even though he was quite a bit older than she was, he had a great body. Under different circumstances, and if he didn't have to talk, she might be open to a brief fling. Just a night of fun between consenting adults. That's as far as she ever took it.

But she hadn't come here to meet men. And sleeping with him to get information was a repulsive thought. She sipped some wine and concentrated on gathering information the old-fashioned way.

"So, how did it go with Karla today?" he asked. "She's quite a trip, *ya?*" He laughed at his own joke.

"Let's just say it was an interesting morning," Alicia said.

"I'll bet. But I'll give her one thing, she knows her sh— uh, her stuff."

"Yeah, it looks like it."

"She's built," Collins said and took a long drink of beer. Alicia couldn't figure out if "she's built" was good or bad.

"So," she said, changing the subject away from Karla. "How long did you say you've been coming here?"

"About a year."

"I have to tell you, I was blown away when you showed me that before photo of you."

"Come on, I didn't look that bad, did I?"

"Oh, yes, you did."

They both laughed.

"Yeah, I know," he admitted. "I'll tell you what, if I hadn't come here, there's no telling what would've happened with my work situation."

"What do you mean?"

"TV's a visual medium. And it's a young person's medium."

"That's a sad thought."

"Sad or not, that's the reality of it," he said. He drank some more and said, "You know about the golden rule, right? He who has the gold makes the rules."

"That's not exactly how I learned it," she said.

"That's how it is in my business. I have to play by their rules or I'm off the air. Simple as that. And if that happens, what am I supposed to do? AM radio? No way. I'd rather take out my *tanto* and do like the samurai."

"Take out your what?"

"*Tanto*. That's the small sword that samurai warriors carry for close combat."

"Oh, so you're going to stab the station manager," she said jokingly.

Collins laughed. "That's not a bad idea, but I was talking about running it through my own heart."

"Oh, my God," she said. His bringing up suicide suddenly brought back the horrible memory of Nikki falling to her death. "Let's talk about something else, okay?"

"Hey, it's all about honor," he went on, not getting the message that she didn't want to talk about this. He had to make his stupid point. "Rather than being captured alive and bringing shame on his people, a samurai would run his *tanto* through his heart. It's a sign of courage."

"People don't kill themselves unless there's something really wrong." She was getting angry and defensive. "Someone has to drive them to it."

"You don't understand the samurai culture like I do. It's an amazing culture once you get to understand where they're coming from."

She didn't want to understand where they were coming from. And she didn't want to talk about this anymore, or even think about it. What this subject did was strengthen her resolve to prove that someone here was responsible for Nikki's death.

"Anyway," she said, "looks like you've gotten your money's worth from this place. I never would have thought that hormones and diet and exercise could do so much."

He swallowed some more beer then turned to her and gazed into her eyes.

Uh-oh. She'd made a big mistake. Her pseudocompliment went straight to his inebriated head. No doubt he was trying to figure out a way to get her into bed. She was trying to figure out a way to get out of here. She wasn't going to learn anything pertinent from him.

She faked a yawn. "It's getting kind of late," she said.

"Hang on." He glanced around the lounge, making sure no one was near enough to hear. Then he leaned in close to her, so close that his cheek brushed hers. She had to inhale the beer fumes of his breath. She had the sickening feeling that he was going to proposition her. "Can you keep a secret?" he whispered.

She was suspicious where he was going with this. "Why?" she asked.

"Let's just say the best therapies here are the ones not listed in the brochure." He stopped to let that sink in and to finish off his beer. Then he whispered, "That's where I get my money's worth."

Suddenly she was interested in what he had to say. "What do you mean?" she asked. Was there a therapy that the clinic was keeping secret? Could Nikki have been on that? Could that have had something to do with her killing herself?

Collins glanced around again. Now his nervousness was hidden behind a look of power, of control. He seemed to realize that he had her where he wanted her.

"This isn't the best place to talk about it," he whispered. He stood up. "Let's find a more private place where we can talk."

Alicia shuddered as she watched Collins unlock the door to his bungalow. Sleeping with someone to get information was not something she'd ever done in the past, on any of the cases she'd ever worked. And it certainly was not something she wanted to do now. But this was not just another case. This was Nikki.

Collins stepped aside to let her go in first. *This is important,* she reminded herself as she walked past him into the bungalow. Maybe he didn't want sex. Maybe he just wanted to show her whatever it was he was talking about.

He came in behind her and closed the door. The lights were still off. He left them that way and drew the blinds on the window. She was only deluding herself. He was interested in only one thing now—and it wasn't weather or Japan.

"This place looks pretty much the same as mine," she said, her nervousness speaking.

"Yeah. I've stayed in a few of them. They're all alike. Good beds, though."

He came up close behind her and gently touched her shoulders. She turned quickly, not wanting her back to him. She needed the safety of seeing him, even in the dark room.

"How about a drink?" she asked. *Give him something to do with his hands other than touch me.*

"Good idea."

He brushed past her and walked to a small refrigerator in the corner. She had to slow him down so she could get what she wanted before he got what he wanted. While he was mixing screwdrivers, she turned on the lamp beside the bed.

The sudden light surprised him. "Man, that's bright," he said, shielding his eyes. "We don't need that."

"I like a little light, if you don't mind."

"Afraid of the dark, are you?" He snickered and came over with the drinks. "I'll protect you." He gave her a glass and sat on the edge of the bed. She was still standing, feeling very uncomfortable and unsure of what to do.

"Sit down," he said. He took hold of her free hand and coaxed her down beside him. "There. Isn't that better?"

She took a sip. Mostly vodka, barely any orange juice. His intentions were clear.

"So," she said, "I'd really like to know what you meant about there being therapies that aren't in the brochure."

"Well," he said, taking his time. He took a drink, downing half the glass. Then he grinned and said, "The ones in the brochure are the FDA-approved ones."

"And there are other ones, not FDA approved?"

"Are you hot?" he asked. "It's really hot in here, isn't it?"

"No, I'm fine. You were saying there are therapies that aren't FDA approved?"

"I'm hot," he said. He began unbuttoning his shirt.

Oh, shit. She was in trouble. She had to get him to talk, fast.

"If that's what's going to get me results," she said, "that's what I want to know about."

"The FDA isn't all-knowing," he said. "They don't have a monopoly on what's effective and what isn't." He swallowed the rest of his drink then stripped off his shirt, revealing a muscular chest, bristly with light brown hair. "Sometimes," he said, whispering again, "obscure little clinics in the Florida Keys have answers the FDA doesn't."

"Like what?"

"Are you sure you're not hot?" he asked. He gently brushed his hand against her face. "You feel like you're sweating."

"I'm fine." She wasn't only sweating, she was squirming

inside, too. She wanted desperately to get away from this pig. But she had to stay and get him to talk. "Tell me about the therapy the FDA hasn't approved."

He fingered her hair. "Or is it being so close to me," he asked, ignoring what she said, "that's making you sweat?"

"Yeah, it is kind of hot. You mind opening the window?" At least that would give her some breathing room.

"That's not exactly what I had in mind," he said. He lowered his hand and brushed his finger over the top button on her blouse.

He wasn't going for the window trick. "I'm really interested in the other therapies," she said.

He smirked. "The secret therapy?"

"Yes." Now she was getting somewhere. "Tell me about it."

He slid his fingers past the buttons on her blouse and brushed her bra. She pulled away quickly.

"What's wrong?" His tone was a mixture of surprise and resentment. "What's your problem?"

"Nothing. I just wanted to hear what you were saying."

His ire melted into one of his lecherous grins. "And I just want to eat you up whole," he said.

He made his move, grabbing her by the shoulders and pulling her against him so he could kiss her. She snapped her head to the side and jumped up off the bed. She couldn't do this. She rushed toward the door.

"Hey, what the hell's your problem?" he said.

She wasn't going to sleep with him for information. No way. She'd find some other way to get it. She pulled open the door and rushed out into the night. She hadn't gotten the information she hoped for. But she knew one thing she hadn't known earlier. There was a secret therapy. And every instinct in her body told her that it was what drove Nikki to kill herself.

21

ETHAN WENT INTO his laboratory, locked the door, and gathered what he needed.

Zack needed Rejuvenol. Rejuvenol needed further testing before he could give it to Zack. He needed to know how it would work on Zack's specific cell line. Since testing it on Kenny and Pete wasn't possible, he decided to test it on the only other genetically suitable candidate. Himself.

He filled an infusion bag with 500 ml of Rejuvenol solution, 6.25 ml per kilogram of body weight. With most of the patients he'd tested it on in the past, he'd used a dose of 3.75 ml/kg. The dose he gave to Doug Collins yesterday was 5.5 ml/kg. He'd always given them an intentionally low dose, fearing what too strong a dose would do. But gradually he'd been increasing the dosage to see how much the central nervous system and the body's immune system could tolerate. He'd have to give Zack the maximum safe dosage. And he'd probably only get one chance to do it.

He tied off his left arm and located a vein. He inserted the IV port into his arm, then attached the infusion bag. He was using stem cells he'd harvested from himself months ago. They'd already been cultured with glion-2 and primed with progenitor cells. This should give him a good idea how it would affect Zack on a cellular level.

He opened the flow.

He felt a hot sensation, first in his arm, then seeping up his torso and finally swelling in his head. Suddenly he couldn't sit still. He was overcome with an adrenaline-like rush. He shot up from the chair. His heart started beating rapidly. Cold fear shivered through him. His whole body felt strange.

Oh, God, what's wrong? Is the dose too high?

Carrying the infusion bag still attached to his arm, he rushed to the window. He needed air. His head was pounding. Yes, he must have taken too high a dose. What would happen? His first thought was Zack. If he OD'd, what would become of Zack? Who would take care of him? That was why he'd been reluctant to test Rejuvenol on himself before now. If something happened to him, Zack would be the one to suffer. But now the full weight of that fear came down on him. Had he done something foolish that would ultimately hurt his son?

The bag was empty. He took out the IV and held a gauze pad over the puncture wound. Could he take something to stabilize himself? He began searching the laboratory, trying to figure out what he could take. A vasodilator? Something to slow his heart? A benzo for the anxiety? All he could do was treat the symptoms. Then he thought he should run to Zack, a protective instinct. But that made no sense.

His thoughts began to whirl in a frenzy. What had he done to himself? Zack's deteriorating health. Paul's loyalties. Beth and her kids. Karla's demands. Money problems. Someone asking about the dead model. His head felt like it was going to explode!

He dropped onto a chair, squeezing his head in his hands. The inside of his head felt like a radio tuned to static, with the volume turned up all the way. *Damn it! Stop!* He felt an urge to run screaming from the lab. He held it in. He forced himself to sit still. The "noise" made his skull hurt—actually, physically hurt. He was growing angry—at himself, at life, at everything. Why couldn't he have a little goddamn peace of mind? Why couldn't he have some relief from the pressures that had been heaped upon him for a decade? Why was it only getting worse? *Why, goddamn it? Why?*

Suddenly the noise stopped. Just stopped. The radio

turned off. His head went silent. He was still gasping for breath, soaked in sweat, but he felt his body slowly calming down. His heartbeat was leveling off. He sat still for a few moments, breathing deeply, settling himself.

Was it just an anxiety attack, brought on by all the pressures he was under? Or was it too high a dose of Rejuvenol? He wasn't sure. Maybe the combination of the two. He just couldn't be sure.

But what mattered was that the sensations passed; they'd disappeared as suddenly as they had appeared. That would fit with a panic attack. But if it was caused by Rejuvenol, and he gave it to Zack, what would this kind of reaction do to him? Considering his fragile condition, it could kill him.

Ethan was more reluctant than ever to give the treatment to Zack without fully testing it. He had to be sure it was safe. And he had to make sure it would help him. It was foolish to take the risk without being certain that there'd be a benefit.

If only Beth wasn't so protective of her sons. If only there was a way to convince her that they'd be all right. Zack needs this to live, damn it!

But she'd never understand. She'd never allow it. Imagine what would happen if Kenny or Pete felt the same momentary rush that he'd just felt. Beth would freak out. She'd call 911, the CDC, the FDA. No, she'd never go along.

Ethan still had to figure out what to do. And he had to do it soon.

Right now he had a patient to see. The one Karla told him about last night. He locked up everything having to do with Rejuvenol, then left the lab and headed to the exam room, anxious to find out who Alicia Fernandes was and what she was doing here.

22

ALICIA WAS NERVOUS. She sat in the examination room waiting for Dr. Granier. Everything she'd learned so far pointed to some kind of therapy that had to have come from him. Karla might know about it, but Ethan Granier had prescribed it. This meeting was the most important of her life.

Finally he arrived. "Good morning, Miss Fernandes," he said, shaking her hand. His palm was sweaty. He looked strange. The word that came to mind was "spent," kind of frazzled, like a college student who'd just pulled an all-nighter, hopped up on caffeine.

He rechecked her blood pressure, listened to her lungs and her heart, tested her strength. He examined the skin around her eyes closely, stretching it out with his fingers then watching it retract. Altogether, the physical exam lasted five minutes. Then he reviewed the results of her blood tests from yesterday, made a few notes on her chart, then sat at the small desk in the corner of the office.

"So, what brings you to De Leon?" he asked, tapping the desk with his pen. He seemed antsy, like he wanted to get on with this, and that annoyed her. Already she didn't much like him. "What are you hoping to achieve?" he asked.

I'm hoping to find out if you're responsible for Nikki's death.

"I guess the same thing everyone else is hoping for," she

said. "To look younger." That was why Nikki had come here.

"How did you learn about us?" he asked.

The question and the tone with which he asked it seemed out of place. She wondered if he already suspected she had a different motive. Perhaps Karla had said something to him. She had to be careful.

"I met an actress who told me about you guys," she said. "Then I found your website on the internet." In case he already knew that she'd asked Karla about Nikki, she needed to be consistent. Changing her story would give her away.

"Who was that?" he asked.

"I think her name was Quinn. I met her on a flight from Los Angeles to San Francisco. We got to talking and she told me about this place." Now the tricky part. "Well, not this place exactly," she added. "Just that she went to a clinic that prescribed hormones and things like that. She didn't tell me the name, but from your web page, I just assumed this was it. Do you know her?"

"No," he said flatly. "It must have been a different clinic." He lied well, better than Karla. "But we get quite a number of patients who are referred by other patients," he said. "I think that speaks favorably of what we do here."

"I guess that's better than having patients speak badly of you," she said with a chuckle.

He didn't even crack a smile. Did he buy her story? She couldn't tell for sure. But he still looked worried. Something was bothering him.

Being on the receiving end of questions made her nervous. She was much more comfortable being the one asking. She quickly took that role before he could ask her anything else.

"So, do you think you can help me?" she asked.

"I do think so, yes," he said. "Judging from the blood tests and from the physical examination, I'm very confident that you would benefit from a complete program of antiaging therapies."

"Even at my age?" she asked. "Am I too young for this stuff?"

"Thirty-five is young, I agree. But it's actually the ideal time to begin treatment. It is much easier to halt the onset of aging than it is to reverse it. It's the difference between doing maintenance on a car and repairing it once something breaks. The programs we design here at De Leon can work in repairing damage, but the results are going to be better when we can concentrate more on maintenance. Does that make sense?"

"Sure."

"Imagine feeling like a thirty-year-old for the next twenty years," he said. "That's our goal with you."

Alicia didn't believe medical science could possibly do that. It would be great if doctors could do that, but that was too tall an order. Still, she had to act like she was buying into this. And she could note the improvement in Doug Collins. So she asked, "And how do you do that? Make me look and feel young forever?"

"We have a unique three-tier approach to restoring youth," he explained. He reiterated the same spiel that was in the brochure. "I specialize in hormone therapy."

Now they were getting to the area that interested her. Could the hormone therapies drive a person to commit suicide? How was she going to find out? She couldn't just come right out and ask him.

She glanced around the examination room. There must be patient files somewhere. If she could get her hands on them, she might be able to find the truth. But she'd have to do that after hours, when the building was empty.

"Can you explain more about the hormonal part?" she asked. "What do you prescribe and are there any dangers?"

He told her he'd start her on human growth hormone, DHEA, melatonin, and testosterone. Same as Nikki. Maybe she should try them, see how she reacted, see if she felt an urge to kill herself. It might come to that if she couldn't find physical evidence here. But the thought of taking them made her very uneasy.

"Isn't testosterone a male hormone?" she asked.

She equated testosterone with steroids. Could that make a person violent, like steroids? Or suicidal?

"Both men and women secrete testosterone in their bodies," he explained. "The levels are higher in men, but women need testosterone as well. The dose I'd prescribe for you will increase your lean body mass, but it will not cause you to develop male characteristics, if that's what you're concerned about."

"What about the human growth hormone?" she asked. The name alone conjured up images of Soviet bloc athletes, with huge bodies and misshapen faces. *Karla?*

"Again, growth hormone is something that occurs naturally in all of our bodies," he said. "Our goal here is to restore the level of growth hormone to what it was when you were younger. By doing that, we can bring you back to the same level of energy, strength, clarity of mind, and so forth that you experienced when you were younger."

"You can do that with hormones?"

What about the secret therapy Collins mentioned? She wanted to get him to talk about that. But he probably needed to get to know her better, to trust her the way Nikki must have trusted him. He did not seem like an easy person to get to know, though.

"Absolutely," he said. "The change is not only in your outward appearance, but also in the way you feel internally."

"So it does affect the way a patient feels mentally?" she asked. *In other words, can it drive a woman to kill herself?*

"Patients do feel better *internally,*" he said, obviously choosing that last word specifically, using it instead of the word *mentally.* He went back to the sales pitch, talking about "having more energy." All good. No adverse side effects.

She pushed a little harder. "But have you had any patients who've had bad reactions to the hormones?" she asked. "Or any of the other therapies?"

"Not really, no," he said. He looked annoyed that she'd asked that.

"Not *really*?" she said.

He hesitated, looking not only more irritated, but also unsure of how to answer. "I wouldn't word it as adverse reactions," he said. "Not that strongly. Some patients may experience minor agitation, sometimes minimal anxiety or melancholy. It's very rare. And we can easily reverse any such response by simply adjusting the doses."

He was obviously doing his best to minimize it, but Alicia had serious doubts. She knew what hormones could do to mood. She just needed clear evidence that these particular hormones, or whatever the "secret therapy" Collins referred to, could bring some people to such emotional depths that they'd want to end their lives.

The patient charts. That was the next place to look.

"Well, it all sounds encouraging," she said. "Is it okay if I think about it a little before I make a decision? It's a lot to digest."

"Certainly. Just let me know what you decide." The sales pitch was over. He stood up to leave. As he headed for the door, he said, "How did it go with Karla Weiss and Dr. Tobin?"

"Well, Karla's going to work up a program for me. She's supposed to have that ready today."

"Very good." He opened the door to show her out. "And Dr. Tobin?" he asked. "Did you discuss surgical options with him?"

"I did. He advised against it," she said.

Granier looked shocked. "He did?" His interest in leaving suddenly vanished. Now he was focused on her again. "Didn't you indicate on the patient questionnaire that you wanted liposuction and a laser peel?"

He riffled through her chart, muttering, "Not that I think you're fat, don't get me wrong, but . . . Here it is," he said, glaring at the paper she had filled out. He seemed to lose all interest in being inoffensive as he said, "Dr. Tobin recommended you *not* have the surgery?" He couldn't believe it. "Are you sure you understood him correctly?"

"Of course."

She felt offended by his questions. Not only was he saying she needed fat sucked out of her hips and butt, but he didn't think she was intelligent enough to understand something as simple as a doctor's recommendation.

Granier snapped shut her chart and muttered something under his breath. He finally regained control enough to thank her for coming before he stormed out.

23

PAUL WAS IN his office, reviewing the questionnaire from a new patient he was scheduled to see shortly, when his assistant buzzed him.

"Doctor. There's a Beth Tobin on line two."

Paul snatched up the receiver and jabbed the button beside the blinking light. This was the first time she had called him since his arrival; he'd always been the one initiating contact. This was good—her wanting to talk to him. Even if she was calling for something inconsequential, the fact that she was initiating contact, which she would not have done in the past no matter what, filled him with excitement and hope.

"Good morning, Beth. How are you?"

"Is this a bad time to call?" she asked. Her voice was flat, unreadable. He couldn't tell how she felt about talking to him. "This will only take a moment," she said.

"No problem, I can talk." He glanced at his watch. He only had a minute or two before he was supposed to see his first patient of the day, but he'd be late if it meant building a closer relationship with Beth. "What's up?"

She hesitated, which wasn't like her. He wondered if something was wrong. Could something have happened to one of the boys?

"Is everything all right?" he asked, starting to worry.

"Yes," she said. "I was just thinking . . ." She sighed. This was not a casual call for her, and not easy. "We haven't had a chance to talk to each other in quite some time," she said. "Even when I drove down there with the boys, we didn't really talk much. It was kind of a strained time."

"I know it was." It had been a start, which was all he could have asked for.

"By the way," she said, "the boys truly enjoyed themselves that day."

"I'm glad to hear that. I wasn't so sure about Kenny. He was kind of standoffish most of the time. Until the Jet Skis, anyway. Pete seemed to have a good time, though."

"They both did."

"I definitely want to spend more time with them," he said. This seemed to be going well, so he went for broke. He said, "I was thinking about maybe taking them camping sometime."

"I think that's a good idea," she said, which surprised him.

In the past, she had been against the boys being exposed to him. She'd called him a dismal role model. Obviously the brief visit a few weeks ago had done what he'd hoped, left a good impression. He couldn't drop the ball now. He could not let her and the boys down again.

"Maybe you'd like to come along, too?" he asked.

She was silent again. Was she actually considering it? That would be great.

Finally she said, "I think you and I should sit down together and really talk, Paul."

"I agree," he said. "We should talk."

"How about tonight?" she said. "Can you come up here? We can have dinner."

"Sure." He answered without even considering how he would get to Palm Beach. With bad credit and little cash, he hadn't been able to buy a car yet. Maybe he could rent one. If he had to, he'd take a taxi. Hell, if he really had to, he'd swim it. This was a chance he could not pass up.

They made arrangements for him to pick her up at seven. She knew a quiet place where they could talk. She would make the reservations.

When they hung up, Paul felt pleased with the way the

conversation had gone. He was getting what he'd wanted, a chance to make things right. After all this time apart, this was the beginning of his family being reunited. He was very hopeful about tonight.

Realizing there was a patient waiting for him, he grabbed the chart and started to leave. When he opened the door, he saw Ethan coming up the hallway toward him.

"Slumming this morning?" Paul said, wondering what brought Ethan to the surgical building.

"Don't leave," Ethan told him. "We need to talk." His tone was hard, all business.

"I have a patient waiting. Can we do this later?"

"The patient can wait."

Ethan sounded angry. He came close, blocking the doorway, as if to keep Paul here. He stood there, glaring at Paul, a patient's chart tucked under his arm. This wasn't Ethan's personality. Something must really be wrong.

"Is everything all right?" Paul asked.

"No, everything isn't."

He continued staring, saying nothing, waiting for Paul to turn around and go back into the office. Obviously it was important. Paul went back into the office. Ethan followed him in and quickly closed the door. Before Paul could say a word, Ethan blasted him.

"What the hell is wrong with you? What the hell is going on in that head of yours? Do you know what this place is? Do you have any idea what we do here?"

Paul didn't know what to say. He was flabbergasted. He had never seen Ethan this irate before.

"Ethan, what's wrong?" he asked.

"What do you think is wrong?"

"I honestly don't know."

"No? Maybe that's the goddamn problem! Maybe if you had an inkling of an idea of how to do your job, there wouldn't be anything wrong! Why the hell do you think I brought you here? Jesus Christ, what the hell is the matter with you?"

"Ethan, calm down and tell me what's wrong."

"You want me to calm down?" Ethan lowered his voice

but the anger was still there, simmering, getting ready to explode at any second. He shoved the patient file he'd been holding into Paul's hands. "Explain this!" Ethan said.

Paul still didn't understand. He read the name on the chart. Alicia Fernandes. He remembered her from yesterday. There hadn't been anything remarkable in her chart then; he wondered if there was something new. He started to skim through it but Ethan quickly grabbed it away.

"Who the hell do you think you are?" Ethan shouted.

Paul's confusion was turning to irritation. He didn't like the way Ethan took the chart away and he didn't like the way Ethan was talking to him. But he managed to keep his cool as he said, "Would you kindly explain what is going on?"

"Did you tell her not to have surgery?"

"Is that what this is about?"

"Did you?" Ethan screamed.

"Yes!" Paul screamed back. He quickly reined in his anger. "I recommended against it, yes. So . . . ?"

"You're not here to talk people *out* of having surgery! That's not your goddamn job!"

"It is if she doesn't need surgery."

"Who the hell are you to determine that?"

"The surgeon, that's who the hell I am!" Paul was shouting again. He couldn't hold it in any longer.

"Don't give me that power crap," Ethan said. "I pulled a lot of strings to get you your goddamn medical license, and I didn't do it so you could refuse to operate on patients."

"I didn't ask you to do that."

"You sure as hell accepted it, didn't you?"

"Not if it comes with a price, no."

"Cut the crap. Everything in life comes with a price. This practice is first and foremost a financial endeavor. It's bad enough you're doing this Dominican kid for free. You're also doing Karla for free. Did I say anything? No. Whatever you two have going between you, that's your business. But finally we get someone who's willing to pay and you don't want to operate. What the hell, Paul! We're here to make money. Remember?"

"Not if it means recommending surgery to a patient who doesn't need it. I won't do that!"

"*Need* it? You're not doing brain surgery or heart bypass. You're not saving lives here. No one *needs* it. You're doing goddamn face-lifts and liposuction. Basic elective cosmetic surgery. For God's sake, if they want it, give them the damn operation!"

Ethan's contempt for his specialty angered Paul, but he wasn't going to continue the shouting match. "It's not that simple," he said in a normal tone.

"It *is* that simple!" Ethan said. "If they want surgery and they're healthy enough to have it, your job is to give them the surgery. That is what you do here, you know. You operate on patients. You're supposed to be a surgeon, not a parent."

"Ethically, I have to—"

"Don't you dare throw that up in my face!" Ethan said. "I'm not asking you to do a single goddamn unethical thing. I'm just saying that if a patient wants the fat removed from her hips, she's entitled to have that done, regardless of whether you think she's fat or not."

"But I do have a responsibility to use my professional judgment to form an opinion regarding the patient's needs—"

"That's bullshit! That's not your responsibility. It isn't even any of your damn business. It doesn't matter what your opinion is. It's what the patient thinks that matters. If she thinks she's fat, then goddamn it, she's fat! If she doesn't like her nose, just give her a goddamn new nose! For God's sake, it's her nose, not yours!"

Paul just stared, speechless. This all seemed so surreal to him—Ethan standing there, screaming at him about fat and noses. Could they really be having this conversation? Ethan's anger about it made it even more strange, more unbelievable.

Ethan must have seen this in Paul's eyes, must have realized it himself. A confused look came over his face, replacing the anger. His eyes darted around the room. He looked like someone who had been awakened from a nightmare and needed desperately to get his bearings. He looked at Paul again.

Paul saw something strange in his eyes. It was there only an instant, but it was very clear. Ethan was as surprised and shocked about his losing control as Paul was. But more than that, he was afraid.

Ethan took a breath and regained his composure.

"I just want you to remember something, Paul," he said, calm, controlled. "It costs a lot of money to run this place. We can't turn business away."

"That isn't what I did. I don't know what Miss Fernandes told you, but when I saw her she wasn't at all set on having surgery. She asked my opinion. I couldn't lie. I told her what I thought. I didn't talk her out of it, Ethan."

"You didn't talk her into it, either."

Paul was surprised Ethan would say that. "You know I can't do that," he said.

"That's not what I meant," Ethan said, looking confused now, and desperate. "I'm just saying that we need to bring in money in order to keep this place running. That's not just for me, that's for you, too. If we don't bring in enough money, we're both out of work. And we both have other considerations. We both have families to consider, children who depend on us financially. We can't let them down. That's all I'm saying."

Paul moved closer and put his hand on Ethan's shoulder. He wanted him to know that they were on the same side. He needed this to be a success, too. He couldn't bear to fail again.

"If she really wanted surgery, she would have gotten it," he said. "She didn't want the surgery, Ethan."

Ethan let out a long, tired breath. His outburst left him completely spent.

"Just keep in mind what I said, okay?" Ethan asked.

Paul didn't answer. He didn't know what to say. He'd already made it clear that he wouldn't do anything unethical, but was that what Ethan was asking? Paul had always had great respect for Ethan, for his professionalism, for his ethics. Ethan was under enormous stress with Zachary.

Watching your son die has to take its toll. That would explain the outburst. Paul couldn't hold this single incident against him. Ethan had principles, as he showed when he resigned from Manhattan General over the incident three years ago. He would never do anything unethical, or ask Paul to.

"Ethan," he said, "I'm not going to let you down. I promise."

Ethan nodded then opened the door. "You have a patient waiting," he said. "You better get going."

Paul walked down the hallway, realizing that for this to work, he was going to have to find a delicate balance between what was right and what was necessary. He was sure it was something he could pull off.

24

ETHAN LEFT THE surgical building, still feeling strange. It was a nebulous thing, what he was feeling. He couldn't really put it into words. Disoriented wasn't it, exactly. He wasn't sick, he just felt . . . *off,* not himself.

The sunshine on his face and the warm breeze coming off the water helped bring him back. He heard voices coming from the pool area as he made his way toward his house. It distracted him a little, but the confrontation with Paul was still on his mind. The thing about it was, he felt an odd distance from the argument, as if he had been more of an observer than a participant. He had calmed down quite a bit since then, but he couldn't forget the rage that had swept through him, the uncontrollable anger. He had never felt anything like it before. In his mind, Paul's actions had been a threat to Zack, and that was all he had been able to see.

That rage had subsided, but he remained upset and troubled. Had it been a mistake bringing Paul here? He needed him to bring in money to keep the research going—not to cause problems. If Paul did anything to jeopardize Rejuvenol, the one who would suffer was Zack.

He still felt a sense of guilt over what had happened to Paul in New York, and he wanted to do his best to make it up to him. But regardless of that, Zack's well-being would always take precedence over Paul. Even if it meant withdrawing the help he was giving Paul to get back on his feet.

Even if it meant doing something to harm him.

Ethan suddenly stopped walking, shocked by his own thought. *Where on earth did that come from? Do something to harm Paul?* He didn't want to harm Paul or anyone else. He stood under the hot sun, sweating, confused, worried. *Fire Paul, yes.* If Paul did anything to interfere with Rejuvenol, Ethan would fire him in a heartbeat. Harm him that way. But not physically.

Ethan still felt strange. Light-headed . . . sort of. Edgy. It must be the heat and the stress he was under. He hurried the rest of the way to his house to get out of the sun and rest for a few minutes.

It was noon. The aroma of Carmen's cooking came from the kitchen. He was in time to have lunch with Zack, something he tried to do as often as possible. He walked into the kitchen but it was empty. Zack must have already finished eating. Ethan didn't see Zack outside on the patio or in the den, so he walked down the hallway to Zack's bedroom.

Zack lay in bed, propped up with pillows. Carmen was trying to spoon-feed him finely chopped chicken with rice, beans, and slices of fried plantain. Zack closed his mouth and shook his head—he'd had enough. He was having difficulty just keeping his head up, let alone chewing.

The sight of his son like this hit Ethan hard in the pit of his stomach. Zack had felt well enough this morning to come to the kitchen for breakfast. He'd been weak, but at least he could sit up and eat something. *Now look at him.* His turnarounds were so quick, so severe. Ethan feared one of them would begin the spiral, which Zack would not be able to pull out of.

He went around to the side of the bed and sat opposite Carmen. Zack's face brightened when he saw him.

"Hi, Dad."

"How are you doing, Zack? How was lunch?"

Carmen, trying to sound upbeat, said, "He did pretty well." But when Ethan glanced down at the dish in her hands, he saw that it was full. Zack hadn't been able to eat much. That was making him weaker. Which took away his appetite even more. The spiral . . .

Zack closed his eyes and within seconds drifted off to

sleep. Ethan kissed him on the forehead, feeling a heavy sense of guilt for the way Zack felt. If only he were a better doctor. If only he'd given his son better genes.

He felt sad and frustrated and angry at himself. He turned away and tried to focus on what he could do. Keep Zack comfortable and happy until he could finish the therapy that would give him a normal life.

He looked across the bed at Carmen. "What happened?" he asked. He needed to know if there was another reason for Zack's energy being so low, something other than the progression of his illness. "Did he do something tiring today?" he asked.

"No, Doctor. He sat outside and played with the cat for a few minutes then watched TV."

"Well, maybe the sun was a little too much for him." Ethan was grasping at straws. Anything that would mean that Zack wasn't getting closer to death. He didn't want to face the reality that he was almost out of time.

"I made sure he was in the shade all the time," Carmen said. "I didn't let him stay too long outside. Fifteen minutes."

Carmen took the rest of Zack's lunch back to the kitchen, leaving Ethan alone with his son. He peered down at Zack, listening to the weak sound of his breathing. The hormone therapy had worked for a while, but Zack needed something more. He needed the stem cell therapy. He deserved a chance. He had been through so much in his short life, he deserved better. He deserved to have a full life, just as much as Kenny and Pete did.

Ethan sat on the bed for twenty minutes before he made up his mind. He knew what he had to do. Beth had told him that she was going to meet Paul for dinner and break the news to him. That meant the kids would be alone.

Tonight, he would do what he had to do.

25

PAUL TOOK A taxi to Key West, rented a car at the airport, then drove the four hours to Palm Beach. He arrived twenty minutes early, so he drove past the house once, then parked one street over and waited. He felt like a teenager on his first date with the hottest girl in school.

When it was time, he drove back to the house. The sun was still bright, even at this hour. Perspiration soaked his neck and dripped down his back. He checked his reflection in the car window. He was pleased. His body was fit and trim. His face had more vitality than a month ago, and even though he knew being in the sun was the worst thing a person could do for his skin, he had a tan. This was Florida. He couldn't help it. He wished he had a new suit, though. This one had definitely seen better days.

And worse days. This was the suit he'd worn to the inquiry three years ago. That day had begun the demise of his career in New York, and the downward spiral of his alcoholism. He hoped tonight's outcome would be a lot better.

He rang the bell. Kenny opened the door. He barely showed any emotion, just that same uncomfortable-in-his-body teenage look.

"How are you, Kenny?" Paul asked. He wanted to hug Kenny, but he knew Kenny wanted no part of such displays of emotion. The best Paul could do was a handshake—a man-to-man, father-to-adult-son kind of thing.

"Mom'll be down in a few minutes," Kenny said. He stepped aside so Paul could come in.

When Kenny closed the door, the two of them stood in the foyer for a moment in uneasy silence. Paul needed to break it. "So, how's school going?" he asked. It felt so much like chatting with a stranger that Paul felt ashamed of having let it get to this point.

"School sucks," Kenny murmured and headed into the living room.

He and Paul sat in chairs directly across from each other, staring. More unnerving silence. Again, it was up to Paul to break the stalemate.

"Hey, I was thinking . . . what do you say we do some deep-sea fishing one of these weekends?"

Kenny stared at him, as though Paul had just said something utterly ridiculous.

"What?" Paul asked.

"It's hurricane season. There's three tropical storms out in the Atlantic right now. Even if we survive going out on a boat, the waters are so rough we'll probably spend the whole time puking over the side. Thanks, but no thanks."

"Give me a little credit, Kenny. We won't go when there's a hurricane."

"I'll pass." Kenny's tone was so bitter it sounded like he was saying *Go to hell.*

Just then Pete ran into the room, excited to see his father. "Daddy!" He jumped up onto Paul's lap, squishing the air out of him, and hugged his neck.

"Hey, champ! How are you?"

While he hugged Pete, he looked up and saw Kenny leaving. "Hey, Kenny, wait. . . ."

Kenny glanced back but didn't stop. In his eyes was a look of silent anger—an anger born out of deep pain. Pain Paul had caused. Paul had a lot of work to do restoring his relationship with Beth, but it was going to be just as difficult, if not more so, repairing things with Kenny. Pete seemed to handle it much better. Maybe it was his age, or his temperament. Whatever the reason, he seemed to forgive Paul and welcome him back into his life.

Beth came downstairs now, dressed in a simple but classy skirt and top. He was flattered that she'd dressed up for him. Another positive sign. Tonight was the night he was going to make his intentions clear to her. Tonight he was going to do whatever was necessary to win her back.

She told Pete to be in bed by nine and called upstairs to Kenny to come back down and keep an eye on his brother. Kenny grumbled. Beth left him the name and phone number of the restaurant where they'd be, then she and Paul left.

26

ETHAN EXITED I-95 and headed west, into West Palm Beach. He had one stop to make before crossing the bridge into Palm Beach and going to Beth's house. But he had to hurry. He was up against the clock. Paul and Beth wouldn't be out too long. An hour, ninety minutes max. Barely enough time to do what he needed to do.

Di Napoli's Gelato was famous in West Palm Beach. For as long as Ethan could remember, Enzo Di Napoli had made the best ice cream in the entire county. Ethan had gone there when he was a kid. They'd only had three flavors back then: chocolate, vanilla, and coffee. Enzo's sons ran the place now. They'd added new flavors since Ethan was a boy, but they used the same method of making the ice cream that Enzo had brought from Italy half a century ago.

Beth was too health conscious to take the boys there often. It would be a treat for them tonight. Ethan was counting on them not saying no.

He bought a gallon of double chocolate fudge then drove the last fifteen minutes to Beth's house. He drove past it. Paul had gone to Key West to rent a car for tonight. Besides Beth's SUV, there wasn't any other car in the driveway or on the street. Good—they'd left for the restaurant. Ethan needed as much time as he could get.

He drove to the end of the street, turned the corner, and parked. He checked the street. No one was around. He took the lid off the ice cream container. The smell of chocolate filled the car. He opened his briefcase and took out one syringe, already loaded with lorazepam, and poked the needle into the ice cream. He injected some of the sedative then moved the needle to another spot and injected some more. He'd picked the double chocolate fudge because the flavor and smell were so strong Beth's kids wouldn't realize it was in there. He injected the rest of the syringe into the ice cream, hoping it was enough. He needed the boys to be sleeping quickly if this was to work.

He put the lid back on the ice cream, then removed the two infusion bags from the briefcase and slid them into the inside pockets of his suit jacket, careful not to rupture them. Last, he gathered everything he'd need to set up two IVs from his briefcase and stuffed it all into his pockets. Everything was ready.

He hesitated a moment, wondering if he should do this. Zack's life was at stake. He *had* to do this.

He took a deep breath to steady his nerves, then got out, checking his watch as he walked up to the front door. Seven-fifteen. If Paul and Beth went out at seven, sat down to dinner at seven-thirty, they'd be done by eight-thirty, nine o'clock at the latest, back here by nine-twenty. He'd have to be done and gone by then. That gave him two hours. The clock was ticking.

He rang the bell. After a short wait, Kenny answered the door.

"Uncle Ethan?" he said, surprised to see him.

Ethan glanced past him toward the empty living room. He heard the faint buzz of a television in one of the rooms beyond that. Pete was home, too. Perfect.

"Is your mom around?" he asked Kenny. He already knew the answer, but the question was part of the cover.

Kenny shook his head. "She went out."

He didn't mention with whom. The teenager was clearly having difficulties relating to his father. Ethan felt a tinge of guilt over that. Some of it was his fault. But only *some* of it. Paul's drinking had started getting out of hand before the incident with Wilkenson. Something would have happened eventually. It was inevitable. Ethan had only accelerated it.

"That's too bad," he said to Kenny. "I brought her some ice cream from Di Napoli's. It's going to melt if someone doesn't eat it."

Pete went right to work on the ice cream. Kenny was a harder sell; the lure of ice cream wanes in the teenage years. But at least he hung around.

Ethan talked sports with him. The Dolphins hadn't been the same since Shula and Marino left, he told Kenny. Kenny had no idea who Don Shula was, but he did know Dan Marino. And that gave them something to talk about. More importantly, Kenny finally took a spoonful of ice cream.

It was only a matter of time now.

27

PAUL JUST STARED. Even if he had known what to say, he just couldn't get any words out. Beth's news left him mute, suffocating. Finally he drew in some air and managed to mutter a few words.

"What . . . what do you mean?" He hoped he'd heard her wrong, or misunderstood her somehow. He needed to hear it differently, needed it explained, needed it taken back, needed it to go away.

But she didn't do any of those things. She just peered across the table. He saw that this was painful for her—but that didn't make it any easier. Silence grew like a wall between them. Paul felt a sickening sense of detachment. He was losing her—*forever.*

"Beth . . ." he started to say. But before he could finish, the waiter came with their entrees. Paul fell silent.

It seemed to take the waiter an eternity to place the dishes, offer cheese, refill the water. Paul just stared at Beth, who avoided his eyes now. *This must be a mistake. She can't possibly mean what she said.* She wouldn't do that to him. Did she understand how much he had changed? How could she not? And he began to convince himself that he'd heard her wrong.

Finally the waiter left. Paul was about to tell her that he had obviously misheard what she just said, when she spoke.

"What did you expect from me?" she said with a mortal

edge of condemnation in her voice. Not only was she not taking back what she'd just said, but she was trying to justify it, blaming him.

What did you expect from me? He didn't know how to reply. He couldn't possibly say the truth of what he'd expected—it seemed so naïve and unrealistic now. But he had to say something. He couldn't just let this happen.

"I thought we had a chance . . ." he said.

She let out a breath of exasperation. "We did," she said. She stared back at him, her eyes showing more disappointment than anger. "Nineteen years ago, we had a chance. But we blew it."

"But we still have a chance, Beth."

She smiled a sad smile and shook her head. "No, we don't. I'm getting remarried in December. I'm getting on with my life. You should do the same."

"You're my life. You and the kids."

She sighed, frustrated. "That's the past. I'm in love with another man. The kids are still in your life, but you and I are over."

He shook his head, not willing to believe her. She was just saying that, trying to hide her true feelings, not wanting to be hurt again. And after what he had done, he couldn't blame her for that. But that didn't mean he would just let her get away.

"I know I hurt you, Beth. You and the kids. And believe me, I'm so sorry for that. But I've changed."

"I know you've changed. And I know you're sorry. But that really doesn't change anything, Paul."

"Of course it does," he said. How could it not change things? It changed everything. He wouldn't have committed the last two years to that if it wouldn't change anything. "We can't just throw away all the years we've had together."

"We already did." There was a flash of anger in her eyes, but that quickly dulled behind the glint of a tear. This was very hard for her. And sad. She wiped the tear away and said, "Please, Paul . . ."

He just couldn't let go. He reached across the table and took her hand. "Look me in the eyes," he said, "and tell me you don't love me."

She took a deep breath, looked him directly in the eyes, and said, "I don't love you."

"I don't believe you."

"Don't make this harder than it already is. I'm getting married in December, and Kenny and Pete and I are moving to Paris to live with Eli."

"But what about—"

She held up her hand, stopping him. "Paul," she said, her tone firm, "it's over. It's over."

Looking at the clarity in her eyes, hearing the resolution in her voice, he realized it was, indeed, over.

28

WITHIN HALF AN hour, Pete fell asleep on the couch in the family room, watching TV. Kenny was taking much longer. He hadn't eaten as much of the ice cream, and because of his size, it took more time for the sedative to have an effect. Ethan had to make an excuse why he was hanging around so long.

"I need to have your mom sign some papers," he told Kenny.

"Who knows when she'll be back."

"I drove all the way up here," Ethan said. "Might as well wait a little while longer."

Kenny shrugged. "Whatever."

He went upstairs to his room, making it more difficult for Ethan to know when the drug did its job. He gave Kenny another twenty minutes then went upstairs and stood by his door. He heard music playing inside the bedroom, some noisy rap song that he couldn't understand. He tried to listen for movement behind the door, for any sounds that Kenny was still awake. But all he heard was the heavy bass of the music. Time was passing quickly. Paul and Beth could return at any moment. He needed to get this done.

He couldn't wait any longer, so he knocked on the door. No answer. He eased it open a few inches and saw Kenny lying on the bed in his clothes, his eyes closed.

"Kenny?" No reaction. He walked into the room and gently shook Kenny's arm. Nothing. He was out cold. Finally.

He checked his watch. Almost eight-thirty. He'd been here more than an hour. He had to hurry.

He took everything he needed out of his pockets. He tied off Kenny's arm with the rubber tube, uncapped the IV needle, and inserted it into a vein on Kenny's arm. Once the port was set up, he drew a specimen of blood. He'd need it to establish a benchmark against which to measure the effect of Rejuvenol. He capped the glass tube and stuffed it into his suit jacket pocket.

Next he took out one of the infusion bags containing Rejuvenol and attached the tube into the IV port. As he waited for the fluid to drain into Kenny's body, he began to think about Paul and Beth again. If they knew what he was doing . . . But they'd never find out. Kenny and Pete wouldn't even remember what had happened. One of the benefits of lorazepam. And what he was doing here might ensure that Zack lived.

When the bag was empty, he stuffed it into his pants pocket, took the IV port out of Kenny's arm, and pressed a square of gauze over the puncture to stop the bleeding. He could only give it a minute, then he put the gauze in his pocket and started downstairs to take care of Pete. He was halfway down the stairs when he heard a car pull into the driveway.

No! Not yet!

He rushed to the small window on the landing. A car was in the driveway. Beth got out and headed toward the front door of the house. Paul got out a moment later and followed.

Damn it!

He had to get out of here quickly. He'd never be able to explain why he was here. It had taken too long for the sedative to work on Kenny. He should have been done and gone by now. There wasn't time to inject Pete. Kenny would have to suffice as a test subject.

Ethan rushed to the bottom of the stairs. He was about to cross the foyer and run to the kitchen, thinking he could escape through the sliding glass door, when the front door opened, blocking his route to the kitchen.

29

PAUL FOLLOWED BETH into the house. She had tried to talk him out of coming in, but he insisted on it. She and the boys were going to leave for France in ten days to spend a week with this Eli person, and Paul couldn't shake the feeling that this was the last time he'd see his sons, even though Beth assured him that wasn't the case. Still, he needed to see them tonight, to feel a connection with them before they went away to begin a new life without him.

From the entryway, Paul heard the rattle of laughter coming from the TV in the family room. The boys were still up. He was thankful for that, but he was also nervous because he didn't know what to say.

"Make it short, okay?" Beth said. "It's getting late."

Paul headed toward the family room, thinking again about the boys beginning a new life without him. Isn't that what they'd been doing for the last three years, living a life without him? Was this really going to be any different for them? Probably not. But it was massively different for him. In his mind, the last three years had always been temporary. This . . . this was permanent. The boys would see a new man beside their mother. A new father? Probably not. But in many ways Eli would be filling Paul's shoes. And this before Paul had a chance to make things right with his boys. Before he *made* the chance, that is. Along with the hurt of Beth's words, Paul hated himself for not going to the boys sooner, not trying to fix things until now. He wasn't much of a man after all. Overcoming his drinking meant nothing if he couldn't reestablish a father-son relationship with his boys. What then had all the struggling been for?

He walked into the family room. Pete was sprawled out on the sofa in his pajamas, fast asleep. The flickering light of the TV illuminated his innocent face. How he could still look innocent after all he'd been through amazed Paul. *After all I've put him through.* How would Pete cope with this next trauma?

Seeing how tranquil the boy looked, Paul wondered if it would be a trauma at all for Pete. He'd been through so much already. Perhaps he welcomed this, some stability in his life, a father figure at last, one he could look up to and respect. Maybe this was the best thing for the boys after all. Maybe it was better that they didn't have a close relationship with a weak, alcoholic screwup of a father like him.

"I told Kenny to make sure Pete went to bed by nine," Beth said, shaking her head, sounding annoyed. "Where is Kenny, anyway?"

She picked up the remote control and turned off the TV. In the sudden silence and darkness, Paul felt the sickening sensation of self-pity. Here he was, his children about to embark on a new and difficult life, and he was feeling sorry for himself rather than trying to figure out what he could do to make this transition easier for them. What a loser.

He swallowed hard against the misery welling up in his throat. After all he'd been through, he was no better now than when he was still a drunk. Hadn't he learned a damn thing?

"Pete," Beth said. "Come on, time to go to bed." She shook Pete's shoulder. Pete just moaned quietly. He was too tired to wake up.

"I'll carry him up to bed," Paul said. He scooped Pete up into his arms and followed Beth toward the stairs.

Beth blew out a breath of exasperation and muttered, "Kenny is really trying my patience."

"He's at that age, Beth . . ." Paul said, feeling he should defend his son.

"What's that supposed to mean?" Beth said, irritated.

"Just that the early teens are a difficult time for a boy. You have to cut him some slack, that's all."

"That's easy for you to say. You're not the one who has to deal with it every day."

Her words stabbed at his heart. He didn't know if she said that on purpose, to remind him what a bad father he was, or if she was just voicing her frustration, not realizing the cruelty of her words.

He followed Beth into Pete's room. She turned down the covers, and he placed Pete gently on the bed. Beth went to the door, clearly eager for Paul to leave, but Paul lingered a moment beside the bed, gazing down at his little boy. He couldn't get over the feeling that he wasn't going to see him anymore—at least not as his father. It was as if that part of him was to disappear as soon as he walked away from this bed.

"Come on," Beth whispered. "He needs to sleep."

Paul knelt down beside the bed and kissed Pete lightly on the forehead. "Good night, champ," he whispered.

Pete lay motionless and silent. Paul selfishly wished Pete would wake up, just for a moment. He needed to see his son's eyes, needed to feel some kind of connection. But Pete was obviously exhausted. He did not stir at all. He did not give Paul the tiny bit of relief he needed.

Paul swallowed hard. The next words were more painful to get out than he'd expected.

"Daddy loves you," he whispered.

It was not so much the words themselves that hurt him, but rather the realization which drove him to speak them, that his past actions had not shown Pete this truth.

He left the room, feeling defeated.

Beth followed him into the hallway. "You won't be long with Kenny, will you?" she asked, sounding tired and irritated that he was still here.

He wanted to shout at her that Kenny was his son, too, and he had every right in the world to spend a little time with him, but that would only make matters worse. The truth was, he didn't have every right in the world, according to the divorce court. Beth had all the rights when it came to deciding how much time Paul had with the boys. Besides, Kenny probably wouldn't want to sit and talk with him for more than a second or two.

Paul nodded in silent resignation.

"And if he's still awake," Beth said, starting down the stairs, "tell him I want to talk to him." She didn't wait for a reply. She went downstairs and disappeared into the kitchen.

Paul walked to Kenny's room. The door was closed. He heard the drone of rap music playing inside and felt a tinge of hope that Kenny was still awake. But he also felt nervous. He didn't know what to say to Kenny. If this went anything like their encounter earlier tonight or the day Kenny came to Coral Key, it was going to be a disaster.

He took a deep breath and knocked on the door.

"Kenny?"

No answer.

He knocked again then slowly opened the door. The light was on in the bedroom, the music annoyingly loud now that the door was open. Kenny lay on his back in bed, asleep.

Or faking it? Paul wondered. Maybe Kenny didn't want to talk to him so he was pretending to be asleep. Like father, like son. Avoid the unpleasant. Close your eyes and pretend to be asleep. Or escape into a bottle. Paul couldn't blame Kenny if that was what he was doing.

But he still wanted to connect with him if he could, even if it was just a word or two before he left. So he walked into the room. As he passed the stereo he turned off the music. The sudden silence didn't wake Kenny. He was either in really deep sleep or faking it. Paul went to the side of the bed.

"Kenny," he said. "Kenny?"

Nothing. Maybe he was exhausted like Pete. It was kind of early for a teenager to go to bed, but he might be sleeping. Even if he was faking it, if it meant that much to him not to talk to his father, Paul had to honor that. He turned to leave.

He stepped on something plastic that crackled under his

shoe. He thought it was a CD or something like that, but when he looked down to see what he'd broken, what Kenny would use to hate him even more, he saw a blue safety cap from an IV needle.

Ethan peered through the slats in the closet door, watching Paul, wishing he would hurry up, kiss the kid good night or whatever he intended to do, and leave, so Beth would go to bed and he could sneak out of here himself.

But then he saw Paul bend over and pick up something off the floor. The moment Paul held it up to the light, Ethan realized what it was. *Damn it!* He thought he had been so careful, doing everything possible to cover his tracks. He hadn't realized that he'd dropped the cap. Surely Paul knew what it was. Surely he'd realize what Ethan had done.

Ethan watched him, hoping that somehow Paul wouldn't realize what he'd found and he'd just throw it away. But Paul continued to look at the cap, then down at Kenny, then back at the cap. No, he knew. He understood exactly what he'd found.

Paul leaned closer to Kenny now. Ethan shifted to the side a little so he could see better what Paul was doing. The clothes hanging behind him pressed against his neck. Something was stabbing him in the ear. But he focused on Paul.

Paul examined one of Kenny's arms. Ethan knew exactly what Paul was looking for. And when he saw Paul lean closer and fix his stare on the inside of Kenny's right elbow, he realized that Paul had found it. The mark from the needle. *Damn it!*

He had to think quickly, figure out what to do. Would Paul put two and two together? Would he realize where the mark came from? Would he realize what Ethan had done to his son? Ethan wondered if he should just explain everything, make Paul realize how desperate Zachary was, make him understand that this was a matter of life and death. Was Paul capable of understanding?

Paul started looking closely at something else. Ethan

shifted position again, trying to get a better look. His shoulder knocked one of the hangers off the bar. A coat flopped down, scraping the door.

Paul jolted upright and spun around toward the closet. Ethan froze, peering through the slats at Paul, who was staring straight back at him. Could Paul see him? He didn't see recognition on Paul's face, only concern. He had certainly heard the noise. What was he going to do?

Then Paul started toward the closet.

Ethan looked desperately for a place to hide. Light came through the slats in the door, horizontal wedges of white cutting the blackness. Near his leg, leaning against the wall, illuminated by the light, was a baseball bat. An image flashed into his brain, as sharp and clear as if it were actually happening: the bat swinging at Paul, hitting him in the side of the head, knocking him to the floor in a pool of blood.

Ethan reached over and grasped the handle of the bat. The wood felt hard and cold in his palm. He clutched it tightly and looked back through the slats in the door. Zack's life was at stake. He could not allow Paul to do anything that would endanger Zack's life. Even if that meant hurting Paul. Even if it meant killing him.

Paul was almost upon him now. Ethan's body responded automatically, instinctively. He lifted the bat. The image of the bat smacking Paul's head filled Ethan's brain again. His hands could almost feel the impact.

It felt strangely . . . *good*.

Paul stopped in front of the closet door. Ethan smelled Paul's cologne, the musk that was supposed to win Beth over. What a fool. Ethan heard Paul's breath—the short, rapid respiration of alarm. Paul reached for the doorknob. Ethan tightened his grip on the bat and focused on his target—the left side of Paul's head.

"Look, I want to get to bed."

Beth's voice shattered the silence. Paul spun around, caught by surprise. He peered across the room, where Beth was standing in the doorway, glaring at him. Ethan could see her through the slats. The look on her face, along with the echo of her tone still reverberating through the room, left a very clear message to Paul: *Leave.*

Ethan moved again so he could see Paul. He looked dejected. He had gotten the message loud and clear. Beth didn't just not want him *here,* she didn't want him, period. That was what this whole evening had been about. That realization seemed to hit Paul as hard as any baseball bat. He looked disoriented, confused, overwhelmed. He hesitated a moment, like he wanted to make an appeal, but no words came out. He seemed to forget all about the closet, the cap he'd found on the floor, the needle mark on Kenny's arm. He dropped his head and trudged toward the door, not saying a word.

Beth avoided looking at him as he walked past. Ethan listened to Paul's steps go down the hall and descend the stairs. He watched Beth stand in the door, staring at the floor. She looked as tortured as Paul.

The sound of the door closing downstairs broke the silence. Beth shook her head and let out a long sigh. She knew she was doing the right thing. She turned off the light in Kenny's room, closed the door, and walked away.

Ethan stood in the darkness. He'd wait in the closet until he was sure Beth was asleep before he'd sneak downstairs and out the door.

30

As Paul drove through the empty streets of Palm Beach, a sick feeling filled his stomach. His head throbbed with disgust. How could he have let Beth tell him that it was over? How could he sit there and listen to her talk about remarrying this Eli guy, whoever the hell he was, and not scream and shout and make her change her mind? How could he let their marriage fall away? What kind of a man would do that?

A small, weak, pathetic excuse for a man. A loser. He should have fought his brains out to keep her. He should have done everything under the sun and moon to stop her from marrying another man. That's what he *should* have done. But what did he actually do? He drove the hell away!

He slammed on the brakes. The car skidded to a stop. Paul was going back. He wasn't going to leave until he convinced Beth that he was the one for her. He needed her to know how much he loved her. He needed her to know that he was a different person now, that he could make her happy—happier than any other man could make her.

Headlights glared in his rearview mirror as a car approached from behind, slowed a moment, then steered around him. Paul checked the street to make sure no other cars were coming so he could turn around and go back to Beth's. But then he hesitated. She'd made it clear that she didn't want him there tonight. How would she react if he barged in again? He'd seem like the same irrational, out-of-control drunk he'd been three years ago, like he didn't care about how she felt. She might even feel threatened, like he was trying to run her life. He needed to do this carefully if it was going to work. He needed to show her that he not only loved her but respected her.

He saw a restaurant half a block up the street. He could call first, tell her he needed to talk, ask her if he could come back over. There was no way he was going to take no for an answer; he'd do everything in his power to convince her to let him back in. But at least he'd be doing it in a way that would show her a good side of him.

He pulled into the parking lot and went inside. The restaurant was half empty at this hour. A hostess greeted Paul at the door.

"Is there a pay phone I could use?" he asked.

"Sure. Over there," she answered, pointing toward the lounge.

Paul walked past the bar to the phone and stared at it for a moment, trying to compose his words. How was he going to begin? What was Beth going to say? Would she even answer the phone at this hour? Maybe she was already sleeping. Was it a good idea to wake her up? He had to think this through.

He went over to the end of the bar where no one else was sitting. He needed to be alone with his thoughts. A thin scent of beer permeated the air in here. At the other end of the bar three men sat together, talking and laughing with each other and with the bartender. They looked like they all knew each other well, regulars, like a family. *Like at Cunningham's.* He remembered his days at his old watering hole on West Fifty-fifth Street. All the regulars knew him. He'd been part of the community there, part of that family. He hadn't felt a part of anything since he stopped going there. Not part of the medical community. Not part of De Leon. Worst of all, not part of his own family.

He wasn't Beth's husband—he hadn't been for a very long time. She made that clear tonight. He didn't even feel like he was Kenny and Pete's father. They were really the only group he wanted to be a part of, and the one group he was the farthest from. He had tried to change that, but he'd failed.

He thought again about calling Beth. Would that really change a thing? She'd made it clear that she didn't want him. Maybe that was something he would just have to accept. No matter what he did or said, he could not make her love him.

He sat at the bar, staring at the army of bottles across from him, soldiers he'd once been on a first-name basis with. A heavy sadness sank down on him as he thought about Beth. He felt a lump in his throat and a sickness in his heart. He closed his eyes. Some mistakes you just can't make up for. What he'd done years ago he'd be paying for for the rest of his life.

"How're you doing tonight, buddy?"

Paul looked up. The bartender was standing across the bar from him. He slid a drink napkin in front of Paul.

"You look like you've seen better days," the man said.

Paul let out an exasperated breath. "You've got that right," he said. The words came out so naturally in this setting, so comfortably. Like he was talking to a buddy.

"I know the feeling," the bartender said. "What'll it be tonight?"

Paul didn't know what to say. For two years and three months his answer had been soda water with a twist of lime. That seemed so ridiculous tonight.

Club soda with a twist of lime? What the hell for?

"Johnny Walker, on the rocks," he said. It came out like a gasp of air, a breath he'd been holding underwater.

The bartender brought the drink so quickly Paul didn't even have a chance to reconsider. He reached into his pocket for money to pay the man. He pulled out a folded twenty. As he set it on the bar, the blue cap he'd found in Kenny's room fell out. He'd forgotten about it until now.

The bartender walked away with the twenty. Paul picked up the cap and peered at it, remembering everything he'd found in Kenny's room. The cap. The needle mark on

Kenny's arm. It could only mean one thing. Kenny was doing drugs.

Paul felt a stab of guilt. Had he driven Kenny to this?
The boy's family falls apart because his father is a drunk.
What was a kid supposed to do? Escape, of course. *Like father, like son.* But blaming himself, no matter how much he
deserved it, wasn't going to help anything at this point.
Paul tried to put his feelings of guilt aside for now and
think this through.

From the absence of multiple marks on Kenny's arm,
Paul assumed Kenny hadn't been doing drugs for long.
There'd only been the one mark. Was it possible that he'd
only shot up one time? Maybe he was just experimenting.
Kids his age did that. Maybe Kenny had tried it and de-
cided he didn't like it.

That was wishful thinking and Paul knew it. He couldn't
rely on hopes that Kenny would stop on his own. A real father would do something about this. He hoped he'd found
out early enough to stop it before Kenny hurt himself
badly. But what should he do? With Kenny's obvious animosity toward him right now, confronting the boy would
not only push him farther away from Paul but it might push
him toward the escape of drugs. He had to be careful.

First, he had to find out exactly what Kenny's problem
was. Maybe there was another explanation for the needle
cap and the mark on his arm. Maybe he'd donated blood at
school. Paul couldn't explain away the cap so easily, but
there had to be another logical explanation for its being in
his room. A science class project? If Kenny was innocent, he
would never forgive his prying father for assuming the
worst. But there was so little time—once Beth took the
kids to France, he'd have very limited contact with Kenny.

Paul decided it was premature to tell Beth at this point.
Even though she was the one who was in the best position
to see any changes in Kenny, he decided to wait until he
had more to go on before he mentioned it to her. He didn't
know for sure what was going on. If he told Beth, she'd
panic. That might just make matters worse. She did every-

thing in her power to protect the boys, to make sure they had lives as normal and healthy as possible, to make sure no one else would hurt them the way their father had.

Hurt them the way their father had.

That hit him hard. He had hurt the people he loved the most. Hurt Beth so much that she had to marry someone else—someone she probably didn't love, Paul told himself—in order to have the stability and security Paul had taken away from her. Hurt Kenny so much that he may have had to turn to drugs to escape the reality his father made for him. And Pete? What horrible thing had he done to Pete?

Feeling thoroughly disgusted with himself, Paul lowered his hand and without consciously thinking it through, grasped the glass of scotch. He needed relief from the guilt, from the painful reality he'd made for himself, and he knew how to get that relief.

Like father, like son. . . .

He looked down and saw his hand wrapped around the glass. In his grip was the thing that made him feel the highest and the lowest. The lows had been so bad, but the highs . . . He'd been forced to give them up as well. Now he had only the constant, dull vigilance that got him through the day. If only he could bring the highs back without the lows. That had to be possible. Other people had that. Why couldn't he manage it? It had to be possible.

He looked hard at the amber liquid bliss in his hand.

Like father, like son.

Indeed.

31

ALICIA WAITED UNTIL midnight.

Outside her bungalow, the air was muggy and hot. The wet breeze blowing off the water held the foul smell of rotting seaweed. The night was alive with the screaking of insects. As she made her way down the palmetto-lined path in darkness, thoughts of spiders and snakes flashed into her head. What else might be hidden out there in the blackness? She felt out of her element here. In the clubs and on the streets of Los Angeles, she knew her surroundings and what to do in all situations. But here, she felt very different. This felt like her first investigation, like she really wasn't sure of what she was doing.

And though the strange surroundings were part of it, the feeling came from deeper inside her. In all those other investigations, she'd had nothing personal at stake. It was her job, and though she took it seriously, in the end it was about other people's lives. But now, justice for her sister rested in her hands. She owed Nikki this. If she failed, she'd be failing her sister, and she couldn't bear to live with that.

The beach was empty. A half moon cast fuzzy shadows from the swaying palm trees. She passed the pool area, also deserted at this hour. The lights in the reception building were out, as were the lights in the bungalows that she could see. A few outdoor lights cast illumination in some spots, but she avoided those areas as she made her way toward Ethan Granier's office.

She found the building completely dark, just as she had expected. In the distance was Granier's house. The lights were off there, too. He must be asleep. She hoped there wouldn't be an alarm in his office. She had to count on the remoteness of this place and the feeling of being safe inside his island compound being Granier's primary security system.

She scanned the darkness again. No one was around. She tried the door of the medical building. Locked, as she'd expected. The lock was a standard commercial one, pretty easy to open if she'd had her tools with her. But she hadn't taken them on this trip. They were illegal to have unless you were a licensed locksmith, and she hadn't wanted to risk losing them to airport security.

She searched for another way in. A window could be just as good as a door. All she needed was one left unlocked. She squeezed between some tropical bushes, thinking again about spiders and God knows what else that might be living in these palms, and shimmied along the side of the building, trying each window as she made her way around the corner and down the back wall. Halfway down—*bingo!*—one of the windows slid open.

She glanced around to make sure she was still alone. The beach was behind her, barely visible through the bushes. Waves washed up on the empty sand. Wind rustled the palms. Nothing else was out there. She was alone and safe and well-hidden here behind the bushes.

She turned back to the window. Moonlight gave enough illumination for her to see what she was doing. She reached in and felt a screen. That came out easily. She set it on the ground beneath the window. Some plants were on the windowsill. She carefully set them on the ground, too.

She stuck her head inside. She was at the reception area of Granier's office. Across the room was the hallway that led to the exam rooms. She assumed that the room where patient records were kept was down there, too, along with Granier's private office. Those two rooms were her target.

She'd started to climb through the window when someone grabbed her leg and yanked her back out. She landed facedown on the ground, the wind knocked out of her. Before she could react, she was dragged violently through the sand, her arms and stomach being scraped raw. Then her legs were wrenched sideways and she was jerked over onto her back, her face banging an exposed root.

Karla Weiss leered down at her. She had Alicia's legs in some kind of martial arts hold, putting immense pressure on her ankles and knees. The pain made Alicia slap the ground and grit her teeth to keep from screaming out.

"Let go!" she said.

Karla kept the pressure up. "What are you doing here?" she said.

"Jesus Christ, let go of me!" Alicia said. "That hurts!"

Instead of letting go, Karla applied more pressure. Pain shot up Alicia's leg. She cried out in agony.

Karla eased off on the pressure. "What are you doing here?" she asked again.

"Let go of me. I'll tell you."

Karla applied pressure again. The pain was crippling. Alicia thought her ankles were about to break. She screamed again, longer this time.

Karla let off slightly. "If I have to ask again," she said, "I'll break the ankles, ya?"

Alicia stared up at the heavily muscled body standing over her, at the intense look in Karla's eyes. She realized just how vulnerable she was. Karla could easily break her ankles or just about any other bone she wanted. What was more scary was that Karla looked like she *would* do it. She might even *want to.*

"Okay, okay," she said. She had to think of an excuse quickly. "When I was in Dr. Granier's office earlier," she said, "I think I left my wallet with all my money and credit cards and everything in there. I was just trying to get it, that's all."

Karla stared down, still holding Alicia's legs.

Alicia said, "Can I get up now?"

"How do I know you're telling the truth?" Karla asked.

"Why would I lie? Why else would I want to go in there?"

Karla thought about it for a moment, then said, "If you left your wallet in there, you'd wait until the morning to get it."

"You don't understand. Everything I need is in my wallet. I mean, I can't even make a long-distance phone call without it—my calling card is in there."

"Why didn't you ask someone to let you in if your wallet's in there?"

"I didn't think anyone was up at this hour."

"Earlier."

"I just noticed. I was going to make a call to Los Angeles. It's three hours earlier there. When I went to get my card, that's when I noticed."

Karla mulled it over for a moment, and Alicia thought she had her, but then Karla shook her head and said, "I don't believe you."

"Why would I lie?" Alicia said again.

From the look on Karla's face, Alicia realized that it was a mistake to keep saying this. Karla knew that there was a reason to lie. Whatever was going on here, she knew about it. Whatever had happened to Nikki, she was a part of it. And that realization sent a shiver of fear through Alicia.

"I swear I'm telling you the truth," she told Karla.

Karla hesitated a moment. Finally she let go of Alicia's leg and extended her hand to help Alicia up. Alicia let out a silent sigh of relief. Karla believed her. She was lucky to get through this without anything broken.

Alicia grasped Karla's hand. Karla pulled her up onto her feet with ease. But before Alicia could get her balance, Karla twisted her arm and wrenched it behind her, then spun her around and hooked her arm around Alicia's neck.

Karla pressed her lips to Alicia's ear and hissed, "I don't believe a fucking word you've said, ya?"

Karla's arm pressed so hard into Alicia's throat, she could barely speak. "I'm telling you the truth. I swear."

Karla jerked up on Alicia's arm, sending a spike of pain through her shoulder. At the same time, she flexed her arm tighter around Alicia's throat, so Alicia couldn't make a sound. Alicia realized in horror that she was completely at this woman's mercy.

"Do you know what I could do to you right now?" Karla whispered in Alicia's ear. She let out a hot sigh on the back of Alicia's neck, a strange moaning breath that sent a shiver of fear through Alicia. "Anything I want," she said. "You know that?"

Alicia didn't answer, but she did know it. They were alone here. Alicia couldn't even scream for help. She didn't stand a chance of breaking the hold Karla had her in. Yes, Karla could do whatever she wanted, and that terrified Alicia.

"So, you'll tell me the truth this time, ya?" Karla said. "Or do I start breaking this pretty little body of yours, piece by piece?"

The truth was not going to pacify Karla; it would only make things worse. Alicia would be better off sticking with the same story. Maybe if she was consistent in the face of this threat, Karla would be convinced.

"I am telling you the truth," Alicia said. "I swear."

Karla stood behind her. Her silence unnerved Alicia. What was Karla thinking? Her face was pressed against Alicia's neck, her hot breath on Alicia's cheek. Alicia could not even guess what was going through Karla's head.

Finally Karla whispered in Alicia's ear, "Convince me."

Much of the intimidation and threat were gone from her voice. Instead she spoke in a lewd hiss that made Alicia's skin crawl. It was obvious what Karla was suggesting.

"We can make an . . . arrangement." Karla whispered.

Alicia remained silent. She didn't know what to say that wouldn't inflame Karla.

"Have you ever tasted a woman?" Karla asked.

Alicia shook her head no. She needed to find a way to get free. But how?

"You don't know what you're missing," Karla said.

Alicia knew exactly where this was going, and she was not going there. But maybe there was a way to use this to her advantage.

"Do you like my body?" Karla whispered, and this time,

along with her hot breath, she dipped her tongue into Alicia's ear.

Alicia squirmed inside. But she couldn't let her repulsion show if she was to have any chance of getting away. She had to go along.

She nodded that she liked Karla's body.

"You want to see me naked, ya?"

Alicia nodded again. She was sure this would work. Karla would invite her back to her bungalow. When Karla let go, Alicia would run like hell. Karla could definitely outrun her, but if she could just get out into the open, close to the other bungalows where people could see and hear, Karla would have to leave her alone.

"I know you do," Karla said. She still had Alicia locked up against her, one arm around Alicia's throat, her other hand ready to snap Alicia's wrist. "I saw it in your eyes when we first met," she hissed. "You couldn't keep your eyes off of me."

"You're so right." Alicia couldn't believe these words were coming out of her mouth. She closed her eyes and said, "Let's go back to my bungalow."

Karla tightened her hold, pulling Alicia harder against her. "I have a better idea," she whispered.

Before Alicia realized what was happening, Karla pulled her into the palmettos and threw her onto the sand, coming down on top of her. She pinned Alicia's hands on the ground. She wasn't even trying to be gentle. Before Alicia could say a word, Karla pressed her mouth over Alicia's. The instant Alicia felt Karla's tongue in her mouth, her instincts took over. She squirmed and jerked her head from side to side. "Wait!"

Karla glared down at her, anger flashing in her eyes. She went from passion to the edge of violence in a split second. That sudden change frightened Alicia. This woman was not at all stable; she was even more dangerous than Alicia had realized. She had to think quickly.

"You promised I could see you naked," Alicia said.

Karla's rage quickly faded. Her steel gray eyes filled with lust again. "You want that, ya?"

Alicia had to take advantage of this moment, before Karla snapped back into that violent woman. Karla clearly liked things rough. So Alicia would give her what she wanted. She bobbed her head up quickly and bit Karla's lip. Karla snapped her head away. Blood trickled down her chin. Confusion flashed on her face, and her hold on Alicia's hands tightened. For an instant Alicia feared Karla was going to strike at her. But then Karla seemed to realize that the bite was playful, prurient. Her confusion vanished. Her defenses disappeared. But so did her restraint. She suddenly gave in to her hunger.

She pulled Alicia's hands together above her head so she could hold them with just one hand. With her other hand, she tugged off her own shirt and sports bra. Her washboard abs were dripping with sweat. Above them were small breasts that gave her muscular frame a touch of femininity. A bead of sweat dripped off one nipple and fell onto Alicia's lip. She knew what she had to do. It took all her willpower to open her mouth and lick away the salty drop.

"You like that, ya?" Karla said. "It's going to get better." She started kissing Alicia's neck, her heavy body pinning Alicia to the ground. Alicia began to fear she had made a big mistake. She might not get out of this after all.

Karla kissed her on the mouth again, and Alicia tasted blood from Karla's cut lip. She felt Karla's hot tongue. She twisted her head to the side, momentarily escaping. But Karla let go of Alicia's hands and grabbed her by the hair, holding her head still so she could get what she wanted. She slid her other hand down Alicia's waist and began to undo her pants.

Alicia grabbed Karla's hand. "No, wait."

Karla lifted her head and grinned at Alicia, her left hand gripping Alicia's fly. "Too late to turn back now," she said.

Alicia had to think quickly. "I don't want to turn back," she said.

"Good." Karla ripped open Alicia's fly, shoved her hand under her panties, and entered her roughly with two fingers. Pain rippled through Alicia's body.

"Wait!" she said. She clutched Karla's forearm and tried

to pull Karla's hand away but Karla was too strong. She just grinned again, her fingers churning.

"No!" Alicia shouted.

Anger ignited in Karla's eyes so suddenly and intensely that Alicia shuddered with fear. Those strong fingers could do unthinkable damage. Alicia needed to calm her, quickly.

"Let me do you first," she said.

Karla hesitated a moment, her fingers still deep inside Alicia, the look of rage still burning in her eyes. Finally the intensity of her glare softened. "Ya?" She scraped her fingers over Alicia's clitoris as she slowly took them out. Equally slowly, her eyes on Alicia, she licked each finger clean. Alicia shuddered.

"Show me what you can do," Karla said. She slid off and rolled over onto her back. But she didn't give Alicia a chance to get away. She pulled Alicia on top of her and held her tightly. Alicia couldn't stand to be this close to Karla's face, so she slid down until she was lying over Karla's legs. With one hand, Karla reached down and grabbed her by the hair. Her other hand pulled at her own shorts. She tried to press Alicia's face into her crotch but Alicia resisted. She pried Karla's hands loose and pushed them hard against the sand.

"I'm in control here," Alicia said.

Karla laughed. "Go for it. I like it strong."

"I'll bet you do."

Alicia took hold of Karla's shorts. Karla's hips and waist were extremely narrow, her spandex shorts tight. Perfect. Alicia gave them a quick tug downward. She lost hold of the wet shorts as they hung up on Karla's quadriceps. Karla wasn't wearing panties. Her pubic hair was shaved completely. She had no tan line at all. Alicia hoped to God this worked. She didn't want to think what would happen if it didn't.

She pulled Karla's shorts down over her knees, then over her huge calf muscles. She left them there, binding Karla's legs together at the ankles. She crawled on her hands and knees back up Karla's legs. Karla started to kick her feet now, trying to get the shorts off and free her ankles.

"Don't do that," Alicia said. She braced her own legs against Karla's to stop her. Then, without letting Karla see, she scooped up a fistful of sand.

"I want to wrap my legs around your head," Karla said, "so I can—"

Alicia flung the sand at Karla's face. Karla bellowed in rage, and her hands went quickly to her eyes. Alicia sprung up and ran. Glancing back, she saw Karla struggle to get up, then trip on her shorts, and flop down into the sand.

Alicia ran around the medical building and down the path that led to the bungalows. She glanced back to see if Karla was following. Not yet. But she knew Karla would come. As she turned and continued around a curve in the path, she ran straight into Paul Tobin coming the other way.

32

PAUL'S REACTIONS WERE slowed by the scotch. He didn't move aside in time to avoid a collision. He did brace himself, though, and she took the brunt of the hit. She started to fall but he grabbed her.

"Are you okay?" he asked, holding her by the shoulders. He recognized Alicia Fernandes from the consultation yesterday.

She was filthy, panting, and looked terrified. She pulled away from him. "I have to go."

He noticed the red smudge on her chin. "You're bleeding," he said. "Let me take a look at that."

"I'm okay." She wiped the blood away. "I have to go."

"Wait." He grabbed her arm. "What's going on?"

"Let go of me!" She yanked her arm free.

"I'm not going to hurt—" he started to say but then Karla came running down the path, nearly running into him. He had to reach out and push her away. She wore black spandex shorts but no shirt, so his hands met her bare breasts. Her skin was covered with sweat and sand. Blood was smeared on her mouth and chin.

She glared at Paul. "What are you doing here?" It didn't seem to occur to her she was the one who should answer that question. She was topless, bleeding, and chasing one of the clinic's patients.

Paul glanced at Alicia, who was glaring back at Karla, looking both frightened and defiant. What had Karla done to her?

He turned back to Karla. "What are *you* doing here?" he said.

"I caught her trying to break into Ethan's office."

"I wasn't trying to break in!" Alicia said.

"You were climbing through the window." Karla glared at Paul. "God knows what she was going to do in there."

"I told you, I left my wallet in the waiting room and I needed to get it out."

"That's a lie! You wouldn't have attacked me if that's all it was."

"I didn't attack you!"

"Then why am I bleeding?"

Paul turned to Alicia. Karla had a point. The blood that had been on Alicia's face had obviously come from Karla. The cut on her lip was fresh. Alicia didn't have any wounds on her.

"She attacked me," Alicia told him. "I was defending myself."

"Don't waste your breath," Karla said. She started toward Alicia.

"Just hold on," Paul said, stepping in between them. "What do you think you're doing?" He didn't know what had happened a few moments ago, but it was over now. There wasn't going to be any more violence while he was here.

"I told you, she tried to break into Ethan's office," Karla said. "I'm taking her to see him. He'll probably want her arrested."

"You're not taking her anywhere." Paul trusted Karla about as far as he could throw her. Take Alicia to see Ethan? Fat chance that was going to happen. Karla would more than likely take her back into the darkness and finish what she'd started. Whatever that was.

Karla glared at him. "Don't interfere with me," she said in a threatening tone.

Paul had never hit a woman and didn't intend to start now, but Karla definitely looked ready for a fight. He wasn't sure what he'd do if she did attack him.

"For your information," he said, "I told Miss Fernandes

to meet me outside Ethan's office. I told her I'd let her in to get her wallet." He turned back to Alicia. "Why didn't you wait for me like I told you to?" he said, hoping she would play along.

Alicia hesitated a moment, looking confused. But then she seemed to realize what he was doing. "I didn't think you were going to show up," she said.

"I'm not *that* late." He looked at his watch then faked surprise. "Wow, I am that late." He turned back to Karla. "I told her to meet me there. She wasn't trying to rob the place."

"Do you really expect me to believe that crap?" Karla said.

"Frankly, it doesn't matter to me what you believe," he said.

This angered her even more. She looked seconds away from throwing a punch. Paul didn't flinch. But it did cross his mind how hard she could probably hit.

"She never said she was supposed to meet you," Karla said. She peered at Alicia. "You're changing your story."

"You didn't give me a chance to explain," Alicia said.

"*That* I can believe," Paul said. Before tonight, he would have tried to placate Karla because of her threat to tell Beth what had happened between them on the island. But now it didn't matter anymore. She couldn't hurt him that way. He'd already lost Beth.

"You want me to believe that you two were supposed to meet at this time of night?" Karla said. "You think I'm stupid?"

"Let's just say that you can be a bit single-minded at times," Paul said.

Karla's face reddened with rage. She clenched her fists. Her biceps bulged. "I'm going to tell Ethan all about this," she said.

"Good, tell him. Tell him you've been attacking our patients in the middle of the night. I think he'd like to know about that. And I'd suggest you put on a shirt before you go wake him up. He might not appreciate you parading around like that in front of his son."

Karla glowered at Paul a long moment, steaming mad, then she stepped past him and moved toward Alicia. He thought Karla was going to hit her, and was about to step between them again. But instead of striking at Alicia, Karla leaned close to her and hissed, "You think you've gotten away with something, ya?"

She glared at Alicia. Alicia looked nervous, but she stood firm, staring back. She had guts. Paul was impressed.

"This isn't over," Karla said, and she bumped Alicia hard as she walked away.

After Karla was gone, Alicia let out a long breath of relief. She could still taste Karla's blood, and her body hurt from being thrown on the ground. But it could have been much worse.

"Thanks for sticking up for me," she told Paul.

"Are you okay?" he asked.

She nodded. A bit shaken up, but physically Karla hadn't hurt her. She considered herself lucky. Given the opportunity, Karla could have done some serious damage. Alicia had never seen a woman with so much strength and ferocity, and so little restraint.

She was grateful that Paul Tobin had been here. No one other than Nikki had ever come to her aid before.

"Are you going to get into any kind of trouble with Dr. Granier for defending me?" she asked.

He shrugged. "Depends. Do you want to tell me what that was all about? What really happened back there?"

"You mean did I attack her or did she attack me?"

"I have a pretty good idea who attacked whom. My question is, why were you trying to break into the building?"

Alicia didn't know what to say.

"How about an easier question," Paul said. "Why are you even here?"

She laughed a nervous laugh. "What do you mean, why am I here?"

"Look, it doesn't take a genius to see that you don't belong at a clinic like this. You don't need antiaging therapies. You're not that old and you're not that vain. Ethan and

Karla see dollar signs when they see you, so they don't question your being here. But I see someone who doesn't belong. So I ask again, why are you here? I suspect the reason has something to do with why you were trying to break into Ethan's office tonight. Am I right?"

She wondered if she could trust him. He had lied to Karla for her, put his job on the line for her. She had gotten a sense before, when he examined her for surgery, that he was an honest man, that he might be able to confide in him. His actions tonight reinforced that notion.

She wasn't learning much the way she was going. Having someone with inside knowledge and access to the private aspects of the clinic might be a big help in finding out what happened to Nicole.

"Can we go somewhere and talk in private?" she said.

They went to Paul's office. Here, inside the confines of the small room, she smelled alcohol on him. He didn't seem intoxicated, but he had definitely been drinking. That made her a little uneasy, considering that he was a surgeon. But then she realized that she was being unrealistic. He was allowed to have a few drinks in the evening. It wasn't like he was an alcoholic. . . .

As she sat alone with him, explaining about Nicole, she realized that she felt a physical attraction for him. He was several years older, but he was still a handsome man. Maybe his age gave her a feeling of safety. Or maybe it was because he had come to her aid tonight. Whatever it was, she definitely felt something for him, and that made her uneasy.

She'd never let anyone but Nikki close enough to affect her feelings. Letting someone in, letting herself *feel* put her in danger. That wasn't the way she wanted to live, afraid of connecting with people. But it hurt less than the devastation of loss.

Did she dare risk that?

Funny how easy it was to take risks on a professional level, even to put her life in danger, but how difficult it was to risk her heart.

She reminded herself that this trip wasn't about her. It was about finding out why Nikki killed herself, so she concentrated on that.

She told Paul about her conversation with Doug Collins, and how he'd said that there was a secret therapy some patients were taking. Whatever it was, she believed it was responsible for her sister's suicide.

"Do you have any evidence to support what you're saying?" he asked. "Anything at all?"

"I know my sister, and I know she wouldn't kill herself. Something made her do that, and whatever it is, it's here. So to answer your question," she said, "no, I don't have any evidence. Not yet. But I know it's here and I'm going to find it."

"And you think the evidence you're looking for is in Ethan's office?"

"It has to be. If I could only get a look at Nikki's records, I know I could find out what Granier did to her."

"You know that's a serious accusation," he said.

"I know."

"If you're wrong—"

"I'm not," she said. "I can prove I'm not, if you'll help me."

Paul wasn't sure why he believed her. He was still feeling the effects of the booze, but he hadn't had *that* much to drink, just enough to get a buzz. But had he lost all sense of judgment? Or was he just reacting to what had happened earlier with Beth? Here was a young, attractive woman who needed him. If he could help her, it'd make him feel that he was valuable, maybe even that he was desirable. Was that so bad?

Tonight, he was numb inside—he'd made himself that way. Pain pushed him to shut down his emotions. Drinking was the way he did that. But he realized he shouldn't have started back down that road. He needed to turn around before it was too late. Was he helping her in order to keep his mind off the bottle?

Or was he acting out of fear? Was he worried that if

something went wrong at the clinic, he would be the one blamed, just like three years ago in New York?

Maybe it was all of the above. Or maybe none of the above. Whatever the reason, he decided to see if there was anything to what Alicia Fernandes was saying. If something was going on, if something had caused one of De Leon's patients to kill herself, he owed it to her, to the rest of the patients, and to himself to find out what it was.

He took Alicia back to the medical building. The night air was hot and smelled of the sea breeze, damp, salty, thalassic. Most of the lights around the clinic were off. The only sounds were the rustle of palms in the wind and the yawning of the ocean as waves lapped the shore. Paul peered into the darkness surrounding them, thinking that Karla might still be out there somewhere, watching. He'd never seen her as angry and feral as she'd been tonight. She'd always had a latent sense of threat about her, but tonight it had been right out there in the open, and he was certain that she was not going to let this go. She was his enemy now.

But the night was quiet for the moment, so he unlocked the door and led Alicia inside, to the records room.

Alicia's sister's name was Nicole Quinn. Paul looked through the *Q*s for her chart, but it wasn't there.

"Could she have used another name when she came here?" he asked Alicia.

"No. That's the name Dr. Granier asked for when he called her house a few weeks ago. And when I called originally, before I talked to Dr. Granier, the woman who answered the phone seemed to know the name Nicole Quinn. I'm sure that's the name she used."

"Well, there's no chart here for her," Paul said.

"There has to be."

Alicia began riffling through the files. Paul just watched, wondering if she was telling the truth about her sister. If her sister had been a patient, there'd be a chart. Could she be making all this up? What if Nicole Quinn didn't even exist? He really didn't know much about Alicia Fernandes. What if she was crazy?

Alicia abandoned her search and turned back to him, looking troubled. "Dr. Granier must have taken her chart and destroyed it," she said. "He's definitely hiding something."

Paul was beginning to have serious doubts. He stared at her, trying to assess her mental state. She looked troubled and angry and on the verge of exploding. But crazy? How could you tell?

His face must have given away what he was thinking, because Alicia said, "You don't believe me, do you?"

"It's not a matter of believing you or not. It's just that—"

"You don't believe me!" she said, her anger boiling to the surface. "I should have known you'd side with Granier. You doctors always stick together."

"I'm not siding with anyone. I'm just trying to understand what this is all about."

"I'll tell you what it's all about. My sister was a patient here—I know she was. Whether there's a file or not, she was a patient here. And something they gave her, some secret drug or hormone or whatever, caused her to kill herself. They're obviously trying to hide it."

"You said someone told you about a secret therapy?" he asked.

"That guy who does the weather on TV. Doug Collins. Do you know him?"

Paul did. He decided to check Collins's chart. That might help clear this up. He looked through the files but couldn't find it. That was strange. He wasn't sure about Alicia's "sister," if she really existed, but he knew that Collins existed. His chart should be here. So why wasn't it?

33

FOR THE FIRST time, Alicia didn't feel so alone in this.

Paul Tobin had agreed to help her. He had access to things she didn't. And the missing Collins chart was real evidence that she was no lunatic.

The answer wasn't in the records room, so they left. As they walked across the dark grounds of the clinic toward the bungalows, Alicia watched the shadows for signs of Karla Weiss. Alicia had outsmarted her, made her look bad. Karla did not seem like the type of person who took that well. She'd do something to get back at Alicia. And next time, she wouldn't give Alicia a chance to trick her.

Alicia unlocked the door to her bungalow. It was dark inside. A shiver of fear went down her back. Paul reached inside and flipped the light switch, and the clean bright light inside washed away her sense of immediate danger. She went in. Paul followed, locking the door behind them.

He must have understood what she was thinking because he said, "Karla won't try anything tonight. Not when she doesn't have the numbers on her side. Two against one, she won't do anything."

Two against one.

He was telling her he was staying.

She couldn't sleep. She got out of bed and walked over to the sofa where Paul was lying, staring up at the ceiling.

"You can't sleep either?" she said.

He shook his head. In the glow of moonlight coming

through the window, she saw that his face was damp with sweat. He looked a little pale, too, like he wasn't feeling well.

"Are you okay?" she asked.

"Yeah, I'm fine. I've got a lot on my mind."

Earlier, he'd promised that tomorrow he'd look into Nikki's visits here, see what he could find out from Dr. Granier. She wondered if he was worried about that, about what he might learn. Dr. Granier was his friend. Was he having second thoughts about helping her?

Paul sat up to make room for her on the sofa. She sat beside him.

"I never did ask you . . ." she said. "What were you doing outside before, when Karla was chasing me? It was kind of late to be taking a walk."

"I was in Palm Beach earlier," he said. "I'd just come back."

"What's in Palm Beach?" she asked.

He thought for a moment, then said, "Nothing, really." He sounded bitter. Obviously there was something there. And obviously he didn't want to talk about it. She didn't press him. He'd done so much for her and she was grateful.

"By the way," she said, "I really want to thank you for helping me. And for staying tonight. I feel safer with you here."

"Well, I doubt Karla would have tried anything."

"I don't know. She was pretty angry at me."

"Yeah, I noticed. What did you do to her, anyway? She was the one with the bloody lip. I wouldn't have expected that. Not to underestimate you or anything, but she's pretty tough. What kind of work do you do? Are you a marine or something?"

Alicia chuckled. "Not quite." She stuck with the profession she'd put on the questionnaire she'd filled out when she arrived. "I'm a teacher."

"What do you teach, karate?"

She laughed. "Let's just say, being tough isn't everything. Intelligence matters, too. And I think on that level, I've got her beat."

"I guess so. So what did happen?"

Alicia didn't want to explain it. She didn't even want to think about it. The things she'd done humiliated her. Intellectually she knew she hadn't done anything wrong. She'd practically been raped by Karla—she'd done what she had to, and she'd escaped. But emotionally she still felt deep shame. She should have resisted more. She should have fought back in a different way, used something besides sexuality.

"Who do you think is behind the missing files?" she asked, ignoring his question.

"It could be Karla."

That had been Alicia's first thought, but she had difficulty accepting that Karla was giving patients some kind of secret drug. She couldn't imagine Nikki accepting any kind of medication from her.

"Do you think she's the one giving patients a secret therapy?" she asked Paul.

He remained silent for a moment, considering this. He looked doubtful. "If there is something like that, I think it'd be beyond her ability."

Alicia thought so, too. "So you think it's Dr. Granier?"

Paul shrugged. "I don't want to speculate. I'll talk to him tomorrow. If he's doing anything like that, I'll find out."

Alicia understood his reluctance to blame his friend, even though it was obvious that it had to be him. He and Paul were the only doctors here. And Granier had lied about Nikki being a patient. Whatever was going on, Granier had to be the one behind it.

"You've known him a long time?" Alicia asked.

Paul nodded. "We should probably try to get some sleep," he said. He didn't want to talk about that, just like he didn't want to talk about Palm Beach, and she didn't want to talk about Karla. They sat together in silence.

She didn't want to go back to bed; she knew she'd just lie awake, thinking. So instead, she leaned her head on his shoulder.

He chuckled. "Don't like the bed?"

"There's a draft over there," she said. They both

laughed. It must have been ninety degrees and as humid as hell in here. But he didn't seem to mind. He put an arm around her and shared the couch. The truth was, she felt safer being close to him.

She snuggled against his chest and wrapped her arms around him. It felt so good to hold a man. It helped weaken the shame of what she'd done with Karla. Being with him helped her feel less . . . a bad person. She could make a man happy.

With her face resting on his chest, she breathed in the scent of his body. She drew herself closer to him, needing to wipe the memory of Karla away, to create a new memory. He must have sensed that she needed to be held because he wrapped both arms around her. She felt his strength and the warm comfort of his sigh on her neck. She ran her hand along his shirt, feeling his chest. The sense of his strength around her sent a shiver through her body. She could relax with him here. She was safe.

"Thank you so much," she whispered.

He hushed her and whispered, "You don't have to thank me."

He caressed her hair with the slow gentle strokes of someone who enjoyed touching her. She let her hand sink lower. She traced a line from the bottom of his abs, over his belt, down to his thigh. She saw that he was hard under his pants. He couldn't hide the way he felt. His body told her what she wanted to know, what she needed in order to feel safe and loved and connected to someone who cared, who felt the same thing for her.

She lifted her head. He was gazing down at her. She peered into his eyes. She wanted to say what she was feeling, but not a word came out. She snuggled closer and kissed him on the mouth. His breath had the slight harshness of alcohol. His tongue was dry. But that wasn't alcohol moving his hand down her back. That wasn't alcohol pushing his lips against hers, his tongue against hers. He felt something for her. The way a man feels for a woman. Alcohol didn't feel this way; desire did.

She turned and wrapped her hands around his neck. His

hands gripped her buttocks and pulled her against him with such force that she knew he wanted her. And she needed to be wanted. And she wanted him. She unbuttoned his shirt and kissed his chest. He let out a long breath, one that sounded like it had been locked up inside him for a long time. She knew exactly how that felt.

She continued kissing him, working her way down his abdomen. Then she slowly undid his belt, hesitating, making him wait, before she finally unzipped his pants. As she slid down and wrapped her lips around him, he grabbed her hair and moaned. She took it slowly and went easy at first, stopping when it seemed like he wanted it the most, teasing him with little flickers of her tongue, then going down on him again, full strength, and hearing him groan with pleasure. The power she had over him drove her crazy.

Suddenly he pulled her up, scooped her off the couch, and carried her to the bed. He laid her out on the mattress and pulled down the shorts she'd worn to bed. He did it with the sureness of a man who knew what he wanted and knew what he was doing. His confidence was enough to put her at ease. She could let go with him, something she longed to do.

He was just as good at teasing her as she was at teasing him, and just as good with his tongue. She closed her eyes and let the sensations rush through her. Her whole body tingled. Then he added a finger, stimulating her deep inside along with the motion of his tongue circling her clitoris. He made her come once, a small orgasm that foretold what was yet to come. Then again, slightly more intense. He took his time with her, giving her one more orgasm with his tongue. Then, with the passion of a man who had lost all inhibition, he ripped off her shirt and slid between her legs.

The sudden rush of feeling frightened her. For so long she had not allowed herself to feel deeply. Now she was feeling with every nerve ending in her body and every fiber of her soul. She was making herself vulnerable. She began to think that she should stop this, now. That she might not be able to handle what was coming. That it was a mistake.

But the way he wanted her, the intensity of his feelings for her, the memory of how he had come to her rescue, all weakened her defenses. And she needed this. After the incident with Karla, after a lifetime of holding back, she needed to let go. She needed someone to let her let go. She chose Paul Tobin. She only hoped she wasn't making a mistake.

34

BEFORE GOING TO wake up Ethan, Karla wanted to know who they were dealing with. She'd warned him about Fernandes yesterday and he hadn't done a thing about her. This time she would go to him with proof that she was trouble. He would have to do something now. Or she would take care of it herself.

She went to her bungalow and showered, scrubbing all the sand off her body. Then she checked her lip in the mirror. It had stopped bleeding, but there was still a cut where that bitch had bitten her. Fernandes would pay.

Karla put on clean shorts and turned on her computer. She logged onto the internet. The home page of her service provider was flashing WEATHER ALERT.

Tropical storm Celine, located one hundred miles east of the Leeward Islands, has just been upgraded to a hurricane. If it continues on its current path and at its current speed, it will come ashore in South Florida on Sunday.

The National Hurricane Service meteorologists believe Celine has a 75% chance of turning north before reaching Florida. Still, they have issued an "advisory" for South Florida, Puerto Rico, and the U.S. Virgin Islands.

Click here for more information . . .

Karla ignored the alert. Storms were always forming in the Atlantic this time of year. Most either turned away and went elsewhere or fizzled out before they reached here. Even if this one didn't turn north, it was still three days away. There was plenty of time to worry about it later.

Her home page also provided links to several competitive swimming sites where she could check out her competition for the 2004 Olympics. She usually monitored results from all the major events around the world each day, comparing the times and distances of the winners with her own numbers, making sure she was on course to winning gold in Athens. But tonight she ignored them. She typed in the web address for the search engine Google. She had something far more urgent on her mind.

Alicia Fernandes wasn't just another patient. That much was clear. First asking about the dead model from Los Angeles. Then trying to break into Ethan's office. Karla needed to know just who the hell Fernandes really was and what she was doing here.

Once in Google, she clicked on "Advanced Search" and typed in *Alicia Fernandes*. She narrowed the search parameters to include only the past three months. The results came right away. There were nine matches. She scrolled through them, looking for one that might be *this* Alicia Fernandes.

One link was to the California attorney general's office. Karla clicked it. It connected her to a website that listed all of the state's licensed private investigators. She scrolled down to the *F*s and found Fernandes's name.

So she's a private investigator?

There was no photo to confirm that it was *this* Alicia Fernandes, but Karla had a strong feeling it was her. She wanted more information. She went back to the search results and looked at the other matches. There was a link to an article in the *Los Angeles Times*. She clicked it.

PI CATCHES HOLLYWOOD SLASHER

She skimmed through the text. A private investigator named Alicia Fernandes tracked and captured a man who had been drugging, raping, and murdering women in the Hollywood Hills. The LAPD had been unable to make progress in the case after twenty-three months. Fernandes was on the case for one night. The newspaper seemed to take pleasure in humiliating the cops. Karla wondered what they were leaving out.

Click here for accompanying photo.

Karla clicked it. A moment later, the photo appeared. And there she was. Talking to the police at the scene of the crime. It was definitely *this* Alicia Fernandes.

"Damn it!" Karla said out loud. *I knew she was trouble. Ethan should have taken care of this yesterday. God only knows how much Fernandes had learned since then, especially with Tobin helping her.*

She wasn't the model's sister after all. She was a private investigator. Karla wanted to know who she was working for. She was obviously looking for information on Rejuvenol. But who had sent her? And what did they want to do with the information? Whatever it was, Fernandes was a serious threat. She could interfere with what Ethan was doing, which would interfere with what Karla needed and jeopardize her chances of winning gold in Athens.

She would do whatever it took to keep Fernandes from doing that.

Whatever it took.

35

ETHAN AWAKENED WITH a start, snapping upright in his chair. He had fallen asleep at the desk in his lab, entering the data from Kenny's blood work into the computer. Something had awakened him. Some noise. He looked across the room and saw Karla standing at a lab table, examining the empty infusion bag he'd used for Kenny. She put that down and picked up the notes he'd left there.

"Do his parents know?" she asked.

"What are you doing here?" Ethan said. He hated the idea of her going wherever she wanted, whenever she wanted. Especially here, his home. "How did you get in here?" he asked, angry.

"The security around this place is terrible."

He looked at his watch. It was a quarter after three in the morning. He wasn't going to put up with her at this hour. He'd been up late working on Kenny's blood tests. Whatever she wanted could wait.

"Do you have any idea what time it is?" he said. He turned off his computer and started toward the stairs. He was just going to leave. She'd get the message for sure.

As he walked past her, she pushed a sheet of paper at him.

"What's that?" he asked.

"Read it. It's an article from the *Los Angeles Times*."

"I'm too tired to play games. What is this?"

"Just read it," she said.

He blew out a breath of exasperation. She wasn't going

to leave until he humored her. He skimmed the headline. Some private investigator caught a serial killer. "Yeah, so?" he said. "What's the point?"

"Do you see the name of the private investigator?" she said, jabbing her finger at the article.

"What name?"

Ethan skimmed the article. When he saw what Karla was talking about he was suddenly horrified. "Is that the same Alicia Fernandes who's here?" he asked.

Karla stuck another sheet of paper in front of him, a photograph from her printer. It wasn't a very good image but Ethan could tell that it was definitely the Alicia Fernandes he'd examined today.

"I told you she was trouble," Karla said. "You should have taken care of this yesterday."

"Just slow down," Ethan said, more to calm himself than to calm Karla. He didn't like the idea of a private investigator coming here, but just because that was her profession didn't necessarily mean she had ulterior motives. She could be interested in antiaging therapies, just like everyone else.

Then Karla shattered his illusion. "I caught her trying to break into your office a little while ago," she said.

Oh, my God. Ethan couldn't believe what he was hearing. "Did she take anything?" he asked.

"No, I stopped her before she could get in."

"Thank God."

Ethan quickly went through the possibilities of who she was, why she was here. His first thought was that another researcher or a pharmaceuticals company had hired her. Somehow they found out that he was on the verge of a major breakthrough and they were using her to steal his research. *Just as he'd used Karla to do for him.* The second possibility was that Fernandes had been hired by the dead model's family. She did, after all, ask about Nicole Quinn. The third possibility worried him the most. What if she was working for a law enforcement agency that wanted to know what was going on here?

"There's more," Karla said.

Another shiver of fear ran down Ethan's back. Could it possibly get worse? "What do you mean?"

"Paul Tobin is helping her," she said.

"What are you talking about?" Ethan couldn't believe that. He'd brought Paul down himself; Paul hadn't come here to steal anything. He hadn't even known what was going on.

"When I caught her trying to get into your office," Karla said, "Tobin just *happened* to show up." She made it clear by her tone that she didn't think it was a coincidence at all. "I had her and I would have gotten her to talk, but then Tobin lied to protect her. I'm sure he's working with her."

"I can't believe that," Ethan said. "I gave him a job, got his license reinstated." There had to be an explanation. Paul wouldn't do anything to hurt him, not after all he'd done for Paul.

"Don't be so naïve, Ethan. He's out for himself, that's all. She offers him more than you; he'll sell you out like nothing. He's probably screwing her, too. And that's not something you can offer, ya?"

Ethan didn't know what to believe. He still found it difficult to accept that Paul would betray him, after he'd given Paul a new start, a new life. But the part about Alicia Fernandes was right in front of his eyes. He couldn't deny it. She was a problem.

"Oh," Karla said, remembering something else. Ethan knew it wouldn't be good. "Tobin's drinking again," she said.

Ethan was stunned and horrified. If this were true and Paul operated on someone while he was drinking, and something happened, so much attention and scrutiny would come to the clinic that Ethan would be forced to halt his research.

"Are you sure about the drinking?" he asked Karla.

"I smelled it on him tonight."

"You're positive?"

"I know what alcohol smells like. He was drunk."

Ethan buried his face in his hands. He didn't need this. Any of this. He had enough to worry about with Zack. He was going to have to look into this himself—the drinking, Paul's loyalty, his connection if any to Alicia Fernandes, all of it.

But as far as Alicia Fernandes was concerned, the evidence was clear. She was looking for information. It didn't matter so much why. What mattered was that she not be allowed to jeopardize his efforts to save Zack's life.

"Maybe I can talk to her," he said, thinking out loud. If he told her about Zack, he might be able to appeal to her sense of sympathy and decency, convince her to drop her investigation and keep quiet about everything.

"You can't really believe that'll work," Karla said. "Do you think she gives a damn about your personal problems?"

Ethan knew Karla was more concerned with her own issues, her dream of Olympic glory and the role Rejuvenol played in that. She wasn't worried about Zack's health in the least. But whatever her motives, she was probably right about Fernandes. Confiding in her wasn't a very good option. Something else would have to be done.

As if Karla could read his mind, she leaned close and whispered, "What if she had an accident . . ."

Ethan couldn't believe what he was hearing. *"What?"*

"She and Tobin both. The keys can be a dangerous place. Maybe while they're snorkeling, something happens, maybe they've had too much to drink and they have an accident."

"No." Ethan wasn't even going to listen to the rest.

The last thing Ethan wanted to do was cause anyone harm. Even when he tested Rejuvenol on patients, he was extremely cautious, making certain that the formulation and dosages were safe. After that woman had died in New York three years ago, Ethan had vowed not to repeat his mistake. If anything, he was perhaps overly cautious. That was why perfecting Rejuvenol was taking so long. If he were a bit more reckless, he might have cured Zack by now. That was a conflict he faced daily. But he always erred on the side of caution.

Until last night, that is . . .

"This project is about helping people, not hurting them,"

he told Karla. "I'm not going to do anything to hurt Fernandes or Paul or anyone else."

"Is that why you gave Rejuvenol to Tobin's kid?" she said. "You don't think that'll hurt him?"

"No," he said. But the question made him angry. She had no right to ask that. He wouldn't have given it to Kenny if he thought it would hurt him. She was the one who was thinking only about herself.

"I don't give Rejuvenol to *anyone* if I'm not sure it's safe," he said.

"Then why didn't you tell Tobin?"

He didn't need to defend himself to her. "Look, that has nothing to do with *this*," he said, holding up the article about Fernandes. "This is the problem."

"So what are we going to do about it?"

"I'll take care of it," he said, not sure what he would do but certain that he didn't want to leave it to her.

"That's what you said yesterday and look what happened tonight. You'll do something this time, ya?"

"I said I'll take care of it!"

She leaned in close to him and said, "You better." There was no doubt about her tone. It was a threat. "I sacrificed too much to get to this point. I'm not going to let anyone get in my way." She looked hard into his eyes. *"Anyone,"* she said.

36

PAUL AWAKENED WITH a throbbing headache. His stomach felt like it had been through a paper shredder. His mouth was dry and bristly, like he'd been chewing on asbestos. Horrible. But oddly, it felt . . . right. Like returning home—a dysfunctional home, but home just the same. The place you came from. The place you belonged. Paul had been here so many times before. He knew every inch of the terrain.

The craving . . . There it was, exactly where it should be. It had never really left him. Now here it was, stronger than it had been in years. An old lover. A lover he knew would betray him, but a lover just the same—familiar, desired, irreplaceable.

He knew what was coming. There it was. Hitting him square in the pit of his stomach. *Guilt.* What had he done? More than two years of sobriety, gone. Just like that. *Aw, shit* . . .

He rolled out of bed, leaving Alicia's sleeping form behind. His body was going on instinct now as he walked over to the chair and picked up his suit jacket from last night. The weight of the bottle in the inside pocket told him everything would be all right. He took out the pint of Johnny Walker. It was half full. Enough to take the edge off, get rid of the headache, start a decent buzz going.

He remembered now how the evening had begun, the conversation with Beth. His chances of patching things up with her were lost, forever. His main reason for staying sober, gone.

He twisted off the cap and inhaled deeply. Mr. Walker's breath filled his lungs. Just the scent alone soothed his headache, dulled his feelings of guilt. He stared at the amber medicine, weighing its benefits against its side effects. It had worked for so long . . . *hadn't it?* They'd had some good years together, back when he'd been able to manage it. He was much smarter now. He'd learned a lot. Moderation. Recognizing when it was becoming a problem. Backing off. People managed it every day. Why couldn't he? It had gotten out of control in the past, but that was before he understood it. Now he understood it. So why deny himself the one thing that still gave him pleasure?

He glanced back at the bed, at Alicia's naked body on top of the covers. *Two things gave him pleasure.* He'd felt so alive last night with her. Would he have gone there without Johnny Walker's company? Gazing at her now, remembering what it had been like with her, he thought he probably would have gone for it anyway. But having a buzz on made it that much better. It proved he was normal. He could drink a little, make love, then get up in the morning and be a surgeon.

He walked into the bathroom and closed the door so he wouldn't disturb Alicia. She needed the sleep. She'd had a difficult night. He turned on the light and placed the bottle on the sink. Then he stood in front of it. What damage could half a pint do? He'd had that much last night and he'd been fine. He knew the effects. He knew when to say when. He could still work today. Even the so-called experts were beginning to recognize that people with past drinking problems could still drink in moderation. Half a pint didn't have to become two pints. *Moderation.* It didn't have to be bad. And it did taste so good. . . .

He picked up the bottle. What harm could it do? Maybe not the half pint. Just a taste. *Why not?* He carried the bottle over to the bathtub, sat down on the rim, and set the bottle beside him. He *really* wanted a sip. Just one sip. A sip or two wouldn't make him drunk. A few sips wouldn't mean anything, one way or the other.

He leaned against the wall, crossed his arms, and watched the bottle. What was the worst that could happen? Beth had already dumped him so he didn't have to worry about driving her away. And in moderation, a few drinks weren't going to interfere with his work.

He picked up the bottle and brought it back to the sink. This time he sat on the lid of the toilet seat and stared at the bottle. Things were going well professionally, so he didn't *need* to drink to excess like before. There was no reason he couldn't be like everyone else, go out with friends to a bar and have a drink or two, or enjoy a bottle of wine with dinner. His life wouldn't fall apart.

Anger began to rise inside him. He couldn't sit still. He walked back across the room, this time leaning against the door and peering down at the opened bottle of scotch, his temper simmering.

People were blaming him for things. Accusing him. What the hell did he do? *Nothing. Not a damned thing.* He just wished people would get off his back. Beth. Ethan. The kids. Alicia. He stormed back to the toilet seat and dropped down in front of the bottle. He was doing his best. Look how far he'd come. Look how many obstacles he'd surmounted to rebuild his life, to get back on his feet. Couldn't anyone appreciate how difficult that was? He'd fought his way back, for Beth, for the kids, for a life again. Damn it, look at what he'd done!

He snatched up the bottle. Scotch spilled onto his hand. The smell of the medicine intensified, calling out to his pain. If he was strong enough to put his life back together, he was strong enough to have a few drinks without letting it get out of control. He'd proved that, for God's sake, hadn't he? If Beth and the kids and Ethan and Alicia and everyone else didn't realize that by now, *to hell with them!*

He started to lift the bottle to his lips but his hand was wet with scotch and the bottle slipped. He caught it before it fell, *thank God*. But more scotch spilled, this time on his pants. *Jesus Christ*. He tried to wipe it dry. His hand brushed over a lump in his pocket. He froze. He remembered instantly what it was. The blue needle cap he'd picked up in Kenny's room last night.

It all came back to him now, his fears that Kenny was doing drugs, his guilt over the example he'd set for his sons. He'd fucked up his first chance with them. Now Kenny was paying the price. Would Pete be next?

He peered down at the bottle. Was he going to fuck up any remaining chance he might have with them?

He sprang off of the toilet seat and rushed to the sink, knowing he had to do this quickly, before he changed his mind. He turned the bottle upside down and closed his eyes as the scotch poured down the drain.

He collapsed onto the floor and wept. He could not do that to his boys again.

37

W HEN A LICIA WOKE up, Paul was back in bed with her. He held her for a long while. He said nothing about his predawn struggle. Finally he had to go to work. He told her he'd look into her sister's history here. They'd talk later.

"Do me a favor," he said. "Be careful today. I don't trust Karla."

"I'll be okay. I'm supposed to check out today. I think I'm going to go up to Tampa and talk to Doug Collins."

"Don't do anything until you hear from me, okay?"

She wrapped her arms around him. "I hope to do more than just *hear* from you."

"You can count on it."

Paul went to his office. The first thing he did was call Alcoholics Anonymous. There was a meeting that night in Key West. He made up his mind that he'd go. He should have known better than to stop in the first place. Just because he was working again and seeing his kids didn't mean he was no longer an alcoholic. He'd had a narrow escape, and he knew it.

After he hung up, he headed to Ethan's office. Ethan was at his desk, staring blankly at the computer. He had bags under his bloodshot eyes. He looked exhausted. Rough night with Zack, Paul assumed with sympathy. And he found himself thinking it could have been one of his own sons.

"You look like you could use some coffee," Paul said from the doorway.

Ethan looked up coldly.

So Karla must have given Ethan her version already. Paul decided he might as well be direct, so he came in and shut the door. "Level with me, Ethan," he said. "Is there anything going on here that I don't know about?" He sat down in the chair next to Ethan's desk.

Ethan stared back, still coldly. "Like what?" he said.

"Any therapies that you haven't told me about?"

Ethan folded his arms. His annoyance was turning to anger, but he was holding it back, barely. "Why would you ask that?" he said.

Direct. Truthful. Paul told him about Alicia and her concerns regarding her sister. "Was Nicole Quinn a patient here?" he asked. "Is there a secret therapy?"

Ethan stood up and came around to where Paul was sitting. He leaned on the desk, his face unreadable. Finally he snatched up a couple of sheets of paper from his desk and thrust them at Paul.

"Here's your answer," he said. "Read it."

Paul read the article. He stared at the photograph. He was shocked. Alicia was a liar. She'd tricked him. Not only did he feel humiliated, but he was furious with her.

"Son of a bitch!" he said.

"She was probably hired by another antiaging center," Ethan said. "They want to find out what we're doing and maybe even stir up some trouble for us, eliminate competition. I can't believe you'd fall for that."

Paul couldn't believe it either. He felt like a fool. But she'd seemed so genuine.

Ethan took the papers back and glared down at Paul, still angry. "What do you think she'd do if she found out about your past?" he asked. "What do you think the chances are she'd let it go?"

Paul stared down at the floor, knowing clearly what the answer was. He felt ashamed of himself, not only for letting himself be fooled by her, but for the mistakes that had put him in this vulnerable position.

"We both know that she, or whoever she's working for," Ethan said, "will do whatever they can to blow it way out of proportion. Something like that could really damage the reputation of this place. Maybe damage it so much so that I'd lose the whole practice. Is that what you want?"

"No. Of course not."

"I hope not."

"Ethan, you know me better than that," Paul said, upset that Ethan would think he'd want to hurt him in any way.

Ethan sat on the desk now and stared hard at Paul. "Now let me ask you something," he said. "Were you drinking last night?"

Paul realized that Karla must have smelled the booze on him and told Ethan. He couldn't deny it.

"I had a couple drinks, yes," he said. He explained what had happened with Beth, hoping Ethan would understand. But Ethan's stare wasn't at all empathetic.

"Do you think the alcohol clouded your judgment regarding this Fernandes woman?" Ethan asked.

Paul realized that it must have. That, along with having lost Beth. A young, attractive woman coming on to him while he was intoxicated and feeling lonely. His judgment probably had been impaired. She had played him for a complete fool.

"Listen," Ethan said, "I have a lot at stake with this clinic. I went out on a limb to bring you here. You had no career, no prospects, nothing. Nobody else was going to give you a chance, you know that. Don't forget that. And please, don't make me regret what I did."

Paul nodded silently. He was in Ethan's debt; he never forgot that. What made him uneasy was that Ethan kept reminding him just how much he owed him. He knew he would have to pay Ethan back for everything, and he couldn't help but worry what that payment might be.

38

ETHAN FELT CONFIDENT that he had handled Paul well. Now he had to do something about Fernandes.

He checked her clinic itinerary on the computer and saw that she didn't have any other appointments. She was scheduled to check out today. Still, he worried that she might have found something incriminating. He had always kept the Rejuvenol records in his house. He'd also removed all the regular charts of the Rejuvenol patients from the records room weeks ago, when he'd learned about the model's death in Los Angeles. But what if Fernandes had still found something, somewhere? He needed to make sure she didn't have anything damaging.

He buzzed his assistant. "What time is my first appointment?" he asked.

"Not until eleven, Doctor."

Good. That gave him time to take care of this. "I'm going home to spend some time with my son," he said. That was something he did often, so it wouldn't raise any suspicions.

He stopped by the clinic dining room on the way, hoping Fernandes was at breakfast. That way he'd have a chance to search her bungalow. But she wasn't there. Nor was she by the pool. He hurried to the front lobby and checked to see if she had settled her account. She hadn't. She was still here. Good. He wasn't too late.

He headed back across the pool area toward her bungalow. If she was in there, he wouldn't be able to search her things to see if she'd taken anything incriminating. But maybe he should just confront her. Tell her that he knew who she really was and demand to know what she was doing here. Would she come clean and tell him the truth? Probably not at first. But if he was persistent and refused to accept any lies, he could make her tell the truth. He didn't like being tricked. And he didn't at all like the idea that someone might have come here with the intention of doing something that could harm Zack.

He felt his heart race and blood fill his head as this thought echoed through his brain. There was no way in hell he was going to let her, or anyone else, do anything to hurt Zack.

He knocked on the door of her bungalow. There was no answer. Thinking she was on the beach or somewhere else on the clinic grounds, he took out his master key and unlocked the door. He opened it just a few inches and poked his head in. As he leaned in a little further, he heard the hissing of the shower behind the bathroom door. So she was here after all.

Her suitcase was open on the bed. A few items of clothing were still scattered around. The TV was on, tuned to Fox News, but the sound was muted. On the screen was a weather map and an Asian woman pointing to the hurricane stirring up the Atlantic. A graphic showed two possible paths the hurricane might take. One had it turning up toward the Carolinas. The other had it coming this way.

He came in and closed the door. As long as she was in the shower, she wouldn't hear him search the place. He wanted to make sure she hadn't stolen anything, first. Then he'd confront her.

He went through her suitcase but didn't find anything suspicious in there. He even checked the pockets of her clothes. Then he went through the oversized handbag on the bureau. No patient files. No computer disks. He found her wallet and took a look through it. The first thing that jumped out at him was the photograph of Fernandes with another woman, one he recognized as the model from Los Angeles, Nicole Quinn.

So these two did know each other. Was it possible that they were sisters? Could she have been telling the truth about that? Maybe she hadn't been sent here by a pharmaceutical company or another antiaging clinic or the FDA. Maybe she was just trying to find out if anything bad had happened to her sister here. In one respect, that was good. That meant no large agency was investigating the clinic. But if her reasons were personal, that meant she suspected that something her sister had received here had caused her to commit suicide. That was ridiculous, of course, but it could mean trouble if she started telling authorities.

As long as she didn't have any support for her accusation, no one would take her seriously. He'd prefer she left here satisfied that nothing bad had happened to her sister. He'd prefer she kept her mouth shut. Actually, he'd prefer she disappeared off the face of the earth—but no way that was going to happen. The only thing he could make certain of was that she didn't steal anything to support her suspicions. And it didn't appear that she had.

He put her wallet away and checked the rest of the room. He was almost satisfied, when he saw a note by the phone. On it was written: *Doug Collins. Tonight 7 P.M. 3434 Royal Palm Way. Tampa. 7-E.*

This was bad.

She was going to meet Collins tonight. *Why?* Could she have found out that he was one of the Rejuvenol patients? She didn't just pull his name out of a hat. What did she know? And what would Collins tell her tonight?

Ethan had been very careful in selecting the Rejuvenol patients. He made sure they understood the importance of confidentiality. They were people who desperately needed to look younger, people who had the resources to pay the hefty price he charged, people who would suffer if word got out about what they were doing.

Collins had met the requirements. He wouldn't tell Fernandes anything. *Would he?* What if she took him to bed, the way she probably had Paul? What would Collins tell her then? Fernandes clearly intended to pursue this further with Collins and God knows who else. She was dangerous after all. He had to stop her.

Kill her!

The thought flashed into his head so suddenly, so unexpectedly, that he was stunned. But it was so vivid, so clear, and he could see himself doing it, clubbing her over the head, hitting her repeatedly until he was sure she was dead. The consequences were just as clear: the problem would be gone. Simple as that.

Do it! Kill her! For Zack . . .

It blasted through his head again, not so much a thought or an image this time as a powerful, primal drive. Instinct. Survival. He shifted position so he could see through the door, see her blurred form behind the shower curtain. If he bludgeoned her over the head while she was showering, he could easily make it look like she had slipped, like it was an accident. The threat to Zack would be gone.

Do it! Now! KILL HER!

His hand found the heavy lamp on the table and his fingers closed around the cold metal.

Yes! Do it! This may be the only chance!

He lifted the lamp, feeling its weight in his hands. What she was doing to Zack was the equivalent of hitting him over the head with this. *She* was the violent one. Zack's fragile life must be protected.

Ethan's anger grew as he focused on her wicked form behind the shower curtain. He unplugged the lamp and moved closer to the bathroom door. She had no right to do what she was doing, no right to hurt Zack. She deserved this.

She deserves to die! Kill her before she kills Zachary!

Ethan's heart was pounding. His head throbbed with anger. He felt adrenaline surging through his veins, giving him strength, giving him the will that he needed to do this.

He stepped up to the door and placed his hand on it. It was moist from the steam seeping out of the bathroom. Slowly he began to push it open further.

Suddenly the sound of the spraying water went silent. Fernandes had turned off the shower. Ethan froze, staring at the shower curtain.

Do it! Do it now!

He saw her hand reach out and start to open the curtain.

Hurry! Before it's too late!

She grasped the towel.

Kill her, damn it!

He started to make his move into the bathroom when suddenly there was a knock at the door behind him. He spun around and glared at the door. Then he peered back into the bathroom. He saw Fernandes wrap the towel around herself. Another knock at the door.

Ethan stepped away from the bathroom doorway before she could see him.

"One second!" Fernandes yelled out.

Heavy pounding on the door.

"I said I'm coming!"

Ethan looked back and forth between the front door and the bathroom. Fernandes would be coming out any second. He was running out of time if he was to do this.

Kill her?

As if he'd just awakened from a sleep, he suddenly felt disoriented and confused. Then he felt the cold, heavy lamp in his hand. He looked down at it, finally realizing what he was about to do. He quickly put it back on the table, flinching away as if from a horrible thing. He couldn't believe what he had been seconds away from doing.

More pounding on the door.

"Damn it, I'm coming!" Fernandes yelled from the bathroom.

Ethan spun around, saw the sliding glass back door, and rushed over. He slid it open just as Fernandes came out of the bathroom. She didn't look his way; instead she walked toward the front door, wrapped in the towel. As Ethan ducked out, he glanced back and saw her open the door. Paul Tobin was outside, glaring at her angrily.

Ethan didn't stick around to see what that was all about. He rushed away, still in shock over what he had almost done.

39

ALICIA WAS THRILLED to see Paul. She hoped he'd learned something about Nikki. She also needed to be in his arms again, to be sure that what had happened between them was no mistake.

"Sorry I took so long," she said. "I was in the shower."

He shoved the door open the rest of the way and stormed into the room, nearly knocking her over. She saw how angry he was.

"Paul, what's wrong?" she asked, closing the door and following him in.

He spun around and glared at her. "You're a damn liar!"

She stopped in her tracks, suddenly afraid to come closer. His face showed so much rage that she didn't recognize him. Then it struck her—she really didn't know this man. She'd let herself feel something for him and she had no idea who he was or what he was capable of.

"Did you hear me?" he said, raising his voice.

"Yes. But I don't know what you're talking about."

"I know who you are. I know that you're a private investigator." He spat out the distasteful words.

How did he know that? He must have been checking up on her. What kind of man slept with a woman and then secretly investigated her?

"The clinic never had a patient named Nicole Quinn." He paced the room angrily. "You used me to get whatever the hell it is you're looking for!"

"No, I didn't! And my sister was a patient here!"

"Just who are you working for?"

"I'm not working for anyone. And I do have a sister named Nicole Quinn. And she was—"

"Save it for your next patsy," he said, dismissing her with a wave of his hand. He started toward the door.

She grabbed his arm. "Paul, please, wait!"

His face was cold, but he stopped with his hand on the door. "Why?"

"I want to explain," she said. "Please?"

He leaned back against the door and crossed his arms, sarcastically feigning the gestures of someone willing to listen. "Go ahead. Explain away."

She gestured toward the sofa. "Please, sit down."

"Just talk," he said. He didn't budge. This wasn't going to be easy.

"Okay. It is true that I'm a private investigator," she said. "But I'm not here on a job. I'm not working for anyone. I'm here for myself."

"You're lying. You're about as interested in antiaging therapies as my eight-year-old son is."

"You're right, I didn't come here to get any treatments."

"No shit."

She ignored his growing anger and said, "I came here to find out about my sister."

His sarcasm returned. "Oh yeah, that's right, the imaginary Nicole Quinn."

"Nicole's not imaginary!" It angered her that he was talking about Nikki like that. "She's real. And she's dead now because of something that happened to her here."

Paul rolled his eyes. "Are we back on that fantasy again?"

"It's not a fantasy."

He shook his head in disgust. "Look, I really don't have time for this," he said. "I have *real* patients waiting."

"Paul, you have to believe me."

"Why? Because you've been so honest with me up until now?"

"Call the L.A. medical examiner if you don't believe me."

"I'm not calling anybody. I've wasted enough time on you. I put far more into this than I ever should have."

She could tell that he wasn't just talking about time.

"I understand how you feel," she said, reaching out toward him.

He stuck out his hand to stop her. "Don't bother," he said.

His words and the hostile look on his face stopped her cold.

"I just hope you're happy," he said. "Whatever it is you came here for, I hope it was worth it. Tell me something," he said. "What's the going price these days for integrity?"

His words stung. She bit her lip to keep from crying, unable to speak.

"I thought so," he said. He opened the door and walked away.

40

KARLA HAD SEEN Ethan go into Alicia's room. She waited, curious to find out what he would do. When Paul came around the side of the bungalow, she thought things might get interesting. She hid in the bushes and watched him knock several times. She saw the door open and, at the same moment, saw Ethan slip out through the sliding glass door in the back. He was more wily than she'd thought. He looked frazzled as he scurried across the grounds toward his office.

Karla followed him in a moment later. His assistant told her that Ethan didn't wish to be disturbed. *He already looks disturbed,* Karla thought. But she needed to know what had happened back there, so she told the receptionist he was expecting her and headed toward the door. She'd realized long ago that Ethan's assistant was intimidated by her, and that knowledge came in handy now.

She walked into Ethan's office. He wasn't behind his desk. The bathroom door was open, and she heard the sound of running water. She walked over to the doorway. Ethan was leaning over the sink, splashing water on his face. He looked like he had seen a ghost.

"What happened?" she asked.

Her voice startled him. He jumped up and started to back away. When he saw it was her, he let out a breath of exasperation. "I told Helen I didn't want to be disturbed," he said. He turned off the water and dried his face. He seemed to be trying to hide how distraught he was, but she wasn't blind, and she wasn't stupid. Something had happened in Fernandes's bungalow and it was troubling him. Was Fernandes a bigger problem than she'd thought? Had she already uncovered something dangerous? If so, something had to be done about it. Fernandes was not going to ruin everything.

He put the towel on the rack and started to leave but she grabbed his arm and held him there. "Don't fuck with me, Ethan. Tell me what happened in there."

"Nothing." He tried to pull his arm away but she held tightly, not letting him off that easy. "You found something," she said. It was a statement, not a question.

He hesitated. He tried to look away but she moved so he couldn't avoid her stare. "What?" she asked. "She found some proof of what we're doing, ya?"

"No."

"What then?"

He took a deep breath and sank back against the wall. "She's been contacting Doug Collins," he said.

Karla knew exactly what that meant. Somehow Fernandes had discovered that Collins was on Rejuvenol and she'd hounded him until she got what she wanted.

"What did he tell her?" she asked.

"I don't think he told her anything—*yet.* They're supposed to meet tonight, at his condo in Tampa. I'm going to need to call him, make sure he doesn't talk to her."

Karla shook her head, disgusted. "You have a lot to learn, Ethan." She walked out of the bathroom and into his office. "Collins will tell her everything."

Ethan hurried after her. "Not if I call him," he said. "I'll make it clear that if he talks, he gets cut off immediately."

When did his brain stop working? "Listen to me, Ethan," she said. "Collins will agree not to talk, then he'll talk. Fernandes will use everything she has to make him talk. I know her type. And thanks to you, Collins has too much testosterone in him to resist her. He'll talk. She'll fuck him and he'll talk." It was pretty simple.

"No, he won't talk. I'll make sure. I'll take care of it."

A man who would give an untested therapy to his own

nephew should be able to deal with Collins and Fernandes. But it looked like the duty was falling to her. She couldn't risk having him screw up again.

"That's what you said about Fernandes twice now."

"I know what I'm doing."

"Not when it comes to this," she said. "Better you stick to making the therapy. I'll take care of Fernandes and Collins."

Ethan came closer. "What does that mean?" he said, worried.

"It means exactly what I said. I'll take care of it. I'm not going to let them interfere."

He looked like a frightened mouse. "What are you going to do?"

"*I'll* talk to Collins. I can be more persuasive than you."

"Just talk?" he said.

She shrugged. "That depends on how persuasive I am."

41

ALICIA DROVE NORTH on the Florida Turnpike.

Hours after Paul had stormed out of her bungalow she was still thinking about him. She should have known not to open her heart to him. She knew better. People hurt you—it was as simple as that. The capacity people had to hurt one another was far greater than the capacity people had to deal with that hurt. How unfair life was. How stupid and naïve she'd been for letting her guard down. She wouldn't let it happen again.

She turned the radio to a classic rock station and put the volume up loud, trying to drown out her thoughts. Bob Seger finished singing, then the DJ came on and gave the latest update on Hurricane Celine. The National Hurricane Service was still predicting that the storm would probably change direction and head north, but if it didn't it would hit somewhere along the South Florida coast in two days. Alicia planned to be long gone by then.

Maybe it'll hit De Leon and pay those bastards back for what they did to Nikki.

She was convinced they had done something to Nicole. And she planned to know what it was before the day was through.

She took Interstate 4 westbound, toward Tampa. Clearly she wasn't going to learn anything else at the clinic, now that they knew who she was. They'd be watching her every move. That Amazon, Karla, had been eyeing her as she checked out and paid for the exams. If there hadn't been so many people around, she was sure Karla would have tried something. Alicia was thankful that she'd never see that woman again.

For that matter, she was thankful she'd never see Paul again. He certainly wasn't going to help her. He was probably hiding something himself. People didn't act the way he did unless they were worried about being exposed. Maybe he was involved in whatever they'd done to Nikki. If he was, he'd go down with the rest of them.

He didn't think she had any integrity? Fine. Let him think what he wanted. The only thing that mattered to Alicia was uncovering what they'd done to Nikki. And if that meant sleeping with Doug Collins, so be it. After all, she'd slept with Paul when he obviously had no feelings for her. Sleeping with the weatherman would be easier; at least she wouldn't have any illusions that he cared for her. It'd be purely physical, and this time she'd get something useful out of it. It was quite clear from the way he'd talked on the phone this morning what he wanted.

"I like to take a Jacuzzi after work," he'd said. "Why don't you join me? Then we can talk about whatever it is you have on your mind." And if that wasn't clear enough, before he hung up, he'd said, "By the way, bathing suits are optional."

She knew exactly what he wanted from her. And she'd give it to him, if it meant finding out what happened to Nikki and ensuring that the people responsible paid for what they'd done.

She found the Royal Palm Villas from the directions he'd given her. It was an aging collection of small buildings alongside Tampa Bay. At the entrance to the complex was a kiosk with a security guard who looked all of nineteen years old and as bored as could be. He simply waved to Alicia when she drove by. Great security, she thought.

She drove around until she found building seven. His unit was one floor up. She walked up the stairs. All the doors opened directly outside. With the setting sun beating down on her, she rang the bell.

Her heart started racing as she thought about what she was going to do. She wiped her clammy hands on her pants and tried to calm herself. She felt more nervous than she'd ever felt on any assignment in L.A. But she wasn't going to turn and run like she had two nights ago. If she had gone through with it then and there, she would have found what she needed by now, and wouldn't have opened herself up to being stung so badly by Paul. She wasn't going to make the same mistake twice.

He didn't answer the door, so she rang the bell again. She checked her watch. Six-thirty. He'd said to be here at seven. Maybe he wasn't home from work yet. She waited a few minutes, in case he was in the bathroom and didn't hear the bell, then she rang it again. Thinking he might be in the Jacuzzi already and couldn't hear the bell because of the jets, she knocked hard on the door a few times, then she tried the knob. It was locked.

She'd driven all this way; she didn't want to leave without the information she needed.

She sat in her car until seven. She didn't see him arrive. She went back up and rang the bell again but there still was no answer. So he wasn't here. But that didn't mean the information she needed wasn't here. She'd gone into people's homes without permission before. That was easy. Easier than having to sleep with someone she barely knew.

Since she didn't have the tools she needed to pick the lock, she'd have to find another way in. She walked around to the bay side of the building. A cool breeze blew off the water. Gulls flew along the shore; their cries sounded like children playing. In the distance, a barge slid under the long bridge that connected Tampa to St. Petersburg. Closer, along the edge of the water, a concrete path wound through trees and shrubbery. A few elderly couples strolled hand in hand. One seventy-something woman pedaled by on a large tricycle, waving to people she probably saw every day. But all of these people were a good four or five hundred feet away, separated from the condos by a tennis court that no one was using and a knee-high concrete wall.

No one seemed the least bit interested in what was happening outside this building.

Alicia walked along the building toward Doug Collins's unit. Here, the condos had sliding glass doors opening onto small balconies. The locks on that type of door were usually pretty easy to open; she'd have no problem with that. As for the security guard, the chances of him leaving the comfort of his air-conditioned kiosk and patrolling the grounds were slim to none. So unless Doug Collins had a bar wedged against the door to keep it from sliding, or an alarm, she would get inside his condo in no time.

She'd need a little assistance to open the sliding glass door, so she went back to her rental car, opened the trunk, and found the small pry bar that came with the tire jack. It was supposed to be used to pop off the hubcap, but it would work just as well on Collins's door.

She went back to the bay side of the building. The patio beneath Doug Collins's balcony had two large palms. Perfect cover for what she needed. She walked over, peeked inside the first-floor unit to see if anyone was home, glanced back to make sure no one was paying attention to her, then took one of the lawn chairs and positioned it behind a palm. She checked one more time to be sure it was safe, then stood on the chair and quickly pulled herself up onto Collins's balcony.

She peered through the sliding glass door and into the living room. It was decorated in a Japanese manner, which looked very odd for a single man's place. The only non-Japanese furniture was the huge entertainment center along one wall, with a large-screen TV and a stereo system that looked like it was made by NASA. A blue blazer and blue tie hung over the back of the sofa. Collins was nowhere in sight.

Alicia scanned the inside frame of the door for alarm contacts. None. Nor was there a bar wedged in place to keep the door from opening. This would be easy as pie.

She had the door open in a few moments. She crept inside and slid the door closed behind her. The air in here had a distinct odor, not offensive, just the smell of someone else's place, a scent that reminded her that she was somewhere she didn't belong. The room was quiet, the only sound the faint cries of the seagulls outside and a low hum coming from somewhere in the condo.

She wasn't sure what she was looking for, just something that would help her understand what Collins had meant about therapies not approved by the FDA. If she could find proof that something like that existed, she could force the attorney general or the FDA to investigate the clinic and nail Paul and Ethan Granier for what they did to Nikki.

A small teakwood desk in the corner held a laptop computer and a clutter of papers. The desk was a skeletal thing that didn't have any drawers, just a top and four legs. She flipped through the stack of mail—bills, advertisements, nothing of interest. On the other side of the desk were more papers. She picked up the top one and unfolded it. It was a memo from Channel 10, where he worked. It was dated today.

From: Richard Faine, Station Manager
To: All Staff, Morning News

Content:
As most of you already know, the ratings for the morning news program have been steadily declining for the last three months. Something must be done to reverse this. Therefore, we have found it necessary to make significant changes to the program. Effective next Monday, Todd Hollings will become the morning meteorologist. We believe he will bring a fresh energy to the show. His notoriety on the professional volleyball circuit will help attract a younger audience to our program while his conservative approach to broadcasting will maintain our senior base.

I'm sure you all join management in thanking Doug Collins for his years of excellent service to Channel 10. If he should wish to remain with the station in a different capacity, every effort will be made to accommodate him.

Alicia was stunned. She stared down at Doug Collins's termination notice, sent out in a memo for all to see. Was this how he got the news? Talk about a not-so-subtle way of firing someone. Probably the station manager's way of keeping the rest of the staff on their toes. Fear was a great motivater.

She put the memo down, actually feeling sorry for Collins. She didn't like him at all; his use of the power he had over her disgusted her. But she couldn't help thinking what a blow this must have been for him. How was he going to get another job at his age, even looking as good as he did? There was always someone younger and better-looking coming along. She knew that from her own experience with Kristin.

She thumbed through the rest of the papers and found nothing important, so she turned to the laptop, which Collins had left on. His screen saver was a series of photographs of Japan. She tapped the space bar to get rid of the screen saver and a Word document came on the screen. Another memo.

From: Doug Collins, naïve fool
To: Richard Faine, Station Manager and Dickhead

Content:
Fuck you! Fuck you!

Alicia couldn't help but laugh. "Good for you," she said. She hoped Collins went ahead and sent the memo. Richard Faine deserved it.

She skimmed through the "My Documents" folders, but didn't find anything that seemed like it might apply to De

Leon or any drugs he was taking, so she left the computer and headed into the bedroom.

The bed was unmade. A shirt and pants were on the bed. Shoes, socks, and underwear on the floor. The humming noise she had heard when she first entered the condo was louder in here. She realized now that it was coming from the bathroom.

She stopped. Could Collins be here? Maybe he was in the Jacuzzi and hadn't heard her at the door. She'd have to tell him he'd left the door unlocked, and then do what she came to do.

Dreading what was about to come, she eased over to the half-open door and peered inside. Steam clouded the bathroom. She saw the edge of the large marble bathtub. She leaned in a little further and saw bubbling water. It was dull red. Before her brain registered why it might be red, she leaned further and saw Collins sitting in the tub, a small sword stuck through his chest, his hands still clutching the handle.

42

ALICIA RUSHED OVER to the tub, thinking only of trying to save him. She grabbed the sword by the ornate handle and pulled it out of Collins's chest. When she did, his body slid forward then sank down under the water. She saw his face staring up at her through the dull red, and she knew he was dead.

Her whole body shuddered. She'd seen dead bodies before—exactly two. One died from a heart attack, the other was hit by a car. But she hadn't known those other two men. She knew Collins. She'd planned to *sleep* with him tonight. And he'd stabbed himself like a noble samurai warrior, exactly as he'd told her he would.

Then, despite all her attempts to forget, she remembered that she'd seen one other dead body, another suicide, and *that* had been the worst of all. She'd only been able to look for a split second, but Nikki's body after she'd fallen sixteen stories to the concrete below was the most horrible thing Alicia had ever seen, or ever would see. The memory shocked her enough to make her realize she had to get out of Collins's apartment.

As she turned to leave, she saw a note taped to the mirror. A suicide note, no doubt. But before she could even consider whether or not to read it, she saw her own reflection in the mirror, the bloody sword in her hands. She quickly dropped it on the floor and rushed out, no longer caring what was in his suicide note. The police could read it. She just needed to get out of there.

She ran past Collins's phone and out the front door, not even stopping to close it. Let the stupid security guard earn his pay, she thought as she raced across the parking lot to the kiosk. Let him deal with this.

"Call the police!" she screamed at the kid.

He nearly fell off of his chair. "What's wrong?"

"He's dead. Unit seven-E. He killed himself. Call the police," she said.

"Are you sure?" the kid said, coming out of the kiosk.

"Yes, I'm sure." What an asinine question. "Just call the police."

He reached into the kiosk and grabbed the cell phone from the shelf. "Show me," he said. His face lit up. Surely this was the most excitement he'd ever had on this job.

The door to Collins's condo was closed when she and the security guard arrived. She thought she'd left it open when she ran out, but she couldn't be sure.

"In there," she told the security guard. She had no intention of going back in herself. "In the bathtub. He left a note taped to the mirror."

"I'll check it out." He looked eager to go in. Probably his first dead body. This naïve kid was in for the shock of his life.

He tried to open the door but it was locked. He looked at her, expecting her to unlock the door.

"I don't have the key," she said.

He took out a ring filled with keys and thumbed through them, trying a few keys until he found the one that opened the door.

"I'll be right back," he said. "Wait here." That was fine with her.

She watched him ease open the door and walk in. He went up the hall slowly, as if he expected the body to jump out at him. Finally he came to the bedroom. He turned and hesitated a moment, probably having second thoughts, then he took a deep breath and disappeared into the bedroom.

He'd be in the bathroom in a few seconds, Alicia calculated. How was he going to handle it? Vomit? Run like hell? Or maybe he was one of those morbid kids who didn't mind looking at dead things, possibly even enjoyed it.

She didn't want to think about that, about anything that was happening in that bathroom. She peered down the hall, through the living room, at the sliding glass door through which she'd entered the apartment, trying to distract herself. The Japanese blinds rattled in the wind like a snake.

Something was wrong. Hadn't she closed the sliding door when she came in? Yes, she was certain she had. She remembered thinking that she didn't want anyone to see it open while she was snooping around, didn't want to attract any attention. So how could it be open now?

Just then the security guard stepped out of the bedroom and into the hall. He stared at Alicia for a long moment. Finally he motioned for her to come over. She didn't want to go back in, but obviously there was something bothering him, something he didn't understand. She didn't want to play mother to this kid, tell him how to handle a suicide, but it looked like she was going to have to. But that didn't mean she'd have to go all the way into the bathroom.

She walked down the hall and stopped at the bedroom door. "What is it?"

He was pale, but his voice was steady. "I thought you told me there was a suicide note."

"There is. Taped to the mirror."

"There's nothing taped to the mirror."

She had no choice now but to go back in there and show this stupid kid how to do his job. She pushed past him and made her way to the bathroom, preparing herself psychologically as she went in. She wasn't going to look at the body, just find the note, tape it to this kid's forehead so he'd be sure to find it, then get out.

She went into the bathroom. He was right, the note had fallen off the mirror. She looked in the sink below, but it wasn't there. She checked on the floor. No note. Avoiding the tub, she scanned the room but could not see the note anywhere.

"This doesn't make sense," she said. "I know it was here." She turned back to the kid, who was standing in the doorway, blocking her exit. He stared at her, his eyes full of suspicion.

"Who are you, anyway?" he asked.

"A friend of his." Better to leave it at that.

"And you found him?" the kid asked.

"Yes."

"He was already dead?"

"Yes." She was growing impatient with his stupid questions.

"You don't have a key to the condo," he said.

No kidding, Sherlock. "I know," she said. She'd had enough questioning right now, and she'd stayed long enough in this bathroom. It seemed to be getting smaller and stuffier by the second. The hum of the Jacuzzi was grating at her nerves. The thought of what the hot water was doing to that body made her sick. She needed air.

"Excuse me," she said, pushing her way past him. She crossed the bedroom and went back into the hall, far enough away from the body that she felt better. And out here, she didn't feel so claustrophobic.

The kid followed her. "How did you get in here," he asked, "if he was already dead when you arrived and you don't have a key and the door was locked?"

Oh, Christ. Now the kid was a detective. What made it worse was that she really didn't have an answer for him. So she turned the tables.

"Look, there's a guy in there who committed suicide," she said. "Stop asking stupid questions and call the police."

They were going to ask the same stupid questions, she realized, but she would come clean with them, tell them about the clinic, the secret drug, all of it. They'd understand her sneaking in through the balcony door; this cop wannabe wouldn't. And they might be able to help find out what Ethan Granier, Paul Tobin, and Karla Weiss were doing down there.

"I'll call them," he said, "but you wait here until they come."

"Where do you think I'm going to go?"

"And don't touch anything."

His orders were really annoying her. He was an inexperienced kid. He had no business telling her what to do and not do. "What am I going to touch?" she said, sarcastic.

"That, for starters." He pointed to the pry bar she had used to force open the sliding glass door. It was on the floor in the living room, in front of the door, the door she had closed when she came in, the door that was now open.

Someone had opened it. Just like someone had taken the missing suicide note. Like someone had closed the front door.

Someone has been here since I ran out. Someone must have been in the condo while I was here.

That thought sent a shiver down her spine. Was Doug Collins's death really suicide? But he'd left a note. And he'd told her about the samurai code. It had to be suicide. He'd found out that he was being fired because he was too old, even after spending all the money he'd spent at De Leon. At his age he'd have difficulty getting another job in TV, which meant his career was over. Devastated, he wrote a note and killed himself. Irrational, but it fit.

But then who had been here a few minutes ago? And the note was gone; whoever was here must have taken it. Why?

Suddenly she realized what was happening. She was being set up.

"Exactly where was this supposed note?" the kid asked, his voice heavy with doubt. She noticed that he was staring at her hands. She looked. Collins's blood was smeared on her fingers.

"Let's let the police figure this whole thing out," he said, taking out his cell phone.

Suddenly it didn't seem like a good idea to wait around for the police to arrive. How was she going to explain all of this? What happened if they didn't believe her? She could end up in serious trouble. The suicide note was gone. Her fingerprints were on the weapon that killed Collins, on the pry bar, on the sliding glass door. And Collins's blood was on her hands. And God only knew what this kid was going to say.

She started toward the door to leave but the kid positioned himself to block her escape.

"Let's just wait until the police get here," he said, dialing 911.

"I didn't do anything," she said.

He ignored her and spoke into the phone. "Yes, this is Ron Geddis, security at Royal Palm Villas." As he gave the address, he kept eyeing Alicia suspiciously. Increasingly she felt this was getting out of hand. She needed to get out of here. "There's been a murder here," he told the 911 operator.

"A suicide," Alicia said.

The kid shielded the phone so the operator couldn't hear Alicia's voice and he turned slightly to the side. "I have the suspect here," he whispered.

Alicia had to get the hell out of here. *Now!* She rushed toward the kid, which startled him. He whirled around, unprepared, and dropped the phone. He fumbled to grab the pepper spray on his belt, but before he could get it, Alicia drove her knee into his groin. He doubled over in pain. She locked both fists together, raised them over her head, and brought them down hard on the back of his head. His legs folded beneath him and he crumpled to the floor. She jumped over him to get to the door. He made one last weak attempt to stop her, reaching up and grabbing her leg, but she easily kicked herself loose and ran from the condo.

43

ETHAN PULLED INTO Beth's driveway a little before seven. He still wasn't sure how he was going to get the blood specimen from Kenny. He had two options. Either he could ask Beth, claiming he needed the blood to run some tests that might help Zack, omitting the part about having given Kenny Rejuvenol the other night. Or he could get Kenny away from the house somehow, make up an excuse like asking him to go fishing or shoot some baskets or go get some ice cream. But that depended on Kenny agreeing to go. Then he'd have to sedate Kenny, draw blood, and wait for him to come around.

Neither option seemed like a sure thing, but he was leaning toward the second one.

He tucked the syringe with the sedative into his pocket, along with an empty syringe to draw a blood specimen and a rubber tube to tie off Kenny's arm. Then he went up to the door and rang the bell. Pete let him in.

"We got a dog, Uncle Ethan! We got a dog!"

"Really? That's wonderful!"

"We don't have a name for him but I wanna call him Oreo because he's black and white. Wanna see him? He's out back with Kenny."

"Yeah, I'd like to." Maybe Beth wasn't here. This would be the perfect opportunity to do what he needed to do. "Where's your mom?" he asked Pete, hoping he'd say she was out shopping or having dinner with what's-his-name.

"She's in the kitchen."

So much for that idea. "I'll be outside in a minute, okay?" he told Pete.

"Okay."

As Pete hurried off to play with the dog, Ethan wondered if somehow he could use the dog to get Kenny alone. Maybe he could offer to take it for its shots. No, they'd probably done that first thing—Beth was so careful. He could suggest that he and Kenny go to PetSmart and pick up some supplies, his gift to Beth and the kids.

He went to the kitchen to find Beth and make his pitch.

She was standing by the sink, making a salad.

"Eating a little late?" he said.

"We got tied up getting a dog." She gestured out the back window where the kids were chasing the dog around the pool area.

"I know, Pete told me. But I thought you and the kids were going away in a week or so. What are you going to do with the dog?"

"It needs to be neutered. We'll get that done while we're away. The dog will stay at the vet's." She smiled and said, "Don't worry, I wasn't going to ask you to take care of it."

"I wasn't even thinking that."

"Yeah, right. Anyway, I figured with the move and everything it might be good for the kids to have a dog. We had one when we were their age, remember?"

"I remember. It's a good idea. Hey, I'll tell you what I'll do," he said. "You look busy, why don't I take Kenny down to PetSmart and pick up—"

Just then Pete rushed into the kitchen, screaming, "Mommy! Mommy! Kenny hurt Oreo!"

Beth quickly dropped the tomato and the knife into the sink and rushed to the back door, Pete hurrying alongside her. Ethan ran after them. When they got outside, they saw the dog lying on the pool area patio, licking its rear leg, whining. Kenny was standing over it, breathing heavily, obviously angry.

"What happened?" Beth said, running over.

Kenny whipped his head around and glared at Beth, his anger focused on her now.

"Why do you always blame me?" Kenny said.

"I'm not blaming you. I'm asking you what happened."

"He bit me!" Kenny stuck out his hand, showing a tiny nick on the back of his hand. A bead of blood seeped out. "I'm bleeding, see?"

Beth touched the dog's leg and it whimpered.

"No, no, it's okay," she told the dog. She peered up at Kenny. "What did you do to the dog?"

"Nothing. It just bit me for no reason."

"You kicked it," Pete said.

"That was after it bit me, dickhead!"

"Kenny!" Beth said.

Pete started crying. "Mommy, he called me dickhead!"

"You don't have to repeat it," she told Pete. Then she turned to Kenny. "What on earth is the matter with you?"

"Why is everybody against me? I'm the one who got bit. The stupid mutt bit me!"

"Oreo isn't a stupid mutt," Pete said.

"How would you know, you stupid moron, and its name isn't Oreo."

"Mommy!"

"Kenny!"

"He started it!"

While they were arguing, Ethan gently examined the dog's leg. It was definitely broken. "He's going to need to go to the vet," he told Beth.

She glared up at Kenny again. "You're in big trouble, mister," she said. "Just go to your room. I'll deal with you later."

Kenny wheeled around, kicked a rubber float into the pool, and stormed off, grumbling, "Man, this sucks!"

Ethan carried the dog to Beth's car. Beth knew of a twenty-four-hour animal hospital.

"I want to go," Pete said, hopping into the backseat beside the dog.

Ethan realized this was the opportunity he needed, so before Beth could say anything to him, he said, "I'll stay here with Kenny. I should take a look at that hand of his, just to make sure it isn't going to get infected. And I can talk to him about what he did."

"Thanks. I'd really appreciate that." Beth went around the car and got in behind the wheel. Through the window, she said, "I don't know what's gotten into him lately. All day he's been like this—fighting with Pete, arguing with me, he broke his Walkman when it wouldn't work right, and now this." She shook her head, bewildered.

"Kids go through phases like this," Ethan said.

"Well, I hope to God it's a short phase."

Ethan watched them drive away then he went upstairs to Kenny's room. The music was blasting again. He knocked but Kenny didn't answer so he opened the door. Kenny was lying on his stomach on the bed, moving one foot to the beat of rap music. Ethan called out to him a couple times, but Kenny didn't hear, so Ethan walked over to the bed and tapped him on the leg.

Kenny jumped up, fists clenched. He had a ferocity in his eyes as if he were ready to fight to the death. Ethan stepped back, worried Kenny was going to lash out at him.

"It's only me," Ethan said. "Calm down."

Kenny glared at him for several long seconds. Ethan didn't think the boy even recognized him. Finally his aggression dissolved into a look of irritation. He turned away, plopped back down on the bed, and said, "What do you want?"

Ethan walked over to the stereo and turned the volume down. "I wanted to take a look at your hand." He wanted Kenny to think he was siding with him in the dog incident. "It looked like that dog took a pretty good chomp at you."

"For no reason," Kenny said.

Ethan shook his head, faking disgust. "Some dogs just aren't suited to be around people."

"That one isn't, that's for sure. Not without a muzzle, anyway."

Ethan pointed to Kenny's hand. "Does it hurt?"

Kenny shrugged. "I'll live."

"Let's take a look at it, make sure it's not going to get infected."

Kenny stuck out his hand. While Ethan examined it, Kenny said, "I don't know why Mom blames me for everything."

"She's under a lot of stress right now, with the move and everything."

"So am I, but you don't see me freaking out like her."

"I'll talk to her."

"Like that's going to do any good."

Ethan took Kenny to the bathroom and washed out the bite mark. It wasn't bad at all; the skin was barely broken. But he made a big deal of it to win Kenny over. Also he could use this as an excuse to get the blood specimen he needed.

He bandaged Kenny's hand then said, "I'm going to take a little blood just to make sure the dog didn't give you any bacteria when he bit you."

"They do that?"

"It's just a precaution."

Kenny shook his head in disgust. "That dirty mutt."

Ethan took out the syringe, tied off Kenny's arm so he could get a vein, then took the blood.

"You carry that stuff around with you all the time, Uncle Ethan?" Kenny asked.

"Not always," he said with a chuckle. "I was up here seeing a patient so I had it with me."

When Ethan was done, he said, "Do me a favor, don't tell your mom about this." He pointed to the blood. "You know how she is. She'll start worrying, blow the whole thing out of proportion, and . . . freak out."

Kenny chuckled at Ethan's choice of words. "Yeah, I know."

"I'll let you know if anything turns up, if you need any antibiotics, but I doubt there'll be a problem."

"That's cool," Kenny said.

Ethan slid the blood specimen into his jacket pocket. Now he just needed to wait for Beth to return from the vet so he could get back to De Leon and start running the tests on Kenny's blood. He hoped to have the results by Sunday morning, then he'd know if the dose was safe and effective to give to Zack.

Judging from his observations of Kenny, it seemed to be all right. He wondered about the incident with the dog, though. Could Kenny's violent outburst have anything to do with Rejuvenol? Ethan didn't see how it could. Rejuvenol didn't make people violent; it made them younger. It regenerated cells and organs. No way could that cause someone to be violent. More likely it was the stress Kenny was under, facing a move to another country, a life with a new father figure, the hectic hormonal eruption of puberty. Not Rejuvenol.

Kenny's outburst reminded him of the way he himself had felt this morning, in Alicia Fernandes's bungalow. The sudden rage. The desire to hurt her. But he wasn't a killer. He'd been angry, and afraid for his son. His feelings were natural—just like Kenny's.

44

THE TWELVE-STEP MEETING was held in the basement of a Methodist church a block from the craziness of Duval Street. The room was crowded, which was good. It gave Paul anonymity. He needed that tonight, until he felt comfortable with this group. Returning to an AA meeting was difficult for him. He felt an embarrassing sense of guilt, not only for having drunk last night, but also for having thought he was better than everyone else in here and could stay sober without putting any effort into it. Now here he was, tail tucked between his legs.

He opted not to speak tonight, except when they went around the room introducing themselves. "My name is Paul and I'm an alcoholic," he said, the might of those words humbling him. As he sat in the back and listened to people talking about how they dealt with their addiction and their recovery, he began to feel a warm sense of relief. The thing about these meetings that had worked for him originally was the feeling he got that he was not alone, he was not doing something that had never been done before. If he wanted help, it was here for him. There definitely was a way back.

The meeting also reminded him of how far he had come, how much strength and willpower he had mustered once, and could again. Sure, he'd relapsed last night, but relapse was part of recovery. AA hammered home that point all the time. Just because he'd had a few drinks last night didn't mean he'd blown his future, didn't mean he should resign himself to a life of booze and give up trying. He'd regained control in time, and he was here doing something to minimize the chances of that happening again. That was what mattered most.

He did get a twenty-four-hour chip. It was important. He stuffed it into his pocket and reached in a few times to touch it. It marked the first day of his new sobriety.

By the end of the meeting, he decided he needed to get a local sponsor, someone he could call if he ever again got to the point he'd been to last night. He'd had a sponsor in New York, and it was something he needed again now.

Most of the people at the meeting were open and friendly. Several of them introduced themselves to him afterwards, since he was a new face there, but he didn't find anyone he hit it off with. It would take time to find a sponsor, he knew. He didn't expect to get one tonight. He might have to try several different meetings, different nights, different locations. But this was a start. He definitely felt stronger and better about himself when he left.

Before he returned the rental car and looked for a taxi to take him back to Coral Key, he stopped at the diner across the street from the church hall. He hadn't slept much the night before and he needed a coffee for the drive back. He sat at the counter. The diner had a TV. A baseball game was on. He was surprised to see the Yankees playing. He used to follow them pretty closely. The last couple of years, though, he'd lost interest.

"They got some team this year, huh?"

Paul turned toward the man who spoke. Two seats over was a sixty-year-old man who looked like a skinny Santa Claus. Paul recognized him from the meeting. He'd talked about how he used to drink Listerine and how he still couldn't gargle with mouthwash, even after fifteen years.

"The choice is between relapse and bad breath," he'd said, drawing laughter. "Either way I wasn't going to get a lot of kissin'."

From his accent, Paul knew the guy was a New Yorker. The Bronx.

"I don't know," Paul said, looking back up at the ball game. "I haven't kept up too much this year."

"Take my word for it, they do. In spite of Steinbrenner."

"Well, they're the Yankees. They have a hell of a team every year."

The man extended his hand. He was missing two fingers. "Rocco Tempesta," he said.

Paul shook his hand, trying not to stare at the missing fingers. His first thought was a guy named Rocco, from the Bronx, missing fingers—he must be in the mob, did something wrong, maybe skimmed some money, got his fingers chopped off, then got sent down here to keep low.

"Paul Tobin," he said. "Nice to meet you."

"Likewise."

"I saw you across the street," Paul said.

Rocco looked him over for a moment then said, "You was at the meeting? You didn't say nuthin', right?"

"That was me."

"Forget about it. When you're ready, you'll talk."

They talked a bit about New York. Rocco was a retired carpenter. Paul felt like an idiot for thinking the guy was a mobster. He was direct and funny and kind and smart. They moved over to a booth and the talk switched to their drinking histories. Paul confided in him about last night. Rocco told him stories about losing everything, living on the streets of New York, panhandling for change so he could drink.

"Listo's the way to go," he said. "You can get it anywhere, twenty-four/seven, Sundays, too. And it's fifty proof, you know. Tastes like shit, but who drinks for taste at that point?"

By the time they were on their third cup of coffee, Paul was sure he'd found a sponsor.

The baseball game remained close for a while, so they watched some as they talked. Right after the sixth inning, a news update came on. The anchor talked about the hurricane; it hadn't turned north yet so the National Hurricane Service in Miami issued a watch for all of the keys. The chance of a direct hit was getting better every hour. The station cut to a boring guy standing on the beach in Miami, droning on about the storm.

"We're trying to watch a game here," Rocco shouted at
the TV.

"You think the hurricane's going to be a problem?" Paul
asked.

"I'm living here twelve years. You know how many
times we've been told to evacuate 'cuz a hurricane's coming, and then nothing happens? Lots."

"So the hurricanes usually turn away?"

"They usually hit the Carolinas."

"Didn't Hurricane Andrew hit pretty hard down here?"

"What are you, a troublemaker?"

The weatherman finished and the anchorman started
talking about a murder-suicide in Coral Gables. A woman
had gone to the home of her ex-husband and shot him
dead, then turned the gun on herself.

"The world is going crazy," Rocco said, shaking his
head. He shouted, "How about the ball game!"

The anchor continued. When he said the woman's name,
Paul stared in shock. It was Lita Davis, the patient he was
supposed to operate on in a few days.

"I can't believe she would do that," he said out loud, not
even realizing he was saying it until Rocco responded.

"Me, I believe it. I was married to a crazy broad once
myself."

"That woman isn't crazy. She's one of the sweetest people I've ever met."

"You know her?"

"She's a patient of mine. I don't understand how this
could happen. She wasn't violent at all."

"Well, she was violent as hell today."

Paul dropped off the car and picked up a cab at the airport.
The whole ride back, he thought about Lita Davis killing
her husband and then turning the gun on herself. That was
not the Lita he'd met. He could understand Lita trying to
take revenge against her ex-husband after what he'd done
to her. But killing him? And then killing herself? That
didn't fit at all. She'd been happy about punishing her ex in
the divorce settlement, and looking forward to having sur-

gery to fix the external damage he'd done. Paul hadn't realized how much internal damage the man had done.

But still, murder-suicide? Not Lita.

The cab turned off A1A and headed toward the bridge. The tide was high and waves lapped over the road.

"I'm not driving over that," the cabby said.

"It's okay. It's safe."

"You sure?"

"It's safe," Paul said.

The cabby shrugged and drove ahead. But now Paul started to wonder if it really was safe. Had Ethan hired engineers to do structural tests after the hurricane? Didn't the constant barrage of waves put stress on the bridge?

The cab made it across. Paul put the bridge out of his mind and thought about Lita again. That whole incident got him thinking about Alicia's claims of having a sister who committed suicide. What if she were telling the truth? Was it coincidence that two patients had killed themselves? That didn't sit well with Paul. If Alicia was telling the truth about her sister—and he still didn't know if she was—then there had to be some connection to De Leon.

Would hormone therapy make someone suicidal? He didn't think so. If not that, then what else could it be?

The secret therapy?

Could Alicia have been right?

The taxi let him off by the lobby. Instead of going right to his bungalow, he went to his office. He needed to make a phone call. He checked the time. A quarter to eleven. There was a three-hour time difference. Someone might still be in the office.

A man answered on the third ring.

"Los Angeles County medical examiner."

45

WHEN ETHAN GOT home, Carmen was sitting beside Zack's bed, knitting in the dark. Zack was asleep, oxygen tubes in his nose. Carmen got up and joined Ethan in the hallway.

"What's wrong?" he asked.

"Zachary wasn't feeling well tonight. He wanted me to sit with him."

Ethan's heart began to race. "What happened?" he asked, worried. He felt guilty that he hadn't been here. "What was wrong? How is he?"

"He's okay now. He said he was feeling strange, weak. I checked his vital signs." She showed him the notes she'd taken. "His respiration was a bit slow and his pulse was shallow. I didn't think it was something to call you or nine-one-one about. I brought him to bed, put him on oxygen, and stayed with him, to monitor him."

Ethan peered through the doorway and into the bedroom. His son looked so tiny, fragile, vulnerable. Ethan had stopped crying a long time ago; he had to be strong for his son. But the pain of seeing Zack suffer like this tore fresh wounds in his heart every day.

"Zack's vital signs were a bit better the last time I checked them, about half an hour ago," Carmen said. "I think he's okay."

Ethan sighed, feeling some relief. But the worry didn't go away completely. It never did. And neither did the guilt. Every time he left, even if just to go to the medical building three minutes away, he feared that if something happened to Zack and he wasn't there to help him, Zack would die.

Thank God for Carmen. She treated him wonderfully, as though he were her own son. That was the only consolation Ethan felt about leaving Zack's side. He was in good hands. He borrowed Carmen's stethoscope and went into the bedroom. He rechecked Zack's vitals. His son's breathing was a bit shallow and raspy, but for him this was fairly normal. He listened to Zack's heart. The beats were thready and weak. The predominant danger for children with progeria was heart failure or stroke. Zack was getting so much worse, accumulating so much plaque, that he was becoming extremely vulnerable.

Ethan leaned over and kissed him gently on the forehead. "It won't be long now," he whispered, meaning Rejuvenol. "I promise."

He turned on the audio monitor so he'd hear if anything happened. He thanked Carmen for sitting with him and told her she could go to bed. Her room was across the hall.

He stayed with Zack for a short while before going upstairs to his laboratory. He wanted to get the tests on Kenny's blood started right away. The sooner he knew the results, the sooner he'd be able to give Rejuvenol to Zack. He just hoped to God the results were favorable. There was no telling how much longer Zack could hold out. Weeks. Maybe only days.

He took the syringe of Kenny's blood from his jacket pocket and brought it to the lab table to prepare the culture. He needed every drop of the blood to do the analysis, so he had to be careful pouring it into the test tubes.

He lined up the three tubes he needed and had begun pouring blood into the first one when a hand grasped his shoulder. He spun around, startled, and nearly dropped the syringe. Karla stood behind him, chuckling.

"You're a little jumpy tonight, ya?" she said.

He glared at her. "Don't do that," he said. He knew she'd done it on purpose. Her asinine little game had almost caused him to lose this blood specimen, which could have cost Zack his life.

Karla walked around the lab table, fingering some empty test tubes.

Ethan turned his back to her and took a few deep breaths to steady his nerves. He didn't want her to see that she'd succeeded in disturbing him. That would only encourage her to keep it up. And he couldn't let her disrupt what he was doing tonight. He had to concentrate on his work.

As he went back to preparing the culture, he said, "What do you want? I'm extremely busy tonight."

"That blood is from Tobin's boy?"

He ignored her question and continued working. Once he had the culture prepared, he brought it to the Cultrex machine. Karla slid up close behind him. He knew what she was going to do and he wasn't in the mood.

"What is it you wanted?" he asked.

"You remember Alicia Fernandes?" she asked. She ran her finger up his back and across his neck.

He didn't have time for this. "Karla, please. I told you, I'm very busy."

"How busy?" she asked, starting to massage his shoulders.

He reached back and removed her hands. "Too busy to be wasting time like this," he said. He turned and faced her. "Would you please tell me what it is that you want so I can get back to work?"

She pouted, as if he'd hurt her feelings.

"There was a time when you liked my late-night visits," she said.

He stepped past her and went to his desk. "I really *really* need to get some work done tonight. So unless whatever it is you're here for is urgent, this conversation will have to wait until tomorrow."

"Sure." She started toward the steps.

That was too easy. He waited for the other shoe to drop.

She stopped at the top of the stairs. "I just wanted to let you know," she said, "that Alicia Fernandes is not going to be a problem for us anymore."

Her words sent a chill up his back. "What did you do?" he asked, dreading the answer.

She pretended that he'd hurt her feelings again. "That's pretty rude of you, Ethan, to accuse me of doing something."

"Cut the crap, Karla. Just tell me what happened."

"Well, you were right. She did go see Collins."

"I know that. Did he tell her anything?"

"He didn't say a word to her." She grinned. "He wasn't in the talking mood."

Her vagueness irritated him. "Will you just tell me what the hell happened, Karla!"

She shrugged and very casually said, "Collins is dead."

"What?" Ethan was stunned. "What do you mean?"

"Not breathing anymore. No longer alive. Dead, ya?"

He listened in disbelief as she related the story about how she found Collins dead in his Jacuzzi, a suicide, and about how Fernandes broke into Collins's condo, setting herself up for the police to blame her for his death.

"Why would they blame her for a suicide?" he asked.

"I guess it isn't so apparent to them that it was a suicide," she said.

She explained how she had removed the suicide note from the bathroom and taken the notice from the TV station informing Collins that he was being fired. Fernandes's fingerprints were all over the condo, and in particular all over the sword Collins used to kill himself.

"Why did you do that?" Ethan worried that this was going to impact De Leon and Rejuvenol. "Now the police are involved." And that could only be bad.

"Collins killed himself and Fernandes set herself up to be blamed. What I did was minimal. The police were going to investigate anyway. Better they focus on Fernandes instead of on us."

Ethan didn't like the way this was turning out. "It would be better if the police weren't involved at all," he said.

"I told you, they were going to get involved anyway. I directed their attention to Fernandes. She is stubborn and tricky. She would have continued pursuing this until she found a way to interfere with Rejuvenol. That should be your real concern, ya? Think of your son."

He hated her bringing up Zack. She didn't give a damn about him. Her mentioning him only defiled his name. And that made him irate. "The only one you care about is you," he said. "So stop pretending to care about my son."

She pretended to be offended again. "Ethan, why do you hurt me?"

He didn't even bother answering. He was still angry and worried. "Christ," he said, "how am I supposed to fix this mess?"

"There's no mess. Collins can't talk now. Fernandes is wanted by the police, she doesn't know enough to hurt us, so she can't make any more trouble. See? No mess."

Ethan shook his head in disgust. "You don't understand," he muttered. Maybe it was that Collins had killed himself, just like Nicole Quinn. Maybe it was the possibility that somehow Rejuvenol was involved. Maybe it was the notion of Alicia Fernandes going to jail for a murder she didn't commit. Whatever the reason, he could not rest easy about this.

"This man is dead," he said. "No matter what you say, that's a mess."

"Look, what's important to you, Ethan? Collins and Fernandes or your son?"

He couldn't control his rage. He pushed her backward into the wall. "Don't you dare question my love for Zack!" he shouted in her face.

She grinned like someone who had just won a bet. "That's all I wanted to hear," she said. "You keep working on Rejuvenol, ya? I'll be ready for my injection on Monday."

Rage swept over him again. Her grin. Her selfishness. He couldn't stand it any longer. He clutched her by the throat. An uncontrollable anger burned inside him. He couldn't stop himself. It was instinct now. He started to choke her, wanting desperately to kill her.

His anger and hatred were so focused on her arrogant smirk that he didn't notice what she was doing with her hands until it was too late. She clamped her fist around his testicles and squeezed hard. Pain shot up through his body.

Both arms went limp as he doubled over. He let out a cry of pain. She twisted her hand. His legs buckled beneath him. He collapsed to the floor.

"Don't ever threaten me again," she said calmly.

Ethan squirmed on the floor in the fetal position, his hands holding his crotch in pain. Karla waited, letting the weight of her warning sink in. Finally she turned and headed down the stairs. "I've got to go. I lost a whole day of training already."

She left him in anguish and shame on the floor, his head filled with thoughts of violence.

46

RED AND BLUE lights appeared in Alicia's rearview mirror. A police car sped toward her. *Oh, shit!* She fought the urge to floor the accelerator, the natural instinct to flee. She tried to be logical. They couldn't have ID'd her so quickly. It would take time to trace the car, contact the rental company, find out who had rented it, then check the fingerprints on Collins's *tanto* sword against the fingerprints she'd given when she got her PI license. That all took time. More time than had passed since she fled Collins's condo.

She steadied her nerves and checked the speedometer. Fifty. The speed limit was fifty-five. She kept the speed steady and watched the flashing lights rapidly approach. That cop had to be after someone else. She held tightly to the steering wheel, taking deep breaths to calm herself. Each time she peered into the mirror and saw the lights, she felt the weight of her right foot on the gas pedal. She wanted to floor it.

The lights bore down on her. She thought again about making a run for it. She'd never get away. The brown Highway Patrol car veered to the left and sped past her. She let out the breath she'd been holding. They hadn't ID'd her car yet. But it was only a matter of time before they came looking for her.

She needed to buy herself some time to find out what was happening.

She reached the Tampa airport without coming across any other police cars. She left her car in the loading zone so they'd find it and hurried inside to the ticket counter. A flight left for Los Angeles in half an hour. She bought a one-way ticket with her credit card and ran through the concourse to the gate.

The flight was already boarding. As she got on the plane and headed up the aisle, she scanned the rows, looking for just the right passenger. Alicia spotted her in row 9, an elderly woman, sitting by the window. The other two seats were still empty. She was traveling alone. Perfect.

"Excuse me," Alicia said. "I think you may be in my seat."

"Oh, dear me," the woman said, looking worried. She started to get up.

"No, no, that's okay, don't worry about it," Alicia said, motioning for her to sit back down. "You're already settled in here, I'll sit in your seat. It's okay."

"You don't mind?"

"Not at all. Can I see your ticket, so I'll know where to sit?"

"Yes, of course."

It took the elderly woman a few moments to find the ticket in her pocketbook. She handed it to Alicia.

"Let's see," Alicia said and turned, as though she were looking for the seat she was supposed to sit in. With her back to the woman, she slid the woman's ticket out of the jacket and stuck her own in its place, then she turned back to the woman, gave her the switched ticket, thanked her, and headed forward again, toward the exit.

"I have to get off," she told the flight attendants, who were preparing to close the door. She pretended to be short of breath and shaky. "I thought I could fly but I just can't."

"Are you sure?" one of them asked her.

"I'm sure," Alicia said and hurried up the jetway toward the terminal.

She told the gate agent that she had to get off the flight. The agent took her ticket and removed her name, Milly Finnell, from the roster. As far as the airline knew, Alicia Fernandes was still on the flight. That was what the police would think, too, when they traced her credit card purchase. They'd concentrate their search in L.A.

When she left the terminal, she saw a tow truck hooking up her rental car. She got in a taxi and asked the driver if he knew a quiet, out-of-the-way motel.

The I-4 Motor Inn was a real dive. She checked in under the name Susan Anthony, paid cash in advance, then went to her room. It had a magnificent view of the interstate's off-ramp and the motel's Dumpster. She drew the blinds for privacy. The room had no air conditioner so she had to leave the window open. A warm breeze rattled the blinds. The scent of diesel fuel from the truck stop across the street blew in. Tractor trailer rigs rumbled by constantly. This wasn't a typical tourist spot by any stretch of the imagination, but it met her needs. She figured she could bum a ride from one of the truckers later, once she knew where she was going.

The first thing she needed was information. Her being set up at Collins's condo had to be connected with De Leon. It couldn't be anything else. And that meant three suspects. Ethan Granier. Karla Weiss. And Paul Tobin. She was going to have to find out as much as she could about the three of them.

She dialed Steve Polaski's office back in L.A. She got the machine, which wasn't unusual, so she tried his cell phone and finally reached him. She could hear a PA in the background, an announcement for a train to Barstow.

"It's Alicia," she said.

"I can't talk now," he whispered. He had to be on a case. "I'll call you in the morning."

"It can't wait until morning. I'm in trouble, Steve. I need help."

He was silent for a moment then he said, "Give me your number. I'll call you back in five minutes."

When Steve called back, he was in his car.

"What's going on?" he asked.

She filled him in on what had happened at De Leon and

Collins's condo. "I need to find out as much as possible about Tobin, Granier, and Weiss," she said. "I can't do much at this end, with the police looking for me. Can you help?"

Steve didn't hesitate. "Give me a few hours."

Alicia tried to stay awake but she nodded off. She slept restlessly, tossing and turning through a nightmare in which she was standing naked in Doug Collins's bathroom, staring at the dead body beneath the bloody water of the Jacuzzi. Suddenly the body sprang up and clutched her throat. It wasn't Doug Collins at all. It was Paul Tobin. She woke up, breathless, soaked in perspiration, her heart racing.

It was only a dream, she told herself, and sank back down. She considered calling Steve to see what he'd learned. She checked her watch. It was almost one in the morning, ten P.M. in L.A. Steve would be calling soon. She took a cool shower to wake up and clear her head, then she sat up by the window, watching for the police and waiting for Steve's call. By one-thirty, she couldn't wait any longer. She called and reached Steve in the office.

"Sorry it took so long," he said. "It was a bitch getting the home numbers. I just hung up."

"Whose home numbers? Who did you talk to?"

"The trustees at Manhattan General Hospital in New York."

"Why did you call them? What did you find out?"

"We'll start with Ethan Granier," Steve said. "Nothing out of the ordinary." He detailed Granier's educational and career history and his uncontested divorce, which was in the public record in New York State. The reason was "abandonment." One dependent child, a handicapped boy named Zachary, of whom Granier was granted sole custody. Resigned from Manhattan General three years ago. Impeccable reputation there.

"The guy's pretty clean," Steve said.

"What about the other two?" Alicia asked.

Steve told her about Karla Weiss, a former East German

athlete who won a gold medal in swimming in the 1980 Olympics in Moscow. "That's one of the asterisks years," he said and explained about the U.S. boycott of the Games. Just as with the 1984 Games, when the Eastern bloc countries boycotted the Los Angeles Olympics, some people considered these Games to be of lesser importance, and the medals to be slightly tainted, since the competition was limited.

The rest of the information about Weiss was limited, since she had lived most of her life in the former East Germany.

"There is some interesting history on Paul Tobin," Steve said.

"Really? What did you find?"

"That's the call I just made."

"That wasn't about Granier? I thought you said he worked at Manhattan General."

"They both did. Tobin's rep, however, isn't so impeccable. He was fired from the hospital and the state revoked his medical license."

"What?" Alicia was stunned. She hadn't expected that. Steve went on to explain that Tobin had been blamed for the death of one of his patients. He was accused of negligence. There wasn't enough evidence to prosecute him criminally but the state medical board thought there was enough to bar him from ever practicing medicine in New York.

"Apparently," Steve said, "there was an issue of Tobin being drunk, and that's what may have caused the patient's death. The director of the hospital's trustees, one James Medford, was pretty tight-lipped about the incident. He referred me to their legal department and hung up. Something went on there that no one wants to talk about."

It was a lot for Alicia to digest. She remembered that Paul had smelled of alcohol last night. Could he still have the drinking problem? Could that somehow be causing the trouble at De Leon?

"Tobin and Granier both worked for the same hospital?" she asked Steve. "That can't be coincidence."

"They're brothers-in-law, too."

She was sure now Paul had lied about everything. He was definitely involved in whatever was going on at De Leon. And he'd probably known Nikki. The whole thing last night, intervening when Karla was attacking her, had been for show, a setup. Just like his sleeping with her, pretending he cared. More deception. He was a horrible man. And he was obviously hiding something. He was the one she should be pursuing.

Steve believed the hospital in New York was concealing something about Paul. It might help her understand what he was doing, what had happened to Nikki. She had to go there herself and see what she could learn.

After she hung up with Steve, she checked out of the motel and went across the street to the truck stop. Within thirty minutes she found a husband-and-wife truck-driving team willing to take on a passenger for a hundred dollars. They were going to take turns driving and go straight through the night. She'd be in New York by tomorrow night. She intended to have answers soon afterward.

47

THE MEDICAL EXAMINER on duty confirmed that they
did do an autopsy on a suicide victim named Nicole Quinn.
The woman who actually did it, Dr. Susan Polk, worked
days. He'd have her call Paul in the morning.

Paul hung up, troubled. So Alicia had been telling the
truth—at least about Nicole Quinn having killed herself.
How much of the rest of her story was true? Was Nicole
Quinn her sister? Had she been a patient here? If so, was
one of the therapies she received here responsible for her
suicide?

One step at a time, he told himself. As far as he knew,
De Leon never had a patient named Nicole Quinn. There
was no chart for her. And Ethan denied her ever being here.
So at this point, he had no way to follow up on that.

But there was a chart for Lita Davis. Paul knew that she
existed, that she had been a patient here, and that she'd
done something completely out of character. It wasn't *exactly* the same thing that Nicole Quinn did, but it was similar enough that he could not dismiss it. Was it possible that
something the two of them received here caused them to
behave so erratically?

Outside his bungalow, the grounds of De Leon were deserted. The bungalows lining the beach were dark, as were
the windows of the offices and medical facilities. Paul
headed toward the medical building where Lita's information would be kept. He noticed lights on in Karla's bunga-

low in the distance. What was she doing up at this hour? Working out? Or did she have somebody in there?

The more he knew of her, the more he worried about what she was capable of. Whatever was necessary to get what she wanted, she would do. If there was any truth to what Alicia claimed, Karla had to be behind it. Clearly she was taking steroids. That body didn't happen without some help. She probably took other performance-enhancing chemicals, too.

Could she be selling whatever illegal substances she was taking, convincing De Leon's patients that they should use them if they wanted to be like her? She could be very persuasive. He knew that from personal experience. Was that how she was getting the money she needed to pay for her Olympic dream? Steroids had produced violent outbursts in athletes. Could they also cause someone to commit suicide? Could they cause a woman to murder her husband?

If Lita took steroids and that was what made her violent, they would show up in her blood tests. That would be in her chart. Paul would know the answer to that before the night was over.

He reached the medical building and let himself in. He left the lights off. After what had happened to Alicia last night, he had a feeling Karla might be prowling the grounds again, and he did not want to deal with her tonight. He'd brought a penlight with him. He went right to the D section of the files to get Lita Davis's chart.

It was gone.

He stood in the darkness, staring at the files, confused and growing worried. This made no sense. He searched through the nearby files, thinking it might have been misfiled. He even checked under "L." It was not here.

He'd never seen Nicole Quinn's chart so he didn't know if that existed. But he had seen Lita Davis's chart. His own notes were in it. So why was it missing? Just like Doug Collins's chart. Someone had taken it. But who? Karla? Ethan? One of them for sure. But which one?

Paul left the medical building. The light was still on at Ethan's house. He considered going over there and asking

Ethan about it right now. He and Ethan had a history to-gether; Ethan owed it to him to tell him the truth.

But the only reason Ethan would be up at this hour was if Zack was sick, so this wasn't the time to barge in and question him. Tomorrow would be better.

Paul headed back to his bungalow. As he walked down the path, he saw that Karla's bungalow was dark now. He couldn't confront her tonight either. Not that it would do any good if he did. She was angry at him for last night and surely wouldn't tell him the truth. He wanted to believe that she, not Ethan, was the one behind the missing charts. But it would have to wait until morning.

He went back to his bungalow and sat in the darkness, feeling guilty about having exploded at Alicia this morn-ing. She might have been telling the truth after all. He checked the clock. Two A.M. Eleven at night in California. She might still be up. But what would he say to her? For starters how about I'm sorry? . . .

He debated for a few minutes whether or not to call her, then he finally picked up the phone, got her number from directory assistance, and called. Her answering machine picked up. He left a message, asking her to call him. He waited in the darkness, hoping she'd call tonight.

The phone rang, awakening Paul. He peered at the clock. It was a quarter after nine in the morning. He couldn't be-lieve he'd slept so late. He grabbed the phone, hoping it was Alicia.

"Could I speak with Dr. Tobin?" a woman said.

Paul was disappointed. "Yes. This is Paul Tobin," he said.

"This is Susan Polk, from the Los Angeles Medical Ex-aminer's Office."

She confirmed what Paul already knew, that a woman named Nicole Quinn had committed suicide several weeks ago. But she also told Paul that Ms. Quinn did have a sister named Alicia Fernandes, whom she'd met. Paul described Alicia to Dr. Polk.

"That's her," she said.

Polk was willing to share the results of the autopsy. She hadn't found anything remarkable. Cause of death was trauma from the impact of the sixteen-story fall. The decedent's body had been badly disfigured, but the medical examiner was able to retrieve all of the internal organs. Dr. Polk did an extensive examination. No narcotics or alcohol were on board. No steroids or unusual chemical substances. No obvious fatal illness. There was an indication of a possible bone marrow transplant, which would indicate a past episode of cancer, but that was unsubstantiated at this time. The mark could have been the result of the decedent being a donor for someone else.

"Do you know if she was depressed or had any mental health issues?" Paul asked.

"Obviously that doesn't show up in an autopsy," Polk said. "But according to her sister, the answer is no. The decedent was not depressed or mentally ill."

The tox screens showed elevated hormone levels, which suggested to Paul that Nicole had in fact been a patient here. More of Alicia's story was looking true. But Polk could offer nothing that would support Alicia's claim that some drug her sister had received at De Leon was responsible for her killing herself.

Polk said she'd let him know if she learned anything else, but Nicole's case was not high priority. "There was a witness to her suicide," she said. "Alicia was right there watching when it happened."

Paul was stunned. He hadn't realized that. How horrible it must have been for her to see her sister die. He felt even worse for doubting her. He hoped to see her again so he could apologize.

After he hung up, he sat in his bungalow, running it all through his head again. If Nicole Quinn had been a patient, why had Ethan lied about that? What was he hiding? *A secret therapy?* Alicia said Doug Collins told her such a therapy existed. Could that be true? Could that be the answer to all these questions?

Perhaps it was time to talk to Doug Collins.

Paul was scheduled to operate on Leito Pelez in half an hour. He'd have to wait until afterwards to talk to Collins or Ethan. But before the day was over, he was determined to do both, determined to have some answers.

48

ZACK WAS TOO weak to come out of his room for breakfast, so Ethan brought a bowl of his favorite cereal and a glass of Ensure to the boy's bedroom. He sat beside the bed, sipping his coffee as Zack managed to eat a few spoonfuls of Fruit Loops. He didn't touch the Ensure. He had no appetite this morning, no energy, none of his usual spirit.

It worried Ethan.

Zachary was deteriorating even more rapidly than Ethan had thought. Time was running out.

Just hold on until tomorrow morning. Then he'd have the results of Kenny's blood tests and he'd know if he could give Zack Rejuvenol, and in what dose. *Just a little longer . . .*

Ethan coaxed Zack to drink a few sips of the Ensure. Then Zack wanted to go back to sleep.

"How about sitting outside for a little while?" Ethan said. He thought the fresh air and some mild morning sunlight might do him some good.

Zack just shook his head—he didn't want to leave his bed. He only wanted to sleep. He was already starting to nod off.

It was not like Zack to stay in bed. In the past, no matter how sick he was, he always wanted to get up and do something. He had more fight in him than Ethan had ever seen in anyone else. But today that seemed to be fading.

Ethan checked Zack's vital signs, which were discouraging. He stayed as long as he could, but he had a new patient coming in this morning. He figured the exam and sales pitch would only take an hour or so, and he needed the money to continue caring for Zack. Perhaps later, if Zack slept for an hour, he'd feel strong enough to get up.

Ethan told Carmen to watch Zack closely and call him if he got any worse. He was at the door about to leave when the phone rang.

"I'll get it," he told Carmen.

He answered it in the living room. A familiar voice came over the line. "Ethan, we have to talk."

Ethan was surprised that James Medford would be calling him. Medford was the director of Manhattan General's trustees. He and Ethan hadn't spoken since the blowup over the Paul Tobin incident. What on earth could Medford want now? Ethan had other things on his mind at the moment—Zack, Alicia Fernandes, Karla becoming out of control. He wanted to dispense with Medford quickly.

"Jim, I'm in the middle of something," Ethan said. "Can this wait?"

"No. I really need to talk to you."

The urgency and concern in his voice told Ethan that this was important, at least to Medford. But the two of them probably had far different priorities.

"Why don't you call my office," Ethan said, "and set up an—"

"Please, can we talk now?"

There was a timbre of fear in Medford's voice. Something was definitely troubling him. Maybe it was important. After all, Medford wasn't the type of person to call, especially after the heated argument he and Ethan had had over the incident, unless it was something truly urgent.

Ethan sat down. He'd have to hear Medford out, but he'd make sure it was brief. "What is it, Jim?"

"I got a call last night from a man who claimed to be the medical director of an HMO in Illinois."

Ethan was losing interest already. "Look, Jim—"

"Wait, Ethan. Hear me out. The man wasn't who he said he was. The number on my caller ID was for a private investigator in Los Angeles."

As soon as Ethan heard this, he sprang up off the sofa. The call had to be connected to Fernandes. One of her associates in Los Angeles, no doubt.

"What did he want? Did he ask about me?" Ethan said. He hoped to God Medford hadn't told him anything.

"He didn't ask about you," Medford said. "He was asking about Paul Tobin."

Damn it! That was even worse. If Fernandes dug too deeply, and she was definitely the type of person who would do that, she would learn about Paul's dismissal, learn about Wilkenson, perhaps even uncover the truth about what had happened three years ago. At the very least that would bring attention and pressure on De Leon, interfering with what he needed to do to keep Zack alive. At the worst Ethan could end up in prison. He'd be unable to care for Zack, which would be a death sentence for his son. Ethan couldn't let that happen.

"What did this investigator want to know?" Ethan asked.

"He said he was considering hiring Paul Tobin and he wanted to find out the details of Tobin's dismissal from MGH."

"He knew about the dismissal? That was supposed to be sealed."

"Well, somehow this guy unsealed it."

"What did you tell him?"

"Obviously I didn't tell him anything," Medford said, sounding offended by the question. But Ethan didn't care. He'd offend Medford and whoever else he had to in order to protect Zack.

"Did this guy *unseal* Wilkenson's file just like he unsealed Paul Tobin's disciplinary action?" Ethan asked.

"No, of course not. Those records are secure."

"Are you sure?"

"Of course I'm sure. The problem isn't on *this* end, Ethan," Medford said.

Ethan didn't like the way that sounded. Medford's tone

was accusatory, almost disdainful. "What is that supposed to mean?" Ethan said, challenging him.

Medford hesitated. "It's just that . . . well, your relationship with MGH didn't end on the best of terms," he said, struggling for the right words. "And since you were on the board when the incident with Tobin occurred, and since you were the lone dissenting voice on the board, I just thought . . . if this person calls you about the incident . . ." Medford hesitated again, laboring for a tactful way to broach what was on his mind. "Well, let's just say I didn't know if you were still upset with the hospital over what had happened and if you were at all open to . . ." Medford couldn't find the right word, but Ethan understood what he was saying.

"I'm not looking for revenge," he said. "You didn't fire me. I resigned, remember? I'm not out to get you, if that's what you're worried about."

"I wouldn't put it that way . . . exactly. I just mean, the incident happened a long time ago. We'd just as soon leave it in the past. I guess I wanted to know how you felt about that."

"Don't worry, I don't intend to talk to any investigators."

"Well, I am relieved to hear that," Medford said. "You know," he said, taking on a friendly tone now, "I always had great respect for you, Ethan. I may not have agreed with all of the stands you made but I—"

"I have to go," Ethan said. He didn't have time for Medford's ass-kissing.

"I understand that you're busy. How's the clinic down—?"

Ethan hung up before Medford could even finish the question. He had no time for small talk either. He had a problem. A big problem. Fernandes was still looking into the death of her sister. Karla had said that Fernandes would be preoccupied with what had happened to Collins; the police would keep her busy. Obviously Karla was wrong. Ethan realized that he'd have to take care of this himself.

Fernandes's search had led to Manhattan General. Wilkenson's records were still locked away in that hospital. If she got hold of those records, there was no telling what she'd be able to extract from them. Considering what she possibly learned about her sister from the autopsy, she might be able to put two and two together. She was certainly intelligent enough to figure it out. But was she cunning enough to get to those records? Ethan feared that the answer was yes.

He had to do what he should have done three years ago.

He picked up the phone again and called his assistant. "Reschedule all of my appointments today. I can't see anyone," he said.

"But Mr. Allen is already—"

"Just do it!" he shouted. He calmed himself and said, "Please, just do it. I'm not feeling well enough to see patients today."

"I understand, Doctor."

The next call he made was to U.S. Airways. He booked a seat on the next flight from Key West to New York, and a seat on the last flight back tonight. He talked to Carmen; she agreed to put off her usual weekend trip to Miami until tomorrow. Then he went in to see Zack and explain that he had to take a quick trip.

The last thing he wanted to do was leave his son, even if for only half a day. But he had to take care of this "problem" in New York because it threatened Zack's well-being. It was too important to trust anyone else to do it for him.

49

THE RECONSTRUCTIVE SURGERY turned out to be more complicated than Paul had anticipated. Once he made the incision in Leito's skin and saw that the cartilage damage was more extensive than he'd originally thought, he realized he was going to be here for a while.

Several hours into the surgery a powerful urge to duck out and have a drink came over him. It wasn't just desire; it was utter, desperate need. The few shots the other night had opened a part of him that he'd managed, with over two years of hard work, to close up. Suddenly he felt unsure of himself, fearing his hands were going to become unsteady if he didn't have a shot now.

He tried not to think about it and focus instead on the procedure he was doing, but the craving wouldn't subside. Every fiber in his body said, *Get out and find a bottle!*

He asked Rita, his surgical assistant, to towel off his forehead, using that as an excuse to stop for a moment. He drew a deep breath of the cool air conditioning. *Fight it! Be strong.* But the fear of doing something that would hurt Leito made the impulse to drink even greater. The work he was doing was precise, delicate. If he slipped, even just a bit . . .

Wilkenson.

He stopped again. Rita looked up at him. "Is everything all right, Doctor?"

He nodded. *Get a hold of yourself. You can do this.* He hadn't had the chance to visualize this procedure last night or this morning. He felt like he'd never done this before; suddenly he wasn't sure what to do. What if something unexpected developed? How would he handle it? They were half an hour, at least, from the nearest hospital. What if he killed this boy?

"Doctor?" Rita said again.

He realized he was just standing there, staring, thinking. He took a deep breath. *You can do this,* he told himself again. "Scalpel," he said, reaching out. As Rita placed it in his palm, he looked down at his hand. *Steady.* He remembered the ritual. He held the scalpel out over the surgical area, trying not to be too obvious about what he was doing. He stared at his hand. *Steady as could be.*

He could do this. He swallowed against the dryness in his mouth and throat. The craving for a taste of scotch stayed with him, but he managed to concentrate on the operation. The craving was like a throbbing headache. If ignored, it could be endured—but it wouldn't be appeased and go away.

He finished the surgery late in the afternoon, exhausted. He sat with Leito's parents in the waiting room for a few minutes, assuring them that all had gone well and that their son was going to be fine. When they went into the recovery room to see him, Paul went to his office and collapsed behind the desk.

A moment later Stacy, his office assistant, came in carrying a large envelope containing X rays. She saw Paul slouched in his chair, his head arched back.

"Sorry to disturb you, Doctor," she said. "I have the X rays for tomorrow's surgery. I'll just leave them over here." She put them on the edge of the desk. "You can review them later."

Paul was too tired to sit up. "Thanks." He closed his eyes and sighed. "What time is it scheduled for? I hope it's not too early." He hadn't had a good night's sleep in two days.

"Nine in the morning," she said. "But if you want, I can call Ms. Davis and reschedule it for a little later."

"No, that's all right, I—"

Suddenly the name registered. Paul sat up and grabbed the envelope. "Lita Davis?" he said.

"Yes."

"Is her chart in here?" That would explain why it wasn't in the records room last night. Maybe there wasn't a cover-up going on after all.

"No, just the films you ordered," Stacy said, destroying his illusion that nothing was wrong. "I've sent a request to the records department for her chart. They're having difficulty locating it, but I'm sure they'll send it over soon. Should I call her and see if she can reschedule?"

"No." He opened the envelope and pulled out the X rays. How symbolic. The skeleton of information about her. Nothing of her life. Nothing of the therapies she underwent, trying to make herself happy again. Nothing to explain her tragic end.

"Are you sure you don't want me to try to reschedule?" Stacy asked.

"Ms. Davis won't be coming for surgery tomorrow," he said. "She died yesterday."

"Oh, my gosh. I hadn't heard. What happened?"

"That's what I'd like to know." Paul stared at the X rays, wishing they could somehow tell him about Lita, somehow explain what she had done.

Stacy stood there, not knowing what to say. Finally she said, "I'll notify Rita about the cancellation. And tell the records department to cancel the request for her chart."

"No. If they find her chart, have them send it over anyway." But he doubted they'd find it.

He sat back, still holding the X rays, gazing at the incomplete image of the woman he'd met and admired. How could this be all that remained of her visit here? He was about to put away the X ray when he noticed a dark spot in the frontal lobe area. He walked over to the viewer, turned on the light, and placed the film under the clips.

"What is it?" Stacy asked.

That was what he wanted to know, too. He stared at the film, trying to make sense of that spot on her frontal lobe. *It shouldn't be there.* He removed the film and put up another, a different view of the same area. The same spot was there. *What is it?*

"Is there something wrong, Doctor?" Stacy asked. She peeked over his shoulder, trying to see what it was.

His mind turned this over and over, trying to understand. She had a tumor in her frontal lobe. The center of the brain responsible for emotional stability, for self-control. Was it possible that the tumor could have caused Lita to snap the way she did? He'd need to speak with a neurologist about it to make sure, but he believed it was possible.

What could have caused the tumor?

That was something he was going to have to find out. Could one of the therapies here be to blame?

Stacy lost interest in the X ray. She shook her head and started toward the door, murmuring, "I can't believe it. Two patients dying in one day."

"What?" Her words drew Paul's attention away from the X ray. "What did you say?"

"Two patients dying on the same day?" she said.

"What do you mean?"

"Didn't you hear?" Stacy said. "That TV weatherman from Tampa was found dead in his condo yesterday. It was on the news this morning."

Collins. His chart missing, too. *A secret therapy.* Lita. The tumor. Suicides. Murder. More deaths. The information was coming too quickly for Paul to assimilate, leaving him stunned and confused.

"What happened?" he asked Stacy.

"I don't know too much. The police aren't saying a whole lot—you know how they can be."

"Was it a suicide?" Paul needed to know if it was connected with Lita and Alicia's sister. And if it was suicide, had Collins developed a tumor similar to Lita's? Had Alicia's sister?

"They didn't say if it was a suicide or murder. But the news said he was killed with a sword. I mean, who kills themselves with a sword, right? That's weird. You know what's even weirder? The police are looking for another patient from here in connection with the death."

"Who?"

"Alicia Fernandes."

It can't be true. "Are you sure?" he asked.

"They said it on the news. The police said they want to question her. They won't come out and say it, but I think they think she did it."

Paul had a different take on it completely. And if he was right, there could be a whole lot more similar deaths. He had to find out—*quickly!*

"Do we have any X rays or CT scans on Collins?" Paul asked.

"I don't know. I can call the records department and find out."

"Do that. ASAP, okay?"

"Sure." Stacy came back in a few minutes later. "It's kind of strange," she said. "The records department can't find Mr. Collins's chart."

Paul didn't think it was strange at all. He knew for certain now that something was going on. And though he really didn't want to believe it, he realized who the missing charts and the "secret therapy" had to involve.

He grabbed Lita's X rays and hurried out, hoping Ethan could prove him wrong.

50

ZACK'S NURSE, CARMEN, came to the door. "Dr. Tobin, it's you." She looked worried. Paul wondered if she had been expecting someone else.

"Is Dr. Granier here?" he asked.

"I wish he was. I don't know what to do."

"What's wrong?"

"It's Zachary."

When Paul went into Zachary's room, he found the boy pale and struggling to breathe.

"How are you feeling, champ?"

Zack shrugged. "Tired," he said, his voice scratchy and faint.

Paul touched Zack's forehead reassuringly. Zack was running a fever. Possibly an infection was beginning somewhere. That was troubling.

"Busy day?" Paul said, trying to put Zack at ease and gather information at the same time. Maybe there was an excuse for his weakness. "Had a little too much fun in the sun?" he said.

Carmen whispered, "He was in bed all day."

The last time Paul had seen Zack, he'd had a lot more energy. His days were unusually active for someone with his disorder. Paul hadn't seen him in a couple of weeks, though, and he was surprised at how much the boy had deteriorated.

He borrowed Carmen's stethoscope and listened to

Zack's heart and lungs. Fluid was building up in his lungs. His heartbeat was fast and thready. Paul wasn't sure if this was normal for Zack. He also needed to find out what meds Ethan had him on, what adjustments he could possibly make.

He motioned to Carmen. They went to the side and spoke quietly. "Did you call Dr. Granier?" Paul asked. "Is he coming over?"

"No. He's in New York."

This surprised Paul. "*New York?* He didn't say anything about going away."

"It was an emergency trip. He had to go at the last minute. With him not here, I don't know what to do with Zachary. And he forgot his cell phone in the rush—I found it on his bureau."

"Don't worry. Everything will be all right."

He asked Carmen about Zack's normal vitals and medications. She showed him a chart, detailing Zack's decline over the last few days. His meds were listed on a chart that she had to fill out every time she administered any drugs.

Ethan had Zack on Lasix, a diuretic for the congestion in his heart and lungs. Carmen had given him fifty milligrams an hour ago. The dose was considerable already, but it could safely be raised on a limited basis. It was important to get that fluid out, to keep him from getting pneumonia.

"Let's give him another fifty milligrams," he told Carmen.

One of the other meds Zack was on was Coumadin, for his heart. Paul left that dose alone for now. He really didn't want to do too much without consulting with Ethan.

"Can you think of any way to get hold of Dr. Granier?" he asked Carmen.

"I don't know," she said. "He didn't leave a number. He said he'd call to check in later."

"When?"

"I'm not sure when."

"When is he supposed to return?"

"Late tonight."

The only other thing they could do right now was try to ease Zack's breathing. Paul and Carmen propped him up a little more and repositioned his oxygen tubes.

Paul didn't want to do anything else just yet, not until Ethan called. If Zack got worse before then, he'd have to try something else, but for now he hoped the oxygen and the diuretic would stabilize the boy.

Paul looked down at Zack. He'd done well for a long time, but he was losing the battle now. Before long he'd need to be in a hospital. Ethan might disagree, wanting to keep Zack near him where he could ensure his care, but if Zack deteriorated much further, he'd need intensive care. This was something else Paul needed to discuss with Ethan. Sometimes when someone is right in the middle of a crisis, they cannot see the obvious.

Carmen gave Zack the diuretic with a couple sips of water.

"Not too much water," Paul told her. They needed to get the fluid out, not add more to his system.

Zack struggled to swallow the pill. He peered up at Carmen. "Where's Dad?" he asked.

"Your dad had to go away for a little while," Carmen said. "But Dr. Tobin and I are here and we're going to make sure everything is all right."

Paul sat on the bed beside Zack.

"Is it time for my shot?" Zack asked Paul.

Paul didn't understand. The chart Carmen showed him didn't mention any injections. He looked up at Carmen. She shrugged and shook her head, gesturing that she didn't know what Zack was referring to.

"What shot is that?" Paul asked Zack.

"The special shot Dad's making. The one that'll make me better."

A shiver ran down Paul's neck. *Secret therapy.* Could it really exist? Or was he talking about the hormone therapies that were administered by injection?

"Do you know what the name of it is?" Paul asked. "HGH, testosterone, DHEA? . . . Do you remember?"

"Those are different," Zack said. He settled back down

on the pillow, looking weak from the strain of raising his head and talking. He needed to rest. But if there was another med that Ethan usually gave him, one that might make him better, Paul wanted to know.

He looked over at Carmen. "Where does Ethan keep the meds?" he asked her.

"Right here." She gestured to the table where the charts and pill bottles were. "When they need to be refilled, the pharmacy that the clinic uses delivers them."

"Not the special shot," Zack said, straining to talk.

Paul leaned closer so Zack wouldn't have to struggle to speak. "Where does he get the special shot?" Paul asked.

"In the laboratory."

Paul looked over at Carmen. "What laboratory?"

She hesitated a moment, looking nervous, then finally she said, "I'll show you."

51

ALICIA WATCHED THE truck pull away into the night
traffic. Suddenly she felt alone and vulnerable. She understood what she was up against. Patients at De Leon were
dying, and someone was trying to conceal it. But how far
would they go to stop her from exposing them? They were
already killing patients; it would be nothing to kill her as
well.

She shuddered as she stood on the sidewalk, skyscrapers
rising up around her, strange faces rushing past. Yes, they
would kill her if they had the chance. She couldn't go to
the police for help. Steve could provide a little information, but she couldn't involve him too much. She was on
her own.

She shook off a shiver and stared at the headlights
streaming past her, the clutter of pedestrians hurrying down
the street. She was still dressed for Florida, not for the New
York chill. She thought about buying a sweater but she
needed the little cash she had on her. She didn't dare use
her credit cards; that would tip off the police that she was
here. So she braced herself against the stiff wind and
headed up Lexington Avenue.

She asked an elderly man dressed in a three-piece suit
and walking with a cane where Manhattan General Hospital was. It was several blocks away but easy to find. She
also asked if he knew where there was a hardware store.
Much closer, he said, and he walked with her to a True

Value. She picked out what she needed, paid cash, then made her way quickly to the hospital.

It was a quarter to eight. The receptionist in the lobby told her that visiting hours would be over in fifteen minutes.

"That's okay. I won't be long," she said.

"What's the name of the patient you want to see?"

Alicia crossed her fingers. "Johnson," she said, hoping there was one.

The receptionist typed it into the computer. "Elaine or Sydney?"

Alicia let out a silent breath of relief. "Elaine."

The woman gave Alicia a visitor's pass. "Take the blue elevators at the end of the hall. Remember, fifteen minutes."

"Absolutely."

Alicia hurried down the corridor toward the elevators. She stopped at the hospital directory she passed on the way. Inpatient floors were seven through ten. Her pass was for the eighth floor. The lower six floors plus two floors belowground contained the various specialties—endocrinology, surgery, pediatrics, etc.—as well as the accounting department, human resources, and patient records. The administration offices were listed on the upper floors, eleven through nineteen. That was where Alicia needed to go.

Two of the elevators were blue and were marked FLOORS s2–10. Two gray doors said STAFF ONLY and required a hospital ID with a magnetic strip to open. Visitors came out of one of the blue elevators as Alicia approached. She stood in the corridor and let the doors close. She gave the elevator a moment to head off toward another floor, then pushed the call button. She glanced back at the gray doors, waiting for someone to come down.

At this hour on a Saturday night, trustees would not be working. The floors with their offices should be empty, unless some ambitious assistant was working late, trying to get a promotion. But it was Saturday. Even the most ambitious administrators took weekends off—she hoped. If she could just get into the staff elevator, she could go up there and try to find out what it was Paul Tobin had done to lose his medical license.

The blue doors opened again: more visitors. Alicia moved forward, as if she were going in, but she let the doors close again and waited for the gray elevator. It was five to eight now. She was running out of time. She needed a staff person to come out of one of those elevators. She pushed the call button again. An announcement came over the PA saying that visiting hours were over, all visitors should leave.

Just then Alicia heard a "ding" behind her. One of the staff elevators opened. She glanced over her shoulder. Two nurses came out, complaining about something. Alicia heard, "I've been doing this too long to have to put up with that," as they headed up the corridor. The gray doors started to close. She needed the nurses to turn the corner. *Come on!* She glanced at the doors. Almost closed. *Hurry!* At last the nurses turned the corner. Alicia darted over to the gray doors and stuck her hand through the opening just in time. The doors jolted open again and she ducked inside.

She pushed 12, the floor where the director's office was. As the doors started to close, a security guard came down the corridor. His eyes met Alicia's. He looked concerned. Did he realize she wasn't staff? She smiled and nodded, as though everything were okay, as though she belonged here. He just stared at her while the doors closed. But at least he didn't try to stop her. She sighed as the elevator went up. She'd gotten past him. The rest should be easier.

The doors opened on the twelfth floor. All of the lights were off, all of the offices dark. She took out the flashlight she'd bought at True Value and shined it up the corridor. The first thing she noticed were the horrible sculptures on the walls, long narrow stone pieces that looked like totem poles and had probably cost the hospital a fortune. *No wonder health care is so expensive.* She walked past the ugly sculptures, shining the light on the office doors. They had gold placards on them. *More wasted money.*

She was looking for the gold placard for the director of the trustees, James Medford. Whatever records there were concerning Paul and the incident that got him fired would likely be locked in his office, rather than in some general records room where lots of people would have access to them.

She found Medford's office at the end of the hallway. The sculpture beside his door was the ugliest and probably the most expensive of them all. It was fashioned out of steel and looked like a dinosaur bone with a fracture in it. She looked away from it and tried the doorknob. As she'd expected, it was locked. She was prepared.

She took out the tools she'd bought at the hardware store and went to work on the lock. Five minutes later she was inside the office, searching through Medford's desk and file cabinets for the information she needed.

52

THE ONLY FLIGHT Ethan could get was a connection through Atlanta into Newark. Due to heavy traffic in the Northeast, the plane circled for an hour over New Jersey. Ethan tried to use the Skyfone at his seat to call Florida before Zack went to bed, but there was some problem with the plane's phone system.

Being unable to talk to Zack made him nervous. What if something was wrong? What if Zack needed him? What if there was a problem and—he had to stop thinking that way. He'd only been away a few hours. It wasn't much different from driving to Palm Beach. He'd be back in Florida before the night was over. Everything would be okay.

When the plane finally landed he felt for his cell phone—and realized it was lying uselessly on his bureau at home. He tried to find a pay phone, but his flight wasn't the only one delayed; the airport was a zoo, with crowds clustered around the pay phones. It took him fifteen minutes to find one that wasn't being used. He grabbed it before anyone else could reach in. He tried to dial and then realized why no one else was using it. No dial tone. The numbers didn't work. It was dead.

He slammed it down, frustrated. He needed to hurry up and do what he came here to do or he'd never make the return flight tonight. So he hustled through the terminal and hailed a taxi to take him to New York. He'd call Zack later on. If Zack was asleep, he'd talk to Carmen to make sure everything was okay down there. Right now he needed to focus on this.

He didn't expect any traffic at this hour but the Lincoln Tunnel was closed due to a truck that overturned earlier. The cabby should have taken the Holland Tunnel but before Ethan realized what the guy was doing, he headed north, taking the George Washington Bridge, through the Bronx and Harlem, then down into the city. Ethan didn't arrive at the hospital until almost eight-thirty.

A security guard stopped him at the door. "Visiting hours are over, sir."

Ethan no longer had his MGH ID. He wasn't going to get by this guard without a lot of trouble, and he didn't want that. He wanted to get in, do what he had to do, and get out without attracting any attention. He could have called one of the people he'd worked with when he was here. They'd have gotten him in. But he didn't want to have to explain why he was here.

He turned and walked back up the block and around the corner to the emergency room. This entrance was open twenty-four hours. And there was usually enough confusion there that the comings and goings of one unremarkable man would not be noticed.

The guard in the ER eyed Ethan as he went to the triage desk. He scribbled a name on the pad, Jim Peters, and walked into the waiting room. About a dozen people were seated there. He took a seat next to three women speaking Spanish. Across from him was a homeless man, asleep and reeking of beer. Two other patients came in after Ethan. The triage nurse appeared a few minutes later and called Jim Peters.

Ethan went over and explained that he was having chest pains, he felt weak, and he was having difficulty breathing. He knew she'd assume he was having a heart attack and give him priority. Within two minutes, the ER nurse came out and took him back into the ER unit. He lay on a gurney and continued the act while the nurse took his vitals and hooked him up to a cardiac monitor. When she left to get the attending physician, Ethan quickly disconnected the electrodes, put his shirt back on, and scampered past the normal confusion of the ER to the door that led into the hospital.

The corridor was empty. The only activity came from the imaging room a few doors from the ER. The technician wheeled a patient out and back up the corridor toward the ER. Ethan nodded to the man as they passed each other, acting like he belonged here. He continued down the hallway to the elevators. Since he didn't have his old ID he couldn't take the staff elevator. The visitors elevators didn't go to the floor he wanted so he had to take the stairway.

He pulled open the heavy fire door and started up the twelve flights of stairs.

53

CARMEN TOOK PAUL down the hallway to a door. Paul tried to open it but it was locked.

"I know where Dr. Granier keeps an extra key," Carmen whispered. "It's in his bedroom, in the bottom drawer of the bureau."

"Will you go get it?" Paul asked.

Carmen nodded and hurried up the hallway. She disappeared into the bedroom.

He wondered how she knew the key was there. As the only one Ethan trusted with Zack, she probably saw a lot more than Ethan realized. But right now Paul didn't care; he was interested in getting into Ethan's lab and seeing if there was another medication that would help Zack.

And if there's a "secret therapy" causing patients to kill themselves.

Zack had called it a "special shot." What did that mean? A prescription medication used to treat the symptoms of Zack's disorder? Maybe there was no shot at all. Carmen didn't know about it. If it was something Ethan used regularly, wouldn't she know?

Again he wondered why Ethan had gone to New York so suddenly. Was it connected with the deaths yesterday? How could New York be connected? More likely it was connected to what Alicia was doing. Ethan had been concerned that she'd find out about Wilkenson; he thought that would lead to something damaging to the clinic. That must be his reason for rushing up there.

Just then it occurred to him . . .

Patients dying. Ethan's bringing him down here, out of the blue. Now Ethan's secret trip to New York. *Could Ethan be setting me up?* Wilkenson had been Ethan's patient, too. Ethan had been treating her for years before she came for surgery, and knew her family. It could not have been easy for Ethan to defend the man accused of killing his own patient. He'd resigned his position at the hospital in protest against the way they treated Paul, and that could not have been easy for him either. He'd given up his job overnight, putting his future and Zack's in jeopardy. Ethan had been alone, with no job and no income, and with a son who required expensive care. All because of Paul.

Did he bear a grudge about this? Had he been waiting all these years to take revenge? Was that why he had brought Paul down here? Was that why he was in New York right now?

That's ridiculous, Paul told himself. Ethan was on his side. He'd gone out on a limb for him three years ago, and again now. Giving Paul this job wasn't totally altruistic—Ethan was going to benefit, too. But he could have hired someone else. What it showed was that he didn't hate Paul, didn't want to hurt him. If he had wanted to see Paul hurt, he could have left him as he was, on the brink of bankruptcy, his life in shambles. That would have been the best revenge.

Carmen returned from the bedroom and handed Paul a single key.

She looked worried. "I just don't want anything to happen to Zack," she said.

Paul understood what she was trying to tell him. "I won't say anything to Dr. Granier, don't worry," he said. "As far as I know, I found this place all by myself and let myself in."

He unlocked the door and eased it open. The smell of chemicals seeped out. Stairs were directly in front of the door. He peered up into the darkness above. A shiver ran through him. As much as he tried to rationalize that he was looking for Zack's medicine, he could not suppress the feeling of uneasiness. A mysterious lab. A special shot. A secret therapy. Patients killing themselves, killing others. Missing charts. Something strange was going on. *Is this where it all originates? Is this where all the answers lie?*

He glanced back at Carmen, who was standing a couple feet behind him. She looked more than just worried now. She looked distraught and anguished.

"Why don't you stay with Zack," he said.

She nodded nervously, looking relieved. She hurried down the hallway, glanced back once, then went into Zack's room. Paul turned to the stairwell. A light switch was on the wall at the bottom of the stairs. He flipped it on.

Upstairs, the glow of lights illuminated the hidden room. From here, he still couldn't see what was up there, what he would find, but he had a feeling that it was going to change everything. He took a breath and started up the stairs.

54

THE FILE CABINET locks were a bit more difficult, but Alicia got them open. In one section marked DISCIPLINARY ACTION she found a few dozen large white envelopes with names printed on them. They were in alphabetical order. She flipped through and came to one marked TOBIN, PAUL MD (COSMETIC SURGERY).

She brought it to the desk and turned on the lamp. The flap on the envelope was sealed closed. They were going to know someone had opened it and read the file. But that couldn't be helped.

She picked up one of the gold pens on the desk and jabbed it into the envelope, then tore it open across the top. She pulled the contents out and placed them on the desk. Several X rays, some medical charts, copies of letters from the hospital to Paul and to the New York Board of Medical Licensure, from NYBML to the hospital and to Paul. There were letters from nurses and other doctors to the hospital. And an autopsy report.

Alicia looked first at the autopsy report. The name of the decedent was Linda Wilkenson. She skimmed down to "Cause of Death":

> Shock due to internal bleeding and infection resulting from puncture wound (length .25 cm, depth indeterminate) to left hip bone.

Alicia stared at the last few words, stunned by what she was reading. A puncture wound to the hip bone? That was the one abnormality that the medical examiner in Los Angeles found during Nikki's autopsy. Could it possibly be . . . ?

She nervously read more. Farther down the page was a space marked "Comments." There, the medical examiner had typed

Decedent's medical records (Man. Gen. Hosp.) support autopsy findings (i.e., incision approx. 1.5 cm in length through the dura of upper left leg) that decedent underwent liposuction surgery sixteen days prior to her demise. Track from scar to tear in muscle tissue and tendons to puncture in hip bone, strongly indicative of possible undetected insult by surgical cannula during liposuction procedure. (Autopsy X ray attached.)

Alicia quickly shuffled through the X rays until she found one labeled NYME. The image on it was of the dead woman's left leg. A small section of the X ray was circled with a black marker and an arrow was drawn pointing to a small dark spot on the patient's hip.

Exactly the same as Nikki's X ray!

She was shocked. It was right there in front of her. Paul had killed this woman. Probably by accident, but he was still responsible for the death. He'd made a mistake during the liposuction and killed her. Then he'd tried to cover it up.

And Nikki? Was that what happened to her? Was that what Paul did? He'd said he didn't operate on her, but that had to be another lie. She'd had the same mark as Wilkenson. He had to have performed liposuction on her, and he must have accidentally punctured her hip bone.

He killed Nikki, the same way he'd killed Wilkenson. And he was the one at Doug Collins's condo, the one who set her up to be blamed for murder. He'd slept with her, then lied to her, then betrayed her. He was a monster. How had she ever let him trick her?

Alicia was disgusted with herself. She should have been

smarter. She would be from now on. She'd start by making sure Paul paid for killing Nikki.

Of course, she thought more rationally, Nikki hadn't died of shock from the puncture the way Wilkenson had. Nikki had committed suicide. Maybe she would have died from the surgery if she hadn't killed herself. They'd never know for sure. The fact remained that Nikki was just as dead as Linda Wilkenson. And Alicia had to keep looking until she found out why. Something at De Leon had caused it. Something Paul Tobin knew about and was covering up. This record proved that.

Alicia shuffled through the rest of the contents of the envelope, finding Wilkenson's medical chart from Manhattan General. She skimmed through it. A little more information might help her nail Tobin. Wilkenson had suffered from non-insulin-dependent diabetes. The chart indicated that it was probably caused by her obesity. The doctor recommended diet and exercise and referred her to the hospital's nutritionist. Wilkenson was on medication for her diabetes.

When Alicia saw the name of the physician who had been treating her for that, she was flabbergasted.

Granier, E. M.D.

Both of them. They're in it together.

Whatever was going on in Florida, whatever had driven Nikki to take her own life, had driven Doug Collins and God knows how many other patients to commit suicide, Paul Tobin and Ethan Granier were both part of it.

I never should have trusted him. I was so foolish. So blind. She'd thought he cared about her. She'd even let herself care about him. *So damned stupid!*

She'd never make that mistake again. Never. Not with him or anyone else.

She was starting to stuff everything back into the envelope so she could take it with her, when the silence was broken by the sound of someone slowly turning the doorknob. *Someone was coming!* She snapped off the light and ducked under the desk to hide.

55

PAUL STARED INTO the small laboratory, surprised at how well equipped it was. The chemical analyzer was state of the art. That alone must have cost ten thousand dollars or more. Then there was that massive Cultrex machine, whatever that was. It had probably cost a small fortune. Just about everything up here was top of the line. This place was better equipped than the lab in the medical building.

Whatever Ethan was doing here was more important to him than what he was doing at the clinic. So what was it?

Paul walked between the lab stations, past the equipment, to the desk set up in the rear of the room. Paperwork cluttered the top—computer printouts, compound analyses, chemical diagrams. A stack of patient charts was on one side.

Doug Collins's name was on the top chart. So his chart wasn't missing after all. Ethan had been reviewing it. But why? And why here, rather than in his office?

Paul opened the chart and skimmed through the progress notes. Collins had been on a full battery of Ethan's antiaging hormones. Pretty much what Paul expected. Most of the patients at De Leon were on the same hormones, just in different dosages. Paul looked for X rays to see if Collins had the same frontal lobe tumor as Lita Davis, but there were no X rays in his chart.

Paul closed the chart and went to the next one. The name

on it was COLLINS, DOUG. He stared at it, confused. He looked at the first chart again to make sure he hadn't somehow put it back on top. No, there were two charts with the same name.

He opened the second chart and skimmed the progress notes. The dates on the entries matched what he remembered of the first chart, but the entries themselves did not refer to the hormone therapies most patients were on. Instead there was a word that Paul had never seen before.

Rejuvenol.

Paul read on. He recognized Ethan's handwriting, detailing the dates and amounts of Rejuvenol that he'd given Collins. But what was Rejuvenol? Paul continued reading, trying to find the answer. Apparently there were different types of Rejuvenol, because Collins had received Rejuvenol[4] and Rejuvenol[5]. Both entries were followed by pre- and postinfusion measurements of cardiac output, blood oxygenation, strength tests, bone density, and cell regeneration, along with tests measuring an array of hormones and enzymes in Collins's system.

The improvements with Rejuvenol[4] were remarkable: Collins's numbers improved in most areas, particularly in the capacity of cells to regenerate. The one exception was cardiac output, which was only slightly improved.

The results of Rejuvenol[5] were even better than Rejuvenol[4]. Even the cardiac output had improved dramatically. Cell regeneration, the body's ability to repair itself, was extremely high. It was as if several years of wear and tear had literally been eliminated from Collins's biological clock. Antiaging to the extreme.

Was this the "special shot" Zack mentioned?

Was it the "secret therapy" Alicia said Doug Collins had told her about?

If these data were accurate, Rejuvenol might be advantageous for Zack. The same improvements Collins had seen were exactly what Zack needed. But what was Rejuvenol? He still had no idea. And why was Ethan keeping it a secret? Maybe to protect it from being stolen by other antiaging researchers or some unscrupulous pharmaceutical company. That made sense. Clearly, Ethan was on to something extremely important with this, and potentially quite valuable. Not just as an antiaging therapy, or even a cure for progeria, but for many illnesses. The possible applications of this kind of cell regeneration were endless.

Suddenly it struck him.

Cell regeneration . . . The problem with substances that cause cells in the body to multiply is that if they can't distinguish between types of cells, they can cause more harm than good. If there are cancer cells present anywhere in the body, cells that may be so negligible in number and slow growing that they would never become cancerous in the person's lifetime, the substance that causes cells to regenerate and multiply could accelerate the growth of the cancer cells. Cancer cells that wouldn't have caused a problem could develop into life-threatening tumors.

Could that be what happened to Lita Davis?

Paul told himself not to get carried away. He didn't even know if Lita had been on Rejuvenol.

He started looking through the rest of the files, wondering if hers was up here. It was the fourth one down. And the fifth one. She had two charts as well. He looked in the Rejuvenol chart. Yes, she had undergone the same bone marrow extraction and the infusion therapy. Could Rejuvenol be responsible for the tumor in her brain? And was that tumor responsible for what she had done?

Paul still had very little proof. And he wanted to give Ethan every benefit of the doubt. He'd have to find out if any other patients had the same type of tumor, if they'd done anything like what Lita had done.

Paul flipped through the other charts. He found one marked QUINN, NICOLE. Alicia's sister. So she had definitely been a patient. Alicia had been telling the truth about everything.

Like Lita, Nicole had committed suicide. The chart confirmed that, also like Lita, she'd been given Rejuvenol— Rejuvenol^3, Rejuvenol^4, and Rejuvenol^5, starting six months ago. But unless there was an X ray or CT scan somewhere, he'd never be able to find out whether or not she'd had the same type of tumor.

He needed to find out what was going on. Patients were dying. Why? He'd need more information. He still didn't know what Rejuvenol was. He counted the files on the desk. Eighteen. That meant there were nine patients on Rejuvenol. He needed to talk to them and start piecing together the truth about what Ethan was doing here.

He collected all the files and went downstairs. Carmen met him in the hallway.

"Did you find the medicine for Zack?" she asked, worried.

"No." He wasn't sure Ethan was giving Rejuvenol to Zack. Nothing up there indicated that he was. He didn't even know where the Rejuvenol was. "Ethan hasn't called?" he asked.

"No. What should I do?"

"I have to go check on something. You keep an eye on Zack. If he gets any worse, call an ambulance and get him to a hospital." If he got any worse, an intensive care unit was the only place that could help him.

"Yes, Doctor," Carmen said. She looked relieved that someone else was making such an important decision.

Paul hurried out into the humid night. It was almost nine. He hoped it wasn't too late to call some of these patients and start getting answers. This was too urgent to wait until tomorrow. If something Ethan was giving patients was causing tumors and these tumors were driving the patients to kill themselves or do God knows what else, action had to be taken immediately.

56

KARLA SHUT OFF the lights and locked the door of her studio. She was soaked with sweat. Her muscles felt pumped and tingling. She felt alive with adrenaline. After a hard workout, she always had too much energy to sit still in her bungalow. She needed to burn it off tonight.

She thought about going for a run on the beach or a late-night swim. A good roll in the sack would be better. But where was she going to get that around here?

She headed across the dark grounds of the clinic, trying to remember if there were any patients she'd assessed to-day or yesterday who might be worth getting to know a lit-tle better. The wannabe bodybuilder from Vancouver. He had a killer body and he seemed to be hung like a horse. But the problem with bodybuilders was that they were too into themselves. They developed those great physiques by being obsessed. But that vanity and self-importance made them rotten lovers.

She remembered that skinny, long-haired actor from New York. His body was nothing special but he had mes-merizing eyes and kind of a rock star appeal. Also, his tongue had to be five inches long. Karla wondered what it would feel like being licked by that.

She started toward the guest bungalows. The actor was in number 2. Why not give him a try? As she headed down the path, she saw Tobin scurrying from the direction of Ethan's house. *What was he doing there?* She ducked into the shadows and watched him hurry up the path toward her. Ethan was in New York. Tobin had no business going to his house.

Could he be nailing the sick kid's live-in nurse?

Karla smiled at the thought of Tobin on top of that petite little Latina woman. Tiny as she was, was she a fireball in bed? Did she scream out in Spanish when she came? Karla had never been interested in her, but she was curious what it was like with a Latin lover.

As Tobin came nearer, she saw that he had something tucked under his arm. He came a little closer and she realized what he had. *Patients' charts.* Was that what he'd been doing at Ethan's? If he'd gotten those from Ethan's, they were obviously the ones Ethan didn't want anyone to see, the ones that would expose what they were doing here. That would ruin everything. She couldn't allow him to do that.

An impulse to attack him came over her suddenly, unexpectedly. Not just attack him—*kill him.* Bash him over the head with something. Get rid of a problem. She felt the emptiness of her hands. She glanced around for a weapon but by then he had rushed past her. She'd lost her chance.

She felt a strange letdown when she saw him hurry away, alive. She wasn't accustomed to failing. It really disturbed her. She should have done it.

Damn!

She watched him scurry like a rat to his bungalow then burrow inside, hiding. The lights glowed in the window. She needed to know what kind of trouble he was stirring up in there.

She came out of the shadows, made sure no one else was watching, then glided up to the window of his bungalow. She saw him sitting at his desk. He had the charts in front of him and was going through them. Then he picked up the phone and started dialing. *That rat bastard!*

He was becoming a problem. He was going to do something that would screw up her Olympic destiny. He had to be stopped. Ethan wasn't here to do it. Ethan didn't have the balls to do it anyway. She did. She could handle him. She would eliminate that threat even if it meant killing him with her bare hands. She just needed the opportunity. She'd had it a moment ago, but she'd hesitated and lost the chance. Next time, she wouldn't let it pass her by. Next time, he was hers.

57

ALICIA HUDDLED UNDER the desk, listening to the door creak open. Had they seen the light on in here, or were they just doing regular security rounds? She prayed that they'd see nothing and leave.

The beam of a flashlight sliced through the darkness of the room. First it illuminated the side wall, then it fixed on another doorway that she hadn't noticed before. She didn't know where it went but she wished she'd seen it a moment ago; she would have hidden in there. Too late to try to get out now. All she could do was stay under here and hope to God whoever it was left without looking.

The beam of light panned across the room and stopped on the file cabinet behind the desk, the one she had been searching. She'd left the drawer open. *Damn it!* The light stayed on the file cabinet. They knew someone was here now. They weren't just going to peek in and leave. They'd check under here. She had to do something.

The light swept across the room and now focused on the desk. She stayed perfectly still, holding her breath. She'd need an excuse for being here. What could she possibly say? They'd never believe her, no matter what story she gave them. They'd call the police; she'd be arrested for Collins's death and locked up in jail. How was she going to prove she wasn't a murderer? No, she couldn't let Security catch her. She needed a plan.

What if it isn't a security guard?

She shuddered at that thought. Then she heard footsteps

entering the room. *Oh, shit!* She had to do something. She couldn't just stay here. She peered at the second door again. If she made a sudden break for it, she'd have the element of surprise on her side and might just be able to pull it off. She still didn't know where it went but she didn't have any other ideas. She'd have to try.

The footsteps continued slowly into the room, pausing every couple of steps as the flashlight beam moved around the darkness, checking different spots in the room. She twisted around so she was on her hands and knees, facing the side door. This would have to be fast. She took a deep breath, tucked the envelope containing the evidence under her arm, and listened to the footsteps start, then stop again. When she saw the beam of light sweep away in the opposite direction, she made her move.

She jumped up and dashed toward the side door. The flashlight beam swept around, illuminating her and the door in front of her. She slammed against it and clutched at the doorknob. It twisted easily. She shoved the door open and was about to rush out when a hand grabbed her shirt and pulled her back into the room, flinging her against the wall. She hit hard, smacking the back of her head against the wood paneling. Her legs gave out beneath her and she crumpled to the floor. For an instant, her vision faded out. She was still too wobbly to stand. Finally she peered up at the man standing over her, shining the flashlight in her face.

"Just stay put," he said.

"Can you shine that light somewhere else?" she said, shielding her eyes.

"Nope," he said. "I had a notion when I saw you go in that elevator that something was fishy."

She still couldn't see him because of the glare in her eyes, but she realized who he was. She had to try to talk her way out of this. Hopefully he wasn't too bright.

"You don't belong up here," he said.

"I beg your pardon," she said, filling her voice with indignation. "I'm Mr. Medford's executive assistant. I not only belong here, I was instructed by Mr. Medford to come here and pick up a file for him." She held up the envelope. "I'm supposed to bring it to his house on Long Island before nine-thirty."

"Where's your ID?"

"I left it in my car. If you don't believe me, you can come down there with me and I'll show you. Okay?"

"You were under the desk," he said. "You gonna tell me that's where the files are kept?"

"No," she said, trying to sound like he was the one doing something wrong. "I was under there because I didn't know who the hell you were or what you were going to do. A woman alone has to be careful. Or didn't you know that?" She needed to put him on the defensive. "Why didn't you identify yourself when you came in?" she asked. "That's what you're supposed to do. That would have saved us both a lot of trouble."

What was going on behind that light? He was silent; confused, she hoped. She had to take advantage of it.

She started to get up. "What is your name, anyway?" she asked in a threatening tone.

"Stay right there!" he ordered. He fumbled to draw his pistol. He leveled it at her.

"What are you doing?" she said.

"You're nobody's secretary. You're a thief. And you're not going to move an inch until New York's finest come up here and haul your ass off to jail. Now for starters, I want that envelope you're holding."

He transferred the flashlight to his armpit so he'd have a free hand. He reached toward her. "Hand it over."

She didn't have any choice. She gave him the envelope. There had to be a way out of this. She glanced back at the door, too far for her to try another break for it.

The guard tucked the envelope under his armpit with the light then took out the walkie-talkie that was holstered on his belt. He pressed the call button. The radio beeped. He spoke into the mouthpiece. "This is Armstrong. Central, you there?"

A moment later the radio chirped again and a scratchy voice came through the speaker. "Go ahead, Armstrong."

"Wait," Alicia said. She needed to convince him not to turn her in. Maybe if she explained everything to him, he'd have a little pity. Probably not. Flirting might get her further. "Do you have to do that right away?" She tried to muster a sexy voice and expression.

"Nice try," he said, then depressed the talk button. The radio chirped. "Yeah, listen," he said into the radio. "I've got a—"

It happened so suddenly that Alicia didn't see it coming. All she saw was a blur in the darkness behind the guard, then an object smashing into the side of his head. A ghastly *crack* echoed through the room. The man flopped sideways, dropping the light and gun. The instant before the light hit the floor, Alicia saw the figure of someone standing behind the guard, wielding the sculpture that had hung in the hallway. She couldn't see him clearly enough to make out his face. But she didn't linger long enough to try. She saw the door to the side, sprang up, and stumbled toward it.

When the light smacked the floor it broke. The room went dark instantly. Alicia kept running. She slammed into the door. She ignored the pain and fumbled in the darkness for the knob. The attacker's footsteps clambered toward her. She only had a second. She tugged at the doorknob but her hands slipped off. *Oh, no!* She trembled, realizing she was too slow. She braced herself to be hit.

The attacker snorted. His feet scuffled. Then Alicia heard the thud of a body hitting the floor right next to her. She let out a frightened yelp. He'd tripped over the guard. She saw the vague outline of his body. His hands reached toward her. She grabbed the doorknob again and this time turned it. He grasped her ankle. She kicked herself free and pushed open the door. A conference room was on the other side, dark and empty. Another door was on the opposite side of the room. That had to lead to the hallway. She bolted through the room, flinging the door closed behind her.

When she reached the far door, she heard him throw open the door she'd come in through. She looked back and saw his dark frame limping toward her. She yanked open the door and rushed out into the hallway. The glowing exit sign was at the end of the hall to the left. She sprinted all the way, then glanced back and saw the dark figure stagger out of the conference room. She still couldn't see who it was. She shoved open the door and rushed into the stairwell. To the side of the door was a glass wall box containing a fire hose. She ripped open the door, pulled out the hose, and wrapped it around the doorknob. She wrapped the other around the stairway railing and quickly tied it off. Just then he tried to pull open the door. The hose held it shut.

She rushed down the stairs, her heart still racing, blood and adrenaline coursing through her body. All she could think of was getting away. Not until she was out of the hospital and several blocks away did she realize that she had left behind the evidence that would help prove what Paul Tobin and the rest of the people at De Leon had done to her sister.

58

THE FIRST PATIENT Paul called was a woman living in London. He hadn't even thought about the time difference until the woman's husband answered the phone, obviously awakened from sleep, muttering, "What time is it?"

Paul did the calculation quickly in his head. Six hours ahead. Three-thirty in the morning there. He apologized then asked if he could speak with Darlene Perkins. Mr. Perkins wanted to know why the hell an American man was calling his wife at three-thirty in the goddamn morning.

Paul heard a woman's groggy voice say, "I don't know any Paul Tobin."

"She doesn't know you," Mr. Perkins said, "so don't call back." And he hung up.

The next call was to a man in Arizona. It was only six-thirty there. Paul got the man's answering machine. Figuring the guy might still be at work, Paul left a message, asking him to call back as soon as possible. But Paul couldn't count on that. He had to keep trying other patients.

The third patient was a man in New Jersey. Someone answered the phone, which was a good start, and he didn't sound like he'd been asleep, which was even better. Paul heard the sound of a TV in the background, crowds cheering for some sports event.

"Could I speak with Justin Pike?" Paul said.

"Not here."

"When do you expect him back?"

"I don't. Not anytime soon anyways. 'Bye."

"Wait. This is important."

"Whatever you're selling, he ain't buying."

"I'm not selling anything. My name is Paul Tobin. I'm a doctor at the clinic in Florida where Mr. Pike is a patient."

"Oh, you're his doctor," the man said, his attitude changing completely. "Sorry, I thought you were one of those telemarketers. They're always calling. Anyway, yeah, Justin's not around. I guess you didn't hear?"

Paul braced himself. He knew what was coming. Justin killed himself. "Hear what?" he asked.

"Justin was arrested in Boston a couple months ago. Dude just snapped at the airport and killed his old lady, threw her ass out a damn window."

"What?" The way this guy blurted it out, it sounded ludicrous.

"For real. Talk about being pissed, huh? They got him in jail up there, gonna try him for manslaughter."

Paul couldn't speak. A gale of thoughts swirled around in his head. Another patient of Ethan's, not a victim of suicide, but involved in an incident in which someone was killed. Another patient on Rejuvenol who just snapped. *Snapped.* Like Lita Davis, who killed her ex-husband then killed herself. And Alicia's sister, who jumped from her balcony. All were on Rejuvenol. That couldn't be coincidence.

Snapped. That was the perfect description. That's what it had to be, to do something like throw someone out a window, shoot your husband and yourself, jump from a sixteen-story balcony. All restraint gone, all control lost. Instinct only, going on primal urge. Whatever thought that crossed the mind took over. It couldn't be controlled. Just acted on. *Snapped.*

"What happened?" Paul asked.

"You ask me, I think it was that shit he was taking," the man said.

"What do you mean?" Paul had a pretty good idea what the guy meant but he preferred to let him do the talking. He wondered if this guy, whoever he was, was a Rejuvenol patient, too. Paul started shuffling through the charts again, looking for another patient living in New Jersey.

"By the way," Paul said before the man could respond, "what was your name again?"

"Vinny. I'm Justin's roommate."

There was no chart for a patient named Vinny or Vince or Vincent living in New Jersey or anywhere else. So Pike's roommate wasn't a patient, at least not one taking Rejuvenol. But as Pike's roommate, he might know what Pike was taking. It sounded like he did, and it sounded like he'd figured out that Rejuvenol was what had driven Pike to kill his girlfriend.

"Okay, now what were you saying?" Paul asked.

"Just that Justin was definitely juicing."

"Juicing?" Paul asked.

"Yeah, you know, steroids. That shit can give you a real nasty disposition. But you know that, you being a doctor and all."

Paul knew it. And he'd suspected steroids or something like that. But now he was growing certain that it was Rejuvenol, whatever Rejuvenol was.

Vinny continued. "Justin used to be a really mellow dude. But then he one-eightied."

"One-eightied?"

"Yeah. You know, a hundred-and-eighty-degree change. He became real aggressive and short tempered. He and I got into it pretty heavy a few times, nothing physical, but it got pretty close. And not just with me. I heard him one time light into his agent over the phone. Man, if he could have crawled into the phone and come out the other end, he'd've done it and pounded his agent. So yeah, he changed completely. 'Roids'll do that. And second, a dude's body don't change the way his did unless you're getting chemical help. You know what I mean? He was a pretty scrawny dude eight months ago. All of a sudden he gets buffed, like he's been pumping iron all his life. Steroids, man. Had to be."

"Do you know if he was taking anything else?" Paul asked.

"I know he was doing testosterone. I think that has the same effect as 'roids, right? Makes you look good, but does a number on your personality. He was doing some other shit, too. A whole alphabet of vitamins and hormone supplements. He got them down there in Florida. What the hey, it worked for him, right? He looked a lot better." Then he quickly said, "Not that I'm gay or nothing like that. We're not that kind of roommates."

"I understand."

Vinny went on. "I'm just saying that Justin's all buffed and looking ten years younger, that's all. So that stuff he took did what he wanted. He got a movie role in France, some big-deal modeling gigs, more young tail than you can imagine. But if you ask me, I think it fried his brain. I told him when I talked to him on the phone a month ago or so, to tell his lawyer to plead diminished capacity. Jury might buy it. Lotta liberals in Massachusetts. It's worth a shot, right?"

"How certain are you that he did it?" Paul asked. He needed to make sure this had actually happened, that it was not just alleged. "That he killed that woman?"

"Put it this way, they got about a hundred witnesses who saw him push her out the window," Vinny said. "That's pretty strong evidence."

"Yeah, I guess so."

"But hey, nothing comes without a cost, right? Justin got the body he wanted, but he paid the ultimate price for it."

It sounded like the girl he killed was the one who paid the ultimate price.

Paul called the Suffolk County Jail in Boston, where Pike was being held. They told him prisoners couldn't take calls, even from their doctors. But Pike could have a visit from his doctor if it was related to preparing his defense.

Paul called U.S. Airways. They had a late flight leaving tonight from Key West. If he hurried, he could get there in time to make the flight. He booked a seat then called for a taxi. The dispatcher said the cab would be there in twenty minutes.

He tried Alicia's home and got the machine again. He didn't think she'd be there but he wanted to try anyway. He wanted to apologize. He should have believed her from the beginning. If he had, she might not be wanted for murder right now. He wondered where she was and hoped she was okay.

He'd started to pack a few things for the trip, when he heard a noise outside his window, a sharp snapping sound like someone stepping on a stick. He turned toward the window. All he could see was his own reflection in the glass. But he was sure he'd heard something out there. He went to the window and peered out. He didn't see anyone, didn't hear anything except the sound of the ocean and the noise of insects. All the same he was sure someone was out there, watching him.

59

KARLA GRABBED A coral stone by her feet. In her mind, she could see herself swinging the rock, feel it bashing the side of Tobin's skull. It sent a rush of adrenaline through her body, a strange high. She really *really* wanted to kill him.

She remained crouched behind the scrub palms at the side of his bungalow, watching him as he came out of the doorway and looked from side to side. In the darkness, he couldn't see much. He surely couldn't see her. If there wasn't so much brittle flora on the ground, she could easily sneak up behind him and crack his head open.

He was becoming such a big problem that something had to be done. Now was the time, before Ethan came back. She would do it. At the right instant. As soon as he went to sleep. Yes. She'd let herself into his bungalow and plant this rock deep into his skull. *Bam!*

The problem would be explaining it to the police. But she'd figure out a way to cover it up, make it look like an accident.

Tobin stepped out a little farther and moved toward the window where she'd been standing a few moments earlier, watching him. He moved slowly, cautiously. He was worried about being jumped. The paranoid bastard.

But that gave her an idea. She could claim that an intruder had been prowling around, looking for drugs. Tobin caught him, they struggled, and he killed Tobin. The cops would believe that. Now she just needed the opportunity.

Right now would be fine. If Tobin came closer, she wouldn't even have to wait for him to go to sleep.

He checked the area around the window, bending down and inspecting the ground. Then he looked up and scanned the darkness again. He started toward the side of the bungalow, where she was hiding. This was her chance. *Yes. That's it. Come over here.* . . . She gripped the rock tightly, watching, waiting for just the right moment. *Keep coming. A little closer.*

The phone in his bungalow rang.

He turned and scampered back inside, like he was expecting an important call.

Damn it! So close. That was what made it so aggravating. She stood up and crept to the window. Who was he expecting a call from? She peered in and saw him on the phone. She could barely hear his voice from here.

"Yes, I called for a taxi. Oh, okay, I'll be right there."

He stuffed the last few things into his bag and hurried out. Where was he going? She started around the corner toward the door to jump him but he was already out and running up the path.

She followed him to the reception building and hid around the corner while he got into his taxi. Wherever he was going, it was not good. She should have killed him when she had the chance.

She waited until the taxi pulled out and went over the bridge, then she jumped into her Jeep and followed.

The taxi went all the way up A1A to Key West. Karla kept a safe distance behind, where she wouldn't be noticed. The cab went straight to the airport and let Tobin off at the U.S. Airways terminal. Karla pulled into short-term parking, put on the warm-up suit she kept in the back, grabbed her wallet out of the glove compartment, and went inside through a door farther down the terminal. The place was crowded and noisy. Something was going on. Then she remembered the hurricane. This was the first wave of evacuees.

Tobin was at the ticket counter. She watched while he made his way through the line, got his ticket, and checked his bag. He headed toward the security checkpoint. She needed to know where he was going. Leaving in the middle of the night like this could not be good. All those phone calls. The patients' charts he'd taken from Ethan's house. He was up to something.

She cut to the front of the line, saying, "Excuse me. This is urgent." Some people waiting grumbled but she ignored them and went to the same ticket agent who'd checked Tobin in. "Just a minute," the woman said. She was putting Tobin's bag on the conveyer belt. Karla leaned over the counter and tried to see the tag on the bag. As it crept away, she spotted BOS on it. The ticket agent came over. "Can I help you?"

"What's B-O-S?" Karla asked.

"Excuse me."

"B-O-S. What city is that?"

"Boston."

"Are you the only airline that flies there from here?"

Karla found a flight on Delta that went through Atlanta and arrived in Boston within minutes of Tobin's flight. She had to run to make it. The gate agents were already closing the doors when she got there.

"Wait!"

"It's your lucky day," the guy said to her.

He let her in and she boarded the plane, the last passenger on. It was her lucky day. And it was only going to get better once she took care of Tobin. She had three hours to decide how she was going to do it.

60

ETHAN WAVED DOWN a cab on Fifty-seventh Street, out of breath after running several blocks from the hospital. He scrambled into the cab and slammed the door. He peered back to see if any of the MGH security guards or the police were chasing him. No one. *Yet.* But they would be if he stopped. He had to keep moving.

"Let's go," he told the cabby through the Plexiglas divider separating him from the front seat.

"Go where?" the cabby said.

"Just go!"

The cabby shrugged and pulled out into the light flow of traffic. He peered at Ethan through the mirror and said, "What did you do, rob a bank?"

Ethan trembled. Why would the cabby ask such a thing? "No, of course not," he said.

"It was just a joke," the cabby said. "You know where you want to go yet?"

Ethan didn't know where to go. He was desperate to find Alicia Fernandes. But how? In this city, with the head start she had? Impossible. He peered out the window at the pedestrians on the sidewalks, the lights in the coffee shops, the subway entrances. She was out there somewhere, still a threat.

How the hell did I let her get away? Angry as he was at himself, he rationalized that there was nothing he could do about that now. He shouldn't beat himself up over it. That would only stop him from thinking clearly, from understanding what else she could do to threaten Zack, from figuring out a way to stop her.

He couldn't do anything about the fact that she had gotten away, or anything about the guard back at the hospital. He'd never intended to harm the man, let alone kill him. He didn't think he'd hit him that hard. All he'd wanted to do was to take the guard out of the picture for a few minutes so he could stop Alicia Fernandes from finding out about Wilkenson. He wished the guard had never come up there, wished he could take back what had happened, but there was nothing he could do about it now.

At least he had the envelope Fernandes had tried to take.

He closed his eyes now, trying to think what he should do, where he should go. With his eyes shut, he saw the short hair on the back of the guard's head, saw the sculpture swinging toward it, heard the loud crack, and saw the guard crumple to the floor. Not only saw it . . . he *felt* it, felt the impact, so sweet, like a baseball player connecting with a fastball for a home run.

Strangely . . . it felt . . . satisfying.

And that really troubled him. How could it possibly feel good to kill someone? How could that sensation leave him satisfied? That was very wrong. The guard hadn't been the threat—he'd just been in the way. Did he deserve to die?

Does Zack?

That's what it always came down to. Zack's well-being or someone else's? . . . He'd always choose Zack's.

"Yo," the cabby said. "Did you hear what I asked? Where you want to go?"

Ethan peered out the front window. The cars, the lights, the people—too much stimulation. He needed a moment to get his thoughts in order. "Go into the park," he said.

The cabby made a face. "At this hour?"

Ethan didn't even bother to answer. The cabby shrugged and said, "It's your dime, pal."

The taxi pulled into Central Park. The dark emptiness gave Ethan a sense of safety. Fallen leaves were blowing across the road. Ethan looked at the envelope in his hands. He'd gone back for it after Fernandes had escaped. Good thing, too. As soon as he saw Paul's name on the outside, he knew what it was. Exactly what he'd feared she'd find. But at least he had it now, and this was the only evidence the hospital possessed regarding the Wilkenson incident. The Medical Examiner's Office and the state licensing board probably still had some records, but only the hospital had the whole thing, only the hospital had enough to expose him. All he had to do now was destroy the evidence, something he should have done three years ago.

The cab was passing through a section of the park where some benches were set up near trees. Someone had dragged a trash barrel near to them and made a fire in it. The fire was out now but the barrel was charred black.

"Pull over," Ethan told the cabby.

"What do you mean? Here?"

"Yes. Pull over."

The cabby shrugged and pulled over. "I've had stranger fares," he murmured.

"Do you have a lighter?" Ethan asked.

"You tellin' me we stopped 'cuz you want to smoke? You should have said so. We didn't have to stop for that. You can smoke in the cab." He shifted the car into drive to pull away.

"No. Stay here."

The cabby let out an annoyed breath as he strained to slide his hand into his pants pocket and pull out a lighter. He passed it through a tiny opening in the Plexiglas.

Ethan shook it. It was full of fluid. Good. "I need to keep it," he said.

"That's the only one I got."

Ethan took out his wallet and pushed a five-dollar bill through the opening in the divider. "I need to keep it," he said again.

The cabby shrugged and stuffed the money into his pocket. "You see anything else you wanna buy," he said, "let me know."

"Keep the meter running," Ethan said.

He got out, envelope in hand, and walked across the grass toward the benches. He shivered in the icy wind. He wanted to run, get it done, and run back to the warmth of the cab. He scanned the darkness near the trees as he made himself walk to the trash barrel. He could smell the dead fire, but the can was cold. It had been out a while.

Inside the barrel were ashes and a couple of empty vodka bottles. This would work fine. He took out the contents of the envelope he'd taken from MGH. First, he crumpled the sheets of paper into balls and set them in the barrel. Then he placed the X rays on top. He rolled the envelope into a long, narrow wand and lit the end. While it was still burning, he hit the lighter on the edge of the barrel twice, stopping when he saw that the plastic was cracked. Then he held it over the crumpled papers and the X ray and broke it open, pouring the fluid onto the evidence. He then brought the flame to the papers. The instant the fire touched the fluid-soaked paper, it all flared up.

"Aaahhhh!" A man leaped up from the darkness behind one of the benches, screaming, apparently frightened by the fire. Ethan lurched backward. The man, dressed in rags, his hair and beard tangled from years of neglect, snatched a blanket off the ground and started to beat out the flames.

"No!" Ethan shouted and lunged at the guy. He tackled him to the ground, smelling excrement and beer. The man squirmed beneath Ethan, struggling to get away. *To get back to the fire and put it out.* Ethan couldn't let him do that. He pinned the man down and began punching him in the face. The man brought his arms up to protect his head, unable to fight back. Ethan felt how emaciated the man was, how defenseless. But he could not stop himself. He kept striking, landing blows against the man's sticklike arms, most getting past to his head. The man shrieked like a wounded animal, but he did not have the strength to get away.

"Hey! Hey! Get off him!" The cabby rushed over and grabbed Ethan from behind, trapping his arms. "You hurt him enough already. Leave him alone." He tugged at

Ethan, trying to pull Ethan off the homeless man. All Ethan could think of was that the cabby was stopping him from destroying the evidence, stopping him from protecting Zack.

Ethan sprang up and wheeled around. He snapped his arms free and swung at the cabby, clipping him in the side of the head. The cabby lurched back. The hit wasn't hard, but it shook up the cabby enough that he scrambled away toward his cab.

"You psycho!" he shouted at Ethan. "You're not getting back in my cab. I'm gonna call the cops."

The cops? No! That was more trouble. Ethan rushed toward the cab to stop the man, but the man ducked inside and closed the door before Ethan could reach him. Ethan grabbed at the door handle. The cabby slapped the lock, threw the car into gear, and sped away, the car bumping Ethan and knocking him to the pavement.

Ethan got up as quickly as he could, his right hip and leg sore. He was ready to go after the taxi but it was already too far away. A moment later it was just red taillights in the darkness. Then it was gone. Ethan turned back around and saw the homeless man staggering away across the park. The fire was still burning in the can. Ethan limped over. The heat of the fire on his skin felt good, safe. He watched as the X rays melted and the sheets of paper turned to ash. He was still pumped with adrenaline. He felt like doing something—striking out, releasing his aggression, something physical. He felt incomplete. As if he'd been stopped in the middle of some strong emotion.

Had he done enough to protect Zack?

He stood alone in the darkness for several minutes after the fire went out, breathing deeply, waiting for the restless feeling to abate. By now he was feeling the chill of the night again. The sweat he'd worked up beating on the homeless man left his skin cold.

The evidence was gone forever. They couldn't use that against Zack anymore.

He looked down. His hands were covered with blood. He'd beaten that man more severely than he'd thought. He knelt down and wiped his knuckles on the grass, trying to get the blood off.

My God, what's happening to me? He dropped his face into his hands and squeezed his head, as though he could rid his memory of what he'd just done. It seemed so strange, so out-of-body. He closed his eyes and saw himself beating that man, as though it had been another person doing the hitting, not him. If that cab driver hadn't pulled him off, he would have killed that man whose only crime was that he was startled from sleep and frightened by the fire.

And I would have killed him . . .

Like I killed the guard.

He peered down at his hands. Some blood still spotted his fingers and nails. He'd killed a man with these hands. And almost killed another. He'd never thought he was capable of doing such a thing. As he sat on the cold ground, a brutal wind scraping over him, darkness closing in around him like a prison cell, he realized that he was very capable of killing again. He had the capacity to lose all self-control. That wasn't like him. But now it *was* him.

The thought crossed his mind . . . *Can it be Rejuvenol?*

No, several patients had taken it and none of them had killed anyone. It couldn't be Rejuvenol. Rejuvenol *saved* lives. But two patients had killed themselves—Nicole Quinn and Doug Collins. Could that be about loss of self-control? Could that be Rejuvenol? *That's different. That's very different.* They'd killed themselves, not other people. They were depressed because of situations in their lives; they were not violent. No, Rejuvenol was good. Rejuvenol was going to keep Zack alive. Rejuvenol was not the problem.

I killed a man. . . .

"No!" he shouted into the empty night.

He looked around again and shivered. He needed to get out of here. This place only made his thoughts race, stopped him from thinking clearly. And if that cabby did call the police, Ethan didn't want to be here when they arrived. How was he going to explain the blood or what he had burned? How was he going to explain the MGH guard? How could they possibly understand about Zack and all the rest?

No, he had to get out of here. Zack was deteriorating. He needed to get back to Florida, review the results of Kenny's blood work, and give Zack the treatment he desperately needed.

He got his bearings by the high-rise buildings in the distance and headed across the darkness.

When Ethan reached Newark, it was shortly after eleven. He paid the cab driver and went inside. The ticket agent told him he'd missed the last flight of the night. Ethan checked the other airlines but none had a flight out before morning. He'd have to wait until six A.M.

He had seven hours to wait. He considered hanging around the airport, but he hadn't slept much the previous night and he was exhausted. That was probably part of why he felt so strange today. He decided to get a hotel room so he could rest and be ready to get right to work when he got back to De Leon tomorrow.

Before he went outside to look for the shuttle, he stopped at a pay phone and dialed his number in Coral Key. Zack would be asleep at this hour, but Carmen should still be up.

There was no answer.

That was strange. Ethan dialed again, thinking he might have dialed it wrong the first time, but still no one answered. He was beginning to worry. Could Carmen be in the bathroom? He waited five minutes, standing beside the pay phone, then called again. Still no answer. *Something is wrong!*

He searched through his wallet for the piece of paper he'd written Carmen's cell phone number on. He found it and dialed that number. On the third ring, Carmen answered.

"Carmen, it's Dr. Granier," he said.

"Oh, thank God you called." She sounded worried. "I didn't know how to reach you."

"What happened? What's wrong?"

"It's Zachary."

61

ALICIA FELT SAFE down in the subway. She'd boarded the first train that stopped, not knowing where she was, not caring where the train was going. She just wanted to get far away from whoever was trying to kill her. Hours later, she was still down there, moving from one train to the next beneath the city, trying to understand what was going on and what she should do now.

The police were probably going to find her fingerprints in Medford's office and blame her for the guard's murder. They already wanted her for Doug Collins's death. Her only way out of this was to prove what was going on at De Leon and who really killed the guard.

Who really killed the guard? She didn't know.

The envelope she'd found would have gone a long way to showing that Paul Tobin was doing something unsavory down in Florida, that he was responsible for Nikki's suicide and Collins's suicide. Could he be the man in the darkness who killed the hospital security guard? Possibly. After all, he was trying to stop anyone from finding that information and connecting it to the deaths at De Leon. Florida was only a plane ride away.

But she'd dropped the envelope back at the hospital so she no longer had the evidence. She needed to find something else. Maybe not a paper trail or X rays, like the evidence from the hospital. Possibly a witness, someone who could fill in the pieces.

That mark on Nikki's hip, the one that matched the mark

on Linda Wilkenson's hip, that was the key. She didn't understand how it had made Nikki kill herself, but she knew it was the link. And that was what Paul was trying to conceal. Odds were that Collins had the same mark. But what did that mark mean? Was it just bad surgery? That didn't make sense. That wouldn't affect a person's state of mind to the point of suicide. There had to be some other significance to it.

It came back again to what Collins had said. The secret therapy. Collins knew, Collins was going to tell her, and now Collins was dead. She needed to find another patient who knew what was going on. Collins couldn't be the only one.

But she didn't know any other patients. And she couldn't go back to De Leon after all that had happened. So how was she going to—?

Then she remembered. She did know one other patient. Rather, she knew *of* another patient. Nikki's agent had mentioned him: the man who had told Nikki about De Leon. Nikki's agent had said that he'd moved back east. She needed to find him. He was her only chance.

Alicia left the warmth of the subway somewhere in Greenwich Village. The night seemed to have gotten colder in the last couple hours. She shivered as she hurried up the sidewalk, looking for a pay phone. She found one outside a small bodega. Two men were huddled by the door, smoking and speaking in a language she didn't recognize. The smell of harsh tobacco made her eyes tear. She didn't feel safe enough to turn her back to them, to the smoke, so she endured it and placed a collect call to Steve's cell phone.

He was sitting in traffic on the Santa Monica Freeway. "I need your help again," she said.

"The LAPD called me," he said. "The cops in Florida contacted them, thinking you were back here. Something about a plane ticket."

"Good. The New York police may call you, too."

"Alicia, what's going on?" He sounded concerned, like a parent, more worried about her than he'd ever been on any of the assignments she'd done for him. "Are you okay?" he asked.

She glanced at the two men by the door. She didn't want them to hear so she covered her mouth and whispered, "They're killing patients, Steve. And they're willing to kill anyone who threatens them."

"You should go to the police."

"They're not going to believe me unless I have proof of what's going on at that clinic. And I can't get the proof if I'm in jail."

"Do you want me to go down to Florida?"

She appreciated his offer but she didn't think that would do any good. "They already know someone's investigating," she said. "They've destroyed the evidence they had and they're definitely on the lookout for someone else showing up."

"What can I do to help, then?"

"I need you to call Nikki's agent for me." She explained what she needed.

"Sure, no problem," he said. He paused a moment then said, "Can I ask you something, Alicia?"

"What?"

He stalled again. Finally he took a breath and said, "You didn't really kill anybody, right?"

The question hurt her. "What do you think?" she said. But then she realized that he had the right to ask; he was putting himself on the line helping her. "No," she said. "I didn't kill anybody."

"I shouldn't have asked," he said. "Call me back in an hour. I'll see what I can find out."

62

KARLA'S PLANE LANDED at Logan Airport at two-thirty in the morning. Terminal C concourse was nearly deserted. All the gift shops and food places were closed. It was autumn up here, and the few people in the terminal had on boots and coats. It was too cold for the light warm-up suit she had on. But she didn't intend to stay here long. Just as long as it took to kill Paul Tobin.

His flight had landed only two minutes ago. She had to find his gate. A Delta agent told her that U.S. Airways used terminal B. A shuttle outside baggage claim would take her there. She ran to the exit. When she stepped outside, the damp, freezing Boston wind bit into her skin. Not since she'd left Germany three years ago had she been in this kind of weather. She hated the cold. Another reason Tobin deserved to be punished, for forcing her to come up here.

Staving off a shiver, she peered past the taxis and hotel shuttles picking up passengers and tried to spot the airport bus. A skycap was leaning on a signpost, smoking a cigarette. She asked him where the bus to terminal B stopped.

"Right here, but you just missed it," he said, pointing to a bus in the distance. "Another one'll be around in fifteen minutes or so."

"Fifteen minutes?"

"This time of night, yeah. Massport doesn't run as many this late."

She couldn't wait that long. Tobin would be gone by then. "Where is terminal B?" she asked.

He pointed off into the darkness. "That way."

"I have to get there in five minutes."

"Is that a joke? It takes the bus a lot longer than that. It's gotta stop at each terminal along the way and let people off and on."

"Can I get there on foot?"

"In five minutes?" He thought about it. "How fast can you run?"

She raced through the central parking garage, following the signs. She crossed the bridgeway over the airport road, then into the smaller parking annex for terminal B. It was half empty now, the cold air smelling of gasoline. She rushed to the crosswalk. U.S. Airways baggage claim was across the street. She started to cross, then saw Tobin come out through the automatic doors of the terminal. Before he noticed her, she ducked behind the Jersey barrier separating the parking garage from the roadway and watched him.

He stood there, waiting. She looked around to see if someone was meeting him. No one was going over to him. Why had he made this trip? She was torn between waiting to find out why he was here and killing him at the first opportunity she had. Some passengers, skycaps, and taxi drivers were scattered across the sidewalk right now. Too many witnesses for her to sneak up behind him and snap his neck here, no matter how badly she wanted to do that. She'd have to wait awhile, at least until he left the airport.

A shuttle bus for the Airport Hyatt came down the roadway. Tobin waved it down and got in. The hotel wouldn't send a shuttle at this hour unless he'd called for it and booked a room. So he was going to a hotel right now, probably to sleep. Whatever he came here to do, he was going to wait until morning to do it.

She watched the shuttle drive off. She didn't bother following. She could find the hotel later. She went inside the terminal, to the first car rental desk she came to. Following Tobin would be much easier if she had a car.

• • •

She drove to the Hyatt a few minutes from the airport. She found a space in the parking lot from which she could see the front door. Now all she had to do was wait until Tobin came out, then take care of him once and for all.

63

IT WAS THE longest night of Ethan's life. He never did leave the airport to find a hotel. Instead he stayed by the pay phone, calling the hospital every half hour to speak with the physicians treating Zack. Key West Community Hospital was a small facility, fine for treating jellyfish stings and sunburn, but not the best place for anything serious. Certainly not the best place for Zack.

The only good thing about that hospital was that it was close to De Leon. Ethan's plane was scheduled to land in Key West a few minutes after nine in the morning. By ten o'clock, he could have Zack back home and receiving an infusion of Rejuvenol. That was what Zack needed.

Ethan was glad that the hospital's staff wasn't sophisticated enough to figure out what he was doing. They wouldn't give him any trouble. They'd discharge Zack to his care. They'd probably be relieved to have a very sick patient taken off their hands. Zack just had to hang on through the night.

The ER attending was the first—and most incompetent—doctor Ethan spoke with. He'd ordered IV Lasix in such a high dose that it would have dehydrated Zack to the point of kidney failure. Zack would have died before the night was over. Ethan had managed to talk some sense into the idiot. Fortunately he was green enough to realize he was in over his head, so he listened. But then the on-call cardiologist, a Dr. Pine, got into the middle of it all. He thought he knew everything and wouldn't listen to a word Ethan said.

"You're a hematologist and you're in New York," he told Ethan. "I'm a cardiologist and I'm here in the hospital with the patient. Let me do my job."

Ethan fired back. "That patient is my son! I'm going to have a say in how you treat him!"

They argued every time Ethan called. Ethan knew this man wasn't going to be able to do anything to help Zack; Ethan just needed him not to do any harm. Zack's only chance lay in Rejuvenol. If the results on Kenny were positive, Ethan would give it to Zack as soon as he arrived in the morning.

But what if Zack couldn't wait that long?

He had an idea. Aside from him, Karla was the only other person who knew about Rejuvenol. Could she give the first dose to Zack, just enough to keep him alive and strong until he could arrive? He could explain exactly what to do. She knew where his lab was, knew where the serums were stored. She was accustomed to injecting herself with hormones and steroids, and she'd seen him administer Rejuvenol to her several times. She should be able to manage.

Yes, he would have her do that.

But he still didn't know if the latest formulation of Rejuvenol worked. He had to find out the test results from Kenny's blood. Karla could do that for him, too. The equipment did most of the work. He could easily talk her through a simple blood analysis.

He dialed the number of her bungalow. The phone rang and rang with no answer. He looked at his watch. It was four-twenty in the morning. She never went into work this early. Could she be training? He dialed the number of her weight lifting room. There was no answer there, either. *So where is she?* He needed her help desperately.

He waited fifteen minutes, thinking she might have been in the shower or out running, then he dialed both numbers again, neither time finding her. He slammed down the phone, frustrated and angry. *Damn her!*

He stared across the empty airport terminal, trying to

figure out what to do. A man in the distance was vacuuming the carpet by another gate. A young couple with backpacks were sleeping on the floor beside one of the windows. Outside, the airport was black, dotted with a series of tiny blue lights. He felt so remote here, so distant from his son, so helpless to do what Zack needed. He couldn't let Zack die.

Paul.

Paul was his friend. He could explain the whole situation, then ask Paul to test the blood. He wouldn't tell him it was Kenny's, not right now, not over the phone, not while he needed Paul to be on his side one hundred percent. If the analysis was positive, he'd ask Paul to go to the hospital and give Zack the infusion.

But could he trust Paul with the knowledge of Rejuvenol? Ethan believed he could. More than he could trust Karla, as it turned out, and he'd told her everything. After all, he was the one who'd given Paul a second chance. Paul would agree to help him—it was the least he could do.

Ethan dialed Paul's bungalow. The phone rang continuously, with no answer. *Son of a bitch!* Ethan grew angrier with each ring that echoed in his ear. *What the hell is going on there?* First Karla, now Paul. *Can't I leave for one day without everything going to hell?*

He hung up the phone and dialed Paul's office, hoping he'd gone in to work early. Again, no answer.

"Damn it!" Ethan said aloud, slapping the receiver back into the cradle. The sound echoed through the deserted terminal. He heard the vacuum cleaner turn off, looked, and saw the maintenance man staring at him. That guy had no idea what he was going through, no idea what it was like to have a son dying and be unable to help him.

He turned back to the phone and tried to figure out what to do.

There was one other person he could call. He dialed Carmen's cell phone. She answered. She was in the hospital, staying with Zack the whole time.

"How is he?" Ethan asked.

"He's resting."

Ethan appreciated all she was doing for Zack. She wasn't just a hired nurse; she genuinely cared. And he knew that Zack appreciated her as well. Ethan was reluctant to let anyone who didn't actually *need* to know about Rejuvenol in on what he was doing, but he decided he could trust Carmen. And he did have to let her in on it, if she was to help him save Zack.

"I need you to go back to the house for me," Ethan said.

"You mean leave Zachary alone here?" she said, sounding worried.

"Just for a little while. This is really important."

He gave her thirty minutes to drive back to the house, then he called her cell phone again. She was just driving over the bridge.

"The water is getting high, Doctor. It's washing over the top of the road."

Ethan didn't give a damn about the water. He managed to hold his temper and told her about the key he kept in his desk drawer. She went inside and got it, then unlocked the door and went upstairs.

"Okay, I'm here," she said, sounding nervous. Almost guilty.

"What's wrong, Carmen?" he asked.

"Nothing."

Something was bothering her, but he didn't have the time to pursue that at the moment. He'd sit and comfort her some other time. Right now what mattered was saving Zack's life.

Behind him in the airport terminal, businessmen were slowly collecting. An airline agent opened the counter at a nearby gate for a commuter flight to Boston. He tried to tune out the noise and focused on telling Carmen what to do.

"Do you see the large machine against the back wall?" he asked.

"Yes, I think. It says Cultrex?"

"Yes. That's it. I want you to open the metal door and remove the culture tray inside."

"Okay." He heard the scrape of metal. "I have it," she said.

"Good. Now take it to the lab table near the window."

"Yes, Doctor." She took a deep breath. She sounded very unsteady.

"Carmen," he said, "please be careful with that. Don't drop it, okay?" Or he'd never know if he could give it to Zack or not.

"I won't," she said.

He told her, step by step, how to run the analysis of the blood. He heard the equipment humming as she did what he told her. Now he just had to wait for the computer to do the analysis that would tell him whether it would save Zack's life.

64

PAUL ONLY SLEPT a few hours. He awoke at five and lay in bed, thinking about the patients who had killed themselves, about Justin Pike who had killed his girlfriend, about Alicia who had trusted him, asked him for help, and whom he had let down. And he kept wondering what Ethan was doing.

His troubled mind wasn't going to let him get any more sleep, so he got out of bed and sat by the window, staring out at the city skyline in the distance. Being here felt so unreal. Investigating Ethan felt so unreal. So deceitful and hypocritical. Three years ago, Ethan had believed him, no questions asked, despite the very clear mark on Linda Wilkenson's hip bone. And now here he was, taking a secret trip in the middle of the night, trying to find out if Ethan was responsible for some suicides. And he had no clear evidence to base this on, nothing but speculation and conjecture. And this was after Ethan had given him a second chance at life.

Paul couldn't help but feel guilty. He dropped his eyes in shame and stared down at the hotel parking lot below. Even if Rejuvenol was causing tumors, and if the tumors were impairing patients' ability to control their actions—and Paul still wasn't positive about any of it—maybe Ethan didn't *know*. Ethan deserved the benefit of the doubt until there was definitive proof that he was culpable. Until then it was all speculation.

In a few short hours, Justin Pike could change that.

Paul took a long shower, trying to clear his head. At seven he couldn't wait any longer. He got dressed, went downstairs for a cup of coffee in the hotel restaurant, then left in one of the taxis waiting by the front door.

The Suffolk County Jail was in downtown Boston, a fifteen-minute drive from the Hyatt. The Sunday morning traffic was light going through the Sumner Tunnel and across the Central Artery. The Nigerian cabby looked at Paul sympathetically when they stopped at the jail. He probably figured Paul was visiting a relative.

Paul paid him and hustled up the steps toward the entrance. The morning air was chilly and damp, with a cutting wind off the river. Paul wasn't dressed for the north, wasn't prepared for this cold after the two months in the Florida heat. The hormones he was taking left him feeling stronger and more energetic, but the time in the sunshine had weakened his tolerance for the cold.

As he opened the door and ducked into the warm building, he found himself wondering about the therapies Ethan had put him on. Was there a chance that it wasn't Rejuvenol after all that caused the tumors? Could it be the hormone combination he was taking? Could he be developing the same tumor that had driven the other patients to suicide and homicide?

He shook his head, needing to clear that nonsense away. He wasn't here to get paranoid. He was here to gather information so he could determine if Rejuvenol was causing people to become violent or suicidal. If he kept thinking this way, he was going to spend the rest of his life inside an MRI machine worrying about developing a brain tumor.

Paul was let into a small room with a wooden table to the right and a chair on each side. The metal door behind him closed. He sat in one chair. Across from him was a glass door, behind which prisoners were mulling around, all wearing identical gray jumpsuits, white socks, plastic sandals. A few minutes later, a guard opened the glass door, and a tall, blond man who looked to be in his late twenties came in. Paul remembered from Pike's chart that he was in his early forties. How much of his looks was genetics and how much was Rejuvenol?

The guard behind Pike gave Paul a disgusted look then closed the door. He stood behind the glass, watching. Pike stood across the table, staring suspiciously at Paul.

"Justin Pike?" Paul asked, standing up and extending his hand.

Pike nodded and reluctantly shook Paul's hand. "I didn't know Mr. Callahan was sending a doctor today," he said, still not sitting down. His voice was soft, almost timid. Paul had a hard time imagining him as a killer.

"Your lawyer didn't send me," Paul said.

Pike looked confused. "Then who are you?"

"My name's Paul Tobin. I'm a surgeon at the De Leon Center in Florida."

That didn't clear up the look of confusion on Pike's face; in fact it only perplexed him more. "I don't understand," Pike said. "Why are you here?"

Paul gestured to the chair. "Can we talk?"

Pike looked worried. "I'm not sure if I'm supposed to or not."

"I promise you, I'm not trying to do anything that could hurt your defense. There's a chance that it might even help."

"Help how?"

Paul gestured to the chair again and said, "Please."

Pike reluctantly sat. "Okay. So tell me how you can help my defense."

"I'm not sure that I can. I said there might be a chance."

"How?"

"You were a patient at De Leon, correct?" Paul asked.

Pike stared for a moment without answering. Finally he reluctantly nodded.

"And you were taking a therapy called Rejuvenol?" Paul said.

This time a look of worry whitened Pike's face. He didn't answer. But he didn't have to. His expression was answer enough. He'd been taking it and he knew it wasn't a regular, legal therapy.

"If you came here to ask me a bunch of questions," he said, "I don't see how that's going to help. Maybe I shouldn't be talking to you." He started to get up.

"Wait," Paul said. "I'll talk. You just listen."

Pike sat back down, hesitant and distrustful.

"I know that Dr. Granier has a therapy called Rejuvenol," Paul said. "And I know it's not one of the regular antiaging therapies he uses. He only gives it to special patients who promise not to discuss it with anyone. Right?" Paul was speculating, but how else could the therapy have remained such a secret? Paul went on guessing. "He probably explained that it wasn't FDA approved and if it ever got out that you were taking it, you'd get into as much trouble as he would. Right?"

Pike didn't answer, but he was still sitting there, still listening, so Paul assumed he was right so far.

"And he probably charged quite a bit for it, too," Paul said. "And since the results are good, it's worth the money and the secrecy. And the results *are* good. And Dr. Granier assured you that it was safe."

Pike leaned forward and finally spoke. "Is it?" he whispered.

"That's what I'm trying to find out. There may be some evidence that it may have caused one patient, perhaps others, to act violently."

"You're saying that's what made me kill Britany?" Pike said, suddenly looking hopeful.

"I don't know that for sure. That's what I'm here for, to try to find out. I was hoping you could help me. Maybe we'll end up helping each other."

"How can I help?"

"What do you know about Rejuvenol?"

"Nothing, really."

"Dr. Granier didn't tell you what it is?"

Pike shrugged. "Something he does with the blood."

Paul didn't understand. "Can you tell me anything more specific?"

"He kind of explained it once, but I don't remember all the technical details."

"Tell me what you do remember." Paul hoped he'd be able to piece it together.

"Well, I know he uses stem cells," Pike said. "You know what they are, right?"

Paul knew. And now it began to make a little more sense. The unbelievable results some of the antiaging patients were getting weren't from hormones, they were from cell regeneration. Stem cells had long been thought to have the capacity to regenerate cells, all cells, from all organs. Theoretically they were like raw cellular building material that could repair whatever parts of the body were worn out or damaged—the heart, the lungs, skin, brain cells that had diminished with age. *Theoretically.*

Only it wasn't so theoretical anymore. If Pike was telling him the truth, Ethan was on to something extremely important. He had devised a way to use stem cells to reverse the degenerative effects of aging.

The special shot. Did it also work the same way for Zack's disorder? Cell regeneration might keep him alive. Was that what Ethan was doing? The possibilities of this kind of cell regeneration therapy were endless.

Paul's excitement was tempered by one thing. Anything that caused cells to multiply and reproduce could accelerate the growth of cancerous cells. Could that be what happened to Lita Davis? He was growing more certain of it the more he learned. And he was beginning to suspect that something similar had happened with Doug Collins and Nicole Quinn.

And probably the man sitting across the table right now. Paul stared at Pike's forehead, wondering if there was a tumor growing behind there as they spoke.

"What else do you remember about the therapy?" Paul asked.

"Just that Dr. Granier did something genetically to the stem cells after he took them out. Then he put them back in. He said it was safe. You don't think it was, huh?" he asked Paul. "You think that's what made me do what I did?"

"There may be some evidence of that, yes," Paul said.

"My lawyer should know this."

"I'll talk to him, tell him what I've found. I suggest you have a CT scan or an MRI."

"What for?"

"It may help your case." He didn't want to get into the details right now, not until he knew all the details. He told Pike he'd explain it all to his lawyer and the lawyer could relate it to him.

"I do have another question," Paul said. "Where did the stem cells come from?"

Pike pointed to his hip. "Right here," he said. "Dr. Granier poked a needle into my hip bone and took out bone marrow. It hurt like hell. But that's where they came from. Is that important?"

Paul stared, unable to answer.

He had blocked out as many of the details from the incident three years ago as his brain would allow. But the nightmare had never really left him. No matter what he did, the bad dream had remained in the back of his memory, waiting for some incident to draw it out to torment him again. And this was it.

The puncture in her hip.

That's what Linda Wilkenson had died from. Paul had been certain that he couldn't have done it, that he hadn't accidentally nicked her during surgery. But there had been no other explanation. She'd undergone no other procedure. And with his drinking, he'd begun to doubt himself.

But now . . .

Nicole Quinn had a puncture mark on her hip. Justin Pike had had a needle poked into his hip. Lita Davis? Doug Collins? Did Ethan do that to them, too?

Ethan had killed Linda Wilkenson three years ago. Paul was certain of it. She'd been his patient, too. In fact, he had been the doctor who referred her for surgery. Had he been developing Rejuvenol back then? The mark suddenly made sense. Ethan was responsible for her death, knew he was responsible, and still he let his friend and brother-in-law take the blame for it. He had watched Paul's life go down the drain, all the time knowing full well that he himself was responsible.

Paul's shock turned to anger. How could Ethan have done that to him? He'd ruined his career, broken up his family, destroyed his life. Paul wanted to scream and cry and hit something. But he held it inside. For now. He was definitely going to take this up with Ethan when he returned to Florida. And God have pity on Ethan when he did.

65

ALICIA AWOKE WHEN the bus pulled into South Station. She'd managed a couple hours of sleep on the ride from New York but she was still tired. Her neck hurt from sleeping with her head tilted sideways. She would have liked nothing better than to find a warm bed and a bottle of Motrin. But that wasn't going to happen anytime soon.

She only had a few dollars left. She bought a small cup of coffee at Dunkin' Donuts in the bus terminal, then walked over to the train station next door. There she spent another dollar on a token for the T, Boston's subway. She headed toward the escalator to the subway level but stopped when she saw a *New York Times* on a bench. She flipped through it quickly until she found the two-paragraph story about the break-in at Manhattan General Hospital and the security guard who was killed.

Alicia trembled as she read it. She remembered being there, seeing that poor man fall dead to the floor. The image was branded into her brain. Paul Tobin had murdered him.

How could she have been so wrong about him? He was a cold-blooded killer. Even if he hadn't known that what he was doing at De Leon would drive patients to kill themselves, he'd found out when Nikki died and had done nothing to prevent it from happening again, with Doug Collins and God knows who else. And then last night, the undeniable truth of who he was, what he was. There was nothing accidental or unintended about that. Paul killed that man.

He was evil. How could she have made love to him? The guilt and humiliation made her sick.

She took the Red Line to Science Park. A subway worker pointed out the tall brick building that was the Suffolk County Jail, a few blocks from the T station. She walked toward the jail in a cold wind. She wasn't sure how Justin Pike could help her, but he was the only other patient she knew. He might be able to tell her something useful. He might know something that would incriminate Paul. That seemed unlikely, but she had to try. At least he might be able to send her in the right direction to find the proof herself. She had no other leads to pursue.

As she drew nearer to the brick building, she realized the real reason she was here was more personal. He had known Nikki. For that reason, she felt a strange affiliation with him, even though she'd never met him. It felt right to talk to him. Even if he didn't know anything about what Tobin was doing, he might be able to tell her something about Nikki, and that alone would make the trip worthwhile.

She reached Nashua Street. The jail was still a couple hundred feet away. She paused to take a breath, needing to steel herself before going in. His connection to Nikki was going to make this difficult emotionally. But it was something she needed to do.

She was about to cross the street when the front door of the jail opened and Paul Tobin stepped out.

Rage came over her. She'd let him inside her body and inside her heart a few nights ago, and all the while he was the one who had taken away her sister, her only family, her whole world. No one could have hurt her more.

What in God's name was he doing here? The same reason she was here, no doubt. Justin Pike. He was trying to cover his tracks, the son of a bitch. He'd gotten to Pike first. Could he have convinced him to keep his mouth shut? She'd make him talk. No matter what she had to do, Paul Tobin was going to pay for what he did.

He saw her now, too. She didn't care. She glared straight at him, not showing any fear. He didn't budge. He stood blocking the doorway. Did he think he could stop her from going inside? No way! He couldn't do a damn thing to stop her, not here, out in the open, on a public street in the middle of Boston. She'd march right up to that door and go in. And maybe on the way spit in his face.

She started to cross the street.

It all happened so quickly Paul didn't have time to react.

He saw Alicia step into the street, saw the car come speeding toward her. He started to move and shout to her but it was too late. The car didn't try to stop. Alicia spun toward it, startled. She made an effort to leap to the side but she wasn't fast enough. She only got partway to the sidewalk when the car rammed into her.

"Noooo!" Paul shouted.

Alicia bounced off the fender and dropped to the pavement. Paul was still far away. In shock, he stopped for an instant. He thought about rushing back inside the jail and telling someone to call an ambulance. But he couldn't control the instinct to run to her and try to help her. He started running toward her, and the car door opened and the driver jumped out.

A woman wearing a blue warm-up suit rushed over to Alicia, bent down beside her, and lifted her up off the ground. She carried Alicia so easily toward her car that Paul thought it was a man, maybe an off-duty paramedic trying to get Alicia to a hospital. But then Paul saw the driver's face for the first time.

Karla!

She looked up at him from across the street, no surprise at all on her face. She stalled for a moment, staring at him, and then he could have sworn he saw her grin. He sprinted toward her, wanting to make her pay for hurting Alicia. She must be the one behind all the deaths, not Ethan.

Karla shoved Alicia into the front seat of her car, then she slid in beside her and slammed the door shut. As Paul reached the street and bounded the last few yards toward the car, Karla floored the accelerator. The tires spun, kicking pebbles at him. He grabbed for the rear fender, wanting to jump onto the trunk, but the car sped away before he could get hold of it.

Karla would kill Alicia if he didn't stop her. He didn't have a car to chase after her. He looked around, desperately looking for a car he could take, but he didn't see any. He looked down the road. Karla had to hit the brakes as she came to an intersection. She barely missed one car, then continued on. But she had to drive slowly because of the traffic and construction in the area.

He did the only thing he could. He took off after her on foot.

66

KARLA FELT A rush of adrenaline as she sped up the street, swerving around the cars and construction barrels. Horns blared at her. She ignored them and kept going. These people in their meaningless little lives had no idea what was at stake.

She glanced down at Fernandes, still unconscious on the seat beside her. Some blood seeped through the scrape on Fernandes's forehead. Her left arm was also bloody, along with the whole side of her left leg. The impact had felt so good, so satisfying. The power in her hands. The thump when Fernandes's body hit the car. Karla felt the same rush again now, just thinking about it. The hollow smack of Fernandes's bones against the steel fender. The way Fernandes flew. Then lay there, defenseless. A rag doll. A broken toy. It was so vivid in Karla's mind, so sensory, so right.

Fernandes was still breathing, but she looked banged up and broken. *Poor rag doll.* Karla laughed out loud. Fernandes was supposed to be some kind of private investigator. Her name in the paper. Big hero who saved Los Angeles. *Ha!* It had been so easy to take her down. *Some great investigator.* She was nothing. She thought she was hot shit the other night back at De Leon, playing her little tricks. *We'll see who laughs last.*

Karla peered up into the rearview mirror. In the distance Paul Tobin came running down the street, chasing the car.

"Perfect," she said out loud. "Keep coming, hero, ya?"

She'd assumed he would have found a car to chase her.

Maybe she'd overestimated him. Didn't matter. This was good enough. In a car, on foot, even on the damn bus—it didn't matter. Her plan would work just the same. It just meant she had to drive more slowly, so she wouldn't lose him.

But she needed to make it look like she *had* to slow down. He wasn't a total idiot. If it was too obvious, he'd catch on. He'd still keep coming—he was one of those morons who always had to save the damsel in distress. But he might be too cautious, which might prolong the inevitable. She didn't want anything to go wrong. She just wanted to do what had to be done and leave Boston with both of these nuisances eliminated forever.

She reached the next intersection. Orange construction barrels were set up, forming new lanes that detoured to the left. Orange detour signs were everywhere. To the right was an unfinished road, still unpaved and blocked off with more barricades. It went under the elevated highway bisecting downtown, and wound around concrete piers and into a new tunnel that was also still under construction.

Karla swerved hard to the right, through the construction barrels. The car bounced off the pavement and onto the dirt road. Through the cloud of dust behind her she saw the pathetic figure of Paul Tobin still running, struggling to keep up.

New elevated roads were being built all around. Mammoth cranes rose out of the construction site that stretched through the heart of the city. Karla maneuvered around one of the mounds of fill dirt. The crews weren't working today, giving the area an eerie, abandoned feel. The road dropped a foot suddenly. The car bounced, sending Fernandes off the seat and onto the floor. The impact jarred her awake. She moaned and raised her head.

"Did you sleep well?" Karla asked, grinning at her.

Fernandes was still dazed. She stared up, obviously not understanding at all what Karla meant or where she was or what was about to happen to her.

"Go back to sleep," Karla said.

Fernandes just looked at her strangely, no idea what was

coming. Karla drew her fist back then jabbed at Fernandes's face, one quick, hard blow. Fernandes's head snapped back. Karla felt the soft flesh of lips and cheek against her knuckles, then the delicate, brittle bones of Fernandes's pretty little face distorting. *Oh, it felt so good!* Fernandes flopped back down, moaning like a wounded goat. Karla felt a deep urge to do it again. She needed that release. So much anger and aggression and betrayal and anxiety had amassed inside her that the only way to get relief was to let it out. She needed to hit Fernandes again, to feel the control, the supremacy that gave her. For so long she had felt the situation was ruling itself, that she wasn't able to direct things the way they needed to be directed. That was all changing now.

She peered up into the mirror again. Tobin was barely visible in the cloud of dust behind her. But he was there, running down the dirt road like a third-rate sprinter struggling for last place. He was losing speed, though, running out of strength and energy. It was going to be so easy to finish him off. This was turning out much better than she'd expected.

When she lowered her eyes from the mirror, she was startled to see Fernandes on her knees and coming at her. She tried to land another punch, but Fernandes was already too close, flailing and scratching and shrieking like a rabid cat. There wasn't enough space between them for Karla to throw a punch. The street was too rough with too many obstacles for her to let go of the wheel and unload everything she had on this annoyance. She managed to push Fernandes back and hold her away with one hand, giggling at how easy, how weak and useless Fernandes and her punches were. She was a joke. This scrawny thing couldn't possibly hurt her.

With one hand, Karla steered around a parked dump truck and drove toward the tunnel entrance. Somehow Fernandes squirmed past her arm. She lunged, screaming and swinging. One of her hands got through and scraped Karla's face. A finger poked her eye, ripping at the lid. Suddenly rage burned in Karla. She wrapped her hand behind Fernandes's head and instead of pushing her away, pulled her head down, smacking her face into the steering wheel. She felt blood spray onto her arm. Fernandes went limp in her hand. She shoved Fernandes's face down on the seat and stiffened her arm, holding Fernandes down.

"Bitch!" Karla hissed. "You're going to pay."

Karla floored the accelerator. The car bounced onto the ramp that descended into the tunnel. She glanced into the mirror and noticed that she was losing Tobin, but she didn't give a damn. He'd catch up eventually. What mattered more right now was making this bitch pay for all the trouble she had caused.

Karla kept her foot to the floor and sped past the parked trucks and construction equipment, deep into the dark tunnel. At this speed and with so many obstacles it was difficult steering with one hand while holding Fernandes down with the other. But at least Fernandes had stopped resisting. She just lay there like a—

Fierce pain suddenly shot through Karla's thigh, pain so severe that she couldn't control the scream of anguish. Instinct took over. Both hands reached toward the pain. She took her eyes off the roadway, to see what hurt so much, and saw a screwdriver sticking up from her thigh. The words TRUE VALUE glared at her. Blood oozed out onto her pants. Fernandes sprang up, another screwdriver in her hand. She jabbed at Karla's arm. The angle was off and this time the screwdriver scraped her biceps but didn't go in.

Karla turned her rage toward Fernandes. She pounded her hard in the jaw, knocking her down to the seat, then she reached down to strangle the last breath of life out of her.

Fernandes reached up. Karla swatted her arm to the side, thinking Fernandes was trying to stab her again. But this time Fernandes grabbed hold of the steering wheel and pulled it, sending the car swerving into the concrete wall.

The impact came suddenly. Karla felt Fernandes slip out of her grasp and fly toward the floorboard. Karla herself flew up off the seat. The airbag burst and knocked her sideways. She banged her head into the side window.

•   •   •

When the fog in Karla's head began to clear, she smelled gasoline, saw blurred broken glass all around her. She blinked the focus back into her eyes and looked down at the floorboard for Fernandes.

She was gone.

Karla straightened up. Pain burned in her shoulders and neck and leg. She peered through the broken windshield and into the darkness of the tunnel. *There she is!* Fernandes—staggering away. All Karla could think of was catching her and literally beating the life out of her. She struggled to climb through the broken windshield and out onto the hood of the car. The metal was hot against her hands. She rolled off the side and onto the pavement. The instant she put weight on her right leg, a dagger of pain cut into her quadriceps.

The screwdriver was still sticking out of her thigh. She gripped the handle, clenched her teeth against the pain, and ripped it out. She screamed in agony. Blood poured out. She slapped her hand over the hole in her leg. Nothing had ever hurt so much. But she couldn't let that stop her.

She took a step. Her leg gave out beneath her. Pain shot through her body again and she screamed again. Fernandes must have hit a muscle. That would ruin everything. How was she going to qualify in a few weeks with a punctured quad muscle? *I have to make it to the Olympics. I have to!* To get this far and not even get past the qualifiers, not even get to Athens, not even get the chance to fix all the injustices that had been done to her. No, she couldn't let that happen.

She took another step, feeling the muscle moving under her hands. The pain felt right in the center of her thigh, right in the muscle. It was as bad as she feared. She was going to kill Fernandes for this. Not just kill her, but make her suffer, make her feel the pain of what she had done. It would take hours to give her what she deserved. But Karla was going to do it, she was going to repay Fernandes every last bit of it.

She started limping after her, her entire being writhing with pain and anger and hate. The pain stopped registering as adrenaline pumped through her body. The puncture in her leg became more like a weight slowing her down. It was still there, a nuisance, a reminder of what Fernandes had done, but that was all. Her only conscious thought was for vengeance, the feverish passion to see Alicia Fernandes dead.

67

ALICIA COULD BARELY stand up, let alone run. Her leg and hip and ribs burned with pain. Her senses were hazy. The world swayed around her. Everything was out of focus. She took a step and missed the ground. As she started to fall, she glimpsed the wall and reached desperately for it. Her hands hit the cold, wet concrete, sending a spike of pain up her arm and into her shoulder.

In a howl of anguish, she collapsed against the wall, struggling to find the strength to endure the pain and move on. As the pain reverberated through her body, she began to remember. *The car in front of the jail.* She'd been hit. But how did she get here? And where was *here?* So dark. *But isn't it morning?* The air held the smell of mildew and was thick with a strange dust. And the quiet. The unearthly silence, broken only by the steady hiss of water somewhere close by. And her own breathing. She struggled to draw in each breath.

Confused and lost, she managed to push herself upright again and continued hobbling. As her senses slowly cleared, she noticed a strange sensation on her face. She patted the skin around her nose and mouth. *More pain!* And wet. The smell of blood began to choke her. She realized her nose and mouth were bleeding. *Punched in the face! By Karla!*

It all began to come back to her now. Karla beating her in the car. The lock-picking tools she had bought in New York. Stabbing Karla's leg. The car crashing. Crawling out.

She stopped and looked behind her. Still blurry. She blinked and squinted, trying to focus. Then she wiped her eyes and felt the slimy wetness of blood there, too. A shiver of terror went all the way down her back to her legs, weakening her. She realized how much danger she was in. Karla was trying to kill her.

She wiped the rest of the blood from her eyes and saw a point of light in the distance behind her. The way out was that way. She'd been going the wrong way, deeper into this dark grave.

Much closer behind her was the silhouette of the wrecked car. Before she could move or even figure out what to do, she saw another silhouette, this one moving, the shape of someone staggering from the car and coming in this direction. Someone hunched over and moving with a feral, simian gait. Whoever it was looked more like an ape than a human. But even in silhouette, the person looked dangerous.

Karla!

Alicia tensed with fear. First she couldn't move, not knowing what to do. Then adrenaline rushed through her, firing her instinct to flee. She was too badly hurt to put up a fight. And Karla was too strong. She had to find another way out.

She wheeled around, moving so quickly that she almost fell again. She caught herself on the wall and staggered away from Karla and deeper into the darkness. But her legs were weak and each step sent pain up her back. She clenched her teeth and kept going. She glanced over her shoulder and saw Karla fifty feet behind her, gaining quickly. Alicia summoned all the strength she had and staggered ahead.

The tunnel curved to the right. As it did, it split into two narrower tunnels—the four lanes of traffic becoming two two-lane roads. The one on the left curved sharply. Alicia thought it might be an exit. She looked back over her shoulder again. *Oh, God!* Karla was closer now and coming faster. Alicia had to hurry. Steadying herself, she staggered down the road to the left and prayed it was a way out.

As she came around the curve, she saw another straight roadway tunneling deeper into the darkness. No light ahead. Not a way out at all. She was only going deeper, burying herself further beneath the ground, further into danger.

Her eyes were growing accustomed to the darkness, enough that she could see the dark outlines of construction equipment littering the roadway. She couldn't get out, and she certainly couldn't outrun Karla. But maybe she could hide. Her only chance was to hide and hope someone came before Karla could find her.

With each step Karla took, she felt a slice of pain in her right thigh. Her anger at Fernandes grew fiercer with the pain. She couldn't run at all. Her Olympic chances were vanishing. Fernandes would pay for this. Pay dearly.

Karla saw the venomous reptile up ahead, limping deeper into the darkness. Tricky and evil, but stupid, just running blindly like a frightened mouse. *Keep going. You're just making it easier for me to kill you!* Karla pushed herself, desperate to get her hands around Fernandes's throat. That was the one thing that would soothe the pain.

The tunnel divided up ahead. Fernandes went to the left, picked up speed a little, then suddenly vanished. Terror struck Karla. *Could that be an exit? She's escaping! No!* Karla pressed her hand hard over the hole in her thigh and broke into a run, desperate to get to Fernandes before she could get out. Blood poured down her leg. The pain returned, so sharp that she wailed each time she planted her right foot. But she kept going. Like an animal caught in a trap, she'd sacrifice her leg or any other part of her body, just to satisfy her primal instinct—not to live, but to kill.

As she rounded the curve and saw only blackness ahead, she slowed to a walk. This wasn't an exit after all. *Good.* Fernandes wasn't getting out. She was trapped. *You're mine now.*

On the road in front of her were several trucks and pieces of heavy construction equipment. She didn't see

Fernandes running down the road. That meant the little snake was hiding. Could she really be that stupid, thinking she wouldn't be found? Karla let out a sardonic laugh. It was only a matter of time now, a matter of hunting her down.

Very soon, Fernandes would be dead.

When Paul reached the car, he was out of breath from running. He fell against the fender and leaned in through the broken windshield.

"Alicia?"

The car was empty. Glass fragments littered the seat and floorboard. Paul saw a lot of blood and he grew more frightened for Alicia. What had Karla done to her? How badly was Alicia hurt? Was she even still alive?

He pulled out of the window and peered around the tunnel. "Alicia!" he called out. His voice echoed through the silence of the tunnel. No answer. No other sound at all.

Where is she? Where are *they?* He didn't see anyone in the darkness. He looked at the car again. Blood was smeared on the hood, too. He followed the smear off the edge of the hood and down the fender. He knelt down on the road and found splotches of blood soaking the pavement. A trail of blood headed deeper into the tunnel.

"Alicia!" he called out as he jumped up and hurried down the road, hoping to God he wasn't too late.

68

OVER THE PHONE, Ethan heard the analyzer stop humming.

"What does it say?" he asked Carmen, eager for the data.

She slowly read off the values on the display screen and as she did, he felt a warm sense of relief and joy rush through him. *It worked!* Zack would be all right.

"I need you to do one more thing," he told Carmen. "I need you to prepare an infusion bag."

He explained to her exactly how to prepare Rejuvenol for Zack. While she was getting it ready, he called the hospital to see how Zack was doing. It had been almost an hour since he'd last spoken with the doctor. Pine's assistant paged him.

Here in Newark, the airline had opened his gate and people were already lined up to board. He checked his watch. He only had a few minutes to get everything straightened out. He could not miss that flight.

Dr. Pine came on the line. "I'm glad you called, Dr. Granier."

Cold fear shivered through Ethan. "What's wrong?"

"There's no change in your son's status. I just wanted to let you know about the hurricane."

"I know about the hurricane." Ethan didn't want to talk about the weather. All he cared about was what they were doing for Zack.

"Then you know it was supposed to turn north."

"Look, I'm not interested in that."

"It's pertinent because the hurricane hasn't turned away, so we've been ordered to evacuate."

"What?" Ethan couldn't believe it.

"We're transferring all of our patients to facilities in Miami."

"What are you talking about? When?"

"We've already started. There's a helicopter coming for Zack shortly. He's being transferred to Jackson Memorial Hospital. They're better equipped than we are to care for him, anyway," Pine said.

"No, I don't want him transferred."

That would ruin all his plans. Carmen would be leaving the clinic soon, bringing Zack the Rejuvenol. That was what Zack needed, far more than any care a hospital in Miami could give him.

"He can't stay here," Pine said. "All the patients are being evacuated."

"Then discharge him to my nurse."

"We can't do that. Not in the condition your son is in."

"I'll take full responsibility."

"You're not even here, Doctor. You don't know your son's condition. I can't take that risk."

"I'm not going to sue you, for God's sake!"

"That's not my concern. I'm only trying to do what's best for your son."

"Look, I'll be there in a few hours," Ethan said. "Let my son stay until I get there."

"The hospital will be closed in a few hours."

"Just wait for me to get there, okay?"

"I can't. We don't have any choice. The authorities are evacuating the keys. All of our patients are being transferred—no exception."

"At least wait until my nurse arrives. I don't want Zack to go alone."

"We don't have much choice in when he goes. When the helicopter is available, he has to go. I'm sure you can understand how difficult it is evacuating an entire hospital."

"Just wait until my nurse gets there," Ethan said again. Zack didn't stand a chance without Rejuvenol. "She'll be there soon. Please. I'm begging you."

Pine let out a breath of exasperation. "When will she arrive?" he asked.

"Half an hour, forty-five minutes at the most."

"I thought you meant a few minutes. We can't wait that long. The helicopter is already on the way. It'll be here any minute. With the weather deteriorating the way it is, the helicopter won't wait."

"Please. Just keep my son there. I'll take responsibility."

"I'm sorry, Doctor, but we can't. My hands are tied."

Ethan argued with the man for a few more minutes, this time threatening that he would sue if they moved Zack, but it was to no avail. Pine would not relent. Ethan felt trapped and helpless and unable to protect his son from so far away. He wanted to punch the wall or tear the phone out of the metal box, anything to get some of the anger and aggression out of his system. Instead he just slammed down the receiver.

"Hey, be careful with that," a man behind him said. "I want to use the phone next, so don't break it."

Ethan glared at the man. "Mind your own business," he said.

"It is my business. Those are public phones. I'm part of the public."

Ethan turned his back to the man and ignored him. He called Carmen. "Are you almost done?"

"Almost."

"You have to hurry. They're moving Zack. You have to get there before the helicopter leaves. He needs that infusion or he'll die."

"I'm hurrying, Doctor," she said, her voice cracking under the pressure.

He hung up and stared at the phone, trying to figure out what else he could do to keep Zack there long enough for Carmen to bring the medicine.

"You about done there?" the man behind him asked.

Ethan ignored him and picked up the receiver again. He called the hospital. There had to be a way to reason with Pine. He could tell him that the altitude of the helicopter would jeopardize Zack's life. Pine might buy it, or at least check into it. That might stall the transfer long enough to allow Carmen to arrive.

Pine's assistant told Ethan that Dr. Pine was too busy to come to the phone.

"Get him right now, or I swear to God I'll sue him and that hospital!" he shouted. "And you, too," he added, "for every goddamn cent you have!"

The man behind him chuckled. "That doesn't work," he told Ethan.

His voice was irritating. His mere presence behind Ethan was annoying the hell out of him. "Just shut the fuck up," Ethan told him.

"I will when you finish your calls."

"I'm not leaving, so go find another phone."

"Come on, pal. It's a public phone."

Over the PA he heard the announcement that all passengers for his flight were to report to the gate agent. He peered past the man behind him and strained to see the gate. Passengers were gathering around the check-in counter. He couldn't tell what was going on.

"Just let me make one damn call," the man behind him said.

Ethan ignored him and tried to see what the agent was telling the passengers, but he couldn't figure out what they were doing. Then, over the phone, Pine's assistant finally came back on.

"I'm sorry, Dr. Granier," she said in a whiny, I-don't-give-a-damn-about-you-and-your-problems voice, "but Dr. Pine is with a patient and he—"

Ethan slammed the phone down, unable to listen to her lies anymore. "Son of a bitch!" he said out loud.

"Come on, man, I asked you not to break that," the man behind him said. "I need to call my—"

Ethan snapped. Unable to restrain himself, he grabbed

the receiver and began banging it against the front of the phone. "There!" he barked at the man. "You like that?" He kept banging it, hoping the man would take a swing at him so he could start banging the receiver on the guy's head. "See what I'm doing? See? You got a problem? Huh?"

The man glared at him, looking shocked and nervous. "Man, you're crazy," he said, backing away.

"That's it, go bother someone else," Ethan said.

He turned back to the phone and calmed himself as much as he could. It was all mounting—the idiot behind him, the airline doing something about his flight, Pine's assistant, Zack's health. And Carmen. He needed to talk to her, to make sure she was on her way to the hospital.

He called her cell phone to see how far she was from the hospital. He might be able to stall Pine a little longer if he could give Pine a better estimate of when she'd arrive.

"I'm still at the house," she said when she answered the phone. "I'm not finished preparing the infusion yet."

"Damn it!"

"I'm sorry, Doctor. I'm going as fast as I can."

"Just hurry, Carmen. Please. Hurry."

He slammed down the receiver again, frustrated and growing more angry that he couldn't do what he needed to get done.

"Hey!"

Ethan turned around and saw an airport security guard staring at him. Behind the guard was the man who had been pestering him for the last few minutes.

"What's your problem, pal?" the rented uniform said.

"Nothing." Ethan turned his back to the guard and dialed the hospital again.

"Those phones don't belong to you," the guard said.

Ethan ignored the guard. The guy had about as much authority as a crossing guard. He was another nuisance interfering with vital efforts to keep Zack alive. Over the PA, the airline again called all passengers on his flight to go to the gate. He looked over as he listened to the phone ringing at Key West Community Hospital. The door to the jetway was closed. No one was boarding. So why were all the passengers there?

Pine's assistant came on the phone again, her voice distracting Ethan from the activity in the airport. Again she told him that Pine was with a patient.

"This is urgent," he said. "I must talk to him."

"You have to understand that we have an emergency situation here."

"So do I!"

The guard tapped him on the shoulder. "Listen, pal."

Ethan wheeled around and glared at the guard. It took all his restraint to keep from swinging at that fat, stupid head. The guard saw the threatening look in Ethan's eyes and he took a step back.

"Just leave me alone!" Ethan said.

"I'm just telling you that if you break that phone—"

"All right, you've told me, now leave me the hell alone."

He turned his back to the guard and faced the phone. "Page him, do whatever you have to do, just get him on the phone."

Pine's assistant put him on hold. He waited impatiently, constantly checking the time and glancing back at the activity in front of his flight's gate. He couldn't miss that plane or he'd never get down there in time to save Zack. In his ear was the inane music they played when putting someone on hold. *Come on, someone pick up the damn phone!* Behind him, the guard kept babbling about something. Ethan tuned him out. He heard the gate agent call his flight again. Then the hold music disappeared.

"Hello? Hello?"

No response. A moment later a voice came on and said that if he wanted to place a call, he should hang up and dial again. He'd been cut off. "Fuck!" he shouted and threw the receiver against the phone.

"Hey!" the guard said. "If you break that—"

Ethan pushed past him and hurried to the gate, needing to find out what was happening with his flight. The passengers were heading away. *Could they have changed the gate?* He went up to the counter. The gate agent was helping another passenger, typing into her computer, looking for something.

"What's going on?" Ethan asked a man in line.

"They canceled the flight to Key West," the man said.

"What?" Ethan couldn't believe what he was hearing. He rushed to the side of the counter, close to the agent. "You can't cancel the flight," he said. "I have to get down there."

She finally looked up. She looked tired and frustrated. "Sir, there's a hurricane down there," she said. "The airport is closed. It's probably going to be closed all day. We're trying to reroute people to nearby airports, but no one's going to be flying into Key West today."

"But I *have* to go there!"

The woman looked unconcerned. "You need to go to the ticket counter so they can try to find an alternative destination for you."

"I don't want an alternative destination. I want to go *there,* where I'm supposed to go! Now type that into your computer and find a way for me to get there!"

"I'm helping this gentleman at the moment," she said.

"Goddamn it!" he shouted and pounded on the counter. "If it was your son down there, you'd sure as hell make sure the goddamn plane flew into Key West!"

The same security guard who had harassed him at the phones ran over, asking the airline agent if Ethan was causing trouble. Other airline agents joined them. They told Ethan he had to calm down or he would not be allowed on any of the flights. But he couldn't calm down. He couldn't even try. He was too angry and anxious.

Why can't anybody understand how critical it is that I get to Zack?

He argued with the airline agents, threatened to sue them. But it was to no avail. They kept telling him that the Key West airport was closed and there was nothing they could do. He finally threw his worthless ticket at the supervisor and stormed off.

He found an unoccupied pay phone and called the hospital again. This time he got Pine on the line. Pine told him that Zack had just left in the helicopter. It was too late to help him in Key West. Zack's only hope now was that he receive Rejuvenol at the hospital in Miami.

Ethan called Carmen, who was just getting ready to leave the house. He could hear rain on the other end of the line as the skies opened up in Florida.

"I need you to drive the medicine to Miami," he said. "To the hospital where they moved Zack. Can you do that for me, Carmen?"

"The weather is getting pretty bad." She sounded apprehensive. "The roads aren't so good, Doctor. Miami is a long drive."

"Carmen, if Zack doesn't get that medicine, he'll die. You're the only chance he has. Do you understand that?"

She sighed. "I'll do it, Doctor."

He called Beth in Palm Beach and asked her to go quickly to Miami and meet Zack's helicopter at the hospital. He didn't want his son to be alone. After he hung up, he ran across the airport to the ticket counter, desperate to get on a flight to Miami.

69

PAUL HURRIED DEEPER into the darkness. He could no longer see if there was blood on the ground. But the tunnel only went one way.

Then he came to a fork in the tunnel. The right side seemed to go straight. He peered through the darkness. He couldn't see anything. He stopped and listened for footsteps or voices. Nothing but silence.

"Alicia!" he called out. His voice echoed through the tunnel. But there was no answer.

He looked down the left side. This tunnel curved around so he couldn't see very far in that direction. He called again but didn't hear anything down there either. He knelt on the ground and felt along the pavement for blood. His hand passed through a small spot of something wet but in the darkness he couldn't tell if it was blood or water or motor oil or something else altogether. More of it was going to the left. It was all he had to go on, so he got up and hurried down that tunnel.

He followed the curve as it took him to an area cluttered with trucks and generators and large paving equipment. He slowed to a cautious walk now. If they were in this area, they could be hiding. Karla could have Alicia behind or inside one of the trucks, threatening to kill her if she opened her mouth. She had probably heard him call to Alicia. So she knew he was here. But could she see him? And was she armed?

He walked past the first few pieces of equipment, strain-

ing to see in the darkness. He heard the faint rumble of
traffic above. The air here smelled of petroleum and fresh
asphalt. He also thought he smelled a hint of perfume. He
stopped and drew in a deep breath. It was gone now, if it
had even been there at all. Maybe he'd imagined it.

He walked a little farther and checked behind a pickup
truck filled with barricades. No one there. He peeked into
the cab. Empty. He saw several large concrete pipes lined
along the wall. They weren't large enough for a person to
crawl inside, but he checked on the ground behind them.
No one. He stepped around a collection of sledgehammers,
pry bars, picks, and jackhammers and stopped at an asphalt
roller. He was about to look behind it when he heard a
sound behind him.

He spun around. No one was there. Just darkness. But he
was sure he'd heard it. Something like a shoe scraping the
sandy pavement.

"Alicia?" he called out in a whisper. "Alicia, it's Paul."

"Paul?"

It was Alicia's voice. And it came from behind him, behind the roller. He spun back around. Sound must be distorted in the tunnel, he realized; it was echoing off the
concrete surfaces. The noise he'd thought came from the
direction of the pipes and tools had actually come from behind the roller.

"Alicia?" he called again.

Her head poked up from behind the roller. When he saw
her, his entire body slackened with relief. She was still
alive. "Are you okay?" he said.   ·

"Yes, but be careful because—" Her face suddenly registered fright. "Look out!" she screamed.

It happened so quickly. Paul sensed movement behind
him, glimpsed something slashing toward his head. He
started to turn and raise his arm to protect himself, but he
didn't react in time. The metal pry bar slammed into his
shoulder, then bounced up and hit him in the side of the
head. It was as if something exploded inside his skull. Instantly, he lost all sense of balance and flopped over, landing hard on the pavement. Pain throbbed through his head

and down his spine. He couldn't move, couldn't see. All he heard was the echo inside his skull and a faint scratching sound. It took a few seconds to realize that the scratching was Alicia's voice, screaming in terror.

He managed to open his eyes. His vision was blurred. The tunnel swayed and shifted. He blinked and squinted and finally focused on Karla swinging the pry bar at Alicia. Alicia dodged it, but tripped when she did, falling to the ground. She scrambled on the pavement to get away, screaming. Karla went after her.

Paul tried to get up, to stop Karla, but he could barely move. He only managed to roll over before Karla swung at Alicia again. The bar hit her this time across the back and Alicia collapsed facedown on the roadway.

"No!" Paul shouted, managing to get up onto one knee.

Before he could stand, Karla wheeled around toward him, rushed over, and swung the bar toward his head. He ducked. The bar streaked above him, glancing his scalp. He lunged forward, grabbing the thick muscles of Karla's legs and tackling her to the pavement. The bar clanged to the ground a few feet away—she'd lost hold of it. She squirmed out from under him, kicking him as she crawled across the ground. He spotted the bar. She was crawling toward it. He was closer.

He struggled up onto his feet, his head still ringing, his body still unbalanced, and staggered toward the bar. As he started to reach down to get it, she came under him and drove her fist up between his legs, crushing his testicles. All strength left him in an instant. He doubled over in pain. She whipped the bar off the ground and scrambled to her feet. He tried to straighten up, to defend himself, but she attacked too quickly, bringing the bar down hard on his back. He crumpled to the ground, facedown. Then she landed on his back, slid the bar under his neck, and pulled up. At the same time she pressed down on his back with her knee. The pressure of the bar against his throat cut off all his air. She pulled hard, forcing his head back so far that it felt like his neck was going to tear.

"You ruined everything!" she screeched, straining to

speak as she put all of her strength into pulling back on the bar. "Son of a bitch! Look at my leg! *Look!*" She jerked the bar harder. "I'm going to kill you! Both of you!"

Paul could barely see Alicia off to the side, still flat on the pavement. Karla would go after her next for sure. She wasn't rational. She was going purely on emotion, with no ability to temper herself, no restraint. It had to be Rejuvenol.

He had to do something. He reached up and gripped the bar. He tried to pull it away so he could breathe but she jerked back on it, pressing it harder into his Adam's apple.

"You shit!" she shouted. "Coming up here, trying to make trouble, to hurt me! At least I do it to your face. Not like you. Not like Ethan. I want you to know it is me!" She pulled back harder on the bar and leaned forward, so he could see her face. "You see? I look you right in the eye. And I do it to you. I don't go behind your back, I don't use your son, test things on your son."

Her words didn't make sense. He was losing all oxygen. He was beginning to surrender consciousness.

"See, you didn't know," she said. "That's right. Ethan is testing Rejuvenol on your son Kenny. How do you like that?"

Her words shivered through him, like ice seizing every part of his body. Ethan had given it to Kenny? *No! My God, no!* Unable to breathe, he began to lose recognition of where he was. The only thing clear to him was the horror of what would happen to Kenny.

The tunnel began to fade. . . . The last thing he saw was a strange blur.

Suddenly the pressure on his neck vanished. He flopped forward and his face smacked the pavement. He heard the clang of the bar on the ground. Karla was off him. He tried to shake away the chaos in his head. He blinked and squinted, struggling to see through the blur.

He lifted his head and saw Karla on the ground. Alicia was on top of her, screaming and flailing her arms, hitting Karla on the back of the head and shoulders. Karla covered her head, deflecting the blows. Alicia kept at it, but she wasn't doing much damage. Karla mustered the strength to push herself up onto her hands and knees.

Paul knew he had to do something. Alicia was no match for Karla. He had to get there while Karla was still on the ground. He tried to get up, but his equilibrium was still off. He got onto one knee then lost his balance and tumbled over. He saw Karla throw Alicia off her and begin beating her viciously. Her knees were on top of Alicia's arms so Alicia couldn't even cover her face, couldn't protect herself at all.

"You stab me in the leg!" Karla screamed, swinging at Alicia's face. "I can't swim now! I can't swim!" She clutched Alicia by the throat and began choking her. "You like it, ya?" she screamed. "This is what it feels like to me! Die!" she yelled at Alicia. *"Du stirbst!"*

Alicia's face was covered with blood and she wasn't moving.

Paul mustered enough strength to push himself up onto his legs. He had to get over there. He was wobbly and unsteady. The tunnel swayed around him. He staggered toward them and fell onto Karla. She shrugged him off and kept choking Alicia. Her rage gave her incredible strength. Paul grabbed her arms and tried to pull her hands off Alicia's throat but her skin was slick with sweat and his hands slipped off.

She didn't even care that Paul was there. Her entire being was focused on killing Alicia. Desperate, he wrapped his arm around her throat and began choking her as she was choking Alicia.

"Let go of her!" he shouted.

She ignored him. He tightened his hold on her, trying to pull her off at the same time. Karla resisted, fighting his efforts to pull her backward, squeezing harder at Alicia's neck. Paul heard Karla begin to choke. Alicia's mouth gaped open as she desperately tried to get air. She peered past Karla at Paul, her eyes begging for help.

"Let go of her or I'll kill you!" Paul shouted at Karla.

Karla ignored him still. Paul wasn't even sure she heard him. It was as if the only thing that existed to her was Alicia, and she was going to kill her no matter what.

Paul squeezed her throat as tightly as he could. He heard her wheeze as she struggled for air.

"*Du stirbst. . . .*" Karla's voice was faint and failing.

Alicia was turning purple. Her eyes were wide and began to lose focus. Paul gathered all the strength he could to tighten his hold on Karla, to save Alicia.

"*Du . . .*"

Suddenly Karla went limp in Paul's hands. He threw her aside and knelt beside Alicia. She wasn't breathing. He checked her pulse. Nothing. *Damn it!* He quickly began CPR, begging her not to die.

It only took two rounds of compressions and rescue breathing before she began breathing on her own. He felt her carotid. She had a pulse. She was alive.

70

CARMEN PREPARED THE infusion bag just as Dr. Granier had told her. She didn't understand what this was, how it would help Zachary, but she believed Dr. Granier knew what he was doing. He had done so much good for Zachary over the years. She was convinced that if he had been here when Zachary got sick, Zachary never would have gotten as bad as he was now.

She needed something to carry the special medicine in, not wanting to rupture the bag during the long trip to Miami. She was worried about the roads. Not just because the rain was coming down heavily and she didn't like driving in this kind of weather, but the roads and bridges across the miles of keys were pretty narrow. Many had no shoulders, not much room for mistakes. They made her nervous in normal weather, when she drove to Miami to see her family every weekend. In a storm like this, they terrified her. But she'd do it if it meant helping Zachary.

She went downstairs to her room and got the small cosmetics bag she used every Sunday when she drove to Miami. She emptied it and placed the infusion bag inside. She went to the window and looked out. The rain was coming down even heavier now. Lightning streaked across the gray sky. An explosion of thunder unnerved her. She took an umbrella out of the closet, tucked the cosmetics bag under her arm, and made a break for her car.

The wind ripped the umbrella away. She held tightly to the cosmetics bag and kept running. She pulled open the

car door and ducked inside, soaking wet. She wiped the
water out of her eyes. The engine started up right away,
which was a relief. As the wipers swished back and forth
across the windshield, she looked for a safe place to put the
cosmetics bag. She didn't want it sliding around, maybe
falling off the seat. She ended up tucking it on the floorboard, under the passenger's seat.

The battery of her cell phone was low so she plugged the
phone into the lighter and put it on the seat beside her, in
case Dr. Granier called again. She wiped her wet hands on
the seat then shifted the car into drive and headed toward
the bridge that connected Coral Key to the rest of the keys.

The island seemed eerie with all of the patients and staff
evacuated. She was the only one here. A heavy blanket of
gray-black clouds shaded out most of the light. A shiver
ran down her back as she drove past the darkened buildings
and bungalows. She had a strange feeling. Nothing she
could put her finger on, just a bad sense . . .

Her grandmother in Costa Rica had been extremely superstitious. She had always warned Carmen to listen to
those inner feelings. *Those are the spirits talking to you.*
But Carmen never would have come to the United States
and become a nurse if she had listened to the spirits, or to
her grandmother.

She reached for the heater. Some warm air would be
much more useful than her grandmother's superstitions.
The windows were already fogging up from her breathing.
She had been rushing so much, and was so nervous about
transporting something so important and driving in these
conditions, that she was practically hyperventilating. *Calm
down.* She took a few deep, slow breaths and steadied herself. Then she turned on the defogger. The fan whined as it
blew hot air at the glass. It wasn't clearing the windshield
quickly enough so she wiped it with her hand, clearing a
small streak of visibility. She steered around the reception
building and headed up the drive toward the bridge. The
wind was blowing strong, howling as if it were angry, trying to push her car off the pavement. The palm trees lining
the roadway swayed, straining at their shallow roots. She

saw the bridge ahead. Waves lapped up on the roadway. She shivered again, uneasy about driving over it.

The windshield fogged again. She wiped it one more time, then wiped the side window so she could see around her. She was leaning sideways and reaching across the seat to wipe the passenger's side window when a palm frond blew across the road and slammed into the hood of her car.

It made a loud crashing sound that frightened her. She screamed. The palm bounced off the radiator and flew toward the windshield. Carmen threw up her hands, terrified that the glass was going to break and spray her face. The palm hit the windshield and scraped over the roof, disappearing behind her.

She lowered her hands in time to see a huge chunk of the bridge in front of her gone. She mashed the brakes but it was too late. The tires skidded on the wet road and the car slid toward the gap in the bridge and the churning gray water beneath.

71

ETHAN LANDED IN Miami. The airport was a mess with diverted flights. It took half an hour to get a taxi. When he finally got to the hospital, he raced inside and up to ICU. Beth was standing in the door of the waiting room, anxiously watching the hallway. When she saw him she rushed over and hugged him.

"Thank God you're here," she said, looking worried.

"Thanks for coming, Beth."

"You don't have to thank me."

"How is Zack?" Ethan held his breath, terrified she might say he was too late.

"They said he's stable for now, but . . ." She lowered her voice to a whisper. "Ethan, he's really ill."

Ethan knew that. If only he had been here last night, he could have prevented it. But at least he was here now; he could help him now.

"Where's Carmen?" he asked. He needed Rejuvenol. The sooner Zack received it, the better.

Beth shrugged. "Is she supposed to be here? I haven't seen her, and we arrived a few hours ago."

Ethan checked the time. He'd spoken to her over four hours ago. "She should have arrived by now," he said.

"She was coming from Coral Key? Maybe she got caught in the traffic. They're evacuating the keys, you know."

"I know." He'd call Carmen on her cell phone in a

minute, find out where she was, how soon she'd arrive. But first he wanted to see Zack.

Beth's two sons were slumped on a couch in the waiting room, staring at the TV, looking bored and unhappy about being here. There was a news special on TV. STORM WATCH 7 was superimposed on the bottom of the screen. The volume was turned all the way down so Ethan couldn't hear what was being said but he knew it was about the hurricane. They had an aerial view of A1A, the only highway leading in and out of the keys. The lane leaving the keys was bumper to bumper with traffic. The other lane was wide open except for an occasional police car.

He hoped to God Carmen wasn't stuck in that.

He went into the ICU alone. The room was strangely cold and still, the silence broken only by the faint blip-blip-blip of the first bed's cardiac monitor. Ethan shivered as he walked past that patient, an old man who looked close to death. He felt like he was walking through a morgue. He forced that thought from his mind and moved toward Zack's bed.

He was shocked by what he saw. Zack lay beneath a tangle of tubes and monitor cables. He looked so tiny, so vulnerable. His chest was pocked with electrodes that streamed up to a cardiac monitor. The tracer line showed an extremely weak, irregular beat. Zack's heart was terribly damaged. He was barely alive.

Ethan leaned close to Zack. His eyes were shut. His skin was yellowish, jaundiced. His liver was failing, too. A ventilator breathed for him. The brusque, stop-and-go hiss of the machine sent shivers of fear through Ethan. The longer Zack was on this, the more dependent on it he'd become. There was also the danger of infection, of pneumonia, of a profusion of opportunistic diseases. A bag hung below the bed, scant with rust-colored urine. Zack already had a urinary infection. Ethan feared that his kidneys were starting to fail, as well.

An IV dripped medicine into Zack's arm but Ethan

knew that nothing they had here could help his son. He needed Rejuvenol. Now that he knew he had the right formulation, he was confident that he could save Zack. But he had to do it quickly. There was no telling how long Zack could hold on.

Carmen, where the hell are you?

"Zack," Ethan whispered. "It's Daddy."

Zack didn't react at all. Ethan's heart ached terribly to see his son in this condition. He'd spent the last twelve years of his life doing everything he could to prevent Zack from ever reaching this point. And now here Zack was, suffering so much. Zack had counted on him, and he'd let the boy down. First by giving him the faulty genes that caused him to live such a horrible life. Then the constant setbacks with Rejuvenol; he should have had it ready months ago— *years ago!* The little progress he had made wasn't nearly enough. If all he'd done was prolong his son's life in order to make him suffer so much now, then he had done nothing at all. And he'd let Zack become so ill, let him suffer so horribly.

"I'm so sorry," Ethan whispered.

He dropped his face against Zack's chest and began to weep.

After speaking with Zack's physician, Ethan realized that the doctors here had no idea how to help Zack. Their efforts were directed more toward making him comfortable than saving his life. They were surprised that Zack had lived this long. To their way of thinking, Ethan should be grateful for having had his son as long as he did.

Ethan was not willing to give up on Zack, as they were. He knew he could save Zack's life.

He hurried into the waiting room to use the phone. Kenny and Pete were arguing over what to watch on TV. Kenny wanted the ball game. Pete a cartoon.

"Shut up, brat!" Kenny said. "We're watching the game!" He yanked the remote control away from Pete and shoved him off the couch.

"Mom!" Pete whined.

Beth hurried over. "Kenny! I told you before not to hit your brother!"

"He started it," Kenny said.

Ethan tried to block out the arguing as he picked up the phone and dialed Carmen's number.

"Why are you acting like that?" Beth said to Kenny.

"I'm not acting like anything."

Ethan covered his ear and focused on the phone call. He got Carmen's voice mail. After the tone he left a message. "Carmen, it's Dr. Granier. Where are you? I need that medicine."

Beth came over and asked, "What medicine?"

"Call me as soon as you get this," Ethan said into the phone. He read off the number on the phone he was using. "This is extremely important, Carmen. Call me."

"What medicine?" Beth asked him again.

"Ooouch!" Pete screeched. On the couch, he and Kenny were going at it again. "Mom. Kenny poked me."

"I did not, you little brat."

"Did, too."

Ethan couldn't take it anymore. "Will you two stop it, for God's sake!" he yelled. The frustration of not being able to reach Carmen, of not being able to help Zack, mixed with all the noise and confusion, made him explode. "Keep quiet or go somewhere else!" he shouted.

Both boys fell silent immediately and just stared at Ethan, shocked. Beth stared at him, too, surprised but also sympathetic. She turned to the boys.

"Kenny, take your brother to the cafeteria and both of you get a Pepsi or something."

Kenny frowned. "Do I have to take him?" he said. "He always embarrasses me."

"Just do it," Beth insisted.

Kenny trudged out. Pete hurried behind him.

Beth turned back to Ethan and gently held his hand. "Are you all right?" she asked. "I've never seen you explode like that before."

"My son is dying in there! How am I supposed to act?" He didn't mean to snap at her, but he couldn't help it. And he couldn't stop himself from going on. "Jesus, I don't need more stress, Beth." He wanted to stop, but it was as if the anger had a mind of its own. "If you have to bring your kids, at least keep them under control. Holy Christ!"

"I'm sorry, Ethan," she said. "I shouldn't have brought them. Kenny's been real difficult lately. I don't know what's wrong with him. He's—"

Ethan held up his hand to stop her. "Please," he said. "I have enough problems right now. Don't add Kenny."

Beth fell silent. She looked hurt. But what the hell did she expect? Did she want sympathy because her son had a behavioral problem? Discipline the kid, for God's sake. Take a strap and beat some sense into him. Ethan had *real* problems to worry about. Like saving his son's life. He needed Rejuvenol. Carmen should have been here by now.

"Where the hell is she?" he murmured. He picked up the phone and dialed Carmen's number again.

"What medicine were you talking about a minute ago?" Beth asked.

The phone rang several times then he got her voice mail again. Ethan slammed the phone down, which startled Beth. She took a step back.

"Ethan," she said in a scolding tone—the way she should be scolding her sons, not him.

"Where the hell is she?" he grumbled, his anger building. "How difficult is it to pick up a bag and drive here with it?"

"A bag of what? What medicine?" Beth asked again.

"A special medicine for Zack," Ethan said. He didn't have the patience to explain it to her. "She should have been here by now. I should have done it myself. Damn it, I should have done it myself."

He checked his watch again. He needed that medicine. He should have flown into Key West and picked it up himself. But the damn airline wouldn't go. Everybody was against him, against Zack. To hell with them all—he didn't need anybody else. Neither did Zack. They had each other and that was all they needed.

Except he needed Carmen. He'd had no choice but to

rely on her for one simple thing. Which she was screwing up. She wasn't here when she was supposed to be. And she wasn't even answering her damn cell phone.

"Where the hell is she?" he said.

"Can they get the medicine here?" Beth asked.

Such an asinine question. "No, they can't."

She looked at him in disbelief. "Really? What kind of medicine is it?"

"It's something special that Zack takes."

"And the pharmacy here can't—"

"Look, they don't have it here!" he said, snapping at her. "Okay? I have some at the clinic. Carmen was supposed to bring it. I don't know where the hell she is. And I don't need the fifth degree from you. So just drop it, will you?"

Beth looked shocked that he would talk to her like that. He couldn't deal with her temperament along with everything else. He blew out a breath of exasperation, turned his back to her, and grabbed the phone. He called Carmen again. Again the voice mail. The sound of Carmen's voice telling him to leave a message, when she was supposed to be here giving him the medicine that would save Zack's life, angered him so much that he whacked the receiver against the table several times, yelling, "I don't want to leave a fucking message! Where the fuck are you!"

The plastic receiver broke into pieces. He threw it down, growing more angry and frustrated.

"Ethan, calm down," Beth said.

He wheeled around and glared at her. "Don't tell me to calm down! If it was one of your sons in there," he said, pointing toward the ICU, "you sure as hell wouldn't be calm, so just leave me the hell alone."

Beth just stared at him, stunned into silence.

Ethan saw the broken phone and realized that the number Carmen was supposed to call wasn't going to work. *"Shit!"* He headed out into the hallway, looking for another phone.

He found a pay phone and called Carmen again. Again her recorded voice. He left the number of this phone and hung up. But he realized he couldn't count on her to call back or even to show up. What if he waited and waited and she never came? Zack would die. He couldn't allow that to happen. He never should have entrusted Zack's life to someone else in the first place. This was something he should have taken care of himself.

He still had time. But he had to hurry.

"Give me your car keys," he told Beth.

"Why? Where are you going?"

He clenched his teeth and used all his strength to keep from smacking her in the head. "Beth," he said, "my son is dying in there. I have to go back to my clinic and get the medicine for him. Unless you want him to die, give me your car keys."

"You can't go there. There's a hurricane coming, Ethan. They're evacuating the entire area. It's too dangerous."

"Give me the fucking keys!" he screamed. She let out a frightened yelp and backed away. He grabbed her purse away from her, found her keys inside, and threw the purse back to her. She stared at him, obviously wanting to say something.

"Don't," he warned her, and then he stormed out.

72

AFTER PAUL REVIVED Alicia, he sat her up against the wall and went over to Karla. He felt her throat for a pulse. Her skin was cold. She had no heartbeat. He tried CPR but she did not respond. The shocking realization of what he'd done sank in. He'd killed her with his own hands.

"How is she?" Alicia asked, several yards away.

Paul looked back at her and shook his head. Alicia understood. She let out a somber breath and said, "You had no choice, Paul."

He knew that, but he still felt sickening guilt.

He came back over to Alicia. Her face was smeared with blood. Her nose had stopped bleeding; the cut on her lip was still bleeding a little. She had scrapes on her forehead and arms that seeped blood.

"How do you feel?" he asked.

"I've been better."

He checked her leg and hip as well as he could without an X-ray machine. She didn't appear to have any broken bones from being hit by Karla's car. She was still sore, though. As he did what he could to clean up her face and stop the bleeding on her lip, she stared at him, something obviously troubling her. She looked like she wasn't sure whether to trust him or not.

"What is it?" he asked.

"I need you to tell me the truth about my sister," she said.

"I told you, I didn't know your sister. I wasn't even sure

you had a sister until last night, when I found her chart. I'm sorry I didn't believe you."

She shook her head, looking disappointed. "Paul, I know you operated on her. I was hoping you'd tell me the truth."

He was stunned that she was saying this. "Alicia, I didn't operate on your sister. I told you, I never even met her."

"I know you operated on her," she said. "I saw the X ray of that woman in New York. The one who died because of the mistake you made. Nikki had the same mark on her as that woman, Linda Wilkenson. You did it when you operated on her. I wish you'd stop lying about it."

"Alicia, I swear to God, I didn't operate on your sister. I never even met her. That mark is from a bone marrow extraction."

"Nikki didn't have cancer."

"I know. Ethan did it. Dr. Granier." He explained everything he knew.

She stared into his eyes, taking it all in with difficulty. Finally she said, "You're telling the truth this time, aren't you?"

He let out a sigh, relieved that she believed him. "Yes," he said. "Finally."

Faint sirens broke the silence. Somebody must have seen them come in here and called 911. They'd be arriving any minute.

"The police are going to arrest me," Alicia said.

Paul remembered that she was wanted in Tampa in connection with Doug Collins's death. Yesterday, when he'd heard about it, he didn't want to believe she did it. He still didn't believe it now. But the police wouldn't be so open-minded. About that or about Karla's death.

"I'm sure they'll take us both in," he said. They'd probably want to question them for hours, if not days.

"What should we do?" Alicia asked.

Paul glanced back at Karla. Was it true what she'd said about Ethan giving Rejuvenol to Kenny? Paul suddenly remembered the blue safety cap he'd found on the floor in Kenny's room. *Oh, God.* Karla was telling the truth. Kenny was in danger.

He looked at Alicia. "Do you think you can walk?" he asked.

"I'm sure I can."

"Let's get out of here."

When they got to Logan, Paul couldn't find a flight to Palm Beach anytime soon. There was a flight to Miami, already boarding. He bought two tickets for that flight and they ran through the concourse to make it on time. They reached the gate just before the door was closed and locked.

As soon as the plane was airborne and the pilot said it was okay to use the phones, Paul picked up the Skyfone at his seat. He needed to warn Beth, make sure she watched Kenny closely until he could get there. No one answered at Beth's house so he dialed her cell phone number. She answered on the first ring.

"Beth, it's me, Paul."

"Oh." She sounded disappointed. He assumed she was expecting *him*—Eli. "Where are you?" she asked.

"I'm on a plane. I just left Boston; I'm heading to Miami."

She let out a breath of relief. "I didn't know if you were stuck in the keys. With the hurricane and everything, I was worried," she said.

"No, I'm fine. Look, where's Kenny?"

"Right here with me," she said. He could hear a television in the background; it sounded like a ball game. "We're at Jackson Memorial Hospital, in Miami."

Paul's breath seized. His worst fears were coming true. "The hospital? Why? What happened to Kenny?"

"Relax. Kenny's fine. It's Zachary." She lowered her voice. "Hold on a second," she said. Then it sounded like she was moving. Finally she came back on. "I just wanted to go into the hall so the boys wouldn't hear. Zachary took ill last night. They transferred him here."

Paul was sorry to hear the news. Zack had been doing poorly yesterday when he'd seen him. "How is he?" he asked Beth.

"I don't know what to say." She hesitated. "It doesn't look very good," she whispered.

"Where's Ethan?" Paul asked. "Is he back from New York?"

"Oh, yeah. He's back."

Alicia heard Paul and grabbed his arm. "Dr. Granier was in New York?" she asked.

He covered the phone. "Yeah. Why?"

"Then it must have been him who hit that guard. He tried to kill me," she said.

"Paul, are you there?" Beth said on the phone.

Paul was shocked into silence by what Alicia said. Testing a therapy in order to help his son, not realizing that it would hurt someone, that fit Ethan's personality. But going out and intentionally trying to kill someone, that was not the Ethan Paul thought he knew.

But neither was setting up his brother-in-law to take the blame for a death he had nothing to do with. Or giving a dangerous substance to Kenny. Paul reluctantly accepted that he really didn't know Ethan at all.

"Paul?" Beth said again.

"Yes, I'm here," he said. "Look, can I talk to Ethan?" Surely Ethan was going through hell with Zachary, but Paul still wanted to talk to him, to find out if what Karla had said about Kenny was true and if there was something they could do to reverse the effects.

"Ethan left a little while ago," Beth said. "He had to drive back to Coral Key to get some special medicine for Zachary."

Rejuvenol?

"So Kenny is okay?" he asked Beth.

"Why do you keep asking about him? He's fine," she said. "A bit of an attitude lately, but he's a teenager. I guess he's going through a phase. He's been kind of difficult and aggressive. He broke the dog's leg the other day—he said it was an accident. And he's been fighting with Pete a lot."

A shiver of fear ran up Paul's neck. *It was true.* He didn't want to believe it.

"Beth, this is really important," he said. If Ethan had injected Kenny with anything, she had to have known about it. Ethan may have told her he was doing something else,

but he wouldn't have been able to do it without her knowing. "Do you know if your brother did anything that—"

Suddenly Beth screamed, and he heard the phone fall.

"Beth? What's going on?"

He heard her yelling to someone. Running footsteps.
More screaming.

"Beth! Beth! What's going on?"

Alicia squeezed his arm again. "What is it?"

"I don't know."

The commotion continued. Finally he heard the scraping of the phone being picked up, and Beth's horrified
voice came on.

"Oh, my God!" she said.

"Beth! What is it? What's happening?"

"It's Kenny. Paul, Kenny has Pete out on the ledge and is
threatening to kill them both!"

73

THE RAIN WAS coming down so heavily the wipers could barely keep up. Wind blew palm fronds across the road. One hit the side window of the Explorer, startling Ethan. He jerked the SUV to the side. The tires slipped off the pavement and onto the sandy shoulder. He steered hard back onto the road and sped toward Coral Key.

The Florida Highway Patrol had stopped him once up near Marathon. They told him that the keys were being evacuated and he couldn't go any farther. He explained that he was a doctor, showed them ID, and told them it was a medical emergency. They were much too busy corralling the traffic to spend time verifying what he was saying. They waved him on.

That was many miles back. Here, the roads were deserted. He turned off A1A and drove up the road toward the bridge to Coral Key.

He was desperate to know how Zack was doing, but getting to De Leon and preparing another dose of Rejuvenol was his top priority. He didn't have time to stop and find a phone. Every minute counted. He could call from the house and talk to Beth while he prepared the infusion bag.

The road in front of him came in and out of view with the sweep of the wipers. He knew it well enough that he could make it without seeing clearly. The De Leon sign appeared for a moment in front of him, then disappeared be-

hind a sheet of rain. When the wipers cleared the windshield, he was already out on the bridge. A sheet of rain ob-
structed his vision again. He knew the bridge was narrow
and he had to be careful. But he was reluctant to slow
down. He was so close to the house, to getting Rejuvenol,
that he felt the urge to speed up instead. It was an urge he
could not control.

He pressed hard on the accelerator. The wipers swept
across the windshield, clearing a momentary view of the
bridge, just long enough for him to confirm that he was
centered in the roadway. He pressed the accelerator a little harder, speeding up. Within minutes he'd be at the
house preparing Rejuvenol, and on the phone finding out
how Zack was doing. The rain washed out his view
again.

The wipers swept across the windshield again. Ethan
was suddenly disoriented. The bridge in front of him was
gone. He saw only the gray churning water. He slammed
on the brakes. The Explorer slid across the wet pavement
toward the gap in the bridge in front of him.

He wasn't going to stop in time! He stomped on the
brake pedal and threw up his hands instinctively, bracing
himself for the crash. The front of the SUV dropped
abruptly as the tires left the pavement. Then there was a
loud, grating clang—the undercarriage scraping the roadway. Ethan lurched forward, smacking his forehead on
the steering wheel. He bounced backward as the SUV
ground to a stop, half on the bridge, half suspended over
the water.

The engine was still running, the front tires spinning in
midair. The windshield wipers scraped across the glass,
clearing a momentary view of Carmen's car, nose down in
the water in front of him. Only the trunk and a little of the
roof were above the waves. A sheet of rain covered his
view of the car again. Cold fear went right to his heart. *Is
the Rejuvenol in there, destroyed?*

The wipers cleared the windshield again. The car
seemed to sink deeper in that brief second. He gave only a

moment's thought to Carmen's being inside. As the rain obscured his vision again, he realized he had to get inside that car and see if she had the supply of Rejuvenol. If he couldn't find it, he'd have to formulate another dose from scratch and that would take hours. He wasn't sure Zack would last that long.

He threw open the door. The water was right beneath him. He slid out and splashed into the rough surf, sinking toward the bottom. The water was warm but extremely salty. As he came up and poked his head above the water, he drew in a breath of air. A wave washed over his head. He swallowed a mouthful of the brine. Coughing and spitting, he swam over to Carmen's car.

He drew a deep breath and ducked under the water. Here the world was suddenly silent, dark, blurry. Weighted down by his soaked clothes, he sank onto the hood of the car. The windows were rolled up, the doors still closed. Through the windshield he saw Carmen's body still strapped in place by the seatbelt. Her face was swollen, her mouth wide open. Dead eyes stared up at him.

Seeing her dead angered him. He had counted on her to do something important for Zack and she'd failed. She might even have destroyed the dose of Rejuvenol. He never should have entrusted such a critical job to her.

He kicked himself to the surface and drew in a deep breath of air. Rain pelted down on his head like bullets. The noise from the rain and wind and churning waves heightened his sense of urgency and anger. He ducked down and swam underwater to the driver's side door. He tugged on it, pushing his foot against the back door for leverage. The door slowly came open. He swam inside.

Where would she put a bag of Rejuvenol? He found her purse floating near the dashboard. He opened it and pulled everything out. No bag. He then checked the pockets of Carmen's clothing. He couldn't find the bag anywhere. He was running out of air. He swam deeper and opened the glove compartment and pulled out the papers and the owner's manual. No bag of Rejuvenol. *Where the hell is it?*

He needed air. He swam out and resurfaced. Gasping at the wet air, he grew angrier by the second. He was running out of time. Zack needed him to bring Rejuvenol. He needed to find that goddamn bag. Where the hell did Carmen put it?

He went under again and swam into the car. He felt around on the seat, then he unstrapped Carmen and pulled her out so he could check more thoroughly. She floated away from the car and the current slowly carried her off. Ethan swam out of the car and felt the sand beneath it, thinking the bag might have fallen out. He couldn't see much in the water; it was dark and clouded with sediment and stung his eyes terribly. He struggled to hold his breath and went back inside the car.

When he couldn't hold his breath any longer, he swam out of the car and kicked himself to the surface. Gasping for air, he treaded water, realizing he was not going to find the infusion bag down there. He had no choice but to go back to his lab and prepare another dose. It would take some time, but he had to do it.

He swam to shore. His clothes felt like lead weights on him and the wind was ferocious. He struggled to run up the road toward his house. He tried to shake the sense of doom but it would not leave him. Everyone had abandoned De Leon. He felt he was battling the world.

When he got into the house, he tried to turn on the lights but they did not work. The storm must have taken out the power lines somewhere. He found a candle and hurried upstairs to his laboratory. The first thing he did was pick up the phone to call Miami and see how Zack was. There was no dial tone.

"Damn it!" He slammed down the phone. He found his cell phone and tried to place a call but there was no signal. The hurricane must have blown down the tower.

No lights was one thing. Not being able to find out how Zack was doing was much more difficult. He felt more worried, more rushed. He had to do this quickly. He had to get back to Zack. If he couldn't save his son's life, he'd have no reason to live himself.

He hurriedly began working.

74

THE AIRPORT IN Miami was total chaos. Flights to Key West were being diverted here. Passengers were stuck. The concourse was wall-to-wall people.

Paul and Alicia raced through the terminal. Outside, a light steady rain was coming down. The sky was dark gray, a reminder that a hurricane was coming ashore in a few hours.

They tried to get a taxi but there were more people than taxis. It would take hours. Paul ran back inside and rented a car. It seemed to take the agent forever to print up the contract and get the keys. The woman started to explain the usual terms but Paul grabbed the keys, scribbled his name and initials in the spots she indicated, and ran off to get the car. He and Alicia sped through the traffic to the hospital.

Six police cars were in the parking lot, lights flashing. They had cleared an area in front of the building, marked it off with yellow tape. A few dozen people were standing in the rain, staring up. Paul left the car in a fire lane and jumped out. When he peered up and saw his two sons on the ledge ten stories up, his breath left him.

Desperate, he ducked under the tape and ran toward the hospital door.

"Hey! You! Stop!" a cop yelled.

Paul ignored the man. He heard Alicia tell the cop, "It's okay. He's the boys' father." Then she ran inside behind him.

The lobby was chaos. The hospital had evacuated all

nonessential people from the tenth floor. The patients and staff were still up there, but everyone else was down here, whispering and speculating about what was happening. A security guard by the elevators asked them what floor they were going to. Paul ignored him and pressed 10. He wasn't going to let anyone stand in his way.

A police officer waiting outside the elevator on the tenth floor tried to stop them. "Those are my sons!" Paul said and pushed past. Alicia followed.

They got to the waiting room where police officers and firemen were gathered around Beth. A fireman was leaning out of one window, saying something to Kenny. Two policemen had their heads stuck out of another window, watching.

"Paul!" Beth cried when she saw him. She ran over and fell into his arms.

"It's going to be okay," he said. "We're going to get them off of there, don't worry."

"I don't know what's happened to him! Why would he do such a thing?"

Paul did know what happened to him. Ethan's Rejuvenol. "It's going to be okay," he told her again. He eased her over to the couch and coaxed her down. He gestured to a female officer, who came over and tried to comfort her. He went to the window where the policemen were and told them to let him talk to his son.

Paul stuck his head out. Rain slashed at his face. He glimpsed the ground ten stories down and the image of his sons falling terrified him. If he made a mistake now, it would be the worst mistake of his life, one he'd never be able to recover from. There was no detox or AA for killing your children.

He looked over at Kenny, who had Pete in a headlock. They were standing on a foot-wide ledge, soaking wet, their backs pressed against the wall. Pete looked terrified; tears were running down his face and he was frozen still, possibly in shock. He didn't budge or make a sound.

Kenny just looked angry. His thoughts seemed somewhere else. He didn't look scared at all, or even aware of the consequences of what he was doing. Paul had seen the same look on the face of Karla this morning, when she was trying to kill him and Alicia.

On the other side of Kenny and Pete, the fireman was trying to talk him into coming inside. Kenny wasn't listening.

"Kenny," Paul said. "It's me, Dad."

Kenny snapped his head around and glared at Paul. His eyes were wide and white. He glowered at Paul, looking enraged. He spit out an angry laugh. *"Dad?"* he said, mocking the word. "Yeah, right . . ."

"Kenny, I know things haven't been that great between us the last few years—"

"There's been *nothing* between us the last few years! Half the time I saw you you were drunk! The other half, you were just pathetic. You killed a patient, you screwed up your life and our family, and you abandoned us. And I'm supposed to think of you as my dad?" He spit out another mocking laugh.

Paul wanted to crawl under a rock and never come out. What Kenny was saying was true. He had screwed up their lives. He didn't kill Wilkenson—he knew that now. And he didn't abandon them—he'd fought constantly with Beth and with the judge who granted her sole custody. But this wasn't the time to defend himself. Now he had to be the father he should have been all along.

"Please don't do this, Kenny," Paul said.

"Don't do what?" he snapped back.

"Don't jump from there. Come back inside. We'll talk about what's bothering you. Things will be better, I promise you."

"Yeah, right."

Paul didn't know how to overcome the effects of Rejuvenol. Kenny wasn't thinking straight because of it. Paul didn't know if it would wear off and he'd be able to reason with Kenny or if the only way to get him off the ledge was to go grab him and pull him inside.

The boys were about four feet away. Paul doubted he could reach them from where he was and grab them. He had to get Kenny to come closer.

"Listen, Kenny," he said. "I know everything seems hopeless right now. I know that all you can think of is what's bad, what's wrong. But believe me, things are not what they seem."

"How do you know?" Kenny said. "You don't even know what 'things' are!"

"Why don't you tell me, then."

"Why? You don't care."

"Yes I do. Of course I do."

Behind Kenny, the fireman pulled his head back inside the building. A second later, Alicia stuck her head out. Kenny didn't notice her, though. He was focused intensely on Paul.

She and Paul exchanged glances. She gestured that she was almost close enough to Pete to grab him. Paul wasn't sure what good that would do. Maybe she could hold Pete, *if* she could get hold of him. But she couldn't reach Kenny, and even if she could, he was too heavy for her to hold.

It still depended on him, on their father. He had to get them off this ledge alive.

"Please, Kenny, talk to me," Paul said. "Tell me what's going on with you."

"I hate you, that's what's going on with me! All right? What do you have to say about that . . . *Dad?*"

"Well, I think you have good reason to feel that way about me," Paul said. "I have let you down. But I'm trying to change that. Haven't you seen that over the past few months?"

"No. All I see is a loser. And now I have to move to France. Plus I have this twerp to take care of," he said, tightening his hold on Pete. Pete gagged and tried to press himself flatter against the wall. "What reason do I have to live?" Kenny said.

"You have lots of reasons."

"Name one."

"You have a lot of people who love you. Your mother, me, your brother—"

"Oh, please," he groaned, unimpressed. "Like that's supposed to be something good."

"Kenny, you're young, you have your whole life ahead of you."

Kenny rolled his eyes. "Do me a favor, will you? Just go back to your life and leave me alone."

"I won't do that."

"Then I'm jumping. Right now!" he said, suddenly raising his voice and becoming irate. "Leave me alone!"

Behind him, Alicia reached carefully toward Pete. Paul saw that if she stretched herself, she could get her hand pretty close to Pete's leg. But Kenny was still out of reach of both of them. He had an idea.

"No, I won't leave you!" he told Kenny.

"Then I'm jumping!" Kenny screamed.

"Then I'm jumping with you!" Paul said and started to climb out the window.

"Stop!" Kenny shouted, backing away from Paul, closer to the window Alicia was leaning out. "Stop or I swear to God I'm going to jump!"

Paul stopped, one leg on the ledge. The rain was spraying his face now. He felt the wind trying to pull him and the boys to their death. But he was closer to his sons now, and that felt good. He wasn't sure, but he thought he could reach Kenny if he had to.

Alicia nodded to him. Now that Kenny had backed toward her, she was definitely able to get a good hold of Pete. It was up to Paul now.

"Kenny," he said, perched half out of the window, "don't you understand? If you and Pete die, I have no reason to live anymore."

"That's a lie!"

"What other reason do I have to live?"

Kenny didn't have an answer. He looked frustrated and he finally screamed, "This isn't about you! Why can't everybody just leave me alone?"

"Is that what you want?"

"Yes. Go! Leave me alone!"

"No, I don't mean here, now. I mean, is that what you want when you come back inside?"

"I'm not coming back inside!"

"What would get you to come back inside with Pete?" Paul asked.

"Nothing!"

"There's got to be something. You're out here for a reason."

"You think it's because of the TV, don't you?" Kenny said, suddenly defensive.

"I don't know what it's because of."

"I'm not stupid! It's not just the TV. It's lots of things. Why do I always have to put up with this twerp?" His anger flared again and he started to shake Pete. When he did, he turned and noticed Alicia within reach.

"Get away!" he screamed.

Paul knew he had to act now. He slid through the window and out onto the ledge. Kenny turned and saw him. Alicia grabbed Pete by the leg. Kenny saw this and tried to pull away. He lost his footing and started to fall. Paul stretched out toward him and grabbed his jeans, pulling him toward the window. Alicia had a good enough hold on Pete to pull him inside.

Paul only had one hand on Kenny as he fell from the ledge. But he held on tightly and stopped his fall. Kenny dangled from the side of the building, screaming.

"Help! Help! Dad, help me!"

"I got you, Kenny."

Paul held with all his strength. He felt himself start to slide over the ledge. Someone grabbed him around the waist. One of the policemen squeezed through the window beside him and grabbed Kenny's arm. Together, they pulled Kenny inside.

The hospital staff sedated Kenny. It was hard for Paul to see his son in restraints but he knew it was necessary. Pete was in another room, traumatized by what had happened. He'd been unable to speak, unable to sit still. The psychiatrist had been forced to sedate him, too. Now both of them were resting. But Paul knew that this was going to affect both boys for a long time to come.

And Beth, too. She was shaking in the waiting room.

Alicia was trying to calm her. Paul came over and held Beth, assuring her that everything was going to be all right. Inside he was seething at what Ethan had done to his son. He wanted desperately to make him pay for this.

"Where's your brother?" he asked Beth quietly, not wanting to let out how angry he was at Ethan. "Is he in ICU with Zachary?"

"He didn't come back from his house yet."

"How long ago did he leave?"

"A couple hours, I think."

He couldn't wait around. He needed to find Ethan. He assured Beth that the boys would be all right and told the doctor that Beth needed something to calm her down as well. The doctor agreed.

When Paul told Alicia that he was going to De Leon to find Ethan, she insisted on going with him. Ethan had done the same thing to her family as he'd done to Paul's, only the consequences had been worse—her sister had died. She was going to De Leon, either with him or on her own.

As they were about to leave, a doctor came up to them and asked if they were with Zachary Granier.

"His father's not here, but I'm his uncle," Paul said. "Why?"

"I'm sorry, but Zachary passed away a few minutes ago."

75

RAIN POURED DOWN so hard Paul could hardly see the road ahead. Darkness was closing in. His headlights only illuminated the wall of rain in front of the car. He stopped and strained to see the road sign swaying in the wind.

"Can you read it?" he asked Alicia.

"No."

Neither could he. The sign was flailing wildly, and it was out of focus in the rain and darkness.

"I'm pretty sure this is the road," Paul said.

He turned off A1A and drove slowly ahead. On the radio, the newscaster droned on about the storm, how fast the sustained winds were, how quickly it was moving, what class storm it was. Paul tuned out most of that. His thoughts were on Kenny and Pete back in Miami. And on Ethan. Was Ethan even still here? He could have left hours ago. The whole drive in, they'd tried to watch the road for Beth's Explorer going the other way, but they hadn't seen it. He just hoped they hadn't missed him.

Ethan might know how to reverse the effects of Rejuvenol on Kenny. Even if he didn't, Paul still needed to confront him.

The radio said the eye of the storm was centered fifty miles west of Key West, not a direct hit but close enough to the keys to cause major damage. The way the trees were bending in the wind, Paul couldn't imagine what a direct hit would have been like. A gust of wind blew across the road. Paul held the wheel tightly with both hands to keep the car under control.

They came to the sign that said DE LEON CENTER. Paul saw the bridge ahead. Beth's SUV was stopped halfway across, blocking the road.

"Is that his car?" Alicia asked.

"That's it."

Something about it looked strange from this angle, but it was difficult to see under the veil of rain. Paul drove ahead slowly. As they got closer, Paul noticed that the front was dipping down. He strained to see. Alicia saw at the same moment.

"The bridge collapsed!" she said.

The front axle of Beth's SUV was hanging over the water, where the bridge had given out. A shiver ran through Paul. Their car was on the bridge as well. Was it safe?

He stopped the car and they got out. The rain drenched them immediately. They slowly approached Beth's SUV and peered into the window. It was empty.

"Look!" Alicia said, pointing.

Paul looked to where she was pointing. He saw the rear end of a car sticking up from the rough water. It looked like Carmen's car.

"Oh, my God," he said. Did she get out in time? Did somebody rescue her? Or was she still in there, dead?

He had to check.

"Wait here," he told Alicia as he walked to the edge of the bridge.

"Where are you going?"

"To see if anyone's in there."

"I'm going with you."

"No. Wait here. The water's too rough. It's too dangerous. I'll be right back."

He jumped into the current. It tried to pull him to the side but he fought it and swam the short distance to Carmen's car. Before he could check inside, he heard a splash behind him. He turned and saw Alicia fighting the current. He reached out and grabbed her hand then pulled her over.

"I thought I told you to wait there."

"I forgot," she said.

They both ducked under the water and checked the car. The driver's door was open, the car empty. Carmen must have gotten out. Thank God.

They came to the surface and caught their breath.

"Do you think he's still here?" Alicia asked.

"I don't know." Beth's car was here, but Ethan might have left another way. Paul peered toward the island. There were no lights. It looked deserted. "The hurricane's nearly here," he said. "It's not safe. He must have left. We should go, too."

"I want to get the evidence of what he's doing before we leave," Alicia said. "I want to be able to prove what he did to my sister."

"We can come back after the hurricane's gone."

"What if the records get lost in the storm? No, I'm going to get it all now."

There was no sense arguing with her. She was probably right, they should get whatever was here now, just in case the island didn't withstand the storm.

"Let's do it quickly," Paul said.

They climbed up on the trunk of the car and pulled themselves onto what remained of the bridge. They had to battle the wind as they walked. It tried to push them back off the island. The rain slashed at their faces, stinging as if the drops were razors. They hurried to Paul's bungalow and tried the lights, but weren't surprised when they didn't work. The power lines were probably one of the first casualties of the storm.

Even without lights Paul found the files on the desk where he'd left them. He and Alicia collected them, then found a plastic bag and wrapped the files so they wouldn't get ruined in the rain. When they went back outside, the storm seemed to have grown more intense. The wind whipped palms across the grounds. No one had taken in the patio furniture before they evacuated the clinic, and now some of it was tumbling across the pool area.

In the wind, Alicia could barely steady herself. Paul was heavier than she and a little more stable; he held on to her as they started to make their way back across the grounds.

Then Paul saw the flicker of candlelight in the upstairs window of Ethan's house.

Ethan must still be here.

"Listen, go back to the car," he told Alicia, giving her the files. "I'll meet you there in a few minutes. There's something I need to do."

"What?"

"Don't worry about it. Just go back to the car. I'll be there in a few minutes."

Exactly what he'd do to Ethan he still didn't know, but he did have to see him. And he also knew that Ethan couldn't stay here. It wouldn't be safe when the hurricane hit full strength.

"What are you going to do?" Alicia asked.

"Never mind. Just go."

Alicia saw the light in Ethan's window. She understood right away. "I'm going with you," she said.

"No, you're not."

"Are we going to keep this up all day?" she said. "Look, he's responsible for my sister being dead. I'm going in there to get him."

"It's not a lynching," Paul said. "I just want to talk to him."

"Fine, you talk to him. I'm going to lynch him."

"I mean it, Alicia."

"So do I," she said and hurried toward Ethan's house, leaving Paul behind.

He ran and caught up with her and they went in together.

They closed the door of the house behind them, sealing out the wind and rain. But he still heard the storm pummeling the island outside. The house creaked. The barrage of rain on the roof and walls sounded like the house was under attack. And in a way, it was.

The downstairs was dark. A glow came from the doorway leading upstairs. Paul heard Ethan moving around above. He remembered how dangerous Karla had been and he wondered if Ethan was on Rejuvenol himself. As good as he looked, he had to be. Would he be as out of control as Karla?

"I don't suppose it would do any good to tell you to wait here," Paul said to Alicia.

"Right, it wouldn't do any good."

"Just let me go first."

He didn't know what to expect as he went through the doorway and up the stairs. When he got to the top, he saw Ethan at one of the lab tables, sealing an infusion bag. Ethan looked up and saw them. His face did not register surprise or any other emotion. He just looked at them.

"What are you doing here?" he asked, nothing in his voice, not a hint of what he was thinking or feeling. He peered at Alicia and said to Paul, "Why did you bring her?"

"We were looking for you," Paul said.

Ethan looked down and focused on what he was doing. He finished sealing the bag then said, "Do you have a car here?"

Paul nodded. He tried to assess Ethan's demeanor. Ethan seemed strange, not himself. But Paul couldn't put his finger on what it was about him that was different. Rather than being out of control, the way Karla had been, Ethan seemed to be in total control, emotionless, almost robotic.

"Good," Ethan said. "The car I came in is stuck."

"We saw it," Paul said.

"I'm ready to go." He held up the bag. "Zack needs this."

"That's Rejuvenol?" Paul asked.

"I know you found out about it," Ethan said. He gestured toward Alicia. "You shouldn't have told her. I thought I could trust you, Paul."

"He didn't have to tell me," Alicia said. "I found out myself. That's what killed my sister."

Ethan shook his head. "Your sister killed herself."

"No! *You* killed her!" Alicia shouted. "*That's* what killed her," she said, pointing to the bag. She started toward Ethan but Paul grabbed her arm and pulled her back. She tried to yank herself free but he held tightly. "Let go of me!"

Paul glared at Ethan. "How long did you think you could keep it a secret, Ethan?"

"Long enough to keep my son alive."

"And what about my son?" Paul's anger began to grow. "You gave that to Kenny," he said. "You didn't give a damn about what happened to him. Is your son more important than mine?"

"Your son is fine."

"He almost killed himself and Pete!"

Alicia tried to pull herself free again and get to Ethan. "My sister isn't fine!" she said, tears streaking down her face now. "She's dead because of you! Is your son more important than her?"

Paul held her tightly. He knew how she felt, knew she had every right to take out her anger and pain on Ethan, but he also knew that wouldn't do any good. And he still needed to find out from Ethan if there was something that would reverse the effects of Rejuvenol on Kenny.

Ethan struggled for something to say to Alicia. Finally he just stuffed the bag into his pocket and said, "I don't have time for this. I have to get back to Miami. Zack needs me."

Ethan started toward the steps. Alicia became passive now. Paul understood why. They both were thinking the same thing. Ethan had to be told about Zack. And as angry as they both were at him, they knew this news was going to devastate him.

Paul held out his hand and stopped Ethan.

"I have to go," Ethan said, glaring at Paul.

"Ethan," Paul said quietly, "Zack is dead."

Ethan stood there, staring. It seemed to take a few moments for it to sink in. "What?" he asked in a whisper.

Paul nodded. "He died a few hours ago."

"No," Ethan said. "He can't be."

"I'm sorry."

Ethan's jaw dropped open. His eyes began to water. His skin lost all color. "Zack really is . . . ?" He couldn't say the last word.

Paul nodded and again said, "I'm sorry, Ethan."

Suddenly Ethan's face seemed to change. The sheet of pale gray anguish vanished, replaced by a flush of red anger. He glared at Paul. His body tensed. He clenched his fists. Paul was sure he was going to lash out at him.

But then he looked past Paul and glared at Alicia with a wild look in his eyes. "If I hadn't gone to New York because of you," he shouted, "I would have been here to save Zack. I wasn't here because of you!"

Before Paul could say a word, Ethan lunged at Alicia. Paul pulled her behind him, then grabbed Ethan and shoved him away, into a lab table. A microscope tumbled over. Test tubes smashed on the floor. Ethan sprang up and rushed toward them, ramming into Paul and Alicia with such force that he knocked them both to the floor. Paul fell hard, smacking his head on the wood. He lost his senses for an instant. When he came to, Ethan was swinging wildly, hitting him and Alicia with a barrage of punches. Ethan had more strength than Paul would have imagined. His body was solid; his fists felt rock hard.

Ethan pounded Paul in the face. The hit echoed inside his skull. He swung blindly at Ethan, landing a feeble blow to his shoulder. Ethan pushed him down then turned to Alicia and drove his fist into her stomach. She gasped, the wind knocked out of her, her face contorted in pain. Paul punched at Ethan's ribs, slowing his attack only momentarily. Ethan cocked his arm back and drove his fist into Alicia's chin. The cracking sound when it hit echoed through the room. Alicia's head snapped back against the floor. Ethan's hand drew back for another hit, but this one Paul managed to grab, stopping him.

Alicia lay motionless, helpless. Ethan turned his attack on Paul now, swinging wildly. Paul threw up his arms to deflect the punches. He rocked sideways, enough to tip

Ethan off balance. Then he pushed Ethan off him and tried to get on top and hold him down. But Ethan fought back. The two of them grappled on the floor, rolling and punching. Paul got in several solid hits. He was getting the better of Ethan when suddenly a tree came smashing through the window a few feet away.

It sounded like an explosion. Glass sprayed down on them. Rain poured in. The wind churned up the papers and blew rain everywhere. The candle went out, leaving them in sudden darkness. Ethan jabbed up into Paul's chin, then scrambled out from under him and ran down the stairs.

He was leaving. Paul realized that he and Alicia needed to do the same thing. This house wasn't safe. The whole island probably wasn't safe. He remembered what Ethan had told him about the hurricane that had hit here several years ago. Many of the buildings hadn't survived. Much of the island had been underwater. They definitely needed to get out of here.

He crawled over to Alicia. She was unconscious but breathing. He scooped her up into his arms and started toward the stairs. Just then part of the roof ripped off. Rain and wind lashed down at them. The house creaked and howled under the strain of the wind. There was no telling how much longer it would hold up.

Paul staggered down the stairs, carrying Alicia and struggling to steady himself against the wind and the sheet of water on the steps. He got downstairs and didn't see Ethan anywhere. More of the roof ripped off above. The noise of the storm and of the house being torn apart was deafening.

Alicia came to. "What happened? What's going on?"

"We have to get off the island! Can you walk?"

"I think so."

He put her down, and the two of them limped through the house to the front door. Just then one of the windows imploded, spraying glass across the room, several shards biting into Paul's side. Alicia cried out as three tiny dag-

gers stuck into her shoulder and arm. Paul pulled the glass
out. Blood streaked down her arm. They'd have to take
care of that later. So, too, the glass in Paul's side. It stung,
and he could feel warm blood seeping beneath his shirt, but
they didn't have time to stop and tend to it now.

"Ready?" he asked Alicia.

"Let's go!"

As soon as he pushed open the front door the wind
grabbed it and ripped it off the hinges. It flew across the
yard. Paul and Alicia hadn't even stepped outside yet and
still they could feel the wind trying to knock them over. It
had gotten much stronger since they came in. But was it
too strong for them to go out there? Could they fight their
way back to the car? How were they going to get across the
water?

As if on cue, the house creaked again. More of the roof
ripped off. Something crashed upstairs. Another window
blew in. Paul knew they couldn't stay here either. But outside the noise alone was terrifying. It sounded like the entire world was collapsing. Waves crashed against the shore
right beside the house. When the storm surge came, it
could cover the island completely, wash them away if they
were still here. The wind roared and screamed as if it were
a living entity, an enemy waiting for them to step outside
so it could attack them.

Then thunder exploded outside, so loud that the house
shook. Lightning flashed, momentarily illuminating the
grounds of the clinic. In the glare of light Paul saw the wall
of rain in front of them. Palm bushes bounced across the
grounds, slamming into buildings. Chunks of wood and
stucco from the bungalows slashed about.

Paul was trying to figure out what to do, whether to go
out there or not, when another blast of thunder resounded.
In the flash of lightning he saw Ethan outside, struggling
against the wind to return to the house. He must have tried
to escape but realized it was impossible.

They were going to have to stay in here and try to ride
out the storm. He hoped Ethan had calmed down and re-

gained control of himself, because they were all in this together. He watched Ethan stagger closer. It seemed to take
all of his strength to anchor himself to the ground and not
let the wind carry him away. A few times, a gust pushed
him off line but he managed to fight his way back toward
the house. But he was struggling. Paul wasn't sure he'd
make it.

Then Alicia said, "What's he got with him?"

Paul hadn't noticed until now that Ethan was carrying
something. Another flash of lightning. Paul saw that Ethan
had something in his right hand, partially hidden at his
side. It was about a yard or so long, but Paul couldn't see
what it was.

Ethan got to the end of the walk, saw them in the doorway, and stopped. He glared at them, still angry. Paul realized that Ethan wasn't going to come in if they were there.
He was going to endanger his own life out of hatred for
the two of them.

"Ethan!" Paul shouted, taking a step out into the rain
and wind. He extended his hand to Ethan. "Come on, get in
here!"

Ethan stood there, fighting the wind. "Move!" he said.

Paul didn't understand. Then he realized that Ethan was
looking past him, trying to get a clear view of Alicia, who
was standing in the doorway.

"Come on inside with us," Paul said.

Ethan stepped to the side so he could see Alicia, then he
raised his right arm. Paul saw now what it was he was
carrying. *A speargun!* He pointed it past Paul, at Alicia.

"You killed my son!" Ethan shouted.

Paul jumped in front of Alicia, blocking Ethan's aim.
"Ethan! Don't!"

Ethan tried to step to the side to get a clean shot at Alicia
but Paul moved with him, shielding her.

"Get out of the way, Paul. I don't blame you. I blame
her. She has to pay for killing Zack."

"She didn't kill Zack."

"Move!" Ethan shouted.

He stepped sideways again. Paul moved, too, blocking him again.

"Don't make me shoot you!" Ethan warned. "I will if I have to!" Ethan started to move again.

"Alicia!" Paul shouted. "Watch out!" Then he started to rush toward Ethan.

Ethan fired at Alicia, but Paul moved into its path and the spear sliced into his thigh. The pain sapped Paul of all his strength. He spun from the momentum of the spear and collapsed to the ground. Alicia rushed over and grabbed him. She was starting to pull him inside when Ethan loaded another spear into the gun and pointed it at her head.

Struggling against the wind, he took a step toward her. "You killed my son!" he screamed.

"You killed my sister," she said.

"Shut up!"

"Ethan, listen to me," Paul said.

"No! She has to die! She killed Zack! Now I'm going to kill her!" Ethan's body tensed. He screamed in rage and pulled the trigger.

"Ethan, no . . . !" Paul shouted.

Just then a huge chunk of roof blew across and crashed into Ethan. The gun went off and the spear veered to the side, clacking into the wall. Ethan tumbled over and flopped to the wet ground. He struggled to his feet, shaken from the blow. The wind nearly knocked him down again. He reached into his belt and pulled out his diving knife, then he staggered toward them.

Paul couldn't stand. Alicia tried to pull him into the house but Ethan came on quickly. He was right there in seconds. He screamed and lunged with the knife. Paul tried to slide over and shield Alicia, but she scrambled out from behind him, and before he realized what she was doing, she ripped the spear out of his thigh. Pain shot up through his body. As Ethan came down toward her, she flipped the spear around and thrust it into his chest.

Ethan gasped and staggered backward. The knife fell out of his hands. His mouth fell open. Blood poured out.

He tried to speak but could only gurgle. He stared up at them then crumpled to the ground, dead.

Alicia dragged Paul inside the house. They huddled in a corner as the storm pounded the island.

EPILOGUE

PAUL WAS WAITING at the gate, staring down the concourse. Behind him passengers boarded the Air France jet. He'd have to board himself in a few minutes. Where was she? He didn't want to leave without seeing her.

Finally he spotted Alicia weaving through the crowd, running toward him. He hurried over to meet her. She nearly knocked him over as she fell against him and wrapped her arms around him.

"Sorry I'm late," she said.

"I was afraid you weren't going to make it."

"The freeway was a mess. Next time you fly to Paris, can you not go during rush hour? You ever try to get from downtown L.A. to here at four o'clock in the afternoon?"

"Complain, complain, complain," he said. "You should have left earlier."

"Some of us have to work, you know. Not like others who can just go flying off to Europe at the drop of a hat."

"Oh!" Paul said, remembering. He took the letter out of his pocket to show her.

"What's that?" she asked, unfolding it and quickly skimming through. Her mouth fell open. She was stunned.

He grinned, proudly. "You're looking at California's newest licensed plastic surgeon," he said.

She hugged him again and kissed his neck. "You got it!"

"In today's mail."

"All right! I just wish we could celebrate together."

"We will, when I get back," he said.

Her excitement waned. She held him tightly and whispered, "I wish I could go with you."

"I wish you could, too. I just don't think Kenny and Pete are ready for their dad having a girlfriend yet. They're still getting used to having a dad again."

"Their dad's girlfriend?" She grinned. "Is that what I am?"

He pulled her close again. "You're a lot more than that."

He'd spent the last five months with her. They'd helped each other get through the pain and trauma of what had happened in Florida. The events they had experienced together had given them an immense closeness, as well as a strong sense of trust.

He had helped her deal with the death of her sister, helped her finally let her sadness come to the surface and vent. And she had used her connections in the investigative world to help him prove to the licensing board in New York that he was not at fault for Linda Wilkenson's death. Their reinstating of his license was essential to his getting a license in California.

Paul had moved to California to be with her. They still kept separate apartments, but they spent most of their time together. Paul wasn't sure if they'd get married; it was still too soon to know that. But he felt a love for her that he hadn't thought he could ever feel for anyone but Beth.

"The boys are going to spend the summer with me this year," he told her. He wanted them to get to know her, to accept her in his life and in their own lives. But that would take time. They still had to adjust to living in France and to get over the trauma of what had happened in Miami. Maybe by summer . . .

"How are they?" Alicia asked.

That was a difficult question to answer. "Kenny seems to be back to normal," he said. He shrugged and said, "Well, as normal as a teenager can be. The last MRI showed no abnormality in his frontal lobe." The operation to remove the small tumor had been successful.

"Pete still has nightmares," Paul said. "But Beth tells me they're not as frequent or as scary as before. I think he's going to be all right."

"Children are resilient," she said.

Paul remembered her telling him about the trauma she'd endured as a child, her parents dying. That had shaped her life ever since. She still hadn't overcome it completely. He hoped Kenny and Pete would fare better.

"They're good kids," Alicia said. "And they have good parents. They'll get through this."

Paul hoped so.

The gate agent announced that all remaining passengers for the Air France flight to Paris should board.

Alicia hugged Paul again. She gazed into his eyes and said, "I'm really going to miss you. I've gotten used to having you around."

He knew that this kind of talk didn't come easily to her. Over the months that they'd been together, he'd watched her struggle so much to let her emotions out, and to let him inside her heart, to let herself feel. He too had difficulty opening up to her, risking loving her. But they both had taken it gradually, and helped each other, and that made their bond so much stronger.

"I'm going to miss you, too," he said.

"Call me?"

"Of course. Every night."

The last passengers boarded. The gate agents were preparing to close the door to the jetway.

"You better get going," she said.

He grabbed her, pulled her against him, and kissed her. "I love you," he said.

"I love you, too. Hurry back."

He ran to the door, waved one last time, then went down the jetway toward the plane. For the first time in a long time, he felt good about life. Terrible things had happened in Florida, but in the end, he'd proven to himself how strong he could be. He'd settled everything that had been unresolved in his life. And he'd found a true new beginning in Alicia.

As he took his seat and waited for the plane to taxi, he thought about De Leon. The hurricane had left almost nothing standing. All of Ethan's research was lost. His files, everything. Whatever benefit might have come from Rejuvenol was lost, too. But so was the harm it could do.

Paul felt some relief.

But one thing continued to trouble him. Had there been other patients on Rejuvenol that he didn't know about? Somewhere out there might be more time bombs. He'd never know for sure. As he began his new life he held on to some of the hard-won wisdom of AA, which just now reminded him, take it one day at a time.

DON DONALDSON
DO NO HARM

"Full of twists and turns, and brimming with chillingly authentic medical details...takes the reader on a lively ride." —Tess Gerritsen

Dr. Sarchi Seminoux, a Memphis pediatric resident, gets a call from Marge, her nephew's adoptive mother, that they are bringing Drew into the emergency room. Drew can't move or talk, but all his vitals are OK, blood tests are all normal. Dr. Latham is a brilliant brain surgeon who seems to think that he can help Drew, but the doctor refuses to go into any details with Marge or Sarchi. Drew gets his operation, but Sarchi notices some side effects. Sarchi decides to look into Dr. Latham's practices, but as she does, Dr. Latham tries to ruin Sarchi's reputation.
Can Sarchi make the hospital and the other doctors see what Dr. Latham is and how he is harming patients?

❑ 0-515-12650-0

Available wherever books are sold or to order call 1-800-788-6262

JOHNNY CARSON

MEL BROOKS

TOM STOPPARD

LOUISE BROOKS

SIR RALPH RICHARDSON

"Together they make up a royal flush of talent. Each has a style that is as inimitable as a finger-print. Last and far from least, they all rank high on the list of people whom I would invite to an ideal dinner party."
—KENNETH TYNAN

"QUITE A DINNER PARTY IT WOULD BE. TYNAN...COMMUNICATES HIS OWN PASSION FOR GENIUS IN A SPLENDID FLOW OF WORLDS!"
—*Atlanta Journal-Constitution*

"HE IS NEVER DULL!"

—*Time*

KENNETH TYNAN

*Profiles
in
Entertainment*

SHOW PEOPLE

BERKLEY BOOKS, NEW YORK

The text of this book appeared originally in *The New Yorker*.

The author is grateful for permission to reprint the following excerpts:
From Christopher Logue's poem (page 99), reprinted by permission of
Alfred E. Knopf, Inc., from *New Numbers*, © 1969 by Christopher Logue.
From T. S. Eliot's "Love Song of J. Alfred Prufrock" (page 67), reprinted
by permission of Harcourt, Brace, Jovanovich, Inc., from *Collected Poems
1909–1962*, © 1962 by T. S. Eliot, and by permission of Faber and Faber,
from *Collected Poems 1909–1962* by T. S. Eliot.

This Berkley book contains the complete
text of the original hardcover edition.
It has been completely reset in a type face
designed for easy reading, and was printed
from new film.

SHOW PEOPLE:
Profiles in Entertainment

A Berkley Book / published by arrangement with
Simon and Schuster

PRINTING HISTORY
Simon and Schuster edition / February 1980
Berkley edition / July 1981

ISBN: 0-425-04750-4

A BERKLEY BOOK® TM 757,375
Berkley Books are published by Berkley Publishing Corporation,
200 Madison Avenue, New York, New York, 10016.
PRINTED IN THE UNITED STATES OF AMERICA

Contents

Foreword

THIS BOOK consists of word portraits of five people who have two qualities in common—(1) they all work in show business, and (2) I admire them enormously.

I have called these portraits "profiles." Until a few decades ago, they would have been described as "essays," but in recent years "essay" has become a dirty word in certain literary circles. Many critics maintain that the essay is an inferior form; and many publishers believe that modern readers care only for long-distance, marathon writing, and that there is no room left for such middle-distance, eight-hundred-metre stuff as essays. Out of the window—if these experts are right—goes Montaigne. To the bonfire with William Hazlitt, closely followed by Max Beerbohm, Sainte-Beuve and John Aubrey. A brusque kiss-off to Francis Bacon, Charles Lamb, La Bruyère and the best of Mencken, not to mention Suetonius's *Lives of the Caesars;* and into the garbage goes Samuel Johnson's *Lives of the Poets*, perhaps the finest book of profile-essays ever written. The list could be indefinitely extended. Any theory that regards works like these as second-class literature is transparently dotty. It is as if art critics were to judge pieces of sculpture by their bulk.

I am not, of course, claiming a place for myself among the masters I have named above. (Although, when Lamb is at his most whimsical, I sometimes feel I could go a couple of rounds with him and not make a total fool of myself.) I have spent much of my life as a literary sprinter, writing thousand-word reviews of plays and movies. But I have also aspired to be a middle-distance man, and the pieces that follow are my latest efforts in this genre.

Their subjects are show people, inhabitants of the over-lapping worlds of theatre, cinema, and television which I have professionally observed for the past three decades. Together, they make up a royal flush of talent—talent to which, over the years, I have happily responded and which I have felt the need to define in print. Not with the comprehensive detail of a biography, nor yet with the epigrammatic brevity of a thumbnail sketch, but in the space of twenty thousand words or so, enough to convey the essential facts of a man's life and to explore the nature of his gifts.

My chosen quintet includes a great actor (Sir Ralph Richardson), a great television virtuoso (Johnny Carson), a great screen beauty (Louise Brooks), a great comic creator (Mel Brooks), and a uniquely inventive playwright (Tom Stoppard) who has more than once been within hailing distance of greatness and may, any season now, earn a permanent niche in the dramatic pantheon. Each of them has a style that is as inimitable as a fingerprint. All but one (the exception being Stoppard) are performers—a fact that reflects my abiding obsession with the skills that enable a man or woman to seize and hold the rapt attention of a multitude. Last and far from least, they all rank high on the list of people whom I would invite to an ideal dinner party.

KENNETH TYNAN

At three minutes past eight
you must dream
—RALPH RICHARDSON

SIR RALPH RICHARDSON celebrated his seventy-fourth birthday on December 19, 1976, the day after Harold Pinter's *No Man's Land*, in which he co-starred with his old friend Sir John Gielgud, ended its Broadway run at the Longacre. Sir Ralph played Hirst, a wealthy Englishman with an awe-inspiring thirst, incessantly slaked, for vodka and Scotch. Hirst is also a famous writer, although we do not discover this until page 67 of the published text (which ends on pages 95)—a little late in the day, some may think, for such an important disclosure. Some, indeed, would get downright shirty if another playwright were thus to withhold essential information that could easily have been revealed in the first ten minutes; but when Mr. Pinter does it, audiences marvel at what they have been taught to recognize as his skill in creating an atmosphere of poetic suspense. At all events, Hirst, protected by a pair of sinister servants called Foster and Briggs, lives in a palatial Hampstead house, where he is bearded by Spooner, a threadbare poetaster (played by Sir John) whom he may or may not have cuckolded—Mr. Pinter leaves us in poetic doubt—on the eve of the Second World War. Spooner, who seeks employment as Hirst's secretary, is under pressure throughout the play to quit the household. I don't propose to offer an interpretation of *No Man's Land*, but it may not be irrelevant to point out that all of its four characters are named after English cricketers who flourished around the turn of the century. Mr. Pinter is known

1

to be a fanatical lover of cricket—a game in which a batsman
(e.g., Spooner) invades the territory of the opposing team (e.g.,
Hirst, Foster, and Briggs), which then attempts, by a variety
of ploys that include bluff, deceit, and physical intimidation,
to dismiss him from the field. The dialogue, garlanded with
bizarre non sequiturs, is often hilarious. Whether the play is
more than a cerebral game is a decision that will have to wait
until we see it performed by second-rate actors. Fortunately
for Mr. Pinter, the English theatre is well equipped with senior
players who can bestow on whatever material comes their way
a patina of seignorial magic.

Sir Ralph is one such. Devotees of the Richardson cult—
who had last seen their idol on Broadway in 1970, when he
appeared (also with Sir John) as a benevolent lunatic in David
Storey's *Home*—observed with relief that immersion in Pin-
terdom had left his professional trademarks unchanged. There
was the unique physical presence, at once rakish and stately,
as of a pirate turned prelate. There was the balsawood lightness
of movement, which enabled him to fall flat on his face three
times in the course of a single act—a rare feat for septuagen-
arians. There was the peculiar method of locomotion, whereby
he would spring to his feet and, resembling a more aloof and
ceremonious Jacques Tati, propel himself forward with the
palms of his hands turned out, as if wading through waist-deep
water. There was the pop-eyed, poleaxed look, with one eyebrow balefully cocked, whenever he was faced with a remark
that was baffling or potentially hostile. Above all, there was
the voice, which I once described as "something between bland
and grandiose: blandiose, perhaps." Or, as I wrote in another
context, when he played *Cyrano de Bergerac* in 1946:

> His voice is most delicate; breath-light of texture; more
> buoyant even than that of M. Charles Trenet. . . . It is a
> yeasty, agile voice. Where Olivier would pounce upon
> a line and rip its heart out, Richardson skips and lilts
> and bounces along it, shaving off pathos in great flakes.

A personal note: The noise that Sir Ralph makes has sometimes struck me as the vocal equivalent of onionskin writing
paper—suave, crackling, and resonant. This curious associa-

tion is no doubt strengthened by my memories of his definitive performance as Peer Gynt, in 1944—specifically, of the scene in which Peer tries to find his true identity by symbolically peeling an onion, only to discover that beneath the last layer of skin there is no core of selfhood but, simply and literally, nothing. Sir Ralph has often been at his best when playing men in whose lives, gamely though they keep up appearances, there is a spiritual emptiness, a certain terror of the void. One of his greatest regrets is having turned down Samuel Beckett's *Waiting for Godot* in the early nineteen-fifties, when he and Alec Guinness were invited to play the two Godot-forsaken tramps. They were dissuaded in part by Gielgud, who decried the play—in a phrase of which he is now thoroughly ashamed— as "a load of old rubbish." Sir Ralph, then appearing at the Haymarket Theatre in London, asked Beckett to come and discuss the script with him. "I'd drawn up a sort of laundry list of things I didn't quite understand," Sir Ralph recalls. "And Beckett came into my dressing room—wearing a knapsack, which was very mysterious—and I started to read through my list. You see, I like to know what I'm being asked to do. March up the hill and charge that blockhouse! Fine—but I wasn't sure which was the hill and where the blockhouse was. I needed to have a few things clear in my mind. But Beckett just looked at me and said, 'I'm awfully sorry, but I can't answer any of your questions.' He wouldn't explain. Didn't lend me a hand. And then another job came up, and I turned down the greatest play of my lifetime."

Richardson became an indisputably great actor in the latter half of 1944. Since then, despite some wildly misguided choices of roles, he has continued to ripen. Today, both as a man and as a performer, he is more expansive in his uniqueness and his eccentricity than ever before. He is the eldest of a formidable trio of English actors—the others being Gielgud and Laurence Olivier, his juniors, by respectively, two and five years—who were born early in the century, and whose careers, which have frequently crisscrossed, form a map that covers most of the high points of English theatre in the past five decades. (Richardson and Olivier were knighted in 1947; Gielgud had to wait for his accolade until 1953.) Gielgud and Olivier, from their earliest days in the profession, were that

godsend to critics, a pair of perfect opposites. You could list
their qualities in parallel columns:

GIELGUD	OLIVIER
Air	Earth
Poet	Peasant
Mind	Heart
Spiritual	Animal
Feminine	Masculine
John Philip Kemble	Edmund Kean
Introvert	Extrovert
Jewel	Metal
Claret	Burgundy

Concerning the great Shakespearean parts that both actors
have played, the critical consensus is that Gielgud has defeated
Olivier as Hamlet and Romeo, while Olivier has knocked out
Gielgud as Othello, Antony, and Macbeth. King Lear has
outpointed both of them. But where does this all leave Sir
Ralph? Very much the odd man out. Many of his greatest
Shakespearean successes have been in parts like Falstaff, Caliban, Bottom, and Enobarbus, which the other members of the
triumvirate have never attempted. In 1960, he contributed a
series of autobiographical pieces to the London *Sunday Times*,
in one of which he wrote, "Hamlet, Lear, Macbeth and Othello
are the four glorious peaks of dramatic literature." Of Macbeth,
a role he played in 1952, he said, "I couldn't do it for nuts—
not for a second did I believe in the air-drawn dagger, and if
I couldn't, no wonder no one else did." In 1938, he failed as
Othello, though he cannot have been much helped by his Iago:
Olivier, who elected to play the part along Freudian lines, as
a man consumed by a smoldering homosexual passion for the
Moor, but who neglected to inform Sir Ralph that he intended,
in the course of the performance, to kiss him full on the lips.
James Agate, the leading London critic of the time, headed his
review "Othello Without the Moor." In it he sombrely con-
cluded:

The truth is that Nature, which has showered upon this
actor the kindly gifts of the comedian, has unkindly

refused him any tragic facilities whatever. His voice has
not a tragic note in its whole gamut, all the accents being
those of sweetest reasonableness. He cannot blaze.

As for Hamlet and Lear, Sir Ralph has avoided them both—
wrongly, I think, as far as the latter role is concerned, but this
is a point to which I'll return. "Clearly," he wrote in 1960,
"I don't belong to the first division. It could be that my place
is in doomed second." Alternatively, it could be just that he
lacks the traditional (but now surely outdated) attributes of the
tragic hero—the rumbling voice, the aquiline nose, the high
cheekbones, the profile of ruined beauty. Critics have written
of his "round, sober cheese-face," his "broad moony countenance," which has also been likened to a "sanctified potato."
Interviewed on British TV in 1975, he said, "I don't like my
face at all. It's always been a great drawback to me." He is
utterly sincere about this, the proof being that although he has
been working in the cinema since 1933, he has never seen any
of the rushes. "It discourages me," he says of his physical
appearance. "I lose confidence in myself." Yet, despite this
alleged handicap, and despite his failure to conquer the tragic
Big Four, he has remained, both in and out of the classics, a
star with an assured place in the Big Three—a wine to be
judged on the same level as Burgundy and claret, even if
nobody can quite manage to locate the vineyard.

To explain his continued presence in the top trio, a special
category had to be invented for him. Ralph Richardson, it was
said, represented not the Tragic Hero or the Poetic Hero but
the Common Man. I once asked him how he differed as a
performer from Olivier. He ruminated for a moment and then
replied, "I've not his size or range. I'm a more rotund kind
of actor. Laurence is more the spiky sort. I haven't got his
splendid fury." Fury, of course, takes many forms that are not
explicit, and hearty bluffness can veil many kinds of desolation
and misanthropy. To this matter, too, I shall return. During
the thirties and early forties, it became an article of theatrical
faith that Richardson was Everyman, the chap you cast when
you wanted an embodiment of commonplace decency, of ster-
ling (if slightly tongue-tied) honesty—in short, a sort of human
dobbin. Not everyone was deceived. Barbara Jefford, a handsome classical actress with whom he has worked at the Old

Vic, once said to me, "People called him the epitome of the
ordinary man, I suppose because of his round face. They were
absolutely wrong. I can imagine him as a kind of Thomas
Hardy hero—a plebeian type transmogrified and exalted. But
he could never be your average worker." In 1963, she went
on, she appeared with Sir Ralph in Pirandello's *Six Characters
in Search of an Author*. He played the father, a fictitious creature permanently condemned to a twilit half existence, since
the play-within-a-play of which he is the protagonist is never
completed. "And, of course, he was superb," Miss Jefford
said, "*because he was playing a ghost*. That's the point about
Ralph. There's always something spectral about him. He really
is a man from Mars." In 1957, he scored a great hit in *Flowering
Cherry*, Robert Bolt's first stage success, as a dowdy suburban
husband with delusions of grandeur. His performance gave the
lie to the theory that he was Everyman reborn in Surbiton.
"To any role that gives him half a chance," I wrote at the time,
"he brings outsize attributes, outsize euphoria, outsize dismay.
Those critics who hold that he excels in portraying the Average
Man cannot, I feel, have met many Average Men. . . . He gives
us fantasy, not normality."

If Sir Ralph was not Everyman, what was he? Two quotations may be helpful. One is from George Jean Nathan:
"Drama is a two-souled art: half divine, half clownish." The
other is from Sir Ralph himself: "The ability to convey a sense
of mystery is one of the most powerful assets possessed by the
theatre." If Sir Ralph was the odd man out, the operative word
was "odd." Mystery, clownishness, oddity: all of them forms
of protective carapace—smokescreens, layers of the onion.

First Interlude: 5 P.M. on June 14, 1976. Interview between
Sir Ralph and me at his London house, which is extremely
grand—designed by Nash and overlooking Regent's Park. The
meeting has been easy to fix: strangely, for a man so deeply
private in other respects, he does not bother to have an unlisted
telephone number. I have known him slightly for twenty-odd
years: Will he remember that I described him in *Macbeth* as
"a sad facsimile of the Cowardly Lion in *The Wizard of Oz*"
and as "the glass eye in the forehead of English acting"? I
ascend by lift (still a great rarity in London houses) to wait in

a resplendent L-shaped living room with floor-to-ceiling windows. My qualms are allayed when he bursts in beaming and asks if I'd care to join him in one of his special cocktails. I accept with thanks. He pads across to a well-stocked drinks table, selects two half-pint tumblers, and pours into each of them three fat fingers of Gordon's gin, followed by a huge slug of French vermouth. I reach out for my drink. He shakes his head and adds a lavish shot of Italian vermouth. I repeat business; he repeats headshake. Into each glass he now pours three *thumbs* of vodka. "That," he says gravely, "is what makes the difference." I can well believe him. Three things are known about Sir Ralph's relationship with alcohol. One: He enjoys it. Two: On working days he restricts himself, until the curtain falls, to a couple of glasses of wine, taken with luncheon. Three: He is never visibly drunk. I recall a story told me by a former director of a famous classical repertory theatre, who wanted Sir Ralph to join the company and went to his home to discuss what parts he might play. "There was this long mahogany table," my informant said, "Ralph sat at one end and put a full bottle of gin in front of me. 'That,' he said, 'is for you.' Then he got another full bottle and placed it at his end of the table. 'And that,' he said, 'is for me.' Then he sat down. 'Now, my dear fellow,' he said, 'what do we want to talk about?'"

I stealthily consult some notes I have made about his career, but before I have framed my first question he says, "I've no idea what we're going to say to each other. After all, where did we come from? Did you ever have a vision of the place we came from before we were born? I did, when I was about three years old. I used to dream about it a good deal. I even drew pictures of it." He leans forward confidentially. *"It looked rather like Mexico,"* he says with quiet emphasis. Wind utterly removed from sails, I am silenced: Who else would start a conversation like this? I sip his lethal cocktail, which he leaps up to replenish as soon as the level falls more than half an inch below the rim of the glass. From life before birth it is a short step to life after death. "I've been very close to death," he muses. "It's like dropping into an abyss—very drowsy, rather nice." Is he referring to wartime experiences in the Fleet Air Arm or to the motorbike on which, pipe in mouth, he habitually

zooms around London? In a conversation recently recorded in
the London *Observer*, Gielgud said to Sir Ralph, "The last
time you took me on the pillion, I practically had a fit. I was
a stretcher case." Sir Ralph nodded and esoterically replied,
"I have been killed several times myself." Meanwhile, he pur-
sues his metaphysical speculations: "God is very economical,
don't you think? Wastes nothing. Yet also the opposite. All
those galaxies, stars rolling on forever..."

By a mighty effort, I turn the conversation to contemporary
realities. What does he think, after all these years, of his old
partner Olivier? He springs from his seat, arms outstretched
above his head. "I *hate* Larry. Until I see him. Then he has
more magnetism than anyone I've ever met. Except Alexander
Korda. I had a film contract with Korda from 1935 until he
died, in 1956. I would go to see him with a furious speech
about what I wanted, and what I'd do if I didn't get it. And
all the time he'd be staring at my feet. When I'd finished, he'd
say, 'Where did you get those marvellous shoes? I'd give
anything to have shoes like those.' And I would be defeated."
He subsides into a chair. "I admire anyone who has a talent
that makes me tingle. Like Chopin, or Conrad, or Pinter, or
Beckett. Though not the later Beckett. I am sadly literal-
minded, and in Beckett's recent work I find obscurity instead
of mystery. And, of course, I worship Ethel Merman."

We talk about Peter Hall, who succeeded Olivier as artistic
director of Britain's National Theatre, and for whom Sir Ralph
has lately worked in Ibsen's *John Gabriel Borkman* as well as
in *No Man's Land*. A few months earlier, Hall confided to his
associates that Sir Ralph was "the greatest poetic actor alive,
with perhaps two or three good years left in him," adding that
it was their duty to make sure that he spent these precious days
at the National. Accordingly, Hall acquired the rights to *The
Kingfisher*, a new play written for Sir Ralph by the popular
boulevard dramatist William Douglas Home and originally intended for presentation in the commercial theatre. Hall's in-
genious plan was that after a token run of a few weeks at the
National the play should be moved to the West End. The
director (Hall) and any stars in his cast would then be remu-
nerated at West End levels, which are considerably higher than
those at the National, since they include percentages of the

box-office gross. A profitable operation for all concerned—
though there were purists who doubted whether the true function
of a national theatre was to stage commercial productions for
quick moneymaking transfers to the West End. Sir Ralph makes
no claims for the play as a part of art: "*The Kingfisher* is two
bits of cobweb stuck together with stamp edging and sticking
plaster. It's about two elderly people—Celia Johnson plays the
woman—who very nearly had an affair when they were much
younger but didn't quite. He's now an old novelist, and her
husband has just died. They try to begin again where they left
off all those years ago. Things like that happen all the time.
When I was, oh, about twelve, I met a girl named Francesca.
I never kissed her, never even touched her, doubt if I saw her
more than a couple of times, but as long as I live I shan't
forget her." Topping up our drinks, he lowers his voice. "Don't
you think Peter Hall has something *Germanic* about him? I do
hope he doesn't get Germanic with the Willie Douglas Home
play, because if he does we shall all go down with the Titanic."
Pause. Then a broad, beatific smile: "Or the Teutonic." (Since
this conversation took place, Hall has had a change of heart.
Influenced, perhaps, by the increasingly vocal doubts of the
purists, the National has relinquished the play to the commercial theatre, where it will be staged by another director, with
Sir Ralph still in the lead, but without the aid of public subsidy.)

Before we part, he reminisces about his pet ferret. He really
used to have a pet ferret. He washed it every week in Lux soap
flakes. (There were rabbits, too, and hamsters. "Whether it's
a ferret or a motorbike or a firework," said Barbara Jefford,
"he concentrates entirely on his extraordinary enthusiasms. It's
a boy we're talking about, a great boy.") "Goodbye, my dear
chap," he says, waving me into the lift. I leave feeling (a) that
I have known this man all my life, and (b) that I have never
met anyone who more adroitly buttonholed me while keeping
me firmly at arm's length.

Sir Ralph once said, "I've never given a good performance,
that has satisfied me, in any play." Is this false modesty or
genuine diffidence? A young actor I know appeared with Sir
Ralph in a recent production. One evening, as they stood in
the wings awaiting their entrance, Sir Ralph turned to my friend
and murmured, "I had a little talent once. A very little talent.

If you should ever come across a tiny talent labelled R. R., please let me know." Then the cue came, and he surged imperiously into the spotlight.

Ralph Richardson was born in 1902 in the intensely respectable West Country town of Cheltenham. His mother was a devout Catholic and his father a Quaker—according to Sir Ralph, "a shortish man with a beard and cold blue eyes," who wore bright-colored waistcoats and taught art at the local Ladies' College. Ralph had two elder brothers, of whom—as of Cheltenham and, indeed, of his father—he remembers very little, since when he was four his mother ran away from home, taking him with her. When he is asked why she bolted, he maintains a silence that may betoken either tact or ignorance. On a minute allowance of two pounds and ten shillings a week, provided by his father, they lived at Shoreham-by-Sea, in Sussex, in a pair of disused railway carriages standing side by side on the beach and joined together by a tin roof. This meant that they had, in Sir Ralph's words, "a front door and a back door, as well as about twenty side doors." Their neighbors were few. "I had one friend for a time," Sir Ralph has written, "until I was accused of murder." It seems that when he was idly twirling an iron hoop on a stick it flew off and accidentally struck his friend, a small girl, on the head. Unfortunately, her mother was an explosive pioneer feminist on a very short fuse, who came storming out of her nearby bungalow and howled, "You brute. You have killed my daughter." He had in fact merely grazed her scalp. Since his mother had hopes of grooming him for the priesthood, he was sent to several Catholic schools; one of them was a seminary, from which, to her great disappointment, he ran away. Academic subjects bored him: "I was not passionate enough and had not the character to be rebellious. I think I was just a big oaf."

He recalls from his school days only one moment of fulfillment, when a teacher called on him to get up and recite a passage from Macaulay's *Lays of Ancient Rome*. He accepted the challenge and astounded himself. "It frightened the life out of the class, and it frightened the life out of me. They were horrified, they were electrified. It was really very good. I never read again. No one ever asked me to." Around 1910, he and his mother moved to South London, and thence to Brighton, living in a succession of cheap flats, hotels, and boarding houses. "I had no education at all, really," he later told a TV interviewer. "I was sort of professionally ill when I was a little boy." He was forever catching things—mumps, scarlet fever, diphtheria—and his mother, a lonely and possessive woman, as well as an expert hypochondriac in her own right, saw to it that he stayed at home as much as possible. There was money on the Richardson side of the family, which included prosperous leather manufacturers in Newcastle-upon-Tyne, but Ralph's father had forfeited his share of the fortune by abjuring commerce and taking to the arts. Even so, the boy remembered his paternal grandfather, controller of the dynastic loot, with fondness:

> He came to take me out in London one day when he was about eighty. Wonderful white beard and very ironic, like a pirate in a good mood. It was my day, he said, and we'd do exactly what I liked. I took him to the Crystal Palace and we spent hours on the switchbacks; he never turned a whisker. I was told afterwards I might have killed him.

What follows could easily be a novel by H. G. Wells modulating into a novel by J. B. Priestley. In 1919, young Richardson is employed as an office boy in a Brighton insurance company. Being a sprightly lad with a taste for heights and none for his job, he amuses himself one day by shuffling his way around the office building on a narrow outside ledge, vertiginously overlooking Brighton High Street. Crowds gather on the sidewalk, watching him in horror. (He later admitted that he was partly motivated by exhibitionism; after all, "the Alpine climber's audience is sparse.") He has timed his exploit to coincide with a period when the boss will be out of the building. His timing is off. The boss reenters his office to find Richardson passing slowly by outside his window, and freezes in the act of removing his hat. Richardson smiles and waves in a friendly manner. Receiving no response, he puts his head in over the top of the window and affably explains, "I was chasing a pigeon." His employer, too nonplussed to take disciplinary action, nods vaguely and makes a mental note: "Richardson is not reliable."

Soon afterward, Richardson's Newcastle grandmother died—a wealthy woman he had hardly met. When he was six, she summoned him to visit her. He took with him a pet mouse named Kim. The servant who met him at the station shook her head and said, "You'll never be allowed to take that creature up to the big house." "Why not?" said Ralph. "I've been invited to see my grandmohter, and I never travel without Kim." "She won't let it in the house," said the servant. "In that case," said Ralph, "when's the next train back to Brighton?" He stood his ground, and the matriarch was forced to capitulate; but she was so impressed by his stubbornness that she remembered him in her will. In fact, she left him five hundred pounds—a sum large enough to change the course of his life. "Kim cost me sixpence," he reflected later. "It was the happiest buy I ever made."

He gave up insurance and enrolled in Brighton School of Art. But not for long. A few months afterward, Sir Frank Benson and his renowned Shakespearean company appeared at the Theatre Royal, and Richardson went to see them in *Hamlet*. This was "the decisive moment that moved my compass," he wrote later. "I suddenly realized what acting was and I thought: By Jove, that's the job for me." He abandoned painting and applied for work with a semiprofessional troupe run in Brighton by a stubby, hooknosed actor-manager named Frank R. Growcott. He chose as his audition piece a speech by Falstaff. Growcott was appalled. "That is quite awful," he said. "It is shapeless, senseless, badly spoken. . . . You could never, never be any good as Falstaff." (This diatribe burned itself into Richardson's mind. When Olivier, a quarter of a century later, asked him to play Falstaff, his first reaction was to say that he couldn't possibly do it.) Nonetheless, Growcott agreed to hire him for six months. During the first half of the engagement he would pay Growcott ten shillings a week, after which Growcott would pay him the same sum. In the following year, 1921, he achieved full professional status. He joined a touring repertory company led by a now forgotten Irish actor called Charles Doran. The Doran productions were rehearsed in London, so Richardson—who until then had never seen a play on the West End stage—was able to study the work of people like Charles Hawtrey ("I think the best actor I've ever seen") and Mrs. Patrick Campbell ("who knocked me flat"). For three years, he toured with Doran, building a solid Shakespearean technique on the basis of parts like Orlando, Macduff, and Bottom. A fellow member of the troupe was Muriel Hewitt, whom he married in 1924, and later summed up as "the perfect example of the natural actress." They went on to work together at the Birmingham Repertory Theatre, which was then the most adventurous regional ensemble in Britain, and in 1926 Richardson made his West End debut, in *Yellow Sands*, a Birmingham success by Eden and Adelaide Phillpotts that moved to London and ran for over six hundred performances, with Cedric Hardwicke in the leading role. Richardson's wife was also in the cast. In his own words:

> Her career on the stage was brilliant but brief, and her courage was terribly tested, for after a few years of work she fell under some rare nervous attack, perhaps akin to polio, and some years later she died.

"Ralph's first wife contracted some kind of sleeping sickness in Croydon," John Gielgud told me recently. "Her death was long and painful." It finally took place in 1942. "They were devoted to each other," Gielgud added.

Richardson's first real blossoming began in 1930 at the Old Vic, where, over a period of two years, he played a full range of classical roles, among them Prince Hal in *Henry IV*, part I, Caliban, Bolingbroke, Iago, Tony Belch, the Bastard in *King John*, Petruchio, Kent in *King Lear*, Enobarbus, and Henry V. Gielgud remembers "his marvellous performances of shaggy-dog faithfulness—the kind of part Shakespeare wrote so well," and says, "He was unforgettable as the Bastard and Enobarbus and Kent. And he always gave them a touch of fantasy. But he couldn't bear fights. When I played Hotspur to his Hal, and he had to kill me, he used to count the strokes out loud. 'Come on, cockie,' he'd say. 'One, and two, and three, and four . . .' I never really felt his heart was in it."

By the midthirties, he was an established star in modern plays (*For Services Rendered* and *Sheppey*, both by Somerset Maugham, and J. B. Priestley's *Eden End*) as well as the classics. In 1935, Broadway saw him for the first time, playing the Chorus and Mercutio in *Romeo and Juliet*, with Katharine Cornell as the Capulet heiress. A year later, back in London, he plunged into the title role of *The Amazing Dr. Clitterhouse*, a long-running thriller, in which he was supported by Meriel Forbes, who subsequently became—as she still is—his wife. Thus far, he was a thoroughly respected actor, versatile and dependable, yet somehow earthbound. Agate had written of "his solid, inexpressive mien, altogether admirable . . . in all delineations of the downright," and the phrase epitomized what up to that point most playgoers felt about him. His stage persona, however, did not reflect the combustible *bizarrerie* of the man within.

Second Interlude: November 5, 1937 or 1938. (None of the surviving participants is quite sure of the year.) It is Guy Fawkes Day, on which the British let off fireworks to celebrate the discovery (and frustration) of a Catholic plot to blow up the Houses of Parliament. It is also Vivien Leigh's birthday. She and Olivier—as yet unmarried, because Olivier's divorce from his first wife, Jill Esmond, is not final—have moved into a tiny house in Chelsea. Miss Leigh has spent months and a great deal of money turning it into (Olivier's phrase) "a perfect little bandbox," full of costly trinkets, with a minuscule garden behind. Instead of giving a large housewarming party, they decide to invite only two old friends—Ralph Richardson and Meriel Forbes, the latter known by the nickname of Mu. What follows is Sir Ralph's account of the festivity, as he recalled it for me last year: "I took great trouble and care. I arrived at the house with Mu and a huge box of fireworks that I had bought with loving joy. I took the biggest rocket out into the garden—it was one of the kind you use to attract attention if your ship is sinking—and there I set it off. It came straight back into the dining room and burned up the curtains and set the pelmet on fire." According to Olivier, it also wrecked a lot of priceless antique crockery and left him and Vivien, who were cowering behind the sofa, blackened about the face like Al Jolson. "I knew that Vivien had taken great trouble with her decorations, and that her pelmet was unpleasantly burned. But it was my *benevolence* that had caused it all. 'Let's get out of here.' I said to Mu. 'These people don't understand us.' I grabbed the doorknob, and through no fault of mine it came off in my hand. I have to admit that I was very hurt, next day, when nobody rang me up to say, 'How kind of you, Ralph, to have thought of bringing those fireworks.'"

Some years later, Sir Ralph mentioned to Olivier that he had given birth to a splendid idea for the National Theatre, should it ever come into being. Every night (he said), as the curtain went up, a synchronized rocket should rise from the roof of the theatre, to inform the populace that an event of national significance was about to take place. It would be known as Ralph's Rocket. This suggestion was adopted, and in March, 1976, when the National Theatre finally moved into its new home, on the south bank of the Thames, the first rocket was duly launched. Sir Ralph himself lit the fuse.

It was not until 1944, after five wartime years spent as a pilot in the Fleet Air Arm, that Ralph Richardson's great period began. He outgrew his humility, burst the bounds of sobriety that had theretofore constrained him, and started to allow his fantasy free flight. "He had always wanted to be a matinee idol," Gielgud says, "and felt inadequate because he couldn't be." Or, as Barbara Jefford puts it, "he was always a wonderfully flexible film performer—better in many ways than Gielgud or Olivier—but he never had the obvious good looks you expect of The Great Actor." Now that he had entered his forties, this lack of physical glamour began to seem less important. He joined the revived Old Vic company, which was to be temporarily housed at the New Theatre, in the West End, since its original (and much humbler) home, south of the Thames, had been gutted by German bombs. Richardson shared the artistic directorship with Olivier and a promising newcomer named John Burrell, and launched the inaugural season, on August 31, 1944, by playing the title role in *Peer Gynt*. Tyrone Guthrie directed, with assistance "in grouping and movement" from Robert Helpmann, then at the height of his powers as dancer and choreographer. Sybil Thorndike, Margaret Leighton, and Olivier (in the small but spine-chilling part of the Button-Molder) were in the supporting cast; and Richardson, as the peasant who circumnavigates the globe in fruitless search of self-fulfillment, gave the most poetic performance of his life—volatile, obsessed, constantly surprising. (He has said that Peer Gynt, who is a "little mad," is his favorite part.) In the same season he played Bluntschli, the pragmatic soldier in Shaw's *Arms and the Man*; Richmond to Olivier's overwhelming Richard III; and Uncle Vanya in the tender, unsparing play of that name. In the autumn of 1945, he opened as Falstaff in both parts of Shakespeare's *Henry IV*. These were the productions that—coupled with those left over from the previous season, and augmented by the flabbergasting double bill in which Olivier played Sophocles' Oedipus and (after the intermission) Mr. Puff in Sheridan's *The Critic*—established the highwater mark of English acting in the twentieth century.

"Falstaff," Sir Ralph wrote in 1960, "proceeds through the plays at his own chosen pace, like a gorgeous ceremonial Indian elephant." As an undergraduate at Oxford, I said of his performance, "Here was a Falstaff whose principal attribute was not his fatness but his knighthood. He was Sir John first and Falstaff second." I continued.

> The spirit behind all the rotund nobility was spry and elastic.... There was also, when the situation called for it, great wisdom and melancholy. ("Peace, good Doll! do not speak like a death's head: do not bid me remember mine end" was done with most moving authority.) Each word emerged with immensely careful articulation, the lips forming it lovingly and then spitting it forth. In moments of passion, the wild white halo of hair stood angrily up and the eyes rolled majestically; and in rage one noticed a slow, meditative relish taking command... it was not a sweaty fat man, but a dry and dignified one.... He had good manners and also that respect for human dignity which prevented him from openly showing his boredom at the inanities of Shallow and Silence.... He was not often jovial, laughed seldom, belched never.... After the key-cold rebuke [from Prince Hal, once his fellow-boozer, now his monarch], the old man turned, his face red and working in furious *tics* to hide his tears.... "I shall be sent for soon at night."

But we know, of course, that he will not. Of the preceding scenes, lyrically comic, set in a twilit Gloucestershire orchard, where Falstaff basks in the sycophantic adulation of Justice

Shallow (Olivier), a shrivelled drinking crony of his youth, I
see no reason to revise what I wrote thirty years ago: "If I had
only half an hour more to spend in theatres, and could choose
at large, no question but I would have these." In the 1946–47
season, Sir Ralph's exuberent, opportunistic performances as
Cyrano de Bergerac and Face, the scheming servant in Jonson's
The Alchemist, set the seal on his new reputation. Always
excepting Olivier, no actor in England was riding higher.

Third Interlude: The summer of 1946. Ralph and Meriel
Richardson are motoring down to spend the weekend at Notley
Abbey, in Buckinghamshire. The Oliviers have recently acquired the fifteenth-century abbot's lodge, and converted it,
at ridiculous expense, into a stately home. Stopping his car on
the brow of a hill that overlooks the abbey and its domain,
Richardson turns to Mu and says (they both recall the exact
words), "I hope to God I don't put my foot in it this time."
Since the Chelsea holocaust, purely social contacts between
the two couples have been limited—mainly because the war
has kept them apart but also because of a lingering sense (on
Mrs. Olivier's part) that there is something inherently hazard-
ous, almost poltergeistic, about Richardson's presence.
The day passes sweetly. The guests are shown over the
estate. Across a candlelit dinner table, good stories are told,
and plans made for the future of the Old Vic. Richardson
conducts himself with extreme caution, a man walking on
eggshells. Olivier talks of the abbey's history, and of some
remarkably preserved frescoes painted by the monks on beams
in the attic. Wouldn't the Richardsons (he suggests after dinner)
like to come up and see them? Mu declines the invitation; her
husband, the model guest, accepts. The men having left, the
wives chat over their coffee. Mrs. Olivier feels obscurely uneasy, but after five, ten, fifteen minutes have passed without
incident, she is ready to scoff at her qualms. At this moment,
there is a prolonged splintering noise from above, followed by
a colossal crash that makes the whole house shake. The women
dash upstairs, where, in the main guest room, lovingly decorated under Mrs. Olivier's personal supervision, they find Richardson flat on his back and covered in plaster, on a bed that
has collapsed under his weight. Above it there is a gaping hole
in the ceiling, through which he has evidently fallen. It emerges

that the attic has no floor and can be traversed only on narrow rafters. Olivier had brought a flashlight, with which he directed Richardson's attention to the paintings on the beams above their heads. Two versions exist of what happened next. According to Sir Ralph, "Larry said to me, 'Why don't you take a step back to see the pictures better?'" Olivier denies this, saying, "Ralph just whirled round in pure wonderment and toppled off." At all events, Mrs. Olivier was seen to be foaming with rage, like a Cassandra whose prophecies of doom have gone unheeded.

"I felt pretty dogsbody, I can tell you," Sir Ralph remarked to me later. At the time, he thought himself slightly more sinned against than sinning, but now he admits that his hostess had some cause to be upset. "There was a rational basis to Vivien's fury, which we must salute," he said to me the other day. "If you prod a tigress twice in her lair, you must not expect her to purr."

Knighted (along with Olivier) in 1947, his film career thriving, Sir Ralph was at his perihelion when, in a fit of collective paranoia, the governors of the Old Vic did an extraordinary thing. Fearing that the company had lost its identity as a people's theatre offering high art at low prices, and was in danger of becoming a gilded playground for West End stars, they fired the entire directorship at a stroke, without warning, in the middle of the 1948–49 season. "We felt rather badly treated," Sir Ralph told me years afterward, with the stoicism of hindsight, "but a fired butler doesn't complain of his master."

Burrell, Olivier, and Richardson were jobless overnight. It did not, of course, take them long to find other employment; but the three men, despite differences of temperament, had formed a spectacularly successful and cohesive team, like a jazz trio in which contrasting styles coalesce into a whole that is greater than the sum of its parts. The decision to axe them changed the course of theatrical history in England, and during the years that followed, Sir Ralph, bereft of the stimulation that group leadership can provide in the theatre (for the leaders no less than the led), sometimes looked a little lost. Something he said of his colleagues in the Fleet Air Arm may also apply to his co-directors at the Vic: "They brought the best out of

you by being so absolutely certain you'd got the best in you."
He continued, of course, to have his triumphs—as Peggy Ash-
croft's glacially possessive Papa in *The Heiress* (adapted from
Henry James's *Washington Square* and directed by Gielgud)
and as Vershinin, the philosopher-philanderer in Chekhov's
The Three Sisters. But the creative interplay, the artistic checks
and balances, the argumentative crosscurrents of the Old Vic
days had gone forever. Thenceforward, Sir Ralph was on his
own.

His plague year was 1952, in which he went to Stratford-
upon-Avon to play Prospero, Macbeth, and Volpone, and failed
in all three. He said himself, "I don't know which was the
worst." The night I saw his Volpone, many of the lines eluded
him, and replacements were smuggled in from other plays. At
one point, he stunned his fellow actors by addressing them as
"Ye elves of hills, brooks, standing lakes, and groves," and
went on (since there was clearly no going back) to favor us
with the rest of the famous speech from *The Tempest* which
begins with that phrase. In 1953, having seen him in *The White
Carnation*, a puny play by R. C. Sherriff, I wrote:

> He has taken to ambling across our stages in a spec-
> tral, shell-shocked manner, choosing odd moments to
> jump and frisk, like a man through whom an electric
> current is being intermittently passed.

The year 1956 brought us a most erratic *Timon of Athens*,
containing "gestures so eccentric that their true significance
could be revealed only by extensive trepanning." But even at
his most aberrant he remained supremely watchable. Once the
curtain had risen, you could never be sure (nor, it seemed at
times, could he) what he would do next. A moment of pure
dottiness might be followed by a flash of revelation. More and
more, he was bringing the aura of his own private world onto
the stage with him, like a glass bell with which to protect
himself from the audience—for whom, in any case, he had
never felt any overpowering fondness. "I'm rather inclined,"
he told a man from *The Guardian* last year, "to think of them
as a cage of bloody tigers that will bite you, and will put you
out of the stage door if they can. . . . You must never let them
command." (Even the theatregoers of Brighton, to whose ap-

plause he had so often bowed during his apprenticeship, he described in 1975 as "very dangerous.") A master of all the stratagems of self-protection, he has always been extremely wily if he suspects that an attempt is being made, in Hamlet's phrase, to pluck out the heart of his mystery. Not long ago, he and Gielgud were photographed by Jane Bown, of the London *Observer*. She had hardly arrived when Sir Ralph began to profess amnesia about his identity. "The trouble is I can never remember who I am whenever I'm photographed. Who *am* I? I find I'm no one in particular."

"However close you get to him, he's still distant," Barbara Jefford says. "In life and onstage, he has a kind of remote intimacy. When you're acting with him there's no eye contact. He never looks at you. And he never touches people onstage. I played his stepdaughter in *Six Characters in Search of an Author*, and there's a big scene where he's supposed to grope me. He never even touched me. And yet I'm told the audience got a very sensual impression from the whole scene." The play was staged by the American director William Ball. Miss Jefford recalls, "The most typical thing that Ralph did happened during rehearsals. One morning, Bill called the company together and said, 'Today, I want us all to throw away our scripts and improvise our way through the play.' Ralph didn't say a word. He was perfectly polite. He just quietly rose and left the room. Oh, he was *about*, he didn't leave the building, but he didn't come back to that room. He couldn't bear the thought of *exposing* himself like that."

In 1964, as part of the festivities in honor of the quartercentenary of Shakespeare's birth, the British Council sent Sir Ralph on a tour of Mexico (his prenatal homeland), South America, and Europe, playing Shylock in *The Merchant of Venice* and Bottom in *A Midsummer Night's Dream*. Miss Jefford went along as Portia and Helena. Lady Richardson, although she had never before appeared in Shakespeare, decided at the last moment to volunteer her services as Titania. I saw *The Merchant* before it left England. It had a lot of very old-fashioned sets, with equally old-fashioned blackouts between scenes, and was memorable chiefly for Sir Ralph's physical appearance. He wore a bright yellow skullcap, set off by lurid green makeup, and he brandished what I took to be a shepherd's crook. "He looks like the Demon King in a pantomime," a junior member of the cast had told me, with awe in his voice, before the performance. I paid a brief visit to Sir Ralph's dressing room afterward. When I asked about the shepherd's crook, he explained although he based his interpretation on the assumption that Shylock was "a gent," it was vital not to forget that "the Jews were a race of nomadic shepherds." He added, "Shylock knows all about breeding sheep. Look at his speech about Jacob and Laban and the ewes and the rams—typical piece of Shakespearean illumination." The notion of a pastoral Shylock was something I was not quite ready for, and, as I remember, our conversation ended there. During the months that followed, however, I often thought of this strange, glaucous, eerily imposing apparition, and what the citizens of Lima or Buenos Aires must have made of it as it came looming at them over the Andes. Miss Jefford has vivid memories of Sir Ralph off duty during the three-month tour. "In Latin America, he became intensely English, very much the squire, with a yellow waistcoat and a panama hat at a jaunty angle." In another vignette, he is standing beside her in the wings, watching his wife—an excellent actress in modern roles—tackling Titania. "She tries very hard," he muses. "But"—and here he mimes the gestures of a violinist—"she hasn't got the *bowing*."

He and Miss Jefford met in 1956 when they were at the Old Vic together, though not in the same plays. "He was only in *Timon*, so I didn't know him at all, but one night he came to see me as Imogen in *Cymbeline*. Next day, I got one of his beautiful little notes, written in exquisite script, so delicately arranged on the page, with wide, wide margins all covered with little sketches. He said that in the bedroom, when Iachimo creeps out of the trunk to examine me, he thought my *sleep* was especially convincing. Rather an odd tribute, considering that I didn't move a muscle throughout the scene. But I appreciated it." A great Richardson fan, Miss Jefford concedes that he was below his best as Shylock. She says shrewdly, "He's not good at portraying *mundane* sins and desires. There isn't enough poetry in Shylock for Ralph." She agrees with me that he ought to have a crack at King Lear. There's no doubt that he would be heartbreaking in the final exchanges with Cordelia:

We too alone will sing like birds i' the cage:
When thou dost ask me blessing, I'll kneel down,
And ask of thee forgiveness.

In these passages, Lear has fought his way through to a
simplicity and an emotional sanity that lie on the far side of
complexity and madness. (It is the early Lear, the capricious
and egocentric despot of the opening scene, who is truly mad.)
I have heard it objected that Sir Ralph lacks the vocal firepower
for the "Blow, winds, and crack your cheeks" aria on the storm-
blasted heath; but the point, nearly always forgotten, about this
speech is that Lear is not attacking the storm or trying to shout
it down. Its fury confirms his misanthrophy: *he is on its side*.
Played thus (as I have yet to see it played), the speech would
be well within Sir Ralph's compass.

At 5 P.M. on January 11, 1976, I visit Sir John Gielgud in
his suite at the Drake Hotel in New York. My host is spruce,
poker-backed, voluble, eyes wickedly gleaming—a lighthouse
spraying words instead of candlepower. "It's true that Ralph
is wary about the audience," Sir John says. "He watches it like
a hawk. Quite often he'll say to me, 'Did you notice that man
in the fifth row groping that girl during the second act?'" We
talk about *No Man's Land*: "I always think that Hirst, the
character Ralph plays, is very much like Hamm, the hero of
Beckett's *Endgame*—a sort of tyrant who's dominated by his
domestic staff. Did you know, by the way, that Larry wanted
to play the part? I think Ralph is so marvellous in the second
act, when he's doing his bland-clubman stuff. In some ways,
he's the great successor to A. E. Matthews." (Not, perhaps,
the most overwhelming of tributes: Matthews, a brilliantly
accomplished light comedian who went on acting into his
eighties, was never regarded as a player of the first rank.) Since
the two knights co-starred in *Home* seven years ago, they have
been endlessly interviewed and photographed together, and are
frequently mistaken for one another on the street. "We're like
the Broker's Men in *Cinderella*," Gielgud says, referring to
a pair of slapstick clowns in traditional English pantomime.
For interview purposes, he and Sir Ralph have evolved what
amounts to a double act, in which certain routines and catch

phrases (including the one about the Broker's Men) ritually recur. There's usually a formal exordium, such as the following, taken from the London *Observer* in October, 1975, during the West End run of *No Man's Land*:

SIR RALPH: You're looking very well, by the way.
SIR JOHN: Thank you.
SIR RALPH: I haven't seen much of you lately.
SIR JOHN: We meet in costume.
SIR RALPH: We meet as other people.

These encounters, normally held in restaurants at lunchtime, seldom pass without providing opportunities for Sir Ralph, a fervent and mercurial gourmet, to leap into action. Here are three examples:

I love bread so much; I want it to be taken out of my temptation. I have made a vow. I am going to give up my beautiful rolls. (*The Guardian*, November, 1976).

It has been my experience, in the past, that most of the wine served in American restaurants is cat's urine, disguised in French labels. (Luncheon with present writer, though without Gielgud, November, 1976).

SIR RALPH (*suddenly jumps, points to his plate dramatically. Waiters surround him):* What is THAT?
SIR JOHN: I think it's a bit of liver, Ralph.
SIR RALPH: Never touch it. Take the liver away ...Bear the offending liver away. (*The Observer*, October, 1975).

This confirms what Gielgud now tells me—that Sir Ralph, though a superb host, is not a good guest. "I eat out of tins, but Ralph always insists on the best." From the same *Observer* interview, Gielgud recalls Sir Ralph's response when Peter Brook was mentioned as a director of world renown:

SIR RALPH: What was that *terrible* production Brook did?...That *ghastly* thing. You were in it.

He was referring to Seneca's *Oedipus*, directed by Brook for the National Theatre, in which Gielgud played the protagonist. It was far from ghastly, at least in my opinion; I was working for the National at the time and selected the play for its repertoire. I don't deny, however, that there were unusual elements in Brook's staging, notably in his handling of the chorus. Let Sir Ralph continue:

> SIR RALPH: When I went to see the production, somehow I hadn't got a programme. So I said to Mu, 'Leave it to me.' And I went down the aisle to a chap, but he was lashed to a pillar. I didn't know what was going on. It turned out that he was in the show. I think he was one of the chorus. But the show hadn't started yet. Mu said, 'Did you get a programme?' And I had to say it wasn't possible because all the programme-sellers were lashed to the dress circle. Very strange.
>
> SIR JOHN: But what did the poor actor who was lashed to the pillar say to you?
>
> SIR RALPH: Well, of course, when I asked him for a programme all I got were these strangled sounds. He was gagged, you see. The whole experience upset me very much. I'm a very *square* man.

Gielgud first appeared with Sir Ralph in 1930, and has enormous respect for his old confrere. "He loves the craftsmanship of his art. He prepares his work and exhibits it with the utmost finesse. It's like Edith Evans—she used to open a window to her heart and then slam it shut, so that you'd come back the next night to see more. My own tendency, on the other hand, is always to show too much. Ralph says he never thinks anything he does is a success. He doesn't even want to repeat his Falstaff. I wish he would; it's his greatest performance. And he was wonderful as John Gabriel Borkman at the National last year. I shall never forget the noise he made when Borkman died. As if a bird had flown out of his heart."

We sip white wine while Gielgud recalls Sir Ralph as he first knew him: "He had a very unhappy early life as an actor. He used to walk with his behind stuck out, and thought he was terribly unattractive to women. He was very poor, and then there was his first wife's dreadful illness. But now he's acquired such a control of movement, such majesty. Of course, he does have a violent side to his nature—a powerful sadistic streak, sudden outbursts of temper. But you have to remember that he went through a really wretched time before he was able to marry Mu." Gielgud smiles. "He used to expect her to be the perfect hostess during dinner, and then, after coffee was served, to kick up her legs like a chorus girl. It must have been difficult at times, to reconcile those two demands."

Fourth Interlude: 1:45 P.M. on November 11, 1976. Luncheon with Sir Ralph at the Algonquin Hotel. He arrives late, bustling through the crowded restaurant, mustache bristling, eyes moist with apology. We talk first about the honorary D. Litt. he received from Oxford University in 1969. It was bestowed by Harold Macmillian, the Chancellor of the University and former Prime Minister, who delivered a Latin oration. "What he said, in essence, was that the gods have been graceful and lucky for you, and that we of this university wish to add to their smiling," Sir Ralph says. When we have ordered, I ask Sir Ralph whom he would invite to an ideal dinner party, given free choice from the living and the dead. His list, like a good deal more about him, is highly idiosyncratic. "Samuel Butler, demolisher of Victorian fathers. Robert Louis Stevenson. Joseph Conrad, provided that he admired Shakespeare. Scott of the Antarctic. And another explorer, Shackleton, to whom I'm distantly related. Einstein, definitely, And, above all, David Lloyd George, that rascally fellow-actor, that bandit, that savior of our country, without whom Kaiser Bill might even now be walking through Buckingham Palace waxing his mustache." Sir Ralph eats for a while in silence, apparently— and to my great relief—with pleasure. "I've just been reading some of Freud's lectures. Amazing how these tiny little childhood things can have repercussions like the atomic bomb. I wouldn't mind having him at our dinner table. He had such a great sense of humor." Another pause for eating. "I've always been intrigued by his picture of life—the sex down there, the caretaker up here. But I wouldn't put sex ace high, No. 1, the thing that winds up the whole clock. I think murder is more basic. Before you get the woman, you must kill the man who possesses her. Hunger is the first impulse of all. But then I must *possess* something. And then I must *enjoy* something. And that may involve destroying somebody else. For reasons of policy and politeness, of course, we put the brakes on."

It is getting late, and the room has emptied. The waiters are laying tables for dinner. For a moment, Sir Ralph watches them. Then he says, "I wouldn't mind running through this restaurant and smashing all those glasses. I see them glittering there." A pause. "One is putting the brakes on all the time." While we wait for the check, his mind reverts to *No Man's Land:* "Hirst is capable of murder, you know. I believe he was responsible for the drowning of a girl in a lake, although Mr. Pinter might not necessarily agree. He is certainly capable of killing Spooner. We all have original sin. Hirst has it. *I* have it." Sir Ralph's eyes are blazing. As I escort the former altar boy (for such he was in his papist youth) to his limousine, he says, "I would much rather be able to terrify than to charm. I like malevolence. What an enjoyable lunch."

In September, 1975, Sir Ralph went on London Weekend Television and gave a sixty-minute interview by which (his finest stage performances apart) I would not mind remembering him. He was freewheeling and free-associating, seeming artless in his candor, yet laying artful diversionary smokescreens whenever anything central to his privacy appeared to be threatened. We were watching a master mesmerist. No great lover of publicity for its own sake, he had undertaken this chore at the behest of the National Theatre, by whom he was currently employed. His interlocutor was Russell Harty, a dapper North Countryman, who runs the most popular chat show on the British commercial channel. The setting was the usual studio mockup—in this case, a semicircular arrangement of window draperies with nothing behind it, and a low window seat and a pair of tulip-shaped chairs (one of them occupied by Harty) in front of it. A packed house applauded as Harty urged it to welcome "one of the most distinguished actors in the British theatre."

Sir Ralph enters around one side of the draperies, wearing a tweed suit, a pink satin tie, and bright-yellow socks. Instead of taking his expected place in the empty chair, he walks straight past it (and Harty) toward the audience, before whom he halts, bounteously beaming. He seems in a genial frame of mind. Cameras whirl round to keep him in shot, none too successfully.

> SIR RALPH *(to Harty, over his shoulder)*: You've got a very nice place here, haven't you? It's a great deal bigger than my place, where you came to see me the other day.
> HARTY *(left high and dry, but keeping his cool)*: Yes, but it's not as posh as yours.
> SIR RALPH: No, but you've got a lot more friends than I have.

In his voice we note a false bonhomie, as of a Dr. Watson—played, of course, by Nigel Bruce—behind whose slightly fatuous facade a canny, Holmeslike intelligence is at work.

> SIR RALPH: Are they friends of yours? Or are they enemies?
> HARTY: Well, we don't know.
> SIR RALPH: Shall I address them? Ladies and gentlemen of the jury, I assure you that this man Harty is innocent.

Who said he was guilty? Already Sir Ralph has taken control.

> SIR RALPH: You've got a lot more cameras in your place than I've got in mine. Cameras always make me rather nervous. They sort of prowl in on you. Of course, you know them. You probably feed them. What do they eat? Celluloid and chips?

Thus far, he has been strolling around inspecting the technology. He now wanders past Harty, still glued to his tulip, toward the window seat. On this he sits, and he peeps gently through the draperies at what we know perfectly well is the wall of the studio.

> SIR RALPH: I say, what a wonderful view you've got here. I mean, you could see anything from here, couldn't

you—the Tower of London, Buckingham Palace, the Post Office Tower? I'll bet you could.

Consenting at last to occupy a chair, Sir Ralph immediately begins to interview Harty, asking him about his past career and whether his parents have secure and pensionable jobs. Some time passes before Harty manages to sneak in a question about the Pinter play.

SIR RALPH: There isn't any plot. But that never bothers an actor. And the characters are never really rounded off. They don't quite know who they are. But that's rather natural in a way. We don't know exactly who we are, do we? We hardly know anybody else, really completely. We none of us know when we're going to die.... We're a mystery to ourselves, and to other people.

He goes on to say that acting is never boring, because the audiences are always different.

SIR RALPH: In music, the punctuation is absolutely strict, the bars and the rests are absolutely defined. But our punctuation cannot be quite strict, because we have to relate it to the audience. In other words, we are continually changing the score.... For me, what gives our work its special fascination is the challenge that has to do with time. If you're a writer or a painter, you write or paint whenever you want to. But we have to do this task at a precise moment. At three minutes past eight, the curtain goes up, and you've got to pretend to believe, because no one else will believe you unless you believe it yourself. A great deal of our work is simply making ourselves dream. That is the task. At three minutes past eight you must dream.

HARTY: Do you dream when you go to bed?

SIR RALPH: Yes, I dream a lot. I lead a fairly sheltered life. Things are fairly peaceful, and nobody tries to murder me much.... Fortunately, I am able to remember my nightmares. They help me in my work. When I'm asleep,

I'm earning my living if I have a nightmare. I get murdered a good deal. I get stabbed quite a bit.

Harty suggests that Sir Ralph doesn't much like his own body. Conceding the point, Sir Ralph proposes that they might swap. Perhaps feeling cornered, he fires a sudden question at Harty: "Do you hate your face?" Commendably unfazed, Harty replies that he hates not only his face but his name and his body from the waist down. "Oh, really?" says Sir Ralph. "I can't see anything the matter with it." Harty now tries yet again to seize the initiative.

HARTY: I wondered whether you'd gone into acting because you weren't satisfied with your face or your body.

SIR RALPH *(not to be drawn)*: There are lots of reasons why people become actors. Some to hide themselves, and some to show themselves. As for my face, I've seen better-looking hot cross buns.

Before long, Sir Ralph, back in the driver's seat, is asking Harty what kind of people he finds the easiest to talk to. Having given a long and honest answer, Harty reverses the question.

SIR RALPH: I like talking to engineers best. They build bridges, they're very precise, they're very disciplined, yet I find they have roving minds. They can talk about anything. My other favorite people are explorers and potholers. To *choose* to be brave is a great sign of character, I think. They have great accuracy, and also great fantasy.

Harty shows a clip from Sir Ralph's latest film, *Rollerball*, and afterward points out to the viewers that throughout the excerpt Sir Ralph busied himself with lighting his pipe and carefully averted his eyes from the screen. Emitting clouds of smoke, Sir Ralph resumes the questioning. Does Russell Harty like his own name? Harty says that he doesn't. Sir Ralph hastens to reassure him.

SIR RALPH: I think Russell Harty is a jolly decent name. . . . I'm very fond of Russell because half my family are Russells. My mother was a Russell, so I'm very used to the name. And I don't mind Richardson. I think it suits me, because it's rather plain.

Here he drifts off into free association, before the eyes of approximately twelve million viewers.

SIR RALPH: How weird it is, the way people's names seem to suit them—how they get a name and grow up to be like it. . . . Shakespeare, for instance—it's an arresting, an aggressive word. You can see the man. . . . And Velazquez—how the name suits the painter! It's a delicious sound; you can feel him laying on the paint, you could almost eat the paint itself. And Rembrandt—he's an old ruminative man, drawing old things with long memories. . . . But I tell you, I like the name of Richardson, and I like the name Russell. . . .

HARTY: Are you viewing the prospect of old age with regret or happiness?

SIR RALPH: I'm amazed that I'm as old as I am. I always had the idea that when I was old I'd get frightfully clever. I'd get awfully learned, I'd get jolly sage. People would come to me for advice. But nobody ever comes to me for anything, and I don't know a thing.

Later, as if it were a matter of trifling consequence, he remarks that he has "never been particularly afraid of dying." Finally, at Harty's gentle instigation, he goes to a lectern and brings their conversation to an end by reading Keat's "To Autumn," that being the season of the year.

As I watched, I remembered him, thirty years ago, as the dying Cyrano, sitting in a convent garden, with autumn leaves twirling and floating around him. Sir Ralph looked even then, very odd, and absentminded, and solitary, and absurd, and noble, and desolate. When he spoke, he sounded at once defiant and merciful. There has always been in his voice a mixture of challenge and benison.

Like Gielgud, I wanted to see him again as Falstaff, a role of which W. H. Auden once wrote:

Falstaff never really does anything, but . . . the impression
he makes on the audience is not of idleness but of infinite
energy. He is never tired, never bored, and until he is
rejected he radiates happiness as Hal radiates power, and
this happiness without apparent cause, this untiring devotion to making others laugh becomes a comic image
for a love which is absolutely self-giving.

Very delicately, Auden goes on to suggest nothing less than
that Falstaff is a comic symbol of Jesus Christ. When the
Christian God presents himself on earth, "the consequence is
inevitable," as Auden points out. "The highest religious and
temporal authorities condemn Him as a blasphemer and a Lord
of Misrule, as a Bad Companion for mankind." Which, of
course, is what happened to Falstaff. Quite apart from its fun
and its lunatic grandeur, there was a charity about Sir Ralph's
performance, a magnanimity and a grief, that made you wonder
whether Auden's audacious hint might not be the simple truth,
after all.

In fact, to take a step further, if a playwright were to revive
the anthropomorphic conception of the deity and write a play
about God himself, and if he were then to ask my help in
picking an actor for the central role, I know exactly in which
direction I would point him. I would find it entirely credible
that the creator of the universe as we know it was someone
very like Sir Ralph. This does not mean either that I accept
the Christian hypothesis or that I approve of the current state
of the world; but if we imagine its maker as a whimsical,
enigmatic magician, capable of fearful blunders, sometimes
inexplicably ferocious, at other times dazzling in his innocence
and benignity, we are going to need an actor who can imply
metaphysical attributes while remaining—to quote C. S. Lewis
on God—"a positive, concrete, and highly articulated character." Someone, in short, who is at once unapproachable and
instantly accessible. Sir Ralph's number, as I have said, is in
the book.

[1977]

Withdrawing with style
from the chaos
—TOM STOPPARD

IN *Jumpers*, a play by Tom Stoppard, whose other works include *Rosencrantz and Guildenstern Are Dead*, *Travesties*, and *Dirty Linen*, a man carrying a tortoise in one hand and a bow and arrow in the other, his face covered with shaving cream, opens the door of his apartment. Standing outside is a police inspector bearing a bouquet of flowers. There is a rational explanation for this.

In *After Magritte*, a much shorter play by the same author, we learn that a one-legged blind man with a white beard, who may in fact have been a handicapped football player with shaving cream on his face, has been seen hopping, or perhaps playing hopscotch, along an English street, wearing striped pajamas, convict garb, or possibly a West Bromwich Albion football jersey, waving with one arm a white stick, a crutch, or a furled parasol while carrying under the other what may have been a football, a wineskin, an alligator handbag, or a tortoise. (One of the characters, discounting the hypothesis that the man was blind, scornfully inquires whether it was a seeing-eye tortoise.) There is also a perfectly rational, though much longer, explanation for this.

In "The Language of Theatre," an address delivered by the same author in January, 1977, at the University of California at Santa Barbara, the lecturer began by stating that he was not going to talk about the language of theatre. ("That was just a device to attract a better class of audience," he said, eying the spectators. "I see if failed.") Instead—and among other things—he told a story about a man he knew who bought a peacock on impulse and, shortly afterward, while shaving in his pajamas, observed the bird escaping from his country garden. Dropping his razor, he set off in pursuit and managed to catch the feathered fugitive just as it reached a main road adjoining his property. At that moment, a car flashed by, middle-aged husband at the wheel, wife at his side. For perhaps five seconds—*vrrooommm*—they caught sight of this perplexing apparition. Wife: "What was that, dear?" Husband: "Fellow in his pajamas, with shaving cream all over his face and a peacock under his arm." There was, as we know, a perfectly rational explanation. (Stoppard went on to say that several of his plays had grown out of images such as this. He added that when he tried the peacock anecdote out on the members of a literary society at Eton College, it was received in bewildered silence. He soon realized why: "They all *had* peacocks.")

In none of the same author's plays will you find any reference to (or echo of, or scene derived from) the following singular, and partly equivocal, story. During the nineteen-thirties, there lived in Zlin—a town in Czechoslovakia that is now known as Gottwaldov—a middle-class physician named Eugene Straussler, who worked for a famous shoe company. Either he or his wife (nobody seems quite sure which) had at least one parent of Jewish descent. In any case, Dr. Straussler sired two sons, of whom the younger, Thomas, was born on July 3, 1937. Two years later, on the eve of the Nazi invasion of their homeland, the Strausslers left for Singapore, where they settled until 1942. The boys and their mother then moved to India. Dr. Straussler stayed behind to face the Japanese occupation. He died in a Japanese air raid, or in a prisoner-of-war camp, or on a Japanese prison ship torpedoed by the British (nobody seems quite sure which). In 1946, his widow married a major in the British Army, who brought the family back with him to England. The two Straussler scions assumed their stepfather's surname, which was Stoppard. Thomas, who claims to have spoken only Czech until the age of three, or possibly five and a half (he does not seem quite sure which), grew up to become, by the early 1970s, one of the two or three most prosperous and ubiquitously adulated playwrights at present bearing a British passport. (The other contenders are Harold Pinter, who probably has the edge in adulation, and Peter

Shaffer, the author of *Equus*, whose strong point is prosperity.)
There is no perfectly rational explanation for any of this. It is
simply true.

Preliminary notes from my journal dated July 24, 1976:
Essential to remember that Stoppard is an émigré. A director
who has staged several of his plays told me the other day,
"You have to be foreign to write English with that kind of
hypnotized brilliance." An obvious comparison is with Vla-
dimir Nabokov, whom Stoppard extravagantly admires. Stoppard said to me not long ago that his favorite parenthesis in
world literature was this, from Lolita: "My very photogenic
mother died in a freak accident (picnic, lightning) when I was
three." He is at present adapting Nabokov's novel *Despair* for
the screen; Rainer Werner Fassbinder, who commissioned the
script, will direct. Stoppard loves all forms of wordplay, especially puns, and frequently describes himself as "a bounced
Czech." Like many immigrants, he has immersed himself beyond the call of baptism in the habits and rituals of his adopted
country. Nowadays, he is *plus anglais que les anglais*—a
phrase that would please him, as a student of linguistic caprice,
since it implies that his Englishness can best be defined in
French. His style in dress is the costly-casual dandyism of
London in the nineteen-sixties. According to his friend Derek
Marlowe, who wrote the bestselling novel *A Dandy in Aspic*,
"Tom goes to some very posh places for his clothes, but he
finds it hard to orchestrate all his gear into a sartorial unity.
The effect is like an expensive medley." (Told of this comment,
Stoppard protests to me that Marlowe is exaggerating. "Derek,"
he says, "is a fantasist enclosed by more mirror than glass.")
Because Stoppard has a loose, lanky build, a loose thatch of
curly dark hair, liver tinted lips, dark, flashing eyes, and long,
flashing teeth, you might mistake him for an older brother of
Mick Jagger, more intellectually inclined than his frenetic sib-
ling.

Stoppard often puts me in mind of a number in *Beyond the
Fringe*, the classic English revue of the sixties, in which Alan
Bennett, as an unctuous clergyman, preached a sermon on the
text "Behold, Esau my brother is an hairy man, and I am a
smooth man." The line accurately reflects the split in English
drama which took place during (and has persisted since) this

period. On one side were the hairy men—heated, embattled, socially committed playwrights, like John Osborne, John Arden, and Arnold Wesker, who had come out fighting in the late fifties. On the other side were the smooth men—cool, apolitical stylists, like Harold Pinter, the late Joe Orton, Christopher Hampton (*The Philanthropist*), Alan Ayckbourn (*The Norman Conquests*), Simon Gray (*Otherwise Engaged*), and Stoppard. Earlier this year, Stoppard told an interviewer from the London weekly *Time Out*, "I used to feel out on a limb, because when I started to write you were a shit if you weren't writing about Vietnam or housing. Now I have no compunction about that. . . . *The Importance of Being Earnest* is important, but it says nothing about anything." He once said that his favorite line in modern English drama came from *The Philanthropist*: "I'm a man of no convictions—at least, I *think* I am." In *Lord Malquist and Mr. Moon* (1966), Stoppard's only novel to date, Mr. Moon seems to speak for his author when he says, "I distrust attitudes because they claim to have appropriated the whole truth and pose as absolutes. And I distrust the opposite attitude for the same reason." Lord Malquist, who conducts his life on the principle that the eighteenth century has not yet ended, asserts that all battles are discredited. "I stand aloof," he declares, "contributing nothing except my example." In an article for the London *Sunday Times* in 1968, Stoppard said, "Some writers write because they burn with a cause which they further by writing about it. I burn with no causes. I cannot say that I write with any social objective. One writes because one loves writing, really." On another occasion, he defined the quality that distinguished him from many of his contemporaries as "an absolute lack of certainty about almost anything."

Seeking artistic precedents for this moral detachment, this commitment to neutrality, I come up with four quotations. The first is from Oscar Wilde:

A Truth in art is that whose contradictory is also true.

The second is from Evelyn Waugh's diary:

I . . . don't want to influence opinions or events, or expose humbug or anything of that kind. I don't want

to be of service to anyone or anything. I simply want
to do my work as an artist.

Then these, from John Keats's letters:

It struck me what quality went to form a Man of
Achievement, especially in Literature, and which Shakespeare possessed so enormously—I mean *Negative Capability*, that is, when a man is capable of being in
uncertainties, mysteries, doubts, without any irritable
reaching after fact and reason. . . .
The only means of strengthening one's intellect is to
make up one's mind about nothing—to let the mind be
a thoroughfare for all thoughts, not a select party.

In Stoppard's case, "negative capability" has been a profitable thoroughfare. When I asked him, not long ago, how
much he thought he had earned from *Rosencrantz and Guildenstern Are Dead*, his answer was honestly vague: "About—
a hundred and fifty thousand pounds?" To the same question,
his agent, Kenneth Ewing, gave me the following reply: *"Rosencrantz opened in London in 1967. Huge overnight success—
it stayed in the National Theatre repertory for about four years.
The Broadway production ran for a year. Metro bought the
screen rights for two hundred and fifty thousand dollars and
paid Tom a hundred thousand to write the script, though the
movie was never made. The play had a short run in Paris, with
Delphine Seyrig as Gertrude, but it was quite a hit in Italy,
where Rosencrantz was played by a girl. It did enormous business in Germany and Scandinavia and—oddly enough—Japan.
On top of that, the book sold more than six hundred thousand
copies in the English language alone. Up to now, out of Rosencrantz I would guess that Tom had grossed well over three
hundred thousand pounds."
And now, on this sunny Saturday afternoon, to Gunnersbury
Park, in West London, where a cricket match is to be played.
Cricket, to which I am addicted, is a pastime of great complexity and elegance. Shapeless and desultory to the outsider,
it has an underlying structure that only the initiate perceives.
At the international level, a match may last five days, end in

a draw, and still be exciting. Cricket may seem to dawdle, to meander, to ramble off into amorphous perversity; but for all its vagaries and lapses into seeming incoherence there is, as in a Stoppard play, a perfectly rational explanation. Not surprisingly, Stoppard is a passionate fan of the game—an enslavement he shares with many British writers of the cool school. Generalization: Cricket attracts artists who are either conservative or nonpolitical; e.g., P.G. Wodehouse, Terence Rattigan, Samuel Beckett, Kingsley Amis, Harold Pinter, and Stoppard, all of them buffs who could probably tell you how many wickets Tich Freeman, the wily Kent spin bowler, took in his record-breaking season of 1928. Leftists, on the whole, favor soccer, the sport of the urban proletariat. It's hard to imagine Wesker, Arden, Trevor Griffiths, or the young Osborne (the middle-aged Osborne has swung toward right-wing anarchism and may well, for all I know, have taken up the quarterstaff) standing in line outside Lord's Cricket Ground. As a cricket-loving radical, I am an anomaly, regarded by both sides with cordial mistrust.

Today's game is an annual fixture: Mr. Harold Pinter's XI versus the *Guardian* newspaper's. The field, rented for the occasion, is impressively large, with a well-equipped pavilion, inside which at 2:30 P.M., the advertised starting time, both teams are avidly watching another match—England versus the West Indies—on television. Eight spectators, including two children and me, have turned up. The *Guardian* XI looks formidably healthy, featuring several muscular typesetters and the paper's industrial correspondent. The Pinter squad seems altogether less businesslike. To begin with, only nine of the players are present, the principal batsman having discovered on his arrival that he had left his contact lenses at home. Since he lives in an outlying northern suburb, the game may easily be over by the time he returns. Moreover, Skipper Pinter, inscrutable as always, has decided at the last moment to absent himself, thereby leaving his lads leaderless. Among the nine remaining are a somewhat bald fortyish publisher, a retired Chelsea football player, Pinter's teenage son Daniel (already a published poet, who has lately won a scholarship to Magdalen College, Oxford), and—by far the most resplendent, in gauntlets of scarlet leather and kneepads as blindingly white as Pitz

Palu—Tom Stoppard, the team's wicketkeeper, who swears to me that he has not played cricket for over a year.

He asks me to take the place of the myopic batsman. I refuse, on the ground that I have no white flannels. Characteristically, Dandy Tom has brought a spare pair. I counter by pleading lack of practice, not having put bat to ball for roughly twenty years, and am grudgingly excused. Why, I wonder, has Pinter let down the side? The answer, gleaned from his teammates, is that his estranged wife, the brilliant but temperamental actress Vivien Merchant (who made no secret of her vexation when, a year earlier, Pinter left home to live with Lady Antonia Fraser, the biographer of Cromwell and Mary Queen of Scots), has announced her intention of watching the game, ostensibly to see her son in action. Anxious to avoid a scene, the captain has retired to a nearby Thames-side pub, where—doubtless biting his nails, for he is a deeply competitive man—he will await the result. (As it happened, he need not have worried: Mrs. Pinter failed to show up until the game was over.) Many amateur cricket teams have specifically designed ties; I learn from Stoppard that the Pinter outfit does not. "But if it had," he adds, alluding to the pauses for which Pinter's plays are famous, "the club insignia would probably be three dots." The *Guardian* XI, having torn itself away from TV and won the toss, has elected to bat first; it is time for the Pinter XI (reduced to IX) to take the field. Stoppard goes out, managing as he does so to drop a smoldering cigarette butt between kneepad and trousers. "There may be a story here," he calls back to me. "'Playwright Bursts Into Flames at Wicket.'"

Having no fast bowlers, who are the match-winning thunderbolts of cricket, the Pinter team is forced to rely on slow spinners of the ball, oblique and devious in their approach. To hazard an analogy: Pinter onstage is a masterly spinner, but his surrogates on the field, lacking his precision, are mercilessly bashed about by their opponents. The tough and purposeful *Guardian* team scores eighty-three runs, and the figure would be much higher if it were not for the elastic leaps and hair-trigger reflexes of Stoppard behind the stumps, where (in the role that approximates the catcher's in baseball) he dismisses no fewer than four of the enemy side. This leaves room for hope—though not for all that much, as we realize when the Pinter IX starts to bat. Its acting captain, the somewhat bald publisher, holds his own, scoring with occasional suave deflections, the picture of public-school unconcern; but the *Guardian* bowlers have muscle and pace, and wicket after wicket falls to their intimidating speed. The game is all but lost when Stoppard ambles in to bat, with the score at sixty and only two men to follow him. Within ten minutes, in classic style, he has driven three balls to the boundary ropes for four runs apiece. Six more graceful swipes bring his personal total to twenty, thereby making him the top scorer and winning the game for his side. He is welcomed back to the pavilion with cheers.

We repair to the riverside pub, where Skipper Pinter, accompanied by Lady Antonia, has just heard the news. Bursting with pride, he embraces Stoppard and buys expensive drinks for the whole team. (Lady A. sips chilled cider.) He has been informed of certain crass errors made in the course of play, and sharply chides those responsible. It is like listening to Wellington if an attack of gout had kept him away from Waterloo. (Pinter's record commands respect: turning out every Saturday afternoon, he has a batting average that has seldom dipped below seventy, which is very high indeed.) In T-shirt and slacks, this sun-drenched evening, he looks dapper and superbly organized behind his thick horn-rimmed spectacles. Pinter has two basic facial expressions, which alternate with alarming rapidity. One of them, his serious mask, suggests a surgeon or a dentist on the brink of making a brilliant diagnosis. The head tilts to one side, the eyes narrow shrewdly, the brain seems to whirr like a computer. His stare drills into your mind. His face, topped by shiny black hair, is sombre, intent, profoundly concerned. When he smiles, however, it is suddenly and totally transformed. "Smile" is really the wrong word: what comes over his face is unmistakably a *leer*. It reveals gleaming, voracious teeth, with a good deal of air between them, and their owner resembles a stand-up comic who has just uttered a none too subtle sexual innuendo. At the same time, the eyes pop and lasciviously swivel. There seems to be no halfway house between these two extremes, and this, as Pinter is doubtless aware, can be very disconcerting.

Pinter's absence from the field, which might have spelled disaster, has in fact made no difference at all, thanks to Stoppard's dashing performance. Where a lesser man might have been nettled, Pinter is genuinely delighted. Team spirit has triumphed: the leer is positively euphoric. Stoppard makes his farewells and departs (to keep a date with his wife), leaving the skipper surrounded by disciples. One might, I suppose, discern a kind of metaphorical significance in the fact that while the top-ranking English playwright's back was turned the runner-up nipped in and seized the victor's crown. But, as Noël Coward said in *The Scoundrel*, I hate stooping to symbolism.

Back home after the match, I decided that for Stoppard art is a game within a game—the larger game being life itself, an absurd mosaic of incidents and accidents in which (as Beckett, whom he venerates, says in the aptly entitled *Endgame*) "something is taking its course. We cannot know what the something is, or whither it is leading us; and it is therefore impermissible for art, a mere derivative of life, to claim anything as presumptuous as a moral purpose or a social function. Since 1963, when the first professional performance of a script by Stoppard was given, he has written one novel, four full-length plays, one miniplay (*Dirty Linen*) that was cheekily passed off as a full-length entertainment, five one-acters for the stage, and ten pieces for radio or television. Thus far, only one of his performed works (*Jumpers*, to my mind his masterpiece, which was first produced in 1972) could be safely accused of having a moral or political message; but the critics are always sniffing for ulterior motives—so diligently that Stoppard felt it necessary to announce in 1974, "I think that in future I must stop compromising my plays with this whiff of social application. They must be entirely untouched by any suspicion of usefulness. I should have the courage of my lack of convictions." In another interview, he said he saw no reason that art should not concern itself with contemporary social and political history, but added that he found it "deeply embarrassing . . . when, because art takes notice of something important, it's claimed that the art is important. It's not." Hating to be pinned down, politely declining to be associated with the opinions expressed by his characters, he has often remarked, "I write plays because dialogue is the most respectable way of contradicting myself." (Many of his apparent impromptus are worked out beforehand. Himself a onetime journalist, he makes a habit of anticipating questions and prefabricating effective replies. Indeed, such was his assurance of eventual success that he was doing this long before anyone ever interviewed him. When he read the printed result of his first conversation with the press, he said he found it "very déjà vu." Clive James, the Australian critic and satirist, now working in London, has rightly described him as "a dream interviewee, talking in eerily quotable sentences whose English has the faintly extraterritorial perfection of a Conrad or a Nabokov.")

Philosophically, you can see the early Stoppard at his purest in *Lord Malquist and Mr. Moon*, which sold only four hundred and eighty-one copies in 1966, when it was published. Malquist says:

> Nothing is the history of the world viewed from a suitable distance. Revolution is a trivial shift in the emphasis of suffering; the capacity for self-indulgence changes hands. But the world does not alter its shape or its course. The seasons are inexorable, the elements constant. Against such vast immutability the human struggle takes place on the same scale as the insect movements in the grass, and carnage in the streets is no more than the spider-sucked husk of a fly on a dusty window-sill.

Later, he adds, "Since we cannot hope for order, let us withdraw with style from the chaos."

When Moon, his biographer and a professed anarchist, attacks Malquist's antihumanism on the ground that whatever he may say, the world is made up of "all *people*, isn't it?" Malquist scoffs:

> What an extraordinary idea. People are not the world, they are merely a recent and transitory product of it. The world is ten million years old. If you think of that period condensed into one year beginning on the first of Jan-

uary, then people do not make their appearance in it until
the thirty-first of December; or to be more precise, in
the last forty seconds of that day.

Such trivial latecomers sound barely worth saving.

Though Stoppard would doubtless deny it, these pronounce-
ments of Malquist's have a ring of authority which suggests
the author speaking. They reflect a world view of extreme
pessimism, and therefore of conservatism. The pessimist is
necessarily conservative. Maintaining, as he does, that mankind is inherently and immutably flawed, he must always be
indifferent or hostile to proposals for improving human life by
means of social or political change. The radical, by contrast,
is fundamentally an optimist, embracing change because he
holds that human nature is perfectible. The Malquist attitude,
whatever its virtues, is hardly conducive to idealism. I recall
a conversation with Derek Marlowe about Stoppard's private
beliefs. "I don't think," Marlowe said, "that there's anything
he would go to the guillotine for." I found the choice of in-
strument revealing. We associate the guillotine with the de-
capitation of aristocrats. Marlowe instinctively identified Stoppard with the nobility rather than the mob—with reaction rather
than revolution.

There are signs, however, that history has lately been forcing Stoppard into the arena of commitment. Shortly after I
wrote the above entry in my journal, he sent me a typescript
of his most recent work. Commissioned by André Previn, who
conducts the London Symphony Orchestra, it is called *Every
Good Boy Deserves Favour*—a mnemonic phrase familiar to
students of music, since the initial letters of the words represent, in ascending order, the notes signified by the black lines
of the treble clef. Involving six actors (their dialogue inter-
spersed with musical contributions from Mr. Previn's big
band), it had its world première in July, 1977, at the Royal
Festival Hall, in London. It started out in Stoppard's mind as
a play about a Florida grapefruit millionaire, but his works
have a way of changing their themes as soon as he sits down
at his typewriter. The present setting is a Russian mental home

for political dissidents, where the main job of the staff is to persuade the inmates that they are in fact insane. What follows is a characteristic exchange between a recalcitrant prisoner named Alexander and the therapist who is assigned to him:

> PSYCHIATRIST: The idea that all the people locked up in mental hospitals are sane while the people walking about outside are all mad is merely a literary cliché, put about by the people who should be locked up. I assure you there's not much in it. Taken as a whole, the sane are out there and the sick are in here. For example, *you* are here because you have delusions that sane people are put in mental hospitals.
> ALEXANDER: But I *am* in a mental hospital.
> PSYCHIATRIST: That's what I said.

Alexander, of course, refuses to curry Favour by being a Good Boy. Beneath its layers of Stoppardian irony, the play (oratorio? melodrama?) is a point-blank attack on the way in which Soviet law is perverted to stifle dissent. In the script I read, Alexander declares, at a moment of crisis, "There are truths to be shown, and our only strength is personal example." Stoppard, however, had crossed this line out, perhaps being reluctant to put his name to a platitude, no matter how true or relevant it might be. Simplicity of thought—in this piece, as elsewhere in his work—quite often underlies complexity of style. *E.G.B.D.F.* rests on the assumption that the difference between good and evil is obvious to any reasonable human being. What else does Stoppard believe in? For one thing, I would guess, the intrinsic merits of individualism; for another, a universe in which everything is relative, yet in which moral absolutes exist; for a third, the probability that this paradox can be resolved only if we accept the postulate of a presiding deity. In 1973, during a public discussion of his plays at the Church of St. Mary Le Bow, in London, he told his interlocutor, the Reverend Joseph McCulloch:

> The whole of science can be said, by a theologian, to be operating within a larger framework. In other

words, the higher we penetrate into space and the deeper
we penetrate into the atom, all it shows to a theologian
is that God has been gravely underestimated.

Nietzsche once said that convictions were prisons—a remark that the younger Stoppard would surely have applauded.
Later, I shall try to chart the route that has led Stoppard, the
quondam apostle of detachment, to the convictions he now
proclaims, and to his loathing for the strictly unmetaphorical
prisons in which so many people he respects are at present
confined.

Stoppard's childhood was full of enforced globe-trotting.
Much of it was spent on the run from totalitarianism, of both
the European and the Oriental variety. By the time he was five
years old, he had moved from his Czechoslovakian birthplace
to Singapore and thence—with his mother and elder brother—
to India. His father, as we have seen, stayed in Singapore,
where he died in circumstances that remain obscure. (Not long
ago, I asked Stoppard why this question, like that of his
family's Jewish background, could not be cleared up by his
mother, who, together with his stepfather, nowadays lives in
the Lake District. "Rightly or wrongly, we've always felt that
she might want to keep the past under a protective covering
so we've never delved into it," he said. "My father died in
enemy hands, and that's that.") Stoppard attended a multiracial,
English-speaking school in Darjeeling. There his mother managed a shoe store and met Major Kenneth Stoppard, of the
British Army in India, whom she married in 1946. By the end
of the year, Major Stoppard had brought his new family back
to England. Demobilized, he prospered as a salesman of machine tools, and Tom went through the initial hoops of a traditional middle-class education. From a preparatory boarding
school in Nottinghamshire he moved on to "a sort of minor
public school" in Yorkshire. He summed up his extracurricular
activities for me in a recent letter:

> I wrote a play about Charles I when I was twelve.
> It was surprisingly conventional: he died in the end. I
> edited no magazines but I did debate. I remember being

completely indifferent as to which side of any proposition I should debate on.

In 1954, aged seventeen, he left school to live with his family in the West Country port of Bristol, where they had settled a few years earlier. He bypassed higher education and plunged into local journalism, first at the *Western Daily Press* and later at the Bristol *Evening World*, in a variety of posts, including those of news reporter, humorous columnist, feature writer, and reviewer of plays and films. For a while, although he was unable to drive, he held down the job of motoring correspondent on the *Daily Press*. ("I used to review the up-holstery," he says.) He rejoiced in the life of a newspaperman, relished "the glamour of flashing a press card at flower shows," and had no higher ambition than to make a gaudy mark in Fleet Street. He did not contemplate becoming a playwright until the late nineteen-fifties, when a new breed of English authors, led by John Osborne, began to assert themselves at the Royal Court Theatre, in London. Simultaneously, a new breed of actors emerged, to interpret their work. One of the latter, the then unknown Peter O'Toole, joined the Bristol Old Vic—probably the best of Britain's regional repertory companies—and in the course of the 1957–58 season he played a series of leading parts, among them the title role in *Hamlet* and Jimmy Porter in Osborne's *Look Back in Anger*. (This was the unique and original O'Toole, before he submitted his profile to surgical revision, which left him with a nose retroussé and anonymous enough to satisfy the producer of *Lawrence of Arabia*.) Years later, at a seminar in California, a student asked Stoppard, "Did you get into the theatre by accident?" "Of course," he said innocently. "One day, I tripped and fell against a type-writer, and the result was *Rosencrantz and Guildenstern*." In reality, it was O'Toole's blazing performances—and the plays they adorned in Bristol—that turned Stoppard on to theatre. By the end of the season, he was incubating a new vocation.

Meanwhile, he stuck to journalism, writing two columns (both pseudonymous) in every issue of the *Daily Press*. "They became a bit tiring to read, because they were a little too anxious to be funny," he says nowadays. "At the end, I was desperate to be printed in *Punch*. I was overextended." During this period, Bristol was a seedbed of theatrical talent. Geoffrey Reeves, who directed the first performance of *After Magritte* and collaborated with Peter Brook on several of the latter's productions, was then a research student in Bristol University's Drama Department. He recalls Stoppard as "a cynical wit in a mackintosh, one of the very few sophisticated journalists in town—though I would never have thought of him as a potential playwright." Peter Nichols (the author of *A Day in the Death of Joe Egg*) and Charles Wood (who wrote the screenplays of *The Knack, How I Won the War*, and *The Charge of the Light Brigade*) were both growing up in Bristol when Stoppard was there. Wood remembers Stoppard as "a sort of Mick Jaggerish character, who wrote some rather unfunny newspaper columns," and adds, "He wasn't a part of our world." Nichol's recollections are similarly tinged with waspishness: "Tom was a great figure in Bristol, to be mentioned with bated breath. His comings and goings were reported as if he were Orson Welles." When Nichols told me this, he had just returned from Minneapolis, where one of Stoppard's works was being performed. With a glint of malice in his voice, he continued, "Tom is very big in Minneapolis. Unlike a lot of modern British drama, his stuff travels well. No rough edges on Tom. None of those awkward local references. There never were." During the nineteen-sixties, Stoppard's *Rosencrantz and Guildenstern*, Wood's *H* (a chronicle of the Indian Mutiny of 1857), and Nichols's *The National Health* were all to be presented at the National Theatre, thereby provoking rumors of a Bristolian conspiracy to dominate British drama. *H*, stunningly written but structurally a mess, was a box-office failure; the Nichols play, in which a hospital ward symbolized the invalid state of the nation, had a great success with British audiences; but Stoppard's was the runaway smash, at home and abroad, with critics and public alike.

His career as a playwright began in 1960, when he wrote a one-act piece called *The Gamblers*, which he described to me in a recent letter as "*Waiting for Godot* in the death cell— prisoner and jailer—I'm sure you can imagine the rest." (It was staged in 1962 by Bristol University undergraduates, and has never been revived.) Later in 1960, he spent three months writing his first full-length play, *A Walk on the Water*. It was so weightily influenced by Arthur Miller and by Robert Bolt's *Flowering Cherry* that he has come to refer to it as "Flowering Death of a Salesman." He said in 1974 that, although it worked pretty well onstage, "it's actually phony because it's a play written about other people's characters—they're only real because I've seen them in other people's plays." A few years afterward, indulging in his hobby of self-contradiction, he told a group of drama students, "What I like to do is take a stereotype and betray it, rather than create an original character. I never try to invent characters. All my best characters are clichés." This is Stoppard at his most typical, laying a smoke screen designed to confuse and ambush his critics. Run the above statements together and you get something like this: "It's wrong to borrow other writers' characters, but it's all right as long as they're clichés." *A Walk on the Water* is about George Riley, a congenital self-deceiver who declares roughly once a week that he is going to achieve independence by leaving home and making his fortune as an inventor. Never having won more bread than can be measured in crumbs, he is entirely dependent—for food, shelter, and pocket money—on his wife and their teenage daughter, both of whom are wearily aware that, however bravely he trumpets his fantasies of self-sufficiency in the local pub, he is sure to be back for dinner. For all his dottiness (among his inventions are a pipe that will stay perpetually lit provided it is smoked upside down and a revolutionary bottle opener for which, unfortunately, no matching bottle top exists), Riley has what Stoppard describes as "a tattered dignity." This attribute will recur in many Stoppard heroes, who have nothing to pit against the hostility of society and the indifference of the cosmos except their obstinate conviction that individuality is sacrosanct. C. W. E. Bigsby says in a perceptive booklet he wrote on Stoppard for the British Council:

While it is clear that none of his characters control their own destiny ... it is equally obvious that their unsinkable quality, their irrepressible vitality and eccentric persistence, constitute what Stoppard feels to be an authentic response to existence.

The first performance of *A Walk on the Water* (and the first professional production of any Stoppard play) was given on British commercial television in 1963. Considerably rewritten, and retitled *Enter a Free Man*, it was staged in the West End five years later, when *Rosencrantz and Guildenstern* had established Stoppard's reputation. Both versions of the text are indebted not only to Miller and Bolt but to N. F. Simpson (the whimisical author of *One Way Pendulum*, a gravely surreal farce that contains a character whose ambition is to train a team of speak-your-weight machines to sing the "Hallelujah Chorus"), and both pay respectful homage to P. G. Wodehouse and to British music-hall comedy, especially in the exchanges between Riley and a saloon-bar companion named Brown. In one of these, Riley insists that Thomas Edison was the inventor of the lighthouse. Brown, anxious to avoid a row, hints at the probable source of his friend's misapprehension by gently singing the opening lines of the well-known folk song: "My father was the keeper of the Eddystone light and he met a mermaid one fine night." This causes "a terrible silence," after which:

RILEY: Your father was what?
BROWN: Not my father.
RILEY: Whose father?...Whose father was a mermaid?
BROWN: He wasn't a mermaid. He *met* a mermaid.
RILEY: Who did?
BROWN: This man's father.
RILEY: Which man's father?
BROWN *(testily)*: I don't know.
RILEY: I don't believe you, Jones.
BROWN: Brown.
RILEY: This is just sailors' talk, the mythology of the seas. There are no such things as mermaids. I'm surprised at a grown man like you believing all that superstitious rubbish. What your father saw was a sea lion.
BROWN: My father didn't see a sea lion!
RILEY *(topping him):* So it *was* your father?

Both scripts are flawed by a running gag that the passage of time has tripped up. The invention that is supposed to demonstrate Riley's invincible stupidity beyond all doubt—viz., an envelope with gum inside and out, so that it can be used twice—has since been widely adopted as an efficient method of sending out bills. (Hazards of this kind are endemic to humorists who mistrust the march of science. Cf. the English wit J. B. Morton, who convulsed his readers in the nineteen-thirties by predicting the advent of an electric toothbrush.) Wherever the 1968 text differs from the original, the changes are for the better, as witness the addition of Riley's crowning fancy—a device that supplies indoor rain for indoor plants. From Stoppard's deletions, however, we learn something crucial about the nature and the limitations of his talent.

"Tom cares more about the details of writing than anyone else I know," Derek Marlowe told me. "He's startled by the smallest minutiae of life. He'll rush out of a room to make a note of a phrase he's just heard or a line that's just occurred to him. But the grand events, the highs and lows of human behavior, he sees with a sort of aloof, omniscient amusement. The world doesn't impinge on his work, and you'd think after reading his plays that no emotional experience had ever impinged on his world. For one thing, he can't create convincing women. His female characters are somewhere between playmates and amanuenses. He simply doesn't understand them. He has a dual personality, like the author of *Alice in Wonderland*. His public self is Charles Dodgson—he loves dons, philosophers, theorists of all kinds, and he's fascinated by the language they use. But his private self is Lewis Carroll—reclusive, intimidated by women, unnerved by emotion."

Geoffrey Reeves agrees with this analysis: "However abstract Beckett may seem, he always gives you a gut reaction. But Tom hasn't yet made a real emotional statement."

This is not to say that he hasn't tried. In the telecast of *A Walk on the Water*, as in the stage version, Riley's daughter is horrified to discover that her lover, who she thought to be unmarried, has a wife. Before the play reached the theatre, however, Stoppard excised the following outburst, addressed by the girl to her mother:

> He said he loved me. Loved me enough to have me
> on the side, didn't he? For his day off. . . . I asked him

if he'd meant it, about loving me, really, and he said,
he liked me a lot. It's murder. . . . If I was king, I'd hang
people for that. Everybody saying they love each other
when they only like each other a lot—they'll all be *hung*
and there'll be no one left except hangmen, and all of
them will say how they love each other when they only
like each other a lot, until there's only one left, and he'll
say—That's everybody, king, except me, your only true
and loving hangman. And I'll say, you don't love me,
you only like me a lot, and I'll *hang* him, and I'll be
king, and I'll like myself a lot.

There was more in that vein, which playgoers were luckily
spared. Not long ago, I asked Stoppard what he thought of
Marlowe's charge that his plays failed to convey genuine
emotion. He reflected for a while and then replied, "That criticism is always being presented to me as if it were a membrane
that I must somehow break through in order to grow up. Well,
I don't see any special virtue in making my private emotions
the quarry for the statue I'm carving. I can do that kind of
writing, but it tends to go off, like fruit. I don't like it very
much even when it works. I think that sort of truth-telling
writing is as big a lie as the deliberate fantasies I construct.
It's based on the fallacy of naturalism. There's a direct line
of descent from the naturalistic theatre which leads you straight
down to the dregs of bad theatre, bad thinking, and bad feeling.
At the other end of the scale, I dislike Abstract Expressionism
even more than I dislike naturalism. But you asked me about
expressing emotion. Let me put the best possible light on my
inhibitions and say that I'm waiting until I can do it well." And
what of Marlowe's comment that he didn't understand women?
"If Derek had said that I don't understand *people*, it would
have made more sense."

(A word on Stoppard and women. It is felt by some of his
friends that his sexual ambitions, compared with his professional ambitions, have always been modest. He has been twice
married. He met his first wife, a nurse called Jose Ingle, in
London in 1962; Derek Marlowe remembers her as being
"svelte and sun-tanned." Their marriage produced two sons,
who bear the Dickensian names of Oliver and Barnaby. But

the dramatic change in Stoppard's way of life that followed the triumph of *Rosencrantz and Guildenstern* in 1967 was more than Jose could could cope with, and that familiar show-business phenomenon—the ditching of the presuccess partner—took its sad accustomed course. According to one observer, "Jose was a feminist before her time, and she got bloody-minded about being overshadowed by Tom." At all events she finally suffered a nervous breakdown. Now fully recovered, she lives in a flat on the northern outskirts of London and is studying at a technical college for a teaching diploma. Divorce proceedings began when Stoppard left home, in 1970. Shortly afterward, he set up house with Miriam Moore-Robinson, a dark-haired pouter pigeon of a girl, buxom and exuberantly pretty, whom he had known, on and off, for about four years, and whose marriage to a veterinary surgeon was already at the breaking point. Miriam was the same age as Stoppard, and her ancestry included a Jewish grandparent who was born in Czechoslovakia. A qualified doctor, she worked for a pharmaceutical company that specialized in birth-control research, and has gone on to become its managing director. She has also made vivacious appearances on popular-science programs on British TV, answering questions on biology, zoology, and sex. Since 1972, when she and Stoppard were married, she has given him two more sons, William and Edmund. In matters of emotion, Stoppard is one of nature's Horatios; you could never call him passion's slave, or imagine him blown off course by a romantic obsession. He thrives in the atmosphere of a family nest. "I can't work away from domestic stability," he once told me.)

To revert to chronology: In 1960, the text of *A Walk on the Water* landed on the desk of Kenneth Ewing, the managing director of a newly formed script agency, which now represents such writers as Michael Frayn, Charles Wood, Adrian Mitchell, and Anthony (*Sleuth*) Shaffer. Ewing sent Stoppard an encomiastic letter; the two men lunched in London; and Ewing has ever since been Stoppard's agent. "When I first met him, he had just given up his regular work as a journalist in Bristol, and he was broke," Ewing says. "But I noticed that even then he always travelled by taxi, never by bus. It was as if he knew that his time would come." In 1962, Stoppard heard that a new magazine called *Scene* was about to be launched in London;

he applied for a job on the staff and was offered, to his amazement, the post of drama critic, which he instantly accepted.
He then left Bristol for good and took an apartment in Notting
Hill Gate, a dingy West London suburb. Derek Marlowe lived
in the same dilapidated house. "Tom wrote short stories, and
smoked to excess, and always worked at night," Marlowe recalls. "Every evening, he would lay out a row of matches and
say, 'Tonight I shall write twelve matches'—meaning as much
as he could churn out on twelve cigarettes." *Scene* made its
debut early in 1963. Virulently trendy in tone and signally
lacking in funds, it set out to cover the whole of show business.
In seven months (after which the money ran out and *Scene* was
no longer heard from), Stoppard reviewed a hundred and thirty-
two shows. Years later, in a sentence that combines verbal and
moral fastidiousness in a peculiarly Stoppardian way, he explained why he thought himself a bad critic: "I never had the
moral character to pan a friend—or, rather, I had the moral
character never to pan a friend."

Since the magazine was ludicrously understaffed, he filled
its pages with dozens of pseudonymous pieces, most of which
he signed "William Boot." The name derives from Evelyn
Waugh's novel *Scoop*, in which William Boot is the nature
columnist of a national newspaper who, owing to a spectacular
misunderstanding, finds himself shipped off to cover a civil
war in Africa. (As things turn out, he handles the assignment
rather well.) Boot took root in Stoppard's imagination, and
soon began to crop up in his plays, often allied to or contrasted
with a complementary character called Moon. As a double act,
they bring to mind Lenin's famous division of the world into
"Who" and "Whom"—those who do and those to whom it is
done. In Stoppard's words, "Moon is a person to whom things
happen. Boot is rather more aggressive." Early in 1964, BBC
radio presented two short Stoppard plays entitled *The Disso-
lution of Dominic Boot* and *M is for Moon Among Other Things*.
The leading characters in *The Real Inspector Hound* (1968) are
named Birdboot and Moon. Apropos of the eponymous heroes
of *Rosencrantz and Guildenstern*, the English critic Robert
Cushman has rightly said:

> Rosencrantz, being eager, well-meaning, and con-
> sistently oppressed or embarrassed by every situation in

which he finds himself, is clearly a Moon; Guildenstern, equally oppressed though less embarrassed and taking refuge in displays of intellectual superiority, is as obviously a Boot.

Cushman once asked Stoppard why so many of his characters were called Moon or Boot. Stoppard crisply replied that he couldn't help it if that was what their names turned out to be. "I'm a Moon, myself," he went on. "Confusingly, I used the name Boot, from Evelyn Waugh, as a pseudonym in journalism, but that was because Waugh's Boot is really a Moon, too." Having thus befogged his interviewer, he added a wry etymological touch. "This is beginning to sound lunatic," he said.

In 1964, a cobbler sticking to his last, Stoppard wrote a ninety-minute TV play called *This Way Out with Samuel Boot*, which he equipped with a *pair* of Boots, who represent diametrically opposed attitudes toward material possessions. Samuel Boot, a fortyish man of evangelical fervor, preaches the total rejection of property. Jonathan, his younger brother, is a compulsive hoarder of objects, unable to resist mail-order catalogues, who fills his home with items bought on credit which are constantly being repossessed, since he never keeps up the payments. ("It's like Christmas in a thieves' kitchen," Samuel cries, surveying a room stacked with vacuum cleaners, goggles, filing cabinets, miners' helmets, boomerangs, knitting machines, miniature Japanese trees, and other oddments.) At one point, a salesman comes to deliver a hearing aid for a week's free trial. Having fitted the device into Jonathan's ear, he shouts into the box, "There! That's better, isn't it?" "You don't have to shout," says Jonathan sharply. "I'm not deaf." He demands to know who told the salesman that he suffered from this infirmity.

SALESMAN: It was an assumption.
JONATHAN: If I told you I'd got a wooden leg, would you assume I was one-legged?
SALESMAN: Yes.
JONATHAN: Well, I have. And you may have noticed I'm wearing skis. You seem to be making a lot of nasty assumptions here. You think I'm a deaf cripple.

This *reductio ad absurdum* is pure Stoppard. An unreason-
able man uses rational arguments to convince a reasonable man
that he (the latter) is irrational. The salesman flees in panic,
but Jonathan still has the hearing aid. Though both brothers
are Boots by name, Samuel turns out to be a Moon by nature.
He ends up defeated by his own innocence. When he claims
to have found an exit from the commercial rat race, Jonathan
brutally demolishes his dream:

> There's no out. You're in it, so you might as well
> fit. It's the way it is. Economics. All this stuff I've
> got . . . people have been paid to make it, drive it to the
> warehouse, advertise it, sell it to me, write to me about
> it, and take it away again. They get paid, and some of
> them buy a carpet with the money. [He has just had a
> carpet repossessed.] That's the way of it and you're in
> it. There's no way out with Samuel Boot.

Jonathan has a vast collection of trading stamps. Samuel
steals them and holds a public meeting at which he proposes
to give them away. He is mobbed and killed by a crowd of
rapacious housewives. "He died of people," says one of his
disciples, a young deserter from the army. "They trod on him."
To this, Jonathan replies, "That's what it is about people. Turn
round and they'll tread on you. Or steal your property." The
deserter delivers Samuel's epitaph:

> He was a silly old man, and being dead doesn't change
> that. But for a minute . . . his daft old crusade, like he
> said, it had a kind of dignity.

Whereupon he picks up, as a souvenir of Jonathan's acquisitive way of life, a newly delivered vacuum cleaner. Rising
to the defense of property, Jonathan shoots him dead with a
mail-order harpoon gun.

Samuel Boot is patchily brilliant, an uneasy blend of ab-
surdist comedy and radical melodrama. I have dwelt on it
because (a) it is the last Stoppard play with a message (i.e.,
property is theft) that could be described as leftist, and (b) it
is one of the few Stoppard scripts that have never been per-

formed in any medium. Kenneth Ewing offered it to a London commercial-TV company and took Stoppard with him to hear the verdict. It was negative. "Stick to theatre," he advised his dejected client on the way back. "Your work can't be contained on television." Then Ewing's thoughts moved to Shakespeare, and for no reason that he can now recall, he brought up a notion he had long cherished about *Hamlet*. Quoting the speech in which Claudius sends Hamlet to England with a sealed message (borne by Rosencrantz and Guildenstern) enjoining the ruler of that country to cut off Hamlet's head, Ewing said that in his opinion the King of England at the time of their arrival might well have been King Lear. And, if so, did they find him raving mad at Dover? Stoppard's spirits rose, and by the time Ewing dropped him off at his home he had come up with a tentative title: *Rosencrantz and Guildenstern at the Court of King Lear*. A seed had clearly been planted. It pleases Ewing to reflect that agents are not necessarily uncreative.

In the spring of 1964, the Ford Foundation awarded grants to four British playwrights (or would-be playwrights) enabling them to spend six months in West Berlin. The senior member of the chosen quartet was James Saunders, then thirty-nine years old and very much in vogue as the author of *Next Time I'll Sing to You*, a lyrical-whimsical play that seemed to some critics anemic and to others a near-masterpiece. The remaining grants went to Derek Marlowe, Piers Paul Read (son of Sir Herbert, the illustrious poet and critic), and Stoppard, an avowed admirer of Saunders, by whose penchant for fantasy and wordplay his own work had been visibly affected. The four authors were installed, courtesy of Ford, in a mansion on the shore of the Wannsee. "We were there as cultural window dressing," Saunders says, "to show the generosity of American support for European art." They were all eager to see Brecht's Berliner Ensemble, in East Berlin, and three of them immediately did so. Stoppard alone hung back, and did not make the trip until his stay in Berlin was nearly over. He had never set foot in Communist territory, and the prospect of crossing the border repelled him. Although his passport was British, it stated that he was born in Czechoslovakia, and this had planted in him a superstitious fear that, once in East Berlin, he might never be allowed to return.

In the house by the Wannsee, he wrote a one-act comedy in verse, *Rosencrantz and Guildenstern Meet King Lear*. His work, like that of his colleagues, was performed by English amateur actors in one-night stands at a theatre on the Kurfürstendamm, with no decor apart from a large photograph of the author. Saunders, having seen Stoppard's *jeu d'esprit*, urged him to expand it into a full-length play. In his spare time, Stoppard was recruited by a young Dutch director to appear in a low-budget film based on a short story by Borges. He played a cowboy, and Marlowe has vivid memories of a sequence that showed Stoppard belligerently twirling a pair of six-shooters in front of the Brandenburg Gate. While Stoppard was in Germany, a Hamburg theatre presented the first stage production of *A Walk on the Water*, and he flew from Berlin for the premiere. The performance passed off in silence but without incident; and when the curtain fell Stoppard's German agent rashly urged him to go onstage and take a bow. He did so, with a cigarette between his lips—perhaps in emulation of Oscar Wilde, who had once used the same method of showing his indifference to audience reaction. He was greeted, for the first time in his life, by a storm of booing. It was directed, as he readily admits, at the text, not the tobacco.

Summing up his impressions of Stoppard, in Berlin and afterward, James Saunders says, "Diffident on the surface, utterly unworried underneath. He's extremely cautious about being thought too serious. I've heard him quote Auden's famous remark to the effect that no poet's work ever saved anyone from a concentration camp. Well, that may be true, but it's terrible to *admit* that it's true. After all, the writer's job is constantly to redefine the role of the individual: What can he do? What *should* he do? And also to redefine the role of society: How can it be changed? How *should* it be changed? As a playwright, I live between these two responsibilities. But Tom—Tom just plays safe. He enjoys being nice, and he likes to be liked. He resists commitment of any kind, he hides the ultimate expression of his deepest concerns. He's basically a displaced person. Therefore, he doesn't want to stick his neck out. He feels grateful to Britain, because he sees himself as a guest here, and that makes it hard for him to critcize Britain. Probably the most damaging thing you could say about him is that he's made no enemies." Since Berlin, Stoppard's star has risen while Saunder's has tended to decline. I asked Saunders how this had affected their relationship. He smiled, and quoted a well-known British dramatist who had once told him, "Whenever I read a rave review of a young playwright in the Sunday papers, it spoils my whole day." He continued, "When Tom first became famous, he gave a series of expensive lunches at the Café Royal to keep in touch with his old pals. I thought that was pretty ostentatious behaviour. Meeting him nowadays I do feel a sort of cutoff." He made a gesture like a portcullis descending. "I don't think that he's overrated, as much as that many other writers are underrated. He has distracted attention from people who have an equal right to it."

(A word on Stoppard and friendship. Most of those who know him well regard him as an exemplary friend. "He actually drops in unannounced, which hardly anyone does in London," says a close female chum, "and he usually brings an unexpected but absolutely appropriate present. And he mails huge batches of postcards, which are not only funny but informative and helpful. He really works on his friendships." When Derek Marlowe wrote a novel entitled *Nightshade*, Stoppard, who knew that Marlowe venerated Raymond Chandler, sought out an antique pulp magazine containing a Chandler story called "Nightshade," and arranged for it to reach Marlowe on publication day.)

After Stoppard returned from Berlin, he shared a flat in Westminster with Marlowe and Piers Paul Read. "At this period, his idol was Mick Jagger," Marlowe says. "He looked like him, he dressed like him, and he was thrilled when he found out that Jagger loved cricket as much as he did." Stoppard transmuted *Rosencrantz and Guildenstern* from verse into prose, and turned out a couple of short plays for television; but for the greater part of 1965 "he lived on the Arabs," as Kenneth Ewing puts it. "For some unfathomable reason, the BBC hired him to write the diary of an imaginary Arab student in London, which was then translated into Arabic and broadcast on the Overseas Service. He alternated with another author, and every other week he was paid forty pounds for five episodes. As far as I know, he had never met an Arab in his life. But the job kept him going for about nine months." Eager to scan the results of this bizarre assignment, I approached the BBC for permission to consult its files. I was told that no copies of the scripts were in existence—a body blow to theatrical history but conceivably good news to Stoppard.

Early in 1965, the Royal Shakespeare Company took a twelve-month option on a play that was by then called *Rosencrantz and Guildenstern Are Dead*. The company failed to fit the play into its repertoire, and after the option expired the script went to several other managements, all of which rejected it. In the summer of 1966, the president of the Oxford Theatre Group walked into Kenneth Ewing's office and asked for permission to present an amateur production of the play on the Fringe of the forthcoming Edinburgh Festival. (The Fringe is Edinburgh's Off and Off-Off Broadway.) At first reluctant, Ewing eventually consented. He did not regret his decision. The opening night got a handful of bad notices, but over the weekend the momentous, life-changing review appeared. Ronald Bryden, writing in the *Observer*, described the play as an "erudite comedy, punning, far-fetched, leaping from depth to dizziness," and continued, "It's the most brilliant debut by a young playwright since John Arden's." At the time, I was working for Laurence Olivier as literary manager of the National Theatre, whose company was housed at the Old Vic. Minutes after reading Bryden's piece, I cabled Stoppard, requesting a script. Olivier like it as much as I did, and within a week we had bought it. Directed by Derek Goldby, it opened at the Vic in April, 1967. Very seldom has a play by a new dramatist been hailed with such rapturous unanimity. Harold Hobson, of the *Sunday Times*, called it "the most important event in the British professional theatre of the last nine years"; that is, since the opening of Harold Pinter's *The Birthday Party*. Stoppard, who had subtly smoothed and improved the text throughout rehearsals, found himself overnight with his feet on the upper rungs of Britain's theatrical ladder, where several hobnailed talents were already stamping for primacy.

When *Rosencrantz and Guildenstern* had its London triumph, Vaclav Havel was thirty years of age, just nine months older than Stoppard. He wore smart but conservative clothes, being a dandy in the classic rather than the romantic mode. Of less than average height, he had the incipient portliness of the gourmet. His hair was trimmed short, and this gave him a somewhat bullet-shaped silhouette. He both walked and talked with purposeful briskness and elegance. He drove around Prague (where he was born on October 5, 1936) in a dashing little Renault, bought with the royalties from his plays—for in 1967 Havel was the leading Czechoslovakian playwright, and the only one to have achieved an international reputation since Karel Capek wrote *R. U. R.* and (with his brother Josef) *The Insect Play*, between the wars. Havel's family connections were far grander than Stoppard's. Vera Blackwell, a Czech émigrée who lives in London and translates Havel's work into English, has said that "if Czechoslovakia had remained primarily a capitalist society Vaclav Havel would be today just about the richest young man in the country." One of his uncles was a millionaire who owned, apart from vast amounts of real estate and a number of hotels, the Barrandov studios, in Prague, which are the headquarters of the Czech film industry. All this was lost in the Communist takeover of 1948, and during the dark period of Stalinist rigor that followed, Havel's upper-class background prevented him from receiving any full-time education above grade-school level. Instead, he took a menial job in a chemical laboratory, spending most of his off-duty hours at evening classes, where he studied science. In 1954, he began two years of military service, after which he made repeated attempts to enter Prague University. All his applications were turned down. His next move was to offer himself for any theatrical work that was going. He found what he was looking for in the mid-sixties, when he was appointed *Dramaturg* (i.e., literary manager, a post that in Europe quite often means not only play selector and script editor but house playwright as well) at the Balustrade Theatre, which was Prague's principal showcase for avant-garde drama.

We nowadays tend to assume that the great thaw in Czech socialism began and ended with the libertarian reforms carried out by Alexander Dubcek's regime in the so-called Prague Spring of 1968. By that time, artistic freedom had in fact been blooming for several ebullient years: a period that saw the emergence of filmmakers like Milos Forman, Ivan Passer, Jan Nemec, and Jan Kadar; of theatrical directors like Otomar

Krejca and Jan Grossman (who ran the Balustrade); and of a whole school of young dramatists, at whose head Vaclav Havel swiftly established himself. In one sense, he was a traditional Czech writer. Using a technique that derived from Kafka, Capek, and countless Central European authors before them, he expressed his view of the world in nonrealistic parables. His plays were distorting mirrors in which one recognized the truth. Stoppard belongs in precisely the same tradition, of which there is no Anglo-Saxon equivalent. Moreover, Havel shares Stoppard's passion for fantastic word juggling. Some critics have glibly assigned both writers to the grab bag marked Theatre of the Absurd. But here the analogy falters, for Havel's Absurdism is very different from Stoppard's. Vera Blackwell says:

> Havel does not protest against the absurdity of man's life *vis-à-vis* a meaningless universe, but against the absurdity of the modern Frankenstein's monster: bureaucracy . . . . The ultimate aim of Havel's plays . . . is the improvement of man's lot through the improvement of man's institutions. These, in their turn, can become more "human" only insofar as the individual men and women who invent and people these institutions are prepared to be fully human—i.e., fully responsible for their actions, fully aware of their responsibility.

If Dubcek's policies represented what Western journalists called "Socialism with a human face," Havel's work gave Absurdism a human face, together with a socially critical purpose.

Like Stoppard, he had his first play performed in 1963. Entitled *The Garden Party*, it was staged by Grossman at the Balustrade. The hero, Hugo Pludek, is a student whose consuming interest is playing chess against himself. "Such a player," says his mother sagely, "will always stay in the game." His parents, a solid burgeois couple, base their values on a storehouse of demented proverbs that they never tire of repeating; e.g., "Not even a hag carries hemp heed to the attic alone," "He who fusses about a mosquito net can never hope to dance with a goat," "Not even the Hussars of Cologne would go to the woods without a clamp," and—perhaps the most incontrovertible of all—"Stone walls do not an iron bar." They worry about Hugo, since he shows no inclination to apply for work in the ruling bureaucracy. Under their pressure, he attends a garden party thrown by the Liquidation Office, where he poses as a bureaucrat so successfully that before long he is put in charge of liquidating the Liquidation Office. From a high-ranking member of the Inauguration Service—the opposite end of the scale from the Liquidation Office—he learns the Party line on intellectual dissent: "We mustn't be afraid of contrary opinions. Everybody who's honestly interested in our common cause ought to have from one to three contrary opinions." Eventually, the authorities decide to liquidate the Inauguration Service, and the question arises: Who should inaugurate the process of liquidation—an inaugurator or a liquidator? Surely, not the former, since how can anyone inaugurate his own liquidation? But, equally, it can't be the latter, because liquidators have not been trained to inaugurate. Either liquidators must be trained to inaugurate or vice versa. But this poses a new question: Who is to do the training? At the end of the play, driven mad by living in a society in which all truths are relative and subject to overnight cancellation, Hugo feels his identity crumbling. He knows what is happening to him, but, good bureacrat that he now is, he cannot resist it. In the course of a hysterical tirade, he declares:

> Truth is just as complicated and multiform as every-
> thing else in the world—the magnet, the telephone,
> Impressionism, the magnet—and we are all a little bit
> what we were yesterday and a little bit what we are
> today; and also a little bit we're not these things. Any-
> way . . . some of us are more and some of us are more
> not; some only are, some are only, and some only are
> not; so that none of us entirely is, and at the same time
> each one of us is not entirely.

This was Absurdism with deep roots in contemporary anxieties. The play was an immediate hit in Prague, and went on
to be performed in Austria, Switzerland, Sweden, Finland,

Hungary, Yugoslavia, and West Germany. Meanwhile, Havel composed a series of "typographical poems" to amuse his compatriots. One of them, labelled "Philosophy," went

```
!!!!!!!!!!!!!!!!!!!!!!!
!!!!!!!!!!!!!!!!!!!!!!!
!!!!!!!!!!!!!!!!!!!!!!!
!!!!!!!!!!!!!!!!!!!!!!!
!!!!!!!!!!!!!!!!!!!!!!!
!!!!!!!!!!!!!!!!!!!!!!!
!!!!!!!!!!!!!!!!!!!!!!!
```

Another, wrylý political, was printed thus:

```
              FORWARD
      FORWARD           FORWARD
      FORWARD           FORWARD
      FORWARD           FORWARD
      FORWARD           FORWARD
      FORWARD           FORWARD
      FORWARD           FORWARD
      FORWARD           FORWARD
      FORWARD           FORWARD
      FORWARD           FORWARD
              FORWARD
```

And the following is Havel's succinct comment on the role of humor under Stalinism:

```
100% 100% 100% 100% 100% 100% 100%
100% 100% 100% 100% 100% 100% 100%
100% 100% 100% 100% 100% 100% 100%
100% 100% 100% 100% 100% 100% 100%
100% 100% 100% 100% 100% 100% 100%
100% 100% 100% 100% 100% 100% 100%
100% 100% 100% 100% 100% 100% 100%
100% 100% 100% 100% 100% 100% 100%
100% 100% 100% 100% 100% 100% 100%
100% 100% 100% 100% 100%  99% 100%
100% 100% 100% 100% 100% 100% 100%
100% 100% 100% 100% 100% 100% 100%
```

It is captioned "Constructive Satire."

Authentic satire operates on the principle of the thermos flask: it contains heat without radiating it. Havel's second play, *The Memorandum* (1965), was a splendid example: burning convictions were implicit in a structure of ice-cold logic and glittering linguistic virtuosity. His target was the use of language to subvert individualism and enforce conformity. Josef Gross, the managing director of a huge but undefined state enterprise, grows unsettled when he discovers that, on orders from above, the existing vernacular is being replaced by a synthetic language called Ptydepe, uncontaminated by the ambiguities, imprecisions, and emotional vagaries of ordinary speech. Its aim is to abolish similarities between words by using the least probable combinations of letters, so that no word can conceivably be mistaken for any other. We learn from the Ptydepe instructor who has been assigned to Gross' organization, "The natural languages originated . . . spontaneously, uncontrollably, and their structure is thus, in a certain sense, dilettantish." For purposes of official communication, they are utterly unrealiable. In Ptydepe, "the more common the meaning, the shorter the word." The longest entry in the new dictionary has three hundred and nineteen letters and means "wombat." The shortest is "f" and at present has no meaning, since science has not yet determined which word or expression is in commonest use. The instructor lists several variations of the interjection "Boo" as it might be employed in a large company when one worker seeks to "sham-ambush" another. If the victim is in full view, unprepared for the impending ambush and threatened by a hidden colleague, "Boo" is rendered by "Gedynrelom." If, however, the victim is *aware* of the danger, the correct cry is "Osonfterte"—for which "Eg gynd y trojadus" must be substituted if *both* parties are in full view and the encounter is meant only as a joke. If the sham-ambush is seriously intended, the appropriate expression is "Eg jeht kuz." Jan Ballas, Gross's ambitious deputy, points out to his baffled boss that normal language is fraught with undesirable emotional overtones: "Now, tell me sincerely, has the word 'mutarex' any such overtones for you? It hasn't, has it? You see. It is a paradox, but it is precisely the surface inhumanity of an artificial language that guarantees its truly human function." Gross's problems are compounded by the fact that he has received an official memorandum in Ptydepe, but in order to get a Ptydepe text translated one must make an application in Ptydepe, which Gross does not speak. "In other words," he laments, "the only way to know what is in one's memo is to know it already." Ever willing to compromise (and this is Havel's underlying message), he does not complain when he loses his job to Ballas; and it is through no effort of his own that he regains it at the end. The authorities have observed that, as one of their spokesmen resentfully puts it, wherever Ptydepe has passed into common use, "it has automatically begun to assume some of the charactertistics of a natural language: various emotional overtones, imprecisions, ambiguities." Therefore, Ptydepe is to be replaced by a new language, Chorukor, based on the principle not of abolishing but of intensifying the similarities between words. Gross, reinstated to spearhead the introduction of Chorukor, remains what he has never ceased to be: a time-serving organization man.

This small masterpiece of sustained irony was staged throughout Europe and at the Public Theatre, in New York, where it won the 1968 *Village Voice* award for the best foreign play of the Off Broadway season. In April of that year, Havel's next work, *The Increased Difficulty of Concentration*, opened in Prague. If the logical games and verbal pyrotechnics of *The Memorandum* suggested analogies with Stoppard, there were aspects of the new piece which anticipated a play that Stoppard had not yet written; namely, *Jumpers*. Havel's central character is Dr. Huml, a social scientist engaged (like Professor Moore in *Jumpers*) in dictating a bumbling lecture on moral values which goes against the intellectual grain of his society. He is interrupted from time to time by a couple of technicians bearing an extremely disturbed and unreliable computer with which they propose to study his behavior patterns. Here are some telescoped samples of Huml at work, with Blanka, his secretary:

HUML: Where did we stop?
BLANKA *(reads)*: "Various people have at various times and in various circumstances various needs—"

HUML: Ah yes. *(Begins to pace thoughtfully to and fro while dictating to Blanka, who takes it down in short-hand)*—and thus attach to various things various values—full stop. Therefore, it would be mistaken to set up a fixed scale of values—valid for all people in all circumstances and at all times—full stop. This does not mean, however, that in all of history there exist no values common to the whole of mankind—full stop. If those values did not exist, mankind would not form a unified whole—full stop. . . . Would you mind reading me the last sentence? . . . There exist situations—for example, in some advanced Western countries—in which all the basic human needs have been satisfied, and still people are not happy. They experience feelings of depression, boredom, frustration, etc.—full stop. In these situations man begins to desire that which in fact he perhaps does not need at all—he simply persuades himself he has certain needs which he does not have—or he vaguely desires something which he cannot specify and thus cannot strive for—full stop. Hence, as soon as man has satisfied one need—i.e., achieved happiness—another so far unsatisfied need is born in him, so that every happiness is always, simultaneously, a negation of happiness.

Can science help man to solve his problems? Not entirely, says Huml, because science can illuminate only that which is finite, whereas man "contains the dimensions of infinity." He continues:

   I'm afraid the key to a real comprehension of the individual does not lie in a greater or lesser understanding of the complexity of man as an object of scientific knowledge. . . . The unique relationship that arises between two individuals is thus far the only thing that can—at least to some extent—mutually unveil their secrets. Values like love, friendship, compassion, sympathy, even mutual conflict—which is as unique and irreplaceable as mutual understanding—are the only tools we have at our disposal. By other means we may perhaps be able to explain man, but never to understand him.... The fundamental key does not lie in his brain, but in his heart.

Meanwhile, the computer has broken down, and emits a shrill bombardment of imbecile questions, endlessly repeated:

> Which is your favorite tunnel? Are you fond of musical instruments? How many times a year do you air the square? Where did you bury the dog? Why didn't you pass it on? When did you lose the claim? Wherein lies the nucleus? Do you know where you're going, and do you know who's going with you? Do you urinate in public, or just now and then?

On August 21, 1968, the Soviet Union, alarmed by the experiment in free socialism that was flowering in Czechoslovakia, invaded the country and imposed on it a neo-Stalinist regime. One of the first acts of the new government was to forbid all performances of Havel's plays.

By the summer of 1968, Stoppard had had his third London premiere within fourteen months. *Enter a Free Man*, which I've already discussed, had opened to mixed notices at the St. Martin's Theatre in March, and *The Real Inspector Hound*, to which I'll return later, had been more happily received (the *Observer* compared it to a Fabergé Easter egg) when it arrived at the Criterion Theatre, in June, just two months before the Russian tanks rolled into Prague. *Rosencrantz and Guildenstern* remained a great drawing card in the repertory—a hand already stacked with aces—of the National Theatre. A couple of weeks before its first night, in 1967, I had written a piece on the performing arts in Prague. In it I said that the new Czech theatre was "focussing its attention not only on man vs. authority but on man vs. mortality," and that "the hero is forced to come to terms not merely with the transient compulsions of society but with the permanent fact of death." Under liberal governments, I added, authors tend to concern themselves with "the ultimate problem of dying as well as the immediate problems of living." With the benefit of hindsight, I realize that every word of this might have been written about *Rosencrantz and Guildenstern*: it fitted perfectly into my group portrait of Czech drama. (Perhaps the most memorable speech in the play occurs when the former and dumber principal character asks, "Whatever became of the moment when one first knew about death?"—that shattering instant, surely inscribed on everyone's memory, which for some reason no one can remember.) Of course, one can also spot Western influences. The sight of two bewildered men playing pointless games in a theatrical void while the real action unfolds offstage inevitably recalls Beckett. Stoppard has said, "When *Godot* was first done, it liberated something for anybody writing plays. It redefined the minima of theatrical validity. It was as simple as that. He got away. He won by twenty-eight lengths, and he'd done it with so little—and I mean that as an enormous compliment." When Guildenstern says, "Wheels have been set in motion, and they have their own pace, to which we are . . . condemned," we think once more of Beckett's doom-laden slogan, "Something is taking its course." The debt to Eliot's "Love Song of J. Alfred Prufrock" is equally transparent:

> No! I am not Prince Hamlet, nor was meant to be;
> Am an attendant lord, one that will do
> To swell a progress, start a scene or two . . .
> Full of high sentence, but a bit obtuse;
> At times, indeed, almost ridiculous—
> Almost, at times, the Fool.

"Prufrock and Beckett," Stoppard has said, "are the two syringes of my diet, my arterial system." But has anyone noticed another mainline injection? Consider: Rosencrantz and Guildenstern are unaccountably summoned to a mysterious castle where, between long periods of waiting, they receive cryptic instructions that eventually lead to their deaths. They die uncertain whether they are the victims of chance or of fate. It seems to me undeniable that the world they inhabit owes its atmosphere and architecture to the master builder of such enigmatic fables—Franz Kafka, whose birthplace was Prague, and who wrote of just such a castle.

Stoppard is nothing if not eclectic. His play even bears

traces of Wittgenstein, according to whose *Philosophical Investigations* (1953) it is conceivable that:

> . . . two people belonging to a tribe unacquainted with chess should sit at a chessboard and go through the moves of a game of chess. . . . And if we were to see it, we would say they were playing chess. But now imagine a game of chess translated, according to certain rules, into a series of actions which we do not ordinarily associate with a *game*—say, into yells and stamping of feet. And now suppose these two people to yell and stamp instead of playing the form of chess that we are used to. . . . Should we still be inclined to say they were playing a game? What *right* would one have to say so?

Stoppard's twin heroes are clearly involved in "a series of actions which we do not ordinarily associate with a game." They are caught up in a strict and ferocious plot—both onstage and off, people are being killed—but the total experience, however unplayful it looks, may still be a kind of game, as formal in its rules as chess.

Again, Oscar Wilde (a good fairy, in the elfin sense of the word, who has more than once waved an influential wand over the *accouchement* of a Stoppard work) supplies an apt quotation, from *De Profundis*:

> I know of nothing in all Drama more incomparable from the point of view of Art, or more suggestive in its subtlety of observation, than Shakespeare's drawing of Rosencrantz and Guildenstern. They are Hamlet's college friends. They have been his companions. . . . At the moment when they come across him in the play he is staggering under the weight of a burden intolerable to one of his temperament. . . . Of all this, Guildenstern and Rosencrantz realise nothing.

Which they prove in the funniest speech of Stoppard's play, when, having been told to "glean what afflicts" Hamlet, the two spies quiz each other about his state of mind and come up with the following conclusion:

ROSENCRANTZ: To sum up: your father, whom you love, dies, you are his heir, you come back to find that hardly was the corpse cold before his young brother popped on to his throne and into his sheets, thereby offending both legal and natural practice. Now why exactly are you behaving in this extraordinary manner?

Wilde goes on:

They are close to his secret and know nothing of it. Nor would there be any use in telling them. They are little cups than can hold so much and no more.... They are types fixed for all time. To censure them would show a lack of appreciation. They are merely out of their sphere: that is all.

Despite its multiple sources, *Rosencrantz and Guildenstern* is a genuine original, one of a kind. As far as I know, it is the first play to use another play as its decor. The English critic C. E. Montague described *Hamlet* as "a monstrous Gothic castle of a poem, full of baffled half-lights and glooms." This is precisely the setting of *Rosencrantz and Guildenstern*: it takes place in the wings of Shakespeare's imagination. The actor-manager who meets the two travellers on the road to Elsinore says that in life every exit is "an entrance somewhere else." In Stoppard's play, every exit is an entrance somewhere else in *Hamlet*. Sometimes he writes like a poet:

We cross our bridges when we come to them and burn them behind us, with nothing to show for our progress except a memory of the smell of smoke, and a presumption that once our eyes watered.

And at other times with fortune-cookie glibness:

Eternity is a terrible thought. I mean, where's it going to end?

But we are finally moved by the snuffing out of the brief candles he has lit. Tinged perhaps with sentimentality, an emotional commitment has nonetheless been made. To quote Clive James:

> The mainspring of "Rosencrantz and Guildenstern Are Dead" is the perception—surely a compassionate one— that the fact of their deaths mattering so little to Hamlet was something that ought to have mattered to Shakespeare.

The Real Inspector Hound, which joined *Rosencrantz and Guildenstern* on the London playbills in June, 1968, need not detain us long. It is a facetious puzzle that, like several of Stoppard's minor pieces, presents an apparently crazy series of events for which in the closing moments a rational explanation is provided. Two drama critics, Birdboot and Moon, are covering the premiere of a thriller, written in a broad parody of the style of Agatha Christie. At curtain rise, there is a male corpse onstage. Stoppard unconvincingly maintains that when the play was half finished he still didn't know the dead man's name or the murderer's identity. (How did he find out? "There is a God," Stoppard says when he is asked this question, "and he looks after English playwrights.") Toward the end, the two critics implausibly leave their seats and join in the action. In the dénouement, Moon, who is the second-string critic for his paper, is killed onstage by the envious third-string critic, who, posing as an actor in the play within a play, has previously slain the first-string critic (the curtain-rise corpse) and rigged the evidence to frame Moon. (A general rule about Stoppard may be stated thus: The shorter the play, the harder it is to summarize the plot without sounding unhinged.) People sometimes say that Stoppard, for all his brilliance, is fundamentally a leech, drawing the lifeblood of his work from the inventions of others. In *Rosencrantz and Guildenstern*, he battens on Shakespeare, in *Inspector Hound* on Christie, in *Jumpers* on the logical positivists, in *Travesties* on Wilde, James Joyce, and Lenin. The same charge, of course, has been levelled against other and greater writers; in 1592, for example, the playwright and pamphleteer Robert Greene accused Shakespeare of artistic thievery, calling him an "upstart crow, beautified with our feathers."

Allegations of this kind do not ruffle Stoppard's feathers. "I can't invent plots," he admitted in a public discussion of his work which was held in Los Angeles earlier this year. "I've formed the habit of hanging my plays on other people's plots. It's a habit I'm trying to kick." Apropos of borrowings, I may as well reveal my suspicion that a hitherto undetected influence on *Inspector Hound* is that of Robert Benchley. At one point, when the stage is empty, a phone rings, and the critic Moon gets up to answer it: Surely this calls to mind the legendary moment during a Broadway premiere when a phone rang on an empty stage and the critic Benchley, remarking, "I think that's for me," rose and left the theatre. Nor is Stoppard's play the first in which a drama critic has been seen dead onstage. Back in 1917, seeking material for a newspaper article, a writer lately employed as the drama critic of *Vanity Fair* played the role of a corpse in *The Thirteenth Chair*. His name, guessably, was Robert Benchley.

Jumpers, produced in 1972, was the next milestone in Stoppard's career; but something should first be said of his work for radio, a medium he has used more resourcefully than any other contemporary English playwright. In *Albert's Bridge* (1967) and *Artist Descending a Staircase* (1972), both written for the BBC, he explores two of his favorite themes. The first is the relativity of absolutely everything. (It all depends on where you're sitting.) The second is the definition of art. (Is it a skill or a gift? Is it socially useful? Or does that, too, depend on where you're sitting?) Albert, in the earlier play, is painting a lofty railway bridge that will have to be repainted as soon as he has finished painting it. Despite the repetitious and mechanical nature of his job, he loves it, because it has a symmetry and coherence that are lacking in his life on the ground. He is joined by Fraser, a would-be suicide, who has climbed the bridge in order to jump off. The world below, Fraser explains, is doomed:

> Motor-cars nose each other down every street, and
> they are beginning to breed, spread, they press the people
> to the walls by their knees, and there's no end to it,
> because if you stopped making them, thousands of people
> would be thrown out of work, and they'd have no money

to spend, the shopkeepers would get caught up in it, and the farms and factories, and all the people dependent on them, with their children and all. There's too much of everything, but the space for it is constant. So the shell of human existence is filling out, expanding, and it's going to go bang.

After a while, however, he changes his mind. Seeing it all from above, at a distance, he finds order in the chaos. "Yes," he says, "from a vantage point like this, the idea of society is just about tenable." So he descends; but shortly afterward he returns, convinced that he was right the first time. The bridge finally collapses, with both men on it, when a massed phalanx of assistant painters march across it without breaking steps. It is a fine catastrophe, but also a neat escape hatch for Stoppard, who is thus absolved from the responsibility of telling us which view of life we should espouse—the long shot or the closeup.

Artist Descending a Staircase has a plot that starts out backward and then goes forward. I shall not take up the challenge to summarize it, except to say that it concerns the careers and beliefs of three artists, one of whom is dead and may have been murdered by either of the others, or by both working in cahoots. The title derives from Marcel Duchamp's painting "Nude Descending a Staircase," and the play contains plenty of evidence that self-cannibalism is not alien to Stoppard. For example:

The artist is a lucky dog. . . . In any community of a thousand souls there will be nine hundred doing the work, ninety doing well, nine doing good, and one lucky dog painting or writing about the other nine hundred and ninety-nine.

Slightly compressed, this superb speech reappears in *Travesties*; and there are references to Lenin and Tristan Tzara (and their joint sojourn in Zurich during the First World War) which look forward to the same play. Stoppard leaves us in no doubt about his attitude toward twentieth-century art in its more extreme manifestations, which he calls "that child's garden of easy victories known as the avant-garde." Again:

Skill without imagination is craftmanship and gives us many useful objects such as wickerwork picnic baskets. Imagination without skill gives us modern art.

He also takes a sharp sideswipe at an artist who, having gone through a period of making ceramic food, realizes that this will not help to fill empty bellies. The artist decides instead to sculpture edible art out of sugar. One of his colleagues says, "It will give Cubism a new lease of life." I think we can take it that Stoppard is expressing his own feelings in the following definition, which recurs unchanged in *Travesties*:

An artist is somewho who is gifted in some way that enables him to do something more or less well which can only be done badly or not at all by someone who is not thus gifted.

I once told Stoppard that, impressive though his dictum sounded, it could equally well be applied to a jockey. He wandered out of the room for a full minute, presumably to ponder, and then wandered back. "That's exactly what I meant," he said. "In other words, a chap who claims to be a jockey and wears a jockey's cap *but sits facing the horse's tail* is not a jockey."

During the four years that separate *Inspector Hound* from *Jumpers*, the total of new work by Stoppard consisted of three one-acters and a short play for television. This apparent unproductiveness was due partly to distracting upheavals in his private life (the collapse of his first marriage, the cementing of his new relationship with Miriam) and partly to an ingrained habit of preparing for his major enterprises with the assiduity of an athlete training for the Olympics. Or, to use Derek Marlowe's simile: "For Tom, writing a play is like sitting for an examination. He spends ages on research, does all the necessary cramming, reads all the relevant books, and then gestates the results. Once he's passed the exam—with the public and the critics—he forgets all about it and moves on to the next subject." Moreover, the second play is always a high hurdle. Although *Inspector Hound* came after *Rosencrantz and Guildenstern*, it didn't really count, being a lightweight diversion, staged in a commercial theatre. The real test, as Stoppard knew, would be his second play *at the National*.

Early in 1970, he told me, over lunch, that he had been reading the logical positivists with fascinated revulsion. He was unable to accept their view that because value judgments could not be empirically verified they were meaningless. Accordingly, he said, he was toying with the idea of a play whose entire first act would be a lecture in support of moral philosophy. This led us into a long debate on morality—specifically, on the difference between the Judeo-Christian tradition (in which the creator of the universe also lays down its moral laws, so that the man who breaks them is committing an offense against God) and the Oriental tradition represented by Zen Buddhism (in which morality is seen as a man-made convention, quite distinct from God or cosmogony). Only with Stoppard or Vaclav Havel can I imagine having such a conversation about a play that was intended to be funny. A few days later, Stoppard sent me a letter in which he said that our chat had "forced me to articulate certain ideas, to their immense hazard, which I suppose is useful," and went on, "All that skating around makes the ice look thin, but a sense of renewed endeavour prevails—more concerned with the dramatic possibilities than with the ideas, for it is a mistake to assume that plays are the end-products of ideas (which would be limiting): the ideas are the end-products of the plays."

The theatrical image that triggered *Jumpers* came from an exchange in *Rosencrantz and Guilderstern*, when Rosencrantz says, "Shouldn't we be doing something—constructive?" and Guildenstern replies, "What did you have in mind? A short, blunt human pyramid?" Stoppard subsequently told an interviewer:

> I thought, How marvellous to have a pyramid of people on a stage, and a rifle shot, and one member of the pyramid just being blown out of it, and the others imploding on the hole as he leaves. . . . Because of the success of "Rosencrantz" it was on the cards that the National Theatre would do whatever I wrote, if I didn't completely screw it up. . . . It's perfectly true that having shot this man out of the pyramid, and having him lying

on the floor, I didn't know who he was or who had shot
him or why or what to do with the body. Absolutely not
a clue.

Cf. Stoppard's virtually identical and identically unper-
suasive statement about a similar situation in *Inspector Hound*.
However, play it again, Tom:

> At the same time, there's more than one point of
> origin for a play, and the only useful metaphor I can
> think of for the way I think I write my plays is conver-
> gences of different threads.... One of the threads was
> the entirely visual image of the pyramid of acrobats, but
> while thinking of that pyramid I knew I wanted to write
> a play about a professor of moral philosophy.... There
> was a metaphor at work in the play already between
> acrobatics and mental acrobatics, and so on.

In December, 1970, I got a note from Stoppard saying that
the new piece would not be ready until the following autumn.
In the late summer of 1971, I called him and begged him to
give us some idea of its substance, since within a couple of
weeks we had to fix our plans for the forthcoming season. He
replied that, although he had nearly finished the first draft, he
could not possibly get it typed so soon. Might he therefore
read it to us himself? Acting on this suggestion, I arranged a
singular audition at my house in Kensington. The audience
consisted of Laurence Olivier, John Dexter (then associate
director of the National Theatre), and me. The time was late
afternoon, and Olivier had come straight from an exhausting
rehearsal. Stoppard arrived with the text and a sheaf of large
white cards, each bearing the name of one of the characters.
We had a few glasses of wine, after which Stoppard announced
that he would read the play standing at a table, holding up the
appropriate card to indicate who was speaking. What ensued
was a gradual descent into chaos. *Jumpers* (which was then
called *And Now the Incredible Jasmin Jumpers*) is a complex
work with a big cast, and before long Stoppard had got his
cards hopelessly mixed up. Within an hour, Olivier had fallen
asleep. Stoppard gallantly pressed on, and I have a vivid mem-

ory of him, desperate in the gathering dusk, frantically shuffling his precious pages and brandishing his cards, like a pan-
icky magician whose tricks are blowing up in his face. After
two hours, he had got no farther than the end of Act I. At that
point, Olivier suddenly woke up. For about thirty seconds, he
stared at the ceiling, where some spotlights I had recently
installed were dimly gleaming. Stoppard looked expectantly
in his direction: clearly, Olivier was choosing his words with
care. At length, he uttered them. "Ken," he said to me rum-
inatively, "where did you buy those lights?" Stoppard then
gave up and left. Next day, it took all the backslapping of
which Dexter and I were capable to persuade him that the play
was worth saving.

Jumpers turned out to be something unique in theatre: a
farce whose main purpose is to affirm the existence of God.
Or, to put it less starkly, a farcical defense of transcendent
moral values. At the same time, it is an attack on pragmatic
materialism as this is practiced by a political party called the
Radical Liberals, who embody Stoppard's satiric vision of socialism in action. They have just won an election (the time,
unspecified, seems to be the near future), and no sooner are
the votes counted than they take over the broadcasting services,
arrest the newspaper proprietors, and appoint a veterinary surgeon Archbishop of Canterbury. A prominent Rad-Lib—and
the villain of Stoppard's piece—is Sir Archie Jumper, vice-
chancellor of an English university and an all-round bounder,
who holds degrees in medicine, philosophy, literature, and
law, and diplomas in psychiatry and gymnastics. Archie encourages the philosophers of his staff (mostly logical positivists) to be part-time athletes, and it is they who form the human
pyramid, perforated by a bullet, with which the action begins.

The killing takes place during a party thrown at the home
of George Moore, professor of moral philosophy—a middle-
aged word-spinner and resolute nonacrobat, who is implacably
opposed to Archie's values, or lack of them. This is Stoppard's
hero and it is not the least of his problems that he bears the
same name as the world-famous English philosopher (d. 1958)
who wrote *Principia Ethica*. However, being one of Stoppard's
unsinkable eccentrics, he does not let this mischievous coincidence get him down. On hearing that the veterinarian Clegthorpe is the new Primate, he ironically observes, "Sheer disbe-

lief hardly registers on the face before the head is nodding with all the wisdom of instant hindsight. 'Archbishop Clegthorpe! Of course? The inevitable capstone to a career in veterinary medicine.'" (The use of a rare word like "capstone" instead of the more obvious "keystone" or "climax" is typical of Stoppard. Nabokov, another exile with a taste for verbal surprises, might have made the same choice.) George's role, one of the longest in the English comic repertoire, is devoted mainly to the composition of a hilarious, interminable, outrageously convoluted lecture designed to prove that moral absolutes exist—and closely analogous, as I've said, to the address dictated by Dr. Huml in Havel's *The Increased Difficulty of Concentration*. Theatrically, it disproves the philistine maxim that intellectual comedy can never produce belly laughs.

Seeking to demonstrate that purely rational arguments do not always make sense, George cites the Greek philosopher Zeno, who concluded that "since an arrow shot towards a target first had to cover half the distance, and then half the remainder, and then half the remainder after that, and so on *ad infinitum*, the result was . . . that though an arrow is always approaching its target, it never quite gets there, and Saint Sebastian died of fright." To underline his point, Saint George actually uses a bow and arrow, just as he employs a trained tortoise and a trained hare (both of which escape) to refute another of Zeno's famous paradoxes, "which showed in every way but experience . . . that a tortise given a head start in a race with, say, a hare, could never be overtaken." Hare, tortoise, arrow, and bow come together at the play's climax, which is one of the supreme—tragicomic is not quite the word, let us say tragifarcical—moments in modern theatre.

George sums up his beliefs in a discussion with Archie:

When I push *my* convictions to absurdity, *I* arrive at God. . . . All I know is that I think that I know that I know that nothing can be created out of nothing, that my moral conscience is different from the rules of my tribe, and that there is more in me than meets the microscope—and because of *that* I'm lumbered with this incredible, indescribable and definitely shifty *God*, the trump card of atheism.

He dismisses Archie's supporters as "simplistic scoreset-tlers." George versus Archie is Stoppard's dazzling dramati-zation of one of the classic battles of our time. Cyril Connolly gives a more dispassionate account of the same conflict in *The Unquiet Grave*, his semiautobiographical book of confessions and aphorisms:

> The two errors: We can either have a spiritual or a materalistic view of life. If we believe in the spirit then we make an assumption which permits a whole chain of them, down to a belief in fairies, witches, astrology, black magic, ghosts and treasure-divining.... On the other hand, a completely materialistic view leads to its own excesses, such as a belief in Behaviourism, in the economic basis of art, in the social foundation of ethics, and the biological nature of psychology, in fact to the justification of expediency and therefore ultimately to the Ends-Means fallacy of which our civilisation is per-ishing. If we believe in a supernatural or superhuman intelligence creating the universe, then we end by stock-ing our library with the prophecies of Nostradamus, and the calculations on the Great Pyramid. If instead we choose to travel via Montaigne and Voltaire, then we choke amid the brimstone aridities of the Left Book Club.

In that great debate there is no question where Stoppard stands. He votes for the spirit—although he did not state his position in the first person until June of this year, when, in the course of a book review, he defined himself as a supporter of "Western liberal democracy, favouring an intellectual elite and a progressive middle class and based on a moral order derived from Christian absolutes."

The female principle in the George-Archie struggle is rep-resented by George's wife, Dotty. Some ten years his junior, she is a star of musical comedy who has suffered a nervous breakdown (and gone into premature retirement) because the landing of men on the moon has destroyed her romantic ideals. She says:

Not only are we no longer the still centre of God's universe, we're not even uniquely graced by his footprint in man's image. . . . Man is on the moon, his feet on solid ground, and he has seen us whole . . . and all our absolutes, the thou-shalts, and the thou-shalt-nots that seemed to be the very condition of our existence, how did *they* look to two moonmen with a single neck to save between them?

We already know the answer. Captain Scott, the first Englishman to reach the moon, has a damaged spaceship that may not make it back to earth. To reduce the weight load, he has kicked Astronaut Oates off the ladder to the command module, thereby condemning him to death. What is moral has been sacrificed in favor of what is practical. Remember that we are still dealing with a high—a very high—comedy. In this context, Geoffrey Reeve's opinion is worth quoting:

> "Rosencrantz" is a beautiful piece of theatre, but "Jumpers" is *the* play, without any doubt. The ironic tone perfectly matches the absurd vision. It's far more than an exercise in wit; it ends up making a fierce statement. Not necessarily one that I would agree with—politically and philosophically. Tom and I have very little in common. But it's a measure of his brilliance that in the theatre I suspend rational judgment. He simply takes my breath away. People sometimes say he has a purely literary mind. That's not true of "Jumpers." It uses the stage *as* a stage, not as an extension of TV or the novel.

Jumpers went into rehearsal at the Old Vic in November, 1971. Diana Rigg played Dotty, and Michael Hordern, as George, had the part of his life: quivering with affronted dignity, patrolling the stage like a neurotic sentry, his face infested with tics, his fists plunging furiously into his cardigan pockets, he was matchlessly silly and serious at the same time. Ten days before the premiere, however, the play was still running close to four hours. I begged Olivier for permission to make cuts. He told me to approach the director, Peter Wood, who said he was powerless without the author's approval. Stoppard felt that alterations at this stage would upset the actors. Faced with this impasse, I took unilateral action. The next afternoon, just after the lunch break, I nipped into the rehearsal room ahead of the director and dictated to the cast a series of cuts and transpositions which reduced the text to what I considered manageable length. They were accepted without demur, and the matter, to my astonished relief, was never raised again. *Jumpers* opened in February, 1972, to resounding acclaim. B. A. Young, of the *Financial Times*, spoke for most of his colleagues when he wrote, "I can't hope to do justice to the richness and sparkle of the evening's proceedings, as gay and original a farce as we have seen for years."

Two months later, the London *Sunday Times*, whose regular critic had given a rhapsodic account of the first night, unexpectedly published a second review of the play—written by Sir Alfred Ayer, Wykeham Professor of Logic at Oxford and, by general consent, the foremost living English philosopher. He had made his name (which was then plain A. J. Ayer) in the nineteen-thirties as the precocious author of *Language, Truth and Logic*, probably the most masterly exposition in English of the principles of logical positivism. Thus, Ayer represented, in its most Establishment form, the philosophical tradition that Stoppard had set out to undermine. George tells us in the play that his next book will be entitled *Language, Truth and God*, and Dotty summarizes the archfiend Archie's views on morality in a speech that might have been borrowed from Ayer:

Things and actions, you understand, can have any number of real and verifiable properties. But good and bad, better and worse, these are not real properties of things, they are just expressions of our feelings about them.

It seemed on the cards that Ayer-Archie would resent being cast as Stoppard's villian. But nothing of the sort: he "enormously enjoyed" the evening, and "came away feeling the greatest admiration for its author and for the actor Michael

Hordern, who takes the leading part." If he identified himself with any of the characters, it was not Archie but George, in whom "I thought, perhaps conceitedly, that I occasionally caught echoes of my own intonations"—though not, needless to say, of his ideas. He analyzed the play's philosophical content with detached but devastating aplomb:

> The argument is between those who believe in absolute values, for which they seek a religious sanction, and those, more frequently to be found among contemporary philosophers, who are subjectivists or relativists in morals, utilitarians in politics, and atheists or at least agnostics. . . .
>
> George needs not one but two Gods, one to create the world and another to support his moral values, and is unsuccessful in obtaining either of them. For the creator he relies on the first-cause argument, which is notoriously fallacious, since it starts from the assumption that everything must have a cause and ends with something that lacks one. As for the view that morals can be founded on divine authority, the decisive objection was beautifully put by Bertrand Russell: "Theologians have always taught that God's decrees are good, and that this is not a mere tautology; it follows that goodness is logically independent of God's decrees." This argument also shows that even if George had been able to discover his second God it would not have been of any service to him. It would provide a utilitarian motive for good behaviour, but that was not what he wanted. It could, more respectably, provide an object for emulation, but for that imaginary or even actual human beings could serve as well. . . .
>
> The moral of the play, in so far as it has one, seemed to be that George was humane, and therefore human, in a way the others were not. This could have been due to his beliefs, but it did not have to be. Whatever Kant may have said, morality is very largely founded on sympathy and affection, and for these one does not require religious sanctions. Even logical positivists are capable of love.

After reading Ayer's review, Stoppard invited him to lunch, and the two men became close friends.

We now flash forward to an entry in my journal for October 19, 1976, when Stoppard and I motored to New College, Oxford, to be Ayer's guests for dinner at High Table. An English drama critic once said, "Stoppard, who never went to a university, writes more like a University Wit than any graduate dramatist now practising." The trip to New College would be Stoppard's initiation into Oxford life, and he would be going in off the top board, since, of all the dons currently teaching at the university, Ayer is the reigning superstar:

En route to Oxford, Tom and I lunch at the Waterside Inn, plush French restaurant forty minutes west of London by car. The Thames idles past our table, visible through plate glass and weeping willows. Tom talks of how, earlier this year, he lunched with the Queen at Buckingham Palace: "Everything you touch is beautiful, and the food is superb. The other guests were writers, athletes, accountants—all kinds of people. Don't expect me to knock occasions like that. I'm very conservative. As a foreigner, I'm more patriotic than anyone else in England except William Davis." (Davis is the German-born editor of *Punch*.) I ask whether there's any living person he especially longs to meet. Three names cross his mind: Marlon Brando, Alexander Solzhenitsyn, and Sugar Ray Robinson. We discuss his view of politics in general and British politics in particular: "I don't lose any sleep if a policeman in Durham beats somebody up, because I know it's an exceptional case. It's a sheer perversion of speech to describe the society I live in as one that inflicts violence on the underprivileged. What worries me is not the burgeois exception but the totalitarian norm. Of all the systems that are on offer, the one I don't want is the one that denies freedom of expression—no matter what its allegedly redeeming virtues may be. The only thing that would make me leave England would be control over free speech." Of his plays he says, "My characters are all mouthpieces for points of view rather than explorations of individual psychology. They aren't realistic in any sense. I write plays of ideas uneasily married to comedy or farce." Has he got any manuscripts hidden away in a bottom drawer? He grins and answers, "No—with me everything is top drawer." We talk about James Joyce's exuberantly erotic letters to his wife, which have recently been published for the first time. If Tom had read them before writing *Travesties*, in which Joyce is a leading character, would he have made use of them? "I wouldn't have dreamed of it. I'm interested in Joyce the author of *Ulysses*, not Joyce the husband. Nor, by the way, do I think of him as a biochemical parcel consumed by worms. I believe there is something of him that is still around, still capable of suffering because of the revelations made public by Faber & Faber."

After lunch, coffee at the large nondescript Victorian house that Tom bought four years ago in the nearby village of Iver, in Buckinghamshire. The garden, though spacious, is a bit too close for comfort to a traffic roundabout. In his book-upholstered study, he shows me his most prized possessions, among them a first edition of Hemingway's *In Our Time* and a framed letter, written in January, 1895, at the Albemarle Hotel, London, in response to an insolent request for an interview, a photograph, and a job as the addressee's literary agent.

Sir,—I have read your letter and I see that to the brazen everything is brass.

Your obedient servant,
OSCAR WILDE

What would Tom do if he found a gold mine under his garden and never needed to work again? "Nothing spectacular. I love books—nonfiction for preference. If I had a gigantic windfall of bullion, I'd take a six-month sabbatical, pluck out of my shelves the two or three hundred books I haven't opened, and just read. The secret of happiness is inconspicuous consumption." For such a wealthy writer, he leads a comparatively simple life. He enjoyed his first secretary only a year ago ("I got the idea from Harold Pinter") and knows little about his financial affairs, which are handled by his brother, a professional accountant.

Thence to Oxford, an hour's drive away, and the back quad of New College, where Freddie Ayer, scholastically gowned, gives us sherry in his rooms. A busy, bright-eyed man, short of stature and formidably alert, he tells me that C. S. Lewis, the great critic, novelist, and Christian apologist, described him after their first meeting as "a cross between a rodent and a firefly." He shares Tom's passion for cricket. "I used to captain the New College Senior Common Room XI," he says proudly. "The first time I played for the team, I was fifty-three years old and I scored seventy-five"—a highly respectable total. We then pass through the ritual stages of an Oxford banquet.

Phase I: We meet the Warden of the College at his lodgings, where the other dons and their guests are assembled, making about forty in all. More sherry is consumed, with champagne as the alternative option. "My taste in theatre is mainly classical," Freddie says, adding that the twentieth-century playwrights he most admires are Pirandello, Coward, Maugham, and Sartre. "I vastly prefer Sartre's plays to his philosophy. Existentialism works much better in the theatre than in theory."

Phase II: We march in procession to take our place at High Table, set on a dais overlooking hundreds of already seated undergraduates. Tom and I sit on either side of Freddie. Food forgettable; wines exceptional (hock, Burgundy, Sauternes). "Tom is the only living dramatist whose work I would go to see just because he wrote it," Freddie says. "There was a time when I would have said the same about John Osborne, but now—well, let's say I would wait to be taken by other people. With John, the rhetoric runs away with the context. Tom plays with words and makes them dance. John uses them as a sledgehammer."

Phase III: We move on to a panelled, candlelit chamber and are seated at tables where port, Madeira, and Moselle are circulated. Tom tells me a story of how he attended a performance of *Travesties*, at the Aldwych Theatre, in London, in order to be introduced to the proposed French translator of the play. In the intermission, he presented himself at the manager's office, where a group of people were sipping drinks. Before long, they were joined by a foreign-looking stranger with flaring nostrils. Taking the newcomer into a corner, Tom embarked on a detailed explanation of the major linguistic problems posed by the text. The man seemed a little perplexed, but he nodded politely, and Tom pushed ahead for fully five minutes. Suddenly, a thought shot through his mind: What an odd coincidence that I should have a French translator who looks exactly

like Rudolf Nureyev. At that moment, there was a knock on
the door, and in came a little man in a beret, smoking a Gau-
loise....

Phase IV: We end up in a common room for coffee and/or
brandy. Here Tom amazes me. Either he has put himself
through a refresher course (which is by no means impossible)
or he is even cleverer than I suspected. He shows himself
splendidly equipped to hold his own with Freddie and his colleagues in philosophical debate. With scintillating skill, he
defends such theses as the following: (a) that Wagner's music
is not as good as it sounds, and (b) that there are *fewer* things
in heaven and earth than are dreamed of in philosophy. I am
also impressed by his ability, under whatever pressure, to quote
Bertrand Russell verbatim, especially after five hours of steady
alcoholic intake. At one point, I interject a tenative reference
to Eastern philosophies, but Freddie pooh-poohs them with
Hegelian vehemence, dismissing Taoism, Confucianism, Hin-
duism, and Buddhism in a single barking laugh. "They have
some psychological interest, but nothing more than that," he
adds. "For the most part, they're devices for reconciling people
to a perfectly dreadful earthly life. I believe there were one or
two seventh-century Indians who contributed a few ideas to
mathematics. But that's about all." I expect Tom would agree.

By 1972, the year of *Jumpers*, the voice of Vaclav Havel
had been efficiently stifled. The ban on Czech productions of
his work had remained in operation since 1969. Censorship
had returned to the press and the broadcasting stations as well
as to the theatre and the cinema; and in January, 1969, Gustav
Husak (Dubcek's successor as Communist Party Secretary)
made an ominous speech in which he said that the time had
come to "strengthen internal discipline." He issued a strong
warning to those who held "private meetings in their apartments
for inventing campaigns" against the regime. Havel and Jan
Nemec, the film director, at once sent a courageous telegram
to President Ludvik Svoboda, protesting against Husak's
threats and predicting (with melancholy accuracy) that the next
step would be police interrogations and arrests. Later in 1969,
Havel received an American foundation grant that would enable
him to spend a year in the United States. The Czech government
responded by confiscating his passport. Productions of his play

outside Czechoslovakia had been effectively forbidden, because the state literary agency, through which all foreign contracts had to be negotiated, refused to handle Havel's work,
on the ground that it gave a distorted picture of Czechoslovakian life. This meant that thenceforward there was no officially sanctioned way for anything by Havel to be performed
anywhere in the world. The authorities, however, were far
from satisfied. What irked them was that they could drum up
no evidence on which to bring him to court. He had engaged
in no antistate activities, and nothing in his plays could be
construed as seditious. They recognized in him a stubborn
naysayer, a noncollaborator; but dumb insolence was not a
criminal offense. One of the archetypes of Czech literature is
the hero of Jaroslav Hasek's novel *The Good Soldier Schweik*,
who drives his superior officers to distraction by practicing
passive resistance beneath a mask of pious conformity. Like
many Czech dissidents before him, Havel had learned from
Schweik's example.

He continued to write. In 1971, the first draft of his latest
play, *Conspirators*, translated by Vera Blackwell, reached my
desk at the National Theatre. It is set in an unnamed country,
conceivably South American, where a corrupt dictatorship has
just been overthrown and replaced by a cautious and indecisive
democratic government. A group of five staunch patriots (including the chief of police and the head of the general staff)
hear rumors of a conspiracy to reinstate the deposed tyrant,
now living in exile. Fearful that the new regime will be too
weak to prevent a coup, they plan a countercoup of their own.
One of them says, "In order to preserve democracy, we shall
have to seize power ourselves." Their plot necessitates the use
of violence, but whenever they meet they learn that their opponents are preparing to commit acts of comparable, if not
greater, ferocity. This compels them to devise even more
bloodthirsty countermeasures. The process of escalation continues until we suddenly realize what is actually happening.
The rumors they hear about the exiled conspirators are in fact
quite accurate accounts of their own conspiracy—reported by
a government spy in their midst and then fed back to them by
one of their own agents in the Secret Service. In other words,
as Havel put it in a letter to me, "they have been plotting to

save the country from themselves." He warned me not to suppose that because the play dealt with politics it was a political play:

> I am not trying either to condemn or to defend this or that political doctrine. . . . What I am concerned with is the general problem of human behavior in contemporary society. Politics merely provided me with a convenient platform. . . . All the political arguments in the play have a certain plausibility, and in some circumstances they might even be valid. . . . The point is that one cannot be sure. For truth is not only what is said: it depends on who says it, and why. Truth is guaranteed only by the full weight of humanity behind it. Modern rationalism has led people to believe that what they call "objective truth" is a freely transferable commodity that can be appropriated by anyone. The results of this divorce between truth and human beings can be most graphically observed in politics.

I was ready to recommend the play for inclusion in the National Theatre's repertoire as a pirated, unauthorized production (thereby keeping Havel legally in the clear), but the script needed extensive revision, and the author, trapped in his homeland, could not come to London to work on it. For this reason, we decided regretfully to shelve the project. Around this time, his German publishers (coincidentally, the same as Stoppard's) decided to thwart the Czech veto by acting as his agents in the Western world. The state literary agency retaliated by intercepting and withholding all royalties sent to Havel by Western producers of his work. As far as I know, *Conspirators* remains unrevised and unperformed.

In 1974, Havel's savings began to run out, and he took the only employment he could find—a post in a brewery at Trutnov, about eighty miles from Prague. Apart from the income it provided, he welcomed the opportunity of meeting Czech citizens who were not members of the secret police. Havel's job consisted of stacking empty beer barrels. This period of his life yielded two short plays, both of them patently autobiographical. In *Audience*, thinly disguised under the name of

Ferdinand Vanek, he is summoned to an interview with the
head maltster of the brewery, a chain drinker and experienced
compromiser, who jovially offers him a chance to better himself. Wouldn't it be more seemly for an intellectual like him
to have a post in the stock-checking department, where no
manual labor would be involved? All that Vanek has to do to
be thus upgraded is to submit a weekly report on his thoughts
and activities, and to bring a certain actress (much admired by
the maltster) to an office party. Vanek is quite happy to invite
the actress, but he politely explains that he cannot see his way
to informing on himself. This provokes the maltster into a self-
pitying alcoholic tirade against intellectuals and their so-called
principles: "The thing is, you can live on your flipping principles! But what about me? All I can expect is a kick in the
pants if I so much as *mention* a principle." And so on. Vanek
gravely lets the storm pass over his head. The maltster then
falls into a stupor, from which, a few moments later, he briskly
recovers. Having erased the confessional outburst from his
memory, he starts the interview over again as if nothing had
happened.

Audience is Havel's vignette of life among the workers.
Private View, its companion piece, takes a similarly ironic look
at life among the intelligentsia. Vanek/Havel is invited to dinner by a sophisticated middle-class couple who are eager to
show off their newly redecorated apartment, with its stereo
deck, its costly clutter of modern and antique furniture, and
its crates of bourbon, picked up on a trip to the States. All this
douceur de vivre, they point out, could be his. Why does he
insist on burying himself in a brewery? If only he would stop
associating with people who criticize the regime ("Commu-
nists," his hostess disdainfully calls them), he could easily get
a well-paid job in a publishing house. Like the maltster, the
couple feel personally affronted (and accused) by his perverse
reluctance to make the few small adjustments that could gain
him such shining privileges. "You're an egoist!" his hostess
shrieks. "Disgusting, unfeeling, inhuman egoist. Ungrateful,
stupid, bloody traitor." But her diatribe, like the maltster's,
ends as abruptly as it began, and when the curtain falls she
and her husband are entertaining their guest with the very latest
pop single from New York. (The two plays were broadcast on

BBC radio in April, 1977. The role of Vanek was played by Harold Pinter.)

In 1974, the year Havel started stacking beer barrels, Stoppard's third major work, *Travesties*, opened at the Aldwych Theatre, presented by the Royal Shakespeare Company and directed (as *Jumpers* had been) by Peter Wood. The play had its origin in Stoppard's discovery that James Joyce, Lenin, and Tristan Tzara, the founder of Dadaism, had all lived in Zurich during the First World War—a conjunction of expatriates that made instant comic connections in his mind. In addition, he had long wanted to write a leading role for his friend John Wood, a tall aquiline actor who had a matchless capacity for delivering enormous speeches at breakneck speed with crystalline articulation. From Richard Ellmann's biography of Joyce, Stoppard learned that during his stay in Zurich Joyce had been the business manager of a semiprofessional troupe of English actors, whose inaugural production was *The Importance of Being Earnest*. The part of Algernon Moncrieff was played by a young man named Henry Carr, who held a minor post at the British consulate. Carr bought a new pair of trousers to embellish his performance, and later sued Joyce for reimbursement. Joyce counterclaimed that Carr owed him the price of five tickets for the show, and, for good measure, accused him of slander. Stoppard sought to link this story, true but implausible, with the hypothesis, plausible but untrue, that Joyce, Tzara, and Lenin had known one another in Zurich. He hit on the idea of filtering the action through the faulty memory of Henry Carr in old age, a querulous eccentric in whose mind fact and fantasy were indissolubly blended. With Henry myopically at the wheel, Stoppard was off to the races. Clive James said of the play in *Encounter*:

> Before John Wood was halfway through his opening speech I already knew that in Stoppard I had encountered a writer of my generation whom I could admire without reserve. It is a common reaction to "Travesties" to say that seeing it is like drinking champagne. But not only did I find that the play tasted like champagne—I found that in drinking it I felt like a jockey. Jockeys drink

champagne as an everyday tipple, since it goes to the head without thickening the waist. "Travesties" to me seemed not an exotic indulgence, but the stuff of life. Its high speed was not a challenge but a courtesy; its structural intricacy not a dazzling pattern but a perspicuous design; its fleeting touch not of a feather but of a fine needle.

There were many such panegyrics, not only in London but on Broadway, where the play won Stoppard his second Tony award. (The first had been for *Rosencrantz and Guildenstern*.) I gladly concede that the grotesque rhetorical ramblings of Henry Carr, whether in soliloquy or in his long first-act confrontation with Tzara, are sublimely funny; but at the heart of the enterprise something is sterile and arbitrary. As Ronald Hayman, a devout Stoppard fan, put it, "there is no internal dynamic." Stoppard imposes the plot of Wilde's play, itself thoroughly baroque, upon his own burlesque vision of life in wartime Zurich, which is like crossbreeding the bizarre with the bogus. Following Wilde's blueprint, he gives Carr (Algernon) and Tzara (Jack Worthing) a Cecily and a Gwendolen with whom, respectively, to fall in love; while James Joyce stands unconvincingly in for Lady Bracknell. In an interview with Hayman, Stoppard said he was particularly proud of the scene in the first act between Joyce and Tzara:

It exists almost on three levels. On one it's Lady Bracknell quizzing Jack. Secondly, the whole thing is actually structured on [the eighth] chaper in *Ulysses*, and thirdly, it's telling the audience what Dada is, and where it comes from.

All of which is undeniable, and the well-read playgoer will happily consume such a layer cake of pastiche. But cake, as Marie Antoinette discovered too late, is no substitute for bread. To change the metaphor, the scene resembles a triple-decker bus that isn't going anywhere. What it lacks, in common with the play as a whole, is the sine qua non of theatre; namely, a narrative thrust that impels the characters, whether farcically or tragically or in any intermediate mode, toward a credible state of crisis, anxiety, or desperation. (Even the two derelicts in *Waiting for Godot*, so beloved of Stoppard, are in a plight that most people would consider desperate.) In *Rosencrantz and Guildenstern, Inspector Hound,* and *Jumpers*, acts of homicide are committed—acts insuring that a certain amount of pressure, however factitious, is exerted on the characters. They are obviously in trouble; they may be killed, or, at least, be accused of killing. Trying, as Stoppard does in *Travesties*, to make a play without the magic ingredient of pressure toward desperation is—to lift a phrase from *Jumpers*—"tantamount to constructing a Gothic arch out of junket."

The opening speech, for instance, is made up of words that Tristan Tzara has silently cut out of an unidentified newspaper and drawn from a hat. He arranges them at random, and recites them in the form of a limerick. It concludes:

> Ill raced alas whispers kill later nut east.
> Noon avuncular ill day Clara.

To French-speaking members of the audience, the lines sound roughly the same as:

> *Il reste à la Suisse parce qu'il est un artiste.*
> *"Nous n'avons que l'art,"* il déclara.

Which means, roughly Englished:

> He lives in Switzerland because he is an artist.
> "We have only art," he declared.

No translation or explanation, however, is offered in the text. Nonspeakers of French are thus left in outer darkness, while French-speakers who have not read the published version are unaware that what they have just heard is a linguistic joke. The result is that nobody laughs. This seems to me unadulterated junket.

As for the arbitrary element in the play, I once asked Stoppard what he would have done if Joyce's company of actors had chosen to present Maxim Gorky's *The Lower Depths* instead of Wilde's comedy. He breezily replied that he would probably have based his plot on Gorky. I have since fed into his mind what I regard as a perfectly corking scenario. During the Second World War, Arnold Schönberg, Swami Prabhavananda, and W. C. Fields were simultaneously working in Hollywood. Cast that trio in *The Lower Depths*, and who knows what monument of junket you might come up with?

The hard polemic purpose of *Travesties* is to argue that art must be independent of the world of politics. Carr says to Tzara, "My dear Tristan, to be an artist *at all* is like living in Switzerland during a world war." Tzara is the target for Stoppard's loathing of the avant-garde. He is made to describe himself as "the natural enemy of bourgeois art" (which Stoppard cherishes) and as "the natural ally of the political left" (which Stoppard abhors). By lending his support to the anti-bourgeois forces, Tzara has pledged himself to the destruction of art. At one point, he rounds on Joyce and says:

Your art has failed. You've turned literature into a religion and it's as dead as all the rest, it's an overripe corpse and you're cutting fancy figures at the wake. It's too late for geniuses!

What's needed, the zealous Dadaist goes on, is vandalism and desecration. Having set up Tzara in the bowling alley, Stoppard proceeds to knock him down with a speech by Joyce, which was not in the original script (it was suggested by the director) but which Stoppard now regards as "the most important . . . in the play." Joyce begins by dismissing Tzara as "an overexcited little man, with a need for self-expression far beyond the scope of your natural gifts." This, he says, is not discreditable, but it does not make him an artist: "An artist is the magician put among men to gratify—capriciously—their urge for immortality." If the Trojan War had gone unrecorded in poetry, it would be forgotten by history. It is the artists who have enriched us with its legends—above all, with the tale of "Ulysses, the wanderer, the most human, the most complete of all heroes." He continues, "It is a theme so overwhelming that I am almost afraid to treat it. And yet I with my Dublin Odyssey will double that immortality, yes by God *there's* a corpse that will dance for some time yet and *leave the world precisely as it finds it*."

So much for any pretension that art might have to change, challenge, or criticize the world, or to modify, however marginally, our view of it. For that road can lead only to revolution, and revolution will mean the end of free speech, which is defined by Lenin, later in the play, as speech that is *"free from bourgeois anarchist individualism."* Stoppard's idol—the artist for art's sake, far above the squalid temptations of politics—is, unequivocally, Joyce. The first act ends with Henry Carr recounting a dream in which he asked Joyce what he did in the Great War. "'I wrote *Ulysses*,'" he said, 'What did you do?'"

The implication of all this—that Joyce was an apolitical dweller in an ivory tower—is, unfortunately, untrue. He was a professed socialist. And this is where Stoppard's annexation of the right to alter history in the cause of art begins to try one's patience. (A minor symptom of the same sin occurs when Carr says that Oscar Wilde was "indifferent to politics"—a statement that will come as a surprise to readers of Wilde's propagandist handbook *The Soul of Man under Socialism*.) In a recent essay in the *New York Review of Books*, Richard Ellmann has pointed out that Joyce's library in Trieste was full of works by leftist authors; that the culmination of his political hopes was the foundation of the Irish Free State; and that Leopold Bloom, in *Ulysses*, is a left-winger of long standing who annoys his wife by informing her that Christ was the first socialist. Moreover, Ellmann quotes a speech from the quasi-autobiographical first draft of *A Portrait of the Artist* in which Joyce addresses the people of the future with oratorical fervor:

> Man and woman, out of you comes the nation that is to come, the lightening of your masses in travail, the competitive order is arrayed against itself, the aristocracies are supplanted, and amid the general paralysis of an insane society, *the confederate will* issues in action.

The phrase I've italicized can only mean, as Ellmann says, "the will of like-minded revolutionaries." It is all very well for Stoppard to claim that he has mingled "scenes which are self-evidently documentary . . . with others which are just as evidently fantastical." The trouble with his portrait of Joyce is that it is neither one thing nor the other, neither pure fantasy nor pure documentary, but is simply based on a false premise. When matters of high importance are being debated, it is not pedantic to object that the author has failed to do his homework.

The second act of *Travesties* is dominated by Lenin. Stoppard quotes him fairly and at length but cannot fit him into the stylistic framework of the play. Somerset Maugham once said that sincerity in society was like an iron girder in a house of cards. Lenin is the girder that topples *Travesties*. Stoppard fleetingly considered making him the equivalent of Miss Prism, the governess in *The Importance*—"but that," he wisely concluded, "would have killed the play because of the trivialization." On the other hand, he did think it would be funny to start Act II with a pretty girl (Cecily) delivering a lecture on Lenin. "And indeed it *was* funny," he told an interviewer, "except that I was the only person laughing." (I wonder, incidentally, what he found so comic about the idea of a pretty girl taking Lenin seriously.) At all events, the lecture stayed in, funny or not, together with the ensuing scenes, which deal with Lenin and his plans for revolution. Too frail a bark to bear such weighty cargo, the play slowly capsizes and sinks.

A footnote from Derek Marlowe: "With Tom, words always precede thoughts. Phrases come first, ideas later. The Stoppard you find in *Travesties* doesn't sound any older than the Stoppard of *Rosencrantz and Guildenstern*. You'd think that nothing had happened to him in the intervening seven years. But, by God, a great deal has."

After *Travesties*, a literary circus of a play in which historical figures jumped through hoops at the flick of Stoppard's whim, it was clear that he had spent long enough in the library. The time had come to turn his attention to events in the outside world. Not unexpectedly, the field he chose to explore was the treatment of political dissidents in Eastern Europe and the Soviet Union. First, however, he had to fulfill an obligation to Ed Berman. Berman is an expatriate American, bursting with bearded enthusiasm, who came to London in 1968 and set up a cooperative organization called Inter-Action, which presents plays in schools, remand homes, youth clubs, mental hospitals, community centers, and the streets. Inter-Action also runs a thriving farm in the dingy heart of a London suburb and launched the Almost Free Theatre, in Soho, where the price of admission is whatever you think the show will be worth. Berman produced the world premiere of two one-acters by Stoppard (*After Magritte*, in 1970, and *Dogg's Our Pet*, the following year), and not long afterward Stoppard, learning that Berman had applied for British citzenship, promised to give him a new play if the application was successful. It was, and *Dirty Linen*, Stoppard's deadpan farce about sexual misconduct in the House of Commons, opened at the Almost Free Theatre in April, 1976. It was an instant hit. The Czech émigré had done honor to his American counterpart, welcoming him to membership in the Western European club.

Simple chronology may be the best way to set out the convergence that subsequently developed between the lives, and careers, of Stoppard and Vaclav Havel.

August, 1976: Stoppard addresses a rally in Trafalgar Square sponsored by the Committee Against Psychiatric Abuse, from which he joins a march to the Soviet Embassy. There he attempts to deliver a petition denouncing the use of mental homes as punishment camps for Russian dissidents. "The chap at the door wouldn't accept it," he told me afterward, "so we all went home."

October 5, 1976: Havel celebrates his fortieth birthday at the converted farmhouse, ninety miles from Prague, where he and his wife live. The next day, he is officially ordered to quit the place, on the ground, patently false, that it is unfit for human habitation.

January 11, 1977: *Dirty Linen* opens on Broadway, to generally favorable reviews. Walter Kerr, in his Sunday column in the *New York Times*, sounds one of the few discordant notes:

Intellectually restless as a hummingbird, and just as incapable of lighting anywhere, the playwright has a gift for making the randomness of his flights funny.... Busy as Mr. Stoppard's mind is, it is also lazy; he will settle for the first thing that pops into his head.... Wide-ranging as his antic interests are, delightful as his impish

mismatches can occasionally be, his management of
them is essentially slovenly.

One speech that gets an unfailing ovation, however, is the
following tribute to the American people, paid by a senior
British civil servant:

> They don't stand on ceremony. . . . They make no
> distinction about a man's background, his parentage, his
> education. They say what they mean, and there is a vivid
> muscularity about the way they say it. . . . They are al-
> ways the first to put their hands in their pockets. They
> press you to visit them in their own home the moment
> they meet you, and are irrepressibly good-humoured,
> ambitious and brimming with self-confidence in any
> company. Apart from all that I've got nothing against
> them.

On the thirteenth of the month, Stoppard flies from New
York to the West Coast, where he is to undergo a sort of
Southern California apotheosis. At the Mark Taper Forum,
which is the fountainhead of theatrical activity in Los Angeles,
Travesties and *The Importance of Being Earnest* are being
staged in repertory for the first time. *Inspector Hound* is about
to open at a new theatre in Beverly Hills. And the University
of California at Santa Barbara is holding "a Tom Stoppard
Festival, during which I will be carried through the streets and
pelted with saffron rice," Stoppard has told me in a letter,
adding, "That is if I haven't gone out of fashion by then." I
hasten to southern California. Stoppard, whisked from the airport to a press conference at the Mark Taper, where I join him,
fields every question with effortless charm. For example, "I
suspect I am getting more serious than I was, though with a
redeeming streak of frivolity." And "We get our moral sen-
sibility from art. When we have a purely technological society,
it will be time for mass suicide." What American playwrights
does he admire? Sam Shepard, for one; and Edward Albee,
"especially for *The Zoo Story* and *A Delicate Balance*. But my
favorite American play is *The Front Page*—though I might
have to admit, if extremely pressed, that it wasn't *quite* as fine
as *Long Day's Journey into Night*."

January 14, 1977: Vaclav Havel is arrested in Prague and thrown into jail. The real, though unacknowledged, reason for his imprisonment is that he is one of three designated spokesmen for a document called Charter 77, signed by over three hundred leading Czech writers and intellectuals, which urges the government to carry out its promises, made in the Helsinki accords of 1975, to respect human rights, especially those relating to free speech.

On the same day, leaving Los Angeles at dawn, I drive Stoppard to the Santa Barbara campus, which is preposterously pretty, palm-fringed, and moistened by ocean breakers. A silk scarf is knotted round his neck, and he wears flashy cowboy boots. We are met by Dr. Homer Swander, professor of English. A bronzed, gray-haired fan, he proudly informs Stoppard that no fewer than four of his plays will be presented at the university within the next week. In addition, there will be mass excursions to L.A. to see *Inspector Hound, The Importance*, and *Travesties*. During the morning, Tom discusses his work with a class of drama students. "I'm a very conventional artist," he says when someone quizzes him about Dadaism. "I have no sympathy at all with Tristan Tzara. The trouble with modern art, from my point of view, is that there's nothing left to parody."

A girl asks him, "Which of your plays do you think will be performed in fifty years' time?"

He replies, "There is no way I can answer that question without sounding arrogant to the point of mania or modest to the point of nausea."

Lunch with the top brass of the faculty is followed by a tour of the campus. The Mark Taper Forum has paid Tom's round-trip air fare from New York; a thousand dollars is his reward for spending the day at Santa Barbara. His lecture that evening fills a nine-hundred-seat auditorium to overflowing. Dr. Swander introduces him as an author in whom Santa Barbara has long taken a proprietary interest. (This is his second visit to the place in two years.) "We claim him as our own," Dr. Swander declares, to applause, "and I personally acclaim him as the most Shakespearean writer in English drama since Webster."

Stoppard lopes into sight, detaches the microphone from its stand to gain mobility, and lights a cigarette. "I've been brought ten thousand miles to talk to you about theatre," he says, "which I find only slightly more plausible than coming here on a surfing scholarship." Solid laughter. "I should explain that my technique when lecturing is to free-associate within an infinite, regression of parentheses. Also, it's only fair to confess that what you are about to hear is in the nature of an ego trip." To illustrate the problems of dramatic composition, he has brought along two dozen drafts of the blast of invective that Tzara launches against Joyce in *Travesties*. He reads them out, from the first attempt, which begins, "You blarney-arsed bog-eating Irish pig," to the final version, which starts, "By God, you supercilious streak of Irish puke!" What isn't commonly understood, he adds, is that "all this takes *weeks*." He paces for a while, and then notices a heavy glass ashtray that has been thoughtfully placed on a table in front of him. "Writing a play," he continues, "is like smashing that ashtray, filming it in slow motion, and then running the film in reverse, so that the fragments of rubble appear to fly together. You start— or at least *I* start—with the rubble."

Strolling back and forth across the stage, meditatively puffing on his cigarette, he says, "Whenever I talk to intelligent students about my work, I feel nervous, as if I were going through customs. 'Anything to declare, sir?' 'Not really, just two chaps sitting in a castle at Elsinore, playing games. That's all.' 'Then let's have a look in your suitcase, if you don't mind, sir.' And, sure enough, under the first layer of shirts there's a pound of hash and fifty watches and all kinds of exotic contraband. 'How do you explain this, sir?' 'I'm sorry, Officer, I admit it's there, but I honestly can't remember packing it.'" He says he has addressed only one American campus audience apart from the present assembly; that was at Notre Dame, in 1971, and the occasion did not get off to an auspicious start. "I began my talk by saying that I had not written my plays for purposes of discussion," he recalls in Santa Barbara. "At once, I felt a ripple of panic run through the hall. I suddenly realized why. To everyone present, *discussion was the whole point of drama*. That was why the faculty had been endowed—that was why all those buildings had been put up. I had undermined the entire reason for their existence."

There are questions from the floor:

Q.: May I say, Mr. Stoppard, that I think you are less slick this time than you were two years ago?

STOPPARD: Oh, good. Or—I'm sorry. Depending on your point of view.

Q.: Why don't you try directing your own work? Or acting in it?

STOPPARD: Look, I spend only about three and a half percent of my life writing plays. I'm trying very hard to build it up to four and a half percent. That's all I can handle at the moment.

(Tom's modesty is a form of egoism. It is as if he were saying, "See how self-deprecating I can be and still be self-assertive.")

His act has a strong finish. For an hour and a half, he says, he has shared his thoughts with us and answered many of our questions. But what is the real dialogue that goes on between the artist and his audience? By way of reply, he holds the microphone close to his mouth and speaks eight lines by the English poet Christopher Logue:

> Come to the edge.
>   We might fall.
> Come to the edge.
>   It's too high?
> COME TO THE EDGE!
>   And they came
> and he pushed
> and they flew.

A short silence. Then a surge of applause. In imagination, these young people are all flying.

February 11, 1977: Stoppard has an article in the *New York Times* about the new wave of repression in Prague. It starts:

Connoisseurs of totalitarian double-think will have noted that Charter 77, the Czechoslovak document which calls attention to the absence in that country of various human rights beginning with the right of free expression, has been refused publication inside Czechoslovakia on the grounds that it is a wicked slander.

Of the three leading spokesmen for Charter 77, two were merely interrogated and released—Jiri Hajek, who had been Foreign Minister under Alexander Dubcek in 1968, and Jan Patocka, an internationally respected philosopher. (Patocka, however, was later rearrested, and, after further questioning, suffered a heart attack and died in hospital.) Havel alone was charged under the subversion laws, which carry a maximum sentence of ten years. "Clearly," Stoppard says, "the regime had decided, finally and after years of persecution and harassment, to put the lid on Vaclav Havel."

February 27, 1977: Stoppard travels to Moscow with a representative of Amnesty International and meets a number of the victimized Soviet nonconformists, in support of whom he writes a piece for the London *Sunday Times*.

May 20, 1977: After four months' imprisonment in a cell seven feet by twelve, which he shared with a burglar, Havel is released. The subversion indictment is dropped, but he must still face trial on a lesser charge, of damaging the name of the state abroad, for which the maximum prison term is three years. He agrees not to make "any public political statements" while this new case is *sub judice*. The state attempts to make it a condition of his release that he resign his position as spokesman for Charter 77. He rejects the offer. Once outside the prison gates, however, he unilaterally announces that, although he remains an impenitent supporter of Charter 77, he will relinquish the job of spokesman until his case has been settled in court. He returns, together with his wife, to the farmhouse from which they were evicted the previous fall. (In October, when Havel's case came up for trial, he received a fourteen-month suspended sentence.)

June 18, 1977: By now, Stoppard has recognized in Havel his mirror image—a Czech artist who has undergone the pressures that Stoppard escaped when his parents took him into exile. After thirty-eight years' absence (and two weeks before his fortieth birthday), Stoppard goes back to his native land. He flies to Prague, then drives ninety miles north to Havel's home, where he meets his *Doppelgänger* for the first time. They spend five or six hours together, conversing mainly in English. Stoppard tells me later that some of the Marxist signatories of Charter 77 regard Havel primarily as a martyr with celebrity value, and didn't want him as their spokesman in the first place. "But they didn't go to jail," Stoppard adds. "He did. He is a very brave man."

Like Stoppard, Havel asks only to be allowed to work freely, without political surveillance. But that in itself is a political demand, and the man who makes it on his own behalf is morally bound to make it for others. Eleven years earlier, Stoppard's hero Lord Malquist said, undoubtedly echoing his author's views, "Since we cannot hope for order, let us withdraw with style from the chaos." Stoppard has moved from withdrawal to involvement. Some vestige of liberty may yet be reclaimed from the chaos, and if Stoppard has any hand in the salvage operation we may be sure that it will be carried out with style.

Nothing that he writes, however, is likely to give comfort to those who are not content to delegate the administration of liberty to "an intellectual elite and a progressive middle class"—the phrase, as I've already noted, that Stoppard has recently used to indicate where his deepest loyalties lie. He is not a standard-bearer for those who seek to create, anywhere in the world, a society like that which permitted the Prague Spring of 1968 to put forth its prodigious, polymorphous flowering. For that was a socialist society, and, of the many artists who flourished in it, Vaclav Havel was almost alone in not being a socialist. I wonder—or, rather, I doubt—whether Stoppard would seriously have relished living in the libertarian socialist Prague whose suppression by the Soviets he now so eloquently deplores.

July 1, 1977: World premiere, at the Festival Hall, in London, of Stoppard's latest piece, *Every Good Boy Deserves Favour*, acted by members of the Royal Shakespeare Company (including John Wood) and accompanied by the London Symphony Orchestra. Its subject: the use of pseudo-psychiatry to brainwash political dissenters in Soviet mental hospitals. With few exceptions, the reviews are eulogistic. Michael Billington writes in the *Guardian*:

> Stoppard brilliantly defies the theatrical law that says you cannot have your hand on your heart and your tongue in your cheek at the same time. . . . An extraordinary

work in which iron is met with irony and rigidity with a relaxed, witty defiance.

Bernard Levin, in the London *Sunday Times*, pulls out all the stops:

> Although this is a profoundly moral work, the argument still undergoes the full transmutation of art, and is thereby utterly changed; as we emerged, it was the fire and glitter of the play that possessed us, while its eternal truth, which is that the gates of hell shall not prevail, was by then inextricably embedded in our hearts. . . . I tell you this man could write a comedy about Auschwitz, at which we would sit laughing helplessly until we cried with inextinguishable anger.

What is Stoppard's picture of happiness? Work and domesticity, of course, enlivened by friendship and the admiration of his artistic peers. But of the thing itself—pure, irresponsible joy—his work gives us only one glimpse. It is an image summoned up from childhood and scarred by the passage of years. In *Where Are They Now?*, a radio play he wrote in 1969, a middle-aged man attends a class reunion at his public school and recalls a single moment of unalloyed delight. He was seven years old at the time:

> I remember walking down one of the corridors, trailing my finger along a raised edge along the wall, and I was suddenly totally happy, not elated or particularly pleased, or anything like that—I mean I experienced happiness as a state of being: everywhere I looked, in my mind, *nothing was wrong*. You never get that back when you grow up; it's a condition of maturity that almost *everything* is wrong, *all the time*, and happiness is a borrowed word for something else—a passing change of emphasis.

[1977]

Fifteen years of the salto mortale
—JOHNNY CARSON

JULY 14, 1977: There is a dinner party tonight at the Beverly Hills home of Irving Lazar, doyen of agents and agent of doyens. The host is a diminutive potentate, as bald as a doorknob, who was likened by the late screenwriter Harry Kurnitz to "a very expensive rubber beach toy." He has represented many of the top-grossing movie directors and best-selling novelists of the past four decades, not always with their prior knowledge, since speed is of the essence in such transactions; and Lazar's flair for fleet-footed deal-clinching—sometimes on behalf of people who had never met him—has earned him the nickname of Swifty. On this occasion, at his behest and that of his wife, Mary (a sleek and catlike sorceress, deceptively demure, who could pass for her husband's ward), some fifty friends have gathered to mourn the departure of Fred de Cordova, who has been the producer of NBC's "Tonight Show" since 1970; he is about to leave for Europe on two weeks' vacation. A flimsy pretext, you may think, for a wingding; but, according to Beverly Hills protocol, anyone who quits the state of California for more than a long weekend qualifies for a farewell party, unless he is going to Las Vegas or New York, each of which counts as a colonial suburb of Los Angeles. Most of the Lazars' guests tonight are theatre and/or movie people; e.g., Elizabeth Ashley, Tony Curtis, Gregory Peck, Sammy Cahn, Ray Stark, Richard Brooks. And even Fred de Cordova spent twenty years working for the Shuberts, Warner Brothers, and Universal before he moved into television. The senior media still take social precedence in the upper and elder reaches of these costly hills.

One of the rare exceptions to this role is the male latecomer who now enters, lean and dapper in an indigo blazer, white slacks, and a pale-blue open-necked shirt. Apart from two months in the late nineteen-fifties (when he replaced Tom Ewell in a Broadway comedy called *The Tunnel of Love*,) Johnny Carson has never been seen on the legitimate stage; and, despite a multitude of offers, he has yet to appear in his first film. He does not, in fact, much like appearing *anywhere* except (a) in the audience at the Wimbledon tennis championships, which he and his wife recently attended, (b) at his home in Bel Air, and (c) before the NBC cameras in Burbank, which act on him like an addictive and galvanic drug. Just how the drug works is not known to science, but its effect is witnessed—ninety minutes per night, four nights per week, thirty-seven weeks per year—by upward of fourteen million viewers; and it provoked the actor Robert Blake, while he was being interviewed by Carson on the "Tonight Show" in 1976, to describe him with honest adulation as "the ace comedian top-dog talk artist of the universe." I once asked a bright young Manhattan journalist whether he could define in a single word what makes television different from theatre or cinema. "For good or ill," he said, "Carson."

This pure and archetypal product of the box shuns large parties. Invitations from the Lazars are among the few he accepts. Tonight, he arrives alone (his wife, Joanna, has stopped off in New York for a few days' shopping), greets his host with the familiar smile, cordially wry, and scans the assembly, his eyes twinkling like icicles. Hard to believe, despite the pewter-colored hair, that he is fifty-one: he holds himself like the midshipman he once was, chin well tucked in, back as straight as a poker. (Carson claims to be five feet ten and a half inches in height. His pedantic insistence on that extra half inch betokens a man who suspects he looks small.) In repose, he resembles a king-sized ventriloquist's dummy. After winking impassively at de Cordova, he threads his way across the crowded living room and out through the ceiling-high sliding windows to the deserted swimming pool. Heads discreetly turn. Even in this posh peer group, Carson has cynosure status. Arms folded, he surveys Los Angeles by night—"glittering jewel of the Southland, gossamer web of loveliness," as Abe Burrows ironically called it. A waiter brings him a soft drink.

!"He looks like Gatsby," a young actress whispers to me. On the face of it, this is nonsense. Fitzgerald's hero suffers from star-crossed love, his wealth has criminal origins, and he loves to give flamboyant parties. But the simile is not without elements of truth. Gatsby, like Carson, is a midwesterner, a self-made millionaire, and a habitual loner, armored against all attempts to invade his emotional privacy. "He had come a long way to this blue lawn," Fitzgerald wrote of Gatsby—as far as Carson has come to these blue pools, from which steam rises on even the warmest nights.

"He doesn't drink now." I turn to find Lazar beside me, also peeking at the man outside. He continues, "But I remember Johnny when he was a *blackout* drunk." That was before the "Tonight Show" moved from New York to Los Angeles, in 1972. "A couple of drinks was all it took. He could get very hostile."

I point out to Lazar that Carson's family tree has deep Irish roots on the maternal side. Was there something atavistic in his drinking? Or am I glibly casting him as an ethnic ("black Irish") stereotype? At all events, I now begin to see in him—still immobile by the pool—the lineaments of a magnified leprechaun.

"Like a lot of people in our business," Lazar goes on, "he's a mixture of extreme ego and extreme cowardice." In Lazar's lexicon, a coward is one who turns down starring roles suggested to him by Lazar.

Since Carson already does what nobody has ever done better, I reply, why should he risk his reputation by plunging into movies or TV specials?

Lazar concedes that I may be right. "But I'll tell you something else about him," he says, with italicized wonder. *"He's celibate."* He means "chaste". "In his position, he could have all the girls he wants. It wouldn't be difficult. But he never cheats."

It is thirty minutes later. Carson is sitting at a table by the pool, where four or five people have joined him. He chats with impersonal affability, making no effort to dominate, charm, or amuse. I recall something that George Axelrod, the dramatist and screenwriter, once said to me about him: "Socially, he doesn't exist. The reason is that there are no television cameras in living rooms. If human beings had little red lights in the middle of their foreheads, Carson would be the greatest conversationalist on earth."

One of the guests is a girl whose hobby is numerology. Taking Carson as her subject, she works out a series of arcane sums and then offers her interpretation of his character. "You are an enormously mercurial person," she says, "who swings between very high highs and very low lows."

His eyebrows rise, the corners of his lips turn down: this is the mock-affronted expression he presents to the camera when a baby armadillo from some local zoo declines to respond to his caresses. "This girl is great," he says to de Cordova. "She makes me sound like a cross between Spring Byington and Adolf Hitler."

Before long, he departs as unobtrusively as he came.

Meeting him a few days afterward, I inquire what he thought of the party. He half grins, half winces. "Torturous?" he says.

Within a month, however, I note that he is back in the same torture chamber. Characteristically, although he is surrounded by the likes of Jack Lemmon, Roger Vadim, Michael Caine, James Stewart, and Gene Kelly, he spends most of the evening locked in NBC shoptalk with Fred de Cordova. De Cordova has just returned from his European safari, which has taken him through four countries in half as many weeks. The high point of the trip, de Cordova tells me, was a visit to Munich, where his old friend Billy Wilder was making a film. This brings to mind a recent conversation I had with Wilder in this very living room. He is a master of acerbic put-downs who has little time for TV pseudostars, and when I mentioned the name of Carson I expected Wilder to dismiss him with a mordant one-liner. What he actually said surprised me. It evolved in the form of a speech. "By the simple law of survival, Carson is the best," he said. "He enchants the invalids and the insomniacs as well as the people who have to get up at dawn. He is the Valium and the Nembutal of a nation. No matter what kind of dead-asses are on the show, he has to make them funny and exciting. He has to be their nurse and their surgeon. He has no conceit. He does his work and he comes prepared. If he's talking to an author, he has read the book. Even his rehearsed routines sound improvised. He's the cream of middle-class elegance, yet he's not a mannequin. He has captivated the American bourgeoisie without ever offending the highbrows, and he has never said anything that wasn't liberal or progressive. Every night, in front of millions of people, he has to do the *salto mortale*"—circus parlance for an aerial somersault performed on the tightrope. "What's more"—and here Wilder leaned forward, tapping my knee for emphasis—"he does it without a net. No rewrites. No retakes. The jokes must work tonight."

Since a good deal of what follows consists of excerpts from the journal of a Carson-watcher, I feel bound to declare a financial interest, and to admit that I have derived pecuniary benefit from his activities. During the nineteen-sixties, I was twice interviewed on the "Tonight Show." For each appearance I received three hundred and twenty dollars, which was then the minimum payment authorized by AFTRA, the TV and radio performers' union. (The figure has since risen to four hundred and twenty-seven dollars.) No guest on the show, even if he or she does a solo spot in addition to just chatting, is paid more than the basement-level fee. On two vertiginous occasions, therefore, my earning power has equalled that of Frank Sinatra, who in November, 1976, occupied the hot seat on Carson's right for the first time. (A strange and revealing encounter, to which we'll return.) Actually, "hot" is a misnomer. To judge from my own experience, "glacial" would be nearer the mark. The other talk shows in which I have taken part were all saunas by comparison with Carson's. Merv Griffin is the most disarming of ego strokers; Mike Douglas runs him a close second in the ingratiation stakes; and Dick Cavett creates the illusion that *he* is *your* guest, enjoying a slightly subversive private chat. Carson, on the other hand, operates on a level of high, freewheeling, centrifugal banter that is well above the snow line. Which is not to say that he is hostile. Carson treats you with deference and genuine curiosity. But the air is chill; you are definitely on probation.

Mort Sahl, who was last seen on the "Tonight Show" in 1968, described to me not long ago what happens when a guest fails to deliver the goods. "The producer is crouching just off camera," he said, "and he holds up a card that says, 'Go to commercial.' So Carson goes to a commercial, and the whole team rushes up to his desk to discuss what went wrong. It's like a pit stop at Le Mans. Then the next guest comes in, and— I promise you this is true—she's a girl who says straight out that she's a practicing lesbian. The card goes up again, only this time it means, 'Come in at once, your right rear wheel is on fire.' So we go to another commercial. . . ." Sahl is one of the few performers who is willing to be quoted in dispraise of Carson. Except for a handful of really big names, people in show business need Carson more than he needs them; they hate to jeopardize their chance of appearing on the program that pays greater dividends in publicity than any other. "Carson's assumption is that the audience is dumb, so you mustn't do difficult things," Sahl continued. "He never takes serious risks. His staff will only book people who'll make him look artistically potent. They won't give him anyone who'll take him for fifteen rounds. The whole operation has got lazy."

When an interviewer from *Playboy* asked Robert Blake whether he enjoyed doing the "Tonight Show," he gave a vivid account of how it feels to face Carson. He began by confessing that "there's a certain enjoyment in facing death, periodically." He went on:

There's no experience I can describe to you that would compare with doin' the "Tonight Show" when *he's* on it. It is so weird, and so hyped, and so up. It's like Broadway on opening night. There's nothing casual about it. And it's not a talk show. It's some other kind of show. I mean, he has such energy, you got like six minutes to do your thing. . . . And you better be good. Or they'll go to the commercial after two minutes. . . . They are highly professional, highly successful, highly dedicated people. . . . The producer, all the *federales* are sittin' like six feet away from that couch. And they're right on top of you, man, just watchin' ya. And when they go to a break, they get on the phone. They talk upstairs, they talk to—Christ, who knows? They talk all over the place about how this person's going over, how that person's going over. They whisper in John's ear. John gets on the phone and he talks. And you're sittin' there watchin', thinkin', What, are they gonna hang somebody?... And then the camera comes back again. And John will ask you somethin' else or he'll say, "Our next guest is..."

Carson's office suite at Burbank is above the studio in which, between 5:30 and 7 P.M., the show is taped. Except for his secretary, the rest of the production team occupies a crowded bungalow more than two hundred yards away, outside the main building. "In the past couple of months," a receptionist in the bungalow said to me not long ago, "I've seen Mr. Carson in here just once." Thus the king keeps his distance—not merely from his colleagues but from his guests, with whom he never fraternizes either before or after the taping. Or hardly ever: he may decide, if a major celebrity is on hand, to bend the rule and grant him or her the supreme privilege of prior contact. But such occasions are rare. As Orson Welles said to me, "he's the only invisible talk host." A Carson guest of long standing, Welles continued, "Once before the show, he put his head into my dressing room and said hello. The effect was cataclysmic. The production staff behaved the way the stage-hands did at the St. James's Theatre in London twenty-five years ago when Princess Margaret came backstage to visit me. They were in awe! One of Carson's people stared at me and said, 'He actually came to *see* you!'" (Gust of Wellesian laughter.) Newcomers like me are interviewed several days in advance by one of Carson's "talent coordinators," who makes a list of the subjects on which you are likely to be eloquent or funny. This list is in Carson's head as you plunge through the rainbow-hued curtains, take a sharp right turn, and just avoid tripping over the cunningly placed step that leads up to the desk where you meet, for the first time, your host, interrogator, and judge. The studio is his native habitat. Like a character in a Harold Pinter play, or any living creature in a Robert Ardrey book, you have invaded his territory. Once you are on Carson's turf, the onus is on you to demonstrate your right to stay there; if you fail, you will decorously get the boot. You feel like the tourist who on entering the Uffizi Gallery, in Florence, was greeted by a guide with the minatory remark, "Remember, Signore, that here it is not the pictures that are on trial." Other talk hosts flatter their visitors with artificial guffaws; Carson laughs only when he is amused. All I recall of my first exposure to the Carson ordeal is that (a) I had come to discuss a controversial play about Winston Churchill, (b) the act I had to follow was the TV debut of Tiny Tim, who sang "Tip Toe Through the Tulips," (c) Carson froze my marrow by suddenly asking my opinion not of Churchill, but of General de Gaulle, and (d) from that moment on, fear robbed me of saliva, so that my lips clove to my gums, rendering coherent speech impossible. The fault was mine, for not being the sort of person who can rise to Carson's challenge—i.e., a professional performer. There is abundant evidence that comedians, when they are spurred by Carson, take off and fly as they cannot in any other company. David Brenner, who has been a regular Carson guest since 1971, speaks for many young entertainers when he says, "Nowhere is where I'd be without the 'Tonight Show.' It's a necessary ingredient. . . . TV excels in two areas—sports and Carson. The show made my career."

October 1, 1977, marked Carson's fifteenth anniversary as the star of a program he recently called "NBC's answer to foreplay." For purposes of comparison, it may be noted that Steve Allen, who was the show's host when it was launched, in September, 1954, lasted only two years and four months. The mercurial and thin-skinned Jack (Slugger) Paar took over from Allen in the summer of 1957, after a six-month interregnum during which doomed attempts were made to turn the "Tonight Show" into a nocturnal TV magazine, held together by live contributions from journalists in New York, Chicago, and Los Angeles. Paar's tenure of office seems in retrospect longer than it was, perhaps because of the emotional outbursts that kept his name constantly in the headlines; it actually ended after four years and eight months. On March 29, 1962, having resigned for positively the last time, he took his final bow on the program, his face a cascade of tears. *"Après le déluge, moi"* is the thought that should have passed through Carson's mind, though there is no evidence that it did. He was then in his fifth year as m.c. of "Who Do You Trust?" an ABC quiz show that had become, largely because of his verbal dexterity, the hottest item on daytime television. A few months before Paar's farewell, Carson had turned down a firm offer from

NBC to replace its top banana. The gulf between chatting with unknown contestants for half an hour every afternoon and matching wits with celebrities for what was then an hour and forty-five minutes every night seemed unnervingly wide, and he doubted his ability to bridge it. However, when the job had been rejected by a number of possible candidates—among them Bob Newhart, Jackie Gleason, Joey Bishop, and Groucho Marx—either because they wanted too much money or because they were chary of following Paar, NBC came back in desperation to Carson. This time, he asked for two weeks to consider the proposition. Coolly, he weighed the size of his talent against the size of his ambition, decided that the scales approximately balanced, and told NBC that his answer was yes. The only snag was that his contract with ABC did not run out until September. Undismayed, NBC agreed to keep the "Tonight Show" supplied with guest hosts (they included Merv Griffin, Mort Sahl, and Groucho) throughout the summer. On October 1, 1962, Carson took command. His announcer and second banana, transplanted from "Who Do You Trust?" was Ed McMahon, who was already in great demand as the owner of the most robust and contagious laugh in television. The guests were Rudy Vallee, Tony Bennett, Mel Brooks (then a mere comedy writer, though he nowadays insists that he gave a dazzling impersonation of Fred Astaire on that October evening), and Joan Crawford.

Any qualms that NBC may have had about its new acquisition were soon allayed. Star performers lined up to appear with Carson. Even his fellow comedians, a notoriously paranoid species, found that working with him was a stimulus rather than a threat. "He loves it when you score," Woody Allen said, "and he's witty enough to score himself." Mel Brooks has explained to me, "From the word go, Carson could tell when you'd hit comic gold, and he'd help you to mine it. He always knew pay dirt when he saw it. The guys on the other talk shows didn't." There were one or two dissenters. Jackie Mason enjoyed his first session with Carson but reported that during his second appearance he was treated with "undisguised alienation and contempt," and went on to say, "I'd never go back again, even if he asked me." The press reaction to Carson was enthusiastic, except for a blast of puritanism from

John Horn of the *Herald Tribune*, who wrote of Carson, "He exhibits all the charm of a snickering small boy scribbling graffiti on a public wall." He added, in one of those phrases that return to haunt critics in their declining years, that Carson had "no apparent gift for the performing arts."

With the public, Carson's triumph was immediate and nonpareil. Under the Paar regime, the show had very seldom been seen by more than seven and a half million viewers. (One such occasion was March 7, 1960, when the unruly star came back to his post after walking out in a fit of pique, brought on by the network's decision to delete a mildly scatological joke and protracted for several well-publicized weeks.) Under Carson, the program *averaged* seven million four hundred and fifty-eight thousand viewers per night during its first six months. The comparable figure for the same period in 1971–72 was eleven million four hundred and forty-one thousand, and it is currently being seen by seventeen million three hundred thousand. Over fifteen years, therefore, Carson has more than doubled his audience—a feat that, in its blend of staying power and mounting popularity, is without precedent in the history of television. (Between April and September, the numbers dip, but this reflects a seasonal pattern by which all TV shows are affected. A top NBC executive explained to me, with heartless candor, "People who can afford vacations go away in the summer. It's only the poor people who watch us all the year round.") By network standards, the ultimate test is not so much the size of the audience as the share it represents of the total viewing public in the show's time slot. Here, after some early ups and downs, the Carson trend has been consistently upward; for example, from twenty-eight percent in the third quarter of 1976 to thirty percent in the second quarter of 1977. Moreover, his percentage seems to rise with the temperature; for example, in the four weeks that ended on July 15, 1977—a period during which guest hosts frequently stood in for Carson, whose absence from the show normally cuts the audience by about one-sixth—NBC chalked up thirty-two percent of the late-night viewers, against twenty-four percent registered by CBS and twenty-three percent by ABC. These, of course, are national figures. The happiness of Fred de Cordova, as producer, is incomplete unless Carson not only leads the field nationwide but beats the combined opposition (ABC plus CBS) in the big cities, especially New York and Los Angeles. He is seldom unhappy for long. On peak nights, when Carson rakes in a percentage of fifty or more from the key urban centers, de Cordova is said to emit an unearthly glow, visible clear across the Burbank parking lot.

For his first year on the show, making five appearances per week, Carson was paid just over a hundred thousand dollars. His present contract (the latest of many), which comes into force this spring, guarantees him an annual salary of two and a half million dollars. For twenty-five weeks of the year his performances, which were long since reduced from five to four, will further dwindle, to three; and his vacation period will stay at fifteen weeks—its duration under several previous contracts. These details, which were announced by NBC last December, leave no doubt that Carson qualifies for admission to what the late Lucius Beebe called "the mink-dust-cloth set." Whether they tell the whole story is less certain. Carson's earlier agreements with NBC contained clauses that both parties were forbidden to disclose, reportedly relating to such additional rewards as large holdings in RCA stock and a million-dollar life-insurance policy at the network's expense. Concerning Carson's total earnings, I cannot do better than quote from one of his employers, who told me, months before the new contract was signed, "If someone were to say in print that Johnny takes home around four million a year, I doubt whether anyone at NBC would feel an overpowering urge to issue a statement denying it." And even this figure excludes the vast amounts he makes from appearances at resort centers—preeminently Las Vegas—and from Johnny Carson Apparel, Inc., a thriving menswear business, founded in 1970, whose products he models on the show. David Tebet, the senior vice-president of NBC, who is revered in the trade as a finder, keeper, and cosseter of talent, and is described in his publicity handout as being "solely in charge of the Johnny Carson show," said to me recently, "For the past four or five years, Johnny has made more money per annum than any other television performer ever has. And he has also made more money per *week* than anyone else—except, maybe, for a very rare case like Sinatra, where you can't be sure, because Sinatra will sell you a special through his own company and you don't know how much he's personally taking out of the deal." Despite the high cost of Carson, he remains a bargain. The network's yearly income from the show is at present between fifty and sixty million dollars. "As a money-maker," de Cordova says, "there's nothing in television close to it." In 1975, a sixty-second commercial on the program cost twenty-six thousand dollars. In 1977, that sum had risen by half.

I dwell on these statistics because they are unique in show business. Yet there is a weird disproportion between the facts and figures of Carson's success and the kind of fame he enjoys. To illustrate what I mean, let me cite a few analogies. Star tennis players are renowned in every country on earth outside China, and the same is true of top heavyweight boxers. (A probable exception in the latter category is Muhammad Ali, who must surely be known inside China as well.) At least fifty living cricketers are household names throughout the United Kingdom, the West Indies, Australia, South Africa, India, and Pakistan. Movie stars and pop singers command international celebrity; and Kojak, Starksy, Hutch, Columbo, and dozens more are acclaimed (or, at any rate, recognized) wherever the TV programs that bear their names are bought and transmitted. Outside North America, by contrast, Johnny Carson is a non-entity: the general public has never heard of him. The reason for his obscurity is that the job at which he excels is virtually unexportable. (O. J. Simpson is a parallel case, illustrious at home and *nada* abroad; and if the empire of baseball had not reached out and annexed Japan, Reggie Jackson would be in the same plight.) The TV talk show as it is practiced by Carson is topical in subject matter and local in appeal. To watch it is like dropping in on a nightly family party, a conversational serial, full of private jokes, in which a relatively small and regularly rotated cast of characters, drawn mainly from show business, turn up to air their egos, but which has absolutely no plot. Sometimes the visitors sing. Sometimes, though less often nowadays than in the past, they are people of such world-wide distinction that their slightest hiccup is riveting. But otherwise most of what happens on the show would be incomprehensible or irrelevant to foreign audiences, even if they were English-speaking. This drives yet another nail into the coffin lid, already well-hammered down, of Marshall Mc-Luhan's theory that TV has transformed the world into a global village. (Radio is, as it has long been, the only medium that gives us immediate access to what the rest of the planet is doing and thinking, simply because every country of any size operates a foreign-language service.) Only for such events as moon landings and Olympiads does TV provide live coverage that spans the globe. The rest of the time, it is obstinately provincial, addressing itself to a village no bigger than a nation. Carson, in his own way, is what Gertrude Stein called Ezra Pound—a village explainer.

He has spent almost all of his life confined, like his fame, to his country of origin. He served in the Navy for three years, beginning in 1943, and was shipped as far west as Guam. Thereafter, his travels abroad indicate no overwhelming curiosity about the world outside his homeland. Apart from brief vacations in Mexico, and a flying visit to London in 1961, when he appeared in a TV special starring Paul Anka, he has left the United States only on three trips: in 1975, to the ultrasmart Hotel du Cap in Antibes (at the instigation of his wife, Joanna, who had been there before); in 1976, to see the tennis at Wimbledon; and in 1977, when he threw caution to the winds and went to both Wimbledon *and* the Hotel du Cap. He was recognized in neither place, except by a handful of fellow-Americans. This, of course, was the purpose of the exercise. Carson goes to foreign parts for the solace of anonymity. But enough is enough: he is soon impatient to return to the cavernous Burbank Studio, where his personality burgeons in high definition, and where he publicly discloses as much of his private self as he has ever revealed to anyone, except (I assume, though even here I would not care to bet) his parents, siblings, sons, and wives.

"Johnny Carson on TV," one of his colleagues confided to me, "is the visible eighth of an iceberg called Johnny Carson." The remark took me back to something that Carson said of himself ten years ago, when, in the course of a question-and-answer session with viewers, he was asked, "What made you a star?" He replied, "I started out in a gaseous state, and then I cooled." Meeting him tête-à-tête is, as we shall see later, a curious experience. In 1966, writing for *Look*, Betty Rollin described Carson off camera as "testy, defensive, preoccupied, withdrawn, and wondrously inept and uncomfortable with people." Nowadays, his off-camera manner is friendly and impeccably diplomatic. Even so, you get the impression that you are addressing an elaborately wired security system. If the conversation edges toward areas in which he feels ill at ease or unwilling to commit himself, burglar alarms are triggered off, defensive reflexes rise around him like an invisible stockade, and you hear the distant baying of guard dogs. In addition to his childhood, his private life, and his income, these no-trespassing zones include all subjects of political controversy, any form of sexual behavior uncountenanced by the law, and such matters of social concern as abortion and the legalization of marijuana. His smile as he steers you away from forbidden territory is genial and unfading. It is only fair to remember that he does not pretend to be a pundit, employed to express his own opinions; rather, he is a professional explorer of other people's egos. In a magazine article that was published with annotations by Carson, Fred de Cordova wrote, "He's reluctant to talk much about himself because he is essentially a private person." To this Carson added a marginal gloss, intended as a gag, that had an eerie ring of truth: "I will not even talk to myself without an appointment." He has asked all the questions and knows all the evasive, equivocal answers. When he first signed to appear on the "Tonight Show," he was quizzed by the press so relentlessly that he refused after a while to submit to further interrogation. Instead, he issued a list of replies that journalists could append to any questions of their choice:

1. Yes, I did.
2. Not a bit of truth in that rumor.
3. Only twice in my life, both times on Saturday.
4. I can do either, but I prefer the first.
5. No. Kumquats.
6. I can't answer that question.
7. Toads and tarantulas.
8. Turkestan, Denmark, Chile, and the Komandorskie Islands.
9. As often as possible, but I'm not very good at it yet. I need much more practice.

10. It happened to some old friends of mine, and it's a story I'll never forget.

Extract from Carson-watching journal, January, 1976:

There is such a thing as the pleasure of the expected. Opening routine of "Tonight Show" provides it; millions would feel cheated if the ceremony were changed. The close shot of Big Ed McMahon as his unctuous baritone takes off on its steeply ascending glissando "Heeeeeeeere's Johnny." Stagehands create gap in curtain. Carson enters in his ritual Apparel, style of which is Casual Square. Typical outfit: checked sports coat with two vents, tan trousers, pale-blue shirt with neat but ungaudy tie. Not for him the blue-jeaned, open-necked, safari-jacketed Hollywood ensemble: that would be too Casual, too Californian. On the other hand, no dark suits with vests: that would be too Square, too Eastern Seaboard. Carson must reflect what de Cordova possessively calls "our bread-basket belt"— the Midwest, which bore him (on October 23, 1925, in Corning, Iowa), and which he must never bore.

On his lips as he walks toward applauding audience is the only unassuming smirk in show business. He halts and swivels to the right (upper part of body turning as rigid vertical unit, like that of man in plaster cast) to acknowledge Big Ed's traditional act of obeisance, a quasi-Hindu bow with fingertips reverently joined. Then the leftward rotation, to accept homage from Doc Severinsen—lead trumpet and musical director, hieratically clad in something skintight and ragingly vulgar—which takes more bizarrely Oriental form: the head humbly bowed while the hands orbit each other. Music stops; applause persists. In no hurry, Carson lets it ride, facially responding to every nuance of audience behavior; e.g., shouts of greeting, cries of "Hi-yo." When the ecstasy subsides, the exordium is over, and Carson begins the monologue, or address to the faithful, which must contain (according to one of his writers) between sixteen and twenty-two sure-fire jokes.

Tone of monologue is skeptical, tongue-in-cheek, ironic. Manner: totally relaxed, hitting bull's-eyes without seeming to take aim, TV's embodiment of *Zen in the Art of Archery*. In words uttered to me by the late screenwriter Nunnally Johnson, "Carson has a delivery like a Winchester rifle." Theme:

implicitly liberal, but careful to avoid the stigma of leftism. The unexpected impromptus with which he rescues himself from gags that bomb, thereby plucking triumph from disaster, are also part of the expected pleasure. "When it comes to saving a bad line, he is the master"—to quote a tribute paid in my presence by George Burns. Carson registers a gag's impact with instant, seismographical finesse. If the laugh is five percent less than he counted on, he notes the failure and reacts to it ("Did they clear the hall? Did they have a drill?") before any critic could, usually garnering a double-strength guffaw as reward. Whatever spoils a line—ambiguous phrasing, botched timing, faulty enunciation—he is the first to expose it. Nobody spots flaws in his own work more swiftly than Carson, or capitalizes on them more effectively. Query: Is this becoming a dangerous expertise? In other words, out from under how many collapsed jokes can you successfully climb?

This evening's main attraction is Don (The Enforcer) Rickles, not so much the court jester of TV as the court hit man. Carson can cope superbly with garrulous guests who tell interminable stories (whether ponderously, owing to drink or downers, or manically, owing to uppers or illicit inhalations). Instead of quickly changing the subject, as many hosts would, he slaughters the offenders with pure politesse. Often, he will give them enough rope to hang themselves, allowing them to ramble on while he affects attentive interest. Now and then, however, he will let the camera catch him in the act of half-stifling a yawn, or raising a baffled eyebrow, or aiming straight at the lens a stare of frozen, I-think-I-am-going-mad incredulity. He prevents us from being bored by making his own boredom funny—a daring feat of comic one-upmanship. The way in which he uses the camera as a silent conspirator is probably Carson's most original contribution to TV technique. There is a lens permanently trained on him alone—a private pipeline through which he transmits visual asides directly to the viewer, who thus becomes his flattered accomplice. Once, talking to me on a somewhat tattered theme, the difference between stage and screen acting, Paul Newman made a remark that seemed obvious at the time but grows in wisdom the more I ponder it. "On the stage, you have to seek the focus of the audience," he said. "In movies, it's given to you by the camera." Among the marks of a star on television, as in the cinema, is his or her ability to grasp this truth and act on it. Seek, and you shall not find; grab, and it shall not be given unto you. Carson learned these rules early and is now their master practitioner.

Even the best-planned talk shows, however, run into doldrums; e.g., the guest who suffers from incontinent sycophancy, or whose third marriage has brought into his life a new sense of wonder plus three gratingly cute anecdotes about the joys of paternity, or who is a British comedian on his first, tongue-tied trip to the States, or whose conversational range is confined to plugging an upcoming appearance at Lake Tahoe. On such occasions, the ideal solution is: Bring on Rickles, king of icebreakers, whose chosen weapon is the verbal hand grenade. Rickles is an unrivalled catalyst (though I can already hear him roaring, "What do you mean, I'm a catalyst? I'm a Jew!"). Squatly built, rather less bald than Mussolini, his bulbous face running the gamut from jovial contempt to outright nausea, he looks like an extra in a crowd scene by Hieronymus Bosch. No one is immune from his misanthropy; he exudes his venom at host and guests alike. In a medium ruled by the censorious Superego, Rickles is the unchained Id. At his best, he breaks through the bad-taste barrier into a world of sheer outrage where no forbidden thought goes unspoken and where everything spoken is anarchically liberating. More deftly than anyone else, Carson knows how to play matador to Rickle's bull, inciting him to charge, and sometimes getting gored himself. At one point during this program, Rickles interrupts a question from Carson with an authentic conversation-stopper. "Your left eye is dancing!" he bellows, leaning forward and pointing a stubby finger. "That means you're self-conscious. Ever since you stopped drinking, your left eye dances." Even Carson is momentarily silenced. (I did not fully understand why until, at a subsequent meeting, Carson told me that there was one symptom by which he could infallibly recognize a guest who was on the brink of collapse, whether from fear, stimulants, or physical exhaustion. He called it "the dancing-eyeball syndrome." A famous example from the early nineteen-sixties: Peter O'Toole appeared on the show after forty-eight sleepless hours, spent filming and flying, and could not utter

a coherent sentence. Carson ushered him offstage during the
first commercial. "The moment he sat down, I could see his
eyeballs were twitching," Carson said to me. "I recognized the
syndrome at once. He was going to bomb.")

Testimony of a Carson colleague:
My witness is Pat McCormick, who has been supplying
Carson with material on and off for eighteen years and was a
staff writer on the show from 1972 to 1977. Regarded as one
of the most inventive gagmen in the business, he has also
worked for Red Skelton, Danny Kaye, and others of note.
McCormick, at forty-seven, is a burly, diffident man with hair
of many colors: a reddish thatch on top, a gray mustache, and
patches of various intermediate tints sprouting elsewhere on
his head and face. Suitably resprayed, he might resemble a
cross between Teddy Roosevelt and Zero Mostel. I have it on
Ed McMahon's authority that McCormick takes the occasional
drink, and that he once turned up at a script conference declaring, "I have lost my car, but I have tire marks on my
hands." He gives me his account of a typical day on the "Tonight Show." "The writers—there are usually five of us—arrive
at the studio around 9:30 A.M.," he says. "We've read the
morning papers and the latest magazines. Once a week, we all
get together for an ideas meeting, but most days we work
separately, starting out with the monologue. I tend to specialize
in fairly weird, uninhibited stuff. Johnny enjoys that kind of
thing, and I just let it pour out. Like a line I came up with not
long ago: 'If you want to clear your system out, sit on a piece
of cheese and swallow a mouse.' Johnny finds his own ways
of handling bum gags. When he's in a bad situation, I always
wonder how the hell he'll get out of it, and he always surprises
me."

Always? I remind McCormick of an occasion two days
earlier, when a series of jokes had died like flies, and Carson
had got a situation-saving laugh by remarking, "I now believe
in reincarnation. Tonight's monologue is going to come back
as a dog." That sounded to me like *echt* McCormick.

With a blush matching some of his hair, he admits to au-
thorship of the line. He continues. "All the monologue material
has to be on Johnny's desk by three o'clock. He makes the

final selection himself. One of his rules is: Never tell three jokes running on the same subject. And, of course, he adds ideas of his own. He's a darned good comedy writer, you know."

One sometimes detects a vindictive glint in Carson's eye when a number of gags sink without risible trace, but McCormick assures me that this is all part of the act and causes no outbreaks of cold sweat among the writing team. "After the monologue," he goes on, "we work on the desk spot with Ed McMahon, which comes next in the show, or on sketches that need polishing, or on material for one of Johnny's characters."

Accustomed to thinking of Carson the host, we forget the range of Carson the actor-comedian. His current incarnations include the talkative crone Aunt Blabby (Whistler's mother on speed); the bungling turbanned clairvoyant named Carnac the Magnificent; Art Fern, described by McCormick as "the matinee-movie m.c. with patent-leather hair who'll sell *anything*"; and—a new acquisition—Floyd Turbo, the man in the red shirt who speaks for the silent majority, rebutting liberal editorials with a vehemence perceptibly impaired by his inability to read from a TelePrompTer at more than dictation speed. Fans will recall Turbo's halting diatribe against the antigun lobby: "If God didn't want man to hunt, he wouldn't have given us plaid shirts. . . . I only kill in self-defense. What would *you* do if a rabbit pulled a knife on you? . . . Always remember: you can get more with a smile and a gun than you can with just a smile."

Everything for the evening's show must be rehearsed and ready for taping by five-thirty, apart from the central, imponderable element, on which all else depends: Carson's handling of the guests. Briefed by his aides, he knows the visitors' backgrounds, recent achievements, and immediate plans, and during the commercials he will listen to tactical suggestions from confreres like Fred de Cordova; but when the tape is running, he is the field commander, and his intuitions dictate the course of events. As he awaits his entrance cue, he is entitled to reflect, like Henry V on a more earthshaking occasion, "The day, my friends, and all things stay for me." McCormick, who now and then appears as a guest on the show, has this to say of Carson the interviewer: "He leans right in and goes with you, instead of leaning back and worrying about what the viewers are thinking. He never patronizes you or shows off at your expense. If you're getting a few pockets of laughter from the studio audience, he'll encourage you and feed you. He's an ideal straight man as well as a first-rate comedian, and that's a unique combination. Above all, there's a strand of his personality that is quite wild. He can do good bread-and-butter comedy any day of the week—like his Vegas routines or his banquet speeches—but he has this crazy streak that keeps coming through on the show, and when it does it's infectious. You feel anything could happen."

Example of Carson when the spirit of pure, eccentric play descends upon him and he obeys its bidding, wherever it may lead: During the monologue on May 11, 1977, he finds, as sometimes happens, that certain words are emerging from his mouth in slightly garbled form. He wrinkles his brow in mock alarm, shrugs, and presses on to the next sentence: "*Yetserday*, U.S. Steel announced..." He pauses, realizing what he has said, turns quizzically to McMahon, and observes, "'Yesterday' is not a hard word to say." Facing the camera again, he goes on, "Yesterday—all my troubles seemed so far away..." Only now he is *singing*—singing, unaccompanied, the celebrated standard by John Lennon and Paul McCartney: "Now it looks as though they're here to stay. Oh, I believe in yesterday." By this time, the band, which was clearly taken by surprise, has begun to join in, at first raggedly, but soon improvising a respectable accompaniment. Warming to his berserk task, Carson does not stop until he has reached the end of the chorus. He resumes the monologue: "Now, what was I talking about? Oh, yes. Yesterday..." But no sooner has the word passed his lips than Doc's combo, determined not to let him off the hook, strikes up the melody again. Undaunted, Carson plunges into the second chorus. Having completed it, he silences the musicians with a karate chop. There is loud applause, followed by an extended pause. Where can he go from here? Cautiously feeling his way, he continues, "*About twelve hours ago*, U.S. Steel announced..." And successfully finishes the gag. Everyone in the studio is laughing, not so much at the joke as the sight of Carson on the wing. Grinning, he addresses McMahon.

CARSON: That's what makes this job what it is.
McMAHON: What is it?
CARSON (*frowning, genuinely puzzled*): I don't know.

McCormick on Carson the private man: "Don't believe those iceberg stories. Once, when I was going through a bad divorce and feeling pretty low, I was eating alone in a restaurant and Johnny came in with a bunch of people. I'm not one of his intimate friends, but as soon as he saw me he left his guests and sat with me for more than half an hour, giving me all kinds of comfort and advice."

Further notes of a Carson-watcher (random samplings from October and November, 1976):

Where other performers go home to relax after the show, Carson goes to the show to relax. The studio is his den, his living space—the equivalent in the show-business world of an exclusive salon in the world of literature. He instantly reacts to any untoward off-camera occurrence—a script inadvertently dropped, a guitar string accidently plucked, a sneeze from a far corner of the room—as most of us would react to comparably abnormal events in the privacy of our homes. *Mutatis* very much *mutandis*, the show could be seen as a TV version of "The Conning Tower," Franklin P. Adams's famous column in the *Tribune*, which was launched in 1914 and consisted mainly of anecdotes, aphorisms, and verses contributed by F.P.A.'s friends and correspondents. "The Conning Tower," like the "Tonight Show," was a testing ground for new talents, and many of the people it introduced to the public went on to become celebrities.

October 1: Traditional two-hour retrospective to mark the fourteenth anniversary of Carson's enthronement as NBC's emperor of causerie. Choice of material is limited to the period since 1970, for, with self-destructive improvidence, the company erased all the earlier Carson tapes, including Barbra Streisand's first appearance as his guest and Judy Garland's last. Host's debonair entry is hailed with fifty-second ovation, which sounds unforced. I note the digital mannerisms (befitting one who began his career as a conjurer) that he uses to hold our attention during his patter. The right index finger is particularly active, now stabbing downward as if pressing computer buttons, now rising to flick at his ear, to tickle or scratch one side of his nose: constantly in motion, never letting our eyes wander. Thus he stresses and punctuates the gags, backed always by Big Ed's antiphonal laughter.

Well-loved bits are rerun. The portly comic Dom DeLuise attempts a feat of legerdemain in which three eggs are at risk, and carries it off without breakage. But the sight of unbroken eggs—and others on standby—provokes Carson to a spell of riot. He tosses the original trio at DeLuise, who adroitly juggles with them and throws them back; Carson retaliates with more eggs, aiming a few at McMahon for good measure. Before long, in classic slapstick style, he has expressionlessly cracked an egg over DeLuise's head and dropped another inside the front of his trousers, smashing it as it falls with a kindly pat on the belly. "You're insane." the victim cries. "You guys are bananas!" He gives Carson the same treatment; McMahon joins in; and by the end, the floor and the three combatants are awash with what Falstaff would have called "pullet sperm." Looking back on the clip, Carson puckishly observes, "There's something about eggs. I went ape." The whole impromptu outburst would not have been funny it if had been initiated by someone like Buddy Hackett; it worked because of its incongruity with Carson's persona—that of a well-nurtured midwestern lad, playful but not vulgar. ("Even though he's over fifty," Fred de Cordova once said to me, "there's a Peck's Bad Boy quality that works for Johnny, never against him.")

Other oddities from the program's past: Carson diving onto a mattress from a height of twenty feet; splitting a block of wood with his head on instructions from a karate champion; tangling with a sumo wrestler; cuddling a cheetah cub; permitting a tarantula to crawl up his sleeve. We also see Carson confronted by guests with peculiar skills—the bird mimic whose big items are the mallard in distress and the cry of the loon, for instance, and the obsessive specialist whose act (one of the most memorable stunts ever recorded in a single take) consists of seven thousand dominoes arranged on end in a convoluted, interwoven pattern, involving ramps and tunnels, so that the first, when it is pushed, sets off a chain reaction that fells the remaining six thousand nine hundred and ninety-nine, which spell out—among other things—the DNA symbol and Carson's name. In addition, we get the parody of "Dragnet," that triumph of alliterative tongue-twisting in which Jack Webb, investigating the theft of a school bell, sombrely elicits from Carson the information that kleptomaniac Claude Cooper copped the clean copper clappers kept in the clothes closet. Best of all are the snippets from Carson's interviews with people aged ninety and upward, whom he addresses as exact equals, with care and without condescension, never patronizing them, and never afraid to laugh when they get a sentence back to front or forget the punch line of a joke; one such encounter is with a woman of a hundred and three years, who is still a licensed driver. (Paul Morrisey, the movie director, who is watching the program with me, remarks, "Nobody else on TV treats old people with the perfect tact and affection of Carson. He must have a very loving relationship with his parents.") An NBC spokesman chips in with a resounding but meretricious statistic. The Carson show, he says, has already been seen by more than four times the population of our planet. This presumably means that one person who has watched the program a hundred times counts as a hundred people. Either that or NBC is laying claim to extraterrestrial viewers. The ratings war being what it is, anything is possible.

November 12: After days of spot announcements and years of coaxing by the network, Frank Sinatra makes his debut on the show. Received like visiting royalty, he gives the impression of swaggering even when seated. For once, the host seems uneasy, overawed, too ready to laugh. Don Rickles is hurried on unannounced to dissipate the atmosphere of obsequiousness, which he does by talking to the singer like Mafia subaltern reporting to Godfather; at least this is better than treating him as God. (I get memory flash of cable sent to me by Gore Vidal when he agreed to accept my younger daughter as godchild: "Always a godfather, never a god." For many people in entertainment business, Sinatra is both.) When conversation again falters, Rickles declares to world at large, "I'm a Jew, and he's an Italian, and *here*"—he thrusts at Carson a face contorted with distaste, like diner finding insect in soup—"*here* we have . . . *what*?" Rickles wraps up interview by saying that he truly admires Sinatra, because "he stimulates excitement, he

stimulates our industry, and"—fixing Carson with glare of
malign relish—"*he ... makes ... you ... nervous.*"

Not long afterward, Carson had his revenge. While acting
as guest host on the show, Rickles broke the cigarette box on
Carson's desk by striking it with his clenched fist when a gag
fell flat. The next night, Carson returned. As soon as he sat
down, he noticed the damage. "That's an heirloom," he said.
"I've had it for nine years." Informed that Rickles was the
culprit, he picked up the debris and rose, telling one of the
cameras to follow him. (None of this was rehearsed.) He then
left the "Tonight Show" studio, crossed the corridor outside,
and, ignoring the red warning lights, marched into the studio
opposite, where Rickles was at that moment halfway through
taping the next episode of his comedy series "CPO Sharkey."
Walking straight into the middle of a shot, Carson held out his
splintered treasure to Rickles and sternly demanded both res-
titution and an apology. The Enforcer was flabbergasted, as
were his supporting cast, his producer, and his director. Carson
was impenitent. "I really shook him," he said to me later with
quiet satisfaction. "He was speechless."

Testimony from the two NBC associates who are closest
to Carson:

These are Fred de Cordova and Ed McMahon. De Cordova,
who has been Carson's producer for the past seven years, talks
to me in the "Tonight Show" bungalow at Burbank. He is a
large, looming, beaming man with horn-rimmed glasses, an
Acapulcan tan, and an engulfing handshake that is a contract
in itself, complete with small print and an option for renewal
on both sides. Now in his mid-sixties, he looks like a cartoon
of a West Coast producer in his early fifties. His professional
record, dating back to 1933, is exceptional: Ten years in theatre
with the Shubert organization, followed by a decade making
movies in Hollywood. Thence into TV, where he worked
(directing and/or producing) with Burns and Allen, George
Gobel, Jack Benny, and the Smothers Brothers. In the magazine piece he wrote which appeared with notations by Carson,
he said he now had "the last great job in show business,"
because the Carson program was "spontaneous" and "instan-
taneous." He explained that it wasn't technically live, in that

taping preceded transmission; nevertheless, "practically speaking, we are the only continuing live show left." (For accuracy's sake, this phrase should be amended to read, "the only continuing nationwide nighttime quasi-live talk show left, apart from Merv Griffin's.") He went on to compare the program to a ballgame, played "in front of a jammed grandstand night after night." "To me," Carson noted in the margin, "it's like a salmon going up the Columbia River." Trying to define Carson's appeal, de Cordova wrote, "He's somebody's son, somebody's husband, somebody's father. He combines them all." Which sounds very impressive until you reflect that it applies to most of the adult male population. Carson circled this passage and made it slightly narrower in scope by adding to the first sentence, "and several people's ex-husband." De Cordova's most telling point, at which no one could cavil, came later in the article. "We have no laugh track," he said. "We're naked." In an age when canned hilarity has all but usurped the viewer's right to an autonomous sense of humor, it is reassuring to read a statement like that.

On the wall behind de Cordova's desk hangs a chart showing the lineup of guests for weeks, and even months, ahead. Perennial absentees, long sought, never snared, include Elton John and Robert Redford. When de Cordova is asked why the list is so sparsely dotted with people of much intellectual firepower, he reacts with bewilderment: "That just isn't true. We've had some of the finest minds I know—Carl Sagan, Paul Ehrlich, Margaret Mead, Gore Vidal, Shana Alexander, Madalyn Murray O'Hair." This odd aggregation of names sprang from the lips of many other "Tonight Show" employees to whom I put that question, almost as if they were contractually bound to commit it to memory. Nobody, however, denied that there have been few latter-day guests with the political weight of Nelson Rockefeller, Hubert Humphrey, and John and Robert Kennedy, all of whom appeared with Carson in his earlier years. De Cordova continues, "I've heard it said that Johnny is intimidated by witty, intellectual women. Well, just who *are* these women? Apart from people like Shana, who've had a lot of TV experience, they tend to freeze on camera. We've so often been fooled by witty cocktail talkers who simply didn't transfer to television." Carson, he points out, is no numbskull;

he reads extensively, with special emphasis on politics, and has more than an amateur knowledge of astronomy. Also of sports: "Ilie Nastase, Chris Evert, and Dwight Stones have all been very effective guests." But there are, he admits, certain categories of people who are unlikely to receive the summons to Burbank: "We don't have an official blacklist, but Johnny wouldn't have Linda Lovelace on the show, for example. Or anyone mixed up in a sexual scandal, like Elizabeth Ray. And no criminals, except reformed criminals—we turned down Clifford Irving, the guy who forged the Howard Hughes memoirs. Johnny prefers to look for noncelebrities who'll make human-interest stories. We subscribe to fifty-seven newspapers from small towns and cities all over the country, and that's where we find some of our best material." He goes on to say, "In the monologue, Johnny will attack malfeasance, illiberal behavior, constitutional abuses. But then compassion sets in. He was the first person to *stop* doing anti-Nixon jokes." (Ten years ago, Henry Morgan said of Carson, "He believes that justice is some kind of entity that is palpable. He talks about it as if he were talking about a chair.") Does the monologue suffer from network censorship? "The problem doesn't come up, because Johnny has an in-built sense of what his audience will take," de Cordova says. "He's the best self-editor I've ever known." This, as we shall see, was a somewhat disingenuous reply.

Lunch with the bulky, eternally clubbable McMahon in the Polo Lounge of the Beverly Hills Hotel. Born in Detroit, Big Ed is now in his midfifties, and has worked with Carson for two decades, including five years as his announcer on "Who Do You Trust?" NBC gives him eight weeks' annual vacation with full pay, and he makes a great deal of money on the side from nightclub appearances, real-estate investments, and commercials for a variety of products, chief among them beer and dog food. Even so, he is well aware that, as he says to me, "the 'Tonight Show' is my staple diet, my meat and potatoes—I'm realistic enough to know that everything else stems from that." In 1972, when the show moved from New York to Los Angeles, McMahon left his wife and four children, after twenty-seven years of marriage to go with it. (Divorce followed soon afterward; McMahon remarried in 1976.) He has known his place, and kept to it without visible resentment, since 1965, when the notorious Incident of the Insect Repellent showed him exactly where he stood. "Johnny was demonstrating an antimosquito spray," he says, "and just before using it he said he'd heard that mosquitoes only went for really passionate people. Acting on instinct, I stuck out my arm and slapped it. It wrecked Johnny's gag, and I had to apologize to him during the next break. That taught me never to go where he's going. I have to get my comedy in other areas. Before the show, I do the audience warmup, and even there I have to avoid any topical material he might be using in the monologue."

This being a show day, McMahon eats and drinks frugally (cold cuts and beer). Both he and Carson have drastically reduced their alcoholic intake over the past few years. On camera, Carson sips coffee and cream (no sugar), and McMahon makes do with iced tea. McMahon denies the rumor that Carson has become antisocial because of his abstinence: "If it's a big affair, you'll maybe find him in a corner, talking one to one, but in a small group he can be the life of the party, doing tricks, killing everybody." One of the unauthorized biographies of Carson contains a story about a surprise birthday party to which his second wife, Joanne, invited all his close friends. "There were about eight people there," an unnamed guest is quoted as saying, "and I think it was a shock to all of us." Pooh-poohing this yarn, McMahon counters by telling me about a surprise party he gave for Carson in 1962: "I built it up by pretending it was being held in his honor by *TV Guide* and he really had to go. He finally gave in. I said I'd drive him down there, and he began bitching as soon as he got in the car. So I suggested stopping off at my place for a preliminary drink, and he agreed. I'd arranged for the other cars to be parked out of sight, in case he recognized them. What happened was that he walked straight into the arms of about fifty friends and relatives who'd come from all over to see him. He had tears in his eyes. That was the first time I saw him touched."

Professionally, McMahon most enjoys the tête-à-tête at Carson's desk which follows the monologue: "Sometimes he develops a real resistance to bringing out the first guest. I see something goofy in his eyes. It means that he wants us to go on rapping together, so we play back and forth, getting wilder

and wilder, until maybe the guest has gone home and it's time
for the first commercial."

I read to him some remarks made by the columnist Rex
Reed, who described Carson as "the most over-rated amateur
since Evelyn and her magic violin" and continued, "The most
annoying thing about Carson is his unwillingness to swing, to
trust himself or his guests. . . . He never looks at you; he's too
busy (1) watching the audience to see if they are responding,
and (2) searching the face of his producer for reassurance."

McMahon finds these comments inexplicable. "Johnny can
get absolutely spellbound by his guests," he says. "You'll see
him lean his chin on his hand and really drink them in. And
as for that stuff about not swinging—did the guy ever watch
him with Tony Randall or Buck Henry or Orson Bean? He's
always going off into unplanned areas and uncharted places.
Other people have clipboards full of questions and use them
like crutches. Johnny never uses any. And he loves meeting
new comics and feeding them lines, the way he did with Steve
Martin and Rodney Dangerfield when hardly anyone had heard
of them. Naturally, he likes to get laughs himself. That's part
of the job. A few nights ago, Tony Bennett was on the show,
talking about his childhood and how his family hoped he'd
achieve fabulous things when he grew up. Johnny listened for
a long while and then said, quite deadpan, 'My parents wanted
me to be a sniper.' Another time, he asked Fernando Lamas
why he'd gone into movies, and Lamas said, 'Because it was
a great way to meet broads.' I loved Johnny's comeback. He
just nodded and said, 'Nietzsche couldn't have put it more
succinctly.' And, of course, there are the famous ad-libs that
everyone remembers, like when Mr. Universe was telling him
how important it was to keep fit—'Don't forget, Mr. Carson,
your body is the only home you'll ever have'—and Johnny
said, 'Yes, my home *is* pretty messy. But I have a woman who
comes in once a week.'" McMahon confirms my impression
that Carson was daunted by Sinatra. He adds, "And he's always
been a little bit overawed by Orson Welles. But there was one
time when we were both nervous. I came on as a guest to plug
a film I'd just made, and we had a rather edgy conversation.
When the interview was over, Johnny came out from behind
his desk to shake hands and revealed to the world that he had

no pants on. I was so anxious to get off that I didn't even notice." How long, I ask, will Carson stay with the show, "He'll still be there in 1980," says McMahon confidently.

The year 1977, for Carson-watchers, was one in which the "Tonight Show," while retaining all its sparkle and caprice, gained not an inch in intellectual stature. It is one thing to say, as Carson often does, that he is not a professional controversialist. It is quite another to avoid controversy altogether.

February 2: Appearance of Alex Haley to talk about *Roots*. (During the previous night's monologue, Carson used a curiously barbed phrase to account for the success of ABC's televised adaptation of Haley's best-seller. "Give the people what they want," he said. "Hatred, violence, and sex." It was difficult to tell whether the gibe was aimed at the rival network or at the book itself. One wondered, too, why he thought it amusing to add, "My great-great-great-great-grandfather was a runaway comedian from Bangladesh.") In 1967, when Haley was working for *Playboy*, he conducted a lengthy interview with Carson. In the course of it, Carson attacked the CIA for hiring students to compile secret reports on campus subversives, condemned "the kind of corporate espionage and financial hanky-panky that goes on in business," supported the newly insurgent blacks in demanding "equality for all," and said, "It's ludicrous to declare that it's wrong to have sex with anyone you're not married to." Moreover, he summed up the war in Vietnam as "stupid and pointless." He seldom voiced these opinions with much vehemence on the show. Ten years later, with the war safely over, he welcomed Jane Fonda as his guest and congratulated her on having lived to see her views on Vietnam fully justified by history. With considerable tact Ms. Fonda not only resisted the temptation to address her host as Johnny-come-lately, but refrained from reminding him that when she most needed a television outlet for her ideas the doors of the "Tonight Show" studio were closed to her.

To return to February 2: Haley takes the initiative by asking Carson how far back he can trace his own roots. He replies that he knows who his grandparents were, and was personally very close to his father's parents, both of whom survived into their nineties. Of his pedigree before that, he confesses total ignorance. Haley thereupon shakes him by producing a heavy, leather-bound volume with a golden inscription on the cover: "Roots of Johnny Carson—A Tribute to a Great American Entertainer." Haley has signed the flyleaf, "With warm best wishes to you and your family from the family of Kunta Kinte." Carson is obviously stirred. "I was tremendously moved that Alex had found time to do all this research in the middle of his success," he said to me afterward, and I learned from McMahon that this was only the second occasion on which he had seen the boss tearful. Although Haley was the instigator, the work was in fact carried out by the Institute of Family Research, in Salt Lake City. The people there first heard of the project on the evening of Saturday, January 29, when Haley called them up and told them that the finished book had to be ready for presentation to Carson in Los Angeles the following Wednesday. "That gave us two working days to do a job that would normally take us two months," a spokesman for the Institute told me. "What's more, we had to do it in absolute secrecy, without any access to the person involved." A task force of fifteen investigators toiling round the clock for forty-eight hours just managed to beat the deadline. The results of their labors—consisting of genealogical charts going back to the sixteenth century, biographical sketches of Carson's more prominent forebears, and anecdotes from the family's history—ran to more than four hundred pages. The gesture cost Haley (or his publishers) approximately five thousand dollars. Carson lent me the book, a massive quarry of data, from which I offer a few clippings:

(1) Earliest known Carson ancestor: Thomas Kellogg, on the paternal side of the family, born c. 1521 in the English village of Debdon, Essex. The first Kelloggs to cross the Atlantic were Daniel (born 1630) and his wife, Bridget, who settled in Connecticut. By the early nineteenth century, we find offshoots of the clan widely dispersed in Indiana and Nebraska, and it was Emiline, of the Nebraska Kelloggs, who married Marshall Carson, great-grandfather of Johnny. Marshall (born c. 1833) was allured by gold, and staked a profitless claim in the western part of Nebraska. Along with Emiline, he moved to Iowa where by dying in 1922 he narrowly failed to become a nonagenarian. That was the year in which his

grandson Homer Loyd Carson married a girl named Ruth Hook. John William Carson (born 1925) was the second child of this union, flanked by an elder sister, Catherine, and a younger brother, Dick.

(2) On his mother's side, Carson's first authenticated forebear is Thomas Hooke, a seventh great-grandfather, who sailed from London to Maryland in 1668. Most of his maternal roots, however, lead back to Ireland, whence two of his fifth great-grandfathers embarked for the States in the middle years of the eighteenth century.

(3) His family tree is laden with hardworking farmers. Decennial census sheets from 1840 to 1900 show Carson progenitors tilling the land in Maine, Ohio, Indiana, Nebraska, and Iowa.

(4) As far as anyone knows, Johnny and Kit Carson are no more closely related than Edward and Bonwit Teller. Johnny's background nonetheless contains two figures of some regional celebrity. One is Captain James Hook (maternal branch), who is reputed, but not proved, to have served with Washington at Valley Forge. In a private quarrel, Captain Hook lost a sliver of his ear to a man who pulled a knife on him. Being unarmed, Hook riposted by tearing off a much larger piece of his assilant's ear with his teeth. (Carson, of course, is in the business of bending people's ears, but not dentally.) The other Carson ancestor of note is Judge James Hardy (paternal branch), a whimsical but beloved dispenser of justice in midnineteenth-century Iowa.

(5) Judge Hardy's son Samuel, who died in 1933, at the age of eighty-five, was a skilled amateur violinist. Otherwise, in all the four previous centuries of the Carson family saga, there is no sign of anyone with an interest in the arts or a talent for entertainment.

February 10: Significant how many of the failed gags in Carson's monologues miss their target because they are based on the naive assumption that the studio audience has read the morning papers. One often gets the feeling that Carson is doubly insulated against reality. Events in the world outside Burbank and Bel Air impinge on him only when they have been filtered through magazines and newspapers and then subjected to a second screening by his writers and researchers. Hence his uncanny detachment, as of a man sequestered from the everyday problems with which most of us grapple. In fifteen years, barely a ripple of emotional commitment has disturbed the fishpond smoothness of his professional style. We are watching an immaculate machine. Some find the spectacle inhuman. "He looks plastic," said Dorothy Parker in 1966. On the other hand, Shana Alexander told me with genuine admiration, "He's like an astronaut, a Venusian, a visitor from another planet, someone out of 'Star Trek.'"

Two reflections on tonight's monologue. First, drawing on the latest Nielsen report, Carson informs us that during the icebound month of January the average American family watched television for seven hours and sixteen minutes per day. A fearsome statistic. No wonder they have so little time for newspapers. Second, he knocks the Senate for allowing its members' salaries to be raised to fifty-seven thousand five hundred dollars a year. The joke gives off a whiff of bad taste, coming, as it does, from a man who earns more than that every week. Whatever Carson's failing may be, they do not include a lack of chutzpah.

April 1: Nice to hear Ethel Merman on the show, blasting out "Ridin' High" as if calling the cattle home across the sands of D-flat major. But I wonder whether Carson would (or could) have done what Merv Griffin, of all people, did earlier in the evening; namely, devoted most of a ninety-minute program to a conversation with Orson Welles, which was conducted on what by talk-show standards was a respectably serious level. In 1962, when Carson took over the stewardship of the "Tonight Show," America was about to enter one of the grimmest and most divisive periods in its history, marked by the assassinations of the Kennedy brothers and Martin Luther King, the ghetto insurrections, the campus riots, the Vietnam war. It is arguable that during this bad time Carson became the nation's chosen joker because, in Madison Avenue terms, he was guaranteed to relieve nervous strain and anxiety more swiftly and safely (ask your doctor) than any competing brand of wag? Now that the country's headaches have ceased to throb so painfully, its viewers may be ready for a more substantial diet than any that Carson, at the moment, cares to provide.

April 7: Characteristic but in no way exceptional duologue between Carson and Buck Henry, the screenwriter and occasional actor. Whenever they meet on the show, their exchanges are vagrant, ethereal, unhurried, as if they were conversing in a limbo borrowed from a play by Samuel Beckett.

CARSON: Do you believe in plastic surgery?

HENRY: Absolutely. It's important, I think, to move things about judiciously.

CARSON: They're talking about freezing people and then reviving them in hundreds of years' time.

HENRY (*nods for a while, until a thought strikes him*): But suppose you died of freezing to death? (*Pause.*) I think it would be frightening to come back.

CARSON: If you could come back as somebody else, who would it be?

HENRY (*unhesitatingly*): Miss Teenage America.

CARSON: Where do you get ideas for your work?

HENRY: Oh, everyday places. Looking through keyholes.

CARSON: Eugene O'Neill got his ideas from his family.

HENRY: I expect to get a short monograph out of mine. (*Pause*).

CARSON: You have a strange turn of mind.

Carson brings up a newspaper story about a California woman who was recently interred, in accordance with a clause in her will, at the wheel of her Ferrari.

HENRY: Yes. It's reasonable to be married—or I may mean buried—in a Ferrari.

CARSON: How do you want to go?

HENRY (*very slowly*): Very slowly. With a jazz band playing in the background. I want to be extremely old. I want to be withered beyond recall.

CARSON: But if you lived to be a hundred and fifty, how would you kill time for the last seventy years?

HENRY (*contemplatively*): You'd read a lot. I don't

know what the real fun things to do would be after a hundred and twenty. I think the normal activities that come to mind would probably cripple you.

There was also some adagio talk about quarks and their relationship to other subatomic particles, but Henry declined to expand on the subject, perhaps feeling that it might be over our heads.

- May 11: Advice from Carson on longevity: "If you must smoke, don't do it orally." And, more cryptically: "You can add years to your life by wearing your pants backward."

June 15: He chats with someone who has attained longevity. Clare Ritter, an impoverished widow from Florida in her late seventies, discloses that her life's ambition is to make a trip to Egypt. In order to achieve it, she sells waste aluminum, which she collects by ransacking garbage cans.

CARSON: How much is this trip going to cost?
MRS. RITTER: Three thousand dollars.
CARSON: And how much have you saved so far?
MRS. RITTER: About half of it.

Carson volunteers to give her the rest himself. A graceful (and I am assured, unpremeditated) gesture.

July 19: Seated at the desk with McMahon, Carson says, "If you decide to ban your kids from watching TV, here's what they can do instead." He picks up a sheaf of humorous suggestions submitted by his writers, scans the first page, shows by his reaction that he finds it unfunny, and drops it on the floor. (This, like what ensues, is unplanned and impromptu.) He inspects page 2, raises his eyebrows, shows it to McMahon, drops *that* on the floor, goes on to page 3, gives McMahon a glimpse of it, whereupon both men shake their heads, and it, too, ends up on the floor. At this point, Carson starts to chuckle to himself. "How about *this*?" he says, and page 4 is tossed away, to be joined in rapid succession by a dozen, by *two* dozen more pages, falling faster and faster (the chuckle is by now uncontrollable), in a blizzard of rejection that does not stop until he has discarded every sheet of what was obviously planned as a solid five-minute comedy routine. On network

TV, this is just not done. You do not throw away an expensive script in full view of a national audience unless you can ad-lib something funnier to take its place. Carson offers us nothing in exchange except what he alone can supply: the spectacle of Carson being Carson, acting on impulse, surrendering to whim, and, as ever, getting away with it. (No claim is made for the above escapade as archive material, or as anything more than a specimen of Carson in average form on an average night. I record it to illustrate how, in the right hands, pure behavior becomes pure television. Like Shakespeare's Parolles, Carson can say, "Simply the thing I am shall make me live.")

Later in this show, Albert Finney, an actor who has temporarily turned his hand to lyric-writing and his voice to singing, plugs his first LP, declaring with brooding self-satisfaction that his songs derive from "the spring well" of personal experience. The number with which he favors us constitutes more of a threat to English grammar ("What has become of you and I?") than to Charles Aznavour, who seems to be Finney's model. The last guest is Madeline Kahn, who discusses the psychological ups and downs of her career as an actress. Carson responds with a rare flash of self-revelation. "I've had a little therapy myself," he says, "to cut down the hills and get out of the valleys."

August 4: President Carter has recommended that it should not be a criminal offense to be found in possession of an ounce or less of marijuana.

CARSON: The trouble is that nobody in our band knows what an ounce or less means.

DOC SEVERINSEN: It means you're about out.

January 18, 1977: My first solo encounter with Carson. We are to meet at the Beverly Hills Hotel for an early luncheon in the Polo Lounge. I prepare for my date by looking back on Carson's pre-"Tonight Show" career. It is not a story of overnight success. At the time of his birth in Corning, Iowa, his father was a lineman for an electricity company. It was a peripatetic job, and the family moved with him through several other Iowa hamlets. When Johnny was eight, they settled in Norfolk, Nebraska, a town of some ten thousand, where Carson senior got a managerial post with the local light-and-power company. "When one meets Johnny's parents, one understands him," Al Capp has said. "They're almost the definitive Nebraska mother and father. Radiantly decent, well spoken. The kind that raised their kids to have manners. Of all the television hosts I've faced, Carson has the most old-fashioned manners." By contemporary standards, he had a strict—even rigorous—upbringing, not calculated to encourage extrovert behavior. His brother Dick (now director of the "Merv Griffin Show") was once quoted as saying, "Put it this way—we're not Italian. Nobody in our family ever says what they really think or feel to anyone else." Except, I would add, in moments of professional crisis, when Johnny Carson can express himself with brusque and unequivocal directness. In 1966, for instance, the first three nights of a cabaret engagement he played in Miami were spoiled by a backstage staff too inexperienced to handle the elaborate sound effects that his act required. Carson accused his manager, Al Bruno, who had looked after his business affairs for almost ten years, of responsibility for the fiasco, and fired him on the spot. Again, there was the case of Art Stark, who described himself to an interviewer in 1966 as "Johnny's best friend." He had every reason to think so: for nearly a decade he had been Carson's producer, first on "Who Do You Trust?" and then on the "Tonight Show." He was the star's closest confidant, and when, in 1967, Carson embarked on a legal struggle with NBC for control of the show, including the right to hire and fire, he repeatedly assured Stark that, whatever the outcome, Stark's job would be safe. Having won the battle, however, Carson summoned Stark to his apartment and announced without preamble that he wanted another producer, unconnected with NBC. Dumbfounded, Stark asked when he would have to quit. "Right now," said Carson.

When Carson was twelve, he picked up, at a friend's house, a conjuring manual for beginners called *Hoffman's Book of Magic*. Its effect on him has been compared to the impact on the youthful Keats of Chapman's Homer. ("Chapman hit it in the bottom of the ninth to tie the game against Milwaukee," said the man who made the comparison, a former Carson writer. "Little Johnny Keats was standing behind the center-field fence and the ball landed smack on his head.") Carson immediately wrote off for a junior magician's kit. He worked hard to master the basic skills of the trade, and, having tried out his tricks on his mother's bridge club, he made his professional debut, billed as The Great Carsoni, before a gathering of Norfolk Rotarians. For this he received three dollars—the first of many such fees, for the kid illusionist was soon in demand at a variety of local functions, from firemen's picnics to county fairs. As a student at Norfolk High, he branched out into acting and also wrote a comic column for the school newspaper.

Digressive flash forward: In 1976, Carson was invited back to Norfolk to give the commencement address. Immensely gratified, he accepted at once. He took great pains over his speech, and when he delivered it, on May 23, the school auditorium was packed to the roof. In the front row, alongside his wife, brother, and sister, sat his parents, to whom he paid tribute for having "backed me up and let me go in my own direction." He also thanked one of his teachers, Miss Jenny Walker, who had prophetically said of him in 1943, "You have a fine sense of humor and I think you will go far in the entertainment world." In case anyone wondered why he had returned to Norfolk, he explained, "I've come to find out what's on the seniors' minds and, more important, to see if they've changed the movie at the Granada Theatre" (where, I have since discovered, Carson was working as a part-time usher when the manager interrupted the double feature to announce that the Japanese had bombed Pearl Harbor). He went on to recall that he had been chosen to lead the school's scrap-metal drive: "Unfortunately, in our zeal to help the war effort, we sometimes appropriated metal and brass from people who did not know they were parting with it." He continued, "I was also a member of the Thespians. I joined because I thought it meant something else. Then I found out it had to do with acting." In the manner expected of commencement speakers, he offered a little advice on coping with life in the adult world. Though his precepts were homespun to the point of platitude, they were transparently sincere and devoid of conventional pomposity. The main tenets of the Carson credo were these: (1) Learn to laugh at yourself. (2) Never lose the curiosity of childhood: "Go on asking questions about the nature of things and how they work, and don't stop until you get the answers." (3) Study the art of compromise, which implies a willingness to be convinced by other people's arguments: "Stay loose. In marriage, above all, compromise is the name of the game. Although"—and here he cast a glance at his third wife—"you may think that my giving advice on marriage is like the captain of the Titanic giving lessons on navigation." (4) Having picked a profession, feel no compulsion to stick to it: "If you don't like it, stop doing it. Never continue in a job you don't enjoy." (On the evidence, it would be hard to fault Carson for failing to practice what he preached.) A question-and-answer session then took place, from which I append a few excerpts:

Q.: How do you feel about Norfolk nowadays?

CARSON: I'm very glad I grew up in a small community. Big cities are where alienation sets in.

Q.: Has success made you happy?

CARSON: I have very high ups and very low downs. I can all of a sudden be depressed, sometimes without knowing why. But on the whole I think I'm relatively happy.

Q.: Who do you admire most, of all the guests you've interviewed.

CARSON: People like Carl Sagan, Paul Ehrlich, Margaret Mead . . . *(He recites the official list, already quoted, of Most Valued Performers.)*

Q.: In all your life, what are you proudest of?

CARSON: Giving a commencement address like this has made me as proud as anything I've ever done.

The applause at the end was so clamorous that Carson felt compelled to improvise a postscript. "If you're happy in what you're doing, you'll like yourself," he said. "And if you like yourself, you'll have inner peace. And if you have that, along with physical health, you will have had more success than you could possibly have imagined. I thank you all very much." He left the stage to a further outburst of cheers, having established what may be a record for speakers on such occasions: throughout the evening, he had made no reference to the deity, the flag, or the permissive society; nor had he used the phrase "this great country of ours."

After graduating from Norfolk, in 1943, Carson enrolled in the Navy's V-12 program, but training did not start until the fall, so he filled in time by hitchhiking to California. There, in order to gain access to the many entertainments that were offered free of charge to servicemen, he stopped off at an Army-Navy store and prematurely bought himself a naval cadet's uniform. Thus attired, he danced with Marlene Dietrich at the Hollywood Stage Door Canteen. Later, he traveled south to see Orson Welles give a display of magic in San Diego, where he responded to the maestro's request for a volunteer from the audience and ecstatically permitted himself to be sawed in half. That night, he was arrested by two M.P.s and charged with impersonating a member of the armed forces—an offense that cost him fifty dollars in bail. After induction, he attended the midshipmen's school at Columbia University and served in the Pacific aboard the battleship *Pennsylvania*. Never exposed to combat, he had plenty of time to polish his conjuring skills. In 1946, discharged from the Navy, he entered the University of Nebraska, where he majored in English and moonlighted as a magician, by now earning twenty-five dollars per appearance. In need of an assistant, he hired a girl student named Jody Wolcott; he married her in 1948. (To dispose, as briefly as possible, of Carson's marital history: The liaison with Jody produced three sons—Chris, Ricky, and Cory—and was finally dissolved, after four years of separation, in 1963. "My greatest personal failure," Carson has said, "was when I was divorced from my first wife." In August, 1963, he married Joanne Copeland, aged thirty, a diminutive, dark-haired model and occasional actress. They parted company in 1970 but were not legally sundered until two years later, when the second Mrs. Carson was awarded a settlement of nearly half a million dollars, in addition to an annual hundred thousand in alimony. She had by then moved from New York to Los Angeles. Shortly afterward, Carson migrated to the West Coast, bringing the show with him. Between these two events she discerns a causal connection. She has also declared that when, at a Hollywood party, Carson first met his next wife-to-be, "she was standing with her back to him, and he went right up to her, thinking it was me." On matters such as this, Carson's lips are meticulously sealed. All we know—or need to know—is that on September 30, 1972, during a gaudy cel-

ebration at the Beverly Hills Hotel in honor of his tenth anniversary on the "Tonight Show," he stepped up to the microphone and announced that at one-thirty that afternoon he had
married Joanna Holland. Of Italian lineage, and a model by
profession, she was thirty-two years old. They are still together.
It is difficult to see how Carson could have mistaken her, even
from behind, for her predecessor. She could not be sanely
described as diminutive. Dark-haired, yes; but of medium
height and voluptuous build. The third Mrs. Carson is the kind
of woman, bright and *molto simpatica*, whom you would expect to meet not in Bel Air but at a cultural soirée in Rome,
where—as like as not—she would be more than holding her
own against the earnest platonic advances of Michelangelo
Antonioni.)

Carson's post-college career follows the route to success
traditionally laid down for a television—What? Personality-
cum-comedian-cum-interviewer? No single word yet exists to
epitomize his function, though it has had many practitioners,
from Steve Allen, the archetypal pioneer, to the hosts of the
latest and grisliest giveaway shows. In Carson's case, there are
ten steps to stardom. (1) A multipurpose job (at forty-seven
dollars and fifty cents a week) as disc jockey, weather reporter,
and reader of commercials on an Omaha radio station, where
he breaks a precedent or two; e.g., when he is required to
conduct pseudo interviews, consisting of answers prerecorded
by minor celebrities and distributed to small-town d.j.s with
a list of matching questions, he flouts custom by ignoring the
script. Instead of asking Patti Page how she began performing,
he says, "I understand you're hitting the bottle pretty good,
Patti—when did you start?," which elicits the taped reply,
"When I was six, I used to get up at church socials and do it."
(2) A work-hunting foray, in 1951, to San Francisco and Los
Angeles, which gets him nowhere except back to Omaha. (3)
A sudden summons, later in the same year, from a Los Angeles
television station, KNXT, offering him a post as staff announcer, which he accepts, at a hundred and thirty-five dollars
a week. (4) A Sunday afternoon show of his own ("KNXT
cautiously presents 'Carson's Cellar'"), produced on a weekly
budget of twenty-five dollars, plus fifty for Carson. It becomes
what is known as a cult success (a golden phrase, which unlocks

many high-level doors), numbering among its fans—and subsequently its guests—such people as Fred Allen, Jack Benny,
and Red Skelton. (5) Employment, after thirty weeks of "Carson's Cellar," as a writer and supporting player on Skelton's
CBS-TV show. (6) The Breakthrough, which occurs in 1954
and is brought about, in strict adherence to the "Forty-second
Street" formula, by an injury to the star: Skelton literally knocks
himself out while rehearsing a slapstick routine, and Carson,
at roughly an hour's notice, triumphantly replaces him. (7) The
Breakdown: CBS launches "The Johnny Carson Show," a half-
hour program that goes through seven directors, eight writers,
and thirty-nine weeks of worsening health before expiring, in
the spring of 1956. (8) Carson picks self up, dusts self off,
starts all over again. On money borrowed from his father, he
moves from the West Coast to New York, where he joins the
Friars Club, impresses its show-business membership with his
cobra-swift one-liners, makes guest appearances on TV, and
generally repairs his damaged reputation until (9) he is hired
by ABC, in 1957, to run its quiz program "Who Do You
Trust?" on which he spends the five increasingly prosperous
years that lead him to (10) the "Tonight Show," and thence
to the best table in the Polo Lounge, where he has been waiting
for several minutes when I arrive, precisely on time.

He is making copious notes on a pad. I ask what he is
writing. He says he has had an idea for tonight's monologue.
In Utah, yesterday, the convicted murderer Gary Gilmore, who
had aroused national interest by his refusal to appeal against
the death sentence passed upon him got his wish by facing a
firing squad—Utah being a state where the law allows condemned criminals to select the method by which society will
rid itself of them. Thus, the keepers of the peace have shot a
man to death at his own urgent request. Carson's comment on
the macabre situation takes the form of black comedy. Since
justice must be seen to be done, why not let the viewing public
in on the process of choice? Carson proposes a new TV show,
to be called "The Execution Game." It would work something
like this: Curtains part to reveal the death chamber, in the
middle of which is an enormous wheel, equipped with glittering
lights and a large golden arrow, to be spun by the condemned
man to decide the nature of his fate. For mouth-watering

prizes—ranging from a holiday for two in the lovely Munich suburb of Dachau to a pair of front-row seats at the victim's terminal throes—members of the audience vie with one another to guess whether the arrow will come to rest on the electric chair, the gas chamber, the firing squad, the garrote, or the noose.

This routine seems to me apt and mordant, and I tell Carson that I look forward to seeing it developed this evening. (Footnote: I looked in vain. The January 18 edition of the "Tonight Show" contained no mention of Gary Gilmore's execution apart from a terse and oddly sour sentence—"Capital punishment is a great deterrent to monologues"—inserted without buildup or comic payoff in Carson's opening spiel. A couple of nights later, one of his guests was Shelley Winters, who burst into an attack on the death penalty, using the Gilmore case as her springboard. Carson showed a distinctly nervous reluctance to commit himself; indeed, he shied away from the subject, and cut the discussion short by saying, "There are no absolutes." Yet I had seen him writing a piece that implied fairly bitter opposition to the process of judicial killing. What had happened? I called up Fred de Cordova, who admitted, after some hesitation, that he had disliked the "Execution Game" idea and that the network had backed him up. There had been a convulsive row with Carson, but in the end "Johnny saw reason" and the item was dropped. Hence his remark, meaningless except to insiders, about capital punishment's being "a great deterrent to monologues"; and so much for de Cordova's description of Carson as a supreme "self-editor" who never needed censorship.)

A believer in eating only when one is hungry, Carson orders nothing more than a salad and some mineral water. "I gave up drinking a couple of years ago," he says. "I couldn't handle it." He adds that we can chat until two o'clock when he must be off to Burbank. He doesn't know who is lined up to appear tonight. This prompts an obligatory question: Which guests has he coveted and failed to corral? "Cary Grant, of course. But straight actors often get embarrassed on the show. They say they feel naked. Their business is to play other people, and it bugs them to have to speak as themselves. Naturally, I'd be glad to have Henry Kissinger. And it was a great sorrow to me when Charles Laughton, whom we'd been after for ages, died a few days before he was scheduled to appear. But on the whole I'm pretty content to have had a list of guests like Paul Ehrlich, Gore Vidal, Carl Sagan, Madalyn Murray O'Hair . . ." He flips through the familiar roster. "And it gives me a special kick to go straight from talking to that kind of person into an all-out slapstick routine." He runs over his rules for coping with fellow comedians on the program: "You have to lay back and help them. Never compete with them. I learned that from Jack Benny. The better they are, the better the show is." (In more immature days, Carson's technique was less self-effacing. The late Jack E. Leonard told a reporter in 1967, "You say a funny line on Griffin, and he laughs and says, 'That's brilliant.' Carson repeats it, scavenging, hunting all over for the last vestiges of the joke, trying desperately to pull a laugh of his own out of it.") Carson continues, "When people get outrageous, you have to capitalize on their outrageousness and go along with it. The only absolute rule is: Never lose control of the show."

To stay in control is the hardest trick of all, especially when the talk veers toward obscenity; you have to head it off, preferably with a laugh, before it crashes through the barrier of public acceptance. At times, you have to launch a preemptive strike of salaciousness in order to get an interview started. "Not long ago, a movie starlet came on the show with gigantic breasts bulging out of a low-cut dress," Carson says. "The audience couldn't look at anything else. If I'd ignored them, nobody would have listened to a word we said. There was only one thing to do. As soon as she sat down, I stared straight at her cleavage and said, 'That's the biggest set of jugs I ever saw.' It got a tremendous laugh. 'Now that we've got that out of the way,' I said, 'let's talk.'"

High on his list of favorite guests is Don Rickles, though he feels that Rickles has sadly mishandled his own TV career: "He went in for situation comedy and tried to be lovable. He failed every time. What he needed—and I've told him this over and over again—was a game show called something like 'Meet Don Rickles,' where he could be himself and insult the audience, the way Groucho did on 'You Bet Your life.'" Although Carson himself is less acid than he used to be, he is still capable of slapping down visitors who get uppish with him. "There was one time," he recalls, "when we had Tuesday Weld on the program, and she started behaving rather snottily. I finally asked her something innocuous about her future plans, and she said she'd let me know 'when I'm back on the show next year.' I was very polite. I just said that I hadn't scheduled her again quite that soon." Beyond doubt, Carson's least beloved subjects are British comedians, of whom he says, "I find them unfunny, infantile, and obsessed with toilet jokes. They're lavatory-minded." (It is true that British comics sometimes indulge, on TV, in scatological—and sexual—humor that would not be permitted on any American network; but this kind of liberty, however it may be abused, seems to me infintely preferable to the restrictiveness that prevented Buddy Hackett, Carson's principal guest on February 1, 1977, from completing a single punch line without being bleeped.) I throw into the conversation my own opinion, which is that to shrink from referring to basic physical functions is to be truly infantile; to make good jokes about them, as about anything else, is evidence of maturity. It is depressing to reflect that if Rabelais were alive today he would not be invited to appear on the "Tonight Show."

Carson once said, "I've never seen it chiselled in stone tablets that TV must be uplifting." I ask him how he feels about his talk-show competitor Dick Cavett. His answer is brisk: "The trouble with Dick is that he's never decided what he wants to be—whether he's going for the sophisticated, intellectual viewer or for the wider audience. He falls between two stools. It gets so that you feel he's apologizing if he makes a joke." In reply to the accusation that his own show is intellectually jejune, Carson has this to say: "I don't want to get into big debates about abortion, homosexuality, prostitution, and so forth. Not because I'm afraid of them but because we all know the arguments on both sides, and they're circular. The fact is that TV is probably not the ideal place to discuss serious issues. It's much better to read about them." With this thought—self-serving but not easily refutable—he takes his leave.

* * *

February 10, 1977: The Hasty Pudding Club at Harvard has elected Johnny Carson its Man of the Year. There have been ten previous holders of the title, among them Bob Hope, Paul Newman, Robert Redford, James Stewart, Dustin Hoffman, and Warren Beatty. Delighted by the honor, because it is untainted by either lobbying or commercialism, Carson will fly to Harvard in two weeks' time to receive his trophy. While he is there, he will attend the opening night of "Cardinal Knowledge," the hundred and twenty-ninth in the series of all-male musicals presented by Hasty Pudding Theatricals, which claims to be the oldest dramatic society in the United States. I am to travel with Carson on what will be his first trip to Harvard. To give me details of the program of events that the Pudding people have prepared for him, he asks me to his home in Bel Air, where I present myself at 11 A.M. It is roughly five minutes by car from the Beverly Hills Hotel, and was built in 1950 for the director Mervyn LeRoy. Carson bought it five years ago, and, like many places were West Coast nabobs dwell, it is about as grand as a house can be that has no staircase. When you turn in at the driveway, a voice issuing from the wall sternly inquires your name and business; if your reply pacifies it, iron gates swing open to admit you.

I am welcomed by Joanna Carson's secretary, a lively young woman named Sherry Fleiner, part of whose job consists of working with Mrs. C. for a charitable organization known as SHARE—Share Happily and Reap Endlessly—which raises funds for the mentally retarded. (Other than a married couple who act as housekeepers, the Carson have no live-in servants.) Proffering Carson's apologies, Miss Fleiner says that he is out on the tennis court behind the house, halfway through a closely fought third set. While awaiting match point, I discreetly case the joint, which has (I learn from Miss Fleiner) six bedrooms. Except where privacy is essential, the walls are mainly of glass, and there is window-to-window carpeting with a zebra-stripe motif. Doors are infrequent. In accordance with local architectural custom, you do not leave one room to enter another, you move from one living area to the next. In the reading area (or "library") I spot a photograph of four generations of Carsons, the eldest being my host's grandfather, Christopher Carson, who died two years ago at the age of ninety-eight, and I recall Carson's saying to me, in that steely survivor's voice of his, "One thing about my family—we have good genes." On a wall nearby hangs a portrait of Carson by Norman Rockwell, the perfect artist for this model product of Middle American upbringing. Other works of art, scattered through the relaxing, ingesting, and greeting areas, reveal an eclectic, opulent, but not barbarously spendthrift taste; e.g., a well-chosen group of paintings by minor Impressionists; a camel made out of automobile bumpers by John Kearney and (an authentic rarity) a piece of sculpture by Rube Goldberg; together with statues and graphic art from the Orient and Africa. Over the fireplace in the relaxing area, a facile portrait of Mrs. Carson, who deserves more eloquent brushwork, smilingly surveys the swimming pool.

Having won his match, Carson joins me, his white sporting gear undarkened by sweat, and leads me out of the house to a spacious octagonal office he has built alongside the tennis court. This is his command module. It contains machinery for large-screen TV projection, and a desk of presidential dimensions, bristling with gadgets. On a built-in sofa lies a cushion that bears the embroidered inscription "IT'S ALL IN THE TIMING." Coffee is served, and Carson offers me one of his cigarettes, which I refuse. He says that most people, even hardened smokers, do the same, and I do not find this surprising, since the brand he favors is more virulent and ferociously unfiltered than any other on the market. He briefs me on the impending Harvard visit—a day and a half of sightseeing, speechmaking, banquets, conferences, seminars, and receptions that would tax the combined energies of Mencken, Mailer, and Milton Berle—and then throws himself open to me for further questioning:

Q.: When you're at home, whom do you entertain?
CARSON: My lawyer, Henry Bushkin, who's probably my best friend. A few doctors. One or two poker players. Some people I've met through tennis, which is my big-

gest hobby right now—though I'm still interested in astronomy and scuba diving. And, of course, a couple of people who work on the show. But the point is that not many of my friends are exclusively show business.

Q.: Why do you dislike going to parties?

CARSON: Because I get embarrassed by attention and adulation. I don't know how to react to them in private. Swifty Lazar, for instance, sometimes embarrasses me when he praises me in front of his friends. I feel much more comfortable with a studio audience. On the show, I'm in control. Socially, I'm not in control.

Q.: On the show, one of the things you control most strictly is the expression of your own opinions. Why do you keep them a secret from the viewers?

CARSON: I hate to be pinned down. Take the case of Larry Flynt, for example. [Flynt, the publisher of the sex magazine *Hustler*, had recently been convicted on obscenity charges.] Now, I think *Hustler* is tawdry, but I also think that if the First Amendment means what is says, then it protects Flynt as much as anyone else, and that includes the American Nazi movement. As far as I'm concerned, people should be allowed to read and see whatever they like, provided it doesn't injure others. If they want to read pornography until it comes out of their ears, then let them. But if I go on the "Tonight Show" and defend *Hustler*, the viewers are going to tag me as that guy who's into pornography. And that's going to hurt me as an entertainer, which is what I am.

Q.: In private life, who's the wittiest man you've ever known?

CARSON: The wittiest would have to be Fred Allen. He appeared on a show I had in the fifties, called "Carson's Cellar," and I knew him for a while after that—until he died, in 1956. But there's an old vaudeville proverb—"A comic is a man who says funny things, and a comedian is a man who says things funny." If that's a valid distinction, then Fred was a comic, whereas Jonathan Winters and Mel Brooks are comedians. But they make me laugh just as much.

Before I go, Carson takes me down to a small gymnasium beneath the module. It is filled with gleaming steel devices, pulleys and springs and counterweights, which, together with tennis, keep the star's body trim. In one corner stands a drum kit at which Buddy Rich might cast an envious eye. "That's where I work off my hostilities," Carson explains. He escorts me to my car, and notices that it is fitted with a citizens-band radio. "I had one of those damned things, but I ripped it out after a couple of weeks," he says. "I just couldn't bear it—all those sick anonymous maniacs shooting off their mouths."

I understand what he means. Most of what you hear on CB radio is either tedious (truck drivers warning one another about speed traps) or banal (schoolgirls exchanging notes on homework), but at its occasional—and illegal—worst it sinks a pipeline to the depths of the American unconscious. Your ears are assaulted by the sound of racism at its most rampant, and by masturbation fantasies that are the aural equivalent of rape. The sleep of reason, to quote Goya's phrase, brings forth monsters, and the anonymity of CB encourages the monsters to emerge. Not often, of course; but when they do, CB radio becomes the dark underside of a TV talk show. No wonder Carson loathes it.

February 24, 1977: Morning departure from Los Angeles Airport of flight bearing Boston-bound Carson party, which consists of Mr. and Mrs. C., Mr. and Mrs. Henry Bushkin, and me. Boyish-looking, with an easy smile, a soft voice, and a modest manner, Bushkin, to whom I talked a few days earlier, is a key figure in Carson's private and professional life. "Other stars have an agent, a personal manager, a business manager, a P.R. man, and a lawyer," he told me. "I serve all those functions for Johnny." Bushkin was born in the Bronx in 1942. He moved to the West Coast five years ago and swiftly absorbed the ground rules of life in Beverly Hills; e.g., he is likely to turn up at his desk in a cardigan and an open-necked shirt, thus obeying the precept that casualness of office attire increases in direct ratio to grandeur of status. He first met Carson through a common friend in 1970, when he was working for a small Manhattan law firm that specialized in show-business clients. At that time, Carson lived at the United Nations Plaza, where one of his neighbors was David (Sonny) Werblin, formerly the driving force behind the Music Corporation of America and (until 1968) the president of the New York Jets. In 1969, Werblin had drawn up a plan whereby he and Carson would form a corporation, called Raritan Enterprises, to take over the entire production of the "Tonight Show," which would then be rented out to NBC for a vast weekly fee. Rather than risk losing Carson, the network caved in and agreed to Raritan's terms. "As the tax laws were in the late sixties, when you could pay up to ninety percent on earned income, the Raritan scheme had certain advantages," Bushkin explained to me. "But there were handicaps that Johnny hadn't foreseen. Werblin had too many outside interests—for one thing, he owned a good-sized racing stable—and Johnny found himself managing the company as well as starring in the show, because his partner wasn't always there. When a major problem came up, he'd suddenly discover that Werblin had taken off for a month in Europe and couldn't be reached. Around 1972, Johnny decided that the plan wasn't working, and that's when he asked me to represent him. Not to go into details, let's just say that Werblin was painlessly eliminated from the setup. By that time, the maximum tax on earned income was down to fifty percent, and that removed the basic motive for the corporate arrangement. So the show reverted to being an NBC operation. But Johnny went back with a much better financial deal than he had in 1969." When Bushkin came to Beverly Hills, in 1973, his life already revolved around Carson's. "It took about three years for our relationship to get comfortable, because Johnny isn't easy to know," he went on. "But now we're the best of friends, and so are our wives. The unwritten rule for lawyers is: Don't get too friendly with clients. But this is an unusual situation. This is Carson, and Carson's my priority."

Ed McMahon, I remarked, had predicted that Carson would stay with the "Tonight Show" until 1980. "I'll bet you that he's still there in 1984," Bushkin said.

If Carson can hold on as long as that, it would be churlish of NBC to unseat him before he reaches retiring age, in 1990.

5:30 P.M.: We land at Boston. Frost underfoot, Carson, following President Carter's example, totes his suit (presumably the tuxedo required for tomorrow's festivities) off the plane. He murmurs to me, "If someone could get Billy Carter to sponsor a carry-off suitcase, they'd make a fortune." He walks through popping flashbulbs and a fair amount of hand-held-camera work to be greeted by Richard Palmer and Barry Sloane, undergraduate co-producers of the Hasty Pudding show, who look bland, businesslike, and utterly untheatrical; i.e., like co-producers. Waiting limos take Carsons and Bushkins to the Master's Residence at Eliot House, where they are to spend the night. I repair to my hotel.

8:30 P.M. Pudding people give dinner for Carson and his entourage at waterfront restaurant called Anthony's Pier 4. When I annouce destination, my cabdriver says, "That's the big Republican place. Gold tablecloths. Democrats like checked tablecloths. They go to Jimmy's Harbor Side." Decor at Anthony's features rustic beamery and period prints. Tablecloths definitely straw-colored, though cannot confirm that this has political resonance. Carson (in blue sports jacket, white shirt, and discreetly striped tie) sits beside wife (in brown woollen two-piece, with ring like searchlight on left hand) at round table with Bushkins, Pudding officials, and short, heavily tanned man with vestigial hair, dark silk suit, smoke tinted glasses, and general aspect of semi-simian elegance. This, I learn, is David Tebet, the senior vice-president of NBC, whose suzerainty covers the Carson show, and who in May, 1977, will celebrate his twenty-first anniversary with the network. Of the three men who wield influence over Carson (the others being Bushkin and Fred de Cordova), Tebet is ultimately the most powerful. "It's a terrible thing to wish on him," Frank Sinatra once said of Tebet, "but it's too bad he's not in government today." In 1975, Robert D. Wood, then president of CBS-TV, described Tebet as "the ambassador of all NBC's good will—he sprinkles it around like ruby dust." With characteristic effusiveness, de Cordova has declared that the dust-sprinkler's real title should be "vice-president in charge of caring." In 1965, Carson came to the conclusion that he had to quit the "Tonight Show," because the daily strain was too great, but Tebet persuaded him to stay; what tipped the scale was the offer of an annual paid vacation of six weeks. Ten years later, Carson said he had a feeling that when he died a color TV set would be delivered to his graveside and "on it will be a ribbon and a note that says, 'Have a nice trip. Love, David.'"

During dinner, although wine is served, Carson drinks only coffee. He talks about "Seeds," a Wasp parody of Roots, dealing with history of orthodox midwestern family, which was recently broadcast on the "Tonight Show." Concept was his, and he is pleased with how it came out, though he regrets loss of one idea that was cut; viz., scene depicting primitive tribal ceremony at which the hyphen is ritually removed from Farrah Fawcett-Majors.

"He looks so mechanical," mutters a Pudding person on my right. "Like a talking propelling pencil." Same fellow explains to me that the club is divided into social and theatrical compartments. Former was founded in 1795; latter did not develop until 1844, when first show was presented, establishing an annual tradition that has persisted—apart from two inactive years in each of the world wars—ever since. Pudding performers have included Oliver Wendell Holmes, William Randolph Hearst, Robert Benchley (star of *Below Zero*, 1912), and Jack Lemmon. Tomorrow's production, which is to play a month at Pudding theatre, followed by quick tour to New York, Washington, and Bermuda, will cost a hundred thousand dollars. Revenue from box office and from program advertising, plus aid from wealthy patrons, will insure that it breaks even. (Undergraduates provide words, music, and cast; direction, choreography, and design are by professionals.) Publicity accruing from Carson's presence will boost ticket sales; thus, his visit amounts to unpaid commercial for show.

Another Pudding functionary tells me that club also bestows award on Woman of the Year—has, in fact, been doing so since 1951. First recipient was Gertrude Lawrence, Bette Midler got the nod in 1976, and last week Elizabeth Taylor turned up to collect the trophy for 1977. "She is genuinely humble," my informant gravely whispers. After dinner, Carson and wife are interviewed in banqueting salon of restaurant by local TV station. Mrs. C. is asked, "Did you fall in love with the private or the public Johnny Carson?" She replies, "I fell in love with both." Before further secrets of the confessional can be extracted, camera runs out of tape, to her evident relief.

February 25, 1977: Dining hall of Eliot House is crowded

at 8:45 A.M. University band, with brass section predominant, lines up and plays "Ten Thousand Men of Harvard" as Carson (black-and-white checked sports jacket) leads his party in to breakfast. His every move is followed, as it will be all day, by television units, undergraduate film crew, and assorted press photographers. Asked by TV director whether sound system is to his liking, Carson says he has no complaints, "except I thought the microphone under the bed was pushing it a bit." Member of Harvard band achieves minor triumph of one-upmanship by conning Carson into inscribing and autographing autobiography of Dick Cavett.

Fast duly broken, party embarks on walking tour of Harvard Yard and university museums. Hundreds of undergraduates join media people in the crush around Carson, and police cars prowl in their wake to protect the star from terrorist assaults or kidnap attempts. Weather is slate-clouded and icy; Mrs. Carson and Mrs. Bushkin both wear mink coats. Climax of tour is meeting with John Finley, internationally eminent classical scholar and treasure of Harvard campus, Eliot Professor of Greek Literature Emeritus and Master of Eliot House Emeritus, whose study is in the Widener Library. (During previous week, I called Professor Finley to find out how he felt about forthcoming encounter with Carson. "At first, I thought it was an asinine idea," he said. "I've never seen the man on television—as a matter of fact, I've spent most of my life with my nose plunged into classical texts. But, after all, how important is one's time, anyway?") Carson is properly deferential in the presence of this agile septuagenarian. Eavesdropping on their conversation, I hear Professor Finley say, "Writing is like an artesian well that we sink to find the truth." He talks about Aristotle, getting little response, and then tries to clarify for Carson the distinction drawn by Lionel Trilling between sincerity and authenticity, in literature and in life. "President Carter is an example of sincerity," he explains. "But whether he has authenticity—well, that's another matter. I'm not sure that Trilling would have been much impressed." Cannot imagine what Carson is making of all this.

12:30 P.M.: Luncheon in Carson's honor at the A.D. Club, described to me by reliable source as "the second-stuffiest in Harvard." (First prize goes, by general consent, if not by acclamation, to the Porcellian Club. Choice of venue today is dictated by fact that co-producers of Pudding show are members of A.D. and not of Porcellian.) Atmosphere is robustly patrician enough to warm heart of late Evelyn Waugh: sprigs of Back Bay dynasties sprawl in leather armchairs beneath group photographs of their forebears. Club clearly deserves title of No. 2; it could not conceivably try harder. Members cheer as Carson enters, flanked by Bushkin and Tebet. (This is a strictly gag sodality.) About twenty guests present, among them Professor Finley and Robert Peabody, son of former governor of Massachusetts and vice-president of Pudding Theatricals—a bouncing two-hundred-and-fifty-pound lad much cherished by Pudding enthusiasts for his comic talent in drag. Carson, still rejecting grape in favor of bean, wears blue sweater, dark slacks, and burgundy patent-leather shoes. When meal is consumed, he makes charming speech of thanks, in which he regrets that life denied him the opportunity of studying under Prof. Finley. (Later, rather less lovably, he is to tell drama students of Pudding Club that from his lunchtime chat with Finley "I learned a hell of a lot more about Aristotle than I wanted to know."

2 P.M.: Carson is driven to Pudding H.Q. on Holyoke Street—narrow thoroughfare jammed with fans, through whom club officials have to force a way to the entrance. Upstairs, in red-curtained reception room, Carson is to hold seminar with thirty hand-picked undergraduates who are studying the performing arts. This select bunch of initiates sits in circle of red armchairs. Carson takes his place among them and awaits interrogation. Standard of questions, dismal for allegedly high-powered assembly, seldom rises above gossip level; e.g.:

Q.: As a regular viewer, may I ask why you have switched from wearing a Windsor knot to a four-in-hand?

CARSON: Well, I guess that's about all we have time for. (*Questioner presses for reply.*) Just between ourselves, it's a defense mechanism.

Q.: Did Jack Paar have someone like Ed McMahon to work with?

CARSON: No. A psychiatrist worked with Jack Paar. The last time I saw Paar was in Philadelphia. He was sitting on a curb and he had a swizzle stick embedded in his hand. I removed it.

Q.: I've noticed that people don't always laugh at your monologue. Why is that?

CARSON: Well, we don't actually *structure* it to go down the toilet. But we work from the morning papers and sometimes the audience isn't yet aware of what's happened in the news.

Q.: How do you really feel about Jimmy Carter?

CARSON: The Carter Administration is perfect comedy material. And I think he rented the family. I don't believe Lillian is his mother. I don't believe Billy is his brother. They're all from Central Casting.

Q.: Do you normally watch the show when you get home?

CARSON: No. I'd get worn out from seeing it all over again. If we're breaking in a new character, I'll watch.

Q *(first of any substance)*: Has the "Tonight Show" done anything more important than just brighten up the end of the day?

CARSON: I'd say it was quite important to let people hear the opinions of people like Paul Ehrlich, Carl Sagan, Gore Vidal, Margaret . . . *(Vide, supra, passim)*. We've also taken an interest in local politics. One year, there were eleven candidates for mayor of Burbank, and we had to give them all equal time. That was pretty public-spirited. But what's important? I think it's important to show ordinary people doing extraordinary things. Like we once had a Japanese guy from Cleveland who wanted to be a cop but he was too short, so his wife had been hanging him up every night by his heels. And it's important to help people live out their fantasies, like when I pitched to Mickey Mantle on the show, or when I played quarterback for the New York Jets. But a lot of the time TV is judged by the wrong standards. If Broadway comes up with two first-rate new plays in a season, the critics are delighted. That's a good season. But on TV they expect that every week. It's a very visible medium to jump on. And there's another thing that isn't generally realized. If you're selling hard goods—like soap or dog food—you simply can't afford to put on culture. Exxon, the Bank of America—organizations like that can afford to do it. But they aren't selling hard goods, and that's what the "Tonight Show" has to do. [Applause for candor. This is the nearest approach to hard eloquence I have heard from Carson, and he sells it to great effect.]

Q.: What is Charo really like?

This reduces Carson to silence, bringing the seminar to a close.

4:30 P.M. Cocktail party for Carson at Club Casablanca, local haunt crowded to point just short of asphyxiation. Star and companions have changed into evening dress. Carson tells me how Prof. Finley sought to explain to him eternal simplicities of Aristotle's view of life, and adds, "He's out of touch with the real world." Subject for debate: By what criteria can Carson's world be said to be closer to reality than Aristole's? Or, for that matter, than Professor Finley's? Carson group and nonacting Pudding dignitaries then proceed on foot to nearby bistro called Ferdinand's for early dinner. Eating quite exceptional soft-shell crabs, I sit next to Joanna C., who has flashing eyes and a quill-shaped Renaissance nose. Her mother's parents came from nothern Italy; her father's family background is Sicilian. She introduced Carson to what is now his favorite Manhattan restaurant, an Italian place named Patsy's, and her immediate ambition is to coax him to visit Italy. Eying her husband (who must be well into his second gallon of coffee since breakfast), she tells me that the only time she has seen him cry was at the funeral of Jack Benny, who befriended and helped him from his earliest days in TV. She doesn't think he will still be on the "Tonight Show" when he's sixty (i.e., in 1985). "Of course, everybody wants him to act," she continues. "He was offered the Steve McQueen part in *The Thomas Crown Affair*, and Mel Brooks begged him to play the Gene Wilder part in *Blazing Saddles*. He read the script twice. Then he called Mel from Acapulco and said, 'I read it in L.A. and it wasn't funny, and it's even less funny in Mexico.'"

David Tebet, seated opposite, leans across the table and tells me what he does. His voice is a serrated baritone growl.

From what I gather, he is a combination of talent detector, ego masseur (of NBC stars), and thief (of other networks' stars). Has been quoted as saying that he judges performers by "a thing called gut reaction," and that he understands "their soft underbellies." To a thing called my surprise, he adds that these qualities of intestinal intuition help to keep stars reassured. According to an article in the *Wall Street Journal*, a two-thousand-year-old samurai sword hangs over the door of his New York office. Am not certain that this would have reassuring effect on me. It may, however, explain enigmatic remark of Bob Hope, who once referred to Tebet as "my Band-Aid." Razor-edged weapon is part of huge Tebet art collection (mainly Oriental but also including numerous prints and lithographs by Mucha, Klimt, Schiele, Munch, et al.), much of which adorns his NBC suite. Tebet claims this makes actors feel at home. But at whose home?

7 P.M.: Back to Pudding Club for pre-performance press conference. I count five movie and/or TV cameras, eight microphones, about thirty photographers, and several dozen reporters, all being jostled by roughly a hundred and fifty guests, gate-crashers, and ticket-holders diverted from route to auditorium by irresistible surge of Carson-watchers. Bar serves body-temperature champagne in plastic glasses; Carson requests slug of water.

Reporter asks what he thinks of Barbara Walter's million-dollar contract with ABC News.

He replies, "I think Harry Reasoner has a contract out for Barbara Walters."

Press grilling is routine stuff, except for:

Q.:What would you like your epitaph to be?
CARSON *(after a pause for thought)*: I'll be right back.

Laughter and applause for this line, the traditional cliché with which talk-show hosts segue into commercial break. Subsequent research reveals that Carson has used it before in answer to same question. Fact increases my respect for his acting ability. That pause for thought would have fooled Lee Strasberg.

8 P.M.: Join expectant crowd in Pudding theatre, attractive

little blue auditorium with three hundred and sixty-three seats. Standees line walls. In fat program I read tribute to "that performer who has made the most outstanding contribution to the entertainment profession during the past years—Johnny Carson." Article also states that in the fifties he wrote for "The Red Skeleton Show"—ideal title, I reflect, for Vincent Price Special—and concludes by summing up Carson's gifts in a burst of baroque alliteration: "Outspoken yet disciplined, he is a pool of profanity, a pit of profundity." Audience by now buzzing with impatience to hear from pool (or pit) in person.

Co-producer Palmer takes the stage and, reading from notes, pays brief homage to "a performer whose wit, humor, and showmanship rank him among America's greatest—ladies and gentlemen, Mr. Johnny Carson!" Band plays "Tonight Show" theme as Carson walks down the aisle and clambers up to shake Palmer's hand. Standing ovation greets him. Co-producer Sloane emerges from wings and solemnly presents him with small golden pudding pot. Ovation persists—three hundred and sixty-three seats are empty. When it and the spectators have subsided, Carson holds up his hands for silence and then makes speech precisely right for occasion. (Without notes, of course, as befits man who, if program is to be believed, has "liberated the airwaves from scripted domination.") He begins by saying that it is gratifying to hear so much applause without anyone's brandishing a sign marked "Applause." He thanks the club for the honor bestowed on him, even though (he adds) "I understand that this year the short list for the award was me, Idi Amin, and Larry Flynt." He expresses special gratitude for the hospitality extended to his wife and to him by Eliot House: "It's the first time I've scored with a chick on campus since 1949." He has never visited the university before. However, it has played a small but significant role in his family history: "My Great-Uncle Orville was here at Harvard. Unfortunately, he was in a jar in the biology lab." Widening his focus, he throws in a couple of comments on the state of the nation. Apropos of the recent groundless panic over immunizing the population against a rumored epidemic of swine flu: "Our government has finally come up with a cure for which there is no known disease." And a nostalgic shot at a familiar target: "I hear that whenever anyone in the White House tells a lie, Nixon

gets a royalty." End of address. Sustained cheers, through
which Carson returns, blinking in a manner not wholly expli-
cable by the glare of the spotlights, to his seat.

Cardinal Knowledge, the Pudding musical, at last gets under
way. It's a farrago of melodramatic intrigue, with seventeenth-
century setting and plethora of puns; e.g., characters called
Barry de Hatchet and Viscount Hugh Behave. (How far can
a farrago go?) Am pleased by high standard of performance,
slightly dismayed by lack of obscenity in text. No need to
dwell on show, except to praise Robert Peabody, mountain-
ously flirtatious as Lady Della Tory, and Mark Szpak, president
of Pudding Theatricals, who plays the heroine, Juana de Boise,
with a raven-haired Latin vivacity that puts me in mind of the
youthful Lea Padovani. Or the present Mrs. Carson.

10:15 P.M.: Intermission was yet over. Carson at bar, still
on caffeine, besieged by mass of undergraduates, all of whom
receive bright and civil answers to their questions. He has now
been talking to strangers for thirteen hours (interrupted only
by Act I of show) with no loss of buoyancy. "For the first time
in my life," he remarks to me, "I know what it's like to be a
politician."

Midnight has passed before the curtain falls and he makes
his exit, to renewed acclamation. One gets the impression that
the audience is applauding not just an admired performer but—
why shun simplicities?—a decent and magnanimous man.

Two thoughts in conclusion:

(1) If the most we ask of live television is entertainment
within the limits set by commercial sponsorship, then Carson,
week in, week out, is the very best we shall get. If, on the
other hand, we ask to be challenged, disturbed, or provoked
at the same time that we are entertained, Carson must inevitably
disappoint us. But to blame him for that would be to accuse
him of breaking a promise he never made.

(2) Though the written and rehearsed portions of what Carson does can be edited together into an extremely effective
cabaret act, the skill that makes him unique—the ability to run
a talk show as he does—is intrinsically, exclusively televisual.
Singers, actors, and dancers all have multiple choices: they
can exercise their talents in the theatre, on TV, or in the movies.

But a talk-show host can only become a more successful talk-show host. There is no place in the other media for the gifts that distinguish him—most specifically, for the gift of reinventing himself, night after night, without rehearsal or repetition. Carson, in other words, is a grand master of the one show-business art that leads nowhere. He has painted himself not into a corner but onto the top of a mountain.

Long—or, at least, as long as the air at the summit continues to nourish and elate him—may he stay there.

[1978]

Frolics and detours of a short little hebrew man

—MEL BROOKS

ON A WARM NIGHT in October, 1959, I was bidden to a party
at Mamma Leone's, a restaurant on Forty-eighth Street that
was (and is) one of the largest and most popular in Manhattan's
theatre district. Random House had taken it over for the evening
to celebrate the publication of *Act One*, the first volume of
Moss Hart's autobiography, which in no way surprised its
publishers by turning out to be a best-seller. A further excuse
for festivity was the fact that the author's fifty-fifth birthday
was to take place the following day. By any standards, the
guest list—some three hundred strong—was fairly eye-catch-
ing. In addition to a favored bunch of critics and columnists,
it included a representative selection of the show-business celebrities then active or resident in New York, among them
Claudette Colbert, John Gielgud, Jose Ferrer, Margaret Leighton, Ed Sullivan, Alan Jay Lerner, Yves Montand, Simone
Signoret, Ethel Merman, Alec Guinness, Truman Capote, Ros-
alind Russell, and Marlene Dietrich—at which point my memory gives out. A group of Moss Hart's admirers had put together
a floor show in his honor, and this was already under way
when I arrived. Betty Comden and Adolph Green were just
finishing a routine that satirized some of the more disastrous
ways in which *Act One* might be adapted for the screen. During
the applause, I was burrowing through the resplendent mob,
and like many of my fellow guests, I failed to catch the names
of the next performers when they were introduced by the master
of ceremonies, Phil Silvers.

Peering over the heads of a hundred or so standees, in front
of whom the other spectators sat, squatted, or sprawled, I saw
two men in business suits. One, tall and lean, was conducting

an interview with the other, who was short and compact. Their faces were among the few in the room that were not instantly recognizable. Though I took no notes, I recall much of what they said, and the waves of laughter that broke over it, and the wonder with which I realized that every word of it was improvised. The tall man was suave but relentlessly probing, the stubby one urgent and eager in response, though capable of outrage when faced with questions he regarded as offensive. Here, having been shaken through the sieve of nineteen years, is what my memory retains:

Q.: I gather, sir, that you are a famous psychoanalyst?

A.: That is correct.

Q.: May I ask where you studied psychiatry?

A.: At the Vienna School of Good Luck.

Q.: Who analyzed you?

A.: I was analyzed by No. 1 himself.

Q.: You mean the great Sigmund Freud?

A.: In person. Took me during lunchtime, charged me a nickel.

Q.: What kind of man was he?

A.: Lovely little fellow. I shall never forget the hours we spent together, me lying on the couch, him sitting right there beside me, wearing a nice off-the-shoulder dress.

Q.: Is it true, sir, that Mr. Moss Hart is one of your patients?

A.: That is also correct.

[As everyone present knew, Moss Hart had been in analysis for many years, and made no secret of the benefits he had derived from it.]

Q.: Could you tell us, sir, what Mr. Hart talks about during your analytic sessions?

A.: He talks smut. He talks dirty, he talks filthy, he talks pure, unadulterated smut. It makes me want to puke.

Q.: How do you cope with this?

A.: I give him a good slap on the wrist. I wash his mouth out with soap. I tell him, "Don't talk dirty, don't say those things."

Q.: What are Mr. Hart's major problems? Does he have an Oedipus complex?

A.: What is that?

Q.: You're an analyst, sir, and you never heard of an Oedipus complex?

A.: Never in my life.

Q.: Well, sir, it's when a man has a passionate desire to make love to his own mother.

A. (*after a pause*): That's the dirtiest thing I ever heard. Where do you get that filth?

Q.: It comes from a famous play by Sophocles.

A.: Was he Jewish?

Q.: No, sir, he was Greek.

A.: With a Greek, who knows? But, with a Jew, you don't do a thing like that even to your wife, let alone your mother.

Q.: But, sir, according to Freud, *every* man has this intense sexual attachment to his—

A.: Wait a minute, wait a minute, whoa, hee-haw, just hold your horses right there. Moss Hart is a nice Jewish boy. Maybe on a Saturday night he takes the mother to the movies, maybe on the way home he gives her a little peck in the back of the cab, but going to bed with the mother—get out of here! What kind of smut is that?

Q.: During your sessions with Mr. Hart, does he ever become emotionally overwrought?

A.: Very frequently, and it's a degrading spectacle.

Q.: How do you handle these situations?

A.: I walk straight out of the room, I climb up a stepladder, and I toss in aspirins through the transom.

When they stopped, after about a quarter of an hour, the cabaret ended, and that was just as well, for nobody could have followed them. A crowd of professional entertainers erupted in cheers. The idea of a puritanical analyst was a masterstroke of paradox, and the execution had matched the concept in brilliance. Moss Hart was heard to say that the act was the funniest fourteen minutes he could remember. The room buzzed with comment, yet hardly anyone seemed to know who the little maestro was. Diligent quizzing revealed that he was a thirty-three-year-old television writer, that he had spent most of the preceding ten years turning out sketches for Sid Caesar, and that his name was Mel Brooks. Facially, he had one attribute that is shared, for reasons I have never been able to fathom, by nearly all top-flight comedians; viz., a long upper lip. I later discovered that his interrogator was Mel Tolkin, another, and a senior, member of the renowned menagerie of authors whose scripts, as interpreted by Caesar, Imogene Coca, and a talented supporting cast, had made "Your Show of Shows" a golden landmark in the wasteland of television comedy. Tolkin (a harassed-looking man, once compared by Brooks to "a stork that dropped a baby and broke it and is coming to explain to the parents") was standing in at the party for Carl Reiner, a gifted performer who had also been part of the Caesarean operation. Ever since they met, in 1950, Brooks and Reiner had been convulsing their friends with impromptu duologues. The Moss Hart jamboree was an important show-business event, and, the press being present in force, it would have marked their semi-public debut. Unfortunately, Reiner had a TV job in Los Angeles and could not make the date; hence his replacement by Tolkin, who had performed with Brooks on several previous occasions, though never in front of such a daunting audience. I knew nothing of this at the time; Tolkin struck me as a first-rate straight man. All I knew as I left Mamma Leone's that night was that his stubby, pseudo Freudian partner was the most original comic improviser I had ever seen.

We move forward to Hollywood in 1977. Carl Reiner, who has just directed a boomingly successful comedy called *Oh, God!*, recalls for me the events that led up to Brooks's appearance at the Hart party. "During the fifties," he says, "we spent our days inventing characters for Caesar, but Mel was really using Caesar as a vehicle. What he secretly wanted was to perform himself. So in the evening we'd go to a party and I'd pick a character for him to play. I never told him what it was going to be, but I always tried for something that would force him to go into panic, because a brilliant mind in panic is a wonderful thing to see. For instance, I might say, 'We

have with us tonight the celebrated sculptor Sir Jacob Epstone,'
and he'd have to take it from there. Or I'd make him a Jewish
pirate, and he'd complain about how he was being pushed out
of the business because of the price of sailcloth and the cost
of crews nowadays. Another time, I introduced him as Carl
Sandburg, and he made up reams of phony Sandburg poetry.
There was no end to what he could be—a U-boat commander,
a deaf songwriter, an entire convention of antique dealers.

"Once, I started a routine by saying 'Sir, you're the Israeli
wrestling champion of the world, yet you're extremely small.
How do you manage to defeat all those enormous opponents?'
'I give them a soul kiss,' he said, 'and they're so shocked they
collapse. Sometimes I hate doing it, like when it's a Greek
wrestler, because they have garlic breath.' I asked him whether
he was homosexual. 'No, I have a wife.' 'But what's the
difference between kissing her and kissing a wrestler?' 'My
wife,' he said, 'is the only one I know who kisses from the
inside out.' That was pure Mel—a joke so wild it was almost
abstract. I used to enjoy trying to trap him. One night, when
he was doing an Israeli heart surgeon, I said, 'Tell me, sir,
who's that huge man standing in the corner?' 'Who knows?
Who cares?' 'But surely, sir, you don't want a total stranger
hanging around your operating theatre, bringing in germs?'
'Listen, in a hospital, a few germs more or less, what's the
difference?' 'Even so,' I said, 'I'm still curious to know what
that very large gentleman does.' 'Look,' he said. 'He's a big
man, right? With a lot of muscle? You're small and Jewish,
you don't mess around with big guys like that. Let him stand
there if he wants to.' I still wouldn't let him off the hook. 'But
what's that strange-looking machine beside him?' 'You mean
the cyclotron?' 'No, the one next to that.' 'Oh,' he said, 'that
is the Rokeach 14 machine. It makes Jewish soap powder. As
you well know, we Jewish doctors are incredibly clean, and
we try not to soil our patients during the macabre process of
cutting them to pieces. We get through an awful lot of Rokeach
14.' Which is in fact a brand of kosher soap used by orthodox
Jews." (Brooks later told me, apropos of Reiner's attempt to
outwit him, "He was absolutely dazzling. I'd be going along
pretty good, getting laughs, and he would suddenly people the
room with alien characters bearing mysterious devices. What

was I supposed to do? I had to come up with an explanation or die.")

"Another time," Reiner continued, "we created a family consisting of a Jewish mother, a black father, and a homosexual son. Mel was playing all three parts when I threw him a curve. 'Tell me,' I said, 'why is your son white-haired when you are not?' He answered as the mother. 'I told him always to stay inside the building,' he said, 'because it's full of Jews. One day, he went out and saw a whole bunch of Gentiles on the next block and his hair turned white over-night. It was his own fault. He should have stayed indoors.' Sometimes, if a party went on late, Mel would get punchy and forget the name of the character I'd given him. Once, I said, 'Here is Irving Schwartz, author of the best-selling novel *Up*.' We developed that for ten minutes or so, and then I said, 'Your book has a very unusual jacket. It's triangular in shape.' 'I'm glad you noticed that,' he said. 'It's a one-breasted seersucker jacket. The name is on the lapel—Irving Feinberg.' 'I think you've got that wrong, sir. Your name is Irving Schwartz.' 'Wait,' he said. 'Wait till I look at my driver's license.' He pulled out his wallet, looked at the license, and reacted with shock. 'Hey!' he said. 'My name is Mr. William Faversham.' 'Well, Mr. Faversham, could you tell us how you came to write a book under the name of Schwartz?' 'I think somebody stole my wallet.' But if Mel had a specialty, it was psychiatrists. He did dozens of them, maybe because he was in analysis himself between 1951 and 1957. When I made him a Greek psychiatrist, he said he was Dr. Corinne Corfu, the man who analyzed Socrates. And there was one amazing evening when he played eight different psychiatrists simultaneously, without getting any of them mixed up. He was never at a loss."

"Never" may be an overstatement. Mel Tolkin remembers a party at which Brooks, sans Reiner, delivered a soaringly funny monologue but could not find a satisfactory payoff line. He finally broke off in the middle of a sentence and walked out of the room. After the guests had waited for a while in expectant silence, Tolkin went out to look for him. He had gone home in self-disgust, leaving a scribbled note on a table. It read, "A Jew cries for help!"

"In the fifties," Reiner says, "Mel and I performed just for

fun, among friends." Around 1953, Reiner bought a tape recorder on which to preserve some of their routines. One evening, after dinner at his home in Westchester, inspiration
nudged him. He turned on the machine, picked up the microphone, strolled over to where Brooks was sitting, and said,
"Ladies and gentlemen, we are fortunate to have with us tonight
a man who was present at the crucifixion of Jesus Christ." The
curve had been thrown. Brooks rose to the challenge and hit
it out of the park, with repercussions to which we shall return:
enough, for the moment, to note that this occasion marked the
birth of a comic figure indestructible in every sense of the
word; namely, the Two-Thousand-Year-Old Man. "The guy
who gave us our entrée into the celebrity world was a well-
known playwright named Joe Fields," Reiner goes on. "He
heard us performing somewhere in the late fifties and invited
us to eat at his apartment, along with people like Lerner and
Loewe, Harold Rome, and Billy Rose. We became a sort of
upper-bohemian cult. Then, in 1959, I appeared in a movie
called *Happy Anniversary*, and Mel came to the wrap party for
the cast and crew at a restaurant in the Village. Moss Hart was
dining with his wife on the other side of the room. Mel recognized him. All of a sudden, he got up and walked across to
Hart's table and said, very loudly, 'Hello. You don't know
who I am. My name is Mel Brooks. Do you know who you
are? Your name is Moss Hart. Do you know what you've
written? You wrote *Once in a Lifetime* with George Kaufman,
and *You Can't Take It with You* and *The Man Who Came to
Dinner*. You wrote *Lady in the Dark* and you directed *My Fair
Lady*.' And he ran right through the list of Hart's credits. 'You
should be more arrogant!' he shouted. 'You have earned the
right to be supercilious! *Why are you letting me talk to you?*'
He went ranting on like that, and Hart looked petrified. It took
him quite a time to realize that Mel wasn't just a nut case. But
eventually he started laughing, and everything was fine. Later
on, Mel and I did one of our bits. Hart couldn't help hearing
it and that was how we got the invitation to Mamma Leone's."

   In the autumn of 1959, Reiner's career was prospering, both
on TV and in the cinema. As he put it to me, "I didn't need
to sing for my supper anymore." Brooks's position was very
different. Sid Caesar, for whom he had worked at a steeply

rising salary for ten years, had been taken off the air, and Brooks was almost broke. "One day it's five thousand a week, the next day it's zilch," he said in a magazine interview long afterward, "I couldn't get a job anywhere! Comedy shows were out of style, and the next five years I averaged eighty-five dollars a week. . . . It was a terrifying nose dive." Recently, he told me, "At the time of that Random House party, I was on the brink of disaster." Even during the highflying days with Caesar, he had been prone to recurrent fits of depression. "There were fourteen or fifteen occasions when I seriously thought of killing myself. I even had the pills." One of his colleagues on "Your Show of Shows" recalls how Brooks snapped out of a particularly black mood by grabbing a straw hat and cane and ad-libbing a peppy, up-tempo number that ended:

> Life may be rotten today, folks,
> But I take it all in stride,
> 'Cause tomorrow I'm on my way, folks—
> I'm committing suicide!

Mamma Leone's gave me my first sight of Brooks in performance. My last (to date) took place in the summer of 1977, when he was shooting his Hitchcockian comedy *High Anxiety*. In the intervening eighteen years, and most drastically in the last three of them, his life had changed beyond recognition. A trio of successive hits (*Blazing Saddles, Young Frankenstein,* and *Silent Movie*) had made him a millionaire. In December, 1976, the exhibitors of America had placed him fifth on their annual list of the twenty-five stars who exert the greatest box-office appeal—a fantastic achievement for a middle-aged man whose only starring appearance up to that time had been in a picture, *Silent Movie*, that did not even require him to speak. His friend Burt Reynolds, rated sixth that year, grew accustomed to picking up the phone and hearing a jubilant voice announce, "Hello, Six, this is Five speaking." In the 1977 poll, Reynolds rose to fourth position, while Brooks slipped to seventh, but considering that no new film by Brooks had been shown in the preceding year, it was remarkable, as he pointed out to me, that he had retained a place in the top ten. "And in 1978," he said, "I'm sure I'll be No. 5 again."

* * *

I draw on my journal for the following impressions of the Once and Future Five at work (and play) on *High Anxiety*, a quintuple-threat Brooks movie in which he functioned as producer, director, co-author, title-song composer, and star:

July 14, 1977: Arrive in Pasadena for the last day of shooting. By pure but pleasing coincidence, location is named Brookside Park. Temperature ninety degrees, atmosphere smog-laden. Only performers present are Brooks, leaping around in well-cut charcoal-gray suit with vest, and large flock of trained pigeons. As at Mamma Leone's, he is playing a psychiatrist. Sequence in rehearsal is parody of *The Birds*, stressing aspect of avian behavior primly ignored by Hitchcock: Pigeons pursue fleeing Brooks across park, subjecting him to bombardment of bird droppings. Spattered star seeks refuge in gardener's hut, slams door, sinks exhausted onto upturned garbage can. After momentary respite, lone white plop hits lapel, harbinger of redoubled aerial assault through hole in roof. Brooks's hundred-yard dash is covered by tracking camera, while gray-haired technicians atop motorized crane mounted on truck squirt bird excreta (simulated by mayonnaise and chopped spinach) from height of thirty feet. Barry Levinson, one of four collaborators on screenplay, observes to me, "We have enough equipment here to put a man on the moon, and it's all being used to put bird droppings on Brooks." After each of numerous trial runs and takes, pigeons obediently return to their cages, putty in the hands of their trainer—"the same bird wrangler," publicity man tells me, "who was employed by Hitchcock himself." Find manic energy of Brooks, now fifty-one years old, awesome: by the time shot is satisfactorily in can, he will have sprinted, in this depleting heat, at least a mile, without loss of breath, ebullience, or directorial objectivity, and without taking a moment's break.

Each take is simultaneously recorded on videotape and instantly played back on TV screen—a technique pioneered by Jerry Lewis—to be scrutinized by Brooks, along with his fellow-authors, Levinson, Rudy DeLuca, and Ron Clark, who make comments ranging from condign approval to barbed derision. Dispelling myth that he is megalomaniac, Brooks listens persuadably to their suggestions, many of which he carries out. The writers, receiving extra pay as consultants, have been with him throughout shooting, except for three weeks when they went on strike for more money. Brooks coaxed them back by giving up part of his own share of profits not only of *High Anxiety* but of *Silent Movie*, on which he worked with same three authors. Main purpose of their presence is not to rewrite— hardly a line has been changed or cut—but to offer pragmatic advice. In addition, they all play supporting roles in picture. Later, as also happened on *Silent Movie*, they will view first assembly of footage and help Brooks with process of reducing it to rough-cut form. "Having us around keeps Mel on his toes," Levinson explains to me. "He likes to have constant feedback, and he knows we won't flatter him." All of which deals telling blow to already obsolescent *auteur* theory, whereby film is seen as springing fully armed from mind of director. Good to find Brooks, who reveres writers, giving them place in sun: he has often said that he became a director primarily in self-defense, to "protect my vision"—i.e., the script as written. "There's been no interference from the front office," Levinson continues, as Brooks trudges back to his mark for yet another charge through cloudburst of salad dressing. "Nobody from Fox has even come to see us. Mel has free rein. Jerry Lewis once had that kind of liberty, but who has it now? Only Mel and, I guess, Woody Allen."

Am reminded of remark made to me by Allen a few days earlier: "In America, people who do comedy are traditionally left alone. The studios feel we're on a wavelength that's alien to them. They believe we have access to some secret formula that they don't. With drama, it's different. Everybody thinks he's an expert."

Writers and camera crew gather round tree-shaded monitor to watch replay of latest take. Smothered in synthetic ordure, star bustles over to join them:

BROOKS: I stare at life through fields of mayonnaise. (*Wipes eyes with towel.*) Was it for this that I went into movies? Did I say to my mother, "I'm going to be a big star, momma, and have birds shit on me"? I knew that in show business *people* shit on you—but *birds*! Some of this stuff is not mayonnaise, you know. Those are real pigeons up there.

The take (last of twenty) is generally approved, and Brooks orders it printed. Welcoming me to location, he expresses pleasure at hearing British accent, adding, "I love the Old World. I love the courteous sound of the engines of English cabs. I also love France and good wine and good food and good homosexual production designers. I believe all production designers should have a brush stroke, a scintilla, of homosexuality, because they have to hang out with smart people." (Brooks once declared, in an interview with *Playboy*, that he loved Europe so much that he always carried a photograph of it in his wallet. "Of course," he went on, "Europe was a lot younger then. It's really not a very good picture. Europe looks much better in person." He lamented the fact that his beloved continent was forever fighting: "I'll be so happy when it finally settles down and gets married.")

Brooks's version of shower scene from *Psycho*, shot several days before, now appears on monitor. An unlikely stand-in for Janet Leigh, Brooks is seen in bathrobe approaching fatal tub. Cut to closeup of feet as he daintily sheds sandals, around which robe falls to floor. Next comes rear view of Brooks, naked from head to hips, stepping into bath. Star watches himself entranced.

BROOKS (*passionately*): When people see this, I want them to say, "He may be just a small Jew, but I love him. A short little Hebrew man, but I'd follow him to the ends of the earth." I want every fag in L.A. to see it and say, "Willya *look* at that *back*?"

Before lunch break, he takes opportunity to deliver speech of thanks to assembled crew, whose reactions show that they have relished working with him.

Recall another opposite quote from Woody Allen, who said to me in tones of stunned unbelief, "I hear there's a sense of enjoyment on Mel's set. I hear the people on his movies love the experience so much that they wish it could go on forever. On my movies, they're *thrilled* when it's over."

"As you all know," Brooks begins, "you'll never get an Academy Award with me, because I make comedies." This is a recurrent gripe. Brooks feels that film comedy has never received, either from industry or from audience, respect it deserves, and he is fond of pointing out that Chaplin got his

1971 Academy Award "just for surviving," not for *The Gold Rush* or *City Lights*.

BROOKS (*continuing*): I want to say from my heart that you're the best crew I ever found. Of course, I didn't look that hard. But you have been the most fun, and the costliest. I wish to express my sincere hope that the next job you get is—*work*.

Over lunch, consumed at long trestle tables under trees, he recounts—between and sometimes during mouthfuls—how he visited Hitchcock to get his blessings on *High Anxiety*.

BROOKS: He's a very emotional man. I told him that where other people take saunas to relax, I run *The Lady Vanishes*, for the sheer pleasure of it. He had tears in his eyes. I think he understood that I wasn't going to make fun of him. If the picture is a sendup, it's also an act of homage to a great artist. I'm glad I met him, because I love him. I love a lot of people that I want to meet so I can tell them about it before they get too old. Fred Astaire, for instance. And Chaplin. I've got to go to Switzerland and tell him—just a simple "Thank you," you know? [Chaplin died five months later, before this pilgrimage could be made.]

More Brooksian table talk, in response to student writing dissertation on his work:

STUDENT: What's the best way to become a director?

BROOKS: The royal road to direction used to be through the editing room. Today my advice would be: write a few successful screenplays. Anybody can direct. There are only eleven good writers. In all of Hollywood. I can name you many, many screenwriters who have gone on to become directors. In any movie, they are the prime movers.

STUDENT: Have you any ambition to make a straight dramatic film?

BROOKS (*vehemently*): No! Why should I waste my good time making a straight dramatic film? Sydney Pollack can do that. The people who can't make you laugh can do that. Suppose I became the Jean Renoir of America. What the hell would be left for the other guys to do? I would take all their jobs away. It would be very unfair of me.

STUDENT: In other words, "Shoemaker, stick to your last"?

BROOKS: Yes. And in Hollywood you're only as good as your last last.

STUDENT: But don't you want to surprise your audience?

BROOKS: Sure. Every time. I gave them *Blazing Saddles*, a Jewish Western with a black hero, and that was a megahit. Then I gave them a delicate and private film, *Young Frankenstein*, and that was a hit. Then I made *Silent Movie*, which I thought was a brave and experimental departure. It turned out to be another Mel Brooks hit. *High Anxiety* is the ultimate Mel Brooks movie. It has lunatic class.

STUDENT: But what if you had a serious dramatic idea that really appealed to you? Would you—

BROOKS: Listen, there are one hundred and thirty-one viable directors of drama in this country. There are only two viable directors of comedy. Because in comedy you have to do everything the people who make drama do—create plot and character and motive and so forth—and *then*, on top of *that*, be funny.

UNIDENTIFIED BEARDED MAN: Have you ever thought of being funny onstage?

BROOKS: No, because I might become this white-belted, white-shoed, maroon-mohair-jacketed type who goes to Vegas and sprays Jew-jokes all over the audience. A few years of that and I might end up going to England, like George Raft or Dane Clark, wearing trench coats in B movies.

Debate ensues about differences (in style and personality) between Brooks and the other "viable director of comedy," Woody Allen. Both are New York Jewish, both wrote for Sid Caesar, both are hypochondriacs, much influenced by time spent in analysis. There is general agreement at table on obvious distinction—that Brooks is extrovert and Allen introvert.

BARRY LEVINSON: They're total opposites. Mel is a peasant type. His films deal with basic wants and greeds, like power and money. Woody's films are about inadequacies—especially sexual inadequacy—and frailty and vulnerability. Also, like Chaplin, Woody is his own vehicle. His movies are like episodes from an autobiography. You couldn't say that about Mel.

HOWARD ROTHBERG (*slim, dark-haired young man who has been Brooks's personal manager since 1975*): The big difference is that Mel's appeal is more universal. *Blazing Saddles* grossed thirty-five million domestically and *Silent Movie* is already up to twenty million. Woody, on the other hand, appeals to a cult. I love his pictures, but they have a box-office ceiling. They don't go through the roof.

BROOKS (*who has been wolfing cannelloni, followed by ice cream*): No matter how much *High Anxiety* grosses, it won't give me one more iota of freedom. I have the freedom right now to do anything I want. My contract is with the public— to entertain them, not just to make money out of them. I went into show business to make a noise, to *pronounce myself*. I want to go on making the loudest noise to the most people. If I can't do that, I'm not going to make a quiet, exquisite noise for a cabal of cognoscenti.

This is Brooks the blusterer speaking, the unabashed attention-craver who started out as a teenage timpanist and is still metaphorically beating his drum. Can testify that drummer has alter ego, frequently silenced by the din: Brooks the secret connoisseur, worshipper of good writing, and expert on the Russian classics, with special reference to Gogol, Turgenev, Dostoevski, and Tolstoy. Is it possible that—to adapt famous aphorism by Cyril Connolly—inside every Mel Brooks a Woody Allen is wildly signalling to be let out?

STUDENT: I think your films are somehow more benevolent and affirmative than Woody Allen's.

BROOKS: Let's say I'm beneficent. I produce beneficial things. A psychiatrist once told me he thought my psyche was basically very healthy, because it led to *product*. He said I was like a great creature that gave beef or milk. I'm munificent. I definitely feel kingly. Same kind of Jew as Napoleon.

STUDENT: Napoleon was Jewish?

BROOKS: Could have been. He was short enough. Also, he was very nervous and couldn't keep his hands steady. That's why he always kept them under his lapels. I put him in one of my records. [Fans will remember how the Two-Thousand-Year-Old Man took a summer cottage on Elba, where he met the exiled Emperor on the beach—"a shrimp, used to go down by the water and cry"—without at first realizing who he was: "The guy was in a bathing suit, how did I know? There was no place to put his hands."] Anyway, there's something disgustingly egotistical about me. I never truly felt inferior. I never developed small defenses. I never ran scared. Even in comedy, you don't want your hero to be a coward. You want him to go forth and give combat, which is what I do in *High*

Anxiety. Now, Woody makes Fellini-ish, Truffaut-ish films. He starts out with the idea of making art. He feels that his art is his life. And more power to him. The difference is that if someone wants to call my movies art or crap, I don't mind.

Detect, once more, sound of obsessive drumbeating; last sentence, in particular, seems intended to convince drummer himself as much as anyone else. Conversation breaks off as Brooks returns to work. Hear him in distance inviting youthful assistant to take over direction of brief scene in gardener's hut, already rehearsed, where star is deluged anew with bird droppings—"a job," he graciously declares to the grinning apprentice, "fully commensurate with your latent talents."

Finishing my coffee, I mull over recent conversation with Gene Wilder, who has been directed thrice by Brooks (in *The Producers, Blazing Saddles,* and *Young Frankenstein*) and once by Allen (in *Everything You Always Wanted to Know about Sex but Were Afraid to Ask*). According to Wilder: "Working with Woody is what it must be like to work with Ingmar Bergman. It's all very hushed. You and I were talking quietly now, but if we were on Woody's set someone would already have told us to keep our voices down. He said three things to me while we were shooting—'You know where to get tea and coffee?' and 'You know where to get lunch?' and 'Shall I see you tomorrow?' Oh, and there was one other thing: 'If you don't like any of these lines, change them.' Mel would never say that. The way Woody makes a movie, it's as if he was lighting ten thousand safety matches to illuminate a city. Each one of them is a little epiphany, topical, ethnic, or political. What Mel wants to do is set off atom bombs of laughter. Woody will take a bow and arrow or a hunting rifle and aim it at small, precise targets. Mel grabs a shotgun, loads it with fifty pellets, and points it in the general direction of one enormous target. Out of fifty, he'll score at least six or seven huge bull's-eyes, and those are what people always remember about his films. He can synthesize what audiences all over the world are feeling, and suddenly, at the right moment, blurt it out. He'll take a universal and crystallize it. Sometimes he's vulgar and unbalanced, but when those seven shots hit that target, I know that little maniac is a genius. A loud kind of Jewish genius—maybe that's as close as you can get to defining him."

This reminds me of something written in 1974 by the critic Andrew Sarris:

> Allen's filmmaking is more cerebral, and Brooks's more intuitive. In a strange way, Brooks is more likable than Allen. Thus, even when Allen tries to do the right thing, he seems very narrowly self-centred, whereas even when Mel Brooks surrenders to the most cynical calculations—as he does so often in *Blazing Saddles*—he still spills over with emotional generosity.... What Allen lacks is the reckless abandon and careless rapture of Brooks.

Reflect that this positive judgment is not necessarily incompatible with negative opinion I have lately heard from former colleague of Brooks; viz., "Woody has become a professional, whereas Mel is still a brilliant amateur. Amateurs are people putting on parties with multimillion-dollar budgets."

Return to set, where, after nearly twelve weeks' shooting, current party is over. Brooks has brought in picture—budgeted at four million dollars—four days ahead of schedule. Though in buoyant mood, he expresses horror at rocketing cost of filmmaking: "One actor and a few birds, but I'll bet you this has been a twenty-thousand-dollar day." (Studio accounting department afterward confirms that he would have won his bet.) I take my leave. Brooks clicks heels and bows, saying, "Your obedient Jew." He misses no opportunity to brandish his Jewishness, which he uses less as a weapon than as a shield. Remember (he seems to be pleading) that I must be liked, because it is nowadays forbidden to dislike a Jew.

Manager Rothberg accompanies me to parking lot, explaining how much success of movie means to Brooks. I suggest that surely he can afford to make a flop. "Financially, he can," Rothberg says. "Psychologically, he can't."

August 31, 1977: "My beloved, you are guinea pigs." It is a balmy evening seven weeks later, and Brooks is introducing first showing of rough-cut to audience of two hundred (including workers on picture, their friends and relations, and minor studio employees such as waiters, cleaners, and parking attendants) who have crowded into private theatre at Fox. He continues, "There are children present. Some of them may be mine, so I'm not going to do the filthy speech that is customary on these occasions. For the nonce, by which I mean no offense, this movie. is called *High Anxiety*, a phrase that I hope will enter common parlance and become part of the argot of Americana. But what you will see tonight has no music, no sound effects, and no titles. You won't even see our swirling artwork. You will, however, see a lot of crayon lines, which I will explain for the benefit of the editor. They indicate something called opticals. This picture has one hundred and six dissolves, of which you will see *not one*. There are some other very fancy opticals that I am having processed in Cairo right now. There is also one crayon mark that should be on a men's room wall, but we couldn't get it out in time. As you know, it's incumbent on us all to be killed in a Hitchcock movie, and you will see several people being very tastefully slaughtered. I regret to tell you that in casting four crucial roles we ran out of money, so the people who *wrote* the picture are *in* it. Finally, let me say that I wish you well, but I wish myself better."

Screening gets warm response, punctuated by applause. Brooks scampers down front and thanks audience for their attention, their laughter, and their profound awareness that "there are eighteen million Arabs surrounding two hundred and six Jews, and—no, wait, that's from some other speech, at some hospital somewhere." He then requests detailed and candid criticism: Where did movie drag? Which gags failed? Was plot clear? He listens raptly to all answers, asks other spectators for corroboration or dissent, makes careful notes of points on which action should be taken. And goes back to three and a half more months of furious work, polishing the film for a December premiere, in order to qualify for the Academy Award, which, as he repeatedly, belligerently, fate-placatingly asserts, no comedy can ever win.

The man we know as Mel Brooks was born in a Brooklyn tenement on June 28, 1926. To the question "What were you born?" when it was posed by David Susskind on a TV panel show in 1960, he replied, "George M. Cohan." (Later in the program, he admitted that he really had two diametrically opposed selves, that there were two different sides to "the strange amalgam, the marvellous pastiche that is me." Under Suss-kind's remorseless interrogation, he confessed, "The first side of me is Sir Anthony Eden. . . . And the other is Fred Astaire.") In reality, what he was born was Melvin Kaminsky, the young-est of four boys, whose parents were Eastern European im-migrants. His father, Maximilian Kaminsky, came from Dan-zig, and his mother, née Kate Brookman, from Kiev. According to Brooks, one reason for the success of his collaboration with people like Carl Reiner and Mel Tolkin was that they all shared "the same background, the second-generation Russian-Ukrain-ian-Jewish intellectual heritage." He told Susskind that his mother left Kiev in early childhood, never having learned Rus-sian, and that her English was still fairly impenetrable, mainly because the voice of authority, which she took as her model on arrival in New York, invariably belonged to an Irish cop. The result, Brooks said, was that "she speaks no known lan-guage, and speaks it with an Irish accent."

His father, a process server, died suddenly of a kidney disease at the age of thirty-four, when Brooks was two and a half years old. The shock left him with a sense of loss that persisted into adult life. For example, he recognizes that his relationship with Sid Caesar was that of a child clamoring for the attention and approval of a father. When Brooks went into analysis, in 1951, his purpose, he recently told me, was "to learn how to be a father instead of a son." (His six years on the couch, two to four sessions per week, undoubtedly hastened the emergence of Brooks the father figure, patriarchal ruler of movie sets. "He's sometimes my mother hen, and sometimes even my brother," Gene Wilder says, "but most of the time he's my father." On a wall of Wilder's office at Fox, there is a photograph of the two men, inscribed "To my son Gene, with love, Daddy Mel.") Kate Kaminsky, widowed and pen-niless, with four boys to support, took a job in the garment district, putting in a ten-hour day and bringing home extra work in the evening. A miniature dynamo, less than five feet in height, she also found time and energy to keep her children fed, their clothes washed and mended, and their apartment in spotless trim. The roach or bedbug that entered her domain had signed its own death warrant. She exemplified what Brooks said to Susskind of Jewish mothers in general: "Until they die themselves, they *clean* and *kill*." He went on to sum up his feelings about this indomitable woman by declaiming, "If I could, I would go skinny-dipping with my mother." (Still vigorous in her eighty-third year, she nowadays lives in Florida.) Irving and Leonard, the eldest two sons, were sent out to work when they were twelve and, on a family income that averaged about thirty-five dollars a week, ends were precariously made to meet. Mrs. Kaminsky was obsessed with the idea of preserving what Brooks describes as a "certain threshold of dignity," and for this reason she always refused to go on relief. It must be remembered that her husband died shortly before the Wall Street crash and that Brooks spent his childhood in the roughest years of the Depression. To be Jewish, Brooklyn-born, fatherless, impoverished, and below average stature—no more classic recipe could be imagined for an American comedian. Or, one might suppose, for an American suicide.

Not long ago, discussing Brooks with a prosperous Jewish movie producer, I remarked that he had once been prone to suicidal impulses. "Nonsense," the producer said, "that's self-dramatization. Jews don't kill themselves. Look at their history. They're too busy fighting to survive."

When I reported this conversation to Brooks, he said, "You were talking to a rich Jew. Poor people kill themselves, and a lot of poor people are Jews. One evening, when I was a kid, a woman jumped off the top of a building next door to where I lived. She was Jewish. And there were plenty of other Jewish suicides during the Depression." The image of that death is burned into Brooks's memory. He was playing with friends on a nearby street. Hearing screams and police sirens, he ran to see what had happened. A corpse, covered by a sheet so that only the feet were visible, was being loaded into an ambulance, and he was sure he recognized the shoes as a pair belonging to his mother. His own apartment was empty. Unknown to him, Mrs. Kaminsky was working overtime in Manhattan. The hours that passed before she returned were the worst he ever lived through.

Some revealing sidelights on Brooks's relationship with his parents are thrown by the recorded routine in which he plays a two-hour-old baby, precociously endowed with the faculty of speech. Interviewed by Carl Reiner, he declares that he

already knows his mother, though he hasn't yet "seen the outside."

> REINER: Do you hope she's good-looking?
> BROOKS: I don't care what she looks like. I'm not
> going to date her. I'm her child. But I know she's good.
> Because you can tell a person by what they are
> inside. . . . And I was there, I was inside, and I looked
> around. She's great. . . . I remember when I was a tad-
> pole, a little fetus there, swimming around.
> REINER: You remember having a tail?
> BROOKS: Sure. Oh, that was the best part. I loved the
> tail.
> REINER: Were you unhappy when it disappeared?
> BROOKS: When I lost my tail, I got a nose. . . . The
> nose is much more important, because—you can't blow
> your tail, know what I mean?

He has a simple theory to account for the attacks of queas-
iness that women suffer during the early months of pregnancy:

> BROOKS: I think the moment they realize that there's
> a living creature in them, they puke.
> REINER: But why?
> BROOKS: Wouldn't you be nauseous if there was
> somebody running around inside of you? . . . It's a fright-
> ening thing.

His knowledge of world celebrities is extremely limited.
Reiner reels off a list of names including Queen Elizabeth,
Winston Churchill, Fidel Castro, and Pandit Nehru, none of
whom means anything to him. Then:

> REINER: Have you heard of Cary Grant?
> BROOKS: Oh, sure. Everybody knows Cary Grant.

Pressed by Reiner, he explains that while he was still in the
womb his mother went to a lot of Cary Grant pictures, whereas
she never took him to any Pandit Nehru pictures. "But I'm
sure," he generously adds, "that he's a *hell* of an actor."

At one point, he leaps to the conclusion that he is a girl ("That's *adorable*!"), but Reiner gently disabuses him. "That's all right," he says, putting a bold face on it. "I'll play ball and get drunk and things. I'll be fine." He tentatively asks whether Burt Lancaster is a girl. Reiner gives him a negative answer, which seems to relieve him. "That's good," he says, reconciled at last to masculinity. "I'll be like him." It has been established earlier that Baby Brooks's linguistic skill is a freakish and short-lived gift, likely to be withdrawn at any moment. As long as the theme is his mother, he is eagerly articulate. Significantly, the withdrawal symptoms begin to appear in the following passage, when Reiner introduces a new subject.

REINER: I'd like to know what you feel about your father.

BROOKS: I feel that Dad is the kind of guy that will gah-gah-san.

REINER: Will what? I didn't get that.

BROOKS: I feel that my father will always be the kind of a guy that will take me to ballgames, and we'll be buddies, and we'll sy-ny-ny, ny-foy.

REINER: I don't understand you.

BROOKS: I think that my father and I will probably get along well together, since we're both boys. We'll probably run around and play ball and *nah-nah-hah, nah-nah-hah*.

REINER: I do believe he's losing his intelligence.

And the track ends with Brooks regressing into wailing, bawling, frantic inarticulacy. It is quite an unnerving sound. Listening to it, I recall something that an old friend of Brooks, the novelist Joseph Heller, once said to me: "There's a side of Mel that will never be fulfilled, no matter how hard he drives himself, and it all goes back to his father's death."

At P.S. 19, Brooks was bright but unstudious—the kind of disruptive, obstreperous child that teachers slap down on principle, wearily aware that he will bounce right back up. "I wasn't an avid reader," he says. "I was always an avid talker and doer. Reading books seemed too conservative for me to bother with." He quickly established himself as the clown of the classroom. One of his favorite movies was *Frankenstein* (the 1931, James Whale version), and he discovered at the age of eight that he could reduce his closest chum, a boy called Gene Cogen, to uncontrollable hysterics by singing "Puttin' On the Ritz" in the manner of Boris Karloff. "We had *folie à deux*," Brooks told me. "It got so bad that Cogen couldn't hear that song near a window, because he might roll out and fall to his death. I would start to sing and he would collapse. He would have to be dragged to the principal's room by his feet, with his head banging on the steps, still laughing." Thus the infant Brooks achieved what every comic traditionally strives for—a knockdown, drag-out exit. (He stored up this triumph for future use: Peter Boyle performs the same routine in *Young Frankenstein*.) Despite, or perhaps because of, the damage to his head, young Cogen remained a fan of Brooks, and said to him one day, "You're going to be famous when you grown up. I know that because nobody else uses words like 'urchin' in English composition."

On the streets, where Irish, Italian, and Polish gangs roamed only a few blocks away, Brooks was funny in self-defense. He later said to a *Playboy* interviewer, "If your enemy is laughing, how can he bludgeon you to death?" Whenever it was possible, he and his pals would travel in the company of a well-built Gentile. Even today, it is an article of faith with Brooks that "every small Jew should have a tall goy for a friend, to walk with him and protect him against assault." Much of Brooks's humor, as we shall see, is inspired by fear: fear of injury, illness, sex, and failure; and also of unfriendly Gentiles, especially large ones, and most particularly if they are Germans or Cossacks. Fear, too, of predatory animals, though not, apparently, of sharks. My evidence for this is drawn from the Susskind program mentioned previously.

SUSSKIND: Now let's talk about Jewish mothers.

DAVID STEINBERG (*another of the panellists*): Forget about Jewish mothers, let's talk about sharks.

BROOKS (*instantly assuming a lecturer's voice, plummy and pedantic*): A shark could never harm you. The shark is a benign creature of the sea. Of course, if you thrash about in the water or if you wear shiny bracelets, the shark will be attracted to you. On occasion, the shark has followed people out of the water and has gone to their blanket and eaten their beach ball. One time, the shark followed my brother Irving home on the Brighton local, and, upon being admitted to the apartment house, the shark entered his apartment—Apartment 4-B—and ate his entire family and a brand-new hat. Apart from that, the shark is a pussycat.

All the apprehensions that surface in Brooks's comedy have the same eventual source: a fear—or, to put it more positively, a hatred—of death. The noise he makes is literally death-defying. I append some Brooksian reflections on mortality, culled from various conversations over the past year.

BROOKS: The whole business of death is too formal nowadays. Bing Crosby just succumbed to the great spectre at the age of seventy-three, but the way it's covered by radio and television and newspapers it is no longer a calamity. It is worded in correct obituary paragraphs and it becomes a normal and ordinary event. The good shock value is taken out of it. The moments of horrible grief over somebody's death are handled for us so that we don't experience them, and then they stay with us too long because we didn't grieve properly. The media formalize the tragedy, put a quick film of Saran Wrap over it, so that we don't feel, "My God, one of us has suddenly ceased to be," so that millions of people don't ask, "Where did Bing Crosby go?" Well, where *did* he go? Don't just tell me he died. I want to know where he went. And I want to grieve a little bit.

MYSELF: Are you scared of dying?

BROOKS: Not right now, not just this moment, because I'm feeling good, I'm not in a lot of pain. But I always intend to be afraid of it. To pay proper respect and homage to it. When I was nine, my friend Arnold said to me that we were both going to die. I said, "You're obviously not right, you can't be right. We're not going to die, because why were we born? It wouldn't make any sense." He said, "What about your grandfather? He died. And what about fish?" I said my grandfather was *very* old, *exceptionally* old, and fish had nothing to do with us. I thought I sounded very clever. All the same, that was the first time I knew I was going to die.

Again:

MYSELF: Do you believe in life after death?

BROOKS: No, I don't. I think that's silly. And there's no Judgment Day, either. There isn't a day when we all kiss the little fishes and shake hands and walk together into God's green heaven. So what are we doing here? My guess is that we are part of an evolving process that has no knowable purpose. What's happened is that we were given too many brains, and our brains have screwed up our biological evolution. If we didn't think so much, we'd know what it was all about. When one leaf on a tree begins to turn yellow, it doesn't turn to the other leaves and say, "Jesus Christ, all you guys are green and I'm turning yellow! What the hell is this?" They just turn yellow, and then red, and then brown, and then they leave the tree, and it's all proper. But we say, "Look at this gray hair! Look at this wrinkle! And, my God, I'm so tired after I walk up fourteen steps!" We defer far too much to our brains, our logic, our powers of rational thought. That's why we're so vain, so egotistical, so full of complaining. Leaves never complain.

MYSELF: You're saying that we ought to go along with the processes of nature. But science tells us that we live on a dying planet, where everything—leaves and people alike—is ultimately doomed to extinction. If that's correct, surely the best way to obey the laws of nature will be to kill ourselves now and have done with it?

BROOKS: But we don't have to, because we're going to die anyway. And, because of that, let's have a merry journey, and shout about how light is good and dark is not. What we should do is not *future* ourselves so much. We should *now* ourselves more. "*Now* thyself" is more important than "*Know* thyself." Reason is what tells us to ignore the present and live in the future. So all we do is make plans. We think that somewhere there are going to be green pastures. It's crazy. Heaven is nothing but a grand, monumental instance of future. Listen, *how* is good. *Now* is wonderful. (*Catching himself on the brink of sounding pretentious, he retreats to the safety of self-mockery, and adopts the tone of a humorless pseudo intellectual.*)

By this, of course, I do not mean to intimate that I espouse a totally Sartrean position.

MYSELF: But you're in the movie business. You have to plan ahead.

BROOKS: I only look ahead commercially. I never look ahead spiritually.

On his records with Reiner, there was no advance planning; Brooks lived entirely in the moment, wholly committed to *now*. For this reason (which we'll examine later), they may well represent his most personal comic achievements.

A final exchange with Brooks on eschatology:

MYSELF: When you're playing the Two-Thousand-Year-Old Man, Reiner asks whether you and your fellow cave dwellers believed in a superior being. You answer, "Yes. A guy Phil." You used to offer up prayers to him, like "O Philip, please don't take our eyes out." Then, one day, he was struck dead by lightning. Reiner asks how you felt about that, and you say, "We looked up. We said, 'There's something bigger than Phil.'" Is there?

BROOKS: Yes. There *is* something bigger than Phil, and I'm afraid of it. That's where my standards of morality come from—fear. And not only fear of God. I know how strong *I* am, how powerful *I* can be, how aggressive *I* can get. And I don't want a world where that kind of force can be turned against me. It frightens me. That's why we've all got to behave. That's the beginning of civil behavior. Fear of ourselves.

In 1939, the Kaminskys moved to Brighton Beach, where they shared a house a block and a half from the sea. "It was sort of rustic out there," Brooks recalls. "We actually got to see *trees*. I loved it." One of their neighbors was Buddy Rich, Artie Shaw's new drummer, who befriended Brooks and gave him an occasional free lesson in the art of percussion. The following summer, Brooks took a vacation job as a general helper at a hotel in the Catskills, washing dishes, keeping the tennis courts clean, and yelling things like "Mrs. Bloom, your time is up!" at people in rented rowboats. The food supplied to the staff still haunts his nightmares. Of one especially feculent pie, he says, "It lay under my heart for three years. I called it Harold. I used to pat it every morning and ask it how it was—'Remember how you were when I ate you, you little devil?'" He worked out a simple comedy routine, which, as a reward for good conduct, he was occasionally allowed to perform. Clad in a black overcoat and derby hat, and toting two suitcases, the fourteen-year-old Brooks would trudge out onto the high diving board. Pausing at the edge, he would suddenly scream "Business is terrible! I can't go on!" and plunge into the pool.

After two years of seaside life, Mrs. Kaminsky brought her family back to the old neighborhood; the reason, Brooks says, was that "she missed the friendships of the ghetto." He attended Eastern District High School, where he was either an all-talking, all-singing version of Harpo Marx or a major nuisance, depending on whether you were his classmate or his teacher. Through his brother Lenny, he met Don Appell, a Broadway actor who had appeared with Canada Lee in Orson Welles's 1941 production of *Native Son*. Appell introduced him to the social director of a borscht-belt hotel in Ellenville. Brooks made a strong impression and was hired, for the summer season of 1942, as drummer and part-time *tummler*. Two quotations may here be helpful. (1) Brooks to *Playboy*: "Jews don't do comedy in winter. In summer, all right." (2) Brooks to me: "A *tummler* can be defined as a resident offstage entertainer at a Jewish mountain resort, mostly after lunch." He found it hard to decide on a professional name. Melvin Kaminsky was too overtly Jewish for a comedian. David Daniel Kaminsky, also of Brooklyn but unrelated to Brooks, had faced much the same problem a decade or so earlier, and had solved it by billing himself as Danny Kaye. (Just why Jews in the performing arts were—and, for the most part, still are—expected to Anglicize their names is a question worthy of a separate study. To take three cases at random, is it to simplify pronunciation, to enhance euphony, or to disarm bigotry that Emanuel Goldenberg becomes Edward G. Robinson, Benny Kubelsky becomes Jack Benny, and Isadore Demsky becomes Kirk Douglas? The whole rigmarole discredits the public that demands it.) Brooks's first thought was to borrow his mother's maiden name, but Melvin Brookman turned out to be a nonstarter, because, he told me, "I couldn't get it all on my drum." Chopping off a syllable, he settled for Melvin Brooks.

That summer, two events occurred that helped to lay down the course of his future career. In the band at the Avon Lodge, a neighboring Catskill pleasure dome, there was a pretty good saxophone player called Sid Caesar. Brooks met him in off-duty hours, howled at his mimetic gifts, and formed a friendship that was renewed, to the lasting gratitude of TV audiences, after the war. The other significant event took place back in Ellenville. It was a classic demonstration of the First Show-Biz Law of Psychokinetics, according to which major talent, if unfulfilled, acquires the power of temporarily disabling minor talent that comes within its sphere of influence and impedes its development. One morning, in obedience to this law, the regular stand-up comic fell mysteriously sick and had to be shipped back to New York. Brooks, inevitably, was asked to replace him. He went on that night and improvised, using real characters—the manager, staff, and clientele of the lodge—as his points of departure into fantasy. He also found time to prepare a short blackout spot, for which he co-opted a girl assistant. "It was entitled 'S. and M.,' thirty years before anyone had heard of S. and M.," he told me. "The girl and I walked out from the wings and met in the center of the stage. I said, 'I am a masochist.' She said, 'I am a sadist.' I said, 'Hit me,' and she hit me, very hard, right in the face. And I said, 'Wait a minute, wait a minute, hold it. I think I'm a sadist.' Blackout. That was the first sketch I ever wrote." Within a few days, he had composed his own theme song, the climax of which was a rousing plea for sympathy:

> I'm out of my mind,
> So won't you be kind
> And please love Melvin Brooks?

He was not an overnight smash, but he improved with every performance and held down the job for the rest of the season, in the course of which, incidentally, he celebrated his sixteenth birthday.

One night last winter, Brooks dined with me at my rented house in Santa Monica. Although I was the host, he insisted on providing the wine, which turned out to be Mouton-Rothschild 1961. (He makes the same stipulation wherever he eats. Even at the most expensive restaurants in Beverly Hills, Brooks will arrive with a neat leather case that holds two bottles from his own cellar. He does this partly because few wine lists offer items of comparable quality and partly because he sees no reason to pay exorbitant markups if he can avoid it. Thus he exploits his status while restricting his expenditure, since the restaurateurs would rather slim their profits than lose his patronage.) Over dinner, he told me a little-known story, the saga of Brooks at war, which I here reproduce in his own words:

"I came in at the end. I went overseas with the artillery, and we docked at Le Havre, France, in February, 1945. Then I was transferred into the 1104th Combat Engineer Group. We travelled in a big truck through the nation of France on our way to Belgium, and every time we passed through a little town, we'd see these signs—'*Boulangerie*,' '*Pâtisserie*,' and '*Rue*' this, and '*Rue*' that, and rue the day you came here, young man. When we got to our hundred and eightieth French village, I screamed at the top of my lungs, 'The joke is over! English, *please*!' I couldn't believe that a whole country couldn't speak English. One-third of a nation, all right, but not a whole country. There was very little actual shooting in Belgium, but there was plenty of mortar and artillery fire, and it was very noisy, and I thought that I would not want to be in the war very long, because of the noise. The earth was very hard when I was there, and I could not dig a V-shaped foxhole, as I wanted to, and stay down in the bottom of the V for the rest of the war. All these hot fragments of shrapnel and stuff were flying around, and I did not want to die, so it was awful. I remember hiding under a desk in a kindergarten while there were air battles going on above us, and bombs rattling.

"I was a PFC. Once, I was out on patrol with seven other men, and we found a case of German rifles near an old railway siding—beautiful sharpshooting rifles with bolt action. Sure enough, there were some cartridges right next to them. So we had a contest. There were these white insulation things up on the telephone poles, and any man who shot one down won a dollar from each of the others. I was pretty good at that, and I'd made about twenty-one dollars when suddenly we got a strange call on our jeep radio. It said that German werewolves—guerrillas operating behind our lines—had cut all communication between the 1104th and the Ninth Army by destroying the telephone wires. Holy shit, I realized it was us, so we barrelled right back to camp, and they said, 'Did you see anything?' and we said 'Not a thing.' Then I became very brave. I said, 'Give me some men, sir, and I'll go back. We gotta stop these werewolves.' So I was sent out again on patrol to hunt them down. We hung around the railway siding for about four hours and then came back. My colonel offered to make me a corporal on the spot, and I said, 'No, no, sir, I'm not worthy of it.' Because I knew that noncoms and officers got killed and that somehow privates could survive in This Thing Called War.

"Along the roadside, you'd see bodies wrapped up in mattress covers and stacked in a ditch, and those would be Americans, that could be me. And I sang all the time; I made up funny songs; I never wanted to think about it. Some guy would say, 'We're gonna be killed, we'll never get out of this war,' and I'd say, 'Nobody dies—it's all made up.' Because otherwise we'd all get hysterical, and that kind of hysteria—it's not like sinking, it's like slowly taking on water, and that's the panic. Death is the enemy of everyone, and, even though you hate Nazis, death is more of an enemy than a German soldier.

"At the end, it was very sad, because the Germans were sending old men and little boys to fight against us. I was very good about that. I'd say, 'No shooting, throw down your guns and talk to them in Yiddish and German.' Of course, when we ran into pockets of trained German soldiers, genuine SS. *Flammenwerfer* Nazis who wanted to die rather than surrender, I'd hide, because they'd kill you as soon as look at you. But these groups of little boys and old men wanted nothing but just to go to their mothers or their toilets. From around April 25 onward was the worst two weeks of my life. Then it was over, and it was V-E Day. And on V-E Day I hid again, because the Americans all got drunk and fired off every round of ammunition they had, and a lot of people were killed in the festivities. I knew if I went out on the street I'd get shot to death. I was in a village near Wiesbaden, and the May wine was still green. It can make you very drunk, so I found a wine cellar and opened a hundred bottles of it and poured it all over me. I stayed there for twenty-four hours, until the shooting had stopped."

"And then you went back to the States?" I asked.

"No," Brooks said. "You see, I was the barracks character, and they didn't want to lose me. My major said to me, 'Melvin, why not stay with us and travel around providing the boys with entertainment?' I said 'Great!' So he made me a corporal and gave me an old Mercedes, a real beauty. Then I told him I'd need a chauffeur, and he said, 'I can't let you have a military man.' I said, 'Could you spare a few pfennigs for a German civilian driver?' He said 'Fine,' so I found a German fiddle player named Helga, who became my chauffeuse. My official title was Noncom in Charge of Special Services, and I did shows for enlisted men and officers' clubs. Sometimes for a whole division, with tens of thousands of people out front. I told big, lousy jokes. Every time Bob Hope came by, I would write down all his jokes and use them. Nothing frightened me. I sang like Al Jolson. Everybody could do the low Jolson, but I did the high Jolson that nobody else could do—things like 'I love you as I loved you when you were *sweeeet sixteeeen*.' People said they appreciated that. My chauffeuse played the fiddle for them and together we fiddled in the back seat of the Mercedes.

"I used to go to Frankfurt with my special pass and obtain certain rare cognacs and stick them in my car. I shoved them into every orifice that would take them. There wasn't a nineteen-year-old soldier who got drunker than I did. Helga played Brahms's 'Lullaby' beautifully. I'd say, 'Pull over to the curb and play Brahms's "Lullaby."' That dream world lasted for four months. Then they told me my Occupation duties were over and I could go back to civilian life. And I said, 'No, no—let me die in the back of the Mercedes with Helga.' But they sent me home anyway."

Professionally speaking, what he returned to was almost three years of not very much. During his absence, things had been moving fast for his friend Caesar. While serving in the Coast Guard, Caesar had appeared in a recruiting revue called *Tars and Spars*; its director was Max Liebman, a sharp-eyed

impresario who already numbered Imogene Coca and Danny
(Kaminsky) Kaye among his discoveries. Dominated by Caesar's comedy routines, *Tars and Spars* opened in Florida and
then went on a national tour, after which Columbia made a
movie version that retained nothing of the original except the
title and Caesar. His notices when the film was released, in
1946, launched him on a thriving career in nightclubs and
vaudeville houses. Nobody, however, seemed inclined to discover Brooks. To demonstrate the versatility of his face, he
hired a photographer to snap him in four contrasting moods—
Brooks beaming, Brooks scowling, Brooks pensive, and
Brooks aghast—and had the results printed on one page, copies
of which he sent to every agent in town. He once arrived
without an appointment at the headquarters of the eminent
producer Kermit Bloomgarden. "There were dozens of actors
waiting to see him, some of them quite famous," Brooks told
me. "I walked up to his secretary and said, 'Paul Muni is here.
I have to go in three minutes.' She got on the intercom, and
within ten seconds Bloomgarden came running out of his office. He looked at me and said, 'This boy is not Paul Muni.'
I said, 'Muni's name is Harold Gottwald. I am the *real* Paul
Muni.' [Whose *real* name, incidentally was Muni Weisen-
freund.] Then Bloomgarden grabbed me by the collar and said,
'You've got a lot of moxie. I'm going to remember you.' But
he didn't give me an audition."

Under the pressure of need or fear, Brooks was capable of
any audacity. One night during this period, he went out to New
Jersey to see the comedian Ronny Graham, who was a friend
of his, performing in cabaret. After the show, Graham gave
him a lift back to New York. To continue in Brooks's words:
"We stopped off on the way to have a sandwich at a diner. It
was about 3 A.M. and the place was full of enormous truck
drivers. Ronny was still wearing his stage makeup and some
pretty avant-garde clothes, and these big, hairy men all swiv-
elled round and started to stare at us. Some of them even stood
up. While we were eating, everything went very quiet. I was
terrified. Suddenly, I turned on Ronny like a cobra and said,
'I want my ring back.' He said, 'What?' I said, 'You *spoke*
to that *man*. Back at the club. Don't think I didn't see you
speaking to him, because I did. *I want my ring back*. And I'll

tell you something else—*you'll never have my tongue again!*' And we both went into this berserk faggot row. Finally, I picked up my cup of coffee and threw it in his face. Then I flounced out to the car with Ronny right behind me, wiping his eyes and screaming. Some of the truck drivers followed us out to the parking lot. They just stood there, dumbstruck, with their hands on their hips, as we drove off, kissing and making up. I waved at them out of the window."

In the autumn of 1947, Caesar invited Brooks to come and see him at the Roxy, where he was starring in the stage show that accompanied the long-running movie *Forever Amber.* Afterward, in his dressing room, Caesar mentioned that Max Liebman was planning a revue for presentation on television. "What is that?" Brooks claims to have asked, and to have received the reply "It's a thing that takes pictures of you and sends them into people's living rooms."

"Don't do it," Brooks begged him, straight-faced, "It's trafficking in graven images, and there are strict Jewish laws against that. You better stay away from that stuff or you'll never get your image back. The very least that can happen is that you'll be sterilized by the cameras."

A superstitious man, Caesar was thoroughly unnerved by Brooks's little joke. A few months later, however, when Brooks was directing a shoestring production at Red Bank, New Jersey, Caesar called him with the news that he had decided to risk infertility. He had signed with NBC to appear in "The Admiral Broadway Revue," a sixty-minute program, produced by Liebman, that would make its debut in January, 1949. Caesar proposed a deal whereby he personally would pay Brooks a weekly stipend of fifty dollars to supply him with special material. Brooks jumped at the offer.

"The Admiral Broadway Revue," which ran for nineteen sparkling weeks, was an acorn that soon grew into an oak. With many of the same participants—e.g., Caesar and Imogene Coca as performers, Mel Tolkin and Lucille Kallen as principal writers, and Liebman as producer—it reappeared in February, 1950, now expanded into a full-blown, high-budget, primetime, ninety-minute Saturday-night event, entitled "Your Show of Shows." Brooks refused to renew his private arrangement with Caesar, as he put it, "I don't want to be your boy."

Instead, Liebman hired him, at a hundred and fifty a week. His first contribution to the new series was the famous sketch in which Caesar played a jungle boy who is discovered, clad in a lion skin, roaming the streets of New York.

> INTERVIEWER: Sir, how do you survive in New York City?... What do you eat?
> CAESAR: Pigeon.
> INTERVIEWER: Don't the pigeons object?
> CAESAR: Only for a minute.
> INTERVIEWER (*bringing up a recurrent Brooksian obsession*): What are you afraid of more than anything?
> CAESAR: Buick.
> INTERVIEWER: You're afraid of a Buick?
> CAESAR: Yes. Buick can win in death struggle. Must sneak up on parked Buick, punch grille hard. Buick die.

Within a couple of months, Brooks's salary had risen to two hundred dollars, from which it steadily ascended to the peak of five thousand.

Many detailed accounts exist of the writing team that worked on "Your Show of Shows." Not since the Algonquin Round Table has a group of American wits been more extensively chronicled. In addition to Tolkin, Kallen, and Brooks, it eventually included Joseph Stein (who wrote the book of *Fiddler on the Roof*), Larry Gelbart, and Neil Simon, with Michael Stewart (author-to-be of *Hello, Dolly!*) acting as typist, a post in which he was later replaced by "a little red-headed rat"—to cite Brooks's affectionate phrase—named Woody Allen. Carl Reiner and Howard Morris, from the supporting cast, threw in ideas; and Caesar, with Liebman at his side, presided over the collective delirium, a madhouse of competing egos in which nobody could outshout Brooks. According to Miss Kallen, "Mel imitated everything from a rabbinical student to Moby Dick thrashing about on the floor with six harpoons sticking in his back."

Tolkin told me, "He used to bare his teeth like a rodent if you crossed him. Half of Mel's creativity comes out of fear and anger. He doesn't perform, he screams." (By the end of 1950, Tolkin and Caesar were already in psychoanalysis, and it is not surprising that in the following year Brooks also took to the couch. His therapist had been analyzed by Theodore Reik, who had been a protégé of Sigmund Freud. Brooks felt that what he learned, though it might not be straight from the horse's mouth, was at least feedbox noise from the same stable.)

Addressing the American Film Institute in 1977, Brooks said, "We wrote things that made *us* laugh, not what we thought the audience would dig.... What really collapsed us, grabbed our bellies, knocked us down on the floor and made us spit and laugh so that we couldn't breathe—*that* was what went into the script. Except for the dirty portions, which we couldn't do on live television."

A character in which Brooks specialized, and in which his distinctive comic style first began to assert itself, was the German Professor, played by Caesar. He appeared under many names—such as Kurt von Stuffer, the dietitian, or Seigfried von Sedativ, the authority on sleep—always pontificating with the same majestic fraudulence in the same bedraggled and ill-fitting frock coat. His ignorance, exposed by Carl Reiner's questions, was boundless in its scope and variety. How, for instance, do aircraft fly? As Dr. Rudolf von Rudder, aeronautical expert, he spelled out the answer in layman's language: "It's a simple theory. Matter is lighter than air. You see, the motors, they pull the plane forward and they cause a draft, and then it taxis faster down the field and the motors go faster and the whole plane vibrates, and then, when there's enough of a draft and a vacuum created, the plane rises off the runway into the air. From then on, it's a miracle. I don't know what keeps it up."

After a complex buildup, the laugh comes not from a witty, climactic payoff but from a sudden plunge into bathos. We hear exactly what we would expect to hear from this obvious half-wit. Cf. the reply of Dr. Heinrich von Heartburn when Reiner asked him for his advice on keeping one's marriage alive: "Make it interesting.... I showed a friend of mine once how to keep his marriage exciting.... One day he'd come home from work, his wife would open the door, he's a French soldier.... The next day he's a policeman, he comes in, he starts to run around with the handcuffs and the badges, and the next day he don't come through the door, he jumps through the window, he's a clown. He somersaults all over the living room and throws his wife all around the place. [Pause.] She left him. He was a maniac."

A final glimpse of the Professor (for which, as for the preceding quotes from the original scripts, I draw on the lengthy extracts reprinted in Ted Sennett's book *Your Show of Shows*): in the guise of a mountaineering pundit, he is mourning the loss of a colleague, Hans Goodfellow, who gave his life trying to prove that it was possible to climb mountains on roller skates. What should a climber do, Reiner inquires, if his rope breaks?

> CAESAR: Well, as soon as you see the rope breaking, scream and keep screaming all the way down. . . . This way they'll know where to find you.
> REINER: But, Professor, isn't there anything else you can do?
> CAESAR: Well, there's the other method. As soon as the rope breaks, you spread you arms and begin to fly.
> REINER: But humans can't fly.
> CAESAR: How do you know? You might be the first one. Anyway, you can always go back to screaming.
> REINER: Was Hans Goodfellow a flier or a screamer?
> CAESAR: He was a flying screamer, and a crasher, too.

In this exchange, and dozens like it, Brooks was breaking fresh ground, exploring territory that he was eventually to make his own. He was inventing the interview as a new form of comic art.

The last edition of "Your Show of Shows" went out in 1954, by which time Brooks was married to Florence Baum, a dancer in Broadway musicals. They had three children—in order of appearance, Stefanie, Nicholas, and Edward. The youngest is now studying music in Manhattan, while both of the older ones are taking courses in film at New York University. Brooks refers to them as "these nice friends I've grown." Their parents were divorced in 1962. "We had married too young," Brooks said, more than a decade later. "I expected I would marry my

mother, and she expected she would marry her father." Minus
Coca, Caesar returned to the small screen in 1954, starring in
a show of his own called "Caesar's Hour." He was also minus
Brooks, who, determined to go his own way, had rejected the
offer of a top writing job on the new program. Before long,
however, Brooks regretted his decision to quit the nest. His
own way was leading him nowhere but into debt, and after the
show's first season unable to resist the money, he rejoined his
old boss, under whose paternal shadow he stayed until 1959.
Which brings us back to Mamma Leone's.

Although Brooks left a lasting impression on everyone who
saw him at the Moss Hart jamboree, it did nothing to help his
career. He was a brilliant party turn, but what had after-dinner
improvisation to do with professional comedy? In 1960, with
his marriage crumbling and no source of income, he went job-
hunting to Hollywood, where Carl Reiner was already working.
Hearing that they were both in town, the producer Joe Fields
threw a party in their honor, on the tacit understanding that
they would provide the entertainment. Before an audience of
celebrities that included Steve Allen and George Burns, they
got up and did the Two-Thousand-Year-Old Man. When the
applause had died down, Burns said, "Listen, you better put
that on a record, because if you don't, I'll steal it." Allen, who
shared Burns's enthusiasm, had highly placed friends in the
recording business. He made a call to one of them the following
morning.

"A few days later," Reiner told me, "Mel and I walked into
a studio at World Pacific Records and ad-libbed for over two
hours." The edited result was an LP that came out in the spring
of 1961 and sold over a million copies. "That was a turning
point for Mel," Reiner continued. "It gave him an identity as
a performer for the first time." Moreover, it gave him a comic
persona that at once embodied and exorcised his own deepest
anxieties; for the main point about this jaunty survivor—more
than twice as old as Methuselah and still going strong—is that
he has conquered death. By playing a character who was im-
mortal, Brooks may have staked his principal claim to immortality as a comedian.

Gene Wilder summed up for me his mental image of Brooks:

"I see him standing bare-chested on top of a mountain, shouting 'Look at me!' and 'Don't let me die!' Those are the two things that rule his life." They recur throughout his records with Reiner, of which, to date, there are four. Following the run-away success of the original LP, further revelations by the garrulous oldster of his close encounters with "the great and the near-great" of the past two millennia were issued in the fall of 1961, with sequels in 1962, 1963, and 1973. In these classic interviews, Brooks triumphs not only over death, but over another of his besetting phobias, that of the lifelong seeker after father substitutes who fears he will never make a convincing father himself; for what is the Two-Thousand-Year-Old Man if not the most prolific parent on earth? He tells us that he has been married "several hundred times" and that when he looks back on his wives "a thousand violins explode in my mind."

   REINER: How many children do you have?
   BROOKS (*with stoical self-pity*): I have over forty-two
   thousand children, and not one comes to visit me.

But, at least, he misses their company, which is more than can be said for Warren Bland, the Gentile advertising executive who is one of the many other characters Brooks plays on these remarkable discs. Bland lives in the city of Connecticut, Connecticut, "a very exclusive community," where they don't allow children. They *have* children, of course, but "we send them to Hartford . . . to Jewish and Italian families, people who like children." From time to time, Bland goes on, "I might just mosey over to Hartford, say 'Hi, gang!' you know, then speed right back to Connecticut, Connecticut."
As Bland, Brooks's accent is quintessential WASP. As the bimillenarian, it is not Jewish but—Brooks is insistent on this—*American*-Jewish. "Within a couple of decades, there won't be any more accents like that," he said to me. "They're being ironed out by history, because there are no more Jewish immigrants. It's the sound I was brought up on, and it's dying." Beneath the jokes, these recordings are a threnody. Even on the surface, there are odd moments of unexpected melancholy, as when the patriarch reflects, "We mock the thing we are to

be. We make fun of the old, and then we become them."
Although he has foxed the grim reaper, it has often been by
inches. He has led a life dominated by peril and hostility, in
which practically every human activity springs from one motive.

> BROOKS: Everything we do is based on fear.
> REINER: Even love?
> BROOKS: Mainly love.
> REINER: How can love stem from fear?
> BROOKS: What do you need a woman for?... In my
> time, to see if an animal is behind you. You can't see
> alone, you don't have eyes in the back of your head.... The
> first marriages were: "Will you take a look behind me?"
> "OK, how long do you want?" "Forever." "We're mar-
> ried."
> REINER: I see. And you walked back to back for the
> rest of your life?
> BROOKS: Yes. You looked at her once in a while—
> REINER: When you knew you were safe?
> BROOKS: When you were on high ground.

All of which corroborates the spiritual doctrine that perfect
love casteth out fear. (And, I might add, compares very favorably with the behavior of a well-known English writer who
fled London during the wartime blitz, pausing only to explain
to his girlfriend, "Perfect fear casteth out love.") Again, consider the following exchange:

> REINER: What was the means of transportation then?
> BROOKS: Mainly fear.... You would see an animal
> that would growl, you would go two miles in a minute.
> Fear would be the main propulsion.

As for the origins of human speech.

> BROOKS: We spoke Rock, basic Rock.... Two hundred
> years before Hebrew, there was the Rock language. Or
> Rock talk.
> REINER: Could you give us an example of that?

BROOKS: Yes. "Hey, don't throw that rock at me!
What you doing with that rock? Put down that rock!"

In other words—or, rather, in no other words—the need to
communicate arose from the threat of imminent assault. Similarly, the custom of shaking hands "stemmed from fear." In
order to check whether the other fellow was carrying a rock
or a dagger, "you grabbed his hand—'Hi there, Charlie!' 'How
you doing, Bertram?'—and you held that hand, then you looked
and you opened it up and you shook it a little." The primal art
of dance evolved because it was an even more comprehensive
means of self-protection. By dancing with your antagonist, you
immobilize *both* his hands and "you keep the feet busy, so he
can't kick you." Song, too, had its roots in terror. If you were
in real danger, a high-pitched rhythmical yelling was the only
way to make anyone pay attention. The message had to be
simple and ear-catching, as witness the opening lines of the
first lyric ever sung:

> A lion is eating my foot off,
> Will somebody call a cop?

Shortly afterward came national anthems, with which each
group of cave dwellers tried to frighten its neighbors; e.g.:

> Let them all go to hell
> Except Cave Seventy-six.

The old man has immunized himself against death by obeying a number of rules—some pragmatic, some purely superstitious—which he is eager to share with us. Every morning,
for instance, he sinks to his knees and prays "fiercely" for
twenty-two minutes "that the ceiling shouldn't fall on me, and
my heart should not attack me." Among his other precepts for
longevity: avoid fried food; consume nectarines in bulk ("Even
a rotten one is good. . . . I'd rather eat a rotten nectarine than
a fine plum"); never run for a bus; and "stay out of a Ferrari
or any small Italian car." He has also preserved his pep by
using drugs derived from "certain barks of certain trees that
made you jump in the air and sing 'Sweet Sue.'"

His fear of illness, though intense, is more than matched by his fear of hospitals, which are run today, he believes, on principles that have not changed since his troglodytic youth.

REINER: What are these principles?
BROOKS: The principle of people walking past you when you are screaming, and not caring. The same wonderful indifference to the sick and the dying.

Over the centuries, some of this indifference has rubbed off onto his own philosophy. It emerges most vividly when Reiner challenges him to define the difference between comedy and tragedy. His reply, brutally concise, is an aphorism as memorable as any I have heard on this ancient subject: "Tragedy is if I cut my finger. . . . Comedy is if you walk into an open sewer and die."

He drops names like a drunken waiter dropping plates: few great reputations pass through his hands unchipped. Robin Hood "stole from everybody and kept everything"; Shakespeare, though personally "a pussycat," was a terrible writer ("He had the worst penmanship I ever saw"); Sigmund Freud was nothing more than a good basketball player; and, as for Michelangelo's painting, "I thought it stunk," because it showed naked people flying around, and "you can't hang a naked in your living room." Perhaps his most startling disclosure is that he cohabited with Joan of Arc. He volubly describes the ups and downs of their relationship, after which Reiner intervenes.

REINER: How did you feel about her being burned at the stake?
BROOKS (*with instant, understated finality*): Terrible.

For me—and, I have discovered, for Brooks himself—this is the high point of the whole extravagant saga.

Laughter becomes extreme only if it be consecutive. There must be no pauses for recovery. . . . The jester must be able to grapple his theme and hang on to it, twisting it this way and that, and making it yield magically all manner of strange and precious things, one after another, without pause. *He must have invention keeping pace with utterance.* He must be inexhaustible. Only so can he exhaust us.

The words are Max Beerbohm's, the italics mine. The Two-Thousand-Year-Old Man fulfills Beerbohm's demands to the letter. With this verdict Brooks, who is not noted for bashfulness, would probably agree. "Everybody knows," he has said of his work on these records, "that *that* is terrific stuff." It extracts a unique comic euphoria from a fundamentally pessimistic view of life. I've dwelt on it not only as a milestone in Brooks's past (and in the history of comedy) but as a signpost to which, in the future, he is likely to return for guidance.

Early in the nineteen-sixties, Brooks began to acquire a cult following. To the relatively small number of people who buy nonmusical LPs he became, in his own words, "a royal personage, an emperor of comedy." In other respects, he remembers the years between 1959 and 1965 as "that terrible period when I couldn't get anything off the ground." In 1961, Jerry Lewis had an idea for a screenplay, *The Ladies' Man*, and hired Brooks to work on it. To Brooks's furious chagrin, Lewis took the script and had it entirely rewritten, so that few of Brooks's lines survived. (Show business offers few pleasures keener than that of paying tribute to a former foe who happens to be in eclipse. Brooks's present opinion of Lewis is that "he was an exciting, dynamic creature, and I learned a lot from him." He cannot, however, resist adding, "High-key comics like that always burn themselves out. Lewis could do thirty-one different takes [i.e., physical reactions], and when you'd seen them all, that was it. Low-key, laid-back comics like Jack Benny are the ones that last." Moreover, Lewis stooped to sentimentality—something utterly foreign to Brooks. Gene Wilder told me, "There's not much white sugar in Mel's veins. He would never ask an audience for sympathy.") For some time, Brooks had been working on a novel; he now revamped it as a play, called *Springtime for Hitler*. No producer would touch it. *All American*, a Broadway musical with a book by Brooks, was among the more resounding flops of 1962. In the same year, during which his divorce became final, he turned out another screenplay, entitled *Marriage Is a Dirty Rotten Fraud*. Nobody bought it. Meanwhile, most of his colleagues on the Caesar shows were prospering—a fact that neither escaped his attention nor soothed his frustration.

After separating from his wife in 1960, Brooks had spent a bleak and insolvent period in an unfurnished fourth-floor walkup on Perry Street, for which he paid seventy-eight dollars a month. He then moved in with a friend called Speed Vogel, who had an apartment on Central Park West and a studio on West Twenty-eighth Street, where he made what Brooks describes as "direct metal sculpture." Vogel had left his wife shortly before Brooks arrived. The two men cooked for themselves, carried their clothes to the laundromat, rose at conflicting hours (Brooks late, Vogel early), and bickered over practically every aspect of housekeeping—a setup uncannily prophetic of Neil Simon's *The Odd Couple*.

One Tuesday in the summer of 1962, Vogel gave a party at West Twenty-eighth Street. Among his guests were Zero Mostel who had a studio in the same building; Joseph Heller, whose first novel, *Catch-22*, had appeared the previous year; and Ngoot Lee, a painter and calligrapher of Chinese parentage. These three, together with Vogel and Brooks, enjoyed one another's company so much that they decided to commemorate the occasion by reassembling every Tuesday for food and talk. Meetings were held at cheap Chinese restaurants selected by Ngoot Lee, who knew where the best chefs worked, and kept track of their movements from job to job. The nucleus, itself a fairly motley crew, grew steadily motleyer as it swelled in numbers. Brooks introduced a diamond dealer named Julie Green, who could do eccentric impersonations of movie stars. Heller contributed a fellow-novelist, George Mandel, who had a steel plate in his head as a result of injuries suffered in the Battle of the Bulge. "One night," Heller recalls, "Mandel told us in detail how he had been wounded. There was a long pause, and then Mel did something typical. He said, very slowly, 'I'm sure glad that happened to you, and not to me.' He wasn't being cruel, he was being honest. He just blurted out what we were all thinking but didn't dare to say." Mandel, in turn, brought in Mario Puzo, later to become famous as the author of *The Godfather*. These were the charter members of the fraternity. They called themselves the Group of the Oblong Table or, in more pretentious moments, the Chinese Gourmet Club. What bound them together, apart from revelry in conversation, is best epitomized in a statement volunteered to me by Heller. "I'd rather have a bad meal out than a good meal at home," he said. "When you're out, it's a party. Also, I like a big mediocre meal more than a small good one."

The membership list has been closed for many years. Approved outsiders, like Carl Reiner and Joseph Stein, are invited to the Oblong Table from time to time, but merely as "honored guests." The club has strict rules, some of which I learned from Reiner: "You are not allowed to eat two mouthfuls of fish, meat, or chicken without an intermediate mouthful of rice. Otherwise, you would be consuming only the expensive food. The check and tip, and the parking fees, if any, are equally divided among the members. It is compulsory, if you are in New York, are not working nights, and are in reasonable health, to be present at every meeting." He continued, "The members are very polite. Once, I had a seat facing the kitchen door and I looked through and saw a rat strolling across the floor. They immediately offered me a chair facing the other way." Anxious to retain his status of "honored guest," Reiner begged me to quote Heller and Brooks on the subject at greater length than I quoted him.

Brooks recently told an interviewer that the talk at the Oblong Table mainly deals with such weighty subjects as "whether there is a God, what is a Jew, and do homosexuals really do it." Reiner has other recollections. "From the sessions I've attended," he said to me, "I would put that group up against the Algonquin Round Table and bet that, line for line, they were funnier. The speed of the wit is breathtaking. It just flies back and forth." Brooks's comment on this: "I'm sure we're funnier than the Algonquin crowd, but we're not as bright."

Hershy Kay, the composer and Broadway arranger, had a bitter experience that confirmed what Reiner said about the club's rigorous eating procedure. According to Brooks: "Hershy Kay came once as a guest and took the nicest bits of the lobster and the choicest parts of the chicken, including the wings, which I like. He did not touch his rice. He had to go, and he went." There may, however, have been another reason for Kay's rejection. My source here is Heller, who said, "Bear in mind that I am the only tall member of the group. At the next meeting after the Hershy Kay incident, Mel made a little speech. 'Let's face it,' he said. 'Except for Joe, all of us are quite short. Some of us are very short. *Hershy is too short.*'"

Brooks, incidentally, has grave reservations about Heller's own table manners. "From the very start," he declares, "we accepted Joe on Speed Vogel's word that he would behave, and Speed lied to us, because he did not behave. He took the best pieces of everything and laughed in our faces. One Tuesday, we ordered a tureen of special soup full of delicious things, and Joe grabbed it, scooped all the good stuff into his own bowl, and then said, 'Here, let me serve this.' We each got a spoonful of nothing."

Far from denying this story, Heller openly confesses, "I am a greedy man. I'll eat anything. I even use a fork intead of chopsticks, so I can eat faster. I'm known in the club as the plague of locusts." Presumably, his physical bulk protects him against reprisals.

Puzo, the only non-Jewish member other than Ngoot Lee, is tolerated because of his limited appetite. "Being Italian, Puzo is no threat to us," Brooks says. "He doesn't really like exotic dishes. He prefers noodles and rice—things that remind him of home. He is provincial, and that saves us from the rape of our best food." A stickler for party discipline as well as a dedicated glutton, Brooks never misses a club meeting when he is in Manhattan. If business suddenly compels him to fly in from the Coast on a Tuesday evening, his first act on arrival at JFK is to ring every eligible restaurant in Chinatown until he finds the chosen venue. Thither he dashes, straight from the airport; and before saying a word, he heaps a plate with whatever is left.

Despite their differences over matters of etiquette, Heller has a high respect for Brooks. He freely admitted to me that he used a lot of Brooks's lines in his second novel, *Something Happened*, and that in his next book, *Good as Gold*, "the hero is a small Jewish guy, and there's a great deal of Mel in that." In the early seventies, Heller was teaching writing at City College of New York. He had long been aware that Brooks was vulnerable to practical jokes. One evening, Heller casually lied about his salary, saying that it was sixty-eight thousand dollars a year—more than double the truth. A couple of days later, Heller's accountant, who also worked for Brooks, called him up and said, "For God's sake, Joe, what the hell have you done? First thing this morning, Mel was up here screaming, 'Why am I in the entertainment business? Why aren't I teaching and earning seventy thousand a year like Joe Heller?' He was out of his mind!" Having told me this story, Heller went on, "Mel has always had plenty of resentment and aggression that he can sublimate into creativity. He's usually at his best when he's envying people more successful than he is. Now that there's hardly anyone more successful, what will he do?"

I cited a mot attributed to Gore Vidal: "It is not enough to succeed. Others must fail."

"I thought that was La Rochefoucauld," Heller said. "But anyway it doesn't apply to Mel. He likes to see his rivals fail, but not his friends. Provided, of course, that *he's* succeeding."

I asked whether, in Heller's opinion, fame had changed Brooks.

"Not a bit. He's just as nasty, hostile, acquisitive, and envious today as he ever was. Please be sure to quote me on that," Heller said warmly. He went on, "You have to distinguish between Mel the entertainer and Mel the private person. He puts on this manic public performance, but it's an act, it's something sought for and worked on. When he's being himself, he'll talk quietly for hours and then make a remark that's unforgettably funny because it comes out of a real situation. You might say that he's at his funniest when he's being most serious. He has a tremendous reverence for novelists and for literature in general, because it involves something more than gag writing. In his serious moments, I don't think he regards movies as an art. For Mel, the real art is literature."

Brooks staunchly challenges this view: "When Joe says things like that, he's just electioneering for the novel, because that's what he writes. I think *La Grande Illusion* is a good as *Anna Karenina*, and *Les Enfants du Paradis* is in the same class as *La Chartreuse de Parme*. If we're talking about art at the most exquisite level, Joe may conceivably have a point. But I'm a populist. I want color, I want visual images, I want the sound of the human voice."

In February, 1961, Brooks attended a rehearsal of a Perry Como TV special in which Anne Bancroft, then starring on Broadway in *The Miracle Worker*, was making a guest appearance. Brashly introducing himself, Brooks started to woo her on the spot. They were married in 1964 and are still together, now accompanied by a six-year-old son—"Mel in miniature," according to Miss Bancroft—named Maximilian. "On our second date," Brooks told me, "I asked her, 'Where do you keep your awards?' She'd already won two Tonys. She said she gave them to her mother. I said, 'Funny, so do I'—although the only thing I'd won up to then was a Writers Guild Award for 'Your Show of Shows.' Then I asked her, 'Where does you mother keep them?' She said, 'On top of the TV set.' My heart stopped, and I said, 'So does mine.' My mother now has two Oscars and an Emmy. But Annie has something like thirty major awards—Oscars, Emmys, Tonys, Cannes Festival, about everything an actress can win." Miss Bancroft, whose parents were the children of immigrants, was christened Anna Maria Louisa Italiano, and it took Brooks a long time to reveal to his mother that he intended to marry an Italian girl. If we believe (as we can't) the account he gave David Susskind on TV, his mother's reaction when he finally broke the news and announced that he was bringing his lasagna-loving fiancée over to meet her was simply to say, "That's fine. I'll be in the kitchen; my head'll be in the oven."

In the early sixties, Miss Bancroft was continuously working, either on Broadway or in movies. Brooks had many evenings to kill, and she suspects that this may explain why he founded the Chinese Gourmet Club. "But in any case, Mel really loves men, he has a terrific sense of male camaraderie," she said to me recently. "Have you noticed how all his films before *High Anxiety* end up with two men together? His attitude toward women can be very primitive. When we have big rows, he yells, 'No more monogamy with women for me! Next time, it'll be with a man!' He actually threatens me with Dom DeLuise! Once—and only once—I managed to find out where the club was meeting, and I crashed the dinner. As soon as I came in the restaurant, it was as if a blanket had descended on the gathering. Dead silence. Faces falling. I turned around and left, without eating." She smiled and shrugged. "All the same," she said, "whenever he comes home at night the whole place lights up. He's like an incandescent schoolboy. There are no dull moments."

One evening in the spring of 1962, Brooks was sitting in a Manhattan movie theatre watching a dazzling abstract cartoon by the Canadian animator Norman MacLaren. "Three rows behind me," he recalls, "there was an old immigrant man mumbling to himself. He was very unhappy because he was waiting for a story line and he wasn't getting one." Brooks listened hard, and the result of his eavesdropping was that, for the first time, a film based on a Brooks idea actually got made. "I asked my pal Ernie Pintoff to do the visuals for a MacLaren-type cartoon," he says. "I told him, 'Don't let me see the images in advance. Just give me a mike and let them assault me.' And that's what he did. There was no script. I sat in a viewing theatre looking at what Ernie showed me, and I mumbled whatever I felt that old guy would have mumbled, trying to find a plot in this maze of abstractions. We cut it down to three and a half minutes and called it *The Critic*. It opened at the Sutton in New York, later to become renowned as the home of Mel Brooks hits. It was a smash then and has been ever since." In 1964, it won Academy Awards for both Brooks and Pintoff. A fact to remember: the film's comic impact was entirely dependent on something nonvisual—Brooks's mesmeric power of vocal improvisation.

Alan Schwartz, an urbane, silver-haired native of Brooklyn who has been Brooks's legal adviser and friend since 1962, said to me not long ago, "By Mel's standards, an improviser isn't class. He wanted to be classy. Writing is classy. A screenplay is classy." Schwartz's other clients include Peter Shaffer, Tom Stoppard, and Joseph Heller. "Mel is as intelligent as any of them," he says. "He must have a fantastic IQ. But sometimes, if he's with playwrights or novelists, he feels he has to prove that he's a serious literary person. When he met Shaffer, for instance, he kept saying things like 'pari passu' and 'ipso facto.'"

Brooks's return to the affluence of network TV came in 1965, when he collaborated with Buck Henry on "Get Smart," a series of half-hour episodes from the career of Maxwell Smart, a dangerously incompetent secret agent. ABC, which financed the pilot script, found the central character too charm-less and the satiric twists too bizarre. NBC took over the project (which nowadays looks tame enough), and it became a long-running success, relieving Brooks of such urgent financial worries as alimony and child support. It also left behind it a heritage of bad blood between Brooks and his co-author. Buck Henry, who wrote the screenplay of *The Graduate* a couple of years later, resented the billing he received on "Get Smart"—"By Mel Brooks with Buck Henry"—and there were rumors that, once the series was launched, Brooks's main contribution was to arrive at an advanced stage of rehearsals, propose a few radical and impracticable changes, and then disappear. Re-butting the charge of self-aggrandizement, Brooks says that his agent wanted to exclude Henry's name altogether and that it was he who demanded that both names should appear. "Buck envied me because of the hit I'd made with the Two-Thousand-Year-Old Man," Brooks asserts. "I'd galloped like a greedy child, and got ahead and taken off. I had a reputation for being a crazy Jew animal, whereas Buck thought of himself as an intellectual. Well, I was an intellectual, too. I knew that Dante's last name was Alighieri, but I didn't flaunt it. What Buck couldn't bear was the idea of this wacko Jew being billed over him. The truth is that he reads magazines, but he's not an intellectual, he's a pedant."

Time has not softened Henry's reciprocal animosity toward Brooks. "I'll bet you," he said to me in 1977, "that his name appears five times on the credits of *High Anxiety*."

Informed of this, Brooks replied, "Tell him from me he's wrong. The correct number is six."

The Producers, shot in New York in 1967, was the first Brooks script to reach the movie screen. It also marked his debut as a director—a job he undertook out of no sense of vocation but simply to protect his work against the well-mean-ing vandalism of rewrite experts. The script had gone through a strangely protracted gestation period. Brooks had originally conceived it, more than ten years earlier, as a novel. He had never thought of himself as a writer until 1950, when he saw his name on the credits of "Your Show of Shows." "I got scared," he told me, "and I figured I'd better find out what these bastards do. I went to the library, and read all the books

I could carry—Conrad, Fielding, Dostoevski, Gogol, Tolstoy. I decided that Tolstoy was the most gifted writer who ever lived. It's like he stuck a pen in his heart and it didn't even go through his mind on its way to the page. He may not even have been talented. And I said to myself, 'My God, I'm not a writer, I'm a *talker*.' I wished they'd change my billing on the show so that it said 'Funny Talking by Mel Brooks.' Then I wouldn't feel so intimidated." Before long, however, he stifled his fears and embarked on a novel. "One little word at a time, but, by God, I was going to do it."

The title was *Springtime for Hitler*, and the hero was a nervous young accountant called Leopold Bloom. "I stole the name from *Ulysses*," Brooks said to me. "I don't know what it meant to James Joyce, but to me Leo Bloom always meant a vulnerable Jew with curly hair. In the course of any narrative, the major characters have to metamorphose. They have to go through an experience that forces them to learn something and change. So Leo was going to change, he was going to bloom. He would start out as a little man who salutes whatever society teaches him to salute. Hats are worn. Yes, sir, I will wear a hat. Ties are worn. Definitely, sir. No dirty language is spoken in this world. *Absolument, Monsieur*. But in Leo Bloom's heart there was a much more complicated and protean creature—the guy he'd never dare to be, because he ain't gonna take them chances. He was going to play it straight and trudge right to his grave, until he ran into Max Bialystock, the Zero Mostel character. Bialystock is a Broadway producer who's so broke he's wearing a cardboard belt. He sleeps with little old ladies on their way to the cemetery. They stop off to have quick affairs on the leather couch in his office, which charm them so much that they write out checks for any fictitious show he claims to be promoting. Compared with Bloom, Bialystock is the Id. Bite, kiss, take, grab, lavish, urinate—whatever you can do that's physical, he will do. When Bloom first meets him, he's appalled. But then they get embroiled in each other's lives, and they catalyze each other. Bialystock has a profound effect on Bloom—so much so that this innocent young guy comes up with the idea of making a fortune by producing a surefire flop and selling twenty-five thousand percent of the profits in advance to little old ladies. On the other hand, Bloom evokes the first sparks of decency and humanity in Bialystock. It was a nice give-and-take. But after a while all they did was talk to each other. So I said, 'Oh, shit, it's turning into a play,' and I rewrote it, with a big neo-Nazi musical number right in the middle."

At this point (1963), Anne Bancroft was appearing on Broadway in the title role of Brecht's *Mother Courage*. Gene Wilder played the Chaplain, her cynical hanger-on and occasional bedfellow. He is now Brooks's closest friend and most impassioned fan. "Whenever Mel says 'Let's go,'" he told me recently, "I drop anything I'm doing and follow him." They met backstage during the run of the Brecht play. "Anne introduced me to this little borscht-belt comic she was going with," Wilder recalls. "I knew his name from the Caesar shows, which I'd been brought up on. I used to do Caesar impersonations at junior high, and it turned out that all my favorite bits had been written by Mel. Now he started to give me advice on Brechtian acting. The Chaplain has these long ironic speeches and lyrics on war and injustice, and I didn't know how to handle them, with my Actors Studio and Uta Hagen training. Mel said to me, 'Don't try to work them out in terms of psychology and motivation. He's stopped his play to pamphleteer. Step out of character and treat them like song-and-dance routines.' I didn't agree with him then, but I do now. Without knowing it, he was talking pure Brechtian technique. One day, we went out to Fire Island, and he said, 'I've written a play with a terrific part for you.' He read me the first twenty minutes and I was knocked out. Brooks told me, 'You *are* that character, and if it's ever done on stage or screen you're going to play it! But that's an easy promise, because I've never written a play or a screenplay and you've never had a starring role in a movie, so let's just dream together and eat warm pretzels and drink beer and think about reaching the stars. Even so, he made me swear not to take any other job without checking with him. Not long afterward, "I was offered a part in the Broadway production of *One Flew Over the Cuckoo's Nest*. I told Mel, and he made me write a month's release clause into my contract, which I did. Then *three years* passed, during which—nothing. He didn't even call me. Finally, I'm back on Broadway, in Murray Schisgal's play *Luv*. After a matinée, there's a knock on my dressing-room door, and it's Mel. 'You didn't think I forgot, did you?' he says. Then he explains that *Springtime for Hitler* has become a movie and that I'm going to play Leopold Bloom. I took the script home and read it, and at 3 A.M. I called him and said, 'It's magnificent! When do we start?' I didn't ask about my salary, and I don't think I ever did."

What had happened in the lengthy interim was that Brooks had found the action of his play spreading all over New York, spilling out onto sidewalks and rooftops, leaping from place to place with a spatial flexibility for which film seemed the obvious form. Helped by an inventive secretary with the arresting name of Alfa-Betty Olsen, he refashioned it as a movie. Several agents had "run with it"—to lapse into Hollywood patois—and got nowhere. It then fell into the hands of Sidney Glazier, a fund-raiser and contact man who had won an Academy Award for producing *The Eleanor Roosevelt Story*. Brooks describes Glazier, whom he met on Fire Island, as "a crazy man, he drank and he bellowed, he faced the ocean and roared like a sea lion." Glazier ordered Brooks not to read the script to him but simply to tell him the story. "About halfway through," Brooks continues, "Sidney was drinking coffee and he laughed so much it went up his nose. He collapsed on the floor, spitting and snorting and coughing. As he rolled around, he stuck up his arm, and when I reached out for it he grabbed my hand and said, 'We're going to make this movie. It's the funniest thing I ever heard.' And he knew what an impossible deal I was demanding: My first condition was that I had to direct the picture." Glazier budgeted the production at a million dollars, supplied half of it through his own company, and ran with the script around all the major studios. No dice. He eventually appealed to the independent producer Joseph E. Levine, who had just raised what he claimed to be the last cent at his disposal to finance an extremely risky project called *The Graduate*. Like every other moneyman who had seen the script, Levine said that no Jewish exhibitor would put *Springtime for Hitler* on his marquee. Brooks, for his part, rejected the suggestion that it should be retitled *Springtime for Mussolini*. By now, however, he was reluctantly prepared to settle for something as neutral as *The Producers*. There was one major point in Levine's favor: he genuinely liked what Brooks had written. Against this was the fact that he could not see his way to hiring the author as director.

Desperate to resolve these matters, Glazier brought the two men together over lunch. "I ate very nicely," Brooks says. "Nothing dropped out of my mouth. I didn't eat bread and butter, because I didn't know whether you should cut bread or break it. Meanwhile, Joe Levine ate like an animal. Just on top of some trout, he said, 'What would you do if I said yes? Could you direct it? What do you say, kid? Tell me from your heart. Don't lie to me; it may be the end for me.' He was impressed with me because I was cute and funny, so I said 'Yes, I can do it.' And he said 'OK,' and we shook hands." (Long after the film was made, Levine admitted to Brooks, "I was wrong. We should have called it *Springtime for Hitler*." Brooks told me, "Actually, they did call it *Springtime for Hitler* in Sweden. And when *The Twelve Chairs* came out, they called it *Springtime for the Twelve Chairs*. *Blazing Saddles* was *Springtime for the Black Sheriff*, and *Young Frankenstein* was *Springtime for Frankenstein*. I'm big stuff in Sweden. Everything is springtime there.")

Ten years from conception to handshake, and still not an actor signed: such is the life-devouring pace at which the movie business conducts its affairs. A deal with Gene Wilder was quickly concluded, but Zero Mostel, whom Brooks had always wanted for the role of Bialystock, read the script with mounting horror. "What is this?" he bellowed to Brooks. "A Jewish producer going to bed with old women on the brink of the grave? I can't play such a part. I'm a Jewish person." Enlisting the support of Mostel's wife, Brooks finally managed to change his mind, but their working relationship, once shooting (and shouting) began, was not easy. Between takes, Mostel would be found lying in his dressing room like a beached whale, moaning, "That man is going to kill me! He keeps saying, 'Do it again.'"

According to Brooks: "He was wonderful and he was a great friend, and he was a great pain in the ass. It was like working in the middle of a thunderstorm. Bolts of Zero—blinding flashes of Zero—were all around you. When he wasn't *on*, he was very dear, very pensive, very accessible. We had

family feuds. He had a sense of the grandeur of an artist. He
had what I like in an actor—power, stature, and enormous
bravery. I knew that if I could reach the end of the solar system
of his talent, if I could just prod him into some outburst of
insane anger, I could wake up the sleeping emotional depths
of that extraordinary man. And I did, and, although he protested
bitterly, he was fabulous."

The picture took eight weeks to shoot and eleven months
to edit: Brooks was then learning his trade. Nowadays, he gets
through the editing period in about four months. *The Producers*
was brought in under budget, at nine hundred and forty-one
thousand dollars. It opened in 1968 and, despite murderous
notices, acquired a cult reputation that enabled it to creep into
the black within four years. Brooks has little faith in critics,
believing that they always catch up with him one movie too
late. "I never got good reviews in my life and I never will,"
he declares. "They took one look at *The Producers* and said
it stank. Then I gave them *The Twelve Chairs* and they said
it lacked the great chaotic buoyancy of that majestic triumph
The Producers. Then came *Blazing Saddles*, and they said that
everything I'd learned about films had been forgotten in this
disgusting mess."

Badly wounded by the reception of his maiden effort,
Brooks was resoundingly compensated by the members of the
Motion Picture Academy, who, showing an unusual disdain
for the opinions of both the press and the general public,
awarded him the Oscar for Best Original Screenplay of 1968.
It was a bold and unexpected choice. In order to enjoy *The
Producers*, you have to cultivate a taste for grotesque and
deliberate overstatement. In the early scenes, Mostel and Wilder play together like figures out of a Jonsonian comedy of
humors. Cupidity (Mostel) seduces Conformity (Wilder): in
each, a single trait is exaggerated to the point of plethoric
obsession, and beyond. These are cartoon creatures, whose
dialogue seems to be written in capital letters, heavily italicized. To say that this makes it too "theatrical" is irrelevant,
for as soon as we agree to abandon the convention of naturalism, anything goes, and the screen can be as unrealistic as the
stage. (Who complains, after all, that the Marx Brothers' *Co-
coanuts* is merely a photographed stage production?) The film's

peak is the sequence, already a modern classic, in which a chorus of Storm Troopers, shot from above à la Busby Berkeley, sings "Springtime for Hitler"—a lilting melody composed by Brooks—while revolving in swastika formation. Afterward, everything runs downhill. The idea of playing the Führer as a southern red-neck high on flower power and LSD not only mixes up too many incompatible jokes but destroys the bedrock plausibility of plot without which even the looniest farce collapses. Like most of Brooks's work for the cinema, *The Producers* shows him at his best and at his worst.

Academy Award notwithstanding, there was no stampede in the movie industry for Brooks's services. His fame is now so widespread that we tend to forget (though he does not) how recent its origins are. It was not until 1974, with *Blazing Saddles,* that the days of wine and grosses began. His second picture, *The Twelve Chairs,* opened in 1970, nearly three frustrating years after *The Producers,* and crashed to immediate box-office failure. It was based on a satirical Soviet novel of the nineteen-twenties, by Ilya Ilf and Eugene Petrov. Like *The Producers,* it dealt with greed—the prize in this case being a hoard of diamonds concealed in one of a dozen chairs that are confiscated from a palace during the revolution. Again, the characters are raging obsessives, with the difference that here the model is Gogol rather than Jonson. The atmosphere of rural Russia is lovingly evoked, and Brooks himself, making his movie debut, is superb in the minor role of a masochistic, vodka-sodden caretaker with an insatiable yearning for the good old days of servitude. Yet the film as a whole never comes to life; its jokes seem shod with lead, and one watches glumly as, like the wounded snake in Pope's poem, it drags its slow length along. Perhaps excess of ambition was what betrayed it. Alan Schwartz told me, "It was meant to be a great statement about man's relationship to man, and how revolutions fail to work because of human frailty. Mel wanted to be serious and literary."

Two ironic footnotes should be added. (1) In 1945, an updated travesty of the same novel, transplanted to New York and entitled *It's in the Bag,* was shot in Hollywood. Starring Fred Allen, it treats the source material as an excuse for a parade of cameo appearances by well-known names, among them (the roll is worth calling) Victor Moore, Don Ameche, Jerry Colonna, William Bendix, Rudy Vallee, Jack Benny, and Robert Benchley. Though rampantly disloyal to the original, it has many more laughs than the Brooks version, mired in reverence. Benchley, who plays a hotel rat-catcher, must surely have written his own best line. Frock-coated at his son's wedding, he draws the lad aside to calm his nerves with a last-minute word of advice. "In-laws' suits never fit," he says gravely. "Remember that, boy." (2) Nothing in *The Twelve Chairs* is as funny as the account of its making which Brooks gave in an interview with *Playboy*, published in February, 1975. Having explained that shooting took place in Yugoslavia, where he spent nine months, Brooks continued:

> It's a very long flight to Yugoslavia and you land in a field of full-grown corn. They figure it cushions the landing. . . . Now, at night, you can't do anything, because all of Belgrade is lit by a ten-watt bulb, and you can't go anywhere, because Tito has the car. It was a beauty, a green '38 Dodge. And the food in Yugoslavia is either very good or very bad. One day, we arrived on location late and starving and they served us fried chains. When we got to our hotel rooms, mosquitoes as big as George Foreman were waiting for us. They were sitting in armchairs with their legs crossed.

It is tempting to quote more. Brooks's performance throughout the twelve seventy-five-minute sessions he devoted to answering *Playboy*'s questions was a marathon display of his gift for chat in full flower. The printed result deserves a place in any anthology of modern American humor. The Master is back on home ground. Brooks is showing off his own invention—the interview as comic art—and doing so with a virtuosity that makes one wonder how any other form could ever put his talents to better use.

Fifty thousand dollars was Brooks's reward for writing, directing, coproducing, and acting in *The Twelve Chairs*. It consumed three years of his life, and this means that, after taxes, he was subsisting on an annual sum of approximately

eight thousand dollars. Since then—except on one eccentric
and abortive occasion—he has shrunk from writing a film
alone, preferring to test his ideas in the crucible of collaboration. In his words, "I didn't want to go back to the tables
and risk another gambling session with my career." By re-
sorting to teamwork, he has turned out the hits that have established his reputation; in pragmatic terms, he cannot be
faulted. Even so, there are those—Alan Schwartz is one of
them—who feel that the time may now have come for Brooks
to trust his own intuitions and fly solo again. "Mel surrounds
himself with other writers because the screenplay, to him, is
the most important part of a movie," Schwartz told me. "But
I'd like to see him doing his own stuff. He ought to give us
pure, vintage Brooks, not Brooks riding on the backs of a lot
of other people. There's a strange legal phrase that expresses
what I mean. Suppose I'm working as a driver for a guy named
Al. If I run someone over in the course of my duties, Al is
responsible. But if I take the car to the beach and run someone
over, that is called in law a 'frolic and detour,' and *I'm* responsible. I think Mel should go in for more frolics and de-
tours."

In 1970, when *The Twelve Chairs* were pulled out from
under him by critics and public alike, Brooks was forty-four
years old and was still, by his own standards, a failure. ("To
be the funniest has always been my aim"—statement to *News-
week*, 1975.) Unable to resist another fling at the tables, he
plunged into his last frolic and detour to date—a flirtation with
culture which was so alien to his temperament that it seems,
in retrospect, a gesture of self-destructive defiance. He saw
and was impressed by an Off Broadway production of Gold-
smith's comedy *She Stoops to Conquer*. The play struck him
as "Mozartean," and he promptly adapted it for the screen. His
plan was to shoot it in England, with Albert Finney as Tony
Lumpkin. Not long before, Finney had spent several weeks on
a remote Pacific island with only one record, "The Two-Thousand-Year-Old Man," which he played every night. "When I
met him in New York," Brooks recalls, "he was in awe of me,
he couldn't believe I lived, he thought I was God." Finney
listened to the divine proposition and reverently turned it down.
Brooks took his screenplay on the familiar round of agents,

producers, and studios without raising a flicker of interest, and
got ready to face the fact that he was finished in show business.

David Begelman, recently fined for financial misdeeds committed while he was head of Columbia Pictures, here enters
the story. Despite the cloud of scandal over Begelman's head,
Brooks remains his impenitent admirer. "When he took over
Columbia in 1973," Brooks says, "David Begelman turned it
around and made it, by dint of his aggression and his perspi-
cacity and his acumen, a wonderful, working, winning company. I love it the way I love Fox, where I work, because it
is not Gulf & Western, it's not Transamerica, it's Columbia
Pictures." Before Begelman moved to Columbia, he was vice-
chairman of Creative Management Associates, perhaps the
most powerful talent agency in the entertainment industry. One
day in 1972, Brooks was aimlessly trudging the streets of New
York. Begelman spotted him and approached him. According
to Brooks, the following conversation took place:

BEGELMAN: Where are you going?

BROOKS: Nowhere. I am walking in circles.

BEGELMAN: Why is the most talented man in the world
walking in circles?

BROOKS: Because the most talented man in the world
is out of a job and is maybe not the most talented man
in the world.

BEGELMAN: Can I buy you lunch?

BROOKS: Oh, I would be so happy if you would,
because I haven't eaten in days.

(*They have lunch, after which Brooks is whisked off
to Begelman's sumptuous office, where "even the indi-
rect lighting is good."*)

BEGELMAN: The first thing you should do is sign with
me. You're nobody and I'm everybody. It's a good deal.

BROOKS: You're right. (*He signs.*)

Soon afterward, a friend in the script department of
Warner Brothers sent him a treatment by Andrew Bergman of a Western comedy called *Tex X*. Would Brooks
like to rewrite it? Immobilized by self-mistrust, Brooks
passed the script on to Begelman for advice. This led
to another exquisitely lit confrontation.

BEGELMAN: I think this could be very funny. Do you want to do it?

BROOKS: No.

BEGELMAN: All right, you don't want to do it. Fine. You'll do it.

BROOKS: Why do I have to do it?

BEGELMAN: Because you owe a fortune in alimony, because you are in debt, and because you have no choice. You have to do it, and with all the talent you possess.

BROOKS: OK. I'll do it. As long as I can have Andrew Bergman to work with.

BEGELMAN: Swell. I'll make that one of the conditions.

BROOKS: And not only Bergman. (*His mind races to recapture the security of the past.*) I want to do it the way we did "Your Show of Shows." We'll get a black writer, maybe Richard Pryor, and a comedy team like Norman Steinberg and Alan Uger, and we'll lock ourselves up and write it together, fancy-free and crazy.

Through Begelman's mediation with Warners, this group was rapidly assembled. He negotiated a contract whereby Brooks received fifty thousand dollars for the screenplay (his fellow authors split a smaller sum four ways) and a hundred thousand more if the studio liked the result and asked Brooks to direct it. Brooks regards *Blazing Saddles*—his new title for *Tex X*—as "a landmark comedy," a historic blast of derision at the heroic myths of the Old West. "I decided that this would be a surrealist epic," he said to me. "It was time to take two eyes, the way Picasso had done it, and put them on one side of the nose, because the official movie portrait of the West was simply a lie. For nine months, we worked together like maniacs. We went all the way—especially Richard Pryor, who was very brave and very far-out and very catalytic. I figured my career was finished anyway, so I wrote berserk, heartfelt stuff about white corruption and racism and Bible-thumping bigotry. We used dirty language on the screen for the first time, and to me the whole thing was like a big psychoanalytic session. I just got everything out of me—all my furor, my frenzy, my insanity, my love of life and hatred of death."

Warners snapped up the completed script and hired Brooks to direct his first Hollywood movie. There was one stipulation: the campfire sequence, in which the bean-fed cowpokes audibly befoul the night air, must be cut. Brooks and his colleagues stood firm: either the scene stayed or they quit. Here, and elsewhere in the screenplay, they saw no reason to disown what is called "healthy vulgarity" when it occurs in Chaucer, but "childish smut" when it infiltrates the cinema. Eventually the studio gave in, provided that Brooks would consent, as an executive put it, "to for God's sake hold the decibels down." Casting, however, was not without problems. Brooks wanted Richard Pryor to play the black protagonist, whom knavish State Procurer Harvey Korman appoints as sheriff of a white chauvinist community in the hope of destroying its faith in law and order. Warners rejected Pryor, whom they thought too undisciplined. Cleavon Little (a suave performer with no flair for comedy) got the job instead. Dan Dailey was engaged for the role of the Waco Kid, the burnt-out alcoholic gun-fighter whom Little enlists to support him. On the Friday before shooting began, Dailey suffered an attack of qualms and cabled that he was pulling out. With forty-eight hours to go, he was replaced by Gig Young, but when Young arrived on the set it was obvious that he was in no shape to act. Personal problems, it seemed, were oppressing him, and at the end of a wasted day he was discreetly fired.

"It's a sign from God!" Brooks suddenly cried. "Get me Gene Wilder on the phone in New York!" Though Wilder knew the script and was eager to help, he was about to leave for England, where he was due to appear in *The Little Prince*, directed by Stanley Donen. "Nothing's impossible!" Brooks shouted at him. "Call Donen in London now and ask him to rearrange his schedule. If he can let you out for three weeks, or even two, it's enough."

A couple of hours later, Wilder called back with the news that Donen had generously agreed to reshuffle his plans and release Wilder for three and a half weeks. "I'll fly out tomorrow," Wilder said. Brooks met him at Los Angeles Airport and drove him straight to the costume department of Warners, where he was transformed within minutes into something out of *Stagecoach*. Next morning, roughly thirty-six hours after the idea had first come up, Gene Wilder, word perfect, was playing the Waco Kid. "I don't believe in fate," Wilder said to me recently, "but I'm tempted to when I think of my relationship with Mel. If I hadn't been miscast in *Mother Courage*, none of this would have happened. And if two actors hadn't dropped out of *Blazing Saddles* at the last moment, I would never have got the part."

When shooting (ten weeks) and editing (nine months) were over, Brooks and his producer, Michael Hertzberg, held an afternoon showing of their rough-cut for a dozen top executives at Warner Brothers. The occasion was about as festive—to borrow a phrase dear to Laurence Olivier—as a baby's open grave. The jury sat like so many statues on Easter Island and filed out at the end in frozen silence. Brooks was shattered, convinced that he had thrown away his last chance in movies. Hertzberg was more resilient. Grabbing a phone, he instructed his staff that he was going to run the picture again that evening, in a larger viewing theatre, and that he wanted it packed with at least two hundred people: secretaries, janitors, cleaning women, waiters—anyone but studio brass. Let Brooks continue the story: "So 8 P.M. comes and two hundred and forty people are jammed into this room. Some of them have already heard the film is a stinker because of the afternoon disaster. So they're very quiet and polite. Frankie Laine sings the title song, with the whip cracks. Laughs begin—good laughs. We go to the railroad section. The cruel overseer says to the black workers, 'Let's have a good old nigger work song.' Everybody gets a little chilled. Then the black guys start to sing 'I get no kick from champagne. . . .' And that audience was like a Chagall painting. People left their chairs and floated upside down and the laughter never stopped. It was big from that moment to the last frame of the last reel."

Blazing Saddles opened in 1974 and went on to become one of the two top-grossing comedies in the history of the cinema, out-earned only by Robert Altman's *M*A*S*H*. It is a farce with the gloves off, a living proof of the adage that a feast can be every bit as good as enough. We are not invited to smile: we either laugh or cringe. The major gags are blatant to the point of outrage, as when a thug on foot, faced with a mounted adversary, fells his opponent's horse with a roundhouse right to the jaw. Brooks's method is the comedy of deliberate over-kill. The annoyance of Hedley Lamarr (the Harvey Korman character) at being addressed as Hedy is funny the first time and tedious the third, but by the fifth or sixth it is funnier than ever; in a film full of unexpected twists, the expected twist can pay surprising dividends. Though the jokes run wild, the plot is tightly organized, and parts of the script are remarkably literary—e.g., this far from untypical exchange:

Q.: Don't you see it's the last act of a desperate man?
A.: I don't care if it's the first act of *Henry V*.

With *Blazing Saddles*, a low comedy in which many of the custard pies are camouflaged hand grenades, Brooks made his first conquest of Middle America. He told *Playboy* that it was "designed as an esoteric little picture," but the statement simply does not ring true; he had always wanted the big audience in addition to the art-house minority, and now he had both.

Young Frankenstein (1974) started life as a phrase doodled by Gene Wilder during an Easter vacation at West Hampton in 1973. He called Brooks and explained what he had in mind: one of Frankenstein's scions revisits the family castle in Transylvania and revives the monster his ancestor created. Brooks had no time to do more than express interest, since *Blazing Saddles* was already in preparation. A deal was set up with Columbia whereby Wilder would write a first draft and then, after *Blazing Saddles* was finished, work with Brooks on a revised version. Their collaboration was speedy and harmonious, Brooks supplying the broad comic emphases and Wilder the grace notes. Wilder restrained Brooks, who, in turn, liberated Wilder. "Mel has all kinds of faults," Wilder said to me. "Like his greed, his megalomania, his need to be the universal father and teacher, even to people far more experienced than he is. Why I'm close to him is not in spite of those faults but because of them. I need a leader, someone to tell me what to do. If he were more humble, modest, and considerate, he would probably have more friends, but I doubt whether he and I would be such good friends. He made me discover the *me* in Mel. He taught me never to be afraid of offending. It's when you worry about offending people that you get in trouble." (Compare something that Cocteau once said: "Whatever the public blames you for, cultivate it—it is yourself.")

Brooks and Wilder presented their final draft to Columbia before *Blazing Saddles* appeared. The estimated budget was two million two hundred thousand dollars. The studio wanted it reduced to a million and three-quarters. Happy to compromise, Brooks asked, "How about two million?" The answer was an unyielding no. "So we took the script to Fox, and made the picture there for two million eight," Wilder told me. "We were already shooting when *Blazing Saddles* came out and hit the jackpot." Wilder thinks—and is not alone in thinking—that this was the biggest mistake Columbia ever made. Since *Young Frankenstein*, which has so far grossed over thirty-four million dollars, Brooks has remained unshakably loyal to Fox. (In his office on the Fox lot, the wall overlooking his desk is dominated by a large portrait of Tolstoy, hanging alongside a blown-up label from a bottle of Château Latour 1929—"to remind me," Brooks says, "that there are more important things than grosses.") "On the set of *Blazing Saddles*, there was a lot of love in the air," Wilder continues. "But *Young Frankenstein* was the most pleasurable film I've ever done. I couldn't bear to leave Transylvania."

It would be fair to call *Young Frankenstein* the Mel Brooks movie that appeals to people who don't like Mel Brooks. "I like *things* in all his films," Woody Allen said to me cautiously, "but they're a little in-and-out for my taste. *Young Frankenstein* is the most consistent whole." The parts mesh instead of clashing. The pace throughout, audaciously stately for comedy, is modelled on that of James Whale's *Frankenstein;* and Gerald Hirschfeld's black-and-white photography exactly matches Whale's crepuscular visual style. The members of the supporting cast play together with a self-denying temperance unique in Brooks's work: I think particularly of Frau Blücher (Cloris Leachman), the fright-wigged housekeeper, at every mention of whose name we hear the distant whinnying of terrified horses; and of the Transylvanian police chief (Kenneth Mars), with an expatriate accent even less penetrable than the late Albert Bassermann's, and with a prosthetic arm that he uses as a battering ram when he leads the pitchfork-brandishing peasants against the gates of Schloss Frankenstein. In the title role, Gene Wilder—his eyes burning, his voice an exalted, slow-motion tenor—gives the finest performance yet seen in a Brooks picture. In the best sequence, fit to be set beside the "Springtime for Hitler" routine in *The Producers*, Wilder proudly appears before an assembly of grave Victorian scientists to introduce his new, improved monster, who clumps onto the stage and goes into a halting impression of Boris Karloff singing "Puttin' on the Ritz." The spectators instantly subject the zombie and his master to a bombardment of cabbages and broccoli, the underlying joke being that an audience of bearded savants should have come laden with vegetable missiles in the first place. It is not the gags, however, that give the film its motive force. We have seen that Brooks is driven by a fear, amounting to hatred, of mortality; and what is *Young Frankenstein* but the story of a man who succeeds in defeating death?

Brooks now began to savor the delights of power. "It's an achievement of a kind," he told me some time ago, "to know that I can walk into any studio—any one in town—and just say my name, and the president will fly out from behind his desk and open his door. It's terrific, it's a great feeling. My worst critic is my wife. She keeps me straight. She says, 'Are you pleasing that mythical public of yours again, or is this really funny and heartfelt?'" Brooks refers to the byproducts of success under the collective title of the Green Awning Syndrome. He explains what he means in an imaginary anecdote: "Mike Nichols has just made *The Graduate*, and it's a world-wide smash, and he goes to his producer, Joe Levine, and says, 'Now I want to do *The Green Awning*.' 'The what?' '*The Green Awning*.' 'What is that?' 'It's a movie about a green awning.' 'Does any famous star walk under the green awning?' 'No, all unknowns.' 'Are there any naked women near the green awning?' 'No, no naked women.' 'Are people talking and eating scrambled eggs under the green awning?' 'No. It's just a green awning. Panavision. It doesn't move.' 'How long would it be?' 'Two hours. Nothing but a green awning.' Levine sticks out his hand. 'All right, what the hell, we'll do it!' That's the Green Awning Syndrome."

Brooks knew that the syndrome had descended upon him when he proposed *Silent Movie* as his next picture for Fox: given his track record, the studio simply dared not turn it down, though Brooks admits that he helped Fox to be brave by revealing that there would be cameo roles for Liza Minnelli, Anne Bancroft, Paul Newman, James Caan, and Burt Reynolds. The idea for a movie with no spoken words (apart from a resonant "No!" to be uttered by the mime Marcel Marceau) had come from Ron Clark, a laconic playwright and comedy writer. Clark suggested that he and Brooks should collaborate on the script with Rudy DeLuca and Barry Levinson, widely admired as the writers of "The Carol Burnett Show"; and so it worked out. For more than twelve months—very much on and off, to fit in with their other assignments—the four men met in a room at Fox and reduced one another to hysteria. Shooting began in January, 1976, and the film had its premiere before the end of the year.

A string of sight gags linked by captions (the verbals in many instances being funnier than the visuals), *Silent Movie* consolidated Brooks's international fame. No dubbing was required to make its more explosive set pieces as accessible in Bora Bora as they were in South Bend. It spoke softly but carried a big slapstick. Moreover, it established Brooks as a movie star: Mel Funn, the ex-alcoholic director who saves his old studio from conglomerate takeover with a silent movie called *Silent Movie*, was the first leading role he had ever played. The picture was his third comedy hit in three years, and up to the beginning of 1978 it had brought in more than twenty million dollars at the box office. Yet there are times when one not only can but must argue with success. Even as I smiled (which was more often than I laughed) at *Silent Movie*, I knew I was watching an act of supreme perversity. Here was a master of the improvised word devoting more than a year of his life to something speechless and meticulously planned in advance. Do not suppose, by the way, that Brooks is a director who works on impulse, prancing around the set in ecstasies of Felliniesque free association. The final script of *Silent Movie* was the film the public saw, except for a brief but expensive sequence that Brooks described to me afterward: "It was called 'Lobsters in New York,' and it starts with a restaurant sign that reads 'Chez Lobster.' Inside, a huge lobster in maître d's tuxedo is greeting two very well-dressed lobsters in evening dress and leading them to a table. Already we thought this was hysterical. Then a waiter lobster in a white jacket shows them a menu that says 'Flown in Fresh from New York.' They get up and follow the waiter lobster to an enormous tank, where a lot of little human beings in bathing suits are swimming nervously around. The diner lobsters point to a tasty-looking middle-aged man. The waiter's claw reaches into the tank. It picks up the man, who is going bananas, and that was the end of the scene. We loved it; we thought it was sensational. Every time we saw it, there was not enough Kleenex to stuff into our mouths." Nobody else, however, so much as snickered—not even at the sneak previews—with the result that Brooks decided to jettison the whole sequence. Never before had he faced such a setback, and the memory of it still ruffles him. Seeing *Silent Movie* for the second time, I found myself recalling and endorsing something that Gene Wilder had said to me: "Mel has no physical skills, like Chaplin or Fields. His skills are vocal. Not verbal but vocal." And in *Silent Movie*, for all its popularity, rusting unused.

Excerpts from a dinner with Brooks at the Chambord Restaurant in Beverly Hills late in 1977. He is wearing a dark-blue coat, gray slacks, a light-blue shirt, and a striped blue tie; as usual, he has arrived with a leather case containing two bottles of absurdly expensive wine from his own cellar. Neither of them, alas, comes from the case of magnums of Haut Brion, 1961, which Alfred Hitchcock recently sent him as a gesture of gratitude for *High Anxiety*. In reminiscent mood, Brooks speaks: "Just before *Silent Movie* came out in 1976, I was approached by a staff writer from *Time* who asked me whether I'd like to be on the cover. Well, I expected to be described in *Time* as 'Mel Brooks, flinty, chunky Jew,' but nevertheless I said yes. I had no idea what an insane Pandora's box of heartache would be opened by this simple exchange. Reporters followed me around night and day for weeks. They tortured my mother and my children, all the time looking for negative things about me. Everyone I ever knew was called and cross-examined. Everyone eagerly cooperated. Then, a couple of weeks before the cover was due, I was told I'd been dumped and replaced by Nadia Comaneci. So I asked, 'Isn't the election coming up soon?' 'Don't worry,' they said. 'It's you next week for sure.' Next week, Ford gets the cover. I called them up and said, 'I'm disgusted with myself. I feel used and humiliated, and I may hang myself in my cell.' They said, 'Look, if you'll just help us fill in one or two gaps, there's a good chance that next week, perhaps...' Even then I hesitated, but I finally said no."

I asked what seemed the obvious question.

After a pause, Brooks slowly replied, "If I could get a legal guarantee that they wouldn't bother my immediate family, and if that guarantee was signed by every member of the Supreme Court, then the answer is yes, I *would* do it all again for a *Time* cover."

High Anxiety, which featured the same star, director, and writing team as *Silent Movie*, made its debut in the closing weeks of 1977. Sniffed at by some of the critics (though not by the public, which has swept it into the black with a box-office take that so far amounts to about twenty million dollars), it borrows elements from a number of Hitchcock films—in particular, *Spellbound, Vertigo, Psycho, The Birds*, and *North by North-West*—and, having given them all a ferociously farcical twist, arranges them in a way that would make narrative sense to an audience entirely ignorant of Hitchcock. Brooks once told me that for him the Marx Brothers were "the healthiest of all the comics," and it is not fortuitous that the middle initial of Dr. Robert H. Thorndyke, the character he plays in *High Anxiety*, stands for Harpo. The best half-dozen moments in the picture have the antisocial outrageousness that was always the Brothers' trademark—moments when inhibitions evaporate and excesses long dreamed of are allowed free play; e.g., Thorndyke's fulsome impersonation of Frank Sinatra in a hotel nightclub, and his first dinner as the newly appointed head of the Psycho-Neurotic Institute for the Very, *Very* Nervous. In the latter sequence an establishing shot shows us, by night, a mansion like Manderley in *Rebecca*. The script continues:

> *The lights are on in the elegantly appointed dining room.* CAMERA SLOWLY MOVES *toward the lighted window. It* MOVES *closer and closer, until it actually hits the window and crashes through. We* HEAR *the* SOUND *of the window panes breaking. Everybody at the dining table stops eating their fruit cup, their spoons poised in mid-air.*

When *High Anxiety* failed to receive a single nomination, either from the Academy or from the Writers Guild, Brooks was in despair. "He was as low as I've ever known him," his wife said to me.

Despite its virtues, *High Anxiety* fitted into a confining pattern. Brooks had now made four films in succession, all of them based on other kinds of films—the Western, the horror picture, the silent comedy, and the Hitchcock thriller. Nor was he alone in this dependence on incest—or, if you prefer, cannibalism. Barry Levinson remarked to me, "*Rocky* is a remake even though it's never been made before." In the *Times* on September 25, 1977, Roger Copeland dealt with the whole subject of movies about movies:

> Consider, for example, George Lucas's "Star Wars"— a film that makes so many references to earlier films and styles of film-making that it could just as easily, and perhaps more accurately, have been called "Genre Wars."

Among other pictures cited by Copeland were Martin Scorese's *New York, New York*, Brian De Palma's *Obsession*, Don Siegel's *The Shootist*, Marty Feldman's *The Last Remake of Beau Geste*, and Herbert Ross's *Play It Again, Sam* (written by Woody Allen), all of which drew their inspiration from celluloid sources. Nor did he overlook the career of Peter Bogdanovich, an extended act of homage to the achievements of other directors. He concluded:

There are dangers involved; the dangers of decadence, of art feeding so completely on itself that it becomes totally cut off from life as lived.

In 1965, in an introduction to Malcolm Lowry's novel *Under the Volcano*, Stephen Spender wrote, "Someone should write a thesis perhaps on the influence of the cinema on the novel—I mean the *serious* novel." I should say that there was a more urgent need for a study of the influence of the cinema on the cinema—and I do not mean only the serious cinema. It is self-evident that all the arts live off and grow out of their own past. What is new about film is that it is the first narrative art to be instantly accessible, twenty-four hours a day, in virtually every living room. To immerse oneself in drama, opera, or literature, it is necessary, from time to time, to carry out certain errands, like going to a theatre, an opera house, a record shop, a bookstore, or a library; but to become saturated in cinema you do not even have to go to the movies. They come to you. The lover of stage acting will never know exactly how Sarah Siddons or Edmund Kean performed, or what the theatre in Periclean Athens was really like, but for the movie buff such problems do not arise, since the art of his choice is on permanent record, its whole history an open book, visible at the turn of a switch. This explains why so many contemporary novels and plays, as well as films, are swollen with references to, quotations from, and parodies of old movies. A process of artistic colonization is going on. Never before, I believe, has one art form exercised such hegemony over the others; and the decisive factor is not intrinsic superiority but sheer availability.

The first generation of children nourished, via television, on films has only recently reached maturity, yet it's already clear how deeply—in their private behavior, not to mention their work as artists—the movies are imprinted on them. As the amount of exposed and edited film inexorably piles up, its ascendancy will increase, and we may have to cope with a culture entirely molded by cinematic habits and values. Edmund Wilson, I suspect, was hovering over this point as long ago as 1949, when, having seen a pastiche Hollywood musical called *Oh, You Beautiful Doll*, he indignantly wrote to a friend:

"All these attempts to exploit the immediate past show the rapidity of the bankruptcy of the movies as purveyors of popular entertainment."

Brooks, discussing his future plans, sometimes sounds worryingly unaware of the perils involved in continued addiction to the Self-Regarding Cinema. In the past twelve months, I have heard him frothing with enthusiasm about such projects as (1) "a World War Two picture to end all World War Two pictures"; (2) a remake of the Lubitsch masterpiece *To Be or Not to Be*, starring Anne Bancroft and himself; and (3) "a Busby Berkeley-style musical where crazy people sing for no reason," which would be tantamount to self-plagiarism, since the perfect comment on Berkeley already exists in the "Springtime for Hitler" sequence from *The Producers*. Not long ago, he called up Gene Wilder and said, "When we work together again, we're going to have to bring up the big guns, and there are only two—love and death." Which is all very well except for the fact that *Love and Death* is the title of a film by Woody Allen.

Intermittently, however, Brooks will say something that bolsters one's faith in the curious inner compass that guides him. This, for instance: "I've tied myself to no end but the joy of observation. And I need to pass that on. I'm a celebrator. That's why I like the Russians. They'll look at a tree and cry out, 'Look at that tree!' They're full of original astonishments." And, still more reassuringly, this—a remark uttered in a context that had nothing to do with Brooks's own career: "We are all basically antennae. If we let ourselves be bombarded by cultural events based on movies, we won't get a taste of what's happening in the world."

Springtime, 1978: A sunny lunch in Los Angeles with Anne Bancroft, who is, according to her husband, "a strange combination of the serf and the intellectual." They live in a one-story house (no pool) in Malibu. She tells me that Brooks's newest obsession is to make a film called, *tout court*, *The History of the World, Part One*. She likes the idea, because it means, as she puts it, "that he can play any period in which he feels happy." This, of course, was precisely what he did in the footloose days when he was recording "The Two-Thou-

sand-Year-Old Man." The story of mankind would be an ideal
frolic, a definitive detour; and Miss Bancroft agrees with me
that he ought to write it on his own. "One evening, I came
back late from a difficult rehearsal," she says. "Mel had been
working at home all day. I was feeling very sorry for myself,
and I wailed, 'Acting is so hard.' Mel picked up a blank sheet
of paper and held it in front of me. *'That's* what's hard,' he
said. I've never complained about acting again."

[1978]

The girl in the black helmet
—LOUISE BROOKS

NONE OF this would have happened if I had not noticed, while lying late in bed on a hot Sunday morning last year in Santa Monica and flipping through the TV guide for the impending week, that one of the local public-broadcasting channels had decided to show, at 1 P.M. that very January day, a film on which my fantasies had fed ever since I first saw it, a quarter of a century before. Even for Channel 28, it was an eccentric piece of programming. I wondered how many of my Southern Californian neighbors would be tempted to forgo their poolside champagne brunches, their bicycle jaunts along Ocean Front Walk, their health-food picnics in Topanga Canyon, or their surf-board battles with the breakers of Malibu in order to watch a silent picture, shot in Berlin just fifty years earlier, about an artless young hedonist who, meaning no harm, rewards her lovers—and eventually herself—with the prize of violent death. Although the film is a tragedy, it is also a celebration of the pleasure principle. Outside in the midday sunshine, California was celebrating the same principle, with the shadows of mortality left out.

I got to my set in time to catch the credits. The director: G. W. Pabst, reigning maestro of German cinema in the late nineteen-twenties. The script: Adapted by Ladislaus Vajda from *Erdgeist (Earth Spirit)* and *Die Büchse der Pandora (Pandora's Box)*, two scabrously erotic plays written in the eighteen-nineties by Frank Wedekind. For his movie, Pabst chose the title of the later work, though the screenplay differed markedly from Wedekind's original text: *Pandora's Box* belongs among the few films that have succeeded in improving on theatrical chefs-d'oeuvre. For his heroine, Lulu, the dominant figure in both plays, Pabst outraged a whole generation of German actresses by choosing a twenty-one-year-old girl from Kansas whom he had never met, who was currently working for Paramount in Hollywood, and who spoke not a word of any language other than English. This was Louise Brooks. She made only twenty-four films, in a movie career that began in 1925 and ended, with enigmatic suddenness, in 1938. Two of them were masterpieces—*Pandora's Box* and its immediate successor, also directed by Pabst, *The Diary of a Lost Girl*. Most, however, were assembly-line studio products. Yet around her, with a luxuriance that proliferates every year, a literature has grown up. I append a few excerpts:

> Her youthful admirers see in her an actress who needed no directing, but could move across the screen causing the work of art to be born by her mere presence.—*Lotte H. Eisner, French critic.*

> An actress of brilliance, a luminescent personality, and a beauty unparalleled in film history.—*Kevin Brownlow, British director and movie historian.*

> One of the most mysterious and potent figures in the history of the cinema...she was one of the first performers to penetrate to the heart of screen acting.—*David Thomson, British critic.*

> Louise Brooks is the only woman who had the ability to transfigure no matter what film into a masterpiece....Louise is the perfect apparition, the dream woman, the being without whom the cinema would be a poor thing. She is much more than a myth, she is a magical presence, a real phantom, the magnetism of the cinema.—*Ado Kyrou, French critic.*

> Those who have seen her can never forget her. She is the modern actress *par excellence*....As soon as she takes the screen, fiction disappears along with art, and one has the impression of being present at a documentary. The camera seems to have caught her by surprise,

without her knowledge. She is the intelligence of the cinematic process, the perfect incarnation of that which is photogenic; she embodies all that the cinema rediscovered in its last years of silence: complete naturalness and complete simplicity. Her art is so pure that it becomes invisible.—*Henri Langlois, director of the Cinémathèque Française.*

On Channel 28, I stayed with the film to its end, which is also Lulu's. Of the climactic sequence, so decorously understated, Louise Brooks once wrote in *Sight & Sound,* "It is Christmas Eve and she is about to receive the gift which has been her dream since childhood. Death by a sexual maniac." When it was over, I switched channels and returned to the real world of game shows and pet-food commercials, relieved to find that the spell she cast was still as powerful as ever. Brooks reminds me of the scene in *Citizen Kane* in which Everett Sloane, as Orson Welles's aging business manager, recalls a girl in a white dress whom he saw in his youth when he was crossing over to Jersey on a ferry. They never met or spoke. "I only saw her for one second," he says, "and she didn't see me at all—but I'll bet a month hasn't gone by since then that I haven't thought of that girl."

I had now, by courtesy of Channel 28, seen *Pandora's Box* for the third time. My second encounter with the film had taken place several years earlier, in France. Consulting my journal. I found the latter experience recorded with the baroque extravagance that seems to overcome all those who pay tribute to Brooks. I unflinchingly quote:

Infatuation with L. Brooks reinforced by second viewing of "Pandora." She has run through my life like a magnetic thread—this shameless urchin tomboy, this unbroken, unbreakable porcelain filly. She is a prairie princess, equally at home in a waterfront bar and in the royal suite at Neuschwanstein; a creature of impulse, a creator of impulses, a temptress with no pretensions, capable of dissolving into a giggling fit at a peak of erotic ecstasy; amoral but totally selfless, with that sleek jet *cloche* of hair that rings such a peal of bells in my subconscious. In short, the only star actress I can imagine either being enslaved by or wanting to enslave; and a dark lady worthy of any poet's devotion:

For I have sworn thee fair and thought thee bright, Who art as black as hell, as dark as night.

Some basic information about Rochester, New York: With two hundred and sixty-three thousand inhabitants, it is the sixth-largest city in the state, bestriding the Genesee River at its outlet into Lake Ontario. Here, in the eighteen-eighties, George Eastman completed the experiments that enabled him to manufacture the Kodak camera, which, in turn, enabled ordinary people to capture monochrome images, posed or spontaneous, of the world around them. He was in at the birth of movies, too. The flexible strips of film used in Thomas Edison's motion-picture machine were first produced by Eastman, in 1889. Rochester is plentifully dotted with monuments to the creator of the Kodak, among them a palatial Georgian house, with fifty rooms and a lofty neo-classical portico, that he built for himself in 1905. When he died, in 1932, he left his mansion to the University of Rochester, of whose president it became the official home. Shortly after the Second World War, the Eastman house took on a new identity. It opened its doors to the public, and offered, to quote from its brochure, "the world's most important collection of pictures, films, and apparatus showing the development of the art and technology of photography." In 1972 it was imposingly renamed the International Museum of Photography. Its library now contains about five thousand movies, many of them unique copies, and seven of them—a larger number than any other archive can boast—featuring Louise Brooks. Hence I decide to pay a visit to the city, where I check in at a motel in the late spring of 1978. Thanks to the generous cooperation of Dr. John B. Kuyper, the director of the museum's film department, I am to see its hoard of Brooks pictures—six of them new to me—within the space of two days. Screenings will be held in the Dryden Theatre, a handsome auditorium that was added to the main building in 1950 as a gift from Eastman's niece and her husband, George Dryden.

On the eve of Day One, I mentally recap what I have learned of Brooks's early years. Born in 1906 in Cherryvale, Kansas, she was the second of four children sired by Leonard Brooks, a hardworking lawyer of kindly disposition and diminutive build, for whom she felt nothing approaching love. She herself was never more than five feet two and a half inches tall, but she raised her stature onscreen by wearing heels as high as six inches. Her mother, née Myra Rude, was the eldest member of a family of nine, and she warned Mr. Brooks before their marriage that she had spent her entire life thus far looking after kid brothers and sisters, that she had no intention of repeating the experience with children of her own, and that any progeny she might bear him would, in effect, have to fend for themselves. The result, because Myra Brooks was a woman of high spirits who took an infectious delight in the arts, was not a cold or neglectful upbringing. Insistent on liberty for herself, she passed on a love of liberty to her offspring. Louise absorbed it greedily. Pirouetting appealed to her; encouraged by her mother, she took dancing lessons, and by the age of ten she was making paid appearances at Kiwanis and Rotary festivities. At fifteen, already a beauty *sui generis*, as surviving photographs show, with her hair, close-cropped at the nape to expose what Christopher Isherwood has called "that unique imperious neck of hers," cascading in ebony bangs down the high, intelligent forehead and descending on either side of her eyes in spit curls slicked forward at the cheekbones, like a pair of enamelled parentheses—at fifteen, she left high school and went to New York with her dance teacher. There she successfully auditioned for the Denishawn Dancers, which had been founded in 1915 by Ruth St. Denis and Ted Shawn, and was by far the most adventurous dance company in America. She started out as a student, but soon graduated to full membership of the troupe, with which she toured the country from 1922 to 1924. One of her fellow-dancers, Martha Graham, became a lifelong friend. "I learned to act while watching Martha Graham dance," she said later, "and I learned to move in film from watching Chaplin."

Suddenly, however, the discipline involved in working for Denishawn grew oppressive. Brooks was fired for lacking a sense of vocation, and the summer of 1924 found her back in

New York, dancing in the chorus of George White's *Scandals*. After three months of this, a whim seized her, and she embarked without warning for London, where she performed the Charleston at the Café de Paris, near Piccadilly Circus. By New York standards, she thought Britain's Bright Young Things a moribund bunch, and when Evelyn Waugh wrote *Vile Bodies* about them, she said that only a genius could have made a masterpiece out of such glum material. Early in 1925, with no professional prospects, she sailed for Manhattan on borrowed money, only to be greeted by Florenz Ziegfeld with the offer of a job in a musical comedy called *Louie the 14th*, starring Leon Errol. She accepted, but the pattern of her subsequent behavior left no doubt that what she meant by liberty and independence was what others defined as irresponsibility and self-indulgence. Of the director of *Louie the 14th*, she afterward wrote, "He detested all of Ziegfeld's spoiled beauties, but most of all me, because on occasion, when I had other commitments, I would wire my nonappearance to the theatre." In May, 1925, she made her movie début, at the Paramount Astoria Studio, on Long Island, playing a bit part in *The Street of Forgotten Men*, of which no print is known to exist. She has written a vivid account of filmmaking in its Long Island days:

The stages were freezing in the winter, steaming hot in the summer. The dressing rooms were windowless cubicles. We rode on the freight elevator, crushed by lights and electricians. But none of that mattered, because the writers, directors, and cast were free from all supervision. Jesse Lasky, Adolph Zukor, and Walter Wanger never left the Paramount office on Fifth Avenue, and the head of production never came on the set. There were writers and directors from Princeton and Yale. Motion pictures did not consume us. When work finished, we dressed in evening clothes, dined at the Colony or "21," and went to the theatre.

The difference in Hollywood was that the studio was run by B. P. Schulberg, a coarse exploiter who propositioned every actress and policed every set. To love books was a big laugh. There was no theatre, no opera, no concerts—just those god-damned movies.

Despite Brooks's erratic conduct in *Louie the 14th*, Ziegfeld hired her to join Will Rogers and W. C. Fields in the 1925 edition of his *Follies*. It proved to be her last Broadway show. One of her many admirers that year was the atrabilious wit Herman Mankiewicz, then employed as second-string drama critic of the *Times*. Blithely playing truant from the *Follies*, she attended the opening of *No, No, Nanette* on Mankiewicz's arm. As the houselights faded, her escort, who was profoundly drunk, announced his intention of falling asleep, and asked Brooks to make notes on the show for use in his review. She obliged, and the *Times* next day echoed her opinion that *No, No, Nanette* was "a highly meritorious paradigm of its kind." (Somewhat cryptically, she added that the score contained "more familiar quotations from itself . . . than even *Hamlet*.") Escapades like this did nothing to endear her to the other, more dedicated Ziegfeld showgirls, but an abiding intimacy grew up between her and W. C. Fields, in whose dressing room she was always graciously received. Later, in a passage that tells us as much about its author as about her subject, she wrote:

He was an isolated person. As a young man he stretched out his hand to Beauty and Love and they thrust it away. Gradually he reduced reality to exclude all but his work, filling the gaps with alcohol whose dim eyes transformed the world into a distant view of harmless shadows. He was also a solitary person. Years of travelling alone around the world with his juggling act taught him the value of solitude and the release it gave his mind. . . . Most of his life will remain unknown. But the history of no life is a jest.

In September, 1925, the *Follies* left town on a national tour. Brooks stayed behind and sauntered through the role of a bathing beauty in a Paramount movie called *The American Venus*. Paramount and M-G-M were both pressing her to sign five-year contracts, and she looked for advice to Walter Wanger, one of the former company's top executives, with whom she was having an intermittent affair. "If, at this crucial moment in my career," she said long afterward, "Walter had given me some faith in my screen personality and my acting ability, he might have saved me from further mauling by the beasts who prowled Broadway and Hollywood." Instead, he urged her to take the Metro offer, arguing that if she chose Paramount everyone would assume that she got the job by sharing his bed and that her major attribute was not talent but sexual accessibility. Incensed by his line of reasoning, she defiantly signed with Paramount.

In the course of twelve months—during which Brooks's friend Humphrey Bogart, seven years her senior, was still laboring on Broadway, with four seasons to wait before the dawn of his film career—Brooks made six full-length pictures. The press began to pay court to her. *Photoplay*, whose reporter she received reclining in bed, said of her, "She is so very Manhattan. Very young. Exquisitely hard-boiled. Her black hair and black eyes are as brilliant as Chinese lacquer. Her skin is white as a camellia. Her legs are lyric." She worked with several of the bright young directors who gave Paramount its reputation for sophisticated comedy; e.g., Frank Tuttle, Malcolm St. Clair, and Edward Sutherland. Chronologically, the list of her credits ran as follows: *The American Venus* (for Tuttle, who taught her that the way to get laughs was to play perfectly straight; he directed Bebe Daniels in four movies and Clara Bow in six). *A Social Celebrity* (for St. Clair, who cast Brooks opposite the immaculately caddish Adolphe Menjou, of whose style she later remarked, "He never felt anything. He used to say, 'Now I do Lubitsch No. 1,' 'Now I do Lubitsch No. 2.' And that's exactly what he did. You felt nothing, working with him, and yet see him on the screen—he was a great actor"). *It's the Old Army Game* (for Sutherland, who had been Chaplin's directorial assistant on *A Woman of Paris*, and who made five pictures with W. C. Fields, of which this was the first; the third, *International House*, is regarded by many Fieldsian authorities as the Master's crowning achievement. Brooks married Sutherland, a hard-drinking playboy, in 1926—an error that was rectified inside two years by divorce). *The Show-Off* (for St. Clair, adapted from the Broadway hit by George Kelly). *Just Another Blonde* (on loan to First National). And, finally, to round off the year's work, *Love 'Em and Leave 'Em* (for Tuttle), the first Brooks film of which the Eastman house has a copy. Here begin my notes on the sustained and solitary Brooks banquet that the museum laid before me.

Day One: Evelyn Brent is the nominal star of *Love 'Em and Leave 'Em*, a slick and graceful comedy about Manhattan shopgirls, but light-fingered Louise, as Brent's jazz-baby younger sister, steals the picture with bewitching insouciance. She is twenty, and her body is still plump, quite husky enough for work in the fields; but the face, framed in its black proscenium arch of hair, is already Lulu's in embryo, especially when she dons a white top hat to go to a costume ball (at which she dances a definitive Charleston). The plot calls for her to seduce her sister's boyfriend, a feckless window dresser, and she does so with that fusion of amorality and innocence which was to become her trademark. (During these scenes, I catch myself humming a tune from *Pins and Needles*: "I used to be on the daisy chain, but now I'm a chain-store daisy.") Garbo could give us innocence, and Dietrich amorality, on the grandest possible scale; only Brooks could play the simple, unabashed hedonist, whose appetite for pleasure is so radiant that even when it causes suffering to herself and others we cannot find it in ourselves to reproach her. Most actresses tend to pass moral judgments on the characters they play. Their performances issue tacit commands to the audience: "Love me," "Hate me," "Laugh at me," "Weep with me," and so forth. We get none of this from Brooks, whose presence before the camera merely declares, "Here I am. Make what you will of me." She does not care what we think of her. Indeed, she ignores us. We seem to be spying on unrehearsed reality, glimpsing what the great photographer Henri Cartier-Bresson later called "*le moment qui se sauve*." In the best of her silent films, Brooks—with no conscious intention of doing so—is reinventing the art of screen acting. I suspect that she was helped rather than hindered by the fact that she never took a formal acting lesson. "When I acted, I hadn't the slightest idea of what I was doing," she said once to Richard Leacock, the documentary-film maker. "I was simply playing myself, which is the hardest thing in the world to do—if you *know* that it's hard. I didn't, so it seemed easy. I had nothing to unlearn. When I first worked with Pabst, he was furious, because he approached people intellectually and you couldn't approach me intellectually, because there was nothing to approach." To watch Brooks is to recall Oscar Wilde's Lady Bracknell, who observes, "Ignorance is like a delicate, exotic fruit; touch it, and the bloom is gone."

Rereading the above paragraph, I pause at the sentence "She does not care what we think of her." Query: Was it precisely this quality, which contributed so much to her success on the screen, that enabled her, in later years, to throw that success so lightly away?

To return to Frank Tuttle's film: Tempted by a seedy and lecherous old horseplayer who lives in her rooming house, Brooks goes on a betting spree with funds raised by her fellow-shopgirls in aid of the Women's Welfare League. The aging gambler is played by Osgood Perkins (father of Tony), of whom Brooks said to Kevin Brownlow years afterward, "The best actor I ever worked with was Osgood Perkins. . . . You know what makes an actor great to work with? Timing. You don't have to feel anything. It's like dancing with a perfect dancing partner. Osgood Perkins would give you a line so that you would react perfectly. It was timing—because *emotion means nothing*." (Emphasis mine.) This comment reveals what Brooks has learned about acting in the cinema: Emotion *per se*, however deeply felt, is not enough. It is what the actor shows—the contraband that he or she can smuggle past the camera—that matters to the audience. A variation of this dictum cropped up in the mouth of John Striebel's popular comic-strip heroine Dixie Dugan, who was based on Brooks and first appeared in 1926. Bent on getting a job in *The Zigfold Follies*, Dixie reflected, "All there is to this Follies racket is to *be cool and look hot*." Incidentally, Brooks's comparison of Perkins with a dancing partner reminds me of a remark she once made about Fatty Arbuckle, who, under the assumed name of William Goodrich, apathetically directed her in a 1931 two-reeler called *Windy Riley Goes to Hollywood*: "He sat in his chair like a dead man. He had been very nice and sweetly dead ever

since the scandal that ruined his career. . . . Oh, I thought he
was magnificent in films. He was a wonderful dancer—a wonderful ballroom dancer in his heyday. It was like floating in
the arms of a huge doughnut."

What images do I retain of Brooks in *Love 'Em and Leave
'Em*? Many comedic details; e.g., the scene in which she fakes
tears of contrition by furtively dabbling her cheeks with water
from a handily placed goldfish bowl, and our last view of her,
with all her sins unpunished, merrily sweeping off in a Rolls-
Royce with the owner of the department store. And, throughout, every closeup of that blameless, unblemished face.

In 1927, Brooks moved with Paramount to Hollywood and
starred in four pictures—*Evening Clothes* (with Menjou),
Rolled Stockings, The City Gone Wild, and *Now We're in the
Air*, none of which are in the Eastman vaults. To commemorate
that year, I have a publicity photo taken at a house she rented
in Laurel Canyon: poised on tiptoe with arms outstretched, she
stands on the diving board of her pool, wearing a one-piece
black bathing suit with a tight white belt, looking like a combination of Odette and Odile in some modern-dress version of
Swan Lake. Early in 1928, she was lent to Fox for a picture
(happily preserved by the museum) that was to change her
career—*A Girl in Every Port*, written and directed by Howard
Hawks, who had made his first film only two years before.
Along with Carole Lombard, Rita Hayworth, Jane Russell, and
Lauren Bacall, Brooks thus claims a place among the actresses
on David Thomson's list (in his *Biographical Dictionary of
Film*) of performers who were "either discovered or brought
to new life by Hawks." As in *Love 'Em and Leave 'Em*, she
plays an amoral pleasure-lover, but this time the mood is much
darker. Her victim is Victor McLaglen, a seagoing roughneck
engaged in perpetual sexual rivalry with his closest friend
(Robert Armstrong); the embattled relationship between the
two men brings to mind the skirmishing of Flagg and Quirt in
What Price Glory?, which was filmed with McLaglen in 1926.
In *A Girl in Every Port*, McLaglen, on a binge in Marseilles,
sees a performance by an open-air circus whose star turn is
billed as "Mam'selle Godiva, Neptune's Bride and the Sweetheart of the Sea." The submarine coquette is, of course,
Brooks, looking svelter than of old, and clad in tights, spangled

panties, tiara, and black velvet cloak. Her act consists of diving off the top of a ladder into a shallow tank of water. Instantly besotted, the bully McLaglen becomes the fawning lapdog of this "dame of class." He proudly introduces her to Armstrong, who, unwilling to wreck his buddy's illusions, refrains from revealing that the lady's true character, as he knows from a previous encounter with her, is that of a small-time gold-digger. In a scene charged with the subtlest eroticism, Brooks sits beside Armstrong on a sofa and coaxes McLaglen to clean her shoes. He readily obeys. As he does so, she begins softly, reminiscently, but purposefully, to fondle Armstrong's thigh. To these caresses Armstrong does not respond, but neither does he reject them. With one man at her feet and another at her fingertips, she is like a cat idly licking its lips over two bowls of cream. This must surely have been the sequence that convinced Pabst, when the film was shown in Berlin, that he had found the actress he wanted for *Pandora's Box*. By the end of the picture, Brooks has turned the two friends into moral enemies, reducing McLaglen to a state of murderous rage, mixed with grief, that Emil Jannings could hardly have bettered. There is no melodrama in her exercise of sexual power. No effort, either: she is simply following her nature.

After her fling with Fox, Paramount cast its young star (now aged twenty-one) in another downbeat triangle drama, *Beggars of Life*, to be directed by another young director, William Wellman. Like Hawks, he was thirty-two years old. (The cinema is unique among the arts in that there was a time in its history when almost all of its practitioners were young. This was that time.) At first, the studio had trouble tracing Brooks's whereabouts. Having just divorced Edward Sutherland, she had fled to Washington with a new lover—George Marshall, a millionaire laundry magnate, who later became the owner of the Redskins football team. When she was found, she promptly returned to the Coast, though her zest for work was somewhat drained by a strong antipathy to one of her co-stars— Richard Arlen, with whom she had appeared in *Rolled Stockings*—and by overt hostility from Wellman, who regarded her as a dilettante. Despite these malign auguries, *Beggars of Life*—available at Eastman house—turned out to be one of her best films. Adapted from a novel by Jim Tully, it foreshadows the Depression movies of the thirties. Brooks plays the adopted daughter of a penniless old farmer who attempts, one sunny morning, to rape her. Seizing a shotgun, she kills him. As she is about to escape, the crime is discovered by a tramp (Arlen) who knocks at the door in search of food. They run away together, with Brooks wearing oversized masculine clothes, topped off by a large peaked cap. (This was her first serious venture into the rich territory of sexual ambiguity, so prosperously cultivated in later years by Garbo, Dietrich, et al.) Soon they fall in with a gang of hoboes, whose leader—a ferocious but teachable thug, beautifully played by Wallace Beery—forms the third point of the triangle. He sees through Brooks's disguise and proposes that since the police already know about her male imposture, it would be safer to dress her as a girl. He goes in search of female attire, but what he brings back is marginally too young: a gingham dress, and a bonnet tied under the chin, in which Brooks looks like a woman masquerading as a child, a sort of adult Lolita. She stares at us in her new gear, at once innocent and gravely perverse. The rivalry for her affection comes to its height when Beery pulls a gun and tells Arlen to hand her over. Brooks jumps between them, protecting Arlen, and explains that she would prefer death to life without him. We believe her; and so, to his own befuddled amazement, does Beery. There is really no need for the caption in which he says that he has often heard about love but never until now known what it was. He puts his gun away and lets them go.

Footnote: During the transvestite scenes, several dangerous feats were performed for Brooks by a stunt man named Harvey. One night, attracted by his flamboyant courage, she slept with him. After breakfast next day, she strolled out onto the porch of the hotel in the California village where the location sequences were being shot. Harvey was there, accompanied by a group of hoboes in the cast. He rose and gripped her by the arm. "Just a minute, Miss Brooks," he said loudly. "I've got something to ask you. I guess you know my job depends on my health." He then named a Paramount executive whom Brooks had never met, and continued, "Everybody knows you're his girl and he has syphilis, and what I wanted to know is: Do you have syphilis?" After a long and frozen pause, he added, "Another reason I want to know is that my girl is coming up at noon to drive me back to Hollywood." Brooks somehow withdrew to her room without screaming. Events like these may account for the lack of agonized regret with which she prematurely ended her movie career. Several years later, after she had turned down the part that Jean Harlow eventually played in Wellman's *Public Enemy*, she ran into the director in a New York bar. "You always hated making pictures, Louise," he said sagely. She did not bother to reply that it was not pictures she hated but Hollywood.

The Canary Murder Case (directed by Malcom St. Clair from a script based on S. S. Van Dine's detective story, with William Powell as Philo Vance: not in the Eastman collection) was the third, and last, American movie that Brooks made in 1928. By now, her face was beginning to be internationally known, and the rushes of this film indicated that Paramount would soon have a major star on its hands. At the time, the studio was preparing to take the plunge into talkies. As Brooks afterward wrote in *Image* (a journal sponsored by Eastman house), front offices all over Hollywood saw in this radical change "a splendid opportunity . . . for breaking contracts, cutting salaries, and taming the stars." In the autumn of 1928, when her own contract called for a financial raise, B. P. Schulberg, the West Coast head of Paramount, summoned her to his office and said that the promised increase could not be granted in the new situation. *The Canary Murder Case* was being shot silent, but who knew whether Brooks could speak? (A fragile argument, since her voice was of bell-like clarity.) He presented her with a straight choice: either to continue at her present figure (seven hundred and fifty dollars a week) or to quit when the current picture was finished. To Schulberg's surprise, she chose to quit. Almost as an afterthought, he revealed when she was rising to leave that he had lately received from G. W. Pabst a bombardment of cabled requests for her services in *Pandora's Box*, all of which he had turned down.

Then forty-three years old, Pabst had shown an extraordinary flair for picking and molding actresses whose careers were upward bound; Asta Nielsen, Brigitte Helm, and Greta Garbo (in her third film, *The Joyless Street*, which was also her first outside Sweden) headed a remarkable list. Unknown to Schulberg, Brooks had already heard about the Pabst offer—and the weekly salary of a thousand dollars that went with it—from her lover, George Marshall, whose source was a gossipy director at M-G-M. She coolly told Schulberg to inform Pabst that she would soon be available. "At that very hour in Berlin," she wrote later in *Sight & Sound*, "Marlene Dietrich was waiting with Pabst in his office." This was two years before *The Blue Angel* made Dietrich a star. What she crucially lacked, Pabst felt, was the innocence he wanted for his Lulu. In his own words, "Dietrich was too old and too obvious—one sexy look and the picture would become a burlesque. But I gave her a deadline, and the contract was about to be signed when Paramount cabled saying I could have Louise Brooks." The day that shooting ended on *The Canary Murder Case*, Brooks raced out of Hollywood en route for Berlin, there to work for a man who was one of the four or five leading European directors but of whom a few weeks earlier she had never heard.

Pandora's Box, with which I had my fourth encounter at the Eastman house, could easily have emerged as a cautionary tale about a *grande cocotte* whose reward is the wages of sin. That seems to have been the impression left by Wedekind's two Lulu plays, which were made into a film in 1922 (not by Pabst) with Asta Nielsen in the lead. Summing up her predecessor's performance, Brooks said, "She played in the eye-rolling style of European silent acting. Lulu the man-eater devoured her sex victims . . . and then dropped dead in an acute attack of indigestion." The character obsessed many artists of the period. In 1928, Alban Berg began work on his twelve-tone opera *Lulu*, the heart of which—beneath the stark and stylized sound patterns—was blatantly theatrical, throbbing with romantic agony. Where the Pabst-Brooks version differs from the others is in its moral coolness. It assumes neither the existence of sin nor the necessity for retribution. It presents a series of events in which all the participants are seeking happiness, and it suggests that Lulu, whose notion of happiness is momentary fulfillment through sex, is not less admirable than those whose quest is for wealth or social advancement.

First sequence: Lulu in the Art Deco apartment in Berlin where she is kept by Peter Schön, a middle-aged newspaper proprietor. (In this role, the great Fritz Kortner, bulky but urbane, effortless in the exercise of power over everyone but his mistress, gives one of the cinema's most accurate and objective portraits of a capitalist potentate.) Dressed in a peignoir, Lulu is casually flirting with a man who has come to read the gas meter when the doorbell rings and Schigolch enters, a squat and shabby old man who was once Lulu's lover but is now down on his luck. She greets him with delight; as the disgruntled gas man departs, she swoops to rest on Schigolch's lap with the grace of a swan. The protective curve of her neck is unforgettable. Producing a mouth organ, Schigolch strikes up a tune, to which she performs a brief, Dionysiac, and authentically improvised little dance. (Until this scene was rehearsed, Pabst had no idea that Brooks was a trained dancer.) Watching her, I recollect something that Schigolch says in the play, though not in the film: "The animal is the only genuine thing in man. . . . What you have experienced as an animal, no misfortune can ever wrest from you. It remains yours for life." From the window, he points out a burly young man on the sidewalk: this is a friend of his named Rodrigo, a professional athlete who would like to work with her on an adagio act.

Unheralded, Peter Schön lets himself into the apartment, and Lulu has just time to hide Schigolch on the balcony with a bottle of brandy. Schön has come to end his affair with Lulu, having decided to make a socially advantageous match with the daughter of a Cabinet Minister. In Lulu's reaction to the news there is no fury. She simply sits on a sofa and extends her arms toward him with something like reassurance. Unmoved at first, Schön eventually responds, and they begin to make love. The drunken Schigolch inadvertently rouses Lulu's pet dog to a barking fit, and this disturbance provokes the hasty exit of Schön. On the stairs, he passes the muscle man Rodrigo, whom Schigolch presents to Lulu. Rodrigo flexes his impressive biceps, on which she gleefully swings, like a schoolgirl gymnast.

A scene in Schön's mansion shows us his son Alwa (Francis Lederer in his Pre-Hollywood days) busily composing songs for his new musical revue. Alwa is joined by the Countess Geschwitz (Alice Roberts), a tight-lipped lesbian who is designing the costumes. Lulu dashes in to announce her plans for a double act with Rodrigo, and it is immediately clear that both

Alwa and the Countess have eyes for her. She strolls on into
Peter Schön's study, where she picks up from the desk a photograph of his bride-to-be. Typically, she studies it with genuine interest; there's no narrowing of eyes or curling of lip.
Peter Schön, who has entered the room behind her, snatches
the picture from her hands and orders her to leave. Before
doing so, she mischievously invents a rendezvous next day
with Alwa, whom she kisses, to the young man's embarrassed
bewilderment, full on the mouth. With a toss of the patent-
leather hair and a glance, half-playful, half-purposeful, at
Alwa, she departs. Alwa asks his father why he doesn't marry
her. Rather too explosively to carry conviction, Peter replies
that one doesn't marry women like that. He proposes that Alwa
give her a featured role in the revue, and guarantees that his
newspapers will make her a star. Alwa is overjoyed; but when
his father warns him at all costs to beware of her, he quits the
room in tongue-tied confusion.

So much for the exposition; the principal characters and the
main thrust of the action have been lucidly established. Note
that Lulu, for all her seductiveness, is essentially an exploited
creature, not an exploiter; also that we are not (nor shall we
ever be) invited to feel sorry for her. I've already referred to
her birdlike movements and animal nature: let me add that in
the context of the plot as a whole she resembles a glittering
tropical fish in a tank full of predators. For the remainder of
this synopsis, I'll confine myself to the four great set pieces
on which the film's reputation rests.

(1) Intermission at the opening night of Alwa's revue: Pabst
catches the backstage panic of scene-shifting and costume-
changing with a kaleidoscopic brilliance that looks forward to
Orson Welles's handling, twelve years later, of the operatic
début of Susan Alexander Kane. Alwa and Geschwitz are there,
revelling in what is obviously going to be a hit. Peter Schön
escorts Marie, his fiancée, through the pass door to share the
frenzy. Lulu, changing in the wings, catches sight of him and
smiles. Stricken with embarrassment, he cuts her and leads
Marie away. This treatment maddens Lulu, and she refuses to
go on with the show: "I'll dance for the whole world, but not
in front of that woman." She takes refuge in the property room,
whither Peter follows her. Leaning against the wall, she sobs,

shaking her head mechanically from side to side, and then flings herself onto a pile of cushions which she kicks and pummels. Despite her tantrum, she is watching Schön's every move. When he lights a cigarette to calm himself, she snaps "Smoking isn't allowed in here," and gives him a painful hack on the ankle. The mood of the scene swings from high histrionics through sly comedy to voluptuous intimacy. Soon Schön and Lulu are laughing, caressing, wholeheartedly making love. At this point, the door opens, framing Marie and Alwa. Unperturbed, Lulu rises in triumph, gathers up her costume, and sweeps past them to go onstage. Peter Schön's engagement is obviously over.

(2) The wedding reception: Lulu is in a snow-white bridal gown, suggesting less a victorious *cocotte* than a girl celebrating her first Communion. Peter's wealthy friends flock admiringly round her. She dances cheek to cheek with Geschwitz, who rabidly adores her. (The Belgian actress Alice Roberts, here playing what may be the first explicit lesbian in movie history, refused point-blank to look at Brooks with the requisite degree of lust. To solve the problem, Pabst stood in her line of vision, told her to regard him with passionate intensity, and photographed her in closeups, which he then intercut with shots of Brooks. Scenes like these presented no difficulty to Brooks herself. She used to say of Fritzi LaVerne, one of her best friends in the *Follies*, "She liked boys when she was sober and girls when she was drunk. I never heard a man or a woman pan her in bed, so she must have been very good." A shocked Catholic priest once asked her how she felt playing a sinner like Lulu. "Feel!" she said gaily. "I felt fine! It all seemed perfectly normal to me." She explained to him that, although she herself was not a lesbian, she had many chums of that persuasion in Ziegfeld's chorus line, and added, "I know two millionaire publishers, much like Schön in the film, who backed shows to keep themselves well supplied with Lulus.") The action moves to Peter's bedroom, where Schigolch and Rodrigo are drunkenly scattering roses over the nuptial coverlet. Lulu joins them, and something between a romp and an orgy seems imminent. It is halted by the entrance of the bridegroom. Appalled, he gropes for a gun in a nearby desk and chases the two men out of his house. The other guests,

shocked and aghast, rapidly depart. When Peter returns to the
bedroom, he find Alwa with his head in Lulu's lap, urging her
to run away with him. The elder Schön orders his son to leave.
As soon as Alwa has left, there follows, between Kortner and
Brooks, a classic demonstration of screen acting as the art of
visual ellipsis. With the minimum of overt violence, a struggle
for power is fought out to the death. Schön advances on Lulu,
presses the gun into her hand, and begs her to commit suicide.
As he grips her fingers in his, swearing to shoot her like a dog
if she lacks the courage to do it herself, she seems almost
hypnotized by the desperation of his grief. You would think
them locked in an embrace until Lulu suddenly stiffens, a puff
of smoke rises between them, and Schön slumps to the floor.
Alwa bursts in and rushes to his father, from whose lips a fat
thread of blood slowly trickles. The father warns Alwa that he
will be the next victim. Gun in hand, Lulu stares at the body,
wide-eyed and transfixed. Brooks wrote afterward that Pabst
always used concrete phrases to trigger the emotional response
he wanted. In this case, the key image he gave her was "*das
Blut.*" "Not the murder of my husband," she said, "but the
sight of the blood determined the expression on my face."
What we see is not *Vénus toute entière à sa proie attachée* but
a petrified child.

(3) Trial and flight: Lulu is sentenced to five years' imprisonment for manslaughter, but as the judge pronounces the
sentence, her friends, led by Geschwitz, set off a fire alarm,
and in the ensuing courtroom chaos she escapes. With perfect
fidelity to her own willful character, Lulu, in defiance of movie
cliché, comes straight back to Schön's house, where she acts
like a débutante relaxing after a ball—lighting a cigarette, idly
thumbing through a fashion magazine, trying out a few dance
steps, opening a wardrobe and stroking a new fur coat, running
a bath and immersing herself in it. Only Brooks, perhaps could
have carried off this solo sequence—so unlike the behavior
expected of criminals on the run—with such ingrained conviction and such lyrical aplomb. Now Alwa arrives and is
astounded to find her at the scene of the crime. The two decide
to flee together to Paris. No sooner have they caught the train,
however, than they are recognized by a titled pimp, who black-
mails them into accompanying him aboard a gambling ship.

Geschwitz, Schigolch, and the tediously beefy Rodrigo are also afloat, and for a while the film lurches into melodrama—sub-Dostoevski with a touch of ship's Chandler. Rodrigo threatens to expose Lulu unless she sleeps with him; the Countess, gritting her teeth, distracts his attention by making love to him herself—an unlikely coupling—after which she disdainfully kills him. Meanwhile, the pimp is arranging to sell Lulu to an Egyptian brothelkeeper. Anxious to save her from this fate, Alwa frenetically cheats at cards and is caught with a sleeve full of aces. The police arrive just too late to prevent Alwa, Lulu, and Schigolch from escaping in a rowboat. For the shipboard episode, Pabst cajoled Brooks, much against her will, into changing her coiffure. The spit curls disappeared; the black bangs were parted, waved, and combed back to expose her forehead. These cardinal errors of taste defaced the icon. It was is if an Italian master had painted the Virgin and left out the halo.

(4) London and catastrophe: The East End, icy and fogbound, on Christmas Eve. The Salvation Army is out in force, playing carols and distributing food to the poor. A sallow, mournfully handsome young man moves aimlessly through the crowds. He gives cash for the needy to an attractive Army girl, and gets in return a candle and a sprig of mistletoe. Posters on the walls warn the women of London against going out unescorted at night: there is a mass murderer at large. In a garret close by, its broken skylight covered by a flapping rag, Lulu lives in squalor with Alwa and Schigolch. The room is unfurnished except for a camp bed, an armchair, and a kitchen table with an oil lamp, a few pieces of chipped crockery, and a bread knife. Lulu's curls and bangs have been restored, but her clothes are threadbare: all three exiles are on the verge of starvation. Reduced by now to prostitution, Lulu ventures down into the street, where she accosts the young wanderer we have already met. He follows her up the stairs but stops halfway, as if reluctant to go farther. We see that he is holding behind his back a switchblade knife, open. Lulu proffers her hand and leans encouragingly toward him. Her smile is lambent and beckoning. Hesitantly, he explains that he has no money. With transparent candor, she replies that it doesn't matter: she likes him. Unseen by Lulu, he releases his grip on the knife and lets

it fall into the stairwell. She leads him into the attic, which Alwa and Schigolch have tactfully vacated. The scene that follows is tender, even buoyant, but unsoftened by sentimentality. The cold climax, when it comes, is necessary and inevitable. Ripper and victim relax like familiar lovers. He leans back in the armchair and stretches out his hand; she leaps onto his lap, landing with both knees bent, as weightless as a chamois. Her beauty has never looked more ripe. While they happily flirt, he allows her to pry into his pockets, from which she extracts the gifts he received from the Salvation Army. She lights the candle and places it ceremonially on the table, with the mistletoe beside it. In a deep and peaceful embrace, they survey the tableau. The Ripper then raises the mistletoe over Lulu's head and requests the traditional kiss. As she shuts her eyes and presents her lips, the candle flares up. Its gleam reflected in the bread knife on the table holds the Ripper's gaze. He can look at nothing but the shining blade. Long seconds pass as he wrestles, motionless, with his obsession. Finally, leaning forward to consummate the kiss, he grasps the handle of the knife. In the culminating shot, he is facing away from the camera. All we see of Lulu is her right hand, open on his shoulder, pressing him toward her. Suddenly, it clenches hard, then falls, limply dangling, behind his back. We fade to darkness. Nowhere in the cinema has the destruction of beauty been conveyed with more eloquent restraint. As with the killing of Peter Schön, extreme violence is implied, not shown. To paraphrase what Freddy Buache, a Swiss critic, wrote many years later, Lulu's death is in no sense God's judgment on a sinner; she has lived her life in accordance with the high moral imperatives of liberty, and stands in no need of redemption.

After the murder, the Ripper emerges from the building and hurries off into the fog. It is here, in my view, that the film should end. Instead, Pabst moves on to the forlorn figure of Alwa, who stares up at the garret before turning away to follow the Salvation Army procession out of sight. A glib anticlimax indeed; but I'm not sure that I prefer the alternative proposed by Brooks, who has said, with characteristic forthrightness, "The movie should have ended with the knife in my vagina." It may be worth adding that Gustav Diessl, who played the

Ripper, was the only man in the cast whom she found sexually appealing. "We just adored each other," she has said in an interview with Richard Leacock, "and I think the final scene was the happiest in the picture. Here he is with a knife he's going to stick up into my interior, and we'd be singing and laughing and doing the Charleston. You wouldn't have known it was a tragic ending. It was more like a Christmas party." At Brooks's request, Pabst had hired a jazz pianist to play between takes, and during these syncopated interludes Brooks and Diessl would often disappear beneath the table to engage in intimate festivities of their own.

The Berlin critics, expecting Lulu to be portrayed as a monster of active depravity, had mixed feelings about Brooks. One reviewer wrote, "Louise Brooks cannot act. She does not suffer. *She does nothing.*" Wedekind himself, however, had said of his protagonist, "Lulu is not a real character but the personification of primitive sexuality, who inspires evil unawares. She plays a purely passive role." Brooks afterward stated her own opinion of what she had achieved. "I played *Pabst's* Lulu," she said, "and she isn't a destroyer of men, like Wedekind's. She's just the same kind of nitwit that I am. Like me, she'd have been an impossible wife, sitting in bed all day reading and drinking gin." Modern critics have elected Brooks's Lulu to a secure place in the movie pantheon. David Thomson describes it as "one of the major female performances in the cinema," to be measured beside such other pinnacles as "Dietrich in the von Sternberg films, Bacall with Hawks, Karina in *Pierrot le Fou*." It is true that in the same list Thomson included Kim Novak in *Vertigo*. It is also true that we are none of us perfect.

Day Two: My first view of the second Pabst-Brooks collaboration—*The Diary of a Lost Girl*, based on *Das Tagebuch einer Verlorenen*, a novel by Margarethe Boehme, and shot in the summer of 1929. After finishing *Pandora*, Brooks had returned to New York and resumed her affair with the millionaire George Marshall. He told her that a new movie company, called RKO and masterminded by Joseph P. Kennedy, was anxious to sign her up for five hundred dollars a week. She replied, "I hate California and I'm not going back." Then

Paramount called, ordering her to report for duty on the Coast;
it was turning *The Canary Murder Case* into a talkie and required her presence for retakes and dubbing. She refused to
come. Under the impression that this was a haggling posture,
the studio offered ever vaster sums of money. Brooks's de-
termination remained undented. Goaded to fury, Paramount
planted in the columns a petty but damaging little story to the
effect that it had been compelled to replace Brooks because
her voice was unusable in talkies.

At this point—April, 1929—she received a cable from
Pabst. It said that he intended to co-produce a French film
entitled *Prix de Beauté*, which René Clair would direct, and
that they both wanted her for the lead—would she therefore
cross the Atlantic as soon as possible? Such was her faith in
Pabst that within two weeks she and Clair ("a very small,
demure, rather fragile man" is how she afterward described
him) were posing together for publicity shots in Paris. When
the photographic session was over, Clair escorted her back to
her hotel, where he dampened her enthusiasm by revealing that
he proposed to pull out of the picture forthwith. He advised
her to do the same; the production money, he said, simply
wasn't there, and might never be. A few days later, he officially
retired from the project. (Its place in his schedule was taken
by *Sous les Toits de Paris*, which, together with its immediate
successors—*Le Million* and *À Nous la Liberté*—established his
international reputation.) With nothing to do, and a guaranteed
salary of a thousand dollars a week to do it on, Brooks entrained
for a spree in Antibes, accompanied by a swarm of rich admirers. When she got back to Paris, Pabst called her from
Berlin. *Prix de Beauté*, he said, was postponed; instead, she
would star under his direction in *Diary of a Lost Girl*, at
precisely half her present salary. As submissive as ever to her
tutor, she arrived in Berlin aboard the next train.

Lovingly photographed by Sepp Allgeier, Brooks in *Lost
Girl* is less flamboyant but not less haunting than in *Pandora's
Box*. The traffic in movie actors traditionally moved westward,
from Europe to Hollywood, where their national characteristics
were sedulously exploited. Brooks, who was among the few
to make the eastbound trip, became in her films with Pabst
completely Europeanized. To be more exact: in the context that

Pabst prepared for her, Brooks's American brashness took on an awareness of transience and mortality. The theme of *Lost Girl* is the corruption of a minor—not by sexuality but by an authoritarian society that condemns sexuality. (Pabst must surely have read Wilhelm Reich, the Freudian Marxist, whose theories about the relationship between sexual and political repression were hotly debated in Berlin at the time.) It is the same society that condemns Lulu. In fact, *The Education of Lulu* would make an apt alternative title for *Lost Girl*, whose heroine emerges from her travails ideally equipped for the leading role in *Pandora's Box*. Her name is Thymiane Henning, and she is the sixteen-year-old daughter of a prosperous pharmacist. In the early sequences, Brooks plays her shy and faunlike, peering wide-eyed at a predatory world. She is seduced and impregnated by her father's libidinous young assistant. As soon as her condition is discovered, the double standard swings into action. The assistant retains his job; but, to save the family from dishonor, Thymiane's baby is farmed out to a wet nurse, and she herself is consigned to a home for delinquent girls, run by a bald and ghoulish superintendent and his sadistic wife.

Life in the reformatory is strictly regimented: the inmates exercise to the beat of a drum and eat to the tapping of a metronome. At length, Thymiane escapes from this archetypal hellhole (precursor of many such institutions in subsequent movies; e.g., *Mädchen in Uniform*) and goes to reclaim her baby, only to find that the child has died. Broke and homeless, she meets a street vendor who guides her to an address where food and shelter will be hers for the asking. Predictably, it turns out to be a brothel; far less predictably, even shockingly, Pabst presents it as a place where Thymiane is not degraded but liberated. In the whorehouse, she blossoms, becoming a *fille de joie* in the literal sense of the phrase. Unlike almost any other actress in a similar situation, Brooks neither resorts to pathos nor suggests that there is anything immoral in the pleasure she derives from her new profession. As in *Pandora*, she lives for the moment, with radiant physical abandon. Present love, even for sale, hath present laughter, and what's to come is not only unsure but irrelevant. I agree with Freddy Buache when he says of Brooks's performances with Pabst that they celebrated "the victory of innocence and *amour-fou* over the debilitating wisdom imposed on society by the Church, the Fatherland, and the Family." One of her more outré clients can achieve orgasm only by watching her beat a drum. This ironic echo of life in the reform school is used by Pabst to imply that sexual prohibition breeds sexual abberration. (Even more ironically, the sequence has been censored out of most of the existing prints of the movie.) Brooks is at her best—a happy animal in skintight satin—in a party scene at a nightclub, where she offers herself as first prize in a raffle. "Pabst wanted realism, so we all had to drink real drinks," she said later. "I played the whole scene stewed on hot, sweet German champagne."

Hereabouts, unfortunately, the film begins to shed its effrontery and to pay lip service to conventional values. Thymiane catches sight of her father across the dance floor; instead of reacting with defiance—after all, he threw her out of his house—she looks stricken with guilt, like the outcast daughter of sentimental fiction. In her absence, Papa has married his housekeeper, by whom he has two children. When he dies, shortly after the nightclub confrontation, he leaves his considerable wealth to Thymiane. Nobly, she gives it all to his penniless widow, so that the latter's offspring "won't have to live the same kind of life as I have." Thereby redeemed, the former whore soon becomes the wife of an elderly aristocrat. Revisiting the reform school, of which she has now been appointed a trustee, she excoriates the staff for its self-righteous cruelties. "A little more kindness," her husband adds, "and no one in the world would ever be lost." Thus lamely, the movie ends.

"Pabst seemed to lose interest," Brooks told an interviewer some years afterward. "He more or less said, 'I'm tired of this picture,' and he gave it a soft ending." His first, and much tougher, intention had been to demonstrate that humanitarianism alone could never solve society's problems. He wanted Thymiane to show her contempt for her husband's liberal platitudes by setting herself up as the madam of a whorehouse. The German distributors, however, refused to countenance such a radical dénouement, and Pabst was forced to capitulate. The result is a flawed masterpiece, with a shining central performance that even the closing, compromised sequences cannot dim. Brooks has written that during the making of the film she

spent all her off-duty hours with rich revellers of whom Pabst
disapproved. On the last day of shooting, "he decided to let
me have it." Her friends, he said, were preventing her from
becoming a serious actress, and sooner or later they would
discard her like an old toy. "Your life is exactly like Lulu's,
and you will end the same way," he warned her. The passage
of time convinced her that Pabst had a valid point. "Lulu's
story," she told a journalist, "is as near as you'll get to mine."

In August, 1929, she returned to Paris, where backing had
unexpectedly been found for *Prix de Beauté*, her last European
movie and her first talkie—although, since she spoke no
French, her voice was dubbed. The director, briefly surfacing
from obscurity, was Augusto Genina, and René Clair received
a credit for the original idea. Like so much of French cinema
in the thirties, *Prix de Beauté* is a *film noir*, with wanly tinny
music, about a shabby suburban crime of passion. Brooks plays
Lucienne, a typist who enters a newspaper beauty contest. It's
the kind of role with which one associates Simone Simon,
though the rapture that Brooks displays when she wins, twirling
with glee as she shows off her presents and trophies, goes well
beyond the emotional range accessible to Mlle. Simon. Lu-
cienne-Brooks is triumphantly unliberated; she rejoices in being
a beloved, fleshly bauble, and she makes it clear to her husband, a compositor employed by the prize-giving newspaper,
that she wants a grander, more snobbish reward for her victory
than a visit to a back-street fairground, which is all he has to
offer. She leaves him and accepts a part in a film. Consumed
by jealousy, he follows her one night to a projection theatre
in which a rough cut of her movie is being shown. He bursts
in and shoots her. As she dies, the French infatuation with
irony is fearsomely indulged: her image on the screen behind
her is singing the movie's theme song, "Ne Sois Pas Jaloux."
In *Prix de Beauté*, Brooks lends inimitable flair and distinction
to a cliché; but it is a cliché nonetheless.

At this point, when Brooks was at the height of her beauty,
her career began a steep and bumpy decline. In 1930, she went
back to Hollywood, on the strength of a promised contract with
Columbia. Harry Cohn, the head of the studio, summoned her
to his office for a series of meetings, at each of which he
appeared naked from the waist up. Always a plain speaker, he

left her in no doubt that good parts would come her way if she
responded to his advances. She rebuffed them, and the prof-
fered contract was withdrawn. Elsewhere in Hollywood, she
managed to get a job in a feeble two-reel comedy pseudony-
mously directed by the disgraced Fatty Arbuckle; her old friend
Frank Tuttle gave her a supporting role in *It Pays to Advertise*
(starring Carole Lombard); and she turned up fleetingly in a
Michael Curtiz picture called *God's Gift to Women*. But the
word was out that Brooks was difficult and uppity, too independent to suit the system. Admitting defeat, she returned to
New York in the summer of 1931. Against her will, but under
heavy pressure from George Marshall, her lover and would-be
Svengali, she played a small part in *Louder Please*, a feath-
erweight comedy by Norman Krasna that began its pre-Broad-
way run in October. After the opening week in Jackson
Heights, she was fired by the director, George Abbott. This
was her farewell to the theatre; it took place on the eve of her
twenty-fifth birthday.

For Brooks, as for millions of her compatriots, a long period
of unemployment followed. In 1933, determined to break off
her increasingly discordant relationship with Marshall, she
married Deering Davis, a rich young Chicagoan, but walked
out on him after six months of rapidly waning enthusiasm.
With a Hungarian partner named Dario Borzani, she spent a
year dancing in nightclubs, including the Persian Room of the
Plaza, but the monotony of cabaret routine dismayed her, and
she quit the act in August, 1935. That autumn, Pabst suddenly
arrived in New York and invited her to play Helen of Troy in
a film version of Goethe's *Faust*, with Greta Garbo as
Gretchen. Her hopes giddily soared, only to be dashed when
Garbo opted out and the project fell through. Once again, she
revisited Hollywood, where Republic Studios wanted to test
her for a role in a musical called *Dancing Feet*. She was
rejected in favor of a blonde who couldn't dance. "That about
did it for me," Brooks wrote later. "From then on it was straight
downhill. And no dough to keep the wolves from the door."
In 1936, Universal cast her as the ingénue (Boots Boone) in
Empty Saddles, a Buck Jones Western, which is the last Brooks
movie in the Eastman collection. She looks perplexed, dis-
couraged, and lacking in verve; and her coiffure, with the hair

swept back from her forehead, reveals disquieting lines of worry. (Neither she nor Jones is helped by the fact that all the major sequences of an incredibly complex plot are shot at night.) The following year brought her a bit part at Paramount in something called *King of Gamblers*, after which, in her own words, "Harry Cohn gave me a personally conducted tour of hell with no return ticket." Still wounded by her refusal to sleep with him in 1930, Cohn promised her a screen test if she would submit to the humiliation of appearing in the corps de ballet of a Grace Moore musical entitled *When You're in Love*. To his surprise, Brooks accepted the offer—she was too broke to spurn it—and Cohn made sure that the demotion of an erstwhile star was publicized as widely as possible. Grudgingly, he gave her a perfunctory screen test, which he dismissed in two words: "It stunk." In the summer of 1938, Republic hired Brooks to appear with John Wayne (then a minor figure) in *Overland Stage Raiders*. After this low-budget oater, she made no more pictures.

In her entire professional career, Brooks had earned according to her own calculations, exactly $124,600—$104,500 from films, $10,100 from theatre, and $10,000 from all other sources. Not a gargantuan sum, one would think, spread over sixteen years; yet Brooks said to a friend, "I was astonished that it came to so much. But then I never paid any attention to money." In 1940, she left Hollywood for the last time.

The Eastman house stands in an affluent residential district of Rochester, on an avenue of comparably stately mansions, with broad, tree-shaded lawns. When my second day of séances with Brooks came to an end, I zipped up my notes in a briefcase, thanked the curator and his staff for their help, and departed in a taxi. The driver took me to an apartment building only a few blocks away, where I paid him off. I rode up in the elevator to the third floor and pressed a doorbell a few paces along the corridor. After a long pause, there was a loud snapping of locks. The door slowly opened to reveal a petite woman of fragile build, wearing a woollen bed jacket over a pink nightgown, and holding herself defiantly upright by means of a sturdy metal cane with four rubber-tipped prongs. She had salt-and-pepper hair combed back into a ponytail that hung

down well below her shoulders, and she was barefoot. One
could imagine this gaunt and elderly child as James Tyrone's
wife in *Long Day's Journey into Night*; or, noting the touch
of authority and *panache* in her bearing, as the capricious
heroine of Jean Giraudoux's *The Madwoman of Chaillot*. I
stated my name, adding that I had an appointment. She nodded
and beckoned me in. I greeted her with a respectful embrace.
This was my first physical contact with Louise Brooks.

She was seventy-one years old, and until a few months
earlier I had thought she was dead. Four decades had passed
since her last picture, and it seemed improbable that she had
survived such a long period of retirement. Moreover, I did not
then know how young she had been at the time of her flowering.
Spurred by the TV screening of *Pandora's Box* in January,
1978, I had made some inquiries, and soon discovered that she
was living in Rochester, virtually bedridden with degenerative
osteoarthritis of the hip, and that since 1956 she had written
twenty vivid and perceptive articles, mainly for specialist film
magazines, on such of her colleagues and contemporaries as
Garbo, Dietrich, Keaton, Chaplin, Bogart, Fields, Lillian Gish,
ZaSu Pitts, and (naturally) Pabst. Armed with this information,
I wrote her a belated fan letter, to which she promptly replied.
We then struck up a correspondence, conducted on her side
in a bold and expressive prose style, which matched her handwriting. Rapport was cemented by telephone calls, which re-
sulted in my visit to Rochester and the date I was now keeping.

She has not left her apartment since 1960, except for a few
trips to the dentist and one to a doctor. (She mistrusts the
medical profession, and this consultation, which took place in
1976, was her first in thirty-two years.) "You're doing a terrible
thing to me," she said as she ushered me in. "I've been killing
myself off for twenty years, and you're going to bring me back
to life." She lives in two rooms—modest, spotless, and aus-
terely furnished. From the larger, I remember Venetian blinds,
a green sofa, a TV set, a Formica-topped table, a tiny kitch-
enette alcove, and flesh-pink walls sparsely hung with paintings
redolent of the twenties. The other room was too small to hold
more than a bed (single), a built-in cupboard bursting with
press clippings and other souvenirs, a chest of drawers sur-

mounted by a crucifix and a statue of the Virgin, and a stool piled high with books, including works by Proust, Schopenhauer, Ruskin, Ortega y Gasset, Samuel Johnson, Edmund Wilson, and many living authors of serious note. "I'm probably one of the best-read idiots in the world," my hostess said as she haltingly showed me round her domain. Although she eats little—she turns the scale at about eighty-eight pounds—she had prepared for us a perfectly mountainous omelette. Nerves, however, had robbed us of our appetites, and we barely disturbed its mighty silhouette. I produced from my briefcase a bottle of expensive red Burgundy which I had brought as a gift. (Brooks, who used to drink quite heftily, nowadays touches alcohol only on special occasions.) Since she cannot sit upright for long without discomfort, we retired with the wine to her bedroom, where she reclined, sipped, and talked, gesturing fluently, her fingers supple and unclenched. I pulled a chair up to the bedside and listened.

Her voice has the range of a dozen birdcalls, from the cry of a peacock to the fluting of a dove. Her articulation, at whatever speed, is impeccable, and her laughter soars like a kite. I cannot understand why, even if she had not been a beauty, Hollywood failed to realize what a treasure it possessed in the *sound* of Louise Brooks. Like most people who speak memorably, she is highly responsive to vocal nuances in others. She told Kevin Brownlow, the British film historian, that her favorite actress ("the person I would be if I could be anyone") was Margaret Sullavan, mainly because of her voice, which Brooks described as "exquisite and far away, almost like an echo," and, again, as "strange, fey, mysterious—like a voice singing in the snow." My conversations with the Ravishing Hermit of Rochester were spread over several days; for the sake of convenience, I have here compressed them into one session.

She began, at my urging, by skimming through the story of her life since she last faced the Hollywood cameras: "Why did I give up the movies? I could give you seven hundred reasons, all of them true. After I made that picture with John Wayne in 1938, I stayed out on the Coast for two years, but the only people who wanted to see me were men who wanted to sleep with me. Then Walter Wanger warned me that if I

hung around any longer I'd become a call girl. So I fled to
Wichita, Kansas, where my family had moved in 1919. But
that turned out to be another kind of hell. The citizens of
Wichita either resented me for having been a success or de-
spised me for being a failure. And I wasn't exactly enchanted
with them. I opened a dance studio for young people, who
loved me, because I dramatized everything so much, but it
didn't make any money. In 1943, I drifted back to New York
and worked for six months in radio soaps. Then I quit, for
another hundred reasons, including Wounded Pride of Former
Star. [Peal of laughter. Here, as throughout our chat, Brooks
betrayed not the slightest trace of self-pity.] During '44 and
'45, I got a couple of jobs in publicity agencies, collecting
items for Winchell's column. I was fired from both of them,
and I had to move from the decent little hotel where I'd been
living to a grubby hole on First Avenue at Fifty-ninth Street.
That was when I began to flirt with fancies related to little
bottles filled with yellow sleeping pills. However, I changed
my mind, and in July, 1946, the proud, snooty Louise Brooks
started work as a salesgirl at Saks Fifth Avenue. They paid me
forty dollars a week. I had this silly idea of proving myself
'an honest woman,' but the only effect it had was to disgust
all my New York friends, who cut me off forever. From then
on, I was regarded as a questionable East Side dame. After
two years at Saks, I resigned. To earn a little money, I sat
down and wrote the usual autobiography. I called it *Naked on
My Goat*, which is a quote from Goethe's *Faust*. In the *Wal-
purgisnacht* scene, a young witch is bragging about her looks
to an old one. 'I sit here naked on my goat,' she says, 'and
show my fine young body.' But the old one advises her to wait
awhile: 'Though young and tender now, you'll rot, we know,
you'll rot.' Then, when I read what I'd written, I threw the
whole thing down the incinerator."

Brooks insists that her motive for this act of destruction was
pudeur. In 1977, she wrote an article headed "Why I Will
Never Write My Memoirs," in which she summed herself up
as a prototypical midwesterner, "born in the Bible Belt of
Anglo-Saxon farmers, who prayed in the parlor and practiced
incest in the barn." Although her sexual education had been
conducted by the élite of Paris, London, Berlin, and New York,

her pleasure was, she wrote, "restricted by the inbred shackles of sin and guilt." Her conclusion was as follows:

In writing the history of a life I believe absolutely that the reader cannot understand the character and deeds of the subject unless he is given a basic understanding of that person's sexual loves and hates and conflicts. It is the only way the reader can make sense out of innumerable apparently senseless actions. . . . We flatter ourselves when we assume that we have restored the sexual integrity which was expurgated by the Victorians. It is true that many exposés are written to shock, to excite, to make money. But in serious books characters remain as baffling, as unknowable as ever. . . . I too am unwilling to write the sexual truth that would make my life worth reading. I cannot unbuckle the Bible Belt.

Accepting a drop more wine, she continued the tale of her wilderness years. "Between 1948 and 1953, I suppose you could call me a kept woman," she said. "Three decent rich men looked after me. But then I was *always* a kept woman. Even when I was making a thousand dollars a week, I would always be paid for by George Marshall or someone like that. But I never had anything to show for it—no cash, no trinkets, nothing. I didn't even *like* jewelry—can you imagine? Pabst once called me a born whore, but if he was right I was a failure, with no pile of money and no comfortable mansion. I just wasn't equipped to spoil millionaires in a practical, farsighted way. I could live in the present, but otherwise everything has always been a hundred percent wrong about me. Anyway, the three decent men took care of me. One of them owned a sheet-metal manufacturing company, and the result of that affair is that I am now the owner of the only handmade aluminum wastebasket in the world. He designed it, and it's in the living room, my solitary trophy. Then a time came, early in 1953, when my three men independently decided that they wanted to marry me. I had to escape, because I wasn't in love with them. As a matter of fact, I've never been in love. And if I *had* loved a man, could I have been faithful to him? Could he have trusted me beyond a closed door? I doubt it. It was clever of Pabst to know even before he met me that I possessed the tramp essence of Lulu."

Brooks hesitated for a moment and then went on in the same tones, lightly self-mocking, "Maybe I should have been a writer's moll. Because when we were talking on the phone, a few Sundays ago, some secret compartment inside me burst, and I was suddenly overpowered by the feeling of love—a sensation I'd never experienced with any other man. Are you a variation of Jack the Ripper, who finally brings me love that I'm prevented from accepting—not by the knife but by old age? You're a perfect scoundrel, turning up like this and wrecking my golden years! [I was too stunned to offer any comment on this, but not too stunned to note, with a distinct glow of pride, that Brooks was completely sober]. Anyhow, to get back to my three suitors, I decided that the only way to avoid marriage was to become a Catholic, so that I could tell them that in the eyes of the Church I was still married to Eddie Sutherland. I went to the rectory of a Catholic church on the East Side and everything was fine until my sweet, pure religious instructor fell in love with me. I was the first woman he'd ever known who acted like one and treated him like a man. The other priests were furious. They sent him off to California and replaced him with a stern young missionary. After a while, however, even *he* began to hint that it would be a good idea if he dropped by my apartment in the evenings to give me special instruction. But I resisted temptation, and in September, 1953, I was baptized a Catholic."

Having paused to light a cigarette, which provoked a mild coughing spasm, Brooks resumed her story. "I almost forgot a strange incident that happened in 1952. Out of the blue, I got a letter from a woman who had been a Cherryvale neighbor of ours. She enclosed some snapshots. One of them showed a nice-looking gray-haired man of about fifty holding the hand of a little girl—me. On the back she'd written, 'This is Mr. Feathers, an old bachelor who loved kids. He was always taking you to the picture show and buying you toys and candy.' That picture brought back something I'd blacked out of my mind for—what?—thirty-seven years. When I was nine years old, Mr. Feathers molested me sexually. Which forged another link between me and Lulu: when *she* had *her* first lover, she was very young, and Schigolch, the man in question, was middle-aged. I've often wondered what effect Mr. Feathers had on my life. He must have had a great deal to do with forming my attitude toward sexual pleasure. For me, nice, soft, easy men were never enough—there had to be an element of domination—and I'm sure that's all tied up with Mr. Feathers. The pleasure of kissing and being kissed comes from somewhere entirely different, psychologically as well as physically. Incidentally, I told my mother about Mr. Feathers, and—would you believe it? [Peal of laughter.] She blamed *me!* She said I must have led him on. It's always the same, isn't it?" And Brooks ran on in this vein, discussing her sex life openly and jauntily, unbuckling one more notch of the Bible Belt with every sentence she uttered.

The year 1954 was Brooks's nadir. "I was too proud to be a call girl. There was no point in throwing myself into the East River, because I could swim; and I couldn't afford the alternative, which was sleeping pills." In 1955, just perceptibly, things began to look up, and life became once more a tolerable option. Henri Langlois, the exuberant ruler of the Cinémathèque Française, organized in Paris a huge exhibition entitled "Sixty Years of Cinema." Dominating the entrance hall of the Musée d'Art Moderne were two gigantic blowups, one of the French actress Falconetti in Carl Dreyer's 1928 classic, *La Passion de Jeanne d'Arc*, and the other of Brooks in *Pandora's Box*. When a critic demanded why he had preferred this nonentity to authentic stars like Garbo and Deitrich, Langlois exploded, "There is no Garbo! There is no Dietrich! There is only Louise Brooks!" In the same year, a group of her friends from the twenties clubbed together to provide a small annuity that would keep her from outright destitution; and she was visited in her Manhattan retreat by James Card, then the curator of film at Eastman house. He had long admired her movies, and he persuaded her to come to Rochester, where so much of her best work was preserved. It was at his suggestion that, in 1956, she settled there.

"Rochester seemed as good a place as any," she told me. "It was cheaper than New York, and I didn't run the risk of meeting people from my past. Up to that time, I had never

seen any of my films. And I still haven't—not right through,
that is. Jimmy Card screened some of them for me, but that
was during my drinking period. I would watch through glazed
eyes for about five minutes and sleep through the rest. I haven't
even seen *Pandora*. I've been present on two occasions when
it was being run, but I was drunk both times. By that I mean
I was *navigating* but not *seeing*." When she watched other
people's movies, however, she felt no need for alcoholic sed-
ation. As a working actress, she had never taken films seriously; under Card's tuition, she recognized that the cinema
was a valid form of art, and began to develop her own theories
about it. In 1956, drawing on her powers of near-total recall,
she wrote a study of Pabst for *Image*. This was the first of a
sheaf of articles, sharp-eyed and idiosyncratic, that she has
contributed over the years to such magazines as *Sight & Sound*
(London), *Objectif* (Montreal), *Film Culture* (New York), and
Positif (Paris).

The Brooks cult burgeoned in 1957, when Henri Langlois
crossed the Atlantic to meet her. A year later, he presented
"Hommage à Louise Brooks"—a festival of her movies that
filled the Cinémathèque. The star herself flew to Paris, all
expenses paid, and was greeted with wild acclaim at a reception
after the Cinémathèque's showing of *Pandora's Box*. (Among
those present was Jean-Luc Godard, who paid his own tribute
to Brooks in 1962, when he directed *Vivre Sa Vie*, the heroine
of which—a prostitute—was played by Anna Karina in an exact
replica of the Brooks hairdo. Godard described the character
as a "young and pretty Parisian shopgirl who gives her body
but retains her soul.") In January, 1960, Brooks went to New
York and attended a screening of *Prix de Beauté* in the Kaufman
Concert Hall of the 92nd Street Y, where she made a hilarious
little speech that delighted the packed audience. The next day,
she returned to Rochester, from which she has never since
emerged.

Interviewers and fans occasionally call on her, but for the
most part, as she put it to me, "I have lived in virtual isolation,
with an audience consisting of the milkman and a cleaning
woman." She continued, "Once a week, I would drink a pint
of gin, become what Dickens called 'gincoherent,' go to sleep,
and drowse for four days. That left three days to read, write

a bit, and see the odd visitor. No priests, by the way—I said goodbye to the Church in 1964. Now and then, there would be a letter to answer. In 1965, for instance, an Italian artist named Guido Crepax started a very sexy and tremendously popular comic strip about a girl called Valentina, who looked exactly like me as Lulu. In fact, she *identified* herself with me. Crepax wrote to thank me for the inspiration and said he regarded me as a twentieth-century myth. I appreciated the tribute and told him that at last I felt I could disintegrate happily in bed with my books, gin, cigarettes, coffee, bread, cheese, and apricot jam. During the sixties, arthritis started to get a grip, and in 1972 I had to buy a medical cane in order to move around. Then, five years ago, the disease really walloped me. My pioneer blood did not pulse through my veins, rousing me to fight it. I collapsed. I took a terrible fall and nearly smashed my hip. That was the end of the booze or any other kind of escape for me. I knew I was in for a bad time, with nothing to face but the absolute meaninglessness of my life. All I've done since then is try to hold the pieces together. And to keep my little squirrel-cage brain distracted."

As an emblematic figure of the twenties, epitomizing the flappers, jazz babies, and dancing daughters of the boom years, Brooks has few rivals, living or dead. Moreover, she is unique among such figures in that her career took her to all the places—New York, London, Hollywood, Paris, and Berlin—where the action was at its height, where experiments in pleasure were conducted with the same zeal (and often by the same people) as experiments in the arts. From her bedroom cupboard Brooks produced an avalanche of manila envelopes, each bulging with mementoes of her halcyon decade. This solitary autodidact, her perceptions deepened by years of immersion in books, looked back for my benefit on the green, gregarious girl she once was, and found much to amuse her. For every photograph she supplied a spoken caption. As she reminisced, I often thought of those Max Beerbohm cartoons that depict the Old Self conversing with the Young Self.

"Here I am in 1922, when I first hit New York, and the label of 'beautiful but dumb' was slapped on me forever. Most beautiful-but-dumb girls think they are smart, and get away with it, because other people, on the whole, aren't much smarter. You can see modern equivalents of those girls on any TV talk show. But there's also a very small group of beautiful women who *know* they're dumb, and this makes them defenseless and vulnerable. They become the Big Joke. I didn't know Marilyn Monroe, but I'm sure that her agonizing awareness of her own stupidity was one of the things that killed her. I became the Big Joke, first on Broadway and then in Hollywood.... That's Herman Mankiewicz—an ideal talk-show guest, don't you think, born before his time? In 1925, Herman was trying to educate me, and he invented the Louise Brooks Literary Society. A girl named Dorothy Knapp and I were Ziegfeld's two prize beauties. We had a big dressing room on the fifth floor of the New Amsterdam Building, and people like Walter Wanger, Michael Arlen, and Gilbert Miller would meet there, ostensibly to hear my reviews of books that Herman gave me to read. What they actually came for was to watch Dorothy doing a striptease and having a love affair with herself in front of a full-length mirror. I get some consolation from the fact that, as an idiot, I have provided delight in my time to a very select group of intellectuals.... That must be Joseph Schenck. Acting on behalf of his brother Nick, who controlled M-G-M, Joe offered me a contract in 1925 at three hundred a week. Instead, I went to Paramount for two hundred and fifty. Maybe I should have signed with M-G-M and joined what I called the Joe Schenck Mink Club. You could recognize the members at '21' because they never removed their mink coats at lunch.... Here's Fritzi La Verne, smothered in osprey feathers. I roomed with her briefly when we were in the Follies together, and she seduced more Follies girls than Ziegfeld and William Randolph Hearst combined. That's how I got the reputation of being a lesbian. I had nothing against it in principle, and for years I thought it was fun to encourage the idea. I used to hold hands with Fritzi in public. She had a little Bulgarian boyfriend who was just our height, and we would get into his suits and camp all over New York. Even when I moved out to Yahoo City, California, I could never stop by a lesbian household without being asked to strip and join the happy group baring their operation scars in the sun. But although I went through a couple of mild sexual auditions with women, I very soon found that I only loved men's bodies. What maddens me is that because of the lesbian scenes with Alice Roberts in *Pandora* I shall probably go down in film history as one of the gloomy dikes. A friend of mine once said to me, 'Louise Brooks, you're not a lesbian, you're a pansy.' Would you care to decipher that? By the way, are you getting tired of hearing my name? I'm thinking of changing it. I noticed that there were five people called Brooks in last week's *Variety*. How about June Caprice? Or Louise Lovely?"

I shook my head.

Brooks continued riffling through her collection. "This, of course, is Martha Graham, whose genius I absorbed to the bone during the years we danced together on tour. She had rages, you know, that struck like lightning out of nowhere. One evening when we were waiting to go onstage—I was sixteen—she grabbed me, shook me ferociously, and shouted, 'Why do you ruin your feet by wearing those tight shoes?' Another time, she was sitting sweetly at the makeup shelf pinning flowers in her hair when she suddenly seized a bottle of body makeup and exploded it against the mirror. She looked at the shattered remains for a spell, then moved her makeup along to an unbroken mirror and went on quietly pinning flowers in her hair. Reminds me of the night when Buster Keaton drove me in his roadster out to Culver City, where he had a bungalow on the back lot of M-G-M. The walls of the living room were covered with great glass bookcases. Buster, who wasn't drunk, opened the door, turned on the lights, and picked up a baseball bat. Then, walking calmly round the room, he smashed every pane of glass in every bookcase. Such frustration in that little body! . . . Here, inevitably, are Scott and Zelda. I met them in January, 1927, at the Ambassador Hotel in L.A. They were sitting close together on a sofa, like a comedy team, and the first thing that struck me was how *small* they were. I had come to see the genius writer, but what dominated the room was the blazing intelligence of Zelda's profile. It shocked me. It was the profile of a witch. Incidentally, I've been reading Scott's letters, and I've spotted a curious thing about them. In the early days, before Hemingway was famous, Scott always spelled his name wrong, with two "m"s. And when did he start to spell it right? At the precise moment when Hemingway became a bigger star than he was. . . . This is a pool party at somebody's house in Malibu. I know I knock the studio system, but if you were to ask me what it was like to live in Hollywood in the twenties I'd have to say that we were all—oh!—marvellously degenerate and happy. We were a world of our own, and outsiders didn't intrude. People tell you that the reason a lot of actors left Hollywood when sound came in was that their voices were wrong for talkies. That's the official story. The truth is that the coming of sound meant the end of the all-night parties. With talkies, you couldn't stay out till sunrise anymore. You had to rush back from the studios and start learning your lines, ready for the next day's shooting at 8 A.M. That was when the studio machine really took over. It controlled you, mind and body, from the moment you were yanked out of bed at dawn until the publicity department put you back to bed at night."

Brooks paused, silently contemplating revels that ended half a century ago, and then went on. "Talking about bed, here's Tallulah—although I always guessed that she wasn't as keen on bed as everyone thought. And my record for guessing things like that was pretty good. I watched her packing her douche-bag one night for a meeting with a plutocratic boyfriend of hers at the Elysée Hotel. She forgot to wear the emerald ring he'd given her a few days before, but she didn't forget the script of the play she wanted him to produce for her. Her preparations weren't scheming or whorish. Just businesslike.... This is a bunch of the guests at Mr. Hearst's ranch, sometime in 1928. The girl with the dark hair and the big smile is Pepi Lederer, one of my dearest friends. She was Marion Davies' niece and the sister of Charlie Lederer, the screenwriter, and she was only seventeen when that picture was taken. My first husband, Eddie Sutherland, used to say that for people who didn't worship opulence, weren't crazy about meeting celebrities, and didn't need money or advancement from Mr. Hearst, San Simeon was a deadly-dull place. I suppose he was right. But when Pepi was there it was always fun. She created a world of excitement and inspiration wherever she went. And I never entered that great dining hall without a shiver of delight. There were medieval banners from Siena floating overhead, and a vast Gothic fireplace, and a long refectory table seating forty. Marion and Mr. Hearst sat with the important guests at the middle of the table. Down at the bottom, Pepi ruled over a group—including me—that she called the Younger Degenerates, and that's where the laughter was. Although Mr. Hearst disapproved of booze, Pepi had made friends with one of the waiters, and we got all the champagne we wanted. She could have been a gifted writer, and for a while she worked for Mr. Hearst's deluxe quarterly *The Connoisseur*, but it was only a courtesy job. Nobody took her seriously, she never learned discipline, and drink and drugs got her in the end. In 1935, she died by jumping out of a window in the psychiatric ward of a hospital in Los Angeles. She was twenty-five years old. Not long ago, I came across her name in the index of a book on Marion Davies, and it broke my heart. Then I remembered a quotation from Goethe that I'd once typed out. I've written it under the photo: 'For a person remains of consequence not so far as he leaves something behind him but so far as he acts and enjoys, and rouses others to action and enjoyment.' That was Pepi."

Of all the names that spilled out of Brooks's memories of America in the twenties, there was one for which she reserved a special veneration: that of Chaplin. In an article for the magazine *Film Culture*, she had described his performances at private parties:

He recalled his youth with comic pantomimes. He acted out countless scenes for countless films. And he did imitations of everybody. Isadora Duncan danced in a storm of toilet paper. John Barrymore picked his nose and brooded over Hamlet's soliloquy. A Follies girl swished across the room; and I began to cry while Charlie denied absolutely that he was imitating me. Nevertheless . . . I determined to abandon that silly walk forthwith.

For me, she filled out the picture. "I was eighteen in 1925, when Chaplin came to New York for the opening of *The Gold Rush*. He was just twice my age, and I had an affair with him for two happy summer months. Ever since he died, my mind has gone back fifty years, trying to define that lovely being from another world. He was not only the creator of the Little Fellow, though that was miracle enough. He was a self-made

aristocrat. He taught himself to speak cultivated English, and
he kept a dictionary in the bathroom at his hotel so that he
could learn a new word every morning. While he dressed, he
prepared his script for the day, which was intended to adorn
his private portrait of himself as a perfect English gentleman.
He was also a sophisticated lover, who had affairs with Peggy
Hopkins Joyce and Marion Davies and Pola Negri, and he was
a brilliant businessman, who owned his films and demanded
fifty percent of the gross—which drove Nick Schenck wild,
along with all the other people who were plotting to rob him.
Do you know, I can't once remember him *still*? He was always
standing up as he sat down, and going out as he came in.
Except when he turned off the lights and went to sleep, without
liquor or pills, like a child. Meaning to be bitchy, Herman
Mankiewicz said, 'People never sat at his feet. He went to
where people were sitting and stood in front of them.' But how
we paid attention! We were hypnotized by the beauty and
inexhaustible originality of this glistening creature. He's the
only genius I ever knew who spread himself equally over his
art and his life. He loved showing off in fine clothes and elegant
phrases—even in the witness box. When Lita Grey divorced
him, she put about vile rumors that he had a depraved passion
for little girls. He didn't give a damn, even though people said
his career would be wrecked. It still infuriates me that he never
defended himself against any of those ugly lies, but the truth
is that he existed on a plane above pride, jealousy, or hate. I
never heard him say a snide thing about anyone. *He lived
totally without fear*. He knew that Lita Grey and her family
were living in his house in Beverly Hills, planning to ruin him,
yet he was radiantly carefree—happy with the success of *The
Gold Rush* and with the admirers who swarmed around him.
Not that he *exacted* adoration. Even during our affair, he knew
that I didn't adore him in the romantic sense, and he didn't
mind at all. Which brings me to one of the dirtiest lies he
allowed to be told about him—that he was mean with money.
People forget that Chaplin was the only star ever to keep his
ex-leading lady [Edna Purviance] on his payroll for life, and
the only producer to pay his employees their full salaries even
when he wasn't in production. When our joyful summer ended
he didn't give me a fur from Jaeckel or a bangle from Cartier,

so that I could flash them around, saying, 'Look what I got from Chaplin.' The day after he left town, I got a nice check in the mail signed Charlie. And then I didn't even write him a thank-you note. Damn me."

Brooks's souvenirs of Europe, later in the twenties, began with pictures of a burly, handsome, dark-haired man, usually alighting from a train: George Preston Marshall, the millionaire who was her frequent bedfellow and constant adviser between 1927 and 1933. "If you care about *Pandora's Box*, you should be grateful to George Marshall," she told me. "I'd never heard of Mr. Pabst when he offered me the part. It was George who insisted that I should accept it. He was passionately fond of the theatre and films, and he slept with every pretty show-business girl he could find, including all my best friends. George took me to Berlin with his English valet, who stepped off the train blind drunk and fell flat on his face at Mr. Pabst's feet."

The Brooks collection contains no keepsakes of the actress whom she pipped at the post in the race to play Lulu, and of whom, when I raised the subject, she spoke less than charitably. "Dietrich? That *contraption!* She was one of the beautiful-but-dumb girls, like me, but she belonged to the category of those who thought they were smart and fooled other people into believing it. But I guess I'm just being insanely jealous, because I know she's a friend of yours—isn't she?" By way of making amends, she praised Dietrich's performance as Lola in *The Blue Angel*, and then, struck by a sudden thought, interrupted herself: "Hey! Why don't I ask Marlene to come over from Paris? We could work on our memoirs together. Better still, she could write mine, and I hers—*Lulu* by Lola, and *Lola* by Lulu." To put it politely, however, Dietrich does not correspond to Brooks's ideal image of a movie goddess. But who does—apart from Margaret Sullavan, whose voice, as we know, she reveres? A few months after our Rochester encounter, she sent me a letter that disclosed another, unexpected object of her admiration. In it she said:

I've just been listening to Toronto radio. There was a press conference with Ava Gardner, who is making a movie in Montreal. Her beauty has never excited me,

and I have seen only one of her films, *The Night of the
Iguana*, in which she played a passive role that revealed
her power of stillness but little else. On radio, sitting in
a hotel room, triggered by all the old stock questions,
she said nothing new or stirring—just "Sinatra could be
very nice or very rotten—get me another drink, baby—
I made fifty-four pictures and the only part I understood
was in *The Snows of Kilimanjaro*. . . ." In her conversation, there was nothing about great acting or beauty or
sex, and no trace of philosophical or intellectual concern.
Yet for the first time in my life I was proud of being a
movie actress, unmixed with theatre art. Ava is in essence what I think a movie star should be—a beautiful
person with a unique, mysterious personality unpolluted
by Hollywood. And she is so *strong*. She did not have
to run away (like Garbo) to keep from being turned into
a product of the machine. . . . What I should like to know
is whether, as I sometimes fancy, I ever had a glimmer
of that quality of integrity which makes Ava shine with
her own light.

The next picture out of the manila files showed Brooks,
inscrutable and somewhat forlorn in a sequinned evening gown,
sitting at a table surrounded by men with pencil-thin mustaches
who were wearing tuxedos, black ties, and wing collars. These
men were all jabbering into telephones and laughing mania-
cally. None of them was looking at Brooks. Behind them I
could make out oak-panelled walls and an out-of-focus waiter
with a fish-eyed stare and a strong resemblance to Louis Jouvet.
"You know where that was taken, of course," Brooks said.

I was sorry, but I didn't.

"That's Joe Zelli's!" she cried. "Zelli's was the most famous
nightclub in Paris. I can't remember all the men's names, but
the one on the extreme right used to drink ether. The one on
my left was half Swedish and half English. I lived with him
in several hotels. Although he was very young, he had snow-
white hair, so we always called him the Eskimo. The fellow
next to him, poor guy, was killed the very next day. He was
cut to pieces by a speedboat propeller at Cannes."

Whenever I think of the twenties, I shall see that flash-lit hysterical tableau at Zelli's and the unsmiling seraph at the center of it.

From the fattest of all her folders, Brooks now pulled out a two-shot. Beaming in a cloche hat, she stands arm in arm with a stocky, self-possessed man in a homburg. He also wears steel-rimmed glasses, a bow tie, and a well-cut business suit; you would guess he was in his early forties. "Mr. Pabst," she said simply. "That was 1928, in Berlin, while we were making *Pandora's Box*. As I told you, I arrived with George Marshall, and Mr. Pabst hated him, because he kept me up all night, going round the clubs. A few weeks later, George went back to the States, and after that Mr. Pabst locked me up in my hotel when the day's shooting was finished. Everyone thought he was in love with me. On the rare evenings when I went to his apartment for dinner, his wife, Trudi, would walk out and bang the door. Mr. Pabst was a highly respectable man, but he had the most extraordinary collection of obscene stills in the world. He even had one of Sarah Bernhardt nude with a black-lace fan. Did you know that in the twenties it was the custom for European actresses to send naked pictures of themselves to movie directors? He had all of them. Anyway, I didn't have an affair with him in Berlin. In 1929, though, when he was in Paris trying to set up *Prix de Beauté*, we went out to dinner at a restaurant and I behaved rather outrageously. For some reason, I slapped a close friend of mine across the face with a bouquet of roses. Mr. Pabst was horrified. He hustled me out of the place and took me back to my hotel, where—what do I do? I'm in a *terrific* mood, so I decide to banish his disgust by giving the best sexual performance of my career. I jump into the hay and deliver myself to him body and soul. [Her voice is jubilant.] He acted as if he'd never experienced such a thing in his life. You know how men want to pin medals on themselves when they excite you? They get positively radiant. Next morning, Mr. Pabst was so pleased he couldn't see straight. That was why he postponed *Prix de Beauté* and arranged to make *Diary of a Lost Girl* first. He wanted the affair to continue. But I didn't, and when I got to Berlin it was like *Pandora's Box* all over again, except that this time the man I brought with me was the Eskimo—my white-headed boy from Zelli's."

Brooks laughed softly, recalling the scene. "Mr. Pabst was there at the station to meet me. He was appalled when I got off the train with the Eskimo. On top of that, I had a wart on my neck, and Esky had just slammed the compartment door on my finger. Mr. Pabst took one stark look at me, told me I had to start work the next morning, and dragged me away to a doctor, who burned off the wart. If you study the early sequences of *Lost Girl*, you can see the sticking plaster on my neck. I hated to hurt Mr. Pabst's feelings with the Eskimo, but I simply could not bring myself to repeat that one and only night. The irony, which Mr. Pabst never knew, was that although Esky and I shared a hotel suite in Berlin, we didn't sleep together until much later, when *Lost Girl* was finished and we were spending a few days in Paris. 'Eskimo,' I said to him the evening before we parted, 'this is the night.' And it was—another first and last for Brooks."

More fragments of Brooksiana:

I: Do you think there are countries that produce particularly good lovers?

BROOKS: Englishmen are the best. And priest-ridden Irishmen are the worst.

I: What are your favorite films?

BROOKS: *An American in Paris*, *Pygmalion*, and *The Wizard of Oz*. Please don't be disappointed.

I: They're all visions of wish fulfillment. An American at large with a *gamine* young dancer in a fantasy playground called Paris. A Cockney flower girl who becomes the toast of upper-class London. And a child from your home state who discovers, at the end of a trip to a magic world, that happiness was where she started out.

BROOKS: You *are* disappointed.

I: Not a bit. They're first-rate movies, and they're all aspects of you.

Postscript from a letter Brooks wrote to me before we met: "Can you give me a reason for sitting here in this bed, going crazy, with not one god-damned excuse for living?" I came up with more than one reason; viz., (a) to receive the homage of those who cherish the images she has left on celluloid, (b) to bestow the pleasure of her conversation on those who seek her company, (c) to appease her hunger for gleaning wisdom from books, and (d) to test the truth of a remark she had made to a friend: "The Spanish philosopher Ortega y Gasset once said, 'We are all lost creatures. It is only when we admit this that we have a chance of finding ourselves.'"

Despite the numerous men who have crossed the trajectory of her life, Brooks has pursued her own course. She has flown solo. The price to be paid for such individual autonomy is, inevitably, loneliness, and her loneliness is prefigured in one of the most penetrating comments she has ever committed to print: "The great art of films does not consist of descriptive movement of face and body, but in the movements of thought and soul, transmitted in a kind of intense isolation."

As I rose to leave her apartment, she gave me a present: a large and handsome volume entitled *Louise Brooks—Portrait d'une Anti-Star*. Published in Paris in 1977, it contained a full pictorial survey of her career, together with essays, critiques, and poems devoted to her beauty and talent. She inscribed it to me, and copied out, beneath her signature, the epitaph she has composed for herself: "I never gave away anything without wishing I had kept it; nor kept anything without wishing I had given it away." The book included an account by Brooks of her family background, which I paused to read. It ended with this paragraph, here reproduced from her original English text:

Over the years I suffered poverty and rejection and came to believe that my mother had formed me for a freedom that was unattainable, a delusion. Then . . . I was confined to this small apartment in this alien city of Rochester. . . . Looking about, I saw millions of old people in my situation, wailing like lost puppies because they were alone and had no one to talk to. But they had become enslaved by habits which bound their lives to warm bodies that talked. I was free! Although my mother had ceased to be a warm body in 1944, she had not forsaken me. She comforts me with every book I read. Once again I am five, leaning on her shoulder, learning the words as she reads aloud *Alice in Wonderland*.

She insisted on getting out of bed to escort me to the door. We had been talking earlier of Proust, and she had mentioned his maxim that the future could never be predicted from the past. Out of her past, I thought, in all its bizarre variety, who knows what future she may invent? "Another thing about Proust," she said, resting on her cane in the doorway. "No matter how he dresses his characters up in their social disguises, we always know how they look naked." As we know it (I reflected) in Brooks's performances.

I kissed her goodbye, buttoned up my social disguise—for it was a chilly evening—and joined the other dressed-up people on the streets of Rochester.

[1979]

MS READ-a-thon—
a simple way to start youngsters reading

Boys and girls between 6 and 14 can join the MS READ-a-thon and help find a cure for Multiple Sclerosis by reading books. And they get two rewards — the enjoyment of reading, and the great feeling that comes from helping others.

Parents and educators: For complete information call your local MS chapter. Or mail the coupon below.

Kids can help, too!